ALSO BY L. FERGUS

*Angel of Yorq*

(Available in paperback version of *Birthright*)

*Birthright*

*Razor's Pass*

*Project Omega*

(Available in paperback version of *Razor's Pass*)

*Fall and Rise*

*Rebirth*

*Clouds*

*Sarin's War*

*Li've*

## THE NEW ANGELS

**Earth 168**

**BykeChic**

*Earth 832*

(Coming Fall 2020)

NON-KITA BOOKS

*Warmache*

Earth 168 & BykeChic

Copyright © 2020 by L. Fergus

@FallenAngelKita

http://FallenAngelKita.com

THE NEW ANGELS

# EARTH 168

## L FERGUS

The green light from the radio cast harsh shadows inside the 113A3 APC. Private Logine sat on the far end of the pioneer box, her M-16 rifle between her legs. She rested the edge of her helmet against the front sight post as the smell of diesel and oil seeped up through the floorboards. Over the idling of the APC's engine came a rumble—East German artillery falling nearby.

Staff Sergeant Acoine had the radio hand-mic tucked up under his helmet. Logine guessed he was trying to find out why they stopped. They weren't supposed to stop until they reached Fulda. The 11th Calvary Regiment and 3rd Infantry Division had blunted the Soviet advance, and now NATO forces were on the counterattack.

"Hey!" Private Wallace punched Logine's shoulder, right in her 2nd Armored Division patch. Logine adored the nickname: Hell on Wheels. "Quit stewing. We got this. Sapper Steel!"

Logine turned to look at her girlfriend and then banged helmets with her. "You know it."

Logine and Wallace had been together since high school. They'd joined the Army and as a hometown pair, they'd gone through Basic and AIT together and then assigned to the 168th Engineer Battalion at Wiesbaden Army Base, West Germany.

Across from Logine, Specialist Holiday sat on the demolition box. "You girls checked your rifles? Locked and loaded?"

Logine picked up her rifle. It was heavier now with live rounds in it. She checked the safety, magazine, and receiver. Everything was where it was supposed to be. "Good to go, Specialist."

"Same here, Specialist," said Wallace.

"Good. Now, be quiet. I'm trying to listen."

A year in the Army and Logine learned to be patient. The Army was a lot of waiting, punctuated with brief periods of action. She had learned to summon her mind and body from a lull to combat ready at a moment's notice.

Wallace's gloved hand squeezed Logine's thigh. Logine took Wallace's hand

and squeezed it. Logine knew Wallace had her back, and she had hers. They earned a reputation around the infantry and tanker barracks—mess with one, you were going to get the other. A few guys learned the hard way they were fearless and not afraid to fight. They collected a pair of article fifteens for throwing a tanker that wouldn't take *no* for an answer down a flight of stairs and breaking his arm.

"Outlaw Two Six, roger. Outlaw Two Three is moving." Sergeant Acoine tapped Sergeant Fortune standing in the command hatch on the leg, and the APC lurched forward. He put the hand-mic away. "Ok, listen up. We're moving forward. The task force has hit a minefield and has stopped. The platoon is moving forward to breach it. Outlaw Two Two has fired a MICLIC, and the ACE is moving forward to proof the lane. Holiday, grab the demo bag. You're going to proof the lane in case the ACE doesn't make it. The Soviets have overwatch, but the tanks and Bradleys are keeping them busy. Logine, Wallace, you'll mark the lane, just like Grafe, except I'll attach IR chem-lights to the top, instead of cones. Are you girls good?"

"Yes, Sergeant," Logine and Wallace said together.

"Good. Logine, open the troop hatch and untie the pickets. Wallace, get out your picket pounder."

Holiday scooted out of the way so Logine could stand on the demolition box and open the troop hatch. The sounds of battle assaulted her ears. The *booms* of tank cannons and the rapid-fire *cracks* of Bradleys were uncoordinated with the tracers blazing trails through the night air. Swaying with the APC as it moved, Logine undid the tie downs on the pickets. In front of her, Sergeant Fortune fired a few rounds from the APC's 50. caliber machine gun.

The APC passed through the tree line, engine screaming as it raced toward an unseen destination. Logine dropped back down into the APC. Wallace had body slung her rifle and had the picket pounder in her hands. The forty-pound two-handled cylindrical metal picket pounder was hollow on one end and weighed a third of what Wallace did.

The APC came to an abrupt halt, throwing everyone forward.

"Dammit, Freddy," yelled Holiday.

Logine knew PFC Fredrick couldn't hear Holiday, but everyone was thinking the same thing. Fredrick twisted in the driver's seat and pulled the lever to lower the ramp with a *thump* in the dirt.

"Holiday, go!" yelled Sergeant Acoine.

Holiday jumped out of the APC, turned, and disappeared into the darkness.

"Ok, girls," called Sergeant Acoine, "just like we did a month ago. As the track goes down the lane, I'll toss off the pickets. We'll pick you up on the other side. You good?"

"Yes, Sergeant!" they yelled enthusiastically.

"Remember: mission first, do not accept defeat, there is no quitting, and no one gets left behind."

"Yes, Sergeant!"

"Good. Go kick them in the ass!"

Logine and Wallace ran down the ramp and around the side of the APC. Sergeant Acoine passed a six-foot u-shaped metal picket to Logine, and the APC pulled away. Logine stood the picket up, and Wallace put the picket top inside the picket pounder. Each soldier grabbed a handle on the picket pounder, and with synchronized motion, they lifted the picket pounder and slammed it down, throwing all their body weight with it. After four strikes the picket stood. They lifted the picket pounder off and ran toward the next picket.

The ground became rough and broken as they entered the lane cleared by the MICLIC. The plowing by the ACE did little to improve the footing. Logine ran as fast as she could, her protective mask banging against her thigh and her rifle hitting her butt. They reached the next picket and pounded it into the ground. The row of pickets would guide the rest of the task force through the minefield.

As Logine ran, the ground to the left exploded in a shower of dirt, grass, and metal fragments. The force of the artillery impact threw Logine off her feet. She landed in the dirt. Picking herself up, she ran to Wallace. "Hey, you ok?"

Wallace rolled over. There was a cut in her BDU bottoms just above her cargo pocket. She put her hand on it, and her glove came away with blood. "I think I'll be fine. It's just a little scratch." She stood up and grabbed the picket pounder.

They ran forward through the darkness, pounding pickets. A bright fireball lit the far tree line as a T-72 took a direct hit. Logine couldn't see the APC anymore. She didn't worry about it. They would find it on the other side.

After a dozen pickets, Wallace said, "Can you take the picket pounder? It's getting heavy." Logine took it from her, and they found the next picket. A bright flash illuminated the field in front of them. The APC was in flames.

"What do we do?" said Wallace to Logine.

"We keep going. We'll stop and grab what we need off the APC and finish."

"Ok."

They pounded the remaining pickets and ran to the APC. It was mostly intact, and the flames had died down. Logine dropped the picket pounder and stepped up on the APC's track to reach the top. Sergeant Acoine was gone. Sergeant Fortune was slumped against the 50. caliber machine gun. The smell of diesel and burnt flesh permeated the air. Logine grabbed eight pickets from the pile—the amount one of them could carry—and passed them down to Wallace. The box of chem-lights was on the deck behind the command hatch. Logine reached for them. When a hand grabbed her arm, Logine screamed. Sergeant Acoine stood in the troop hatch. Burnt flesh and uniform covered half of his face and body. With his good hand, he pulled two flares from his cargo pocket.

"Open signal," he croaked and then collapsed back into the 113.

Logine grabbed the flares and the chem-lights and stuck them in her cargo pockets. She jumped down and picked up the picket pounder. "Let's go!"

"What's the scream for?" yelled Wallace.

"Sergeant Acoine was still alive. Kind of."

They pounded the next picket. Logine pulled a chem-light from the box, cracked it, and stuck it on top of the picket. They pounded pickets until they came to the smoking ruin of the ACE laying on its side.

"Does this mean the lane's not proofed?" said Logine.

"I don't know," said Wallace. "We haven't seen Specialist Holiday. When we go forward, we'll run side by side and look for mines. We'll just have to push any we find out of the way."

Logine nodded in agreement. They rushed forward a few feet apart but stayed inside the MICLIC's blast lane. The picket pounder was getting heavy.

"We gotta switch this up," said Logine. "It's too heavy."

"I have three pickets left," said Wallace. "I'll take two, you get one, and we'll both carry the picket pounder."

Each soldier took a handle and their pickets, and ran forward. They pounded two more pickets and reached the end of the MICLIC blast. A few yards beyond the blast was a mine.

"I'll pound the picket, you get the mine," said Logine to Wallace.

Logine pounded the picket with all her might. With just her, it took seven strikes to get the picket in the ground. Using her legs and her weary arms, she lifted the picket pounder off, let it fall to the ground, and attached a chem-light. Exhausted, she threw herself down next to Wallace.

"How's it going?"

With her bare hands, Wallace was pulling dirt out from under the mine. "Checking for mousetraps. So far, I got nothing."

Wallace continued to search until they'd pulled most of the dirt from under the mine. "Ok, I think it's good. Let's lift it up and set it aside."

Carefully, they lifted the mine and carried it to the last picket. Setting it down at the base, Logine cracked a chem-light and placed it on top.

"Ok," said Logine to Wallace. "That's it. Let's find a place to lay low until someone picks us up."

"Let's get to the tree line. We can hide there."

Unslinging their rifles, they entered the woods. Logine stopped. "Wait! The flares!" Logine pulled them out of her cargo pocket. She handed one to Wallace.

"Is it one or both?" said Wallace.

"I don't know." Before they had done the lane marking drill in the daylight and used a smoke pot. "What color is yours?"

Wallace turned the flare so she could read the markings on the side. "Green."

"Mine's green, too. Let's fire both. That way the tankers can't miss seeing them."

"How do they work?"

Logine found the instructions. "Hit bottom against a hard surface. Aim toward the sky."

"The ground's too soft," said Wallace.

"Smack it against our knees."

"Huh?"

Logine took a knee.

"Oh, gotcha." Wallace knelt. "Ready? One...two...three!"

Both soldiers slammed the bottom of the flares against their knees. Two pops were followed by loud *wooshes*. Green lights streaked into the air and exploded, bathing everything in a green light.

Logine tossed the used tube away. "Come on, let's go."

They ran into the trees and stopped at the base of a large pine tree.

*"Gunther, bist du das?"*

"Oh, shit," said Wallace.

There was a series of flashes. Wallace's M-16 fell from her hands, and she collapsed.

"Lizzy!" cried Logine.

More flashes lit the area as Logine ducked behind the tree. Leaning out, she fired back but didn't know where to aim. Flashes came from a neighboring tree. Logine fired at the tree, rolled to the other side, and charged the enemy, firing from her hip.

Logine nearly tripped over the East German soldier. He rose to his knees and aimed his AK-47. Using her bayonet training, Logine knocked the AK-47 aside. Raising the butt of her M-16, she smashed it into his face several times. She jumped back and fired twice in the East German's chest.

Logine ran back to Wallace. She fell to a prone position next to her.

"Lizzy! Lizzy!" Logine yelled while shaking Wallace.

Logine received no response. Two dark spots were on Wallace's BDU top. Logine pulled open Wallace's top, and her brown t-shirt was soaked in blood.

"Love, no," whispered Logine as she touched her helmet to Wallace's chest while fighting back tears. "I won't leave you here."

Logine knelt, slung her rifle from her shoulder, grabbed Wallace's arm and leg, and hoisted Wallace onto her shoulders in a fireman's carry. After a wobbly step, Logine marched back toward the lane's exit.

The chatter of AK-47s came from behind Logine. A fist hit her in the kidney. A second punch knocked the wind out of her lungs. Her knees buckled, and she fell forward onto her chest. Wallace rolled off Logine's shoulders. Logine blinked, trying to understand what happened. A whisper turned into a roar as an M1 tank drove by.

"Mission accomplished," Logine whispered. She coughed and her mouth filled with blood. The sounds of battle faded in her ears as her vision became gray. She closed her eyes, and the world slipped away.

---

Logine's blood glowed like embers. A single flame burst forth and spread across the dead soldier's body. Large flames shot skyward and engulfed her.

An unnatural wind swirled, blowing the ash skyward. The ash became a tornado, swirling tighter. There was a flash, and an Angel with black wings appeared. She was dressed in black leather and heavy combat boots, her midsection was bare and heavy bracers with crystal inlays protected her arms, a heavy stud encrusted belt hung from her hip, and thigh pads held an array of throwing stars. A hood obscured her face. She carried a pair of swords on her back. The Angel removed her hood revealing blonde hair and a sad expression in her blue eyes. She knelt next to Wallace.

The Angel rolled Wallace over, undid her helmet, and tossed it aside. She stroked Wallace's cheek. "Brave soldier, you did your duty and the battle's won, but your job is not done." The Angel touched Wallace's nose. "Boop! Rise Sapper."

Wallace convulsed and screamed. The Angel rolled Wallace onto her hands and knees then drew a sword and cut two slits in her BDU top between her shoulder blades and spine. Two fleshy growths grew skyward forming limbs and joints. Buds on the limbs flesh grew and burst, revealing red feathers with white edges. The Angel helped Sapper to her feet.

Sapper looked at the Angel. Her mouth opened in surprise. "Logine, did we get the lane open?"

"Hey, Wallace. Yes, but we died."

"If we're dead, how am I here?"

The Angel smiled. "Death is only the beginning. Come, it's time to go home."

---

APC—Armored Personnel Carrier

    MICLIC—Mine Clearing Line Charge

    ACE—Armored Combat Earthmover

    AIT—Advanced Individual Training

    BDU—Battle Dress Uniform

    IR—Infrared

    PFC—Private First Class

    Picket—Six-foot-tall u-shaped metal stake for creating wire obstacles

    Picket Pounder—A hollow cylindrical tube with a metal plate on one end and handles

    Article Fifteen—non-judicial punishment for minor offenses

# THE NEW ANGELS

# BYKECHIC

## L FERGUS

*For Charlie.*
*I'm glad I made you grin.*

KITA TAPPED HER BLACK PAINTED NAIL AGAINST HER TABLET AS SHE FLIPPED through a stack of greasy fingerprinted papers, counting them. The transport manifest on her tablet said she should have fifteen vehicles, but there were only twelve intake slips from her mechanic, Mickey. She was missing a mustang, a van, and a motorcycle. *How did I lose three vehicles?*

Kita went back to the manifest on her tablet. According to the transport driver, she unloaded fifteen vehicles. Somewhere between the drop-off area and the mechanic's shed, they'd been lost.

Kita leaned back in her chair, her head hitting the ancient faux wood paneling that made her office dark and dirty. *I don't need this tonight. I want to go home and sleep.* The clock on the wall said it was after ten. A pile of orders and receipts sat on her desk, needing to be processed. *They'll have to wait. I don't make any money if I don't have any vehicles.* Kita pushed off the wall with her head and gathered her tablet and phone.

She navigated between the boxes of papers that hid the filing cabinets and shelves full of parts to the door. The lobby contained a counter that was missing pieces of the 70s-style countertop, a wall of cubbyholes for parts, and a tablet attached to the counter so customers could browse her inventory. The double glass doors led to the dirt parking lot. A side door led to the yard.

After locking her office, Kita left via the side door. An overhead cover protected several workbenches where customers could clean up the parts they pulled. She went around the corner, unlocked an electrical box, and flipped a switch. Two dozen lights lit up, revealing the rows of derelict vehicles.

Kita walked down the central row. One side was motorcycles—those made most of her money. She specialized in older vehicles. Over half her inventory was built before she was born. The rest of the yard contained cars, SUVs, and light trucks.

She kept her eyes open for her missing Indian motorcycle. *Maybe Ralph thought the vehicles were finished and put them on the line. I hope not. I'll be here all night looking.* She reached the end of the motorcycle line without finding her missing motorcycle. As she walked, she also looked for a 1976 Dodge ambulance, which should be easy to spot, and a 1978 Ford Mustang.

At the mechanic's shed, Kita didn't see her missing vehicles. She checked Mickey's desk to see if the slips were there, but all she found were fast-food wrappers, soda cans, and muscle car magazines. Kita picked a magazine up. *The girl's hot. Sigh. Like I'll ever have time for that.*

Not seeing the vehicles, Kita resigned herself to her fate of having to walk the yard. *Someone is getting an ass-chewing in the morning.* She hadn't decided who.

As she walked along the back fence, a light shined through the slating in the chain-link fence. *By the Crushing Depths, now what?* Kita jumped on the hood of a car so she could look over the fence. A light was moving back and forth in the old auto parts plant next door. She owned the plant. The goal was to someday expand her parts business into it. *I can't have kids in there. If they get hurt, their parents will sue.*

Kita jumped off the car and hurried to the back gate. She undid the lock and pulled the gate open. There wasn't much space between the plant and the fence —maybe twelve feet. The asphalt was cracked, crumbling, and covered in weeds.

1

The light was in the parts loading area, but the door to the plant was in the opposite direction.

She reached the door and was able to open it after a brief fight with the lock. An old hallway with faded linoleum tiles led into the darkness. Kita pulled out her phone and turned on the flashlight, scaring a rat. *Perfect.*

The hallway ended at a set of double doors that led to the manufacturing floor. Kita knew the layout of the plant well. She'd played inside it growing up. Before she was born, this place turned out parts for Ford around the clock. Now, the old machinery sat frozen in time.

Following a roller belt, Kita passed the packaging and boxing machine. She kicked a piece of pipe, and the *clang* echoed through the room. *Dammit.* The roller belt ended at the stacker, where the boxes were loaded onto pallets and made ready for shipping. She pushed through the doors to the loading area.

The area was dark.

"Hello?" Kita called. "Come out. I know you're in here."

She was met with silence.

"There's only one way out, and I'm standing in front of it. Don't make me call the cops."

Kita waited for a response. "Fine, but if you get hurt, I'll prosecute you for trespassing."

Annoyed, Kita followed a wall to an electrical box, opened it, and flipped the switch. The lights for the loading area came on with a *thunk*. She turned off the flashlight app on her phone and stuck it back in her pocket.

Kita's missing ambulance and Mustang were parked on the other side of the room near the big double bay doors. *How in the Crushing Depths did you get in here?* She approached them cautiously, ready for someone to jump out and yell, "*Surprise!*" *Or worse, they have a gun.*

The white and orange paint job of the ambulance was faded, and rust had eaten away at the rear doors. The license plate said SPRKKT. *That's odd for a service vehicle to have a vanity plate.* Walking along the side, the tires looked brand new, but the rest was as rusted and battered as the back doors.

Next to the Mustang, the ambulance looked brand new. The car's paint job was more rust than faded gold paint. Corrosion had gotten to the chrome, but the tires were brand new. *Who puts new tires on vehicles going to the scrap yard? I better not have gotten charged for them.* The license plate said BRNOOT. The windows were covered in a layer of dirt, making it hard to see inside.

*It would be nice to have you. Some time with the grinder, a new paint job, a couple of replacement parts, and you'd be good as new. I can see us cruising down the coast now. Sigh. Like I could afford to do that. I can't afford you in the condition you're in now. But I'll have Mickey salvage the tires. Those will fetch a nice price.*

Kita walked toward the front of the room and found the Indian motorcycle. It was white—or had been. Now, it was a dull cream color. The front fender was missing, the leather seat split, the headlight cracked, and all the chrome was dull and dirty.

"Damn, you're beautiful," said Kita. The curves of the motorcycle looked like a girl on all fours sticking her perfect butt out. The license plate read VLOSTI. She dragged her hand over the rear fender, seat, and gas tank. *Dad would have loved you.* Kita loved motorcycles, and she recognized a sexy piece of machinery when she saw it, but her true love was racing bikes.

*So, are you my missing vehicles or not? I guess I should check the VINs.* Kita tapped on her tablet and found the delivery manifest. Each vehicle had a Vehicle Identification Number on it somewhere.

Kita looked up on her tablet the location of each number. She started with the Indian. The plate was mounted left of the steering head. The number matched her manifest.

She opened the ambulance's driver's side door. The inside of the ambulance was in worse shape than the outside. The vinyl was cracked and dirty. The seats were torn. There was no carpeting, and rust had eaten through the floorboards. Kita found the VIN plate on the back of the door. It matched as well.

Kita opened the mustang's door and let out a sigh. *So much for that dream.* The interior was a mess. The seats were dry rotted, the floorboards rusted through, the carpeting had large holes, and the dash was cracked and missing foam. She located the VIN plate on the dash.

"The good news is," Kita announced to the vehicles, "you are my missing three. I wish I knew how you got here because now I have to get you out."

In the morning, she and Mickey would have to bring the flatbed over and use the towing cable to load the vehicles. After setting her tablet on the seat of the Indian, Kita went to the double bay doors. Each door was fifteen feet long and heavy. The doors were supposed to be chained shut, and it didn't help the track was fouled with gunk, but somebody had opened those doors to get the vehicles inside. There was a side door to the right of the bay doors. Kita went out it onto the loading dock. The dock wasn't very wide—maybe eight feet. The concrete access in front of the dock sloped down so the trailers' beds would be even with the dock. A ramp with a rusty handrail went up the right side toward the street.

Kita pulled out her phone and turned on the flashlight. She went to the center of the bay doors. On the ground were the lock and chain. She picked them up. *They didn't cut the lock or the chain, but the chain-link looks like it was pulled apart. What in the Crushing Depths does that?*

Kita stood up and looked around suspiciously. She suddenly felt like she was being watched. *Maybe I should get out of here and come back in the morning. Except, I need my tablet.*

She went back to the side door, pulled on the handle, and found it locked. Kita didn't have a key to the door. *Do I make the long walk around and back through the creepy plant, or do I muscle these doors open? As creepy as I feel, definitely muscling the doors.*

Kita returned to the center of the bay doors. She worked her fingers between them and pulled, while at the same time putting her foot on the opposite door and pushed. The doors didn't budge. Kita braced herself and tried harder. The doors suddenly gave eight inches causing Kita to lose her balance and fall.

*Of course, I can't do it without being a super klutz.*

She picked herself up and walked back to the Indian and her tablet. *Should I leave them here? What if something happens to them?* To be safe, Kita took some pictures of the vehicles and the loading area. *Just in case I have to explain this to the cops...or worse, my insurance.*

Satisfied she had done all she could, Kita went to the back of the loading area and turned off the lights. She walked by the vehicles to the bay doors.

A blue and red light flashed through the gap. *It's rare the cops would come out here.* The blue and red lights didn't leave but grew more intense.

"I didn't call the cops, I swear," Kita said to the vehicles. *Someone probably saw the light and reported it. Just what I want to do, explain to some cop what I'm doing in my building.*

Kita hurried out the side door. *Let's hope I don't get shot.* She waved her arms at the police cruiser. It crept closer and didn't turn off its lights. It came to a stop at the foot of the loading dock. Kita could see the officer, but he was looking straight ahead. *That's odd. The car is a mustang. I thought all cruisers were chargers.*

The cruiser's passenger side door opened. Kita didn't see anyone in the passenger seat. She moved across the dock to talk to whoever got out. She didn't find a person, and the driver hadn't moved, but there was a small boombox in the passenger's seat.

*Does the radio not work in the car?* The boombox turned to jelly, and long, spindly legs grew out the bottom. Arms grew out the sides. The speakers lifted and formed eyes, while the CD lid opened, showing rows of sharp teeth.

The boombox sprang from the car, jumped onto the loading dock, and charged Kita. She screamed and backed away, hitting the bay doors, causing her to drop her tablet. Kita scrambled through the double doors, trying to twist through as fast as possible. She fell into the loading area. Terrified, she crawled toward the motorcycle.

The boombox monster made an unintelligible noise as it squeezed through the bay doors. Kita reached the Indian as the boombox grabbed her foot, causing her to roll over.

"No! Get off!" Kita cried while kicking wildly.

Her head banged against the Indian as she flailed her foot. Kita fell on her back, staring at the darkened ceiling. In the flashing red and blue light, she saw a tall, slender humanoid silhouette. The silhouette raised an arm, and a flash of light blinded Kita. The boombox went flying across the room. The silhouette disappeared into the darkness.

Out of the darkness, a pair of arms lifted Kita and placed her on the Indian motorcycle. Kita grabbed the handlebars out of habit. Something yelled in an unintelligible language. At the bay doors, a large, broad humanoid shape shoved the doors apart.

The Indian's clutch went down under Kita's fingers, and the throttle twisted in her hand. Spooked, Kita removed her hands. The Indian's tires squealed as it shot forward much faster than Kita expected. She wrapped her arms around the gas tank. The motorcycle raced through the bay doors and launched over the cruiser. It landed in a shower of sparks on the concrete, sped up the loading dock access, and made a hard left onto the side street. The Indian didn't stop, making a fast right turn onto the highway.

*By the Crushing Depths! What is going on? What motorcycle drives itself? Is it remote-controlled by those things in the loading area? Autonomous? Did I get someone's experiment that has a serious bug? Or is it just simply possessed, and I need to wake up. I don't want anything to do with this…we're not going that fast.*

4

Kita released her death hug of the gas tank and sat up. The force of the wind nearly knocked her off the back of the motorcycle. *Tuck and roll. I've got this. I just have to roll off the side.* Kita threw herself off the motorcycle toward the road's shoulder, which looked to be a soft combination of dirt and weeds.

The motorcycle liquified. A pair of arms extended and caught Kita. They lifted her back onto the seat as the motorcycle reformed.

*Bloody moons! It* is *possessed.* Kita hung onto the tank. *What am I going to do?* A set of flashing lights came up behind her. Kita turned her head to see if it was the police cruiser. *Save me!* Instead, it was the ambulance. It had a driver, but he had the same blank look as the police officer.

The Indian hugged the shoulder as the ambulance raced past, crossing over the centerline. The Mustang roared up behind the Indian; its hippy driver had the same blank look like the others. Through the windows of the Mustang, Kita could see the red and blue flashing lights of the cruiser. The Indian throttled up and shot forward. The Mustang matched speeds, and the two vehicles caught up to the ambulance.

The Mojave Desert nightscape raced by. Kita looked up. The lights of Reading glowed brightly. The Indian crossed the railroad tracks that ran along the edge of the city. The bump caused Kita to fly out of her seat. She scrambled to hold on as the three-vehicle convoy entered a light industrial district.

Here the streets were narrow and full of potholes from all the heavy semi traffic. The ambulance made a hard right down a road lined with warehouses. As they passed another street, the mustang turned left. Two hundred yards back, Kita could see the cruiser. The Indian throttled down hard and took a right, swerving around a series of giant potholes. The street had several metal buildings with yards surrounded by chain-link fencing. The motorcycle turned down an alley between two buildings and pulled in between a pair of dumpsters.

The Indian expanded under Kita. The arms lifted her as the rest morphed into a slender and graceful eight-foot-tall robot. It set Kita down in a corner formed by a dumpster and fence, and then its left hand changed into a double-barreled cannon. Kita cowered in the corner. The robot lowered its head down close to Kita.

"Please, do not be scared," said the robot. "I am Velositi, and I will protect you."

*WHAT IN THE BLOODY MOONS IS A VELOSITI? PROTECT ME FROM WHAT? DID I DO something? I'm so confused.* Kita looked up at the sound of the sweet, reassuring voice with enough computer synthetization to sound alien. The face was angular with big blue eyes that glowed brightly. White diamond-shaped pieces created a mask that framed her curved face. Her white lips smiled at Kita.

"I—I—Don't eat me," whispered Kita.

Velositi laughed. "I am not going to eat you. I do need to eat, though."

"Are you out of gas?"

"Yuck. For me, that would be like you eating dirt. Just because I have a tank does not mean I use it. I need plasma. Therein lies the rub. There is no plasma on this planet."

*It knows Shakespeare?* Kita raised her hands. "Just so you know, I'm totally freaked out right now."

"I am sorry," said Velositi. "I do not mean to scare you, but I did not want you to be caught by Nitstik and Boom-Boom. They would do horrible things to you to find us."

"What are you?"

"I am a Morphicon. A Vehlix specifically. The other two who are with me, Sprokkit and Bernoot, are also Vehlixen. Nitstik and Boom-boom are Neophormes. The two sides have been at war for generations. We are on Earth searching for the Axiom of Command. It will anoint a great leader that will lead their side to victory."

Kita put her head on her knees. Tears fell from her eyes and landed on her jeans.

"Are you ok?" said Velositi. It sounded worried. "You are leaking—crying. Are you injured?"

Kita raised her head. "I want to go home," she whispered. "Why me? I don't have time for this. My yard is failing, and I can't lose it. It's all I have left of my dad. I don't have any money. I'm getting kicked out of my apartment. You don't want me for your war. I'm a failure. I just want to be left alone."

Velositi frowned. "I am sorry, but you cannot go back—at least, not yet. The Neophormes will be searching the area for us—and you. The only safe place for you is with us. I promise no harm will come to you."

Kita sniffed and rested her head against the fence, letting the wire press into her forehead. "That doesn't pay the bank."

Velositi touched Kita's cheek. Even though its hand was metal, it was warm to the touch. "I understand. But we do not make the opportunity for greatness, it finds us. Come with us. We will need your help, and in return, we will help you."

"How can you help me?"

"There is a Vehlix that looks like an armored car."

Kita's head jerked up. "What?"

Velositi chuckled. "I am kidding. But I am sure there are ways we can help."

Kita sighed. *Do I have a choice? If what it says is true, my life's in danger. How do I protect myself from eight-foot-tall robots armed with cannons that can hide as objects? I could be making toast and BAM the toaster becomes a robot and kills me. At least with Velositi, I have a chance. Some chance is better than no chance. But what good am I to them? The most I can do to one of them is take them apart with a wrench—if it'll stand still.*

*Velositi said greatness finds us. Is this my chance to be great? I could be killed, but I'm dead anyway if I walk away. Greatness or death, what a choice. Did other great people have the same kind of decision? What did Granddad say about his time in China during World War Two? 'I did what I had to because I didn't have a choice—do or die. At the time, the deeds were simple, only later were they considered great'. But that was Granddad—he was awesome—and this is me. Was he scared? I bet he never crawled into a corner and cried. Would he be ashamed of me? No. He'd tell me to dry my eyes, stand up, and face my fear—because there is only one way: forward. That sounds simple, but...*

Kita looked into Velositi's blue eyes. The warm glow was inviting and reassuring. She put her hand on Velositi's.

"Ok, I'll go with you. My name is Kita."

"Hello, Kita. I—"

Red and blue lights lit up the buildings lining the alley.

"Nitstik has found us," said Velositi.

"What do we do?"

"Stay here." Velositi crept to the edge of the dumpster and looked down the alley, raising its cannon.

The lights of the police cruiser came closer as it slowly made its way up the alley. When it was close, Velositi fired twice, then sprang from its position, somersaulted in the air, and landed on the other side of the alley firing twice more.

Kita, surprised at how agile and graceful Velositi was, had scooted out of her corner to see.

Velositi ran up along the side of the building, firing as she went. The cruiser, Nitstik, morphed into a ten-foot-tall broad-shouldered, heavyset robot, in stark contrast to Velositi's slender frame. Velositi landed behind Nitstik and shot it in the back, causing the larger Morphicon to pitch forward. Velositi performed a series of handsprings, landing on top of the chain-link fence. It ran along the top, firing. Velositi's shots left fist-sized holes in Nitstik's torso, scattering bits of hot metal slag across the alley. Jumping to the ground, Velositi knelt and fired a double shot into Nitstik's shoulder, spinning it around and knocking it to the ground.

Velositi morphed into the Indian and pulled up next to the dumpster Kita was leaning against.

"Get on," said Velositi.

Kita jumped onto the cracked seat and hugged the tank. Velositi's back tire squealed as it raced down the alley.

"You can grab the handles," said Velositi in an amused voice.

"Aren't you driving?" cried Kita. "I don't want to interfere."

Velositi laughed. "It is just for looks. I can turn it off."

Kita let go of the tank and took the handles. The desert night air hit Kita in the face. Finding the footpegs, she settled in.

Velositi exited the alley onto a street lined with semi-trailers. It made another series of turns, and a stoplight came into view. Velositi sped up, making a left turn and catching the light as it turned yellow.

"How do we get away from Nitstik?" Kita asked Velositi.

"Nitstik is a hunter-killer. It can detect our plasma emissions. The emissions do not last long. The easiest way is to outrun him and let the trail go cold."

"We can't go fast enough on the surface streets."

"It would be easier if we got on the freeway, but I do not know where that is."

"Stay on Mountain View Parkway until you reach Washington Boulevard. There is an on-ramp about half a mile."

"Will do," said Velositi as it sped through traffic, swerving between cars.

"You'll get us killed driving like this."

"I am perfectly capable of driving at high speeds."

"It's not you I'm worried about. It's the other drivers. They're not as skilled or have the reaction time you do."

"We will be caught if I do not."

"We're going to have to stop and get me a helmet," said Kita as strains of her blonde hair blew in her face.

"At these speeds, a helmet will not protect much."

"Thanks for making me feel better."

"You do not think I will not save you?"

"If we get hit, I think you'll be a little busy to save me."

"You will be surprised at what I can do."

"I saw you fight Nitstik. Your moves are awesome," said Kita.

"Thank you. I do not have as much firepower as the heavies, but I am more agile and limber."

"What's a heavy?"

"Morphicons are divided like humans, heavy and light—compared to your male and female."

"So, you have little Morphicons?" Kita said naïvely.

Velositi giggled. "No. We are constructed. Some of us have heavy frames, carry heavier firepower, while others have light frames, and are not as heavily armed. In our language, heavies would be masculine, and lights are feminine."

"So, you're a girl?"

"Equivalent, yes."

"Oh."

"Is there a problem?" said Velositi sounding concerned.

"No—turn here—I, ah, I wasn't expecting that. I don't assign a gender to machines."

Velositi made the turn onto Washington Boulevard. "Does that make something different between us?"

"No, the world of entertainment has not prepared me for the idea of girl robots."

"I am hardly a robot," Velositi said tersely. "Would you like it if I called you a zombie?"

"Oh, sorry. I didn't mean—I mean…you're not…like—"

Velositi laughed. "I am teasing you. Is this the on-ramp?"

"Yes," said Kita, her ears burning.

Velositi raced up the on-ramp and merged onto the freeway. Traffic was moving at the speed limit, which was rare for the 506. It was usually busy round the clock. Velositi merged into the far-left lane and sped past traffic. She wove her way forward in between cars and even passing on the shoulder.

"How do you know when we've outrun Nitstik?" said Kita.

"I do not. We usually keep going for hours."

"What about the others?"

"I have signaled Bernoot and Sprokkit. I was not sure which one of us Nitstik would follow. They are moving this direction and know we are on the freeway. Eventually, we will need to find a place to rally and plan our next move."

"What is your next move?"

"That's what we were discussing when you walked in. I thought I was clever having us transported by the delivery service to hide our movements. Nitstik must have been closer to us than we realized."

"We should take the five-oh-six to the coast. The docks should make a good hiding place."

"Sounds good to me. Do you know how to get there?"

"Ah, kind of. Hang on. Let me get my phone."

Kita pulled her phone from her back pocket. She turned it on, and it flashed a warning—ten percent of her battery was left. *Great. And my charger's in the opposite direction.*

"Velositi?"

"Yes?"

"My phone is nearly dead. I need to get a charger."

"I can charge it when we stop."

"You come with a USB-C plug? I'm pretty sure the USB plug wasn't even thought of when this model of Indian was built."

Velositi laughed. "You let looks deceive you. This bike is just a disguise. It does not dictate what I can and cannot do. I can charge your phone by induction."

"Oh, sorry. I don't mean to belittle you. You're amazing."

"You are cute when you are flustered. I know you do not know what I am capable of. Same that I do not know what you are capable of. I look forward to seeing what you can do."

Kita's face flushed red. She prided herself on her levelheadedness and situational awareness, but with Velositi, she was floundering like a fifteen-year-old boy on a first date. *Velositi's taken it all gracefully and been understanding. I don't want to offend her. Why am I worried? I shouldn't be. Am I falling for her? NO. Well...it has been a long time since anyone paid attention to me. I just don't want her to go away.* Kita huffed and slumped in the seat.

"Something wrong?" said Velositi.

"No. Yes. I just don't want to make a mistake."

"You mean coming with me?"

"No. That was the right choice. I don't want to die, but I don't want to upset you and have you leave."

"You have gotten yourself into a twist, have you not?"

"I'm sorry. I don't mean to dump on you."

Velositi didn't say anything. She changed lanes to the far-right lane, took an off-ramp, and turned onto a two-lane road. Coasting down the hill, Velositi came to a stop on the shoulder.

"What are we doing?" said Kita.

"Get off," Velositi ordered.

Kita dismounted. They were in the middle of nowhere, only a few lights in the distance and the sound of traffic from the freeway.

"Are we safe?" said Kita.

Velositi morphed and sat on the shoulder. "Sit." She patted the ground next to her.

Kita did as instructed. *I knew I'd screw this up. In record time, too.*

"When I rescued you, I knew I would be playing protector. I did not know I would be a psychologist as well."

"Sorry," Kita whispered.

"Everyone has issues. I do not like water or space. I have got scars from a bad relationship. That is why I took the mission to come here. It got me away from her."

Kita's ears perked up. "Her?"

"I prefer lights to heavies. With heavies, it is all about how big their cannons are. What is bothering you?"

"It's nothing."

Velositi cocked her head. "It is not *nothing* if it is bothering you. And I need your head right if this mission is going to be a success. So, talk to me."

Kita sighed. Tears blurred her eyes as fear tingled her toes. "I'm lonely," she blurted out. "Dad died three years ago on the first day of college. I came home, and I've been running the yard ever since. I live in the middle of nowhere—ultra-conservative America—and I don't dare tell anyone I'm a lesbian and look for a date. My business suffers now because I'm a girl—my parts must be crap because I've got boobs. It'll be even worse if they find out who I really am. I had no friends growing up, no dates. College was supposed to be my chance at a normal life. Instead, I'm stuck in a life going nowhere with no way out." Kita fell backward into the dirt, hitting her head on a rock. "And then you come along, and I'm too stupid and scared to take it."

Velositi twisted, so she was looking down at Kita. "But you are here. You did take it."

"I only chose it because I don't want to die. I should have been like '*slag, yeah!*' and jumped on without a second thought. And now that I am here, I'm afraid I'm going to screw it up, and you're going to leave me beside the road because I'm too much trouble."

"Self-preservation is a great motivator. May I ask you a question?"

"Sure."

"Why did you not sell the salvage yard and return to college when your father died?"

"I don't know. It didn't feel right selling the yard. It was his, and he put his heart and soul into it."

"But that is not where your heart and soul lie. Why keep a dead man's dream alive?"

Kita sighed. "It reminds me of him."

"No," said Velositi firmly. She tapped Kita's head. "He is alive in here and is with you always. You stayed at the yard because it was safe and familiar. In that emotional time of losing a loved one, you needed a place like that. Now, you have become stuck. It is time to move on and find your dream."

"I have no idea what I want."

"Then you explore until you find it. I will help you."

Kita turned her head, grinding the rock she was laying on into the back of her skull. *Ouch.* "Why help me?"

"Because you are helping me, and you are my friend."

Kita sat up. "You don't—"

Velositi held up a hand. "I do not want to hear anything self-deprecating. You will be a fine friend—once you get out of your own way. Do not think about it. As Bernoot says, 'Go with the flow.' Do not worry about offending me. I will tell you if you do, and I promise not to leave you beside the road. All I ask is that you listen and adjust accordingly. Fair?"

*She's serious. I'm a mess, and she's not walking out. She does want to be my friend. Do I deserve a friend who cares about me? She makes it sound so easy. Maybe it is that easy. I just have to do it. Fake it until you make it, right? I do deserve her. I do deserve her. I do deserve her.* Kita felt her spirits rise. She looked into Velositi's eyes. "Fair."

"Good. Let us go find your dream."

"What's your dream?"

Velositi smiled. "To win the war and lead the Vehlix to glory."

"Wow. Nothing small then?"

"You get only as big as you dream."

———————✕———————

KITA AND VELOSITI PASSED A MILEAGE SIGN ON THE SIDE OF THE FREEWAY.

"Ten miles to Newport," said Velositi. "Where are we going when we get there?"

"Let me see." Kita pulled out her phone and opened the maps app. "Ok, five-oh-six will T into the five. We go south to exit two sixty-two, and then turn right onto Vermont Street. That will take us into the port area. I don't know after that."

"We look for a place to hole up."

"I'm sure there are some abandoned buildings out there."

"Uh-oh," said Velositi. "I have got flashing lights behind me."

"Nitstik?" Kita said, a lump building in her throat.

"Light pattern does not match. I think it is a highway patrol."

"At this time of night? You think they'd have something better to do. Should we outrun them?"

"We can outrun him, but we cannot outrun his radio. We will just attract more." Velositi changed lanes and came to a stop on the shoulder.

The patrol car pulled in behind them. The patrolman got out of his car, put on his patrol hat, and walked over to Kita. He pulled out his flashlight and shined it in her face.

"Do you know why I pulled you over?" he asked, sounding annoyed.

"Ah...nope," said Kita.

"Where would you like me to start?"

"Ah, at the part where you let me go?"

"Get off the motorcycle."

Kita climbed off and stood before the taller officer.

"Let's start with no helmet."

"I left in a hurry and forgot it."

"Do you know how fast you were going? You hit something going that fast you're dead without a helmet."

"Obviously, I wasn't going fast enough." Kita couldn't see the officer's face because of the light, but she was sure he wasn't happy.

"Texting and driving—which I'm going to up to reckless driving because you didn't have a hand on the handlebars."

"Hey, that takes a lot of skill to do that. I should get applause, not a ticket."

"Ticket? You're going to jail. License and registration."

"Uhm, I have neither."

"Any ID?"

Kita shrugged her shoulders. "Uhm, nope."

"Turn around and put your hands behind your back."

"Wait! I can explain."

"You can tell it to the judge."

"It's a self-driving motorcycle. Totally autonomous."

"I said, turn around." The patrolman grabbed Kita by the arm and spun her. He smacked her across the back of the head with his flashlight hard enough that she saw stars. He exchanged his flashlight for a set of handcuffs, grabbed her wrist, and slapped them on. After cuffing the other wrist, he grabbed her upper arm and yanked her toward the patrol car.

"Let her go!" Velositi ordered.

The patrolman turned around. "What the hell?" he exclaimed.

Velositi fired both barrels of her cannon into the front of the patrol car, causing it to explode, knocking Kita and the patrolman to the ground. Kita rolled to her knees and stood up. The patrolman sat up, rubbing his face.

"See how you like it." Velositi smacked the patrolman in the back of the head, knocking him out. "Let me see the handcuffs," she said to Kita.

Kita did her best to raise her arms. Velositi grabbed the handcuff chain and snapped it.

"You will have to find the key to get the bracelets off," said Velositi.

Kita searched the patrolman's belt and found the key. After undoing the cuffs, she grabbed his radio. "Smash it. That should give us several hours head start."

Velositi brought her foot down on the radio. She morphed, and Kita hopped on. Together, they drove off into the night toward the coast.

KITA WAS UPSET OVER WHAT HAD HAPPENED WITH THE PATROLMAN AS THEY neared the coast. It was her first time in handcuffs. *I thought I'd be handcuffed someday, but not like that.* She'd hoped the humor would lighten her mood, but it just reminded her that she'd never had a girlfriend.

What bothered her were the repercussions. The patrolman was going to wake up and get help eventually. He'd seen Kita's face and Velositi—not that anyone would believe him. But there was the wrecked patrol car.

"Newport port area ahead," said Velositi.

"Huh? Oh, ok."

"Are you ok? You have been quiet."

"Just thinking. I'm uneasy about what happened with the cop."

"He hit you. I hit him back. Does that upset you?" Velositi asked, sounding concerned.

"No. I've never been in trouble before, and it might lead to bigger trouble later."

"We can talk about what to do after we find a safe place to shelter. Do not worry. I will not let anything happen to you."

Kita closed her eyes and sighed. She'd been told that once before. *And, Dad died. I want so hard to believe, but...*

Velositi took an off-ramp, then turned onto the main surface street that led to the port. A side street took them into the warehouse district. All the warehouses they passed had lights on and semi-trailers parked out front. They traveled around looking for something abandoned.

"How about that place? It has broken windows and soot trails from the windows to the roof," said Kita.

Velositi pulled into the lot and drove up the loading ramp to the door. Kita hopped off and tried the roller door. It wasn't locked and went up smoothly.

Kita and Velositi entered the warehouse. Blackened and burnt pallets of merchandise sat in neat rows. The warehouse walls showed signs of flame, and the concrete floor was blackened. A white residue covered everything.

"Definitely a fire," said Kita, looking up at the pipes and sprinkler heads. "Something must have gone wrong with the fire suppression system to let it burn so much."

"Or maybe it did not start small," said Velositi.

They idled through the debris to the back of the warehouse, Velositi's headlamp lighting the way. A large door blocked their path. Velositi morphed and opened it, revealing another section of the warehouse. It was bare, except for a shipping container in the middle and some one-story offices in the corner. The area showed no scars of the fire.

"They wanted just enough to burn, but not all of it," said Velositi.

"Probably insurance fraud, but they can't have gotten away with it if we figured it out," said Kita.

"We have a lower burden of proof to meet."

"Yeah, I guess so. I'm going to go check out the offices and see if there's anything worthwhile."

Kita crossed the cavernous space and tried the door to the offices. It was unlocked and led to a narrow hallway. She found the light switch and tried it.

The overhead fluorescent lights flickered on. The first office contained a desk that partially hid a chair and filing cabinet in the far corner. A window near the desk connected the office to the warehouse. The second door led to a bathroom. Kita tried the faucet and discovered the water was running. She checked the stall. The seat was gross, but there was toilet paper. *I guess I can hover pee.*

The last office was empty, except for some broken down cardboard boxes. Kita yawned. *Sigh. Right now, any kind of bed looks good.* She gathered up the cardboard. Velositi met her at the door.

"Anything we should worry about?" said Kita.

"No. What is the cardboard for?"

"To sleep on. I've been up for"—Kita checked her phone—"almost twenty-four hours. I need to sleep."

"Oh, yes. You do need sleep. The others are a few hours behind us, so we have some downtime."

"Do you sleep?"

"I can go into a low power mode for repairs, cognitive recalibration, and energy conservation. I have been in energy conservation mode for a long time, so I am well rested, so to speak."

"Oh, you can leave me here if you want to go explore."

"No. I will stay here with you and wait for the others."

"Ok." Kita spread her cardboard on the ground.

Velositi sat at the head of it. Kita wrinkled her nose. Velositi didn't leave her much space. Kita sat on the cardboard and curled up on her side.

"You can use me as a pillow," said Velositi as she patted her thigh.

Kita raised an eyebrow; not sure how comfortable a metal pillow would be. She shrugged and rested her head on Velositi's thigh. Surprisingly, it was warm and comfortable.

"Hey, you said you could charge my phone?" said Kita.

"If it has a battery, I can charge it."

Kita pulled her phone from her back pocket and handed it to Velositi. She turned it over in her hand. "I have never seen anything like it. It is much different than the phones I have seen."

"Standard Android cheapo phone."

Velositi placed the phone on her other thigh and then put her hand on Kita's shoulder and turned out the light.

———————✕———————

KITA AWOKE TO LIGHT ON HER FACE FROM A SET OF WINDOWS HIGH ON THE warehouse wall. She slid out from Velositi's arm. Her eyes were dim. Kita's phone was still on Velositi's leg. She picked it up and checked the battery. It was full, so she pocketed it. Bernoot and Sprokkit were parked not far away.

*I must have been out if I didn't hear them arrive.* Kita tiptoed around Velositi and hurried to the bathroom. After testing her leg muscles to use the toilet, Kita checked her hair in the mirror. The ride had left it wind-whipped. She took off her headband, ran her fingers through her hair, then pulled it back, and put the headband back on. *Improvement, yes. Looks good, no.* When she returned, the three Morphicons were awake and talking next to the shipping container.

Bernoot and Sprokkit stood in sharp contrast to Velositi. Sprokkit was twelve-feet-tall. Bernoot was shorter—only ten-feet-tall. Both had broad angular chests, narrow waists, and thick legs.

"Kita, how are you feeling?" said Velositi.

Kita's stomach growled loudly.

"Ah, hungry," she said with an embarrassed smile.

"As are we all," said Sprokkit in a gruff voice.

"I know you are, Sprokkit, but she does have to eat more often than we do," said Velositi.

"I usually only eat ramen once a day," Kita admitted.

Velositi frowned. "Humans are supposed to eat three times a day—and something more nutritious than dehydrated noodles."

*I didn't think she knew what ramen was.* "It's all I can afford."

"I will fix that."

Kita shrugged. It had been so long she'd forgotten what real food tasted like.

"We must take care of ourselves," said Sprokkit. "We are all low on plasma, and we have made no attempt to construct a converter."

"I plan to start finding pieces for it today."

"What do you need?" said Kita.

"Who are you, human?" demanded Sprokkit. "To stick your finger in our business?"

"I, ah—"

"Sprokkit!" snapped Velositi. "Kita, this is Sprokkit, my science and medical specialist. And this is Bernoot. He is a weapons specialist. Team, this is Kita. She has agreed to help us in return for our help."

"Is she a quantum engineer or a particle physicist?" said Sprokkit.

"No, but I can turn a wrench," said Kita softly.

"I need someone who understands the fundamentals of energy and matter. You are no good to us."

*I will not cry. I will not cry. I—Oh, slag.* Kita wiped at the tears forming in her eyes. She turned around and hurried over to her cardboard bed.

"Sprokkit, she has skills that will help us. I know she can help us gather the parts needed for the plasma converter. She knows the area and the people and can go where we cannot. You will have to build the plasma converter yourself."

"You are soft, Velositi."

"No. There is a reason I am the leader, and you are not. Not everything is a mathematical equation to be solved. Our problems require thinking outside the equations. Kita is one of the solutions. She is young, but give her a chance to prove herself. She is crying out for acceptance and approval and will be loyal if we give it to her."

"The human will slow us down."

"How can we be slowed down anymore? We spent forty Earth cycles in hibernation and have barely explored this planet."

"She will end up like Mike."

Velositi said something in an unintelligible language. "You let me worry about

Kita. You worry about what I tell you to. Figure out what you need to build the converter."

"I know what I need to build the converter."

"And what do you need?" said Kita. She sniffed and wiped her nose.

"Four GE five horsepower motors, two microwave ovens, three hand-held calculators, four telephones, an Atari Twenty-six Hundred, and an Apple Two desktop computer."

"Do you know what *century* it is?" scoffed Kita. She took her phone from her pocket. "This has a million times the computing power of all that stuff combined. Plus, the only place you're going to find that stuff is either a museum or some old lady's house."

"Last time it was in cans on the street."

"Yeah, good luck doing that. I'm not dumpster diving for you. You can go to the Crushing Depths for all I care. All of you! I'm going home." Kita stormed toward the interior door that led to the burned-out section of the warehouse.

Velositi looked at Sprokkit, and an eye dimmed. He frowned and took a step back. She pushed by him and caught up to Kita at the door.

"Kita," said Velositi gently.

"What? I'll find my own way home," Kita snarled.

"Kita, please, you are not going home. Ignore Sprokkit. He only sees value in something if he can attach a number to it. I want you to help us. We cannot do it without you."

"He doesn't have to treat me like I'm less than worthless. I've been doing it all by myself for years. He doesn't know me or what I can do. Just because I'm not a rocket scientist or a particle engineer doesn't mean I don't know stuff."

Velositi put her arm around Kita and hugged her tightly. Kita blew out a breath feeling some of the tension release.

"He can design what you need, right?" said Kita.

"I am sure he can. It might take some time for him to come up with alternative parts. It will take weeks of scrounging, but we will find what we need."

"Do you have that long?" Kita said worriedly.

"Plasma levels are low but not critical yet."

"You can use my phone if you want to speed up the search."

Velositi frowned. "Forgive me for sounding ignorant, but how?"

"You can search the internet."

"And what is that?"

Kita turned to look at Velositi. "You don't know about the internet?"

"We have only been active for a few weeks. My knowledge of this planet ended March thirtieth, Nineteen Eighty-One, when we entered hibernation."

"Well, the internet is a combination of everything humanity knows, gaming platform, communication medium, and porn. All available using this." Kita held up her phone. She turned it on.

"Who is that?" Velositi asked.

"Huh? Oh. My wallpaper. Just a pretty girl. Here." Kita tapped the internet icon, and her Google feed appeared. "See? News of the day."

"How is it done without wires? Sprokkit, come here and look at this," ordered Velositi.

Sprokkit stomped over. "Yes?"

"We have the whole of human knowledge at our fingertips. We just have to access it."

"Even for humans, there is not a library big enough."

"It is not stored in a library, but on this," Velositi pointed to Kita's phone.

"It's not technically on the phone," said Kita. "It's just the portal I use to access it. The phone connects to towers that connect to the internet. The internet is a bunch of connected computers storing all the stuff."

"I have detected an enormous increase in electromagnetic activity. May I see the device?" said Sprokkit.

"You break it, I'll break your face," said Kita as she offered it to him.

"She is very hostile."

"My life is on that phone."

"The phone does not look alive to me."

"Figure of speech," snarled Kita. "I mean, there's really important stuff on there that I can't afford to lose."

"Not to worry. I will scan the hardware and software without damaging it." Sprokkit held the phone in his hand. A wire snaked from a finger on his other hand and connected to the USB port. Light from another finger moved back and forth across the phone. Sprokkit grunted. "Not as primitive as I feared. We can emulate the hardware, and the software is crude. I have copied all applications and the operating system. Once I have connected to the internet, I will pass the specifications over to you, Velositi, and Bernoot. I still have not detected life on this phone."

"I don't mean it's alive. I mean, there are critical things on it like business records, phone numbers, text messages, pictures, and all my music. Things that are important to me and my life."

"I see a lot about automobile parts, transactions, and invoices. I do not see anything of what I would classify as personal."

Kita didn't know if she should be ashamed, mortified, or sad that she had such a little life, and what she had of one was consumed by the yard.

"It's all I have," Kita whispered. She walked away, sat against the shipping container, and put her head on her knees. It felt like her biggest secret was exposed, and no one cared. She expected a reaction of some kind, surprise or ridicule. No reaction stung worst of all.

Velositi placed a hand on Kita's shoulder. Kita looked up at her. "You were right. I'm trapped and have been for so long. I don't know what to do. This is worse than high school. At least there people cared enough to pick on me. Now, I'm worse than that."

"Oh, Kita, it is not that way at all. I respect what you have done. For Sprokkit, that was respect. It shows him you work hard and are dedicated. It was not meant to be an insult. You were dealt a harsh blow, and you handled it the best way you could. Life is about seizing opportunities. You took the opportunity to honor your father, and you came with me. Both of those things take courage, dedication, and resilience. You sell yourself short when you do not see the potential in you."

"I'm just being stupid, aren't I?"

"No. You have valid fears and concerns. You have been hiding from them, and now that you are out of your comfort zone, you must face them. It is a process you would have gone through at college."

Kita groaned. "This was destined to happen?"

Velositi smiled. "If you had stayed in the yard, you could have run from them your entire life. But do you really want to be that person?"

"No. I don't want to end up like the rest of the people in that town—clinging to god, guns, or my job to forge my identity."

"Harsh, but I do not know the people in your town. From what you have told me about the way they treated you, I understand why you are."

"Let them rot out in the desert. Well, not Mickey or Ralph, they're good guys, though they didn't know the truth about me."

Velositi touched Kita's hand. "But you shared the secret of your sexuality with me. Why? If you guard it so deeply."

"You were like me. I thought you'd understand."

"I do not understand why your sexuality is such a big deal."

"Because a book and some religions thousands of years old say what I am is bad and people believe it. Not all people are like that, but people who believe the same thing like to congregate. That's why I couldn't wait to go to college. People there are more open and understanding. Those that dislike me are a small minority."

Velositi put her arm around Kita and hugged her. "I am sorry you being a lesbian matters to so many when it is none of their business. I am proud you have accepted yourself. That is the first step to realizing your potential and your goals."

"I tried to be straight once and kiss a boy. I thought if I did, I would grow to like it. When my lips touched him, I freaked out and ran away. The thought of being touched by a guy weirds me out."

Velositi pulled her arm away slightly. "You do not mind me touching you, do you?"

"No. I like it. You're comforting and make me feel good."

"I am glad I can help you. Are you ready to go see if Sprokkit has any questions about your phone?"

Kita sighed. "Yeah."

Velositi helped Kita to her feet.

"You know what's odd?" said Kita.

"No. What?"

"This shipping container. It's the only one in here, and it has a shiny lock on it."

"Maybe it belongs to the building's owner."

"Maybe, but it seems out of place. This place might not be as abandoned as we think."

"We will be careful."

Kita and Velositi rejoined Sprokkit.

"I am finished with the girl's phone," said Sprokkit. He offered it to Kita. She took it and flipped through her screens to make sure her apps and files hadn't changed. Satisfied, she put it in her back pocket. "I have connected to the internet, and I am searching for parts now. I will send you schematics on how to transform your communicators to connect to their network."

"Ah, you're not using my account, are you?" said Kita. "Because I pay by the gig."

"No. I have detected corporate accounts and spoofed users on theirs."

"Yo, Velositi, there are voices outside," said Bernoot through Kita's phone.

Kita looked at Sprokkit. "I modified your phone so that it will work with our communications."

"Everyone morph," said Velositi. "Kita, hide in the office."

KITA SCRAMBLED INTO THE WAREHOUSE OFFICES, FRANTICALLY SEARCHING FOR a place to hide. She ducked her head into the bathroom. Standing on the toilet and closing the door occurred to her, but she was afraid she'd slip on the disgusting seat and fall in. Across the hall in the first office was a desk and a chair. *I bet I can climb under there.*

Pushing the chair out of the way, Kita climbed under the desk. *Oh, gross.* The previous owner had a habit of sticking their gum on the underside of the desk. *Oh, please don't get stuck in my hair.* Kita kept her head down and pulled the chair in front of her.

Through the office window, Kita heard voices.

"Like I said, I saw a girl on a motorcycle come in, and they haven't left," said a man with a thick eastern European accent. "This is the bike."

"What junk," said a man with the same accent but a deeper voice.

"Where did these other two hunks of junk come from?" said a third authoritative voice.

"I dunno. They didn't come in the front," said the first man.

"Really, genius?" snarled the third man. "I bet they came in the cargo bay doors on the side of the building, but who unlocked them?"

"Probably the girl," said the second man.

"And what about the drivers of these two scrap heaps? They didn't drive themselves in here," said the third man. Kita giggled to herself. "Spread out and find them. I want to know who's squatting in my building."

Kita sucked in a breath and held it. *Think silent. Be silent.* The door to the offices banged open. Footsteps stopped outside her office door. *I should have locked the stupid door.* The door slammed open.

"Anyone in here? Come out, now," said an Eastern European accented voice Kita hadn't heard.

*Great, there's more than three.*

"Check behind the desk," said another voice.

*No. Crap.* Kita pushed herself as far under the desk as she could get.

The chair was flung aside, and a head appeared. Instinctually Kita kicked it. The head recoiled.

"Over here."

A set of arms reached for her. She flailed her legs, trying to kick the hands away. A third hand grabbed her leg and pulled. Kita grabbed a leg of the desk. The man pulled her and the desk toward him.

"Let go, bitch."

A swift kick in the kidney caused Kita to spasm and let go. Another kick hit her gut. She curled up in a ball as they dragged her into the center of the room. A man grabbed her by the back of her shirt and pulled Kita to her feet.

"Hey, watch the shirt," said Kita. *This is my favorite My Little Pony shirt.*

"Shut up!" a man snarled and slapped Kita.

The two men wearing almost identical ill-fitting suits grabbed her by the arms and pulled her out of the office area to a man standing next to the shipping container.

"That's her," said a man wearing a skullcap and black turtleneck.

"Where are your friends?" said the man with an authoritative voice. He was dressed in khakis and a white polo shirt.

"Listen, I don't want any trouble," said Kita. "I was just looking for a place to crash for the night. I haven't touched anything. You want me gone, no problem. You'll never see me again."

"You picked the wrong warehouse, bitch. Where are your friends?"

"I'm by myself."

The man punched Kita in the stomach. "Where are they?"

Kita coughed as she doubled over. The two men on either side of her forced her to stand up.

"There's no one here but me."

"Then what are these two pieces of junk doing in my warehouse?"

*Oh, girl. Think fast.* "I—I was going to strip them down and sell them for parts."

"Who would buy this junk?" demanded the man.

"Collectors, dealers, restorers. It's hard to find parts for seventies vehicles."

"You picked the wrong warehouse to set up shop, sweetheart." The man pulled a gun from behind him. He whistled loudly, and five more men trotted over from around the warehouse.

"Oh, come on," said Kita. "I'll give you a cut—ten percent. I just need a few days. I already have contacts."

"Do I look like I need to run a cheap chop shop?"

"Come on. Everyone can use some extra cash. You don't have to do anything. I'll do all the labor and legwork."

"And leave a mess in my warehouse. No, thanks." He raised his gun.

"Give me a broom. I'll clean up. It'll look better than when I got here. It's a win-win for you."

"You want to help me? My boys have been working overtime on this latest shipment. And now, they have to get this junk out of here. I owe them. And I'm going to give them you."

"ME! Trust me, I'm no good. Inexperienced." *Understatement of my life.*

"By the time they're done with you, you'll have all the experience you need. Feel free to knock her teeth down her throat. I don't want to see her again. When you're finished, get this junk out of here."

*By the Crushing Depths, no!* Kita threw herself into the man next to her, knocking him over. She spun and kicked the other man in the crotch. Someone grabbed her from behind. Kita kicked her legs up into the air and drove her heel into his groin. She dropped to the floor and landed on her stomach.

"Velositi!" Kita screamed as another man grabbed her leg. She rolled on her side and kicked at his hand.

Velositi morphed and leaped into the air. She fired at two men, her cannon blasts ripping through their chests. She landed next to the man who had Kita. Velositi grabbed him by the head and slammed it into the concrete floor.

The leader and his surviving men ran out of the warehouse. Velositi ran to the warehouse divider door. She returned to Kita shaking her head. "Sorry, Kita. They got away. Are you ok?"

Kita threw her arms around Velositi and hugged her tight. *I will not cry. I will not cry. Nothing happened. It's just adrenaline. I just need to let it clear my system.*

Velositi put her arms around Kita. After a few deep breaths, Kita didn't feel so on edge. She snuggled against Velositi's black metal midsection. It was layered like armor and was warm.

Kita let out a long sigh of relief and contentment. She looked up at Velositi, who comically craned her neck down so she could look at Kita as her blue eyes glowed brightly.

"I'll be ok. I just have to let the moment pass and regain my equilibrium. I'm sorry. I don't mean to hug you to death."

Velositi chuckled and stroked Kita's back. "I do not think you could crush me. I am glad you feel comfortable enough with me to find solace."

"I'm not too much, am I?" Kita said worriedly.

"Of course not. I am impressed with how you handled the situation. I do not think I would handle being offered as unwilling gratification so well, especially in the presence of so many."

"In my head, I wasn't so calm, but I also knew I had you. I just wish I could have talked my way out of it."

"You offered what you could. I am surprised you did not offer us."

Kita gasped. "Why would I do that? I wouldn't sacrifice you. I'd sacrifice myself first."

Velositi's eyes dimmed.

"Velositi? Are you ok? Did I say something wrong?"

Velositi's eyes brightened. "No," she whispered. "I...It has been a long time since anyone has shown me that level of commitment."

"I think you're great." Kita hugged Velositi.

"I think you are wonderful, too."

Sprokkit and Bernoot rolled over.

"We should be leaving," said Sprokkit.

Kita lifted her head. "In a minute. I want to know what's in this shipping container."

"Sprokkit and Bernoot, watch the entrances," said Velositi. "If the humans come back, we will retreat out the other exit."

As Sprokkit and Bernoot went to the warehouse entrance doors, Kita let go of Velositi and led her to the shipping container.

"Can you smash that?" said Kita, pointing to the bright, shiny lock on the door.

"No problem." Velositi grabbed the lock and pulled it apart.

Kita flipped the lock latch, twisted the handle, and pulled open the door. Inside were stacks of wooden boxes. There was a two-foot gap along the adjacent wall that led to the back.

"What is in the boxes?" said Velositi.

"I dunno, but it must be important. Grab one, and let's find out."

Velositi took down a box from the stack and set it on the concrete floor. Kita tried to open it and pulled at the wooden lid.

"I, ah, don't want to break a nail. Can you?"

Velositi chirped laughter as she dug her metallic fingers in between the lid and box. She pulled the lid and nails out with ease.

Kita pushed aside the paper strip packing material. "Whoa," said Kita as she pulled an AK-74 out. "No wonder he wasn't interested in parts."

"It is a weapon of some kind?" said Velositi.

"Russian AK-74 assault rifle. A very popular firearm sold around the world. If there's fighting going on somewhere in the world, you can bet these are involved." *According to the movies.* Kita checked the receiver and found a spot that looked like someone had ground something away. "Serial numbers are missing. Definitely a gun runner."

"A what?"

"Unlike you, humans don't come equipped with cannons. We make them, and they get sold around the world. A gun runner is someone who does it illegally."

"Why?"

"Money is the main reason for small guys like this. You'd have to ask the Imperial government why they do it. They're the biggest gun runners in the world, and they don't like competition. Let me have a look at what's in the back." Kita shuffled down the narrow gap. "Found some smaller boxes. Says Czechoslovakia five-point-four-five-millimeter rounds. So, buy the guns, get the ammo. I bet that's the real money maker, selling them ammunition." Kita moved to the back. A briefcase sat on a folding desk. Kita grabbed the briefcase and returned to Velositi. "I wonder what's in here? It's heavy."

Velositi smashed the lock, and Kita hit the latches, causing the briefcase lid to open.

"Damn, that's a lot of money," said Kita. "And passports."

She flipped through the passports from countries around the world. They all had the same picture, but different names and information. The currency was from around the world, too. Kita picked up a stack of Imperial dollars.

"There must be ten thousand dollars in this one stack, and there are five of them."

"Could it be useful?" said Velositi.

"Ah, yeah, but it's not mine."

"Why not take it? He is a criminal, and he did threaten you."

Kita shrugged. *I could do a lot with this, and having some cash could help us. Plus, I can get something to eat.* "I just don't have a place to put it."

A compartment on the side of Velositi's chest opened. "Put it in here."

"Ah." Kita turned red.

"Something wrong?"

"I, ah, just feel like you invited me to play with your boob."

Velositi laughed. "Hmmm, well, mine are form, not function. They create extra space for functionality and armor. They are not expected to feed a tiny Morphicon."

Kita giggled. "I'll never be using them for that, but they're good for other things, or so I've been told."

"Like what?"

"An erogenous zone."

"Oh... OH! Sorry, I looked it up on the internet. That makes much more sense for design. I wondered why you would make something so permanent when you are only going to use it for a few years of your life."

"Yeah, otherwise, what's the point of carrying them around?" *Like someday I hope to get some fun out of them.*

"I can put the money in... if you want," said Velositi.

"No, I'll do it. I'm a big girl." Kita pulled off a few bills and stuck the rest in Velositi's compartment.

Velositi moaned softly.

"What?" said Kita as she jerked her hand back and fell on her butt.

"Sorry," said Velositi as she closed the compartment. "It was too good to pass up."

"How did you know how to do that?"

Velositi smiled. "I scanned all two hundred and five thousand results for erogenous zones. Some are quite visual, and that is the sound many female humans make during stimulation and sex."

"I wouldn't know," said Kita dourly.

Velositi put her hand on Kita's shoulder and said in a serious tone, "Like I know. All I know is what I saw. There is no judgment, only humor. I'm just as lost about how humans have sex as you would be about Morphicon interactions."

*Dammit. I've gone and made something that was supposed to be funny and light into something awkward and serious and shows how selfish I am. It's not all about me. Velositi's done a good job of caring for me, and she hasn't had to. I screwed it up again.*

"I'm sorry," whispered Kita as she looked at the ground and frowned. She sat down hard against the shipping container.

"Kita! Do not act like I hit you. I was telling you the truth. I want you to understand that what we do not know about each other goes both ways. We both have a lot to learn. I have a bit of a head start because of the time I spent with Mike, but he was male and spent most of his time with Sprokkit. I know you are insecure about certain parts of your life, and that is natural. I just hope that you trust me enough not to get defensive about them with me. I want to support you, not tear you down. Understand?"

Kita grabbed her head and leaned forward touching her forehead to the floor. *Why does she stick with me? Why doesn't she hate me?*

"I did not know you were that flexible, Kita," said Velositi.

Kita sat up. "Why don't you hate me? I'm absolutely miserable."

Velositi chuckled. "Sprokkit is miserable to be around. You just need time to find your way. You are young. I was young once. I understand what it is like. I do not find you miserable, just charming and amusing."

"Glad I can amuse you," Kita grumped.

"Your antics are quite over the top and fun to watch. It is interesting to see where your mind goes. Nowhere I would have predicted. Just know I will never hate you—no matter what you do."

"I think you're a glutton for punishment."

"Who are you punishing? Certainly not me. If anyone is a glutton, it is you. You do it repeatedly to yourself. And, for what? You know I am not going anywhere. I will not get mad. I know you have confidence. I have seen it. We have money. I can get you laid if you want?"

Kita sputtered, then laughed. "No. I don't want that to be my first time."

"Then what do you want to be your first time?"

"When I was in high school, I had an entire fantasy that involved hot tubs, candles, and a big soft bed. Now, I'd settle for my bed with someone who cares about me. Even the last part I'm beginning to think is optional."

"I care for you," said Velositi. "And I know others will, too."

Kita sighed. "Yeah. Someday."

Velositi stood up and helped Kita to her feet.

"So, what do we do with all these weapons?" said Velositi.

"I'm not letting that asshat have them," said Kita. "Can you blow them up?"

"None of us have that capability, at least not internally. We would have to find explosives."

"Guess I could phone it in to the police, but we don't want to be anywhere near this place when they arrive."

"Why not?"

"Word about the highway patrolman has to have gotten out. They might have left the part about you out, but not me and not the motorcycle. We need to be careful driving around town. That Indian is noticeable. Maybe we can fit you in the back of Sprokkit."

Velositi frowned. "*Or*, we can just change our disguise."

"You can do that? Right. Yes, of course you can."

Velositi chuckled. "What do you want?"

"I get to choose?"

"You are the one who will be riding around on me. Why not?"

"Anything?"

"Anything my frame will fit. So, smaller things. Motorcycles work best. Do you have anything in mind?"

*Yes, but...*

"Ah, yes, but it's your body. You should get to pick."

Velositi put her hands on her hips. "Kita..."

"I know, but what I want is like the complete opposite of you."

"How do you know?"

"You chose that classic Indian look. Deep curves with classic cruiser styling... it looks great, I love it, but it's not what I'm into, and I don't want you not to be you. You can choose another Indian style, or there's Harley-Davidson or BMW. All of them make great cruiser motorcycles."

Velositi bent down at the waist to be eye level with Kita. "For your information, I did not pick that model, Mike did. It's what he wanted. Anything you pick will be much more my style."

"But I don't want it to be my style. I want it to be your style."

"I am flattered, but nothing on this planet is my style. I want you to be happy and comfortable. So, spit out what you want."

Kita bit her lip. "A Kawasaki Ninja H2R."

Velositi's eyes dimmed.

Kita frowned. *I knew she wouldn't like it. I should have gone with a Harley.*

Velositi smiled as her eyes lit. "There is one at a dealership down in Big Surf. Nice choice. I will look good as it."

"Are you sure? We can get a Harley."

"Are you saying you would rather me be a pig than a rocket?"

"No! I just want to make you happy. Not just me."

"Are you not sweet?" Velositi chuckled. "I will be sleek and sexy as this Ninja. That is what I want. Is not that what you want me to be?"

"Yeah. It looks awesome, and it goes fast too."

Velositi laughed. "Wait until you see what I can do as it. I will take supercharged to the next level. But, one question for you."

Kita looked sideways. "Ok."

"Will I still be beautiful?"

"Of course. I mean, you were beautiful when I first saw you, but now that I know you, you're gorgeous."

"Flattery will get you somewhere." Velositi winked.

Kita's face flushed.

"Let me get Bernoot and Sprokkit back in here, and we can travel down the coast."

Kita nodded.

Bernoot and Sprokkit rolled up and morphed.

"After two run-ins with the natives, we need new disguises," Velositi told them. "Kita and I have found a new one for me. You two need to find your own. Bernoot, once you find one, your mission will be to find us a new safe house. Sprokkit, continue updating your plasma converter schematics. Once you have a parts list, pass it to me, and Kita and I will work on acquiring what we can. If the parts are big, we might have to meet you so you can transport them."

"Rules of engagement?" said Bernoot.

"Evade as best you can. You're not known to the police, so you should not have any trouble with them, and we will be gone if our gun runner friends return."

"And Nitstik?"

"If he finds any of us, try to outrun him. I know traffic out there is bad, so if you cannot, contact the rest of us, and we will ambush him."

"We are supposed to blend in, not make a scene," said Sprokkit.

"We will do what is necessary to find the Axiom of Command," said Velositi. "We will do it as stealthily as possible, but if it means making a scene to find it, then we will do it."

"What happened with the police?" demanded Sprokkit.

"I will brief you later. They are looking for Kita and me, not you. Now, let us go. Kita, can you call in this weapons cache?"

"Sure."

"Good. Then we will leave."

Kita pulled out her phone, looked up the address on the map, and then dialed 911. "Hello, operator?"

"What's your emergency?"

"I'm at 1533 Barrot street, and I found a shipping container full of weapons."

"Do you know who they belong to? Any markings?"

"No. The serial numbers are filed off, and I found a briefcase full of money and passports."

"Ok. Officers are en route to that location. You can meet them out front."

"Sorry I can't stay. I know how long it takes for you to respond. I ran into some thugs earlier, and I'm not waiting around for them to come back."

"Wait—"

Kita hung up the phone. "All set."

Velositi morphed, Kita hopped on, and they exited the building headed for the coastal highway.

VELOSITI PULLED TO A STOP AS THE LIGHT TURNED RED. THROUGH THE towering buildings ahead was a thin strip of blue ocean. Apartment buildings with palm trees sticking up out of the sidewalk lined the streets. A warm, soft breeze blew through Kita's hair. She purred at the feeling.

The revving of a bike engine caught Kita's attention. In the side mirror, a bike slowly drove up the center lane, then parked beside her. The guy rode an awesome neon green Kawasaki Ninja 300. He wore shorts, a tank top, and flip-flops. There was an extra helmet with wings painted on the side strapped to the passenger's seat. *Bet he's going down to the boardwalk to pick up chicks. At least he's wearing a helmet. Of course, what good's a pretty face when you have no skin? Maybe he can get a head tank like in Futurama.*

The guy lifted his visor. "Nice bike. A work in progress?"

"It's got it where it counts," said Kita coyly.

"Think you can beat me?"

"I dunno. Race me and find out."

"Cool, but if I win, I get a kiss."

Kita raised an eyebrow. *Does that pickup line work? One kiss and the girls fall to their knees, ha, ha, ha. Put him on his knees. I've got some floors that need scrubbing.* "Ok, you're on. But, if I win, I get that helmet."

"Deal." He revved his high-pitched engine loudly. "The first one to the second light wins."

Kita grinned and turned Velositi's throttle. Her engine was deeper and roared.

"Do you think it is wise racing this fool?" said Velositi.

"You don't think you can beat him?"

"That was not the question. I asked if it was wise."

"We do it, and we get a free helmet. That'll keep my face hidden and keep us from getting pulled over."

The light turned green, and the other bike took off. Velositi took off slowly.

"I thought you said you could beat him!" yelled Kita.

"I can. I am building the suspense."

Kita wasn't sure how much suspense she wanted. It was only an eighth of a mile to the second light. Fifteen seconds at best. Traffic was clear for the first block, but the second light hadn't changed, and cars were lined up waiting to go.

When the other bike passed the first intersection, Velositi kicked it into gear. Kita was thrown back as she gripped the handlebars tightly. It was like riding a rocket. *I can't wait until she's the H2R.*

Halfway down the second block, Velositi caught the other bike. The light still hadn't changed as they approached the waiting cars. The guy looked over at Kita, gave her the thumbs-up, and opened his throttle as he swerved left to dodge traffic. Velositi jerked to the right, her motor roaring as they raced between traffic and the parallel-parked cars.

Kita watched the other bike between cars. "Come on, Velositi! Wahoo!"

Velositi accelerated forward with a roar of her engine. Kita twisted around and blew the guy a kiss. The light turned green as Kita passed the finish line. Velositi swerved to miss a late car and throttled down as the other bike caught up. Kita motioned for him to follow so she could collect her prize.

They turned left onto Beach Front Road, part of Highway 102 that ran the length of the coast, then pulled into a parking lot. Velositi pulled into a spot that had a NO PARKING sign. The guy pulled in next to Kita and pulled off his helmet.

"Damn. I thought I had you beat, then zoom. What do you have in that thing?" he asked, sticking out his hand. "The name's Ryan, by the way."

Kita took his hand and was surprised when Ryan kissed it. "K-Kita." She gulped. "It's all custom work. A friend of mine does it. We've got the engine, and we're going to see about the body today."

"Sweet ride, especially for a chick. I guess this is yours." Ryan turned around and unfastened the spare helmet. He handed it to Kita. "It's got Bluetooth, so you can connect your phone or talk to me."

"Awesome," Kita squealed.

Ryan smiled at Kita. "I guess you're going to have to add Bluetooth to your bike now."

"When we're done, she's going to be amazing. I just got pulled over for not having a helmet last night. So, thanks, you solved a problem."

Ryan laughed. "Glad I could be of service. I, ah, don't suppose I could get that kiss? I did give you a helmet."

Kita winked at him. "Sorry, I only kiss girls."

Ryan clapped his hands. "Of course, the chick with the awesome bike is into girls. When your bike is done, you're going to be some serious competition out here. We'll have to cruise together."

Kita's heart soared. She wanted to jump up and down, scream, and cry all at the same time. *He likes me for who I am. Not only does he not care that I'm a lesbian, he totally wants to be my friend.* "I'm headed to Big Surf if you're going that direction."

"Hey, I'm game for anything. There's a bike shop down that way. I need to get another helmet."

"You really want to go?"

"Of course. Do you want help with your helmet? It's already paired with my bike. You just need to pair your phone."

Kita pulled out her phone and opened the Bluetooth app. "Lots of devices around here," said Kita as she scrolled through the list.

"My helmet is *Ryan's Helmet*, and yours is *Girl Helmet*."

"I'll have to change that." Kita paired the device and changed the name to KITA'S HELMET.

Kita put the helmet on. "Can you hear me?"

Ryan stuck his ear in his helmet. "Yeah, I got you. Can you hear me?"

"Yep. Sweet. Thanks."

"You beat me fair and square. Ready to head down the coast?"

"Slag, yeah. Let's go." Kita hopped on Velositi and backed out.

Together they exited the parking lot and turned onto the highway.

Even though the highway was two lanes, traffic moved slowly. Kita didn't mind. It was a warm, sunny day—perfect bikini weather, and the girls were out in force. Ryan waved to the girls as they went by.

"You should wave to the girls. Let them know you're interested," said Ryan.

"Ah, I'm not dressed for the beach. I left work last night and drove straight here."

"Plenty of bikini shops. You should buy one and paint your bike to match."

*He thinks I should be in a bikini. Ha. I've never worn a bikini in my life.* "When I get the motorcycle fixed, then I'll worry about it. Plus, I'd take my helmet off, and my hair would scare them away."

Ryan laughed. "I thought your hair looked good."

"That's because you're a boy. It hasn't seen a brush in days. If it weren't for my hairband, I'd have a rat's nest."

The beach gave way to the rocky shoreline. Sea lions barked from the rocks. The highway opened up, and traffic picked up speed. A sign said BIG SURF 13.

"How is it going?" said Velositi through Kita's helmet.

"How did you connect?"

"It was easy to crack. I can talk to you or both of you if you want."

"That might be a little weird."

"We will see. I can just be your strange friend on the phone. You are doing good. I am proud of you."

"You think so? I mean, I'm doing my best not to screw this up. I remember what you told me about confidence."

"Soon, your confidence will be so high you will be riding around with just a bikini on."

Kita's face flushed. "I don't know about that," she whispered.

"You would look good in a bikini. The only one you have to impress is you... and me. I am not letting you ride around on me wearing something ugly."

Kita chuckled. "I'm not very fashionable right now."

"That is because I'm not very fashionable, and I picked you up in the middle of the night. It was dark. I did not see what you were wearing. I am ticking down the minutes until I can get you dressed properly."

"What? This is my favorite shirt."

"It has a cartoon on it."

"It's Princess Luna, and she's awesome. She's the princess of the night and ruler of the dream realm. She's—"

"Ok, ok. Forget I said anything. I am sure we can work around it. We will get you some bellbottoms and—"

"What? No way. Bellbottoms went out of style before I was born. Nobody wears those."

"Then, I will have to do some research."

"Why?"

"I am your accessory, and you are my accessory. You picked what I am wearing. I get to pick what you are wearing—or at least have a say."

"But you said it was ok," Kita whined.

"Yes, and you will have final say over what clothes you wear. If you get on me wearing them is another story."

"You're teasing me, right?"

"We will find you something. I am already bookmarking ideas. What do you know about makeup and hair?"

"Oh, come on!"

Velositi giggled. "I am going to turn you from beautiful to gorgeous. Ryan will be too busy looking at you. He will not see any other girls."

"I don't want him looking at me!"

"If he is too busy looking at you, he is not paying any attention to the other girls in the room. You have already gotten rid of your competition without having to do anything other than looking good."

"How do you know all this?"

"On my planet, I am referred to as an *optic turner*. I like to enter a room and have everyone know I am there."

"I'm a girl that likes to hide in the back away from everyone."

"I know. We have a lot to learn from each other," said Velositi.

Kita grumbled.

"It will be fun. I promise. I—Uh, oh."

"What's wrong?"

"There is a pair of white SUVs coming up the road, swerving in and out of traffic."

Kita looked over her shoulder. "There are no lights, so not cops. A government agency, maybe."

"They do not have government tags," said Velositi.

*How can she see that this far away? Another of her awesome skills. Ugh, I hope she doesn't want me in a dress.* "Should we outrun them?"

"I am afraid if we leave, Ryan will not be able to keep up, and they will go after him," said Velositi.

"It might not have to do with us."

"The probability of that is low."

"Then let's switch positions with Ryan. We can at least be between them and him."

"I will drop back a bit, too."

"Ryan!" Kita called.

"Hey, you went quiet. I thought I might have said something."

"No. I was talking to a friend. Some SUVs are coming up behind us. Switch positions with me and stay ahead of me."

"It's not a problem. I've dealt with aggressive drivers before. Thanks for the heads up. I'll watch my tail."

Kita glanced over her shoulder. The SUVs were only two cars behind them and moving up in the left lane.

"Kita, the man in the passenger's seat is one of the men from this morning," said Velositi.

"How the slag did they find us?"

"I do not know. They are pushing hard to catch us."

Kita's stomach knotted. The road ahead was full of traffic. Ryan had some skill as a driver, but Kita doubted he could keep up with Velositi.

"They just passed the last car. What—Gun! Ryan! Kita! Get down," cried Velositi.

"Huh?" said Ryan.

Kita pressed herself against Velositi's gas tank. She heard the sounds of muffled gunshots. "Ryan! Just do it. They're shooting at us!"

The first SUV pulled up behind them as men leaned out the windows and fired. Velositi stopped hard, but the SUV didn't swerve. Instead, its bumper hit Velositi's rear fender. The second SUV pulled alongside the two motorcycles. The SUV's windows rolled down, revealing two men with assault rifles.

"Ryan, get out of here. We'll deal with them," said Kita. *At least, I hope we can.*

Ryan throttled his bike and pulled forward. The second SUV swerved, colliding with him. His motorcycle wobbled back and forth. Velositi raced forward coming up behind Ryan just as his motorcycle lost control. She morphed, tossing Kita into the air. Somersaulting, Velositi plucked Ryan from his bike as it tipped over. The first SUV hit Ryan's motorcycle and ran over it. Velositi's free arm morphed into her cannons, and she fired two rounds into the first SUV's engine. It exploded, blowing the hood off. The SUV fishtailed off the side of the road and flipped over on a dune.

Velositi's cannon morphed into a hand and caught Kita. As Velositi morphed back into the Indian, she put Ryan behind Kita on the fender.

"Keep your heads down," said Velositi as she accelerated between two vehicles.

"What the hell just happened?" said Ryan. He sounded more excited than scared.

"Hi, I am Velositi—Kita's friend." Velositi zigzagged through traffic, then pulled onto the shoulder, passing cars on the eighteen inches of asphalt. Across traffic, the remaining SUV struggled to keep up driving on the paved median between a concrete divider and traffic.

"Is she on the phone?" said Ryan.

"No. She's the motorcycle," said Kita.

"Velositi is the name of your motorcycle? Did you, like, build Alexa into it?"

"Velositi is way better than Alexa."

"I hope so," said Velositi. "I am the leader of a group tasked with finding the Axiom of Command on Earth. We are called Morphicons. We are beings that can change form and disguise ourselves as objects. My disguise is this nineteen seventy-four Indian motorcycle. Kita and I are on our way to get me a new disguise."

"So, I'm talking to the motorcycle?" said Ryan.

"*She* is a race from another planet," said Kita pointedly. "The motorcycle part his how she hides. When she morphs, she has a human-like body and is eight feet tall."

The SUV swerved across the highway into the right lane and came up behind Velositi. Gunmen leaned out the windows and fired.

"Hold tight," said Velositi.

"You're not going to throw me in the air again, are you?" said Kita.

"I caught you, did I not?" Velositi crossed the right lane and accelerated down the centerline between a semi and some cars. "Duck!"

Kita and Ryan flattened themselves as Velositi slid under the semi-trailer onto the paved median. A police car with its lights and siren on went by in the opposite direction.

"We need to get out of here," said Kita, "before we have both cops and crooks after us."

"What's wrong with the police?" said Ryan.

"Besides the fact that Velositi isn't human, and they would take her to a lab and do the Crushing Depths knows what to her? I got more than pulled over last night. We kind of blew up a highway patrol car."

"Oh, man. You play for keeps, don't you?"

Kita shrugged. "He did hit me."

"I have video," said Velositi.

Behind them, the SUV pulled onto the shoulder, and the gunmen fired.

"Velositi, there's some tire pieces ahead," said Kita.

"I see. Hang on." Velositi hopped in the air, and her rear wheel landed on the tire debris, firing it into the windshield of the SUV, causing it to bounce off the concrete divider, swerve, and hit the semi wedging under the trailer. The semi slammed on the brakes. Velositi moved back onto the highway.

"That was awesome," said Kita.

"I hope they're ok," said Ryan.

"They were shooting at us!"

"I always feel bad when people get into a car wreck."

"I don't. That's how I make—made my money."

"What do you do now?" said Ryan.

"I don't know. Whatever Velositi and I can come up with. Velositi and I robbed a gunrunner this morning. That's who was shooting at us."

"What about my bike? It's going to be totaled."

"You are lucky to get away with your life," said Velositi. "Your bike is the least of your worries. You can call your insurance when we get to the safe house."

"I'll probably get a ticket for fleeing the scene of an accident."

"You were being shot at," said Kita. "I think they will understand."

"I was sure I was going to kiss the pavement. How did you get me?"

"Velositi is awesome. She threw me, morphed, got you, fired her cannon, caught me, and morphed back."

"I told you I could do things," said Velositi.

"Hey, I believed you. I'm making a believer out of him."

An ambulance and police cars went by in the other direction, lights and sirens blaring.

"They're going to need a can opener to get those guys out," said Kita.

"Big Surf is coming up," said Velositi.

"New bike, here we come."

"Maybe we should get you cleaned up first."

"Nah, I'm good."

"Fine. Have it your way."

VELOSITI IDLED THROUGH THE KAWASAKI DEALERSHIP WITH KITA AND RYAN. Motorcycles, watercraft, and ATVs sat in neat rows. She parked in an open spot in front of the rectangular glass building. In the window was the Ninja H2R.

"Wow. There it is," said Kita as she took off her helmet and set it on Velositi. She looked at herself in the side mirror. "Whoa. Scary." She took off her headband and ran her fingers through her hair.

"I've never been to a dealership before," said Ryan.

"Where'd you get your bike from?"

"Craigslist. I paid seven-fifty for it."

"Nice. I advertise parts on Craigslist all the time."

"You need to get the bike close to me so I can copy it," said Velositi.

"Then we'll need to take it for a test drive," said Kita as she grabbed her helmet.

"Next time, I am not a table. If you want me to hold something—ask."

"Oh, sorry. I—" Kita's heart sank. *Oh, no...*

"I am kidding, Kita. I'm just teasing you."

"Ugh. Do you know what you do to me?"

"I know. I am toughening you up and trying to teach you to quit jumping to the worst-case scenario first."

Kita slowly nodded her head.

"What are you toughening her up for?" said Ryan.

"If she wants to talk to you about it, that is Kita's business," said Velositi tersely. "Go get the bike."

Kita and Ryan turned and found a young sales rep standing a respectful distance away, waiting.

"Hi, I'm Brian. What's your name?" he stuck out his hand to Ryan.

"Ah, Ryan, and this is my friend, Kita."

"Nice to meet you both. What brings you in today, Ryan?"

*Hey! We're here for me.*

"Not me," said Ryan. "Her." He waved at Kita.

A hint of disdain and greed crossed Brian's face. "What can I help you with?" he said flatly.

"I want to look at the H2R."

Brian looked at Kita, then at Velositi. "The H2R is for serious enthusiasts. Maybe you'd like to look at the 300?"

"I *am* serious."

"It's a fifty-five-thousand-dollar bike. We should stick to your price range. The 300 is five thousand, and we might be able to get you financing."

Kita wrinkled her nose. "I want the H2R. I want to take it on a test drive."

Brian sighed heavily. "You'll have to fill out a credit application, and I need your license and insurance."

"Ah..." *Uh-oh.*

Kita's phone buzzed. She pulled it out and found a message from Velositi, "Your license and insurance are online. Just open the apps and select them."

"I don't have regular motorcycle insurance," Kita typed back.

"I got you some from your insurance company."

"I can't afford that."

"Who said I paid for it? It's good for six months. The internet makes life so much easier. With Mike, everything was done on paper, and he had to do it. Now, in a couple of nanoseconds, I can do it."

Kita rolled her eyes. *Maybe giving them my phone wasn't the smartest move.* She opened the apps and found her license and insurance.

"Ok, Brian. Here are my license and insurance."

"Send them to Dee at Big Surf Kawasaki dot com." Brian took a phone off his belt and pulled up a screen. "Here is the credit application."

Kita sent the documents and took Brian's phone. She scrolled through the application filling it out as she went. She signed it and hit the send button. Kita handed the phone to Brian.

They waited in awkward silence until the phone chimed.

Brian frowned. "Sorry. Your credit score is four twenty-seven. That's not high enough for even a 300."

"But I just want to take it on a test drive," pleaded Kita.

"Sorry, but no. If you have no other business here, please leave."

Kita huffed in frustration. "Just let me ride it!" she yelled.

Brian glared. "No. If you don't leave, I will call the police."

"Come on, Kita," said Ryan as he gently tugged on her arm. "We'll figure something else out."

"This is so not fair!" Kita stomped her foot. She spun and stomped back to Velositi. She sat on Velositi and put her head on the gas tank.

"Are you ready to do it my way?" said Velositi.

"You couldn't have hacked the credit score?" snarled Kita.

"I did. I gave you an eight oh three."

"He said I had four twenty-seven!"

"Did you hack the right one?" said Ryan.

"There is more than one?" said Velositi.

"There are three bureaus."

"Oh. Oops. But, Kita, he was never going to let you ride that bike."

"Why not!"

"Quit yelling and calm down. The reason is you do not look like a fifty-five-thousand-dollar bike owner. You look like what you have. Me."

"But, you're awesome."

"I know, but I do not look awesome. I look like I have sat around for forty years, and a salvage expert found me."

"So what?"

"If you want a certain part in life, you have to take it. One of the steps is looking the part. Another is acting the part. The third is to have enough knowledge to fake what you are talking about. I did not become the leader of my group because I waited for my turn. I wanted it, and I did what was necessary to get it."

"But what's wrong with me?"

"Nothing on the inside. You want a different life. You came with me to get it. Now, we just need to make you look like you have a different life."

"You want me to change my clothes, hair, and face to—"

"Nails."

"Argh. To just be pretty?"

"No. I want you to be pretty for me. I am going to be pretty for you. I am sure Ryan did not roll out of bed and jump on his bike. He spent some time on his appearance so that he could impress the ladies."

Kita glared at Ryan.

"Time well spent. Girls love it. I mean, you gotta do it. Your appearance is like silently introducing yourself. This is what I look like; come check out the rest. It's not like you need a fairy godmother, Kita, you're beautiful. Get you cleaned up, and the girls won't stay away from you. You'll make me feel left out." Ryan's smile dazzled.

"Fine," Kita moaned.

"Ok, now I'm considering leaving you by the side of the road and riding off with Ryan," said Velositi.

"What? Why?"

"You are going to lament getting cleaned up for me? I am hurt. That is all I am asking you to do."

"But...it's just...I...Don't be mad at me, please."

"I am not mad. I am disappointed and very hurt. It is the one thing I ask of you, and you will not even consider it. I do not want you to be a model or a beauty queen, but I want you to look good and be attractive." Velositi sighed. "I am sorry for sounding harsh, but my appearance means a lot to me. I am working with you on getting a new appearance for me, and you will not even meet me halfway on a new look for you." There was a *click* followed by silence.

Kita looked at Ryan.

"I have no idea," he said, "but she seems pretty upset."

"It's just...What's wrong with the way I look?"

"You look like you've been working on your bike all day—ratty jeans, old sneakers, T-shirt, dirty, hair everywhere. You're still beautiful. That's why I hit on you, but if you showed up looking like this on a date, I'd be like WTF."

"But this is how I normally look."

"Hey, if you don't care how you look, that's your thing. But it doesn't sound like it's Velositi's thing. She wants to look good and be seen. It sounds like she really likes you, but—"

Kita huffed. "She can't accept me as I am."

"You can't accept her as she is."

"What? I do too."

Ryan crossed his arms. "She's willing to meet you halfway, and you're refusing to budge."

"I thought we were going to be friends!" Kita yelled.

"Yeah. I'm supposed to be honest. And I'm telling you you're wrong. You're being stubborn. And I don't understand why. Velositi seems great. You want to show her off making her the H2R. Why can't she be allowed to show you off?"

"I don't want to be stared at like a piece of meat."

Ryan hung his head. "Yet you don't care how many people are going to be attracted to her as an H2R? I—" Ryan bent down and ran his hand through a pool of liquid under Velositi. He looked at the blue fluid on his fingers and then sniffed it. "Velositi's leaking something. It's not oil or coolant."

Kita frowned. "Velositi shouldn't be leaking anything." Kita put a hand on Velositi's seat. "Velositi, are you ok? There's some fluid leaking from you."

Kita looked at Ryan, worried when she didn't get an answer. Ryan knelt and looked around Velositi's engine. He traced it up under the gas tank.

"It doesn't smell like gas." Ryan opened Velositi's gas tank and did a double-take. "It's a solid piece."

"She said she doesn't use gas. She needs something called plasma," said Kita.

"Maybe she was wounded out on the highway."

Kita gasped. "Oh, no. I don't know how to repair her. What do we do? I—I can call Sprokkit. He said my phone could contact him."

Kita pulled out her phone and scrolled through her contacts. Finding Sprokkit, she tapped his icon. It rang a few times before the Morphicon's image appeared.

"Human. What do you want? Where is Velositi?" Sprokkit said in a gruff voice.

"She's with me. She's morphed and won't talk to me. She's leaking a blue fluid. I'm afraid she might be injured."

"If she were injured, the wound would be glowing red. A thin blue fluid is normally not anything to worry about, just a byproduct of plasma being consumed at a rapid rate. It concerns because her plasma levels are so low. What happened?"

"We got into an argument."

"Emotional outbursts can consume plasma at a rapid rate."

"So, she's crying?" said Ryan.

"Who are you?" demanded Sprokkit.

"His name is Ryan. We met him earlier," said Kita.

"Is he as useless as you?"

"I'm a graduate student at C-Tech. I study electrical engineering."

Sprokkit's eyes glowed brighter. "You *might* be useful to me." His emphasis made the knot in Kita's stomach churn.

"So, what do I do about Velositi?" demanded Kita.

"Kiss and make up," said Sprokkit harshly as he killed the connection.

"I bet you she's crying," said Ryan.

"But..." Kita said exasperatedly.

"What's more important to you—the clothes on your back or Velositi?"

Kita grimaced. "You know the real reason I don't want to change?"

Ryan raised an eyebrow. "Why?"

"I don't want to get laughed at and have people treat me like an imposter."

"No one will treat you like an imposter," said Ryan.

Kita gulped. "The last time I tried was for the eighth-grade dance. I put on my dress, did my hair and makeup—and no one talked to me the entire night. I could just hear all the snide comments the girls made."

Ryan laughed. "I was a pimple-faced kid with Coke-bottle glasses who never left the wall during a dance. I think the only dances I got were bets and pity dances. I didn't find my way until my junior year of college. I cleaned my face, cut my hair, got contacts, added a tattoo, and suddenly girls were looking at me, and my confidence soared. A makeover might be good for you, Kita."

*Is that what I need? I am making over my life. No more scrap yard, meeting new friends...I guess my look could use an update. It seems to have worked for Ryan. He doesn't have a problem with self-confidence. And I'm supposed to be working on my confidence. This could be the boost I need.*

Kita smiled warily at Ryan. "Ok, I'll do it, but if I don't like it, I'm coming after you."

"Hey, you got to please yourself...and her." He pointed to Velositi.

*Damn. What do I say to Velositi? I didn't mean to make her cry. I didn't know she cared so much about appearance.*

Kita knelt next to Velositi and put her hand on Velositi's gas tank. "Velositi, I'm sorry. I didn't get that appearance mattered so much to you—"

"You matter to me!" Velositi cried. "You are my friend—more than my friend—and I want you to be happy, confident, and safe. I want the *best* for you."

Kita's pulse raced. No one had cared for her this much since her dad died. She didn't know what to say as a pair of tears slid down her face. "Thank you," she whispered as she sat down and leaned against Velositi.

"Hey, girls. We have a problem," said Ryan, motioning to Brian as he exited the doors of the dealership.

Kita wiped at the tears in her eyes.

Ryan moved to intercept Brian.

"I told you to leave," said Brian.

"Yeah, we are," said Ryan. "We just had to fix a leak."

Brian's face puckered. "Someone is going to have to clean it up."

"I guess you should go find the kitty litter then."

"Get out of here," snarled Brian.

"Kita has it about fixed. Hold on."

Kita gulped. "You matter to me, too, Velositi. I'll do whatever you want to make you happy."

"I want us to be happy," said Velositi. "We will work it out—together."

Kita stood up and sat on Velositi as her engine roared.

"Thanks for nothing," said Ryan to Brian.

Ryan sat behind Kita, and they put their helmets on. Velositi idled backward out of the parking spot, drove through the Kawasaki lot, and turned onto the street.

"So, where are we going?" said Kita.

"Downtown," said Velositi. "There are plenty of salons and boutiques there within easy walking distance. I am sure they'll have what we want."

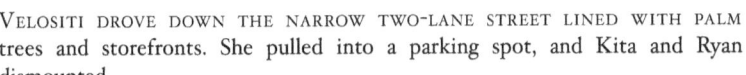

VELOSITI DROVE DOWN THE NARROW TWO-LANE STREET LINED WITH PALM trees and storefronts. She pulled into a parking spot, and Kita and Ryan dismounted.

"According to the internet, everything we need is in this area," said Velositi. "Kita, give Ryan some money for clothes."

Kita dug out the few hundred she had in her pocket.

"He's going to need more than that, and you'll need money from the stash." A compartment in Velositi's gas tank opened.

Kita reached inside for the money hesitantly.

"Expecting me to moan again?" said Velositi.

Kita glanced at Ryan, causing Velositi to laugh. Grabbing the bundle of bills, Kita counted out five thousand. She gave some to Ryan and kept the rest.

"Ryan," said Velositi, "get clothes that are rugged and fashionable. You will need a riding jacket as well."

"Hey, no problem. I'm sure I can find something." He walked off, looking at the shops.

"Come on, Kita," Velositi said from Kita's phone.

Kita sighed quietly.

"The first place we are going is Tranquility Spa. And what is your favorite color?"

"Black."

"We should go well together. I like pink."

———————✕———————

KITA STEPPED OUT OF THE SALON AND SLIPPED HER SUNGLASSES ON, HAPPY that her long ordeal was over. She did feel out of her depth in the salons, spa, and boutiques, but she tried not to show her nerves. Following Velositi's directions helped. She tried to be polite, direct, and confident, even when she had to have something explained to her.

She shrugged on her new black and pink accented leather riding jacket, pulled her low ponytail out from the jacket, and walked back to Velositi. Sitting on a bench nearby was Ryan, reading a book and drinking coffee. Kita stopped in front of him.

"Eh-hem. What are you reading?"

Ryan looked up from the book and held it up. It was titled *Sundered Rock* by Mark Gardner. "Whoa. You look fantastic. Love the hair."

The lady at the salon hadn't done much to Kita's hair—just a trim, layering, cleaning, and conditioning—but it was now shiny and sleek.

"Was it as bad as you thought?"

Kita rolled her eyes. "The waxing and plucking hurt, but the lady doing the waxing said it was a good thing the hair on my legs was long." Kita grinned wickedly as Ryan made a face. "But the clothes, hair, nails, and makeup were fine. I just had to sit there and then pay attention so I can repeat the process. But what do you think?"

Kita opened her jacket, revealing a skin-tight black crop top shirt with Princess Luna surrounded by rhinestones. Over the shirt was a lightweight black and pink flannel she'd tied in the front. She wore black denim skinny jeans, a studded leather belt, and belted riding boots with a two-inch heel. Kita twirled around and held her hand to her pouting baby pink lips to show they matched her black nails French tipped with baby pink.

Ryan looked overwhelmed—like he wasn't sure where to look.

"Does not she look amazing?" said Velositi from Kita's phone. "How do you feel?"

Kita pulled the phone from her back pocket. "I'm trying to match my confidence level to everyone's reactions."

"But how do you feel?"

"With the way you and everyone else has been looking at me, pretty special. It's a little weird. I'm not used to getting so much attention."

"You will get used to it," said Velositi. "How did you do, Ryan?"

He put the book and coffee down, then stood up. Kita held the phone up so Velositi could see that he wore a T-shirt with an eagle on the front with an unbuttoned flannel over it, blue jeans, and fashionable work boots.

"I, ah, got a haircut and a shave, too."

"Very nice, Ryan," said Velositi.

"Here, Kita. I got you some coffee." Ryan picked up the cup and handed it over. "I wasn't sure what you liked, but I didn't think I could go wrong with chocolate mocha."

Kita blushed. "Thanks." She took a sip. It was so much better than the stuff Ralph made at the yard that came out of a can. "Yummy." She gave Ryan an approving smile.

"Now, that we're ready, shall we go get me into something that matches the two of you?" said Velositi.

"Somehow, I don't think your transformation will be as painful as mine."

"I promise you that getting *everything* waxed will be worth it."

VELOSITI PULLED INTO A PARKING SPOT DOWN THE STREET FROM THE Kawasaki dealership.

"Why are we parking here?" said Kita as she took off her helmet and put on her sunglasses. For whatever reason, they boosted her confidence. She didn't care that the sun was going down; she was going to wear them.

"You do not want them to see you riding me. Breaks the image. I pulled in behind this Porsche Cayenne, so it looks like you drove it here. In case anyone was looking. When you are on your test drive, just drive by me slowly, and I will flash the bike."

"Ok. Wish us luck."

"You do not need luck," said Velositi. "You got this."

Kita looked at Ryan. "Shall we go?"

"Sure."

Together, helmets in hand, they walked down the tree and grass-lined sidewalk. Kita made sure to stay on the sidewalk as she entered the dealership. *Sophisticated and polite people don't go crashing through the bushes or cut on the grass.*

The dealership building was lit brightly in the setting sun. Tall lights around the sales lot lit motorcycles, ATVs, and watercraft. Kita had walked four steps onto the lot when a middle-aged man with balding hair in a Kawasaki polo shirt and khakis hurried up to them.

*Uh-oh. They remember us from earlier.* But the man didn't look angry.

"Hi. I'm Tim," he said as he stopped in front of Kita and Ryan. "Welcome to the Big Surf Kawasaki Dealership. It looks like you've come prepared to ride." He stuck out his hand to Kita.

She shook it, noting he didn't give her a limp handshake, nor did he try and crush her hand. Tim shook Ryan's hand.

"So, what brings you in tonight?" said Tim with a high-wattage smile.

Kita returned his smile with a bright one of her own. She shared a look with Ryan.

"Your birthday. You tell him what you want," said Ryan.

*Wow. I'll have to give Ryan some props for coming up with that.* "Yes, it's my birthday in a couple of weeks, and I'm looking for a new toy."

"You've come to the right place," said Tim. "Anything in particular?"

"I'm looking for something fun and exciting. I like to race and hate to lose."

Tim laughed politely. "Who doesn't?"

*Here goes.* "I've had my eye on the H2R."

"You won't lose riding that, I guarantee it," said Tim. "It's the fastest hypersport motorcycle on the planet. Come inside and have a look."

Kita looked at Ryan. He smiled and nodded. They followed Tim inside.

"Can I get you anything? Smart water? Diet Coke? Bubly sparkling water? I've got snacks, too," he asked.

*They give out food? What the slag? I didn't look that bad last time...Well, maybe I did, but they still could have offered a snack. Of course, sophisticated girls don't pig out on free food. So, what would a sophisticated girl get?*

"I'll have a water."

"Sure, no problem. I'll be right back. The H2R is on the stand in the corner. Have a look."

Kita and Ryan walked over and watched the bike turn on the pedestal.

"Are you serious?" Kita hissed at Ryan. "We get all this because we look good?"

Ryan laughed. "Welcome to Cali. It's even prettier up close."

Kita turned back to the reason they were there. The bike was beautiful, sleek, and sexy. Its cowl was gray, with a neon green frame and chrome exhaust.

"It has a 998cc inline four-cylinder supercharged engine, six-speed dog-ring transmission, and the new model has 330mm disc brakes for aggressive braking without overheating at high speeds," said Tim as he walked up. He handed the bottle of water to Kita. "It just set the new speed record at two hundred and forty-nine miles per hour."

"That is impressive," said Kita. "Imagine doing that down the freeway," she said to Ryan.

Tim smiled. "Unfortunately, for the street, the bike has a governor that limits it to one hundred and ninety miles an hour. If you bring the bike to one of our track facilities, we can remove the governor, and you can go as fast as you want on the track. You also get two free sessions with our experts. They'll teach you all you need to know about going fast. But, to really experience it, you need to drive it. Do you want to take it out?"

*By the Crushing Depths, yeah!* Kita decided going with her first impulse wouldn't be prudent. She looked at Ryan. "What do you think?"

"Your birthday. But you won't know if you like it unless you ride it."

Kita nodded. "Ok, Tim, I've got time. Sure."

"Great. Give me a couple of minutes to get it down. In the meantime, I need to collect some information—"

Kita pulled out her phone. "Where do I send it?"

"Please send it to my supervisor— Rick at Big Surf Kawasaki dot com."

"No problem."

"Hang tight," said Tim. "I'll be right back."

Kita leaned against Ryan. "So, this is way better than last time."

Kita's phone buzzed.

"I knew you would like it," texted Velositi.

Kita showed the message to Ryan. "It's all you. I don't get this kind of service when I walk into places."

"I think it's us," said Kita. "We make a pretty good-looking couple."

"That's what I thought when I saw you on the bike."

Kita crossed her arms as Tim and another salesman brought a ramp over to the H2R's pedestal. "I think you were more interested in getting laid."

Ryan smiled sideways. "Maybe when I first saw you. After you beat me, I thought you'd make a good girlfriend. That notion was short-lived, though."

"I can't escape the truth," said Kita apologetically.

"I think someone else is interested in you."

"Who? I haven't been around anyone else but you."

"I'm not going to ruin *her* game. You'll just have to figure it out."

"Ok..." *Who's he talking about? What girl? The only girls I've been around were downtown, and none showed any interest in me.*

"Kita, we're ready," said Tim as he wheeled the bike toward them.

"Awesome," said Kita.

Kita took Ryan's hand and followed Tim outside. He leaned the H2R on its stand. "Hop on."

Kita looked at Ryan, and he waved her on. Kita mounted the bike. *Wow!*

"It has a push-button ignition," said Tim. "You just need to have this fob on you. If it gets out of range, the bike will shut off." He handed the fob to Kita. She tucked it in her jacket. "The bike has a GPS tracker on it, so you can't run away." Kita laughed politely. "Take a left out of the dealership, go up the street, take a right. There will be an on-ramp. Take the freeway to the next exit, use the U-turn to get back on the freeway, and come back here. Any questions?"

"Nope. I got it," said Kita.

Tim started the bike and revved the motor. "Sounds like a jet engine," he said with a smile.

Kita smiled as she pocketed her sunglasses and put on her helmet. After adjusting her ponytail, she closed her visor and took the handles. She revved the engine as her fingers found the throttle, brake, and clutch while her feet found the footpegs, gear-change lever, and brake pedal. Kita gave Tim a thumbs-up and blew Ryan a kiss. She lifted the stand and started forward.

Just the slightest twist of the throttle created a lot of torque. Kita tested the brakes and found them responsive, but with a fair amount of play. Satisfied, she pulled through the dealership lot and turned onto the street. Following Tim's instructions, Kita navigated the busy streets and turned onto the on-ramp.

The on-ramp was clear, and Kita sped up to the elevated freeway. The freeway was full of the remnants of rush hour traffic. *I've got a mile to see what this thing can do—less than sixty seconds. I don't want to waste it in traffic.* She swerved out to the far-left lane where traffic was moving at the speed limit. Not wanting to go the speed limit, she wove in and out of traffic.

The bike handled like a dream. Before Kita knew it, she reached the next exit. With a heavy sigh, she took the off-ramp and followed the U-turn under the freeway back onto the on-ramp. She pulled in behind a crossover that was taking its time. Not wanting to waste a second, she cranked the throttle and passed the crossover on the left shoulder. Kita streaked onto the freeway, using the merge lane to bypass a line of cars. She swerved across the right lane into the middle lane. Gunning the engine to narrowly miss the front end of a semi, Kita passed several cars on the center lane line, before rejoining traffic. She swung across two lanes of traffic and slowed herself as she came to a stop behind a line of cars waiting for the off-ramp light to change.

Kita deviated from Tim's instructions and turned a block early. She followed the street and turned down the side street where Velositi was parked.

"How slow do I have to go?" said Kita to Velositi.

"I just need a second."

Kita throttled the bike down. There was no traffic behind her as she came up to Velositi. As Kita passed, she slowed to a crawl and waved at Velositi. Nothing came from Velositi, which worried Kita. "Did you get it?"

"I got it," said Velositi. "I will see you when you get back."

Kita sped up and turned into the dealership. Tim and Ryan were standing and talking where she'd left them. She pulled up to them, parked the bike, and took off her helmet.

"Have fun?" said Ryan.

"This thing is awesome," said Kita.

"It is a finely crafted piece of machinery," said Tim. "You won't find better anywhere."

Kita dismounted, fixed her hair, and stood next to Ryan.

"So, did you get what you came for?" said Ryan.

"Yes, we're good to go."

"Are you ready to talk finances?" said Tim. "Or will you be paying cash?"

Kita cocked her head to one side. "It'll be cash, for sure, but not tonight. I have a few other bikes on my list I want to check out."

"You won't find better out there."

"I'll have to see how the Lightning LS-218 feels. But I'm ready for dinner." She looked at Ryan and batted her manicured eyes.

Ryan looked at Tim and shrugged. "Never get between a girl and food, right?"

Tim smiled. "Of course, take your time. Here's my card." He dug into his breast pocket and handed it to Ryan.

"Thanks. We'll let you know."

"You folks have a nice evening."

Kita took Ryan's arm in her free hand and let him escort her back to the street.

"You seem to have gotten the hang of rich girl in a hurry," Ryan said with a grin.

"I feel like I'm in the zone. Like part of me was meant to be this way. Now that I'm here, like, I know what to do. Maybe I'm just a good actor. I'll probably wake up and forget everything."

They passed the Porsche, and Kita's jaw dropped. The Indian was gone, and a custom painted H2R stood in its place.

"By the Crushing Depths, Velositi, you look incredible," squealed Kita.

"You like?" said Velositi. "The baby pink matches your nails and lip color."

"You went all out," said Ryan.

"A girl has to coordinate."

Kita ran her hand over the black gas tank with the word Kawasaki in pink. Velositi was beautiful. The cowl and body were glossy black with matte black stripes and pink accents. The bike's frame was pink, and so were the rims. The black seats were trimmed in pink, and the exhaust was matte black. Kita hugged Velositi. "You're amazing," Kita whispered.

"Makes up for this afternoon?"

Kita chuckled. "Definitely...except for maybe the waxing part."

"I'm sure I can make you feel better."

"I'm never going to keep the boys away from you now."

Velositi chirped in laughter. "I belong to one girl."

"She's very lucky."

"Are you ready for dinner?"

"Oh, I'm starving," said Kita.

"Then let's go."

Velositi pulled into the fifties-style diner. It was brightly lit; the outside was decorated in white and red with lots of chrome. Kita and Ryan dismounted and pushed through the double glass door. Booths lined the outside walls, a counter and stools dominated the middle, and a pass-through to the kitchen was on the far wall. A sign read SEAT YOURSELF.

Kita chose a booth and slid into the red vinyl seat. Ryan sat across from her. Four menus were stuck in a holder at the end of the table, along with the condiments. Ryan grabbed two menus and gave one to Kita. She took her phone out of her pocket and put it on the table.

A server in her mid-forties wearing a knee-length skirt, apron, blouse, and white tennis shoes appeared. On top of her head was a peaked paper cap.

"Welcome to Shakes," she said, sounding bored. "Best shakes and burgers in town. I'm Christine. What will you have to drink?"

Kita looked at Ryan.

"Get what you want. I'll have a Coke."

"Ah, water," said Kita.

"Be right back," said Christine as she left.

"Kita, you can get more than water," said Velositi from the phone.

"I don't want to waste our money."

"We have money and will get more. Splurge on something."

"I thought I was by getting a burger and fries."

"There must be something you must want as a treat."

"I don't know. I got you fixed up today."

"A treat for your taste buds. Order something yummy."

Kita sighed. "Ok."

Christine returned with their drinks.

"Can—can I get something else?" said Kita.

Christine raised an eyebrow. "Sure. What?"

Kita wasn't sure what she wanted. She looked around. A placard read BEST CHOCOLATE SHAKES! *That sounds good.* "A chocolate shake?" she said hesitantly.

"No problem. It'll be out in a minute."

"What happened to the confident girl?" said Ryan after Christine had left.

Kita's shoulders slumped. "I don't know. I haven't eaten out in like ever."

"Really?"

"I have no money. I eat ramen once a day."

Ryan laughed. "You sound like a college student."

"Aren't you a college student?"

"Yeah, but I'm a grad student. I get paid to go to school. Seriously, just ramen?"

"Coffee. Sometimes I eat what my staff leaves behind."

"And you never go out?"

Kita shook her head. "Not even before my dad died."

"I promise you the server won't bite."

"I know. Just another thing that feels unnatural. Like, I'm supposed to take care of myself."

"You are taking care of yourself," said Velositi. "Just because you do not cook it. You need to eat more. Eating more would be taking care of yourself."

"I'm fine. I'm like one-oh-four."

"That would be fine if I was looking for a fashion model—those clothes you wore when I found you hung on you like tents. I'm positive you didn't eat this poorly when your father was alive. I understand you are under stress from his death, the business, your sexuality, but even then, you should weigh more. Like around one hundred twenty."

"If I gain weight, my clothes won't fit."

"I'll buy you new clothes."

Christine placed the chocolate shake and leftover shake tin in front of Kita. "You ready to order?"

Ryan flipped the menu over. "Yeah, I'll have the mushroom and swiss burger, medium, no mayo."

Christine jotted it down then looked at Kita.

"I'll have a...ah...burger and fries."

"How do you want it cooked?"

"Ah...medium?" said Kita, remembering that was what Ryan had ordered.

"Everything on it?"

"Sure." *I can pick off what I don't want.*

"So, where are we going now?" said Ryan, once Christine had walked away.

"I do not know," said Velositi. "I have not heard from Bernoot. He is supposed to be finding us a safe house."

"I might know a place—the old C-Tech Rocket Lab. Nobody goes there. It's only used to house old science projects."

"Does it have a bay door big enough for a truck to go through?"

"Yeah. It's how they got the rocket components in."

"Where is it?"

"I can find it on the map."

Kita launched her map app and handed the phone to Ryan. He scrolled around.

"Here we go." He tapped the map dropping a pin.

"I have it," said Velositi. "I will pass along the location to Bernoot. He says he has spent all day cruising up the valley looking for a place. I bet he detoured out to the beach for a bit."

"He hasn't said much," said Kita.

"Once you get to know him, he will not shut up. He is young but experienced. He does what he is told, most of the time, but he loves the beach and water."

Kita took a sip of her shake. It was rich, chocolatey, and creamy. She sucked half of it down in one pull.

"You like it?" said Ryan with a chuckle.

"It's so good." Kita took another long pull.

"Just the spoiling you need," said Velositi.

Kita made a slurping sound when she hit bottom. Unrelenting, she stuck the straw in the leftover shake tin. She quickly emptied it. "Yummy."

"That is what I want to hear."

The burgers arrived, and Kita tried hard not to gobble it up. She took a bite when Ryan did to pace herself. When he wasn't eating the burger, she stuffed the fries in her mouth.

Ryan laughed at Kita when she shoved six fries in her mouth at once. "No one is going to take it from you," he said with a teasing grin.

Kita sighed. *But it's so good.* She did her best to slow down.

When they finished, Kita remembered the bathroom from the night before and decided to use the diner's restroom.

Ryan was waiting when she returned. "I paid the bill, so we're all set. It'll take us almost two hours to get to the university."

"Ok. I know I don't mind, but you're the one who has to hang on."

"I don't mind hanging on to you," he said with a flirtatious wink.

Kita grinned. "Close as you're going to get."

"I might have to borrow Velositi from you for a day. You do owe me a bike."

"You'll have to talk to her. She did save your life."

"Yeah. I have to call my insurance. I don't even know where the bike is. I'll have to contact the sheriff's office to find out where they sent it."

Kita handed him her phone. "You have fun with that. I'm going to enjoy Velositi."

"I'm sure she'll like that," said Ryan as he opened the door for Kita.

KITA'S STOMACH ACHED AND THEN FLIPPED. SHE SWALLOWED THE URGE TO vomit. "We have to pull over," she said meekly.

"Why?" said Velositi.

"I don't feel good. Please."

Velositi swerved across three lanes of traffic to the right shoulder, where she stopped hard. Kita jumped off and scrambled down the shoulder into the grass. She tore off her helmet and fell to her hands and knees. In one motion that started in her stomach and rolled up her body, she vomited. It took her several attempts to control the dry heaves after expelling everything. She spit, trying to rid her mouth of the taste, then collapsed on her side and moaned as tears filled her eyes.

"Are you ok?" said Ryan.

Kita hadn't realized he had followed her. She moaned in reply.

Ryan knelt over her, putting a hand on her shoulder. He pulled a bottle of water from his jacket. "Here, this will help get rid of the taste." He helped Kita sit up and gave her the water with *Kawasaki* on the label.

Kita took a sip and rinsed her mouth.

"Feel better?" said Ryan.

Kita lowered her head and cried. "No."

Ryan sat down next to Kita. "Why are you crying?"

"I ruined Velositi's special treat."

He put his arm around her. "She's not going to care about that. She just wants to make sure you're ok."

"I feel terrible. Figuratively and literally."

"She's not upset. Are you, Velositi?" Ryan called.

"No," said Velositi from Kita's back pocket. "What is wrong with her? I am worried."

"My guess is it was the food."

"The food was bad?"

"No. I'm sure the food was fine. I think Kita's system isn't used to dairy or meat. The human body has specific enzymes for different types of foods. If you don't use them, you lose them. It takes a while to get them back."

"What do we feed her?"

"I'm sure we can find something at the store. Fruits, grains, nuts, vegetables shouldn't be a problem. Sushi would be good for her. But we won't find that until tomorrow."

"Ok. Kita, how are you?"

"Not good. I'm sorry."

"Nothing to be sorry for. I am sorry about the food. I did not know it would upset you. Can you ride? We will put you on the back, and you can hang onto Ryan."

"I'll try."

Ryan helped Kita to her feet. She leaned on him as they climbed the shoulder embankment to Velositi. He helped Kita onto Velositi and sat in front. Kita leaned on him heavily as she put her arms around him. Velositi merged back into traffic, going much slower.

Velositi stopped in front of a gate made of metal bars. A matching fence with signs that read KEEP OUT surrounded the property. An abandoned guard post was on the right. A light pole illuminated the area in yellow light. After a moment, the gate opened.

"Is someone there?" said Ryan.

"That was me," said Velositi. "The gate has remote access."

"Cool. What can you do for door locks?"

"If they are mechanical, not much. I must be able to establish a connection." Velositi killed her lights and idled through the overgrown parking lot around the side of the two-story building to a bay door. She stopped in front of it. "Can you get us in, Ryan?"

"Yeah. There's a door unlocked on the backside because no one can ever find the keys. It'll take me a couple of minutes." Ryan unwrapped Kita's arms from around him. "How are you feeling, Kita?"

She moaned as a response.

"I have to get us inside. I'll help you sit down."

Ryan dismounted, trying to keep Kita from falling. He caught her and helped her off Velositi, then sat her down next to the door. After taking off her helmet, he went around the side of the building.

Kita wrapped her arms around her legs and rested her head on her knees. Her stomach was so upset. A sharp pain was followed by a gurgle. She wanted nothing more than to curl up and die. If that wasn't possible, to sleep.

"Kita," called Velositi. "Kita?"

Kita didn't feel like responding, so she didn't. All she could do was languish in her misery.

"Kita, I am sorry," said Velositi. "I did not know it would make you sick. I just wanted you to feel special."

*Ugh. I feel special all right. Oh, no.* Kita uncoiled and pulled herself to the curb. She heaved up some bile, and dry heaved a few times. When she was done, she rolled over in the scrub grass. Slowly, her vision focused on the few stars visible through the light pollution of one of the largest cities in the world.

Velositi moved over next to Kita. "Kita? Is there anything I can do for you?"

Kita stared at the sky, trying to find some solace. It seemed cruel that she had to wait to sleep. The dirt and grass felt fine. She just wanted it to end.

The bay door opened with a loud set of squeaks as it rolled up its ancient track. Ryan appeared from the door and hurried toward Kita and Velositi.

"What happened?" said Ryan.

"She vomited again," said Velositi.

"Let's get her inside. There are some old army cots she can sleep on." Ryan bent down next to Kita. "Hey, I'm going to pick you up and take you inside. There's a cot you can sleep on."

Kita muttered something unintelligible but didn't fight as Ryan picked her up. She cuddled against him as he carried her through the building. It was mostly empty except for a large concrete pipe with a side missing on the far wall. Scattered around were various objects Kita didn't know the purpose of. They looked like they were electrical. A door leading to a hallway was propped open. Velositi followed behind them.

In front of the concrete pipe was a cot. Ryan lay Kita on it. "Do you want your jacket off?"

Kita grunted, and Ryan helped Kita out of her jacket.

"Do you want it as a pillow?"

Kita curled up in a ball as a reply, so Ryan draped the jacket over Kita.

"Is there anything we can do for her?" said Velositi, sounding worried.

"They sell this pink stuff at CVS, and we should get her some water. That would help her."

"Will she be fine alone? Bernoot is still forty-five minutes away."

"She'll be fine. No one ever comes out here."

"Sleep well, Kita. We will be back shortly," Velositi said to Kita.

Kita mumbled something. But she was more interested in sleeping.

KITA AWOKE TO THE SCREECHING OF THE BAY DOOR WHEELS. IT MOVED quickly, revealing a pair of blinding headlights. She sat up and shielded her eyes.

"Bernoot?" Kita called weakly.

The lights moved forward and stopped. There was the sound of a car door opening. Kita moved to the edge of the cot.

Summoning all the strength she could muster, Kita yelled, "Bernoot?"

Blinding red and blue lights flashed, and a siren blared. *Not Bernoot! Nitstik!* Kita jumped backward. Stumbling over the cot, she knocked it over and fell on top of it. From out of the light emerged Boom-Boom, its jaws snapping at her. Kita scrambled backward, rolled to her feet, and ran toward the hallway.

Behind her, Nitstik squealed his tires and lurched toward Kita. Boom-Boom snapped at her butt. She planted her right foot and kicked Boom-Boom with her left, sending it backward at Nitstik. Turning, Kita sprinted into the hallway and tried the first door she came to, but it was locked. She tried them all as she hurried down the hall. At the hallway entrance, Nitstik sounded his siren, revved his engine, and shined his headlights down the hallway. Boom-Boom rushed Kita, slamming into her and knocking her to the ground. It jumped on top of her, snapping its jaws. Kita raised her arm, and Boom-Boom bit her. She brought a knee up into Boom-Boom's backside, flipping it over her. Scrambling to her feet, Kita kicked Boom-Boom down the hallway. She burst through a wooden bathroom door, slammed it shut, and locked it.

On the other side of the door, Boom-Boom snarled in frustration. Kita could hear a saw and the blows of something striking the door. *The door isn't going to hold for long.*

Kita was in the men's room. Urinals and stalls lined the left wall and sinks lined the right. An old metal trash can sat by the door. On the far wall was a set of high windows. They were too high for her to jump and pull herself up.

Boom-Boom's ax head burst through the door. *Uh-oh. Slag, I have to hurry.* Grabbing the trash can, Kita knocked the top off and flipped it over. She placed it under the windows and climbed on top. Fighting with the ancient lock, she ignored the blood flowing down her arm. The lock turned slowly. Kita grabbed the handle, painstakingly cranking the window open. *How many times do I have to turn this thing?*

When the crank stopped turning, Kita grabbed the windowsill and pulled herself through. The window itself was big enough, but the opening was tight. Kita had to bend and wiggle to get through. There was a nine-foot drop to the ground. *I hadn't thought about that.*

Kita felt something smack her foot. *Slag! Boom-Boom is through.* She kicked her feet and pushed with her arms. Her phone, caught on the window frame, released and pressed into her butt, as Kita slid out of the window, landing hard on her shoulder in the dirt and grass. *That's going to leave a mark.* Kita pushed herself to her feet and leaned against the wall. She was in the rear of the facility and could see the fence, but there was no way she could climb it. The front gate was her only option of getting away. But first, she had to alert the others. *Where the slag is everybody? Why is there not someone here?*

Kita pulled out her phone and tapped Velositi, Bernoot, and Sprokkit's icons. The three answered at once.

"Kita?" said Velositi.

"What?" said Sprokkit.

"Hey, what's happenin'?" said Bernoot.

"Where are you?" Kita said in a harsh whisper. "Nitstik is here."

"What?" said Velositi. "Are you ok?"

"No. He's chasing me around the building."

"Bernoot, where are you?" said Velositi.

"Five minutes out, but I'll slam it into the danger zone."

"Sprokkit?"

"Twelve minutes, but I can go lights and siren."

"I am the farthest, and Ryan is still in the store. Kita, try and hide," said Velositi.

"I tried that. They broke down the door," Kita said agitatedly.

"Try to get out to the road and meet Bernoot."

"Fine." Blue and red flashes appeared from around the corner. "I have to go." Kita hung up and moved in the opposite direction of the lights. Her phone beeped. *Slag. I don't need you to give me away.* As Kita silenced the phone, there was a sync icon on the notifications bar. *Why is my tablet trying to sync? I left it back at the…Oh-no. Nitstik has my tablet, and it knows where my phone is. Ok. Don't panic. How to use this to my advantage?*

Keeping low, Kita hurried to the fence. She moved along it until she found some big rocks. She placed her phone as far away from the fence as she could reach and then put rocks on top of it. *I hope I don't crack the screen.*

From the fence, Kita could see Nitstik's lights moving toward her. In a crouch, Kita sprinted toward the other corner of the building. She followed the building around to the parking lot, where grass grew through cracks in the pavement. Kita hurried across the parking lot to the entrance and the closed gate.

Kita pulled the rickety guard shack door open. It was barren except for a stool, a phone, and a button on a wooden shelf. She pushed the button, and the gate opened. In the distance, headlights were coming up the road. Kita exited the shack, went through the gate, and moved to the shoulder of the road.

*Is that Bernoot?* Not wanting to find out the hard way, Kita crossed the road and lay on the shoulder slope, hidden in the grass.

The headlights were approaching fast and then went out when they came close. A gold 1974 Pontiac Firebird Trans Am skidded to a halt in front of the gate. When the gate opened, the Firebird squealed its tires and drove into the lab's parking lot. The car disappeared in the darkness. Kita didn't feel like chasing after it to see whose side it was on.

As her adrenaline dropped, the pain in her arm registered. She had four deep gashes down her forearm—two on top and two on the bottom. *The damn thing just missed my ulnar artery. I could be dying in that stupid restroom. I'm probably going to need stitches. Like I can afford that. Scars are sexy, right? This was such a stupid idea. Why did I agree to do this?*

Down the road, headlights with flashing red and amber lights appeared. *Could that be Sprokkit? He said he had lights and a siren.* From behind the lab, there were several flashes and an explosion. *That must have been Bernoot. Glad I didn't follow him. Do I follow Sprokkit in or wait for Velositi? Sprokkit will just tell me to get out of the way and to stay put. I might as well not bother him.*

A large yellow emergency four-by-four truck with BULLDOG on the front hood and AMBULANCE on the boxy back entered the lab. It drove around the building and morphed. Sprokkit fired a shot from his cannon and disappeared behind the building.

*At least Sprokkit isn't afraid to fight.* Another explosion lit the night sky. *We're going to attract some attention if they keep this up. I don't want another run-in with the cops. I guess if I went to jail, I'd get out of this mess. Ha-ha. I'm in collusion with aliens. I'll disappear down some government agency hole and never see the light of day again.*

Something landed on Kita's back while making an unintelligible noise. A stabbing pain went into Kita's shoulder. She stood, throwing whatever was on her off. When she turned around, Boom-Boom was struggling to get up.

"You!" Kita snarled. She kicked Boom-Boom, sending it into the bushes. Kita backed up, not sure where it was. Boom-Boom jumped at her from the side and knocked her to the ground. It landed on her chest, driving its pointy legs into her. A leg morphed into a saw and extended toward her face. Kita reached out with her good arm, trying to keep Boom-Boom and the saw off her. With her other arm, she searched for something to hit it with. Kita's hand closed around a fist-sized rock, and she slammed it into the side of Boom-Boom. The Morphicon stumbled as if dazed. Kita rolled to her knees and smashed the rock against the top of Boom-Boom. Its legs gave out, and it crumpled to the ground.

"Die!" Kita snarled as she slammed the rock into Boom-Boom repeatedly. Boom-Boom's saw lashed out, missing Kita by inches. She smashed the rock into the joint of Boom-Boom's body and the leg with the saw. The leg bent and crumpled, and the saw stopped spinning. Kita kept hitting Boom-Boom with the rock, even as pieces flew off. Large parts of Boom-Boom's body glowed red. With one final double-handed blow, Kita drove the rock into Boom-Boom's body. There was a blinding flash, and then the red glowing areas across Boom-Boom's body faded to black. Boom-Boom didn't move anymore.

Kita collapsed onto her back. Weak and drained, she took a few deep breaths and closed her eyes. Slowly, she regained control of her mind and body. The fight or flight response dissipated. Her muscles didn't feel weak. The only thing that registered a complaint was her stomach—it still didn't feel good.

The high-pitched whine of a motorcycle caught Kita's attention. *Velositi and Ryan.* She staggered to her feet, letting the rock fall from her hand. Bending down, she grabbed one of Boom-Boom's legs. She dragged the Morphicon behind her as she climbed up the shoulder's slope onto the middle of the road and waited as Velositi came to a stop. Lit by Velositi's headlight, Kita held up Boom-Boom.

"Kita, are you ok?" called Ryan.

Kita tossed Boom-Boom's body in front of Velositi. "Protect me—my ass!" she shrieked. Spinning on her heel, Kita stormed off down the road.

Ryan caught up to Kita. He grabbed her arm. "Kita, what happened?"

Kita stopped and glared at Ryan's hand. He let go hesitantly. "Don't touch me," she said in a low growl.

"I'm sorry. I just want to make sure you're ok."

"Do I look like I'm ok?" Kita yelled hysterically. "Leave me alone—all of you. I don't ever want to see you again. You can take your slagging war and shove it. I'm done. You can take your clothes, makeup, bike, and the rest of it. I don't want it. I'm going back to the yard. Do you hear me, Velositi? I know you're listening. To the Crushing Depths with all of you." She turned her back on Ryan and walked away.

Kita followed the road until her stomach could take no more. She stumbled down the shoulder next to a tree, sat down, and leaned against it. Resting her head on the bark, what she'd been fighting since she killed Boom-Boom came. Tears silently slid down her face.

*I did what I had to because I didn't have a choice—do or die. But, no one ever said anything about the cost.*

KITA AWOKE TO FOG COVERING THE NEARBY HILLS. SHE ROLLED HER NECK from side-to-side to work the kink out from sleeping against the tree. Her stomach still ached, but not as bad. *It's tolerable. I'll live.* She stretched her legs out into the tall yellow grass. Her jeans were dirty and torn in two places. *Ripped jeans are all the rage, right?* Her right arm was covered in blood and ran down her hand onto her fingers. She only had a little blood on her flannel. The cuts weren't bleeding, so she unrolled her sleeves to hide them. At some point, she would have to find a place where she could clean the cuts and scrub the blood off her.

*I wonder where this road goes?* She didn't have her phone, so she had no maps to navigate by. *Maybe I should sneak back to the lab and get my phone. It's on the outside. I don't have to go near the lab. Otherwise, I'm lost.* She had been too sick last night to know how Velositi got here. *It might be better to go the way we came. At least that way I know there is civilization. I can hitchhike into the city and get a bus ticket home. Hopefully, I have a home to go back to, and Ralph and Mickey haven't screwed things up too bad. Who am I kidding? They won't have done a thing without me.*

Kita sighed and stretched. *Let's make it easy on myself. Find my phone and hitchhike back the way we came until I get into town, then get to the bus station and go home. I'll have to pass the lab, but I can do that without being seen.* Plan in place, Kita stood up and dusted herself off. She turned to climb up the shoulder onto the road and yelled, "What are you doing here?"

Velositi sat on the shoulder and stood when Kita yelled. "I am here to tell you I am sorry. I could not do what I promised. But, please, do not go. We need you."

"Take Ryan," Kita growled as she walked up the shoulder.

"I need you," Velositi said quietly. "Please, come ride with me. You do not have to say a word, and I will not either. Just come with me. Please. When we are finished, I will take you to any place you want to go."

"Take me home?"

"If that's where you wish to go."

"I need my helmet."

"Do you not trust me?"

Kita could hear the pain in Velositi's voice. "Why should I? If last night proved anything, it was only I can save myself."

"No person is an island, Kita. We all need friends, and those friends make mistakes. I made one last night, and you dared to overcome it. I am sorry. I do not know how Nitstik found us. We are investigating our movements, looking for how we made a mistake. It is a major failure, and it nearly cost me you."

Kita crossed her arms. "That isn't your failure. That is mine. They followed my phone using my tablet. They share a connection. I should have remembered. You don't owe me an apology for that. I owe you one. I'm sorry for blowing our cover. I figured it out too late, but I did my best to use it against them. My phone is hidden under some rocks behind the lab."

"Is that why Nitstik was tearing up the fence?"

"Yep. I'm sorry. I should know my stuff better. But you shouldn't have left me alone."

"I am sorry," whispered Velositi. "I thought I was doing what was best for you by getting you the medicine you needed. I should have waited for Bernoot to arrive."

"Did you get some?"

A compartment on Velositi's chest opened. She pulled out a bottle of pink stuff and gave it to Kita. After removing the safety wrapper, Kita opened the bottle and took a long drink.

"Ugh. The stuff tastes awful. I can feel it going all the way down." Kita did feel a soothing sensation in her stomach, and the pain dulled.

"Are you better?" said Velositi as she took the bottle and put it away.

"Ish. Still upset, but I can live with it. It'll take a while to fully work."

"Are you well enough to ride?"

"Still willing to take me home?"

"If that is your desire, but I will not leave you."

Kita raised an eyebrow. "Why such devotion to me?"

"You do not like me?"

"I guess so, but you can be demanding at times. Still, there is liking me and obsessing about me."

"I know what I like, and I want us to be partners."

"But why?"

"You will have to trust me," said Velositi.

"You're not going to use me and dump me, are you?"

"Anything but...To be honest, after the war is over, I want to return here and be with you."

"You like me that much?"

"Yes."

"Little creepy."

"All will be explained in time. For now, you will have to trust me."

Kita sighed. *What do I do? Do I trust her? We both made mistakes. She doesn't seem upset with me over mine. So, is it fair to be mad at her for hers? We all make mistakes, and it doesn't sound like she'll ever leave me alone again. I may regret that. Something is going on with her and with me. I do like her. She does take care of me—no matter how big a pain in the ass I am. She must really care about me. It's been a while since someone has. I forgot how good it feels. I wonder how long she sat out here waiting for me to wake up? I wouldn't have been so patient. I just don't get why she is so protective and absolutely sure I have to be with her. She says to trust her...*

"Ok," said Kita softly. "Where are you taking me to?"

"A drive in the mountains. The scenery is supposed to be spectacular."

"I've never been out there."

"So, you will go?" said Velositi, sounding hopeful.

"Yeah, I'll go."

Velositi climbed onto the road and morphed. Kita hopped on, and Velositi sped off down the road.

---

KITA LET HER MIND BE FREE AS VELOSITI DROVE THE TWISTY NARROW mountain highway. She fell into rhythm with Velositi as she braked, leaned into corners, and accelerated down the straightaways. Kita didn't think, just followed

Velositi's lead like a dance. Velositi hadn't spoken since they left. She seemed to be letting her actions speak for her.

Velositi slowed as they entered the mountain town of Red Feather. It was a small touristy place with several antique dealers, a Christmas store, a bakery, a café, and a walk-up smoothie bar. The town was moderately busy with tourists walking the streets and exploring the shops.

"Are...Are you hungry?" said Velositi.

Kita wiggled her nose as she listened to what her body told her. She was hungry, but she wasn't up for solid food or eating alone in the café. A small smoothie sounded good, though.

"Yeah, I'll grab a smoothie."

Velositi pulled into a spot near the smoothie bar. Kita dismounted and stretched. A breeze blew through her hair and sent a chill up her spine. "Chilly up here." Kita hadn't noticed while they'd been driving.

"Do you want your jacket and phone?" said Velositi.

"You have them?"

A compartment in the side of the bike opened. Kita pulled out her jacket and slipped it on. Checking her pockets, all her makeup and comb were there. She then slipped her phone into her back pocket.

"I guess I'll get cleaned up, too. Seeing as how I'm riding you."

"Thank you," said Velositi quietly.

Kita patted Velositi's fuel tank, then walked to the smoothie bar. Following signs for the restroom around the side of the building, Kita found the door unlocked and went inside. After locking the door, she emptied her pockets onto the sink and shrugged off her jacket. The first thing she did was roll up her right sleeve and wash the blood from her arm and hands. After she cleaned them, she patted her arm dry with a paper towel. The cuts were scabbed over but wide and gnarly. *That's going to take a while to heal. Maybe we should stop and get something to put on it. Probably too late now to be of any use. I might look for something for scars.*

After rolling her sleeve back down, Kita tended to her face—washing, cleaning, and reapplying. When she finished with her face, she combed her hair and tied it back. Satisfied she'd done all she could, she put everything away in her jacket.

Exiting the restroom, Kita went to the bar where a guy with long hair and beard wearing a gray shirt that said ERIN GO BRAGH worked.

"What can I get for you?" he asked.

"A small pomegranate."

"Up from the coast?" he said *coast* like it was a bad word.

"Actually, I'm from the desert."

The guy raised an eyebrow but didn't say anything. *Not a fan of tourists? Maybe he doesn't like pretty people.*

As she waited, Kita checked on Velositi. Two teens had stopped to admire her. *She does attract attention, and she looks good in black and pink. I should talk to her now that I'm not mad at her. Ha. I bet that was her plan all along. Clever girl.*

"Here you go." He set the drink on the bar.

Kita paid for it and walked back to Velositi and her admirers.

"You like her?" Kita said to the teens.

"This is your bike?" a tall, scruffy kid exclaimed.

Kita kissed the air and held out her nails. "Painted to match."

"How fast does it go?" said the shorter and rounder pimple-faced teen.

"*She* is a custom build and is the fastest thing on two wheels. But, it's not about how fast you can go. It's about how you handle the curves...how you lean into them...your precision and control...you have to know what you're doing to make her roar. You can't just twist the throttle."

Kita ran a hand over Velositi's gas tank and seat. She mounted Velositi, and Velositi's engine roared.

"You have to handle her right," Kita said to the teenagers.

"Wow. It must be awesome to ride," said the pimple-faced teen.

"I ride her every day, and she doesn't disappoint."

Velositi backed out of the spot.

"Find us someplace quiet where I can talk to you," said Kita. "The real you."

Velositi responded by turning up a side street. The street climbed up the side of a hill. As they went, the road became more of a patchwork of asphalt and dirt. When they crested the hill, a large oak tree with wide branches came into view. Velositi parked under the tree. Kita dismounted and took a sip of her smoothie. Velositi morphed and looked around.

"It's a nice view," said Kita. "You can see for miles." The hill was mostly yellow grass, but in the distance—on neighboring hills and mountainsides—was a pine forest, scrub trees, and a wide swath of burned grassland. Kita smiled at Velositi. "Sit." Kita pointed to the tree.

Velositi leaned against the tree, leaving one of her legs straight and the other bent. Kita sat in Velositi's lap. Velositi's eyes glowed brightly. Kita leaned against Velositi, laying her head on Velositi's warm chest. It was soft and gave a little. Velositi put an arm around her. Kita took a few sips of her smoothie as she enjoyed being in Velositi's arms and the warmth she put off.

"So, tell me about you," said Kita.

"Me?" Velositi sounded surprised.

"If you want to be an important part of my life, I want to know more about you. I know your favorite color is pink. You like girls. You're in command of this group, and you have a creepy attachment to me."

"I do not mean it to be creepy," said Velositi softly.

"Talk to me, and then maybe it won't be."

"I...When a new Vehlix is constructed, they go before the Oracle and receive a prophecy that will help them in their lives. It is a secret to each Vehlix, and it is the reason I am here."

"Prophecies are always interesting. Are they the kind that no matter what you do it's destined to happen, or are they self-fulfilling and you make them happen?"

"I do not know. I put a lot of work to get here. I am the youngest team leader ever—hand-selected by the Elders. I have fought in many engagements against the Neophormes and distinguished myself. I have led small teams on many missions and have never failed."

"The thing about prophecies is that you'll never know the answer."

"That is an interesting bit of wisdom. No one questions the Oracle."

Kita laughed. "I watch a lot of anime. They're always talking about stuff like that."

"Anime?"

"Cartoons from Japan. They're very philosophical. What do you like?"

"I have always been a soldier. I like pretty things and to be pretty—to get noticed. I spend a lot of time preparing myself for my duties."

"What do you do for fun?"

"I do not know. I do not have much time for fun. Everything I do has a goal."

"You like to drive," said Kita.

"Yes. I like to think I am flying. I think those Vehlixen who can fly are lucky."

"Envy. I like it. I've envied a lot of people—mostly because their lives didn't suck as much as mine."

"I hope to be an improvement on that."

Kita chuckled. "I spoke in the past tense. Life has improved. I just need to catch up to it."

"You seem better, more stable."

Kita sighed. "I've accepted my fate. There is no going back. I almost died, but I made it through. I did what I had to. I may have PTSD from it, but I survived. I will go on, and I'm stronger because of it."

"I was programmed for battle. I do not have any psychological effects from stress."

"I was messed up to begin with. What's one more thing, hey? But, if I have nightmares, I expect you to be there because it's your fault." Kita took a sip of her smoothie.

"It was my failing. I will do whatever you want to make it up to you."

"I don't want you to make it up to me. I want you there to comfort me and make me feel better."

"I can do that. I want to be your friend," said Velositi softly.

"No," said Kita as she sat up in Velositi's lap. "You're more than my friend. In two days, you've changed my entire world. You've shown me more compassion, understanding, and kindness than anyone has since my dad died. You didn't have to. You could have left me." Kita scooted up on Velositi and hugged her, resting her head on Velositi's shoulder. "Thank you." Kita kissed Velositi's cheek.

"I...I..."

Kita touched Velositi's lips with her finger. "I know. I don't know if I'm there yet, but you're very special to me. There's my dad, and then there's you. Give it a little more time. Ok?"

"Ok." Velositi's eyes glowed brightly.

Kita giggled.

"What?" said Velositi.

"Nothing. I'm just happy. For the first time in a long time."

THE RIDE OUT OF THE MOUNTAINS FILLED KITA WITH JOY AND EXUBERANCE. A weight was gone from her shoulders. It was like she was floating, and with the way Velositi was driving, she might as well have been flying. All too soon, it was over. Velositi pulled into the lab's parking lot and stopped in front of the bay door.

Kita hugged Velositi. "That was fun."

"I think I scared some people."

"They're just jealous," said Kita as she dismounted Velositi.

Kita went to lift the door and found it much heavier than she expected.

"Let me," said Velositi. "This door probably has not seen this much use in decades."

"I wonder how the students get it open?" Kita's question was lost in the screeching of the door going up.

Sprokkit and Ryan were hovering over a newly constructed workbench. Bright lights concentrated on whatever they were working on. Bernoot sat leaning against the concrete tube. He had three holes in his chest, each glowing fire-red.

"What's wrong with Bernoot?" said Kita to Velositi.

"Nitstik hit him several times last night. He is powered down to heal."

"Shouldn't we look for a new place to hide?"

Velositi shook her head. "No. Bernoot needs time to heal, and Sprokkit reports Nitstik was also injured badly. By the time he heals, we will be gone."

"I do not think Bernoot has the plasma to heal," said Sprokkit as he turned around.

"Is that not what you are working on?" replied Velositi tartly.

"Yes, and I need parts. The human—"

"His name is Ryan," said Kita.

"I know his name and have been addressing him by it. *Ryan* and I have salvaged parts from the devices stored here, but we need more."

"I told him it shouldn't be a problem," said Ryan, "but we don't have any money to go get them."

"I did not know you would be moving into the production phase so quickly," said Velositi. "We can go and get the parts tomorrow."

"Just send a list of what you need," said Kita.

"We're going to need to take Sprokkit," said Ryan. "What we need won't fit on the back of a bike."

"Then we can all go into the city together. We can look up where we can get the parts tonight."

"Lowes and Walmart will have most of them."

"We can get some other supplies while we're there. I need to find some way of keeping clean and pretty."

"How are you?" said Ryan. "You don't seem so...hostile."

Kita grinned. "Yeah, sorry. But I had just been running for my life, so..." Kita took off her jacket and pushed up her sleeves. She tossed the jacket on a cot.

"What happened to your arm?" said Ryan aghast.

"Huh? Oh, nothing. I was bitten by Boom-Boom."

"Kita, why did you not tell me?" said Velositi.

"Those are not *nothing*," said Ryan. "You should have stitches."

"I cleaned them earlier. They had already clotted."

"They still need to be bandaged and have an antibacterial put on them."

"What are you—a boy scout?" chided Kita.

"Yes," said Ryan. "Hang on. There's a first aid kit at the end of the hallway." He left to retrieve the kit.

"Kita," said Velositi.

"What? I'm fine. Bernoot's the one with three big holes in his chest. I'll heal."

"Please, let Ryan bandage it up."

"Fine." Kita left and went to sit on a cot. She shrugged her flannel off. It was dirty, had some grass seeds stuck to it, and had a hole in the back. *I'm a little rough on clothes. But my shirt looks good.* The shirt had been a present from Velositi. Kita had no idea how she had the shirt custom made and delivered to the boutique in just a few hours. She dug into her jacket and pulled out her comb. After undoing her hair, she brushed it out.

"Ok," said Ryan. "I have the—whoa."

"What?" said Kita.

"Cousin Itt."

"Shut up," said Kita playfully.

Ryan opened the kit and pulled out what he needed. "Arm?"

Kita stopped combing her hair and offered her injured arm.

"These are some gnarly teeth marks."

"It was all I had to keep Boom-Boom away from my face."

"How did you kill it?"

"I beat it to death with a rock."

"You should have heard Velositi."

"What'd she say?"

"More of a sound. Frightened, I think. And worried."

"I bet."

"You two seem to be better."

Kita shrugged. "We talked."

"About what?"

"Girl stuff."

"So, you're staying?"

"Yeah."

"Cool. All done."

Kita's lower arm looked like a mummy. "Thanks. I'll rise from the dead and chase you around later."

Ryan laughed. "Sprokkit and I were going to go get pizza. You want to come?"

Kita shook her head. "No. My stomach is still upset. I think I want to sleep."

"Ok. I'll bring you back a few slices for breakfast."

"Fine. Something light that I can eat. Now, shoo."

Ryan smiled, gathered up the kit, and left.

Kita stretched out on the cot. She looked down at her boots but had to lift her head to see them. *This bra and shirt make my chest look huge. I wonder if that was by design.* She kicked off her boots and gathered her jacket up for a pillow.

Velositi came over and morphed.

Kita reached over and stroked Velositi's cowl. "Night," she whispered.

KITA AWOKE TO VELOSITI AND SPROKKIT ARGUING IN AN UNINTELLIGIBLE language. She sat up, stretched, ruffled her hair, and got up to see what the matter was. She stopped next to Velositi and put her hand on her back. The two Morphicons stopped and looked at Kita.

"What's the matter?" said Kita as she stepped in closer to Velositi to get a hug.

"How do you know something is the matter?" said Sprokkit.

"Arguing sounds like arguing in any language. Plus, both your eyes are glowing brightly. That's how you show emotion."

"She is more perceptive than I thought," muttered Sprokkit. "The issue is our dear leader was filmed morphing, and it is all over the internet."

Kita pulled out her phone and hit the YouTube app. A video entitled "Transforming Motorcycle Saves Driver" was third on the trending list. Kita opened it. It was a dashcam video showing her and Ryan on the highway to Big Surf. A white SUV pulled alongside Ryan and hit him. As Ryan lost control, Velositi morphed, throwing Kita into the air, grabbing Ryan—there was a bump as the dashcam vehicle ran over Ryan's bike—and then Velositi fired at the dashcam vehicle, and the picture was lost in the smoke. The video had over five million views. There was a heated debate in the comments if it was a fake or not.

"That's us," said Kita.

"We are exposed," said Sprokkit. "We must abort."

"We are not aborting," said Velositi. "Just remove the video."

"Sorry," said Kita. "It doesn't work like that. Once something is on the internet, it's there forever. I bet that video has been posted around the world."

"She is correct," said Sprokkit. "The video is all over the world, but the details have changed. Some say it happened in Australia or Canada. There is ample debate if it is real or not."

"With today's video editing software, it's easy to create something like this. I'm sure people are pulling it apart frame by frame looking for any editing errors."

"Can we put some in?" said Velositi.

"Too late," said Kita. "Not only has the video gone around the world, but the file will also have been downloaded, too. We could never get them all."

"You have cost us our mission," snarled Sprokkit as he pointed a finger at Velositi.

"She has not," said Kita. "One video does not mean proof. This will just be an oddity for most people before it becomes fodder for the conspiracy theory nut jobs. It's not time to panic. We have to be a little more careful. The police are probably looking for me, but everybody will be looking for a beat-up old Indian, not a Ninja. I've changed my clothes, look, and have a helmet. No one should recognize me. They don't even know my name. They do know Ryan's. They'll have run his tags to identify his bike. I'm sure they'll pull his driver's license photo and will be looking for him. He's the only solid connection to us."

"We will have to protect him," said Velositi.

"I'm sure he'll be ok going out. He'll just have to stay away from the cops."

"What about me?" said Ryan arriving late. He looked at Kita's arm around Velositi and raised an eyebrow.

"I told you we talked," said Kita. "I was saying you're the only connection people have to us. Did you ever call your insurance company?"

"Yeah. I need a police report."

"You might want to wait on that."

"Why?"

Kita showed him the video.

"It's weird that an SUV that was shooting at us has a dashcam."

"Probably lowers their insurance rate. You can't see anyone in this SUV firing, just the other SUV. But, ah, you might want to send this video to your insurance to prove fault."

"Then, I have to explain Velositi to them."

Kita shook her head. "That's none of their business."

"They'll probably ask why she couldn't save the bike."

Kita looked up at Velositi.

"I only have two hands."

Kita laughed. "And yet you managed to throw, grab, shoot, catch, *and* morph."

"You are teasing me," said Velositi.

"Yes." Kita gave her a playful squeeze.

"Sprokkit, we will be more careful," said Velositi. "But if exposing ourselves helps us get the Axiom of Command, then I will do it."

"We were explicitly forbidden to reveal ourselves."

"You did not care that Mike knew."

"He was useful."

"So are Kita and Ryan," said Velositi tersely.

"Ryan, yes. Kita is your plaything."

"I never complained about your and Mike's relationship."

"Ours was purely professional," growled Sprokkit.

"He was your friend. I am sorry he is gone."

"I do not need your sympathies. What is done is done. I have moved on." Sprokkit stomped away back to the workbench.

"I am sorry, Kita," said Velositi.

"Hey, he feels how he feels. I can't change that it clouds his judgment of me. I just hope he knows I'm not going anywhere."

"That is good. We have a busy day today gathering the items that Sprokkit and Ryan need. He sent you the list."

Kita opened the email on her phone and found the message with a list of a dozen items and where to find them.

"Sprokkit knows he has to come, right?" said Kita.

"I know. I will talk to him. You and Ryan get ready to go."

"Right," said Ryan. "You want me to go with you to talk to him?"

"No. He needs to be reminded of his place."

Kita hugged Velositi and went to find her boots.

---

VELOSITI PULLED TO A STOP BEHIND A HONDA CIVIC AT A STOPLIGHT. MID-afternoon rush hour hadn't even started yet, but all three lanes of traffic were full.

"Gotta love the city," Kita muttered. Riding in this traffic was no fun. The speed limit was forty, and traffic moved at thirty-five. *Velositi's talents are wasted in traffic like this.*

"Kita," said Velositi, "there is a black sedan three cars back on the right. It has been following us since we left Lowes."

Kita checked the side mirror. Lowes had been their first stop of the day, and they had just left Walmart. Sprokkit and Ryan had gone back to the lab, while Kita and Velositi took the long way home so they could ride together. The black sedan was a BMW 750i. *A powerful machine that could keep up with most other vehicles —except Velositi.* Two men wearing sunglasses were in the front.

"Any idea who they are?" said Kita.

"They do not match any of the gunrunner goons."

"Let's see how interested they are. Let's go out to the freeway but cut through a neighborhood. We'll see how long they can keep up."

"I have a route selected. I will surprise them by turning here." Velositi maneuvered between two cars into the double turn lane. She drove up the center of the turn lanes and reached the front just as the light changed. Velositi took off, taking advantage of the clear street to put some distance between them and the intersection.

"Sprokkit," Velositi called.

"Yes? We have not arrived yet if that is what you want to know."

"I'm not calling to micromanage you. You are capable of doing what needs to be done. I am letting you know that Kita and I are making a detour. We think we are being followed. Watch yourself. Only return to the lab if you know it is safe."

"I will monitor traffic more closely, but no vehicle has followed us for more than a mile."

"Just be careful."

"I will proceed with caution." Sprokkit hung up.

"You'd think we hadn't gotten him exactly what he wanted. He should be happy," said Kita.

"He is upset that I reminded him that he might be older, but I am in charge."

"I get that. Mickey and Ralph are always giving me a hard time when I tell them to do stuff. Half the time they don't do it, or they don't do it right. They think they know best, but it's not their ass on the line."

"Exactly," said Velositi. "If this mission fails, it is I who will look bad. Sprokkit will just join another team. I could be sent back to the Cuts."

"What are the Cuts?"

"The Cuts are a network of trenches that ring our planet. They are hundreds of miles wide and hundreds of yards deep. It is where most of the fighting happens on the ground. Even more goes on in the air and space."

"Wow. That must be awful."

"If you are away from the fighting life is not so bad, but life in the Cuts is miserable. The Neophormes are relentless and attack at a moment's notice. They are always attacking somewhere." Velositi turned down a residential street, taking it easy over the speed humps.

"So, you served in the Cuts?"

"Yes. I fought hard and distinguished myself. I proved I could lead and get results. I was moved to special operations conducting small raids and special missions. I excelled there. I was chosen from that group to lead this mission."

"So, you're like a super warrior?"

"I do not have the hubris to think so. I just do my best at the task given to me."

"I think you're super."

"Thanks, but—"

"I wish I knew if you blushed or not. I bet you'd be cute blushing. Or, do your eyes give it away?"

"The eyes are a window to the soul," whispered Velositi.

"They say the same thing about ours, but with yours, I think it's true."

Velositi sped up and made a left turn to join a major street. She maneuvered back and forth, making room for herself in traffic.

"Do you see them?" said Kita, giving Velositi a chance to escape her teasing.

"I do not," said Velositi.

"Let's keep going toward the freeway. We can take the four-ten to the five-oh-one. That'll take us out near the lab."

"Ok. This street will take us to the on-ramp."

Velositi moved at the speed of traffic, passing people when she could. They'd gone almost two miles when Velositi said, "There is another black sedan behind us. Four cars back on the right."

Kita found the car in the mirror. It was the same BWM make, and the drivers wore sunglasses, but she couldn't tell if they were the same men as before.

"Is it the same men as before?" said Kita.

"No. They are different," said Velositi.

"How in the Crushing Depths did they find us?"

"I do not know. Should we make another turn?"

"Nah. Let's just get to the freeway. We'll outrun them."

Velositi pushed more aggressively through traffic. Using Velositi's mirrors, Kita watched the sedan maneuver through traffic, trying to keep up with the nimbler Velositi. As they approached the freeway, Velositi made a right-hand turn from the far-left lane, cutting across three lanes of traffic. She sped up the shoulder of the on-ramp and merged into traffic.

"That should put them behind us," said Kita.

Velositi drifted across the freeway into the far-left lane. Traffic was moving at a steady fifty-five miles per hour.

"I hope the five-oh-one is better than this," said Kita.

"Maybe we should have chosen a police bike and gotten lights and a siren," said Velositi.

"No way. Police bikes are boxy and ugly. I like you as you are—sleek, sexy, and beautiful—even if we have to go slow in traffic. It just means I get more time on top of you."

"I know there is a compliment there, but is there also an innuendo?"

"Maybe..."

"I think your goal today was to make me blush."

Kita laughed. "I don't know if it was my goal, but did I succeed?"

"Yes. Multiple times."

"Good. Someday you can get me to go multiple times."

"I—someone is in a mischievous mood."

"Maybe, but you still like me anyway."

Velositi merged onto the ramp to take them from the 410 crosstown freeway to the 501, which led out to the valley and the lab. Once on the 501, traffic opened up, and Velositi was able to speed up to sixty-five miles per hour.

"Kita, two black sedans are coming up fast," said Velositi.

"Bloody moons. How do they keep finding us?"

"I do not know. I am going to try and outrun them."

Kita agreed with that. She lowered her torso and kept her head up. Velositi sped by cars, weaving around slower traffic. A thirty-foot-long moving truck was in the middle lane between two semis. As Velositi pulled in behind the moving truck, it sped up. The moving truck passed the semi and merged into the right lane. Seeing the opening, Velositi sped forward. As she came alongside the moving truck, it matched her speed.

A door on the side of the moving truck opened, just as the two BMW sedans came up between the semis. A man in a black uniform held a launcher with a claw-like projectile on his shoulder.

"Look out!" said Kita as the man in the moving truck fired.

The claw projectile hit Velositi's cowl just in front of the clutch. A cable connected the moving truck to Velositi.

"Ki—" Velositi's voice filled with static, and she slowed, causing her to wobble.

"Velositi?" said Kita. *If we don't speed up, we're going over.* Kita twisted the throttle, and Velositi responded. *Great. I suddenly have to learn to drive her.* Kita took control and tried to pull free from their attackers as they attached the cable to a winch.

Kita jerked Velositi to the left, trying to pull free of the claw. On her left, a BMW pulled up next to her. It moved toward her, pushing her toward the moving truck. The other BMW pulled in behind her. *The only way is forward.*

Twisting the throttle, Kita burst forward, pulling hard on the cable and claw. Two of the claw's tines came loose. The BMW on her left caught up to her and moved toward Kita. She jerked Velositi right and sped up. The cable became taut, but the claw refused to let go. The maneuver caused Kita to jerk wildly to the right, almost causing them to crash. Kita regained control, but the men on the truck had the winch working, pulling her toward them. They waited with hooked poles. *I hope I'm not their white whale. I have to get out of here.*

The claw twisted but refused to let go. Kita stood up. Velositi slowed from the sudden drag, putting her rear tire within an inch of the BMW. With all the force Kita could bring to bear, she brought her foot down on the claw. It gave way, causing Velositi to veer hard to the left. Kita caught herself and pulled Velositi back to the right.

Free, Kita twisted the throttle to maximum. Velositi shot forward, outrunning the moving truck. The two BMWs tried to keep up with Kita, but she had reached traffic and was weaving her way through. Kita ducked under a semi into a merging lane. She sped along, trying to put as much distance between her and the BMWs as she could.

Kita passed an on-ramp. She looked in her mirror when she heard the siren. *Are they real cops? With the moving van? I'm not going to stop to find out. How am I going to lose them? And how come Velositi didn't come back? Ugh, I don't want to have to call Sprokkit, but what else am I going to do?*

Kita pulled her phone from her back pocket, scrolled through her contacts until she found Sprokkit. She pushed his icon. It rang a few times before he picked up.

"What do you want?" Sprokkit said loudly in Kita's helmet.

"I'm in trouble, and there is something wrong with Velositi."

"What is wrong with Velositi?" he said gruffly.

"She was hit by this metal claw on a cable. I was talking to her when it happened. Her voice filled with static, and she went quiet. She won't respond, and I have to drive her manually."

"I cannot make any definitive answers until I examine her. It sounds like her system cores were overloaded. She might awaken if her systems can make the repairs. If not, then I will have to do it—depending on how damaged her cores are."

"What does that mean?" demanded Kita.

"She might still yet die. That you can operate her, means there is still some life in her. That is a promising sign."

"Velositi can't die!"

"Then, I suggest you bring her to me."

"I... ah... don't think I can right now. I'm being chased by the police."

"Then give yourself up. Bernoot and I will rescue Velositi from the impound lot."

"What about me?"

"You, I will leave to your fate." Sprokkit disconnected the call.

"I love you, too," Kita huffed.

Kita passed another on-ramp. Checking her mirror, the cop was still behind her. Coming up the on-ramp were four more police cruisers. *Uh-oh. This guy might be a real cop. We have a real high-speed chase going on now. Catch me if you can.*

As Kita raced along the freeway, the police stayed at a respectful distance behind her. Close enough to let her know they were there, but not close enough to press her into doing anything. The freeway was mostly clear—much to Kita's surprise. *It's rush hour. The freeway should be packed.* Passing an on-ramp, she saw police blocking access.

As Kita crested a hill, a rolling roadblock was in front of her. The ten highway patrol cars blocked the five lanes and the shoulders. Kita didn't have a choice but to brake. *Do I turn around?* In her mirror, she could see almost a dozen police vehicles stretching across the freeway. *Nowhere to go. I wish I could fly.*

As the highway patrol slowed down in front of Kita, those behind her caught up. The highway patrol came to a stop, and the police behind Kita closed up around her. Kita stopped and put her feet on the ground. Police officers and highway patrol officers exited their vehicles with guns drawn and surrounded her.

*By the Crushing Depths, what am I going to tell them? I can't tell them about Velositi or the others, but I don't want to rot in prison either. Ha. If I tell them about Velositi, I'm going to rot in a much worse place. I'll be sent to Guantanamo Bay and be forgotten. I was just out for a joy ride, that's all.*

"Shut off the bike and get on the ground!" yelled a highway patrol officer.

*That doesn't mean I have to go quietly.* Kita raised her hands.

The officers took a few steps toward Kita.

"Get off the bike and get on the ground!" another officer yelled.

*So, I can make it easier for you to beat me?* An unmarked charger with its lights flashing pulled around the rear line of police vehicles and stopped near the circle of officers. The doors of the charger opened, and a man and a woman got out. They were dressed in a similar style. The man wore a black suit and tie with a white shirt. She wore a black pantsuit with a white shirt and a black tie. Both wore dark sunglasses. *Who are these two? I thought MIBs were a myth.*

"Get on the ground or get tased!" an officer yelled.

*Uh-oh. Getting serious now.*

The MIBs walked to the circle of officers. The man pulled a badge from his coat and held it up.

"IBI," he announced in an authoritative voice. "She belongs to us."

*Oh, slag me. What did I do to get noticed by the Imperial Bureau of Investigation?*

The man walked around the circle of officers showing them his badge. The woman stood in front of Kita. The officers relaxed some, lowering their weapons, but they maintained a perimeter around Kita. The man approached Kita and held up his badge to her.

"IBI, Miss. Shut down the bike and take your helmet off."

Kita gulped. She hit the ignition button on Velositi and removed her helmet.

"What's your name, Miss?"

"Kita Logine," she whispered.

The man reached into his pocket and pulled out a phone. He turned it on and tapped on it a few times. "Is this you?" He held up his phone so that Kita could see.

It was a picture of Kita sitting on Velositi as the Indian, back when the highway patrol pulled her over in the desert.

*Do I lie? It's not a great picture. It could be anyone. But, do I really want to lie to the IBI? Where would that land me? Maybe I can be coy.*

"Kind of looks like me, but it's not my bike."

The man turned his phone around, tapped, and there were a click and flash.

*Oh, slag me!*

He tapped his phone a few more times. Kita waited in uncomfortable silence for what was to happen next. The phone dinged.

"Facial recognition confirms that is you," said the man.

"So, I got pulled over. So, what?"

"Where's the motorcycle at?"

"I traded it in and got a new one."

"You're coming with us."

"I'm not leaving my bike to this goon squad."

"The bike is coming, too," said the man.

*Uh-oh.* "How about you just impound the bike, and I'll grab it later?" said Kita.

"Sergeant," the man called to a police officer. "I need a three-car escort to the Imperial building downtown. We need to get there as fast as possible."

"Yes, sir," said the officer. He called out some names and gave them instructions.

The man looked at Kita. "Follow us downtown." He reached into his pocket, pulling out a device and stuck it to Velositi's gas tank. "If you decide to run, this will go off and kill the bike.

*Slag. Velositi can't take another electrical shock. What choice do I have but to follow?*

Kita followed the unmarked IBI Charger through the underground garage of the Angel City Imperial Building. They descended six stories and stopped before a door with an anti-vehicle barricade. The man stopped at a security kiosk and scanned his badge. The door went up as the barrier sank into the floor.

The Charger pulled forward, and Kita followed into an empty garage area, complete with large MAC toolboxes, power lifts, air compressors, and everything a working garage needed. Kita was envious. *I wish I had half the stuff they have.*

The Charger parked near a door, and Kita pulled in behind it. The two IBI agents exited the charger and walked over to Kita. She took off her helmet and set it on Velositi's gas tank. Slowly, she raised her hands.

"I want a lawyer," said Kita meekly.

"You're not under arrest," said the woman.

"We do have some questions about you and your bike," said the man. "I'm Special Agent Muller."

"And I'm Special Agent Skulls. We're part of the IBI's UXE division."

"What's a UXE?" said Kita.

"Unexplained Events," said Muller. "We investigate strange occurrences and search for their origins."

"You're not going to pull my bike apart while I'm gone, are you?"

"Your bike is safe. You just need to answer our questions. Follow us."

Muller retrieved the kill device from Velositi and walked toward the door. Kita followed with Skulls behind her. Muller waved his badge at a sensor next to the door. They walked down a long hallway lined with unmarked doors. Muller stopped in front of a random door, scanned his badge, and opened it. He led everyone inside. There was a desk with two chairs on one side, a single chair on the other, and nothing else.

"Have a seat," said Muller, waving to the single chair.

Kita sat and put her hands and elbows on the table. "So, if I'm not in any trouble, I can leave at any time, right?"

"You could leave," said Skulls, "but we are the only ones between you and the Cali Highway Patrol. If you cooperate, we can make it go away."

"Why is nobody doing anything about the goons who attacked me on the freeway?" demanded Kita.

"Can you be more specific?" said Muller.

"Are you saying there are lots of attacks on the freeway?" chided Kita.

"What was involved?" said Skulls.

"Two black BMWs and a large moving van. The BMWs followed me through the city. When I got on the freeway, I was passing the moving van when its side door opened, and a goon with a launcher fired a metal claw into my bike. It took forever for me to get loose. That's why I was speeding through traffic to get away from them."

Skulls opened her phone and tapped for a few moments. She showed something to Muller as she swiped back and forth. "I have found when and where you entered the freeway, but nothing happens until the highway patrol lights you up."

"I was attacked," said Kita firmly. "I have the marks in my bike's cowl to prove it. They tried to reel me in like a whale, with hooks and everything."

Muller stood up and exited the room.

"Where's he going?" said Kita.

"Let's talk about the night the CHP pulled you over," said Skulls.

"You know about tonight."

"You were pulled over two days ago outside the city."

"What about it? I didn't do anything. He hit *me* in the back of the head."

"Tell me about this picture." Skulls opened a picture from the highway patrol car camera that showed Velositi, hand morphed into a cannon, standing over Kita and the highway patrol officer.

"What do you want to know?" said Kita with a gulp.

"What is this robot?"

"Science project?"

Skulls gave Kita a dour look. The door opened, and Muller stepped back in.

Kita huffed. "You wouldn't believe me if I told you."

"There are four holes in the cowl of your bike," said Muller. "Either you're lying about how you got them, or the videos are lying. Let's say I believe that you were attacked—why did they attack you? I believed you about your bike. I'll believe what you say about these pictures."

"With evidence," added Skulls.

Kita sighed. *I can't betray Velositi. That makes me sick to my stomach. But I can't leave her injured in their hands. Maybe I should go back to CHP. They'll just throw me in a regular jail and take Velositi to the impound yard where Sprokkit and Bernoot can rescue her.* "Just arrest me."

"If that's what you want," said Skulls. "But we have a warrant for any motorcycle in your possession or that you have ever owned."

*That's a lot of motorcycles.*

"Your bike will stay with us," said Muller. "And we'll pull it apart until we know everything."

*NO!* "Don't hurt my bike," whispered Kita.

"Answer our questions," said Skulls.

*What do I tell them that won't compromise Velositi and the others?*

"It's just a robot. It comes from Silicon Valley. I, ah, stole it."

"A robot that can do this?" Skulls played the video of Velositi saving Ryan on the highway. "This robot started as a motorcycle, became a robot, and reverted to being a motorcycle. A perfect motorcycle—no seams, joints, or gaps. Complete with rust and a faded paint job. It fired two unidentifiable blasts into the hood of the recording vehicle. That is technology nobody on Earth has."

"Please," whispered Kita.

"What are you protecting?" said Skulls. "I will tear apart the bike for answers. What is the connection between the Indian you were riding in these videos and the Ninja you have now?"

*Slag me. I totally botched this. I should have sent them chasing the Indian. Maybe I still can.*

"I just got the Ninja. I don't want it damaged. That's all. The Indian is an alien machine. It can change between a robot-like form and a motorcycle. I found it a few days ago. It came into my shop. I helped it escape another alien like it. That one is bigger and changes into a police cruiser. The Ninja was a reward for helping it."

"Where's the other rider in the video?" said Muller.

"I don't know. He was just a guy I met out riding. He was tagging along with me to Big Surf."

"What was in Big Surf?"

"The Kawasaki dealership. That's where I got my Ninja," said Kita.

"Where did this alien go?" said Muller.

"I don't know. It was running from the other one. I think it was headed south."

"Do you have any way of communicating with it?" said Skulls.

"No, but I know it can connect with the internet. You might look for it there."

"Interesting," said Muller. "Why were you attacked on the highway to Big Surf?"

"Oh," Kita made a face. "So, a couple of nights ago, we took shelter in an abandoned warehouse that turned out to be not so abandoned. It was housing a container full of guns and ammo. We fought with the owners at the warehouse and drove them away. I called the guns into the police. I think they were after us for revenge."

Skulls showed Muller her phone. "I have the nine-one-one call and the police report from Newport Police Department finding a cache of guns and ammunition. Their report states they found three bodies, two with unidentified wounds and the third with his head smashed in."

"That would be the Indian," said Kita. "I told you we had a shootout."

"Do you know of anything that can hurt the Indian?"

*Yeah, me.* "No. Bullets don't seem to bother it."

"What's its energy supply?" said Muller.

"I don't know. It said something about needing to find a power source."

"Are you aware of any others in the area?" said Skulls.

"Robots? Just the two," said Kita.

"We lost track of the Indian in Big Surf. Do you know why?"

"That's where it and I split up. I don't know."

Muller nodded. "Last question: Why does your Ninja and the Indian have the same license plate number?"

Kita's heart froze. "I like it?"

"Want to hear something crazy?" said Muller.

Kita gulped. "Ok."

"I think that Indian somehow became your Ninja. That's why you don't want us to take it apart. We're not the only ones who have figured this out. Whoever attacked you on the freeway has too, and they have the resources to wipe C-Trans' network video. Whatever you're doing with this robot has taken a dangerous turn, and it's going to put the lives of innocent people at risk. I think you know more about this robot then you're telling, but I believe you don't know who attacked you on the freeway."

A furious tear formed in Kita's eye. "I will die before I let you or anyone touch her," she hissed.

"Then tell us the truth!" Muller yelled.

Kita jumped from her chair and slapped the table. "I will not betray her to a life as an experiment!" she yelled. "She's as much a person as you or me."

"If she's intelligent, she'll be treated like it," said Skulls.

"You can't promise that. I've heard about the government. I know what they'll do to her. She means no harm to us."

"She's destroyed two vehicles, assaulted a highway patrol officer, and killed at least five people. I think she means plenty of harm to us."

"She was protecting me!" Kita yelled. "That officer assaulted me first. Those people tried to rape and kill me. She is not a threat. We are."

"We can protect you and...her," said Skulls.

"You'll rip her apart," said Kita.

"That is a last resort," said Muller. "We want her cooperation."

"To do what?"

"She would prove aliens exist."

"The knowledge she possesses could move us ahead technologically," said Skulls.

"She's a soldier," said Kita. "She doesn't know anything."

"Where is her ship?" said Muller.

"What ship?"

"She had to get here somehow."

"I don't know. She didn't say she came in one—"

"IBI humans."

*Sprokkit?* Kita pulled her phone from her back pocket.

"Let Kita go, or I will destroy buildings in the downtown area at random. If you pursue her, I will level a city block."

The lights in the room went out; the only illumination came from Kita's phone. The door clicked.

*Unlocked. Now's my chance to get out of here.* Kita dashed for the door, opened it, and ran down the darkened hallway.

"Kita!" said Ryan over the phone.

"Yeah. What's the plan?"

"Sprokkit has hacked into the building and is controlling the cameras, lights, and door locks. Once you get Velositi, we're waiting near the bottom ramp of the garage."

"Ok. I'm almost there." Kita burst through the door to the garage. The lights came on as she ran to Velositi. She put her helmet on and started the engine. Gunning the throttle, she held the front brake and spun Velositi around. The garage door and the barricade were already down as she hurried out of the IBI garage. In Velositi's headlamp, there was a large armored police four-by-four truck. The truck's passenger-side door opened, and a person wearing a mask waved. Kita pulled alongside the truck. *Oh, I hope this is them.*

"Ryan?" Kita yelled.

Ryan pulled up the mask partway. "Kita! Hey, follow us. We'll lead you out of the city."

"Ok."

Ryan closed the doors, and Sprokkit moved out at a slow pace, climbing out of the parking garage. *Oh, man. We need to go faster, or they're going to catch us.* But Sprokkit lumbered along up the ramps. On the top floor, he picked up speed, crashed through the garage exit gate, and turned hard into the evening traffic.

Kita followed Sprokkit as he turned on his lights and siren. Traffic was light and mostly quick to respond, allowing them to move quickly out of downtown. Sprokkit turned up an on-ramp to the freeway. Kita followed as he wove between cars.

"You still with us?" said Ryan over Kita's helmet.

"Yeah. I'm good. I think I have handling Velositi down. How did you guys find me?"

Ryan laughed. "You were on YouTube. We left after you called for help."

"Sprokkit said he was going to leave me," said Kita unhappily.

"I talked to him and convinced him not only are you good for the team; you're good for Velositi. She puts all her efforts into you and leaves him alone to do what he wants. He was still unsure about it until he heard you in the interview. He liked your conviction and dedication—and I quote, 'Even if it is to Velositi.'"

"I wasn't going to give you guys up. They don't even know about Sprokkit or Bernoot. But we have to be careful. I was attacked on the freeway, and they can erase C-Trans camera footage."

"Don't worry," said Ryan, "Sprokkit's on it. He's hacked into C-Trans mainframe and is blacking out cameras all over the city. There's no way they can track us. What happened on the freeway?"

Kita told the story of the BMWs and the moving truck.

"Damn. You have any idea what the claw was or what it did to Velositi?"

Kita frowned. "No. She was talking to me, and then it was static."

"Don't worry; we'll get her fixed up."

"I hope so," whispered Kita. "Let's worry about getting home."

Kita followed Sprokkit down an off-ramp, through a neighborhood, and to a deserted park. He parked behind some overgrown trees. Kita pulled in beside him.

"What are we doing here?" said Kita.

Ryan jumped down from Sprokkit's cab. "An APB just went out about you on the police radio. Every cop in the city will be looking for you."

"Great. How are we going to get back to the lab?"

"It is taken care of," said Sprokkit. A line of sparkles started at his bumper and moved over him, changing him into the Bulldog ambulance.

*That's how that works. Cool.*

Sprokkit pulled in front of Velositi. He partially morphed, extending his arms to pick up Velositi and put her in the back of his ambulance. Sprokkit reformed into the Bulldog and opened his cab doors. "We should be safe now."

Kita climbed into the passenger's side next to Ryan.

"We should stop and get some food," said Ryan.

Kita nodded. Food sounded good.

---

SPROKKIT PULLED UP TO THE LAB'S BAY DOOR. RYAN AND KITA HOPPED OUT, each carrying a small pizza. They had to go down the valley to find a vegan pizzeria. The smell of the pizza had tantalized Kita the entire ride back. She was hungry and was sure she could eat the whole thing, but she was afraid she'd make herself sick again. *I'll have to go slow—no more than two pieces.*

Sprokkit morphed and unloaded Velositi in one motion. Kita put her helmet on Velositi's seat and rested her hand on her gas tank. It was a small gesture, but Kita hoped Velositi could feel it.

Sprokkit raised the door. "Bring her inside. Bernoot?" he called.

Kita handed her pizza and helmet to Ryan.

"Do you want help?" said Ryan.

Kita shook her head. "No. I got her." Grabbing the handlebars, Kita pushed Velositi into the lab—past all the old experiments—to the workbench. "Where do you want her?" Kita asked Sprokkit.

"There is fine."

Kita stood Velositi up and hugged her, resting her cheek on Velositi's gas tank.

"I cannot work on her if you are draped over her," growled Sprokkit.

"Sorry," whispered Kita. "What do you have to do to her?"

"I have to draw her system cores out. It is a delicate process and time-consuming."

"Anything I can do to help?"

Sprokkit's eyes dimmed. "No. Ryan could be of some help, though. Go consume your dinner and try not to get sick this time."

Kita sighed as her shoulders slumped. She shuffled over to the cots where Ryan was eating.

"He could use your help when you're done," said Kita as she sat down hard on the cot.

"Here's your pizza," said Ryan. "Ok. A few more slices, and I'll go over. It'll be cool to see how they're constructed."

Kita shrugged and opened her pizza box. She grabbed a slice and took a bite, hoping the vegan pizza wouldn't upset her stomach.

"Did you guys finish the plasma converter?" said Kita, trying to take her mind off Velositi.

"I think so. Sprokkit says it's a lot smaller than the last one he built. Still, the thing is the size of a toaster."

"Does it work?"

"We tried hooking it up here, but the outlets are just a hundred and twenty volts. So, we got a minuscule amount. It needs a high voltage power source—like three hundred thousand volts. Some high-power transmission lines run just north of here. We'll need to go to the sub-station and connect."

"How long will that take?" said Kita.

"All of them are low. A couple of hours each—I think—if I understood Sprokkit correctly."

"We'll have to do it at night."

"Yeah. Hopefully, Velositi will be fixed by tomorrow, and we can go tomorrow night. Then, we can find the Axiom."

Kita's ears perked up. "What do you know of the Axiom of Command?"

"Not much. Sprokkit said it's why they're here and that it's hidden somewhere on Earth. Some ancient Morphicons put it here twelve thousand years ago. What do you know?"

"It's supposed to anoint a great leader among them, and that person will lead the Vehlixen to victory. Velositi hasn't told me why they know it's here, but she's determined to find it."

"It's a big world. Maybe we'll get to see some of it."

Kita hadn't thought of that. She'd never traveled outside of the state. Traveling and dealing with other people who didn't speak English sounded intimidating. "Have you traveled?"

"Sure, well, kind of. I've been some of the states and Mexico, Quebec, and Canada."

Kita wasn't sure that counted. Mexico and Canada were territories of the Empire of the United States. Quebec might as well be part of the EUS; they were so closely tied.

"I wonder where we'll get to go."

"I don't know, but I bet it'll be exciting."

Ryan looked a little over-eager for Kita's taste.

"You should get some sleep," said Ryan. "It'll probably take a while to fix Velositi." He put his pizza box down and went over to Sprokkit.

Kita sighed and slowly ate another slice of pizza. She put her pizza box under the cot, stripped off her top layer of clothing, and lay down. Her mind raced with thoughts of Velositi and what could go wrong. *What if I never get to talk to her again?* A tear slid down Kita's cheek. She rolled over and closed her eyes, telling herself everything would be fine when she woke.

KITA AWOKE TO SOMEONE GENTLY SHAKING HER. "WHA-WHAT IS IT?" KITA saw Ryan and came fully awake. "What's wrong? What happened? Is Velositi ok?"

"Whoa," said Ryan, "slow down. Nothing's wrong. We were able to pull Velositi's system cores. They're damaged"—Kita's heart leaped into her throat —"but Sprokkit thinks he can make new ones and transfer her to them."

Kita relaxed some. It wasn't great news, but it wasn't bad either. Velositi was still in limbo. "What do we need to do to make new ones?"

"Sprokkit and I think we've devised a way to do it. The system cores are made of glass, and their programming is etched into them on the quantum level. We have a list of what we need to do it, but we have to make another trip into the city."

"Let me get ready, and I can go."

"I'll be coming," said Ryan.

"But you've been up all night. You should sleep."

"I can sleep while we're on the road. I have to go to make sure we get the right stuff."

Kita shrugged, stood up, and grabbed her jacket. "You're going to need to get real sleep soon."

"Isn't that what being young is all about? Burning the candle at both ends?"

"It's how mistakes are made," said Kita tersely. "And it's my...friend...on the line."

"Sprokkit is doing most of the work. I'm just watching. It'll be fine."

"Ok. Give me a few minutes. You should take some too and get cleaned up."

"Yeah, I guess I should check on my hair. Velositi's lesson is sinking in," Ryan said in a teasing voice.

Kita wrinkled her nose. "I want to look good for her when she wakes up."

Ryan raised an eyebrow but didn't say anything as he followed Kita to the restrooms.

KITA WATCHED TRAFFIC AS SPROKKIT DROVE THROUGH THE VALLEY, BACK toward the lab. They had spent three hours at Fry's Electronics as Ryan and Sprokkit worked out plans with what parts were available. They then spent another hour buying what they selected. The receipt totaled seven hundred dollars. The one-inch glass cubes had been one hundred dollars each—ground and polished to sparkle like diamonds.

Kita wasn't sure how a dozen Blu-ray writable drives, three Raspberry Pis, and four variable power sources were going to etch circuits into the glass cubes, but Sprokkit and Ryan had a plan, and they seemed confident. She wanted them to succeed. It was her...friend...whose life was on the line. *But doubt lingers...*

"Sprokkit," said Kita quietly.

"Hmm, what do you want? I did not think you could stay quiet the whole trip."

Kita made a grumpy face. "You don't have to be mean; you know."

"You are here so that Ryan can get some sleep."

"I paid for your toys, too."

"I believe Velositi found the money."

"No, I did. She helped me bust the lock."

"I have a feeling you will not relent until I give you what you want. So, what do you want?"

Kita sighed. "I'm worried about Velositi."

"Why are you worried about her?"

"What if you can't fix her?"

"Then, I cannot fix her. I will take her system cores back home, and they will be returned to the forge, and a new Vehlix will be forged from her."

Kita burst into tears.

Sprokkit huffed. "What is wrong?"

"I don't want to lose her. I just met her. She's been the best friend ever. I can't imagine my life without her. I'll never get to say goodbye, and you're just going to take her away from me."

"You are being presumptuous and have not given Ryan and I a chance to repair her yet. I am optimistic that she can be repaired. I will not give up on her until I have tried every avenue. She is my comrade, leader, and friend. I have known her much longer than you have. If she ceases to function, your grief will be a pittance next to mine."

Kita slammed her fist on the dash. "Don't belittle how much I care for her!" she screamed, waking Ryan. "I may have only known her for a few days, but I would gladly trade places with her. She means more to me than you'll ever know."

"What's wrong?" said Ryan with a yawn.

"Let me out," Kita demanded.

"Hey, we're almost to the lab. Calm down."

"I will not calm down!" yelled Kita. "I will not put up with someone who belittles my feelings."

Understanding crossed Ryan's face. "Kita, please, relax. Sprokkit, remember what I told you about how Kita and Velositi felt about each other? How they had an intense connection?"

"You called it love."

Kita's mouth fell open.

Ryan sighed. "Yes. Just because they've known each other for a short time, it doesn't mean their bond is weak. Bonds of love can form very fast and be very strong. In humans, love can cause a lot of emotions."

*I know Velositi loves me, but...*

"Her attachment does not diminish mine," said Sprokkit.

"I'm not saying it does," said Ryan. "But, in humans, the significant other is held in the highest esteem. Friends and family are next in line."

"Because she is in love with Velositi, she outranks me?"

*Do I love her?*

Ryan ran his hand through his hair. "Ok, Velositi is your friend, right?"

"Yes."

"And you've been through a lot—mutual respect, friendship, all that?"

"Yes."

"Ok, in humans, there's a step above that. Velositi has picked someone special to her—Kita—to be the one person she opens her heart to and gives everything.

Kita is first among everyone to her. It's not a competition, Velositi is still your friend, but Kita is the one she's chosen to be her most special friend. Does that make sense?"

*She's not human. Can I even love something that's not human? But I care about her. I would rather I die than something happen to her. Does that mean I love her? I want her around always. I like being in her arms. She makes me smile just thinking about her. I like it when she touches me. Velositi protects me, and I protect her.*

"How did Velositi fall in love with Kita?" said Sprokkit.

"Well, Morphicons bond, right?" said Ryan.

"That is correct. We perform better and are more powerful."

"I'm sure Kita and Velositi sparked a mutual attraction in each other and set off the needed chemical or electrical reaction to propagate love or bonding."

Sprokkit sighed. "It does not seem natural."

Ryan laughed. "A lot of people love their cars—motorcycles."

*What is natural? Does it matter? Velositi is special...to me. If I act like I'm in love, why am I afraid to admit it? What's holding me back?*

"Kita?" said Ryan.

"Huh? Yeah?"

"Are you cool?"

"Oh, yeah. Cool. If Sprokkit doesn't like it, he can take it up with Velositi. I'm sure she'll have some words on the subject."

Ryan laughed. "You're in trouble now, Sprokkit. The girls are ganging up on you."

"Velositi is bad enough," grumped Sprokkit.

"Kita's proving to be a powerhouse herself."

Kita gave Ryan a dirty look. "I just refuse to be talked down to or have a male —human or otherwise—pretend to be superior to me."

"Maybe we should stop for coffee and get Kita something sweet."

Kita rolled her eyes, but something sweet sounded good. *I can't wait to get back to the lab and get away from the stupid boys.*

———————✕———————

KITA SAT IN BERNOOT'S PASSENGER SEAT, WATCHING THE CITY GO BY. IT HAD been hours of watching and waiting for something from Sprokkit and Ryan. All the while, her stomach was turning into the Gordian Knot. When Ryan finally came to her, it wasn't with an update, but that he was hungry. So, she *volunteered* to get dinner. A six-pack of tacos and a pair of bean burritos sat in the back seat.

Her mind still wrestled with the idea of love. She didn't question her feelings for Velositi. It was love itself that bothered her. Love came with a lot of commitment that she wasn't sure she could make. It scared her to devote herself to someone else, even Velositi. *What if I screw it up?* She had asked herself that a lot. *Velositi is forgiving and understanding, but what if I stumble into something even Velositi wasn't aware of or if I screw up too many times? Velositi has to have limits.* Love was so hard and was a gamble. *Am I ready to gamble everything? I don't have to make up my mind right this minute. Do I?*

Kita sighed. Velositi was willing to be patient. *I just have to get over myself and accept what everyone else knows. How does everyone else know if I don't know? How does Velositi know that she's in love if they don't experience love...at least not like we do... or maybe they do? I don't know. Maybe Bernoot knows...* "Hey, Bernoot."

"Hey, dudette. You've been quiet."

"Thinking and worrying about Velositi. Can you explain bonding to me?"

"Yo, tall order, but I'll do my best. I've never experienced it myself. But bonding is when a light and a heavy combine to become a single entity. This new entity can morph into wild and powerful stuff."

"Velositi said she bonded with another light."

"Roger that, and that type of bonding is rare, but it creates some of the most radical morphs ever."

"Why isn't Velositi still bonded?" said Kita.

"Blaade was a real square, and Velositi does everything her way. Different charges attract each other, but they can also annihilate each other. That's what happened between Blaade and Velositi."

"So, is it emotional?" said Kita.

"The bonded pair usually has been together for a long time. Their system cores sync up. It's not emotional, like humans."

"Do you know anything about love?"

"Sure. It's like when a man and woman live together, and he buys her stuff while she makes dinner. When we first arrived, I didn't have much to do, so I watched a lot of TV and got to know human customs and culture."

Kita chuckled, then remembered he was watching seventies TV, not the stuff from today. "How does Velositi know about love?"

"It was really weird when we first arrived. Velositi is deep into humans. She studied you—especially what makes you tick. Mike got her all kinds of big books to read. When Mike said he loved Velositi as the Indian, it blew her mind. Like, she became totally stuck on love, wanting to know all about it. Then she started acting weird toward Mike, trying to get his attention, but it whacked him out. Mike was way into Sprokkit. Kind of like Ryan. They were always together. Velositi was majorly upset but wouldn't spill why. Then the Neophormes killed Mike, and Velositi was totally wasted. It was like her spirit was crushed. After that, she ordered us into hibernation. I don't get what happened. It was totally bizarro, but I'm just a soldier. I don't ask questions. I just do and die."

Kita deflated a bit. "So, I'm not the first human Velositi has taken an interest in?"

"Mike found us by accident. He boosted me. I let him get as far as almost chopping me up for parts before morphing and scaring the skin off him. Velositi and Sprokkit came in and saved him. Mike said he could help us, and Velositi believed him."

"Did he?"

"He helped Sprokkit find and build stuff. Mike also ran his chemistry set making some kind of paper tabs. He knew the southwestern EUS, and we searched most of it for the Axiom. He took us all over the place. Every week it was some new city. We'd meet people, and Mike would exchange his tabs for cash and ask them about the Axiom."

Kita slumped in the seat and rubbed the sides of her head. "You've got to be kidding me..."

"It's totally the truth," said Bernoot.

"I don't doubt it, but you guys are so naïve."

"What?"

"Mike was a drug runner and was using you to move his drugs. He didn't care about finding the Axiom."

"What are drugs?"

"Illegal chemicals humans use to alter their state of mind and body."

"Illegal? But Mike said—"

"Yeah, I'm sure he said it was cool. It's not your fault. You didn't know. I'm just sorry you wasted your time. I will do my best to help you find the Axiom."

"Righteous. Thanks."

*I owe that much to Velositi. She's going to be devastated when she finds out the truth about Mike. Will that make her not trust me? I—*

Bernoot's rear skidded to one side. "Hang on. We've got a bandito that wants to play rough."

"By the Crushing Depths," said Kita as she grabbed the armrest handle.

Something hit Bernoot from the other side.

"Two of them," said Bernoot cheerfully. "Gnarly. Let's see if they can keep up."

Bernoot accelerated, throwing Kita into her seat. He zigzagged through traffic on the three-lane boulevard. Kita twisted in her seat to see out the back window. Two black elevated Dodge Rams were following them.

"Bernoot, they don't have drivers."

"Neophorm drones. I wonder how they got here."

"What's a drone?" said Kita.

"Neophormes run two flavors, masters and drones. Most Neophormes are drones—mindless minions that are built by the millions."

"How did they find us?"

"No clue. But they're going to learn not to mess with me, yo."

"Have you been watching TV now?" said Kita.

"TV is old school. I'm watching YouTube."

Kita rolled her eyes. "That's worse than the seventies TV."

"Hey, now, don't be a hater."

Kita chuckled as Bernoot made a hard right onto another boulevard. The pickups followed and closed behind Bernoot as he slowed down due to traffic stopped at a light.

"Time for the danger zone," said Bernoot.

"The what?" cried Kita.

Bernoot morphed, throwing Kita and the food into the air. He jumped backward and fired his cannons into the hoods of the pickups. He caught Kita, she caught the food, and with his free arm, he fired at the closest pickup. The trucks morphed into ten-foot-tall twins. They charged forward, pushing and punching the cars waiting for the light out of the way. Bernoot carefully sidestepped through traffic between rows of cars, firing as he went. When

Bernoot reached the intersection, he morphed and accelerated down an open lane of traffic.

*Maybe those drones will give the IBI more to think about than me.* "Did you alert Sprokkit?"

"Oh, yeah, good idea. He's been nuking the cameras around town for us."

"Did we lose them?" said Kita as Bernoot made another turn down a side street.

"No idea. They're not as dope as Nitstik at sniffing us out. I'll circle back the way we came. That should snooker them good. How are the tacos?"

Kita opened the bag. "They look good to me." Kita didn't plan on eating tacos. She was done with meat. Her vegan diet was treating her stomach well, and she didn't want to ruin it, especially without Velositi around to take care of her.

"Sprokkit says to park for a while, and then come on back to the lab," said Bernoot. He pulled into a parking spot, and the radio turned on. The knob on the seventies-style radio turned as Bernoot scanned the airwaves. He settled on a hip-hop rap station.

Kita made a face, but he was technically driving. She did her best to ignore it and ate a burrito instead.

---

KITA ENTERED THE LAB AS BERNOOT SHUT THE DOOR. "DINNER!" SHE YELLED at Ryan. He and Sprokkit were hovering over the workbench working on something.

He looked up. "Ok, be there in a minute."

*Yeah, which means you'll come over in two hours.* Kita placed the tacos on Ryan's cot and walked over to the workbench. "How's it going?"

Ryan didn't look up as he twisted a screwdriver. "We have the etching rig built and the energy supply calibrated. We're working on aligning the lasers now."

"The dinner you requested is here," Kita said in a not-so-happy tone.

"Ah, thanks. I'll be right over to eat it."

Kita left him and walked over to Velositi. She had five holes in her where Sprokkit had extracted the system cores. The holes were perfectly square and went deep into Velositi. The holes showed Velositi was solid all the way through and not made of motorcycle parts. *What is Velositi's anatomy like? How does she morph? What makes her so warm? I have so much to learn.*

Bernoot approached Sprokkit. "We got a big problem, big dude."

"What?" said Sprokkit gruffly.

"Somebody knew I was leaving and jumped us in the city."

"Hmm, maybe we should scout the surrounding area. Nitstik might have dropped a mini."

"What's a mini?" said Kita.

Sprokkit's eyes glowed brightly. "Neophormes build tiny Morphicons for scouting and infiltration missions. They are not very bright, but they are vicious. Boom-Boom was a mini."

"I think I'll go with you. I need some air."

Sprokkit growled. "You are to stay inside the fence."

"That's fair."

Sprokkit stomped toward the door, waving Bernoot to follow. Kita fell in behind them. Night had fallen, and the lights from Angel City lit the horizon. On the opposite side were a few bright stars. Kita followed Bernoot and Sprokkit around the building as they searched along the fence. Sprokkit stopped.

"Do you hear that?" said Sprokkit to Bernoot.

"A hum is coming from above us."

*I don't hear anything.*

The two Vehlixen searched the skies. Sprokkit stopped, his arm morphed into his cannon, and he took aim and fired. There was a bright flash in the sky.

"I got eyes on it," said Bernoot as he hopped the fence and ran up the rocky and yellow grass-covered hill. He returned, carrying several pieces. "What is it? I've never seen Neophormes use a design like this."

Kita grabbed Bernoot's hand and pulled it lower so she could see. "It's a drone."

Sprokkit huffed. "The Neophormes have never—"

"It's not Neophorm. It's human. The Neophormes have human help. Nitstik followed me here, and now his helpers are watching us. Those human helpers might be who attacked Velositi and me on the freeway."

"That is a big leap in logic," huffed Sprokkit.

"How else did they know to target the bike and not me—and know what to attack Velositi with to cripple her? Think about it. On a normal Ninja, the cowl is plastic and metal. You're not going to disable the bike by hitting it there, but with Morphicon construction, they can hit anywhere. You're one big solid piece of...whatever."

"A liquid metal which changes form when a voltage is applied," said Sprokkit. "That is a logical argument. Time will prove if it is correct. Bernoot, start performing random perimeter checks."

"Right-o, daddy-o."

"I need to return to my work." Sprokkit looked down at Kita. "And you can do whatever it is you do, just stay out of trouble and don't bother me."

Kita smiled sweetly. "Fix my friend, and you won't have to deal with me."

"Hey, Kita," Ryan said in a loud whisper as he tapped her shoulder.

"Huh, what?" said Kita as she woke up slowly.

"Velositi's back together."

Kita was instantly awake. "Is she ok?"

"She hasn't rebooted. Sprokkit thinks she's too low on plasma. We're leaving for the power sub-station in a few minutes."

"Ok. Give me a second to tie my hair back and grab my boots and jacket."

"Sure. No Problem." Ryan walked to his cot and grabbed his jacket.

Kita ran her hand through her hair. It was still damp. *I couldn't have been asleep very long.* With nothing to do after dropping off dinner, she'd bathed and washed her hair in the restroom sink. She changed her underwear out, too. *To the sexiest and functional underwear Walmart carried. I hope I don't scare Velositi.*

After putting on her boots and jacket, Kita met the others outside the bay door.

"You want to ride with Sprokkit and me?" said Ryan with a hopeful grin.

"Shouldn't you be sleeping? Because that's what I'm going to do."

"Yeah. I just haven't seen much of you."

"I'm sure we'll have plenty of time to hang out while we wait for them to recharge. I'll ride with Bernoot."

"Hot diggity dog," said Bernoot.

"But I get to veto the radio station."

Bernoot made a disappointed sound.

"Let us go," said Sprokkit. He morphed, and Ryan climbed aboard.

Bernoot followed suit and morphed into a gold firebird. Kita slid inside the wide door.

Sprokkit exited the lab and turned away from town, and Bernoot followed into the darkness.

"So, how does this work?" Kita asked Ryan as Sprokkit and Bernoot set up the plasma converter in the electrical substation. They stood watching from outside the perimeter fence, as the area was too dangerous for them.

"I don't completely understand it, but by using a series of electromagnetic fields and a heat source, gas is created. The gas is ionized—that's the important part for the Morphicons."

"And they drink it up?"

"I have no idea. Those glass tubes are what they collect it in. I assume they ingest it some way. Sprokkit said it's going to take a while to collect what they need."

There wasn't much around them, mostly tall dry grass and the occasional small tree. A housing development glowed brightly from beyond a neighboring hill. Kita walked around the corner of the substation, and Ryan hurried to catch up.

"Where are we going?" Ryan asked Kita.

"I'm looking for a comfortable place to sit down."

Kita found a rocky outcropping that let her dangle her feet over the edge and allowed her to look out over the lights of Angel City. Ryan sat down next to her.

"Thanks for your help with Velositi," said Kita.

"Hey, no problem. It's been cool. I've learned a lot from Sprokkit. How they construct things is way different than how we do it. Well, we kind of do it their way, just cruder."

"And how do they build stuff?"

"By layers. They lay it down a layer of atoms at a time. Like how we do 3D printing."

Kita had never seen a 3D printer, nor did she know how one worked, but she got the idea from Ryan's description. "I'm glad you're having fun."

"Yeah. I'm sorry about Velositi. I hope we can fix her."

Kita sighed. "Me too. I miss her so much. It's like suddenly the world is empty. I don't get to see her face or her eyes, and I don't get to feel the warmth she radiates. I just can't get over that in one minute I'm riding her and talking to her, and in midsentence she's gone. It was that quick. Every time I go to sleep, I hope that when I wake up, she'll be there, and when she's not, it's like I lose her all over again. I wish they'd taken me instead."

"I know Sprokkit is doing everything he can, but...but, if Velositi can't be fixed, I was hoping you'd consider me."

Kita's brain felt like she'd been slammed into reverse. *I...I...What? No!* "Are—are you serious?" Kita hissed. "I'm pouring my heart out to you about the person I love, and you make a pass at me?" *I guess that's settled.*

Ryan gulped. "It's just in case Velositi can't be fixed. I don't want you to be sad or lonely."

"So, you think you can just come in and take her place?"

"No! Of course not. I understand you love her. I can't replace her, but I can be just as special to you."

Kita ground her teeth while sucking in a breath. She was so angry she was beside herself. "Ryan, I *am* a *lesbian*. It's not something that you can change."

"I just thought you might be willing to try."

"Wow. You have an ego." Kita hopped off the ledge and landed in the grass a few feet below.

"Kita, wait. I'm sorry," called Ryan as Kita walked away, wiping tears from her eyes.

Kita stormed down the hill until she nearly walked into a barbwire fence. *Slag. I guess I shouldn't go far. I don't need Sprokkit after me, too.* She followed the fence and then turned back up the hill.

*Why are boys so stupid? I bet girls have been asking that question since the beginning of time. I liked Ryan. Why would he do this? I thought he got me. Maybe he's been spending too much time with Sprokkit...Ryan wouldn't sabotage Velositi, would he? No. He's not that kind of guy...I hope. But, Sprokkit does most of the work. He must be watching Ryan. Ugh. Conspiracy brain is running wild. Slag. I don't need this. I should be worrying about Velositi, not stupid Ryan.* As she reached the top of the hill, she angled over to the substation and leaned against the fence. Sprokkit and Bernoot were in the process of filling the glass tubes with plasma. *How much longer?*

"Kita?" Ryan said from behind her.

Kita rolled her eyes and turned around. "What?" she snapped.

Ryan grimaced for a moment. "I wanted to tell you how sorry I am. I just didn't want to see you sad and unhappy."

"Why am I not allowed to mourn and have my grief? I love her, and I should be allowed to. I want to be sad, and I want to be unhappy, those feelings tell me she meant something to me. But, that's not what I'm mad about." Kita folded her arms and glared.

Ryan looked sideways. "Then what are you mad about?" he asked in a tiny voice.

Kita's agitation surged. "You can figure out alien technology, but not why I'm mad? Fine. I'll tell you. I thought *you*"—Kita poked a finger in Ryan's chest—"got me. You understood what I am and knew what that meant. Instead, you act like all those conservative slagbags that think if I met the right man, I would change. I will not change for anybody."

"But you changed for Velositi."

"Velositi is a girl."

"Not really. She's a light and doesn't have any of the defining characteristics of a human female."

"Velositi thinks and acts like a girl. She looks delicate, soft, and is lithe and sleek—not a hulking brute like Sprokkit or Bernoot. Do you think I would fall in love with them? Her touch, compassion, and empathy are like a girl. Just because Velositi lacks the physical characteristics of a human girl, doesn't mean she's not a girl."

"But, she's an alien," protested Ryan.

"So what? Is that all they are to you, aliens?"

"They're friendly enough. I like Sprokkit. I can't imagine falling in love with Velositi. It would be like falling in love with a toaster."

"You said people love their cars."

"That's not the same, and you know it."

"So, suddenly, you don't approve?"

Ryan held up his hands. "No, you're allowed to love whoever you want. I just thought if you could change for Velositi, you could change for me," he said quietly.

"When I look at Velositi, I do *not* see a toaster. I see my friend. I don't care that she doesn't look like me. It doesn't matter that she doesn't have the same parts I do. I see a person—an intelligent being capable of love, compassion, and adoration."

"According to Sprokkit, those aren't normal for a Morphicon to have."

"Then, maybe Velositi is unique and has risen to a higher state of consciousness."

"Maybe she's faking it."

Kita smacked Ryan's arm. "She is not. You haven't been around her like I have."

"Look, I like Velositi. I just don't want to see you get hurt."

Kita made a face. "Thanks for your concern, but I'll take my chances with Velositi."

Ryan sighed. "Ok. I'm sorry I said anything. It's your heart."

"And?"

Ryan gave her a blank look.

"What was I mad about?"

"Oh. I'm sorry, I thought I could change you. I respect who you are. I didn't mean anything negative by it. I just want to see you happy."

Kita pulled her ponytail over her shoulder and stroked it. "Fix Velositi, and I will be."

———×———

KITA SAT IN BERNOOT'S PASSENGER SEAT, WATCHING THE ROLLING countryside. Fences lined the narrow two-lane road, and the occasional herd of cows dotted the hillside. Ahead of them, Ryan and Sprokkit carried the plasma. Traffic was light as the sun was just peeking above the hills.

She fought to keep her eyes open—even though she had managed a quick nap at the substation. *I need to stay awake. I wonder if Bernoot has anything interesting to say.*

"How are you feeling, Bernoot?" said Kita.

"Way better. I got a ton of energy, and I feel like I can do anything. Next time I rumble with Nitstik, my cannons will hit harder, and I will heal faster."

"I thought you hit him pretty hard the last time." *I remember the explosions.*

"Nah. I barely hit him. Next time, it'll be a fair fight."

"Sorry about that. I didn't mean to lead him to us."

"Hey, no problemo. It's what I live for. I—doh! Sprokkit says there's a bear ahead."

"A bear? Out here? They're only in the mountains."

Bernoot laughed. "Bear—the po-po—cops."

"Oh." Kita felt foolish.

"I'll slow my roll. We don't want any heat."

Bernoot crested the hill, and a local sheriff was sitting by the side of the road at the bottom watching traffic. In Bernoot's driver's seat, a male driver with scraggly hair and a beard wearing a folded bandana appeared. Kita tried to touch him, but her hand passed through him.

"We need to update your driver's look," said Kita.

"Why? He's dope."

"Ah, no. He looks like he hasn't showered in months and needs a haircut and shave. When we get back to the lab, we'll find you a new one."

As Bernoot passed the sheriff, Kita waved, but the sheriff ignored her. Halfway up the next hill, Bernoot said, "Danger zone," and accelerated up the hill.

"What happened?" said Kita.

"Sprokkit says the po-po called us in. We match a BOLO."

Kita twisted in her seat to look out the back window. The sheriff had turned onto the road, and his lights were on. *I'm getting tired of that sight.* "It's got to be about yesterday."

"We're not stopping. Hold onto your butts!"

*Did he watch* Jurassic Park?

Bernoot crested the hill and passed Sprokkit coming down the other side. Kita opened the maps app on her phone, searching for a way to lead the sheriff away from Sprokkit.

"Bernoot, there is a road coming up on the left that goes up a canyon. It intersects with another road twenty miles up. That road goes back toward the city. Take it, so they don't follow Sprokkit."

"Right-o, pretty lady. I got it in my sights. This po-po is serious. He's right on our butt." Bernoot decelerated and made the turn up the narrow one and a half lane road lined with small oak trees and a creek on the left side.

"Be careful going up this, Bernoot," said Kita. "We don't want to hit someone coming down."

"You want to get away or what?"

"I don't want to end up in the ditch."

"Leave the driving to me."

Kita rolled her eyes. *Famous last words...* She turned around but didn't see the sheriff.

Bernoot took the winding road as fast as he could, sliding around corners and accelerating to top speed when it was straight. Every so often, they would pass a mailbox. *People live up here? I thought it was all cows.*

Bernoot roared past a barricade with a ROAD CLOSED sign.

"Bernoot, what are we going to do?" said Kita.

"Depends on how closed the road is."

"Great."

"Why? You want to turn around?"

Kita didn't like either option. *Known versus unknown. If we go back, we have to get by the sheriff. Forward means getting by who knows what. I've had enough of cops. I'll take my chances with the road.* "Keep going. We'll figure it out when we get there. We should have a big enough lead on him."

Bernoot rounded a bend, and a barricade read BRIDGE OUT.

"Ah, Bernoot, how are we getting around that?"

"We slam it into the danger zone."

"What?"

"Danger zone!" yelled Bernoot.

The road made a shallow bend to the left as the creek crossed the road. It wasn't a long bridge, thirty feet, but the deck was in pieces next to the road. Only the abutments were in place. A short slope led up to the bridge.

"Yee-hay!" yelled Bernoot. "We're going to be like the Duke boys."

"You're going to jump it?" cried Kita.

Bernoot accelerated forward, throwing Kita into her seat. She checked her seatbelt and grabbed the armrests. *Don't tense up. Don't tense up.* Bernoot raced up the slope and launched into the air. To Kita, it felt like forever before Bernoot hit the ground, causing Kita to be thrown forward. Her seatbelt saved her from hitting the dash. *If he bruised my boob, I'm going to be so mad.*

"Yahoo! We belong in Hazzard County," said Bernoot excitedly.

"I *am* not moving to Georgia," snarled Kita.

"But they have jumps all over the place."

"It's not real."

"It's not?"

"Most of TV is not real, especially stuff from the seventies."

"I thought your world was cool. YouTube is real, right?"

Kita laughed. "Ah, define real. Most of the big stuff doesn't represent everyday life."

"How boring is life on your planet?"

"Ah, as boring or as exciting as you want it to be."

"But there are radical things here?"

"Yeah, just different than what's on TV. For most people, TV is an escape from reality. Stories to distract them from real life."

"That's way depressing."

"For a lot of people, those stories are the highlight of their day."

"Did you watch TV?"

"No. I couldn't afford a TV or to pay for it on my phone." Kita saw a big house built up on the side of the canyon and sighed. *It must be nice.*

"How do you escape reality?"

"I didn't. I worked...until I met Velositi, and then my whole life feels like it's from TV."

"So, you mean we're like a TV show?"

"Yeah. It feels that way."

"Gnarly. So, I'm like a star."

"We're sought after, that's for sure."

"Intersection coming up quick," said Bernoot as he turned a corner and accelerated up a steep hill.

Kita turned and looked out the back window. The whole valley of trees and yellow grass stretched behind them. *So pretty. I wish I could see it with Velositi.*

"Wowsers, bear country!"

Kita whipped her head around. Thirty yards in front of them was a roadblock of six sheriffs' cruisers. Two sheriffs' cruisers blocked the canyon road, and two blocked the intersecting road in each direction. Their lights were on, and the sheriff deputies stood behind their cruisers. *I didn't know this county had so many sheriffs.*

Bernoot accelerated.

"Bernoot, what are you doing?" exclaimed Kita.

"This train ain't stopping."

"There's nowhere to go."

"I'll make a hole."

As Bernoot roared toward the deputies, they raised their guns and fired. Kita ducked under the dash in case a bullet passed through the windshield. Bernoot slammed into the gap between the cruisers, pushing between them. He turned hard to the right. His spinning back tires hit the loose gravel of the road, and his rear end spun around going over the edge of the road. Bernoot rolled down a slope, crashing through a barbed-wire fence. He landed wheels up across a small creek.

Kita's head spun as she tried to regain her bearings.

"Bernoot, are you ok?" said Kita.

"That was a major fail."

"Don't do anything. The cops will be here any second. I'll go with them and keep them busy. Let them pull you out of the ditch and take you to the yard. Once it's clear, get a new disguise and get back to Sprokkit."

"You just got out of the clink."

"I know. Hopefully, Sprokkit can fix Velositi, and you can get me out. But you have to get free."

"We can make a run for it."

"We'll just have more cops. You get away, and I'll keep them busy."

"You ok in there?" said a voice.

"Yeah, I'm ok, except for my pride."

"Do you need help out?"

Kita fumbled with the seat belt release. When she found the button, she fell to the roof. Rolling to her feet, she hissed to Bernoot, "Open a window."

The passenger's side window rolled down, and Kita wiggled through to look up at a quartet of deputies. They grabbed her, pulled her to her feet, and escorted her up the hill to a cruiser.

"You have any ID?" said a deputy.

"On my phone," said Kita.

"Let's see it."

Kita tapped on her phone and brought up her driver's license. She gave it to him. He ran it through the computer and came back, scratching his head.

"There's a sealed Imperial warrant out for your arrest. You a terrorist or something?"

"Nope, just a junkyard girl."

The deputy put Kita's phone on the trunk of his cruiser. "Anything else in your pockets?"

Kita emptied her jacket of her comb, makeup, and money.

"You're the prettiest terrorist I've ever seen," said the deputy. "Take off your jacket, put your hands on the car, and spread your feet."

"You have a female here to pat me down?" said Kita as she shed her jacket.

Another deputy whistled. "Don't need to pat you down with those clothes."

Kita rolled her eyes and curled her lip as the first deputy patted her down. *No fight to see who gets to touch me?*

The deputy grabbed Kita's arms and pulled them behind her, placing handcuffs on her wrists. The deputies helped Kita into the back of a cruiser. *Well, now what?*

KITA LAY IN THE JAIL CELL BUNK WATCHING THE CLOCK ON THE WALL. *I THINK that's some form of torture.* She'd arrived five hours ago, and no one had talked to her since they booked her. *I hope Bernoot got away.*

The door to the cell area opened, and multiple footsteps stopped in front of Kita's cell. Kita interlaced her fingers behind her neck and lifted her head to see through the door's window—a deputy escorted Muller and Skulls.

"You think with as bad as you want me, you would have been here before they booked me," Kita chided the pair of IBI agents.

"Interagency communications don't happen that fast," said Muller, "especially out here."

Kita sat up and stretched. "I take it you're the ones behind my mysterious warrant?"

"You're a person of interest to the EUS. Only an Imperial judge can unseal the warrant."

"So, you can arrest me and not tell me why?"

"Yes."

"Great." Kita stood up. "Then, let's go. Do you have my stuff?"

Skulls held up Kita's jacket and an envelope.

"Approach the door," said the deputy.

With a dramatic sigh, Kita walked to the door.

"Place your hands in the slot."

Kita did, and Muller produced a pair of handcuffs and put them on Kita's wrists. The door opened, and Kita stepped out. Skulls draped Kita's jacket over her shoulders. Kita gave her a funny look.

"You look cold," said Skulls.

The agents escorted Kita out of the sheriff's office and put her in the back of an unmarked Charger. Kita settled back for the long ride back to the city.

KITA SAT IN THE SAME INTERVIEW ROOM SHE HAD ESCAPED FROM DAYS BEFORE. The room was empty. Her hands remained handcuffed behind her as she rested her head on the table.

The door opened, and Kita sat up. Muller and Skulls entered.

"I thought you wanted to talk to me," said Kita.

"Late lunch," said Muller.

Kita looked at Skulls. The woman shrugged as she sat across from Kita. Muller took the chair next to Skulls.

"So, you're talkative," said Muller. "You want to tell us about your friends?"

Kita rolled her eyes. "Not really. I know even less today than I did when you first had me."

"It looks like you made a new friend," said Muller as he showed Kita a picture on his phone.

It was Kita and Bernoot tiptoeing through traffic. From the angle, it didn't come from a traffic camera.

"It's the same one," Kita said quickly.

"They don't look the same to me." Muller put a picture of Velositi and Bernoot side by side. "This one"—he tapped the image of Bernoot—"looks much bigger than this one."

Kita huffed. "You should be more concerned with the two Dodge Rams that tore up traffic."

Muller swiped the screen. "These two?"

"Yeah."

"They've disappeared. You're our only lead. What are they?"

"I said they were aliens," Kita said condescendingly.

"Where do they come from?"

"I don't know. I didn't ask."

"Where is she?" said Skulls gently.

"Who?"

"You said the one you were with was a *she*."

Kita shrugged. "I don't know."

"Is there something wrong?"

"Yeah, I'm in handcuffs."

"I mean with her," said Skulls.

Kita bit her lip. "I don't know."

"We have the Firebird," said Muller. "We'll pull it apart to get answers."

"I doubt that," said Kita. "Trying to take him apart will be a bad idea."

"What do you know?" Muller yelled, slapping the table.

Kita flinched. "I'm telling you everything."

"You know more. I want the whole truth."

"You can't handle the truth!" Kita snapped.

"Both of you relax," said Skulls. "We're trying to help you, Kita, and them."

"They don't need help."

"What about you?"

"I'm going to jail forever no matter what I tell you," said Kita dourly.

"Nobody said you were going to jail."

"Sure seems that way."

Muller's phone vibrated on the table. He picked it up. "Damn." He showed it to Skulls.

She looked at Kita. "It seems your friend has gotten away."

Kita let out a sigh of relief.

"Where's he going?" said Muller.

"I don't know," said Kita.

"What are they after? Why are they here?"

"They're looking for something. They mean us no harm as long as you leave them alone."

"What are you to them?" said Skulls.

"Just a friend. I agreed to help them," said Kita.

"But you don't want us to help them?"

"I don't trust that you won't pull them apart," said Kita. "He keeps threatening to," she added, motioning toward Muller.

"We need information," said Skulls. "You're our preferred method, but we will do what is necessary."

Kita shook her head. "You're just two IBI agents. You can't promise me anything. Once the rest of the government gets them, it'll be over. I'd die first."

"That's showing them a lot of loyalty," said Skulls.

"I have my reasons."

"Are they paying?" said Muller.

"No. The only thing I was promised was protection," said Kita.

"Then why betray your own kind?"

Kita blinked. "I'm not betraying anyone. They asked for help finding something. I said, *yes*. They're not attacking the EUS, nor are they stealing anything. They're just passing through."

"We could help them find what they're searching for," said Skulls.

"Again, you can't make that promise."

There was a sharp rap on the door. Muller and Skulls traded looks. Muller answered the door.

"Special Agent Muller?" said a voice.

"Yes? How can I help you, General?"

"I need to speak to you and Agent Skulls."

Muller waved to Skulls. The door closed with a *click* leaving Kita by herself.

*General? Does the IBI have generals? What if Bernoot didn't get away and the military has him? Are they being rewarded for capturing him? What if Bernoot tore up the place and they killed him? What if Bernoot didn't contact Sprokkit? I—*

The door opened, and a stout older man with a silver burr of hair wearing a formal blue military uniform with medals and ribbons entered, followed by a woman with her dark hair in a tight bun wearing a similar blue uniform, except with a form-fitted jacket, pencil skirt, and heels. Her chest didn't have nearly as much crap on it as he did. She carried a leather briefcase in her left hand.

They moved to the opposite side of the table, and he stood before Kita. His nametag read STRIKER, and hers said ADRESTIA.

"Take the cuffs off her, would you, Major?" said Striker.

Adrestia took a key from the briefcase, walked around the desk, and undid the cuffs without releasing the briefcase.

"Thanks," Kita muttered. She rubbed her sore wrists and rolled her stiff shoulders. She put her hands on the table.

Striker cleared his throat. "I am General Striker of the Empire of the United States Air Force. And, you are Kita Logine. Is that correct?"

"Ah, yeah, that's me."

"I understand you've had a long day. You were arrested just after seven this morning."

Kita made a face. "I have no idea what time it is. I haven't eaten or been to the bathroom."

"Do you need to go?"

"No. I haven't had anything to drink either."

"Major, do we have anything she can have?" said Striker.

Adrestia opened the briefcase and took out a bottle of water and a Snickers bar. She placed them on the table in front of Kita. Their eyes met. Adrestia's face remained rigid, but her eyes twinkled. *Not sure if that's good or bad.*

Kita ignored the candy bar but helped herself to the water. "I'm not telling any more than I told those IBI."

Striker nodded. "I know what you told them. I'm here to ask for your help. Let me tell you what I know, and then you can give me your answer."

*Huh?* "Ok..."

"Are you familiar with the Congo War?" said Striker.

"Not really, but I know we didn't win."

"Yes. From nineteen sixty-five to nineteen seventy-four, we were winning until a group of planes and tanks appeared on the north Congolese side that could outfly and outshoot us. These planes and tanks were indistinguishable from the North Congolese Army versions. Reports of robots that wielded incredible firepower came in from the battlefield. They devastated our ranks and drove us out. At the time, these were the only pictures we had of them."

Adrestia put two grainy pictures on the table. Kita recognized the silhouettes as Morphicon heavies. She sat back; her lips were pressed together.

Striker continued, "From the end of the Congo War to nineteen eighty-six, the CIA and other agencies tried to track what these things were and where they came from. They had little success until a Soviet KGB agent, Nikolai Namestnikov, defected and brought with him a file containing everything the Soviets knew about Morphicons—names, objectives, strengths, capabilities, weaknesses—and who they were allied with."

Adrestia collected the two pictures from the table and laid down six more.

"Namestnikov said these Morphicons are known as Neophormes. Nitstik. Wavbreakr. Litsink. Shelbak. Ultranova. Pumel." He pointed to them as he named them.

Kita studied the pictures. They all looked like Morphicons, just uglier and meaner—even the light looked mean. She looked at Striker and raised an eyebrow.

"Nasty crew," said Striker. "The information Namestnikov proved allowed us to build weapons and develop tactics to use against the Neophormes. In nineteen ninety-one, during Jungle Typhoon, we captured Wavbreakr."

Adrestia laid down a picture of Wavbreakr in some kind of restraining apparatus. Nothing seemed to be physically holding the Neophorm in place.

"Studying and interrogating Wavbreakr led to many breakthroughs. He told us of their plan to destroy the Vehlixen and take the Axiom of Command for themselves. We know how they're constructed, how they transform, we can read their system cores—hell, we've even made the body of one. The nineties were good to us—when we met them on the battlefield, we could hold our own. Then in the two-thousands, it changed. In the wars in Iran and the Philippines, we went from fighting five to dozens. And there are more all the time. We need help.

"I am part of a secret government agency tasked by the Emperor himself to find the Vehlixen. You, Miss Logine, are the first lead we've ever had. The Emperor is willing to offer whatever is necessary to secure Vehlixen help. The Neophormes are allied with the Illuminati—a secret global society that includes the USSR, China, and India as members. The Illuminati's power is growing with

Neophorm help. Until a few days ago, we had no proof the Illuminati, or the Neophormes were operating on Imperial soil. Our war against them has come home, and they must be stopped. This is why I need your help to contact the Vehlixen."

Kita leaned back in her chair. *He brought proof, and he brought food. But how do I trust him? If they tortured and killed a Neophorm, what's to keep them from doing it to Velositi or the others? And do they really need Velositi's help? He said they had the weapons to fight back.*

"You have the weapons, so why can't you kill them?" said Kita.

"We haven't killed any, but we can drive them off. We have special teams that deploy when Neophormes are spotted, but we don't have the resources to equip our entire military against them. We plan to help the Vehlixen find the Axiom of Command. Once they have it, they can defeat the Neophorm threat."

"So, you're fighting drones then?"

"We have drones, yes."

"No, I mean, you're fighting Neophorm drones—mindless creatures that just obey orders. Those original six you showed me are masters. These new ones are drones. I was attacked by a pair the other night."

Adrestia laid out a series of images showing Kita and Bernoot running from the Neophorm drones.

"Those two are drones," said Kita, pointing to the two Neophormes.

"And who are you with?" said Striker, tapping on Bernoot.

"I don't trust you," said Kita bluntly. She looked at Striker, then at Adrestia. He sighed, and she moved her head slightly. "I don't trust that you won't do to them what you did to Wavbreakr. They are my friends, and I would die before I give them up."

"Your commitment is admirable, but we are talking about national security," said Striker.

"Then lock me up. Send me to Guantanamo or wherever terrorists go."

Striker looked at Adrestia. "Hand me the tablet."

Adrestia opened the briefcase, pulled out a black tablet, turned it on, and handed it to Striker. He tapped on it and said, "This is General Striker. I have the contact with me, and I need a moment of The Doctor's time."

*Who is The Doctor? Another government official? A madwoman in a box? Who are they going to get to make me trust them?*

"Good evening, Your Highness—"

Kita tried to remember the royal family. They were so far out of Kita's day-to-day existence that she didn't care about them, and they didn't talk to people like her. *I'm just a junkyard girl—*

"Miss Logine?" said Striker.

Kita looked up as Adrestia put the tablet on a stand. On the tablet was a young woman with dark brown hair tied up with a bow, dark eyes, and a smile that melted Kita's heart. *Damn, she's beautiful.* She wore a blue business suit with a flag pin on the lapel. Kita didn't recognize her. *I bet I probably should...*

· "Miss Logine?" said the woman.

Kita felt lightheaded. *Oh, slag. This is what Velositi was preparing me for. Look the part, act the part, and talk the part. Confidence. I can do this. I just have to be friendly and direct. She's not much older than I am.*

Kita gulped. "Yes?"

"Do you know who I am?"

"Ah...No."

The other girl laughed. "Don't worry. I'm Doctor Kimberly Roosevelt. My father is the Emperor. You can call me Kimmy."

"Hi. I'm Kita."

"Nice to meet you, Kita. I understand you've had a busy couple of days."

"Mostly being chased by the cops and sitting in jail."

Kimmy nodded. "I can take care of that for you. General Striker says you and I have some mutual friends you can put *me* in contact with."

*That* me *didn't mean her, did it?* "Everyone's interested in my friends, but I don't trust that they won't be harmed."

"I understand your fear," said Kimmy. "Your friends are vital to the security of the country."

"That's what Striker said. He also showed me a picture of one being held captive."

"What would it take me to convince you that we mean them no harm?" Kimmy smiled warmly.

"Ah..." *What do I tell them? How can I trust them? What can they do?* "What are you a doctor of?" said Kita trying to stall for time.

"General medicine. I volunteer at Walter Reed when I'm not busy with the government. What do you do?"

"I—I used to work in auto salvage out in the Mojave Desert, the little town of Reading."

"What do you do now?" said Kimmy with a curious look.

"I—I'm looking for a new path."

"That is admirable. It takes a lot of courage to give up what you know and strike out to find something new."

*She sounds a lot like Velositi.* "Yeah, it's been an adventurous couple of days. I even got shot at out on the one-oh-two."

"I saw the pictures of you and your friends. That old Indian is nice, but I see why you changed to the H2R. She's very stylish. What's the boy's name?"

"Ah...I bet you already know."

Kimmy smiled. "I do. Ryan Callahan. He's a graduate student at C-Tech. His roommate reported him missing two days ago. The Cali Highway Patrol would also like to talk to him."

"He was pretty upset about what happened to his bike," said Kita.

"I bet. I'll put a note in the file that he's cleared of any wrongdoing, and the Empire will replace the bike."

*Wow. Talk about power. Ryan will be happy.*

"How about your other friend?" said Kimmy. "Who is she?"

"How do you know it's a *she*?"

Kimmy laughed. "I read the Morphicon file. Heavies are masculine, and lights are feminine. She doesn't look like a heavy—much too delicate and agile. But she packs a punch with those guns."

"Yeah," Kita whispered.

"We haven't seen her around for a few days. You've been riding with a different Vehlix. Is there something wrong with her?"

Tears formed at the corner of Kita's eyes. *If they truly want the Vehlixen as friends, maybe they can help Velositi. Striker said they understood them. But what if I'm wrong? Perhaps there is a way.* "If I take you to them, you have to promise you'll help fix her—"

"If she is injured or damaged, we'll provide whatever assistance is necessary. Striker will have the Majestic Twelve labs on standby. Do you know what's wrong with her?"

Tears trickled down Kita's face. "I don't know. During the attack on the freeway, they shot her with something that damaged her system cores. They made new ones and replaced them, but she didn't wake up." Kita wiped at the tears. *I shouldn't be crying in front of royalty.*

"We know a lot about them. She'll have whatever assistance she needs," said Kimmy.

"And you have to be there. Just you," Kita said firmly.

"I can be there, but I don't know if I can shed my security detail."

"That's the deal. You help Velositi, and you, by yourself, have to come with me to meet them."

Kimmy frowned. "They won't let me go unguarded."

"Fine." Kita pointed to Adrestia. "She'll be your bodyguard when we meet them. She's military."

Adrestia's eyes widened.

Kimmy nodded. "My security detail and Majestic Twelve operators will remain outside and form a perimeter but will stay—"

"At the fence," said Kita.

"Where are they?"

Kita shook her head. "I'm not telling until we're en route. It is outside Angel City."

Kimmy sighed. "That's a big area."

"Those are my terms. I'm sorry, but—"

"Don't apologize. You're doing what's right by you. We're the asking party. It will take about five hours to get from D.C. to Angel City. General Striker, get Majestic Twelve mobilized and ready. You have Imperial authority to commandeer whatever you need. Get Kita whatever she wants. I will see you in a few hours. Thank you, Kita. You don't know how much this means to your country."

"Help Velositi," said Kita.

"We will."

Kimmy ended the call.

Kita looked at Striker. "I want some food and a place to rest."

"We'll take care of that. Follow me."

Kita got up and stretched. "Oh, do you have my stuff?"

Adrestia pulled the envelope from the sheriff's jail containing Kita's belongings out of the briefcase. She handed them to Kita. Kita dumped the envelope contents on the table. She made sure her makeup, comb, money, and phone were there. Adrestia raised an eyebrow.

"Yeah, I bet I look a fright," said Kita.

A corner of Adrestia's mouth ticked up.

"All here," said Kita as she pocketed everything. "Let's go."

Kita sat in a black SUV parked in a hangar on Edwards Air Force Base. She had slept the entire ride here. When they'd arrived, Adrestia gave her a pomegranate smoothie she'd ordered before disappearing with Striker. An Air Force Humvee with two stern-looking airmen sat a couple of feet away. *Are they here to protect me or make sure I don't run away?* After slurping down her smoothie, Kita slid out of the SUV and surveyed the hangar. *If I were the bathroom, where would I be?* There was a door to the rear of the hangar. *Looks good to me.*

"Excuse me, Ma'am?" said an airman from the Humvee.

*Here to keep me from going anywhere.* "What?"

"You're not allowed to leave without an escort."

"Then I take it you're my escort?"

"Yes, Ma'am."

"Two things. It's Miss, not Ma'am—I am not old or attached to any man—and where is the bathroom?"

The airman didn't flinch. "This way, Miss."

Kita followed the airman's verbal directions as he trailed her across the hangar, through the back door, to an adjacent building. The starkly-lit hallway had several doors. The airman stopped her in front of a door.

"Here you are, Miss."

Kita smiled. "I'll be right out after I powder my nose."

Kita entered the bathroom and wrinkled her nose. *Smells like boy in here.* After using the restroom, she redid her makeup and brushed out her hair. *If I'm going to meet royalty, I should look my best.*

When she exited the restroom, the airman looked impatient.

"Problem?" said Kita.

"Air Force Three just landed. We need to hurry back to the hangar."

Kita waved him ahead of her. "Lead on. I'm in no rush."

They returned to the hangar and walked to the giant opening. Striker and Adrestia were waiting. Adrestia had changed into an Air Force battle dress uniform and had a pistol on her hip.

More Air Force Humvees lined the tarmac. The lights of a giant plane were visible on the runway. It taxied off the runway and stopped in front of the hangar. Kita couldn't believe how loud it was. A set of stairs drove up to the plane as the back opened, a ramp extended, and three black SUVs exited. The door above the stairs opened, and two men in black suits jogged down the stairs and stood at the bottom. *More MIBs. Not very inconspicuous.*

A trio of women exited the aircraft. Kimmy led the way dressed in jeans, boots, a leather jacket, and camisole. The other two women were dressed in more formal business attire.

The three SUVs parked in front of the hangar as Kimmy and her entourage entered. Striker and Adrestia saluted Kimmy. Kita, unsure of what to do, did nothing. It didn't seem to bother Kimmy.

"General, are you ready?" said Kimmy.

"Yes, Your Highness. The lab is waiting, and personnel are standing by ready to roll out. We just need to know the destination." He looked sharply at Kita.

"Take the five-oh-one up the valley."

"That's not a destination."

"Easy, General," said Kimmy. "I'm sure she'll give us the next waypoint when we get close. Right, Kita?"

"Yes...Kimmy."

Kimmy smiled. "Let's mount up and get going. We have a long drive ahead. Kita, you'll ride with me."

Kita shrugged. One SUV was as good as another. She followed Kimmy. Her aides took the back seat, and Kita and Kimmy sat in the middle. Kita buckled in after the doors closed.

"You don't need your seat belt," said Kimmy. "These are professional drivers."

Kita pulled back her collar to show the bruise that ran across her chest. "I got that from riding with a car that could drive itself."

"Do you need medical attention?" said Kimmy.

"I don't know. It hurts, but I don't think I broke anything. Nobody seems to have cared that I rolled down a hill in a car this morning."

"Take off your jacket and let me see."

*Here? She is a doctor.* Kita took off her jacket.

"Mind if we roll up your shirt?"

"Ok..." Kita rolled up her shirt across the top of her chest.

"Penlight," said Kimmy to an aide. Kimmy took the light and examined Kita's bruise. "It's consistent with a seat belt injury. Does it hurt when I touch it?" Kimmy pressed her hand in various places.

"No, just tickles."

"Take a deep breath. Does that hurt?"

"No," said Kita.

"Good. It's going to be pretty colors for a while. You want a painkiller?"

"No. I'm good. It hasn't bothered me much."

"Ok, then. I hate to be rude, but car rides are one of the only times I get a chance to take a nap. Daisy, wake me when we reach the first checkpoint."

"Yes, Your Highness."

Kimmy leaned against the door and closed her eyes. Kita turned the opposite direction and watched the darkness go by.

---

"ONE MILE TO THE SITE, YOUR HIGHNESS," SAID THE MIB IN THE PASSENGER seat.

"Dan, tell the other vehicles lights out," said Kimmy. "I don't want to spook them."

"There will be a gate you'll have to open," said Kita.

"We'll pause outside to let the teams get set up."

Kita wasn't so sure she liked the idea of armed teams surrounding the lab, but it was out of her control now.

"I see a light up ahead," said the driver.

"That's the entrance," said Kita.

The SUV stopped. MIBs exited the other SUVs and stood next to Kimmy's SUV. Soldiers ran by hurrying into the darkness. Kita and Kimmy got out, letting

Kimmy's aides exit. Adrestia joined Kita and Kimmy. The three women squeezed into the middle seat.

"So, you've given me one name. What are the others?" said Kimmy.

*It won't hurt now.* "The tall heavy is Sprokkit, and the shorter one is Bernoot. He's the one I was riding with yesterday. Sprokkit is their science and medical specialist, and Bernoot is a soldier."

"And Velositi is the leader?"

"Yes. Sprokkit can be gruff and cold. He probably won't like this idea," said Kita.

"I'm sure we can talk him into it. He has to want to fix Velositi."

"Yeah, but he's stubborn."

"I can be stubborn, too," Kimmy said with a smirk.

*Oh, great.*

"We're ready, Your Highness," said the driver.

"Ok, go ahead."

The SUV moved forward slowly up to the gate. The MIB in the passenger's seat got out and hurried to the shack. The gate went up, and the SUV pulled into the parking lot, leaving the other MIBs on the outside of the fence.

Kita, Kimmy, and Adrestia exited the SUV. There was light visible through the lab's windows.

*At least we know they're home.* "Follow me. The entrance is this way." Kita led Kimmy and Adrestia around the back to the partially opened door.

"Dark in here," said Kimmy.

"It's not too far," said Kita as she entered and passed the door Boom-Boom had destroyed.

"What happened here?" said Kimmy.

"A Neophorm mini chased me through the lab. I locked the door, but it cut it down."

"How did you get out?"

"Through the window."

"Is it still around?" said Adrestia.

"No. I killed it with a rock."

"That's not in any reports," said Kimmy.

"Nobody but the Vehlixen and the Neophormes know," said Kita.

"Impressive," said Adrestia.

"I've got the wounds to prove it."

"Are those the cuts on your arm?" said Kimmy.

"Yeah."

"I can bandage them. They should have been stitched."

"I have no money for a doctor, and how was I going to explain them?" said Kita unhappily.

"We will get them attended to—even if I have to do it."

A light showed through the doorway. Velositi was on the workbench as Sprokkit and Ryan worked on her. Bernoot stood next to the bay door. Kita stopped the group a few feet from the door.

"Let me go in first and talk to them," said Kita. "I'm pretty sure they don't expect me back."

"Why not?" said Kimmy.

"Sprokkit rescued me once. I doubt he'd do it again."

"Ok. Wave when you're ready."

Kita walked through the doorway toward the light.

Bernoot saw her first. "Hey, dudette! How'd you escape going up the river?" He trotted over and offered Kita a high five.

Kita returned it with a tired smile. "I, ah, made a new friend."

Ryan and Sprokkit came over. Kita hugged Ryan.

"I thought we'd be breaking you out again," said Ryan with a laugh.

"The same plan would have worked. I ended up back at the same place."

"Back with the mysterious IBI agents?"

"Yeah."

"How did you slip them?" said Ryan.

"I, ah, got paroled by a higher power. How's Velositi?"

"Ah, well," Ryan rubbed the back of his head.

"Still not functioning," said Sprokkit.

Kita's shoulders slumped. "Can I see her?"

"We are working on her. Maybe later."

Kita blinked a tear away. *At least he hasn't given up on her.* "What's wrong?"

"It is above you," said Sprokkit condescendingly.

"Just tell me," Kita growled.

"We're having trouble aligning her system cores," said Ryan. "They don't want to sit right."

"Do we need to make more?" said Kita.

"We have done the best we could with what we have available," said Sprokkit firmly.

"What if I were to tell you I know someone who could help?"

"Like in Silicon Valley?" said Ryan.

"Ah, better."

"This new friend of yours?"

Kita nodded.

"Who is it?"

"Her name is Kimmy. She wants to help." Kita braced herself for Sprokkit's reaction.

"You told someone about us?" yelled Sprokkit. "You said you would die first. You have compromised us completely!"

Kita shook her head. "I'm pretty sure she wants to keep you a secret."

"The mission is over. We will take Velositi and return home."

"No," cried Kita. "You can't. That's not what she would do."

"She is not in charge. I am."

"You're giving up on her so you can be in charge!" yelled Kita.

"I am not. I am following the mission parameters," said Sprokkit firmly.

"That's not your call to make. That's Velositi's!"

"Be quiet. You have no say in this."

"Then you go home, but you leave Velositi," snarled Kita.

"She would not want to stay on this miserable planet."

"That's not true. She said she wanted to return here and be with me."

"You are some weird fixation of Velositi's. You are nothing!" snapped Sprokkit.

"She loves me!" Kita yelled. "And I love her. You can't take her away from me."

"You have no say in the matter."

"I will not be denied!" Kita yelled in frustration. She waved to Kimmy.

"Sprokkit, come on," said Ryan. "We're not done yet."

"We were told not to reveal ourselves to anyone. We have already violated that instruction with you. I will not violate it further."

"What if I told you your enemy already has in a big way," said Kimmy as she walked up with Adrestia.

"Holy mother of—I mean, Your Highness," exclaimed Ryan as he took a knee.

*Is that what we're supposed to do? How does he know who she is?*

"Who are you?" demanded Sprokkit of Kimmy.

"I am Princess Kimberly Roosevelt, daughter of Emperor James Roosevelt of the Empire of the United States. And, I know a lot about your enemies, the Neophormes. My government has been fighting them for the last forty-five years."

"Fighting Neophormes is not our mission," said Sprokkit.

"I know your mission—to find the Axiom of Command. The Neophormes have a huge head start on you. My government can help you find it. We just need to know where to look."

"I do not have that information. Only our leader has it, and she is inoperable."

"We can help you. We have the facilities and the knowledge. With your help, we can fix her."

Sprokkit folded his arms. "I am not giving our leader over to be experimented on."

Kimberly glared. "We've already done our experiments on the Neophorm Wavbreakr. We know how you're constructed, how you use plasma, how you transform, and how your system cores work. Hell, I have one of you on ice that we built, still waiting for system cores. We can put your leader's system cores in it."

Kita didn't like the sound of that. She wanted Velositi's body.

Sprokkit's eyes glowed brightly. "You know nothing about us."

"I know that there are at least two hundred Neophormes on our planet, and that number grows every year. And, the Neophormes are moving in on you. They know where you are, and they have human help. I don't know where you've been for the last forty-five years, but you are not finding the Axiom of Command without my help."

Ryan raised his hand. "Can—can I say something, Your Highness?"

Kimmy nodded.

"Sprokkit, this is our best chance at saving Velositi. With what we have to do, we need the government's labs and technology. We spent all day trying to cobble together something to troubleshoot Velositi's system cores and have gotten nowhere. We just can't get the tech we need. Velositi is your friend. She deserves every chance at fixing her."

"We are not supposed to reveal ourselves," Sprokkit said firmly.

"It's too late, Sprokkit," said Ryan. "Our world knows you're here. Velositi knew you couldn't find the Axiom without human help. Kita and I are nothing compared to what the princess can offer. If you want to save Velositi and find the Axiom, you have to let them help you."

Sprokkit's eyes dimmed.

Kita ground her teeth. She was tired of waiting for Sprokkit and rushed to the workbench. Searching, she found the five glass cubes of Velositi's system cores and snatched them up.

"What are you doing?" said Ryan.

Sprokkit's eyes brightened. "What are you doing, human?" he roared.

Kita put the system cores in her pocket. "I have what I want. So, go home. I don't need you anymore. You're not fixing Velositi anyway."

Sprokkit's arm morphed into a cannon. "Return Velositi's system cores or I will shoot you."

Adrestia jumped in front of Kimmy and raised her pistol.

"You shoot me," said Kita, "and you have to explain to Velositi why you killed me. You think she'll forgive you?"

"You shoot her, and I will deem you hostile," said Kimmy. "My forces will attack and destroy you."

"Your forces are no match for us," snarled Sprokkit.

"My forces have forty-five years' experience fighting Morphicons. They know how to kill you."

Ryan jumped in front of Kita. "Don't do it, Sprokkit. Please, let the princess help you."

"Kita has betrayed us!" yelled Sprokkit.

Kita shook her head. "I would never betray Velositi. She has my best interest at heart, and I have hers. I believe the princess can fix her. I would prefer her in her original body, but I'll take what I can get. You're the one being stubborn, arrogant, and foolish. All things Velositi is not. If you're going to shoot me, shoot me. Otherwise, put it away, pack your stuff and leave or let Kimmy help you."

Bernoot put his hand on Sprokkit's arm. "Hey, big dude, let's do what we came to do. Let's fix our leader, sniff out the Axiom, so we can kick it in our crib. Kita ain't no traitor. She ate one for me. There ain't no shame in our game for getting the human's help. If we sniff it out, no one's going to care how we got it."

"You do not get a say in the matter," said Sprokkit gruffly.

"Velositi ain't pushing up daisies yet. We play by her rules until then. If humans think they can fix her, let them take a spin. I'm not taking my toys and going home until Velositi is toast." Bernoot stood between Sprokkit and Kita.

Kita made a face. She couldn't see around Bernoot and moved to one side. "Think of it this way. If we repair Velositi and find the Axiom, you'll be the one who made the call."

Sprokkit huffed. "I will drag you before the Elders if we fail."

Kita shrugged. "I'm getting used to being interrogated. Bernoot, will you open the door so Striker and his men can come in and help Sprokkit load?"

"You got it, dudette."

Kita moved next to Ryan as Kimmy and Adrestia talked to Sprokkit.

"So, since when are you on a first-name basis with the princess?" said Ryan.

"Ah, since this evening. I'm not hurting these system cores, am I?"

"No, they should be fine, but we should wrap them up in something to protect them."

Kita went to her cot and found her flannel. She wrapped Velositi's system cores in it and tucked them inside her jacket. She gathered up the rest of her things and put them in a plastic bag.

The lab was full of soldiers and scientists. They had come with large Pelican shipping containers and set them in front of the workbench. Sprokkit directed them on what to load. A truck backed into the lab, and Bernoot loaded Velositi into the back. The soldiers scrambled to tie her down.

Kita grabbed Ryan's arm and pulled him over to the truck when the soldiers were finished. Shoving her bag into Ryan's arms, Kita climbed onto the fender.

"Hey, what are you doing?" said a soldier.

"None of your business. If you don't like it, take it up with Kimmy," Kita said as she crawled into the bed of the truck. She put her hand on Velositi's seat, hugged her, and kissed the cowl. "You'll be back to me in no time. I promise." Kita kissed Velositi again as the truck started. Kita jumped down to be face to face with Kimmy.

"If you're ready to go, we can load up," said Kimmy.

"I'm going to ride with Sprokkit," said Ryan. "He'll probably want a sympathetic ear to talk to."

"Maybe you can teach him sympathy," muttered Kita.

"That's not fair," said Ryan. "He believes what he's doing is right and wants to obey the orders he was given. Sprokkit does want Velositi back. I don't think he likes being in charge."

"I don't like him being in charge. If Sprokkit has all his stuff, I'm ready to go," Kita said to Kimmy.

THE SUNRISE GLISTENED OFF THE YELLOW HILLS AS THE CONVOY OF VEHICLES drove away from the lab. Kita ignored Kimmy and her aides as she stared out the window, thinking about Velositi.

"Kita?" said Kimmy.

"Huh? Yeah?"

"I want to thank you for your help. Finding the Vehlixen is a major boost to national security. You'll be well taken care of."

"Thanks, but I want Velositi taken care of."

"We will fix her. I'm going to need her system cores." Kimmy held out her hand.

"I'll, ah, hang on to them. It's no problem. I'll give them to Sprokkit when we get to the base."

"I must insist. You won't be seeing Sprokkit or the other Vehlixen again."

"What? No way. That wasn't part of the deal."

"Kita, you are not a scientist or a soldier. You'll be sent home to go back to your life—a life that will be much better now."

"I am not living without Velositi," snarled Kita. She turned, popped the door lock, and jerked open the door.

"What are you doing?" cried Kimmy.

The MIB in the passenger's seat lunged to grab Kita as she stood in the SUV's door. Using the door's armrest and the seat, she crawled onto the SUV's roof. The driver slowed. Hanging onto the side of the SUV, Kita reached into her back pocket and pulled out her phone. She found Bernoot's icon and called him.

"Hey, dudette! What's up? Did you miss me?"

"Bernoot! I need a pickup. I'm on top of the princess' SUV. They're trying to take Velositi."

"Yo! I'm on my way. Hang tight."

Kita glanced over her shoulder. Bernoot, as a black Corvette with golden racing stripes, swerved out of the convoy and sped up the line of vehicles in the opposite lane. He pulled alongside Kimmy's SUV.

"I'm going to roll off; you catch me," said Kita.

"You got it."

Kita put her phone away, took a deep breath to steady her nerves, and then rolled to her left off the SUV. Bernoot morphed, caught Kita, and morphed back, placing Kita in the passenger's seat.

"Wow, this is nice," said Kita.

"Totally awesome. I blew the original's tires off going down the freeway."

The SUVs at the head of the convoy stopped in a wishbone formation blocking the road. The rest of the convoy stopped, and Kimmy hopped out of her SUV, looking furious. The MIBs jumped out—their guns drawn—and surrounded her. Bernoot rolled to a stop in front of Kimmy. Kita got out, and Bernoot morphed as Sprokkit pulled up with Ryan. Striker and Adrestia ran up behind them.

"Why so serious?" Bernoot asked Kimmy and her MIBs.

Ryan ran up to Kita as Sprokkit hurried to catch up.

"What's going on?" said Ryan to Kita. "Why were you climbing on the roof?"

Kimmy said, "You—"

"She wants to send us home!" Kita exclaimed to Ryan. "And she wants to take Velositi away from me and never let me see her again."

"No one ever said anything about that," said Ryan. "Did she say that to you, Sprokkit?"

"No. We did not discuss your involvement. I assumed you would come with me. Kita would also come. How long she stays depends on Velositi."

"Neither one of you are trained," said Kimmy. "You are a liability."

"Ryan has proved to be an apt pupil," said Sprokkit.

"I have plenty of scientists who can help you."

"He is my friend and an excellent liaison to human culture. I trust him, and I will not be without him. I know Velositi feels the same way about Kita. Though, I understand doubting her usefulness."

Kita made a face at Sprokkit. "I am the one willing to risk my ass to get things done."

"Your knack for finding trouble is becoming legendary."

Kimmy glared at Kita. "Sprokkit, I can give you official liaisons."

"No," said Sprokkit. "Ryan and Kita have earned our trust. They will make sure our dealings with you and your government are fair."

"You don't trust me?"

"Not to the level I trust them. Kita and Ryan have willingly helped us and asked for nothing in return. They have been honest and willing to put our interests ahead of their own. But, above all, I know Velositi. If Kita is not there when Velositi wakes, she will not help you. Velositi will leave to find Kita. Once they are reunited, then Velositi will search for the Axiom."

"What do you have over Velositi?" demanded Kimmy of Kita.

Kita crossed her arms and smiled. "She loves me, and I love her. I refuse to be without her, and she refuses to be without me."

"Fine," snarled Kimmy. "But they will have bodyguards at all times."

Kita remembered the hangar. "To protect me or to keep me from going where I want to go?"

"Kita and Ryan can go anywhere we can go," said Sprokkit. "I expect Ryan to be by my side as much as possible. Bernoot can take Kita until Velositi is ready."

Kimmy's face puckered. "K—"

"I'll take her." Kita pointed to Adrestia.

"She has better things to do than babysit you," snarled Kimmy.

"Like what? Serve coffee? Shuffle papers? Keep his life straight?" Kita hitched a thumb at Striker. "I'm not having a man follow me around."

"Fine. Major Adrestia, you're assigned as Kita's bodyguard. You will get a detailed briefing later. She is to stay with Bernoot until we get to our final destination. General Striker, find a suitable bodyguard for Ryan."

"Yes, Your Highness."

"Where are we going?" said Kita.

Kimmy glowered at Kita. "Area fifty-one. A place where you can't cause trouble."

*You don't get Velositi fixed, and we'll see about trouble.*

———————⟨———————

Kᴉᴛᴀ ᴄʟɪᴍʙᴇᴅ ɪɴᴛᴏ ᴛʜᴇ Hᴜᴍᴠᴇᴇ ᴀɴᴅ ᴡʀɪɴᴋʟᴇᴅ ʜᴇʀ ɴᴏsᴇ. Iᴛ ᴡᴀs ᴅᴜsᴛʏ, bare metal, and only had thin cushions to sit on. She, Ryan, and Adrestia were leaving the DFAC after having lunch. Kita had barely touched it, not sure if her stomach could handle whatever was under the gravy.

Even though they hadn't reached Area 51 and gotten settled until after midnight, Adrestia had woken Kita and Ryan up at five-thirty. Kita made sure Adrestia knew she wasn't happy, was hungry, and needed new clothes. After breakfast, Adrestia took Kita and Ryan to the base supply office and drew them four sets of Air Force battle uniforms. Their civilian clothes were placed in the laundry.

Kita held Velositi's system cores in her lap, still wrapped in her flannel.

"Where are we going now?" said Kita.

"To the bunker. Sprokkit is ready for the system cores," said Adrestia as she turned down a dusty street.

"What is the bunker?" said Kita.

"It's where Majestic Twelve's research happens."

"Good. I can check on Velositi."

"We'll see how busy the scientists are," said Adrestia.

Kita gave her a dirty look. "If I don't like what they're doing, I will stop it."

"I'm sure you will try."

"I'm sure they're not doing anything without Sprokkit's approval," said Ryan.

Kita nodded. "He wouldn't let them hurt her."

Adrestia followed a road off the base proper. A low building with sloped sides and a flat top had several Humvees parked around it. In the near side of the building's wall was a notch. Adrestia parked and led the pair to the notch, which was a reinforced door. She scanned a badge, then her finger, and the door opened.

An airman sat behind a desk with a computer. He had a pistol in a shoulder holster.

"Major Nicole Adrestia with civilians Kita Logine and Ryan Callaghan to sign in."

The airman produced a tablet. "Here you are, Ma'am."

Adrestia signed them in. The airman entered a command on his computer.

"The elevator is active, Ma'am. What floor?"

"Six."

"Yes, Ma'am. Please, step inside."

Adrestia ushered Kita and Ryan into the elevator. The doors closed, and the elevator hummed as it went down. To Kita, it felt like they'd been going down forever when the door opened. Adrestia led them down a short hallway that intersected with a much bigger hallway.

*This is big enough for a Morphicon to walk through.*

The big hallway led them to a set of large double bay doors, with a human-sized door cut in the large right door. Using a control panel, Adrestia opened the human-sized door. Kita stepped through the door into a cavernous room filled with all kinds of computers, equipment, workbenches, and machinery. On the rear wall was a Morphicon body held in some sort of field. It looked alien and unfamiliar.

Over the equipment, Kita could see Sprokkit with his back to her. Without waiting for Adrestia, she hurried over to him, ignoring the looks of the scientists and engineers.

"Sprokkit?" Kita called.

He turned around, and his eyes lit, but he wasn't looking at her but Ryan. "Ryan, I was wondering when they would bring you. I was about to complain."

"Major Adrestia took us to get new clothes and some food. Did I miss something important?"

"Yes. I will have scientist Paulson walk you through how they were able to transform Velositi."

"They morphed Velositi? Where is she?" demanded Kita.

"Behind those screens." Sprokkit pointed to some eight-foot-high plastic sheet panels. "You can move them," he said to the researchers.

Moving the panels revealed Velositi standing. A dozen cables snaked to her, attaching at various points. Her eyes were off, giving her a vacant look. Kita didn't care. She rushed forward and put a hand on Velositi's hip.

"Don't—" said a scientist.

"She will be fine," said Sprokkit.

Velositi was warm under Kita's hand. Kita inspected Velositi, front and rear. Nothing seemed to mar her paint job. Kita grabbed a stepladder and climbed up to be face to face with Velositi. She stroked the smooth dark gray face surrounded by a pink crown, then wrapped her arms around Velositi's neck and hugged her.

"I miss you," Kita whispered. "So much. Come back to me. I have your cores. I'll give them to Sprokkit and Ryan. Just, please, come back to me." She kissed Velositi's cheek, pressed her forehead against Velositi, and squeezed back some tears.

"Hey," said Ryan, gently teasing. "We can't fix her around you."

Kita laughed. "Ok." She climbed down the ladder and handed Velositi's system cores to Ryan. Kita felt her heart soar. It was good to see Velositi's face. She followed Ryan back to Sprokkit and Adrestia with a big smile on her face.

"From your reaction, I understand you approve?" Sprokkit said to Kita.

"Yes. Velositi looks good."

"Then, Ryan and I will start the system core alignment."

"I guess I'll find something to do to keep myself busy. Let me know if you need my help."

Sprokkit's eyes brightened. "You will be the last person I call."

"I used to work on cars, you know. I know my way around a toolbox."

"Have you seen a bolt or a screw on Velositi?"

"Well, no, but..."

"My point," said Sprokkit. "Why not check on Bernoot? He left with some soldiers this morning."

"Ok." Kita looked at Adrestia. The major nodded. "We can do that."

"And find some better clothes—even I can tell those are ugly on you. I am not explaining why you do not look pretty to Velositi."

*No argument there. Velositi thought my old clothes were baggy. Even a woman's small is a tent. And this tan, brown, and green color clashes with my nails.* Kita smiled at Adrestia. "You heard him. Clothes shopping, then Bernoot."

"I'll have to get authorization for the clothes."

"If she wakes up and sees me in this, I'm pointing at you."

Adrestia raised an eyebrow and then waved Kita to follow her.

THE DUST THE HUMVEE KICKED UP WAS ATROCIOUS. *I'M GOING TO NEED another shower, and I'll never get the dust out of my hair.* To keep her mind off the dust, she turned to Adrestia.

"So, is it ok if I call you Nicole?"

Adrestia gave Kita an unhappy look. "Who told you that?"

"You gave your name to the guy guarding the desk at the bunker. Calling you Major Adrestia sounds too formal for someone who's supposed to follow me around wherever I go. Anyway, you call me Kita and not Miss Logine. Fair is fair."

Adrestia seemed to think it over. "Ok, except in formal situations."

"When's a formal situation?"

"Whenever there are other people around."

"That's like always," scowled Kita.

"Fine. Whenever there is someone higher ranking than me around."

"How will I know that?"

"You'll know. General Striker and the princess for sure."

Kita stuck her tongue out. "I hope I don't see her again."

Adrestia smiled slightly.

"What?"

"You have a lot of courage to defy the princess."

"Velositi told me I need to work on my self-confidence," said Kita.

"I would say you have an exorbitant amount."

Kita slumped back in her seat. "Not really. I just don't want to let Velositi down."

"You seem to have a unique relationship with her."

Kita wasn't sure how much she should say. She hadn't explained her love of Velositi to anyone. *But I've demonstrated it plenty.* "She's my...girlfriend."

Adrestia gave her a you-are-crazy look.

"It's not what you think," said Kita defensively. "It's just...It's—Oh, what does it matter. Just drive."

"Answer me this—does she reciprocate?"

"Of course, she does. Do you think I fell in love with a toaster? She fell in love with me first. It's the first attention I've gotten in any form since my dad died three years ago."

"Sorry about your loss."

"It's in the past. Velositi is helping me move on."

Adrestia nodded. "You can't stay trapped in grief."

"Well, I was. I passed it. So, what do you do?"

"I'm a Major in the Air Force assigned to be your bodyguard."

Kita rolled her eyes. "You had to do something before you started getting Striker his coffee and keeping his life straight."

Adrestia smirked. "Before I was assigned to Majestic Twelve, I was in command of the Tenth Security Forces Squadron at the Air Force Academy in Colorado. I did various officer type jobs before that. A long time ago, I was a sniper for the Air Force Security Forces."

"You know how to shoot?"

"Yes. I am in the top five of the Emperor's Hundred." Adrestia tapped a tab on her left shoulder.

Kita shrugged. "What's that?"

"The best one hundred military and civilian shooters are part of this elite group."

"So, you hit the target every time?"

Adrestia laughed, surprising Kita. "It's not whether you hit the target. It's how close you get to the center. We're measured in millimeters."

"Oh. So that pistol is for more than looks?"

"I wouldn't shoot to kill you. I don't want to explain your death to an eight-foot-tall alien that comes with her own cannons."

Adrestia turned into a parking lot with several military trucks parked in a neat row. "We're here." She climbed out of the Humvee.

Kita did the same and dusted herself off.

"You might as well get used to it. That's all that's out here."

"Where's Bernoot?"

"Out on the range with the operators."

Adrestia led Kita along a path, onto a berm, and to the foot of a tower. Bernoot was on the other side of the berm, talking to roughly thirty heavily armed soldiers in various military uniforms.

Kita trotted down the berm and yelled, "Bernoot!"

The group of soldiers turned to look at her. Bernoot's eyes lit as he took a few steps forward. Kita pushed her way through the operators to him.

"Dudette! Where you been hanging? Nice threads. Velositi's going to totally trip." He lowered his hand for a high five.

Kita slapped his massive hand. "My other clothes needed washing, and I got to see Velositi."

"Oh, yeah? How's she hanging?"

"They're working on her. I gave Sprokkit her system cores."

"Awesome."

"How are you doing? Any problems?"

"Everything's cool. I've been swapping tales of the hood with these guys. They've got some gnarly stories about fighting Neophormes, but none as bad as mine. But you got the most badass story of them all."

"What story?"

"You got a lot of stories, dudette. Did you scrub your noodle of Boom-Boom?"

Kita blushed. "That's hardly a story. I spent most of the time running."

Bernoot looked at the operators. "So, get this. Dudette is kicking it by herself at the lab when Nitstik and Boom-Boom roll up. She's got no cannons, just her mind. She leads them on a chase around the lab. Snookers old Nitstik with her phone and lures Boom-Boom across the street where she kills it with her bare hands. True story. I saw Boom-Boom's wrecked body."

"It wasn't quite like that," admitted Kita quietly. "I used a rock..."

The soldiers gave Kita an approving look. Kita glanced at Adrestia. She looked at Kita with respect.

"I'm Captain Jonny Kerr of the Majestic Twelve Anti-Neophorm Team Five. You must be Kita Logine, the liaison I was told to expect."

"Ah, yes...Sir. I'm keeping track of Bernoot until Velositi is repaired. He, ah, hasn't been a problem, has he?"

Kerr shook his head. "No. We've been doing familiarity exercises to so we can judge capability and working on tactics to best use his strength and firepower."

Kita had no idea what that meant. "Ok. I know he can be a bit much and likes to talk, but he's skillful but young."

"Dudette?" said Bernoot.

"Yeah?" said Kita.

"I can't get any TV signals out here or internet connection."

Kita pulled her phone from her pocket and checked the signal strength. She had none. Kita looked behind the group of operators. "Nicole—Major Adrestia?"

Everyone turned to see her standing behind them. Kerr saluted for the group. "Ma'am."

Adrestia returned the salute and moved through the soldiers to Kita. "Area fifty-one is a dead zone. No commercial communication signals allowed in or out. We can go to the bunker and get your phone upgraded. I don't know what we can do for Bernoot."

"Bernoot can reconfigure himself if he knows what to do," said Kita. "Sprokkit is the one who figured out how to emulate my phone."

"I'll check to see if our scientists have anything. I would hate to bother Sprokkit."

Kita nodded. "We'll get it figured out, Bernoot. You might have to visit the bunker."

"Hey, no problemo. But I got to have my shows."

"You'll get them. Right now, why don't you continue working with, uhm—"

"—Captain Kerr," said Adrestia.

"Yeah, these guys. They're going to help find the Axiom, so you have to work together."

"Righto. I'll show them the danger zone."

Kita chuckled. "Good. I'll leave you to it. If you have a problem, stop and tell them you want to talk to me. I'll work it out." She looked at Adrestia, who nodded. "Have fun."

ADRESTIA SAT DOWN NEXT TO KITA IN THE WEBBED SEAT OF THE BOEING C-17. She shoved a cup of coffee into Kita's hand.

Kita glared at Adrestia with tired eyes. "Can you now explain to me why I had to get up at two a.m. and rush to board this flying whale?"

Adrestia's eyes were bright and excited, though her face didn't show it. She was dressed as a police officer and carried an M-4A4 with a scope. Kita guessed it went with the two black and blue armored vehicles with SWAT painted on them tied down in the back behind Bernoot. The Majestic Twelve operators were dressed like SWAT officers to complete the disguise.

"We're going on a mission to raid an Illuminati safe house. Investigators believe it's the same cell that attacked you on the freeway."

*She sounds excited. It's too early to be excited.* "Why do I have to go?"

"You're Bernoot's liaison. You go where he goes."

"I'm not expected to fight, am I?"

"No. We'll be a block to the north, watching." Adrestia sighed.

"You're really into this," said Kita.

"My job is to watch you and keep you safe."

"Watching me isn't what you're excited about."

Adrestia frowned slightly. "I'll do my job. Don't worry."

"Tell me what you're excited about." Kita smiled at Adrestia mischievously. "Tell me, or I'll take you shopping again."

Adrestia sighed heavily, and her shoulders slumped.

Kita hadn't dragged Adrestia to the mall. Instead, they sat in front of a secure computer for five hours as Kita picked out a new wardrobe. Kita had taken her time because she wanted to make sure Velositi would like what she picked. Adrestia was no help—it was either too revealing, which meant it wasn't baggy like a uniform, or frivolous. Kita took her revenge on Adrestia's lack of interest by making her help pick out new underwear from Victoria's Secret, which was prettier and sexier than the underwear issued by the Air Force. Better yet, the government had paid for everything. Kita wanted to see the face of the accountant that got the bill for a thousand dollars at Victoria's Secret.

Area 51 had no parcel service. Everything went to a random location in Vegas and then flown by special courier to the base. The packages arrived the night before, and Kita hadn't gotten a chance to try everything on. She'd thrown her old clothes on for this mission, except for underwear. She'd made Adrestia wait this morning while she picked out a set.

"It wasn't that bad." Kita chuckled. "So, tell me."

"I've always wanted to go on a mission with a team. They're the best in the world."

"So are you."

"I don't have their training. They come from the SEALs, Green Berets, Air Traffic Controllers, Delta Force—groups you need years of training to get into. These people have been in Special Forces for a decade or more."

There was a longing in her voice.

"Why didn't you become one?"

"Special Forces wasn't open to women when I enlisted. That's why I became a sniper for Security Forces—I was allowed to join SWAT units. My career path as an officer led me in a different direction."

Kita touched her shoulder. "We get to be part of the action today. Who knows, you might get to put that rifle to use."

"You better not go running into trouble."

"I go where Bernoot needs me."

BERNOOT ROLLED TO A STOP A BLOCK FROM THE TARGET BUILDING, AND KITA stepped out the driver's side door. The streets were empty. Local police had sealed the surrounding neighborhood.

"Ok, Bernoot, I've got the live feed on my phone. You let me know if you need help or if the operators do something wrong. Got it?"

"I'm on it, dudette. Let's go bust some heads."

Kita looked over at Bernoot and nodded to Adrestia, who had ridden in the passenger side. Kita joined Adrestia on the sidewalk and moved to cover behind a building. Adrestia's radio picked up chatter from the team, the IBI, and the local police.

"Ten David, Phase line alpha reached," said Kerr.

"Roger. Cutting power and turning on the jammers," replied an IBI officer.

The target building was a two-story garage surrounded by a chain-link fence with privacy slats. On the north side, a pedestrian gate led to an entrance. On the backside of the building were a three-stall garage and a small yard. The second story of the building had windows on all four sides, five on the north and south, and three on the east and west. Kita stood on Adams Street, which ran north-south and intersected with Baker Street, which ran east-west along the north side of the building. Adams Street made a jog around the building to the east.

Bernoot and the Majestic Twelve vehicles approached the building. He and the first Majestic Twelve vehicle followed the jog along the building to a gate on the south side of the building.

"Dagger One, in position," called the first Majestic Twelve vehicle behind Bernoot.

"Dagger Two, in position," said the second Majestic Twelve vehicle parked in front of the building.

"At the spot and ready to rock," said Bernoot in front of the south gate.

"Dagger Three, inbound," said the third Majestic Twelve team coming in via helicopter.

"All teams—go," said Kerr.

The back of the second Majestic Twelve vehicle opened, and soldiers jumped out and sprinted toward the pedestrian gate. On Kita's phone, Bernoot crashed the south gate and entered the yard. The first Majestic Twelve vehicle pulled into the yard, and the soldiers deployed and rushed the closed garage doors and a side door to the west.

An operator shot the lock off the pedestrian gate with a shotgun. The team filed through the gate into the narrow space between the building and the fence.

The windows on the second story opened, and men with assault rifles fired down on the Majestic Twelve operators.

"Dagger Two, taking fire from above. Reporting casualties."

From a block away, Kita could see the team was in trouble. The gunmen from the windows were laying down fire, pinning the soldiers down. The Blackhawk helicopter flew in and hovered over the roof, dropping a large rope. The gunmen from the windows split time between shooting at the operators and the Blackhawk.

Kita put a hand on Adrestia's shoulder. "Hey, you think you can shoot those guys in the window?"

"My job is to protect you."

"Does it look like I'm in danger? They need help. You can give it to them. Unless it's too far," Kita added with a sly smile.

"It's not too far. I don't want to ruin their plan."

"It doesn't look like they have much of a plan. The longer we argue, the more they're going to get shot up."

Adrestia rushed into the street and took up a prone firing position. Kita lay beside her.

"Dagger Two, this is Nemesis," said Adrestia. "Identified three targets, second-floor windows firing AKs. Removal in progress."

Adrestia fired a shot. The gunman in the first window slumped down, his rifle falling to the ground. Adrestia shifted slightly and fired, hitting the second gunman. She shifted again, fired, and hit the third gunman.

"Dagger Two, you are clear. No more hostiles in the windows."

"Thanks, Nemesis. Dagger two proceeding to building breach."

"Nemesis, identify. This is Ten David."

Adrestia looked at Kita. "Tell him the truth."

"Ten David, I'm Major Nicole Adrestia assigned to protect Bernoot's liaison."

"Good shooting, Nemesis. I suggest you stick to your primary objective."

"Yes, Ten David."

"You're not in trouble, are you?" said Kita.

"It's a wash. I got a pat on the back and a kick in the ass."

"At least you get to say you helped with the mission."

Adrestia stood up while pulling Kita to her feet. "Come on, back under cover."

Kita returned to the corner of the building. The soldiers of Dagger Two entered the building's lower door. The Blackhawk turned and flew in a circle around the area.

"Dagger Three has entered the second floor," reported the team leader.

A loud boom echoed down the street.

"What was that?" said Kita to Adrestia.

"I don't know."

"It's Nitstik," said Bernoot through Kita's phone.

"Bernoot, are you ok?"

"I'm going to show this punk what's up."

"Let the soldiers help you."

"All Dagger elements, Neophorm spotted. Switch to ECM rounds and bring out the heavy guns," ordered Kerr.

The video feed on Kita's phone showed Nitstik in his robot form trading shots with Bernoot. The soldiers in the yard were moving around, shooting at Nitstik while avoiding being stepped on.

Bernoot and Nitstik came together, wrestling with one another. They rolled on the ground, trading punches and kicks.

"Hey, yo! Watch where you're shooting, man! That stings. Dudette, they're shooting me."

"Hang on, Bernoot. I'll let them know."

Kita looked at Adrestia. "All Dagger elements—check fire. Check fire. Be advised you are hitting Bernoot. Nemesis, over."

"Nemesis, Dagger Six, wilco. All Dagger elements make sure you fire on Nitstik only."

"It should be better now, Bernoot," said Kita.

She didn't get an answer. Bernoot was throwing Nitstik into the building. Bernoot fired his cannon into Nitstik, leaving large holes glowing red. A claw, like the one that had hit Velositi on the freeway, slammed into Nitstik's chest.

"Stay back, Bernoot!" yelled Kita. "Don't touch Nitstik while he's got that thing in his chest."

Bernoot jumped back and fired his cannon at Nitstik. The Neophorm's movements became sluggish, and his cannon shots were now inaccurate. The soldiers continued to shoot Nitstik as another claw slammed into his back. Nitstik collapsed, and the soldiers moved in. Bernoot hovered on the perimeter, his cannon ready.

"Come on," said Kita to Adrestia.

"We haven't gotten the all-safe signal yet."

"How much safer does it have to be?"

Kita jogged down the block and around the building to the south gate. The soldiers were setting up restraining panels around Nitstik. Kita stopped next to Bernoot and put her hand on his leg.

"Are you ok, Bernoot?"

He turned to face her. He had four melon-sized holes in his front, and his left arm hung limp.

"I'll be ok," he said without his usual enthusiasm.

"Do I need to call Sprokkit?"

"Nah, I just need time to chill. Holler at me when it's time to go." Bernoot morphed and went quiet.

Kita called Sprokkit. "Bernoot's been injured. He has several holes, and his left arm isn't working," said Kita before Sprokkit could say anything. "He's very sullen."

Sprokkit's eyes dimmed. "I will need to examine him. He's probably in a great deal of pain. I suggest he return at once."

"Ok, I'll let them know. We secured the site and captured Nitstik."

"That is good. One less Neophorm in our way."

Sprokkit closed the connection. Kita looked at Adrestia. "Bernoot needs to see Sprokkit immediately."

"I'll pass the word up."

"If they don't hurry, this will be the last mission he goes on."

KITA WALKED NEXT TO BERNOOT AS HE BACKED DOWN THE RAMP OF THE C-17. In his car form, he showed no damage, but Kita could tell he was hurting from his slow movement. Kerr met them at the bottom of the ramp. He saluted Adrestia.

"Ma'am, Miss Kita, Bernoot, I would like to invite you to our After-Action Review. It's a little informal ceremony where we go over the day and recognize accomplishments."

"Bernoot needs to see Sprokkit," said Kita.

"I understand."

"Yo! I'll go," said Bernoot. "Warriors stand together."

Kita frowned. "I guess if it's quick, Captain."

"Then follow me, please."

Kerr led them off the tarmac behind a hangar where Team Five was gathered —except one who had been rushed to the hospital due to gunshot injuries. Several other seated soldiers had bandages on arms or legs. The group came to attention, even the injured, when Kerr approached. He, in turn, saluted Adrestia, recognizing she was the highest rank there. Bernoot pulled up to the rear and morphed, taking a knee. Kita and Adrestia stood next to him.

"I'll keep this short," said Kerr. "It's been a long, hard day, but it has been a successful one. For the first time in almost thirty years, we caught a Neophorm. The unit has been put in for an Imperial Citation, and each one of us has been put in for a medal. I know it's one more for the junk drawer, but it's a job well done—all of you. I have an update on Jackson. He's going to make it. They pulled bullets out of his liver and kidney. He'll be gone a few weeks recovering, but he'll be back. Now, who has the game ball?"

Kerr caught a football that came out of the crowd.

"We had a new teammate today, and we wouldn't have been successful without him. He did some hard fighting and took a few hits, but he refused to quit. Today's game ball goes to Bernoot."

The team applauded and gave a rousing *hooah*. Kerr tossed the ball to Kita.

*Oh, slag me! Oh, don't drop it! Don't drop it!* Kita caught the ball in her arms and trapped it against her chest. Kita offered the ball to Bernoot.

Bernoot stood and took a bow. "To all my homies on the street, I couldn't have done it without ya."

The operators laughed. Kerr caught another football.

"I have one more special game ball," said Kerr. "Without this individual, today would have been a lot worse. She came through when we needed help the most and made our mission a success while completing her own. This special game ball goes to Nemesis. Thanks for watching our asses out there, Ma'am."

Kerr tossed Adrestia the ball, and she caught it with ease.

"Happy to be of assistance, Captain."

"You made her dream come true," said Kita as she wrapped an arm around

Adrestia and gave her a warm hug. She felt Adrestia tense and then relax as she touched her head to Kita's.

"That's all I have," said Kerr. "Everyone's dismissed. Take care of your gun, gear, and yourselves. I expect everyone in bed early tonight."

Kita sighed. She wasn't getting to bed early tonight. She and Adrestia waited to one side while Bernoot said goodnight to the operators.

"Do you like your football?" Kita said to Adrestia.

Adrestia had the ball tucked under her arm. "I'm a little shocked I got it. I didn't do much."

"Right place, right time."

"I didn't do anything extraordinary."

"How many years have you spent honing your skills to shoot like that? That's incredible."

"Not as incredible as climbing onto the princess' SUV and then jumping off."

"I didn't have any options, and I knew Bernoot would catch me as long as I held on. That was the hard part."

The corner of Adrestia's mouth ticked up. "I knew you'd be special."

"I'm not special. I used to be a wreck, but then Velositi came along and showed me differently."

"You're confident."

Kita shook her head. "That's only because I have Velositi backing me up. I'd be a mess without her."

"I think that's a crutch you're holding on to. I think you'd be more than fine without it."

Bernoot morphed and rolled over to them. "Where you ladies headed?"

Kita laughed. "The bunker—to get *you* fixed up."

Kita sat at Velositi's feet, trying to keep her eyes open. She wasn't sure how Adrestia did it. She didn't look tired. Sprokkit and Ryan were examining Bernoot. Kita wasn't sure what Sprokkit's different sounds and eye expressions meant as he worked his way through Bernoot's injuries. Kita leaned against Velositi's leg and fell asleep.

"Hey, Kita! Wake up!" said Ryan gently as he tapped Kita's shoulder.

"Huh? What? Did I fall asleep? Did I fall asleep too long?"

Ryan laughed. "A couple of minutes, I think. We're done with Bernoot."

"Is he going to be ok?"

"He needs time to heal. The bullets the Majestic Twelve guys use stun a small area of the Morphicon's cells. He took a lot of them. That's why his left arm isn't working, but the effects wear off. The damage he took from Nitstik isn't as bad. Bernoot is high on plasma, and so it should heal rapidly."

"By the Crushing Depths," snarled Kita. "I warned those slagbags about shooting him. I'll shoot Kerr with one and see how he likes it."

Adrestia raised an eyebrow. "We will report it to General Striker. I'm sure Velositi will have something to say about it, too."

Kita patted Velositi's leg. "I bet she will. So, is Bernoot done for the night?"

"Yeah," said Ryan. "He's watching YouTube."

"Then we should get some sleep," said Kita pointing to herself, Ryan, and Adrestia.

ADRESTIA, WITH THE FOOTBALL TUCKED UNDER HER ARM, WALKED KITA TO her room.

"You don't have to escort me to my door," said Kita.

"I'm to escort you wherever you go outside this building, and I live in this building, too. I just have a nicer room two floors up."

"Must be nice." Kita's room was the size of a large closet. "Are you going to tuck me in too?"

Adrestia laughed. "I think you can handle that. But I do have something for you."

Kita sighed. "What do I have to carry around now?"

"Nothing. It's personal." Adrestia put down the football and hugged Kita.

Kita stiffened in surprise. When Adrestia kissed her cheek, Kita didn't know what to do. *Uhm...Velositi?*

"I know you're busy with Velositi," said Adrestia, "but thanks for making a dream come true."

"No problem," whispered Kita.

Adrestia squeezed Kita's butt, picked up her football, and walked down the hallway.

Kita closed the door and flopped down on the bed, suddenly too awake to sleep.

KITA SET DOWN HER TRAY OF FRUIT AND GRITS ON THE TABLE AND SAT ON THE bench. Across from her, Ryan put his tray down, loaded with eggs, bacon, toast, and waffles. Adrestia and Ryan's bodyguard, a stern-looking lieutenant, sat a table length away.

Kita hadn't spoken to Adrestia. She didn't know what to say or how to react. She tried to pretend it didn't happen. But, how to tell Velositi gnawed at the back of her mind.

"Are you ever going to eat meat or dairy again?" said Ryan with a laugh.

Kita looked up; her train of thought derailed. "Huh? You try puking up chocolate milkshake and hamburger. I don't want to be sick again. I'm safe this way." She grabbed the sugar and poured a mound on her grits.

"I think that's more sugar than grits."

"They taste awful without it."

"Try some eggs," said Ryan holding up a fork full.

Kita wrinkled her nose. "I'll stick with the grits."

"You're going to be a full vegan before you know it."

"At least my tummy will be happy, and I won't be puking my guts out next to the freeway."

Ryan shrugged. "I'd miss meat too much. I'd retrain myself to digest it."

"I—" Kita's phone buzzed. She pulled it from her back pocket. "Hey, Sprokkit. What do you need?"

"Kita. I need you here. Velositi is awake, but they refuse to let me near her."

"What? Ok. I'm on my way." Kita stood up.

"Why would they keep him away from her?" said Ryan.

"I don't know, but we need to go. Major Adrestia!" Kita barked.

Adrestia gave Kita a concerned look. "I'm right here."

"We need to get to the bunker, right now!"

"Why?"

"Velositi is awake, and Sprokkit is in trouble."

Adrestia sighed. "Ok." She shoved a fork full of eggs in her mouth and grabbed some toast, then led the group out of the DFAC.

KITA TAPPED HER NAIL AGAINST A ZIPPER ON HER JACKET. THE ELEVATOR RIDE down to the sixth floor was taking forever. When the door opened, she hurried down the hallway toward the lab entrance. Adrestia and the others rushed to catch up.

After Adrestia opened the small door to the lab, Kita rushed across, sidestepping scientists and researchers or pushing them out of the way. Sprokkit stood by his workbench. Velositi was standing where Kita had left her. Aimed at her were two restraining panels on thin retractable mounts. A pair of airmen armed with rifles stood in front of Velositi.

"Sprokkit! What's wrong?" said Kita coming to a stop in front of him.

"Kita. Velositi was waking up. I alerted the humans, then a group of soldiers came and aimed those devices at her and will not let me near her."

Adrestia and the others arrived, as Sprokkit explained.

"Who ordered this?" Kita demanded of the airmen standing guard.

"General Striker, Ma'am."

"You get Striker down here immediately. This is unacceptable and against our agreement."

"The general's orders are the Morphicon is to be detained until it is deemed safe."

"*She* is safe," snarled Kita.

"Kita, let's go find the general," said Adrestia. "This is protocol. For security, they don't want her waking up and overreacting."

Kita stepped around the airman toward Velositi.

"No one is allowed near it," said an airman.

"She's not an *it*. Let her go!" yelled Kita. "You can't keep her like this."

"Ma'am, please step back."

Kita kicked the airman in the crotch, then lunged forward, shoving him into the other airman, causing them both to fall. *How do I get Velositi free?* A strong hand grabbed Kita's arm. She twisted, shedding her jacket, and spun into one of the panels knocking it and herself over.

"Don't move," said an airman pointing his rifle at Kita as she tried to untangle herself from the panel.

Kita focused on the rifle barrel. It looked three-feet across.

The other airman keyed his radio. "Bunker Security Station, this is guard detail two-one. We need a detainment for a—"

"Let. Her. Go," said Velositi.

Kita looked up from the rifle barrel. Velositi had both arms morphed into cannons aimed at the airmen.

"That's enough," said Adrestia. "Airmen, at ease. Let Kita up."

"Ma'am, our orders are to—"

"I'm the senior officer on the spot, Airman. Let the girl up and stand down. Call Security and have them inform General Striker that the Vehlix's leader is fully functional and wishes to talk to him. Tell him Major Adrestia has taken charge of the situation."

"Yes, Ma'am."

Kita untangled herself from the panel and lunged for Velositi, wrapping her arms around Velositi's middle. "Velositi," Kita said softly. "I missed you."

Velositi morphed her cannons back to hands, and she wrapped her arms around Kita. "I missed you, too. I guess we are not on the freeway anymore."

"No," said Kita as she fought back tears. "I'm afraid I had to tell people about you to save you. Don't be mad."

Velositi released Kita and knelt. She hugged Kita properly. "I am not mad. You did what you thought was right. I am sure it was not an easy decision. I am proud of you—and thank you for saving me."

Kita sniffed. "I didn't want to lose you. I love you, and no one is going to take you away."

Velositi's eyes brightened so much they looked like flashlights. "Oh, Kita, I love you, too. No one is going to take you from me nor me from you. I promise." She stroked the back of Kita's head, causing Kita to nuzzle in closer.

Sprokkit stomped over in front of Velositi and Kita. "Velositi, I must inform you of what has happened. The humans will want to speak with you."

"Of course, Sprokkit." Velositi released Kita, and with some gentle prodding, she moved Kita to one side. She stood up and looked across the room. "I am sure Kita will have lots to tell me, too."

"Yes," said Sprokkit. "She has played a pivotal role in getting us to this point."

As Sprokkit told Velositi of the deal made with Kimmy and the events leading up to Velositi awaking, Kita wiped her tears and tried to regain control of herself. She felt a little put off, but she understood Velositi was in charge and had more to worry about than just her. Kita walked over to Ryan.

"Somebody looks happy her girl is back," said Ryan.

Kita laughed sadly. "Yeah. I missed her. I've been so worried about trying to get her back that I didn't know I missed her so much."

"We'll have to throw a party or at least go out for pizza or whatever your equivalent is."

"I doubt we'll find a vegan pizza out here or even a regular pizza."

"There is a pizzeria on base," said Adrestia coming up to Kita and Ryan. Kita gave her a dirty look.

"You've been holding out on us," teased Ryan. "We could be eating pizza this whole time instead of at the DFAC."

"The DFAC is better for you and cheaper for the government. But I'm sure I can arrange some pizza for you."

"I've got the cash. That's not a problem, but, hey, if you're paying..."

"I want a smoothie," said Kita to Ryan.

"That'll be harder to come by out here," said Adrestia. "You didn't tell me you had dietary restrictions, Kita. They can make something vegan."

Kita shrugged, turned her back on Adrestia, and looked at Velositi.

"Attention!" someone yelled across the room. All the military personnel came to attention. The scientists stopped and waited. Some unknown signal was given, and everyone returned to what they were doing.

"General Striker is here," said Adrestia.

Kita rolled her eyes as the general and his entourage walked up to them.

"Major," said Striker, "I understand you have everything under control?"

"Yes, Sir. The Vehlix's leader, Velositi, is receiving a briefing from Sprokkit now."

"And why is Velositi free?"

"Velositi's liaison set her free. She didn't agree with the containment order."

"And why didn't you stop her?"

"I tried to restrain her, but she slipped out of her jacket and fell into one of the containment generators."

Striker looked around and settled on Kita. He glared at her as he looked in thought.

Kita glared back. *What are you going to do? Lock me up? Try to take Velositi away? See how long that lasts.*

Striker turned to the airmen with him. "Detain her, but don't remove her."

"Stay away from me!" yelled Kita as she backed up into a workbench. She spun around and grabbed a beaker of something. Kita turned to throw when a pair of hands grabbed her around the waist and lifted her.

"You do not know what is in that," Velositi scolded. "It could be an acid."

"I'm not going to let them take me away."

"And I will not let them. Call me, and I will help you. Do not fight. It only makes it worse." Velositi set Kita down, took the beaker from her, and put it back on the workbench. She turned to Striker. "General Striker, I presume?"

"Yes, Vehlix Leader Velositi. I've come to tell you that I'm not authorized to talk to you. Princess Roosevelt is on her way."

"I see. If it was not for Kita, I was to be kept in containment until your princess arrives?"

Striker rolled his jaw. "I can't answer that."

"Not a pleasant way to treat a potential ally."

"No comment."

"But you trust Sprokkit and Bernoot to be free?"

"They have a separate agreement that you could cancel. We couldn't allow that."

Velositi's eyes glowed. "I could cancel it when your princess arrives, and she would be in danger. But I will not cancel it. They will continue as they have been. Since you are not authorized to talk to me, we are wasting each other's time. I wish to speak to Kita in private."

"We have a room you can use."

"I will take her to a place of my choosing."

"I can't allow you outside of the bunker," growled Striker.

"I will not be kept as a hostage, General. I wish to go outside with Kita. I will remain on this installation. When does your princess arrive?"

"In four hours," said Striker.

"That is plenty of time for me to do what I need to do."

"This is a secure installation. Visitors aren't permitted to wander freely."

"I will accept an escort—if they keep their distance when I request it."

Striker looked between Velositi and Kita.

*And, you thought I was bad.*

"Major Adrestia will accompany you on the ground, and there will be air surveillance."

Kita made a face. *I don't want her anywhere near us.*

"Agreed," said Velositi. "I hope the major has her own transportation."

"She has a Humvee."

"And you can contact her to alert me when your princess arrives?"

"Yes."

Velositi's eyes flashed. "Excellent. Major, please take us outside."

Adrestia looked at Striker.

"Go ahead, Major. Make sure they stay out of trouble."

"Yes, Sir. Velositi, Kita, follow me, please."

Kita fell in behind Velositi as they navigated the path to the lab's door. The big door opened as amber warning lights rotated. Adrestia led them down the opposite direction to a two-story, twenty-foot-square lift. As the elevator went up, Adrestia moved close to Kita.

Paranoia, guilt, shame, and anger flooded Kita's mind. "Don't touch me!" Kita yelled as she jumped backward away from both Adrestia and Velositi.

Both Velositi and Adrestia turned to Kita.

"I wasn't going to touch you," said Adrestia.

"Kita, what is wrong?" said Velositi.

Kita broke into tears. "I'm sorry, but...but it wasn't my fault. I didn't want to."

Velositi put a hand on Kita's shoulder. "Want to do what?" She looked at Adrestia. "What did you do?"

Adrestia's face turned hard as she pressed her lips tight. "I don't know what her problem is. She was the one acting friendly yesterday."

"You kissed me," Kita yelled in a combination of fear and anger.

"On your cheek. I meant it as a thank you. I would have given you more if you weren't so hung up on the Morphicon. Now, I'm glad I didn't. I didn't know you'd lose your mind over it."

Velositi's eyes glowed. "You do not approve of our relationship?"

"I get the intellectual attraction. Ryan and Sprokkit have that, but Kita has an emotional attachment to you that I just don't get. Your emotions aren't like ours."

"I think you are transferring what you know of Neophormes onto Vehlixen. We are very different. Vehlixen have a much more versatile range of emotions than Neophormes. A Neophorm only cares about their next victory and do not have friends. Vehlixen care about each other and form attachments. I have learned love and share it with Kita. We have formed a physical connection. I enjoy looking at her, touching her, and showing her affection.

"To be fair to you, Major, Kita is being a little sensitive and melodramatic, but with good reason. She and I have not set boundaries of what is and is not acceptable. I know she does not want to hurt me. I am not upset you kissed her. Whatever she did for you must have been very special. I am sure she will tell me all about it." Velositi turned to Kita and hugged her. "It is ok. I am not mad. What did I tell you about jumping to the worst conclusion?"

"Sorry," whispered Kita.

"I think you owe the major an apology, too."

Kita wiped her eyes and sniffed. She turned in Velositi's arm to face Adrestia. "I'm sorry I overreacted. I spurned your gift, and I'm sorry. Please forgive my inexperience."

The doors of the elevator opened onto the dry lakebed that surrounded Area 51. Desert mountains rose in the distance. Adrestia led Kita and Velositi out and around the bunker's entrance toward the parking lot and regular entrance.

"I remember what it's like to be young," said Adrestia, "and what first major relationships are like. If you're both happy, then go for it. Velositi, you have a puppy pit bull. Kita's going to be dangerous when she gets older."

"I'm not that bad," said Kita quietly.

Velositi laughed. "Kita is learning. I'm proud of how much she has grown already."

Adrestia stopped at her Humvee. Kita opened the rear door and pulled out her helmet, which had been in the Humvee since she arrived waiting for this moment.

"Where are we going?" said Adrestia to Velositi.

"I have not decided yet. I think for the moment I just want to take Kita riding. I have a map of the installation. There are several long straight roads through the desert."

"Just remember a Humvee can do about eighty before it starts to fall apart."

"We will wait for you." Velositi took two steps and morphed.

Grinning, Kita put on her helmet, fixed her hair, and zipped up her jacket. She mounted Velositi.

"Can you hear me?" said Kita.

"Loud and clear," said Velositi.

"Where are we going?"

"I feel the need for speed. You want to have some fun?"

"I am in desperate need of fun."

———————⟩⟨———————

VELOSITI TURNED OFF THE ROAD, DRIVING BEHIND THE ROW OF HANGARS AND past the Humvees, equipment, and supplies sitting outside. Adrestia followed in her Humvee.

"What are we doing here?" said Kita.

"You will see," said Velositi. "This princess must be important. I am monitoring the local communications, and there is much about her security."

"Kimmy is a two-faced bitch," snarled Kita.

"That was a visceral reaction. What do I need to know?"

"She started nice, being helpful, giving me what I wanted when I needed help with you, but as soon as she had you, she tried to kick Ryan and I out and send us home. I had to crawl on top of her SUV and have Bernoot rescue me. Sprokkit demanded that Ryan stay. He said I could stay until either you awoke to take care of me, or he took you home. I don't think he likes me much."

Velositi giggled. "He does not like that you take up more of my time than he does. He likes to feel important."

"He should have his fill by now."

"I am sure he is glad I am back."

Velositi reached the end of the hangars and turned toward the tarmac. Sitting on the tarmac next to the runway was a pair of F-22 Raptors.

"Falcon flight two-zero-eight, you are cleared to taxi to runway one," said a voice in Kita's helmet.

"Just in time," said Velositi as she pulled to a stop.

The two F-22s moved forward onto the runway and turned ready for takeoff.

"Falcon flight two-zero-eight, the runway is clear. You are clear for takeoff."

Velositi lurched forward, catching Kita by surprise. She recovered and held on as Velositi sped across the tarmac onto the runway. Velositi accelerated as she turned down the runway just as the F-22s slipped their brakes and rocketed forward.

*She's going to race them!* Kita hung on tight and lowered herself against the gas tank, keeping her elbows in and her head up.

"Falcon flight two-zero-eight—scramble! Scramble! Scramble! A bogey on the runway approaching from the east," said the air traffic controller as Velositi caught the two F-22s.

The F-22s punched their afterburners and accelerated forward. Velositi hit another gear and blasted ahead to catch the fighters. As the F-22s nose wheels lifted off the runway, Velositi shot past them. Kita glanced at the speedometer: 354 MPH and Velositi was still accelerating. There was a thunderous boom, and the two F-22s streaked off toward the horizon.

"We have company," said Velositi.

Kita turned her head. Air Force Security Forces Humvees were turning onto the runway. She bet one was Adrestia. *She's going to be furious.*

Velositi reached the end of the runway but slowed down only slightly. The runway was elevated, and Velositi soared over the edge, landing on the hard, dry salt lakebed that went on for miles in all directions.

Kita enjoyed the rush. It was like being strapped to a rocket. The ground went by in a blur. Velositi drifted back and forth, adding a new sensation that Kita adored.

Above them, a helicopter circled. Velositi raced up a four-foot incline sending them airborne. Kita held on expecting a hard impact, but Velositi absorbed it as they landed on the second runway.

Velositi accelerated down the runway, leaned into a ninety-degree corner onto the first runway, and swerved from the runway to the tarmac. She decelerated as she passed the row of hangars and made a hard turn onto the road leading away from the airfield.

VELOSITI AND KITA RACED DOWN A DUSTY TWO-LANE ROAD AWAY FROM THE main Area 51 base toward one of the towering mountains. Above them, a helicopter struggled to keep up. Velositi slowed as the road twisted up the mountain. At the top, the road became gravel and ended in a small parking lot among a forest of antennas, satellite dishes, and a missile defense system.

Velositi stopped, and Kita dismounted. She took her helmet off and slicked back her hair.

Velositi morphed. "This is as far away from anybody as I can get us."

Kita grinned. "Nicole is going to hate us."

"Nicole?"

"Major Adrestia. When we started, I wanted something personable and informal."

"I am sure they are telling her where we are." Velositi pointed at the helicopter.

"I'm sorry. I know it's impossible to escape them."

"I am sure I will mind if they interrupt something, but right now, let them have the illusion of control."

*I like the sound of that. No one controls our destiny but us.*

"What do you think of the view?" said Velositi.

"It's spectacular. You can see forever. Too bad it's the desert. I'm beginning to think you like places with a view."

Velositi's eyes lit. "I do. We have nothing like this on my world. Your world is so varied."

"And you've only seen the southwest."

"That is true. I guess it is natural you would have asked what happened to us before."

Kita nodded. "Bernoot told me. It sounded like a rough time for you."

"It was. I made a mistake and learned a lesson. It was hard, and it hurt."

Kita looked into Velositi's eyes. "I got some of it from Bernoot—about you and Mike, and how he rejected you. I'm sure it's a painful story." Velositi's eyes dimmed. "I know it's highly personal. You don't have to tell me."

Velositi's eyes brightened, and she sighed. "No. You deserve to know. When I went before the Oracle, it told me the person I fell in love with would guide us to the Axiom of Command. I did not know what love was until I came here. I studied it, what it was and meant to humans, and even then, I got it wrong. I did not understand humans used the word in so many different ways. My ignorance cost us precious time that has allowed the Neophormes to gain the upper hand."

"Or, it was the time needed to find the one you would fall in love with. Remember, I wasn't around during the seventies."

"That is true. I just feel stupid for thinking it was Mike—and even stupider for thinking the mission was a failure when he died."

Kita took Velositi's hand. "If you thought it was a failure, then why did you stay?"

"I did not want to go home a failure. I chose exile. When you found us, we were on our way home. I just had not told the others. Then I saw you and my world changed. Everything brightened. I felt I could fly. You still do that to me.

Everything feels right when you are around. I want to keep you safe. That is when I discovered the difference in love.

"When Mike said he 'loved me,' I tried to make myself feel all those things. I tried everything I could, but nothing I did made me feel the things that you make me feel."

Kita blushed. "You make me feel good. And, you listen to me, appreciate me, and adore me. I like to be adored."

Velositi giggled. "I could not tell. It is nice to have someone who appreciates my attention."

Kita's smile faded. "I hate to tell you, but Mike was using you."

Velositi's eyes almost went out. "How?"

"It's not your fault; you didn't know. But he was moving drugs around the country. You were free protection as long as he pretended to help you look for the Axiom."

Velositi turned away and gazed off in the distance.

"I'm sorry," said Kita. "I thought you should know who Mike really was."

"It is not your fault. I trusted too easily. I should have known when he kept bringing us to campfire rings."

Kita put an arm around Velositi and hugged her. "Campfire rings?"

"It is part of the clues for the location of the Axiom. A yellow sun, on a blue planet, a notch at the center of a ring of fire."

"Doesn't ring a bell, but there are lots of rings of fire in the world."

"Maybe the humans will know."

"I'm sure they have some good riddle solvers. Kimmy wants badly for you to find the Axiom and get rid of the Neophormes."

"Yes. I do need to hear what happened while I was being healed." Velositi sat, so she looked out over the desert.

Kita crawled into Velositi's lap. "It's a long story—mostly of me sitting in jail."

———————⟩———————

"AND THEN I GOT A CALL FROM SPROKKIT THIS MORNING, AND I CAME AND freed you," Kita said proudly.

"I think we need to work on your problem-solving skills," said Velositi. "Crashing headlong into them and throwing a fit until you get your way is not the best way to resolve conflict."

"I thought I was using leverage and what assets I had."

Velositi chuckled. "You *do* do that, but we should work on lessening the negative options."

"I refused to be without you, and I wouldn't take *no* for an answer."

"You are not always so stubborn."

"Only for things I love."

Velositi stroked Kita's back. "You have grown up so much since I first met you."

"I want to be like you," said Kita.

"No, not like me. You are becoming your own person. We will make a good team. I will need to teach you self-control."

"Yeah!" Kita crossed her arms and pouted.

Velositi giggled and then tickled Kita. She let out a loud squeak and squirmed. Velositi hugged Kita tightly. Kita relaxed and put her head on Velositi's chest. The sound of a Humvee engine and tires on gravel caused them both to look up.

The Humvee parked, and Adrestia got out.

"Oh, she looks mad," said Kita.

Adrestia slung a rifle on her back and marched over to Kita and Velositi. Kita slid out of Velositi's lap, and Velositi stood. Adrestia stopped in front of them, tears gathering in the corner of her eyes.

"Are you trying to get me thrown out of the Majestic Twelve?" Adrestia screamed on the verge of hysterics.

"Ah," Kita looked at the ground. "I'm sorry. We were just having some fun."

"I apologize," said Velositi. "It was just meant to be a prank—to show Striker how little control he has."

"You don't understand!" yelled Adrestia. "For General Striker—the entire goddamn Air Force—it's all about having control. Real or not. They can't punish you, but they will punish *me!* You are my responsibility, and you made me look incompetent. If you wanted to punish me for that kiss—slap me—hit me! Don't ruin my career!"

"It was not retribution for the kiss," said Velositi aghast. "I would never do that. I will not let them punish you over us."

"It's too late," said Adrestia. "They've already recalled me. I was just closer to you than to them. I thought if I brought you with me, I might just get a reprimand. Please, come with me."

"No," said Kita.

"Kita!" said Velositi.

A tear trickled down Adrestia cheek.

"They're not going to listen to us," said Kita. "Once our back is turned, she'll disappear. Even if we convince them to let her stay as my bodyguard, her career's over. They'll stick her guarding some stack of paper somewhere."

"What do you suggest we do?" said Velositi.

Kita walked over to Adrestia and put her arm around her. "Give her to Bernoot. He needs a liaison, and she can do double duty as my bodyguard. What do you think of that, Nicole?"

"They'll never let me."

"Which part?"

"Both."

"I can be pretty persuasive. I'm sure I can convince Kimmy. She wants Velositi's help badly enough."

"Until this is over, and you and I are made to disappear," said Adrestia.

"Velositi won't let that happen. She plans on staying here with me after this is over."

"I'll do it, but..."

Kita squeezed her tightly. "Hey. You got to fight like there's no way out. Don't take *no* for an answer. We have the advantage. They need us. We can always leave with the Vehlixen and find the Axiom on our own."

Adrestia looked at Kita sideways. "Are you sure you're the same girl that was in the elevator this morning?"

Kita took her free hand, and with a finger, she turned Adrestia's face toward her. "What do you think?" Kita kissed Adrestia. Giving Adrestia another reassuring squeeze, her hand dropped and squeezed Adrestia's butt. She then sauntered back to Velositi.

Velositi's eyes were alight as she chuckled. "Soon, your confidence will know no bounds."

"As long as I have you around, I feel I can do anything and take on anyone."

"Let us get Nicole back to the base before she is in any more trouble." Velositi morphed.

Kita grabbed her helmet. "Coming?" she called to Adrestia, who hadn't moved and still looked shocked.

---

"THERE'S KIMMY'S PLANE," SAID KITA TO VELOSITI AS SHE POINTED TOWARD the airfield. The large blue and white Boeing 747 sat on the tarmac.

"That is a big plane."

"Big ego."

Velositi chuckled. "We should beat her to the bunker."

"I was thinking...We shouldn't meet her in the bunker—too many weapons to use against us."

"I am impressed that you are thinking so tactically."

"Is that what you call it? I'm just trying to keep Kimmy from having the upper hand."

"It is a good idea. How about we meet her in the parking lot? I will make sure Bernoot and Sprokkit are also there. I am not as imposing as they are."

Kita giggled. "Until they see you fight."

"The boys are on their way. Bernoot is at the barracks, and Sprokkit and Ryan are at the pizzeria. They should arrive just after we do."

Velositi took her time driving across the base. Most of the one-story buildings were cinder block construction painted white with maroon doors. A few trees provided shade, and lava rock surrounded the buildings connected by concrete sidewalks. The roads were cracked and faded.

Turning onto the road out to the bunker, Sprokkit and a trailing Humvee fell in behind Adrestia. Bernoot caught up to the convoy as they entered the bunker's parking lot. The group parked, and the humans dismounted, allowing the Morphicons to morph.

Kita led everyone around to the large elevator. "Nicole, don't tell them we're here."

"What if General Striker calls?"

"Just tell him we're on our way. We hit traffic."

Adrestia rolled her eyes. Ryan's bodyguard picked up his radio. "Lieutenant, stop. I'll call them when we're ready."

The lieutenant gave her a dubious look but put the radio away. Adrestia's face darkened. "I'm still the ranking officer, Lieutenant. You can keep your comments to yourself."

Kita waved Velositi to bend down to her and whispered, "Can you jam the airwaves? It'll keep them from bringing up the nastiness they have downstairs."

"Sprokkit can do it."

Kita moved to the edge of the building. The trio of black SUVs escorted by a pair of armed Air Force Humvees came down the road. They stopped in the middle of the parking lot. The Secret Service agents exited and formed a perimeter. Kimmy and her aides climbed out of the middle SUV.

"Ok, they're here," called Kita as she waved the others to her.

Kita stepped around the corner of the building and walked toward Kimmy. The agents stopped and raised their weapons as they shielded Kimmy.

"Stop!" someone yelled.

Kita kept walking, helmet in hand. *What? Don't you remember me?* She took a few more steps, and Velositi, Bernoot, and Sprokkit turned the corner, followed by Ryan, Adrestia, and the lieutenant.

The airmen in the Humvees' cupolas aimed their .50 caliber machine guns at the approaching group. "Halt!" came from a speaker system on the lead Humvee.

"What's wrong, Kimmy?" Kita yelled. "I thought we were friends."

Kimmy pushed her Secret Service agents out of the way. "You're supposed to be in the bunker."

"It's stuffy, and Velositi hasn't had a good experience down there."

Kimmy grabbed her aide and whispered something to her. The aide grabbed her phone, tapped on it, put it to her ear, and then looked at it, confused.

Kita grabbed her phone from her back pocket and held it up. "I can't use mine; you can't use yours." Kita stopped a few yards short of the lead Secret Service agents. "Come talk to me, Kimmy. You want the Neophormes gone, here's your chance."

Kimmy glared at Kita as she approached with her agents, their guns drawn.

"Really, Kimmy? No one over here has a gun out."

Kimmy stopped.

"Don't move," the lieutenant said from a few feet behind Kita.

"Lieutenant, put that away," Adrestia ordered.

"Negative, Ma'am. She's a clear and present danger to the princess."

"Human, if you do not drop the weapon, I will take your head off," said Velositi.

"It will be an honor to die for the princess," said the lieutenant enthusiastically.

Kimmy looked amused, making Kita's blood boil. Kita wasn't sure if it was for the lieutenant's death wish or that Kita had been interrupted. *Let's see how amusing this is.* "Hey, Kimmy! You're a slagging two-faced bitch."

As everyone collectively gasped, Kita spun, took a step, and slammed her helmet into the lieutenant's head and shoulder knocking him to the ground. Kita pounced on him.

"You slagging bastard," Kita roared as she smashed her helmet into the lieutenant's face. "Try and kill me!" Kita hit him again, and blood exploded from the lieutenant's nose. "No one threatens me. I will—" As Kita went to swing her helmet, Velositi grabbed her around the waist and hoisted her into the air. "Lemme go!" Kita screamed. "I'm not done."

"Yes, you are," said Velositi. "Calm down, Kita."

"I knew she'd double-cross us!" Kita screamed as she twisted and kicked in Velositi's grasp.

"She has not double-crossed anyone. It was just an overzealous minion. Now, settle down so we can continue. He cannot hurt you. No one can. We will not let them, but you need to be calm."

Kita huffed and ground her teeth as her anger drained. She crossed her arms and pouted, but she was still.

Sprokkit plucked Kita's helmet from her. "If we want them to put their weapons away, we need to put ours away."

"Are you going to be calm?" said Velositi to Kita.

Kita glowered. "Yeah, fine."

"I need your mind clear to help with this negotiation."

"She's probably laughing her ass off right now."

"Do not worry about the princess. Worry about yourself. That is what you control."

"I wish it was her face."

Velositi sighed. "Kita, you need to drop it. It is over. She had nothing to do with it. Your anger is misplaced and is making things worse. I understand what the princess has done in the past, and I will address it, but she had nothing to do with it this time. Take a few breaths, let it go, and collect yourself." Kita did as instructed but kept her arms crossed. "Uncross your arms and stop pouting. You cannot change your mind if you keep the same body position."

Kita rolled her eyes but uncrossed her arms and did her best to look pleasant.

"Better," said Velositi. "I am going to put you down now. Are you going to behave and be reasonable?"

"Yes," Kita said flatly.

"Is the lieutenant going to be ok?" Velositi asked Adrestia.

"He's got a broken nose and maybe his orbital socket is damaged, but nothing life-threatening."

"Ok, good. He can stay there then. Let us go meet the princess."

Velositi put her hand on Kita's shoulder and guided her and the others to the princess. Kita and Kimmy exchanged a glare.

"Should I give you two five minutes to go at it?" said Velositi.

"I said I would behave," said Kita. "But she started it."

"I don't even know what you're mad about," said Kimmy.

"You tried to take Velositi from me!" Kita yelled.

"I was doing what was best for the country and you. You have complicated this whole process. The Vehlixen are fine without two civilians taking up their precious time and my valuable resources."

"You let them decide if I'm a waste of time. That's not your decision."

"You belong to me."

"I don't belong to anyone but Velositi."

Kimmy put her hands on her hips. "You are my subject—like it or not. I have the final say on what happens to you."

144

"I didn't know who the slag you were until Striker called you on the phone."

"It doesn't matter. Your fate is in my hands."

Kita balled her fists and ground her teeth. "Fine. Do it without me." She spun on her heel, pushed her way around Sprokkit and Adrestia, and stormed past the bunker out into the desert. *I don't care if I die out here. I will not let someone else decide my fate. I left that behind, and I won't do it again. I create my own path...even if it leads to my destruction.*

KITA TRUDGED THROUGH THE DESERT WITH HER HEAD DOWN AND HER JACKET open. She slept in the open last night and saw the breathtaking band of stars that made up the Milky Way Galaxy for the first time. It left her in awe.

The heat of the day rose off the dry lakebed creating shimmering horizons. The sound of a helicopter above made her turn and flip it off. It wasn't the first time they'd come looking. *They can retrieve the body.*

Kita kept walking. The mountains never seemed to get any closer. She hadn't thought they were that far away. The helicopter continued to circle. *What the slag do they want? Can't I die in peace? I have to have some slagging Air Force helicopter circling me like a buzzard. Let the real birds peck at my carcass. I bet Kimmy sent it just to remind me that I belong to her. Well, she can't have me. No one owns me. If I can't live free, I'll die—that gives me an idea.*

Using the heel of her boot, Kita scrapped LIVE FREE OR DIE into the salt of the lakebed. *It looks big enough they should be able to read it from the air. Let Kimmy put that in her pipe and smoke it.*

KITA SPENT ANOTHER NIGHT UNDER THE STARS. NOW, SHE WAS HUNGRY, sunburnt, and her lips blistered. *It doesn't matter. I'll die of thirst first.* The mountains appeared bigger today. *I must be getting close. I don't want to die on the salt flats. The mountains seem a much more romantic place.*

As the day wore on, Kita rested more often. She was hot and stripped off her jacket to put over her head to block the sun. *I've stopped sweating. That's not a good sign.* Spots formed in her eyes as the mirages on the horizon became vivid. She tried to enjoy the hallucinations until her dad appeared.

"Daddy?" Kita whispered.

Her father stood only a few feet in front of her. Kita walked to him, but he moved back. She walked faster, but she got no closer.

"Daddy!" Kita screamed. She dropped her jacket and broke into a run, chasing after him. "Don't leave me again!"

Tears fell down her face as she ran until she could run no more and collapsed to her knees. "Daddy! Don't go," Kita wailed. "Don't leave me. I don't want to be alone. Daddy...Please," she whimpered.

Kita flopped on her side and tasted the salty dirt on her lips. She sobbed past the point of having any tears left. Rolling onto her back, she stared up into the sky. Slowly, a gray haze crept into her vision. The haze swallowed her sight to pinholes. Something dark blocked the light, and Kita slipped into blackness.

THE LIGHT WAS BRIGHT. KITA TRIED TO MOVE HER ARMS TO SHIELD HER EYES, but they refused to move. She squinted instead. Medical equipment surrounded her. A soft beeping came from a machine to her right. An IV tree next to the bed held three bags connected to her arm. Under the thin sheet, she wore a set of hospital pajamas. She occupied a corner of a large two-story room. The rest of the room was empty. She was alone.

*Kimmy couldn't let me die. How sweet of her. Now I get to be a prisoner instead. I wonder if there's a way to kill myself. First, I have to lift my arms.*

Kita concentrated on moving her sunburned arms. She succeeded in wiggling her fingers. That led to balling her fists and rolling them around. Moving her elbows was painful. They loosened after opening and closing them a dozen times. She rotated her shoulders and then worked at moving her entire arms. Pain radiated away from her shoulder, down her arm, and across her back. *What did I do? How long have I been out? Or am I just suffering from dehydration?*

Satisfied she could move her arms, she pushed herself to a sitting position and twisted her torso. She was stiff, and the muscles in her back complained, but it was nothing sharp. She just ached. *Ok, I can move. Now, what can I do to kill myself?* There were cords and sheets, but those would require standing, and she didn't think she could tie them high enough. The IV held promise. It would be slow, but no one had come to check on her yet.

Kita undid the tape holding the IV and pulled the needle from her arm. Using her teeth, she bit through the tubing. With her finger, she found the jugular vein in her neck. Biting her lip, Kita shoved the needle in. Blood squirted across her hand. *This might be faster than I thought.*

Lying back, Kita's blood squirted across the sheets and pillow. She closed her eyes and counted backward from a hundred.

*Ninety-one, ninety, eighty-nine, eighty—*

Several sets of hands grabbed Kita. She opened her eyes and found a nurse, a doctor, and two Air Force medics around her.

"No!" Kita yelled as she flailed her arms. To her pleasant surprise, her legs moved.

The doctor pulled a syringe from his pocket.

"Don't you dare!" screamed Kita. With all her might, she kicked and twisted, her blood spraying everywhere. She thrust herself up with her arms and over the rail of the bed. Kita landed in a heap on the floor. Her adrenaline at maximum, she crawled on the floor under the head of the bed and behind the medical equipment. She pushed herself to her feet and dashed across the room to the open door.

Kita entered the two-story hallway. She was in the bunker, so she ran toward the elevator. At the other end of the hallway, a pair of airmen appeared. The medical team exited the room behind her. The elevator was in the middle of the hallway, and Kita reached it first. She jammed the close door button and then hit the surface.

The ride wasn't long. *I must not have been on the sixth floor.* The door opened, and Kita stepped out. The airman guarding the desk blocked her path. Kita ran at him. When she was close, she faked a step to the right. The airman lunged. Kita went left, jumped over the airman's legs, and ran to the door. Slamming her hand down on the door's open button, she pushed it open and ran outside.

Three black SUVs sat parked in the parking lot. *She's here! I can still escape to the desert.* Kita followed the sidewalk around the building. As she turned the corner to the backside, she bounced off Velositi and landed on her butt. Kita scrambled to her feet. Velositi grabbed Kita around the waist and picked her up.

"Let me go!" screamed Kita.

"What are you doing?" cried Velositi in a panic. She grabbed the IV needle out of Kita's neck.

"No! I won't do it. I'd rather die. Kimmy can go to the Crushing Depths!"

"Kita! Calm down. Please. They are trying to help you."

"I won't be a prisoner!" wailed Kita.

"You are not a prisoner. You never were," said Velositi firmly.

"Let me die in the desert."

"Kita, please calm down and let me explain," Velositi said gentler.

"Just kill me!"

"Kita!" Velositi barked. She locked Kita in a firm embrace that kept Kita from moving.

Kita twisted and pulled, trying to break free. When her adrenaline ran out, so did her strength. She slumped against Velositi and cried. "Why can't I?" she said in a small, muffled voice through her tears.

The medical team and a dozen airmen, including Adrestia, arrived.

Adrestia walked up to Velositi and put a hand on Kita's leg. "Is she going to be ok?" Adrestia asked Velositi.

"I do not know. The desert did not take the fight out of her."

The doctor came over. "Can I sedate her?"

Velositi's eyes dimmed. "No. Let me talk to her first."

"Can we examine her neck? She lost a lot of blood."

Velositi held Kita up and looked into her eyes. "Kita, the doctor needs to look at your neck. Please do not fight them."

Kita didn't answer, lost in her tears.

Velositi set Kita on the sidewalk and let the medical team examined her.

"Blood pressure is low," said the nurse.

"She's going to need some blood," said the doctor. "She didn't lose a critical amount, but she needs a unit." He put a small adhesive bandage over the hole in Kita's neck.

"How is she?"

Kimmy's voice made Kita flinch. She tried to move, but the two medics held her down.

"She's lost some blood, Your Highness, but no other physical injuries."

"How much? It looks like most of hers is all over."

"A half-liter, maybe a little more, Your Highness. She's probably feeling a little lightheaded."

Kimmy waved to Velositi, and they knelt in front of Kita.

Kita had stopped crying and was staring at the sidewalk.

"Kita?" said Kimmy.

Kita responded by bringing her legs to her chest and wrapping her arms around them.

"Kita, there are some things Velositi, and I need to tell you. Do you think you can listen?"

Kita put her head on her knees.

"Maybe we should talk to her in private," said Velositi.

"She seems terrified of me," said Kimmy. "Maybe you should talk to her first."

"Yes, but where would be a comfortable place for her?"

"I don't know."

"Nicole, how's she doing?" said Ryan on the perimeter of the gathered group.

Kita lifted her head, stood up, and with a blank face, pushed her way to Ryan.

"Kita, how are you?" said Ryan hesitantly.

Kita put her arms around him and gave him a gentle hug.

Ryan put his arm around her and squeezed her. "Hey, glad to see you're up. Are you ok?"

Kita shook her head. "I'm trapped in a cage," she whispered. "There's no way out."

Ryan gave a questioning look to Adrestia, and then understanding crossed his face. "It might look that way, but have you examined the cage? I bet you'll find the bars aren't real. The bars are only fear in your mind."

"How do I free myself?"

"You just have to listen. Prove the fear wrong, and the bars will evaporate."

"Listen to who?"

"With an open heart, talk to Velositi and Nicole, and then talk to the princess. Give them a chance to show you that your fear is misplaced."

"Ok."

"You can do it. I promise no one means you any malice. Be free of your fear."

Kita let go of Ryan and walked toward Velositi.

"Where did that come from?" said Adrestia to Ryan.

"*Solid Metal Rangers*. It's an anime from ten years ago. That was dialog from the hero's struggle in season three. He goes to the desolate grove to seek counsel from the sage. I adapted it. I didn't know she'd seen the show."

"You are such a nerd."

"My nerdism just calmed the dragon."

Kita stopped in front of Velositi. "Let me change, and we can go."

"Where do you want to go?"

"Back to the top of the mountain. Bring Nicole."

"Of course," said Kimmy.

Kita looked at Kimmy. "I'm sorry for calling you a bitch."

"I'm used to it. Let's get you checked out, and we'll go up the mountain."

Kita sighed, and her shoulders slumped. *Am I admitting defeat? I'm out of strength to fight. What else can I do...but listen—be free. The bars aren't real. Maybe victory lies down another path.*

---

VELOSITI ROLLED TO A STOP IN THE GRAVEL PARKING LOT ON TOP OF THE mountain. It had been a quiet ride up. Kita refused to say a word to Velositi's gentle prodding. Kita dismounted Velositi, took off her helmet, and slicked back her hair. She was dressed in some of the new clothes she bought—a white halter top and skinny black jeans. Kita had even done her makeup in an attempt to look normal.

Adrestia pulled in as Velositi morphed. Kita walked away from them, staring straight ahead. *The horizon seems so far away. I wish I could run to it. I'll never catch it, but could I run from my fear forever? Sigh. I know what Velositi's going to say, and she has every right to say it. She agrees with Kimmy that I should go away. I've caused Velositi a lot of pain, and I'm more trouble than I'm worth. The Majestic Twelve will pair her with somebody calm and professional. Losing her will hurt. And, I'll still be Kimmy's slave. At least when I'm gone, I can kill myself, and no one will care.*

Kita sat on the edge of a concrete slab that formed part of the base of a radio antenna. She hugged her helmet tight. *Will they let me keep it?* She stared at the horizon, dreaming of a perfect place just beyond it. *A place full of Angels and friends where I am free to be me.*

Velositi knelt before Kita. "Kita?"

"Yeah?" Kita said quietly.

"How are you feeling?"

Kita had sucked down two units of blood before the doctor would release her. *But I doubt she means like that.* "Scared. Alone. I just want to run away. I know everyone hates me and Kimmy's right. I'm more trouble than I'm worth. You deserve better. I hope they find someone who will make you happy and find the Axiom. No matter where I go, I'm a slave, and I'd rather die."

Velositi's eyes dimmed. She looked up.

"Please don't. I admire your conviction, but it's misplaced," said Kimmy. "I didn't mean to imply you were a slave. Subject was a poor choice of words. You are a citizen. Every citizen of the Empire has the same rights, duties, and obligations—including me. I have even more duties and obligations that come with running the country. My first obligation is to keep you safe. One of your duties is to do what is best for the country. I'm sure the government was the furthest thing from your mind living out in the desert. Now, you're deep in the inner circle, and people's lives are on the line.

"I talked with Velositi. She told me how important you are to find the Axiom. I didn't know then, and she says you didn't either. It explains her devotion to you—"

Kita burst into tears. *Velositi only loves me because she needs me. It's not fair. Why must I suffer? What did I do to deserve a broken heart?*

"Kita?" said Velositi as she placed her hand on Kita's shoulder.

Kita squirmed away from Velositi's touch and scooted over.

Adrestia sat on Kita's far side, blocking her escape, and she put an arm around her shoulders. Kimmy sat on Kita's near side, placing an arm around her waist.

"Kita," said Adrestia as she stroked Kita's cheek. "What's going on? I know constitutional law is boring—"

Kita sputtered through her tears, "I didn't go to college. My dad died, and I had to run the yard."

Adrestia squeezed Kita. "I'm sorry. That must have been rough."

"Yeah." *I did it once, and I can do it again, maybe I'm just destined to lose all the ones I love. It's not too late to go with dignity.* Kita wiped her eyes and took a deep breath. "Can I keep this?" She held up her helmet.

"Of course," said Kimmy. "It's yours."

"Ok, then. I'm ready to go home now."

"What?" said Velositi.

Kimmy and Adrestia gasped.

Kita sighed. "I'm more trouble than I'm worth, I know it. I know when I'm not wanted. You need professionals and soldiers to find the Axiom, not a junkyard girl. Velositi says she needs me, but I don't want to be used. I've done my part by getting the Vehlixen here."

Adrestia grabbed Kita's arm and spun Kita to face her. "Who said you're not wanted or needed? You haven't talked to Velositi yet. What did Ryan tell you about listening?"

"She agrees with Kimmy," Kita said quietly.

"How do you know?" said Velositi, plasma leaking from her eyes.

"I see how you act. You're friendly with her. You didn't follow me out in the desert. You have what you wanted—a way to the Axiom. You don't need me anymore."

"Of course Velositi and I are friendly," said Kimmy. "We're allies. We didn't start this way. We negotiated long and hard to work out an agreement that would benefit both of us. We discussed your and Ryan's roles. He will be commissioned in the Air Force as a liaison to Sprokkit. I had to come up with a place to put you. You are now a Ward of the Emperor—part of the Emperor's extended family, and all that entails. Your job is to continue being Velositi's liaison.

"I told Velositi not to follow you into the desert and that we would keep an eye on you. I thought your anger would burn out, and you'd sit or turn around, and we'd get you. When we received the report you had collapsed, Velositi was the one who raced across the desert to get you.

"I have never met someone so stubborn. You're making assumptions on outdated information and what you want to hear. None of which is true. You're not going home, and you're staying with Velositi. That I can tell you for sure. How Velositi feels is up to her." Kimmy grabbed Kita by her jacket collar and belt loop and thrust Kita at Velositi. "Go talk to your girl and say you're sorry."

Kita fell into Velositi's lap. Velositi helped Kita up and retrieved her helmet.

*Listen, and the bars will disappear. I haven't done a very good job of listening—Kimmy's right. I'm trying to distract myself from the real reason I'm upset—Kimmy beat me.*

Kita gulped. "Sorry."

"That is a start," said Velositi as her eyes brightened. "Come on." She took Kita's hand, and they followed a path to a missile battery. Kita climbed onto the concrete pad so she could be a little closer to eye level with Velositi.

"Thank you for rescuing me," said Kita, trying to maintain eye contact.

"It was hard not to follow you, but I agreed with Kimmy that your anger would burn off, and you would stop. By the third day, I was panicking because they said you were still walking."

"Yeah, I, uh, Kimmy got to me. She beat me, and I saw death as the only way out. Sorry for the whole blood thing."

"You scared me. We lose from time to time. I understand your reaction. You wanted to escape. I had a similar visceral reaction after Mike died. What hurt is you saying I am only using you to get to the Axiom. I love you. Did I do something to make you think differently?"

Kita brushed a hand through her hair. "You were working with Kimmy. I thought you'd chosen her over me."

"Of course not! I allied with her because of us. I wanted us to be safe and not always on the run. Kimmy has the resources to get us anywhere in the world, and all she wants is to be rid of the Neophormes. Kimmy is a nice person, she cares about her country and people, but I would not choose her over you."

Kita rubbed the back of her neck. "Sorry. I just thought the Axiom was more important than me."

"I will find the Axiom—with you. Not because a prophecy tells me you will take me to it. I love you. I thought I had shown it."

Guilt and regret formed a pit in Kita's stomach. "You have. I'm the bad one. I'm sorry for being a stubborn, selfish, obnoxious girl that only thinks about herself. You deserve better than me."

"I want you. I know there are going to be tough times between us as you grow. Please talk to me. I know we can work it out. Just do not leave me."

Kita felt like crying. She hugged Velositi instead. "I'm not going to leave you. I love you. I don't deserve you."

"Yes, you do. We deserve to be happy. And you make me happy."

Kita squeezed Velositi. "You make me happy."

Velositi picked Kita up. Kita put her arms around Velositi's neck and kissed her.

KITA SCRAPED HER PLATE CLEAN OF THE FANTASTIC BUTTERNUT SQUASH linguine and vegan mac and cheese. Everyone was eating or relaxing around a set of benches behind the DFAC.

"Good?" said Kimmy. She was enjoying a burger.

"Very. I didn't know the DFAC cooks took orders."

Kimmy chuckled. "It came from my chef. Once I'm gone, you'll get your own."

"What am I going to do with a chef?"

"You'll have more than a chef. You'll have an entire staff," said Kimmy.

Kita's jaw dropped. She had always done everything for herself. "How am I going to keep a staff busy? It's just Velositi and me."

"I expect you and Velositi to be busy doing other things besides cooking and cleaning."

"I guess. I thought I'd be living here for the rest of my life," said Kita.

"That would be pretty dull. Even the regular Area fifty-one staff live in Vegas and are flown in every day."

"You'll get used to government life quickly," said Adrestia. She now had the rank of colonel and was dressed in jeans, camisole, and a leather jacket.

"I guess Vegas won't be bad," Kita said with a shrug.

Kimmy laughed. "You'll get your pick of where you want to live, but Velositi will have to remain hidden."

"I don't want to do that." Kita looked up at Velositi.

"Outside of battle, my form does not matter to me. But whatever house you get will have to have high ceilings and wide doorways, unless you want tire marks on the floor."

"Do you leave tire marks?" said Kimmy.

"Not rubber, but I can if I drive through something."

Kimmy tapped Kita on the arm and leaned into her ear. "Can I talk to you?"

"Ah, sure."

"I mean away from everyone else."

"Oh, ok. I'll be back, Velositi," said Kita.

"Of course. I will be here," said Velositi as her eyes brightened.

Kita got up from the picnic bench and followed Kimmy around the side of the DFAC away from the others.

"Did—did I do something wrong?" said Kita.

"No, no," said Kimmy. "You're not in trouble. I am. I—I wanted to apologize for saying I own you. I did *not* mean to drive you into the desert. I was upset because I'm not used to having my authority challenged openly. I'm sorry. I hope you don't hate me."

Kita shrugged. "I don't hate you. It meant a lot that you came up to the mountain with Velositi and Nicole. You didn't have to. It was my problem to get over."

"I—I wanted to make sure you were ok. I...like...you. You're very special, and no one treats me like you do."

"I thought I'd been pretty nasty."

"You were standing up for yourself. You don't see me as *the princess*. You see me as a person, and that means a lot—more than I can tell you."

Kita smiled and looked into Kimmy's chocolate brown eyes. Kimmy smiled back. Kita liked seeing her smile, and her heart skipped a beat. *Whoa, what am I thinking? I'm sure there is a prince somewhere.* "I, ah—you took me seriously and treated me like I was more than a junkyard girl. You look normal to me. Ah, I mean, you're not normal. You're beautiful. I just—"

Kimmy laughed. "I want to be normal, which I know I'll never be, but having someone who sees me as normal means the world to me. I was hoping...we... could be...friends?" Kimmy's eyes looked hopeful.

"Oh, ah, sure. I'm not very sophisticated, though."

Kimmy giggled.

*She's cute when she giggles.*

"I promise not to invite you to any state dinners." Kimmy hesitantly hugged Kita. "Thank you."

"I...no problem." The scent from Kimmy's hair filled Kita's nose. *Ok, so she's really hot, now that I'm not mad at her. I wonder what Velositi is going to say? Will she be angry that I have a friend?*

Kimmy let go, and Kita could breathe again. "I have a surprise for everyone. We should see if they're done with dinner."

Kita followed Kimmy around to the picnic benches.

"So, can I ride in your plane?" said Kita.

Kimmy laughed. "It's not that exciting. It's like an apartment. I'll give you a tour, though."

They stopped in front of the picnic bench.

"If you're done, I have something for you all at the bunker," said Kimmy. "I'll meet you there."

Kita grabbed her helmet, Velositi morphed, and Kita mounted her. They pulled onto the street and drove toward the bunker.

"What did Kimmy want?" said Velositi.

"She apologized for making me mad and asked me to be her friend."

"Do you like her?"

"Yeah, she seems cool, now that I'm not mad at her," said Kita.

Velositi laughed. "Do you want to see her again?"

"I, ah, sure. That's not going to upset you, is it?"

"Of course not. I want you to have friends—I especially want you to have a close friend."

"I don't know if Kimmy and I will be close. I don't know how much I'll see her."

"I want you to try," said Velositi firmly. "I do not care what kind of relationship you have—friend, girlfriend, or married— as long as it is healthy, vibrant, and meaningful."

*But I thought we were cool.* "What about you?" said Kita, shocked. "Are you dumping me?"

"Of course not. I will still be here and still love you. I have limitations and can only give you so much, and you need so much more. You have already been isolated for three years. I am an improvement on that, but I am not the solution. Your brain and mind are magnitudes more complex than mine, and they require more than I am capable of giving."

"I thought you'd done a good job so far."

"I have, but my knowledge of human psychology will only take me so far. What I emulate and what you would get from another human are not equivalent. It does not mean I love you any less. It means if we are to be successful, you will need additional support."

*I don't understand, but I don't know much about psychology either. She says she still loves me, and that's what important. I love her.*

"I guess I'll look for a friend then," said Kita sadly.

"It is for your mental health and happiness."

"Do I need to do anything for you?"

"No. I am happy. I get to spend time with you and talk to you. I find you fascinating, and I especially like looking at you."

Kita blushed. "I'm pretty for you."

"And I appreciate it."

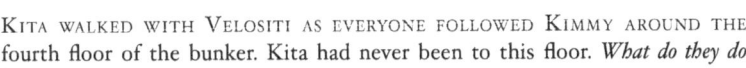

KITA WALKED WITH VELOSITI AS EVERYONE FOLLOWED KIMMY AROUND THE fourth floor of the bunker. Kita had never been to this floor. *What do they do here?*

Kimmy stopped in front of a door. A placard read KITA AND VELOSITI. "I don't know how long we'll be here, so I had these rooms remodeled into apartments fit for both Morphicon and human." She opened the door. "Take a look. I'll show the rest of you to yours."

Kita and Velositi entered the apartment. It was spacious, with polished concrete floors, a table and chair set, and a giant beanbag chair. Scenic images scrolled by on digital picture frames and a high countertop separated the living area and kitchenette. A set of tall double doors led to a bedroom with a queen bed, dresser, vanity, and closet. There was a large empty area next to the bed. A regular-sized door led to a bathroom. Kita opened the closet and found her belongings put away.

"Wow," said Kita. "This sure beats the barracks. I don't have to share a bathroom."

Velositi laughed. "I could look in if you want."

Kita gave her a dirty look. "If you want to see me naked, all you have to do is ask."

"I have never been in a place private enough *to* ask."

"Tonight, you will." Kita gave Velositi a coy look. "Are you going to ask me?" There was a knock at the door. "Too late." Kita left the bedroom and answered the door.

"I'm going to say goodnight," said Kimmy. "Get some sleep, rest, whatever. We start searching for the Axiom at zero nine hundred tomorrow in the briefing room on level one."

"Sure, no problem," said Kita. "Thank you. The apartment is wonderful."

"Glad you like it. I have to make sure the teams are cohesive and working together. Making you comfortable helps achieve that."

"Thanks for putting up with me," Kita said apologetically. "I'm sorry."

Kimmy gave the hint of a sad smile. "I had a rebellious phase not long ago. There was a time I would have joined you in the desert."

"How old are you?"

"Twenty-six."

Kita's eyes widened. "You're incredible for being so young. I don't think I could do what you do."

"I was raised for this. Being in charge happened earlier than expected with my father's stroke and coma, but it was my destiny."

"You sound so sad. Do you want to come in and hang out? You can forget who you are for a while." Kita looked back at Velositi. Her eyes lit up, and she nodded.

"Are—are you sure?" Kimmy sounded hopeful. "I don't know how much fun I'll be, but it would be nice not to be alone."

"You can just relax. I'm sure there's something on TV."

"I haven't watched regular TV in years. Everything is always tuned to Fox News."

"I haven't either. We can explore together," said Kita as she shed her jacket and put it on the counter.

Kimmy did the same and sat in a chair at the table. Her posture was perfect.

Kita laughed. "You're supposed to relax, not be at a formal dinner. Velositi, sit." She pointed to the beanbag chair.

Velositi sat, sinking into the chair. "This is nice."

"Climb on." Kita helped Kimmy sit next to Velositi. "Do you want anything to drink?" Kita called to Kimmy as she opened the fridge. "There's soda, beer, wine, or hard strawberry-lemonade." *Strawberry-lemonade sounds good.*

"Wine, please."

Kita grabbed a bottle and then searched the drawers for a corkscrew. Finding it, she studied it, trying to decipher how it worked. She tried several times to screw in the corkscrew. Once she had it a third of the way in, she tried the handles, but they were in the wrong position. Kita made a face. Kimmy's giggle made her turn away from the offending bottle. "I, ah, have never used one of these before. It's more complicated than it looks."

Kimmy laughed. "If you don't know what you're doing, you'll never get in." She took the bottle, screwed in the corkscrew, and pulled the cork. "Just like that."

"I don't think I can repeat that," said Kita. She opened several cabinets and found a wine glass. She passed it to Kimmy.

Kimmy poured a tall glass as Kita grabbed a strawberry-lemonade. She looked for a bottle opener.

"It's a twist-off," said Kimmy. She took the bottle and opened it.

"I've never had one."

"The manufacturer donates them, and I serve them at the Fourth of July BBQs. They're not bad—sweet—but after the week I've had, wine is what I need."

"Sorry. I know I was a problem. I wasn't trying to make trouble for you."

Kimmy laughed. "You're not a problem. You were the highlight of my week. You brought the Vehlixen. How are you and Velositi?"

Kita smiled. "Ok. We, ah, talked out our differences and set boundaries."

"Good. I'd hate to have to find a couple's therapist to work out here."

Kita giggled. "Velositi is very good at human psychology."

"I could tell. You're very astute, Velositi."

"Thank you. The subject has changed much since I studied it in the seventies —much more insightful now. It has helped me abundantly in my interactions with Kita."

"You do a good job with her."

Velositi's eyes brightened. "I try. Sometimes she defies convention, and I worry about her isolation. I think she forgets how to interact socially."

"She does crave attention." Kimmy gave Kita a wink.

"I refuse to be denied," said Kita firmly.

"I love that you are such a fighter."

Kita blushed. "Why don't we watch TV?"

Kita led Kimmy to the beanbag chair, and they climbed on either side of Velositi.

"What do we want to watch?" said Velositi.

"No idea," said Kita.

Velositi flipped through the guide. "We could compare reality to TV. *Emperor* is about life in the Oval Office."

Kimmy chortled on her wine. "They must have an immense imagination to make my life interesting."

Velositi tuned to the channel. Kita snuggled under Velositi's arm as they watched the program, and Kimmy laughed and served herself more wine.

"From the laughing, the show does not match reality?" Velositi asked Kimmy when it was over.

"I run a tight ship to prevent having those kinds of crises. If I had that many in one day, I'd have someone's head. And, of course, the solutions aren't so neat and tidy. There's a lot of negotiations that last days and weeks leaving everyone unhappy. What I want to know is: Who's having that much sex in the White House?"

"Not you?" said Velositi.

Kimmy slid off the beanbag and poured another glass of wine. She retrieved a strawberry-lemonade for Kita. After tossing the bottle up to Kita, she climbed back up and took a seat.

"No, not me. Men and I don't get along." *No prince?* "When I first ascended, the conservatives demanded that a male be on the throne. There was a big push for me to marry. For three years, I had dates three or four times a week. They were all handsome, wealthy, well-educated men from good families, and I felt nothing for them. Kissing them was like kissing wood. Sex was even worse. Nothing they did turned me on, and I got the reputation of being frigid. I now resent them, the conservative party, for forcing them on me and exposing my inadequacies. Now I don't date, and the conservative party can live with a woman on the throne." Kimmy emptied her glass in a gulp and went to refill it.

"That sounds awful," said Kita.

"It is what it is. I'll be like Elizabeth the First."

"Her reputation was that of a virgin, but history suggests otherwise," said Velositi.

"I might pull it off," said Kimmy as she took a seat and passed Kita another strawberry-lemonade.

*I don't think I can keep up. Does she drink a lot, or is it because she's free to do so?*

"What now?" said Kimmy.

"I have a show I want to watch," said Velositi. She turned to HBO.

"What's it about?" said Kita.

"A lesbian witch."

"Oh," said Kita, having her interest piqued. She settled in and drank her strawberry-lemonade.

Kita watched *Black Pentagram* with interest. Not only was the story of battling demons fun, but there was a lot of graphic sex, which left her horny.

Velositi brought up the lights.

"Wow," said Kimmy. Her face was flush. "That was...wow."

"You look stimulated. Did you experience something?" said Velositi.

"Uhm..."

"You can tell us. Kita is a lesbian."

"You're a lesbian?" Kimmy said with wonder. She looked at Kita as if she'd found a treasure.

Kita shrank. "Yeah. I thought it was obvious with Velositi."

"I knew you loved each other, but I saw it as a human and Morphicon relationship. Not a gender issue."

"It's both," said Kita. "I couldn't love Bernoot. He's cool and all, but...he doesn't act like a girl."

"Can—can I ask you something? You don't have to answer if it makes you uncomfortable."

Kita shrugged. "Sure."

"How do you know you're a lesbian?"

*Ah...I just do?* "I don't know. I'm not attracted to guys. I mean, I know Ryan's good looking, but it does nothing for me. Not like when I see an attractive girl. I notice her hair, face, her body. I like girls' personalities—they're compassionate, smart, shy, positive, and honest."

"Have you ever kissed a boy?"

Kita made a face. "Yeah. I went through a period when I tried to be straight. I kissed him and ran away. It was awful and felt wrong. That's when I knew I'd be alone."

"But you're beautiful. You're...not trapped."

Kita huffed and looked down. "I'm from Reading, Cali—the fringe of conservative America. I didn't dare tell anyone I'm a lesbian. My business suffered because a girl ran it. I don't want to know what would have happened if people found out a lesbian ran it. Being shunned would probably be the best thing."

"Why didn't you move?"

"With what money?" said Kita dourly.

"I know the conservative people, and they aren't bad. Why would they do anything to you?"

Kita pulled out her phone and ran a Google search for news articles on violence against the LGBTQ community. She handed the phone over. "This is the world I live in."

Kimmy took the phone and read. Kita slid off the beanbag and walked her bottles to the sink. Leaning against it, she closed her eyes to get rid of the tears. *I have to remember she's never lived in fear.*

"Kita?" said Kimmy.

Kita opened her eyes. "Yeah."

"I'm sorry. I—This—I've never seen this before."

"Do you not know or not care?"

"Of course I care. This shouldn't happen to anyone. I thought there were laws in place to prevent this. I've never seen anything like this on the news. They would say if this is going on. The conservatives are good people with a strong moral foundation."

"As long as you're one of them. There's more to your country than the conservatives." Kita stepped up to Kimmy. "Maybe...it's time to change your perspective."

"What do you mean?"

"Do you trust me?"

"To do what?"

"Show you what you've been missing." Kita leaned in and kissed Kimmy. She went rigid for a moment, then relaxed and wrapped her arms around Kita.

*I think my heart just floated away.* Kita broke the kiss and leaned back in Kimmy's arms. "Did you feel something?"

"Ah, all the way down to my toes. Is that what's supposed to happen? I thought there was something wrong with me when I got warm fuzzy feelings looking at you. How—how did you know?"

Kita shrugged. "If boys didn't do it for you, why didn't you try girls?"

"If I date a girl, the political backlash would be unreal. My government would fall apart. The conservatives would abandon me."

"Do you believe what they do?"

"I never gave it much thought. That's how it's always been. They say it's wrong, but how can it be wrong if—if I'm gay?" Kimmy blinked. "I'm gay," she whispered and looked at Kita. "What am I going to do?"

Kita rolled her eyes. "You can continue to deny it and be miserable and lonely or embrace it and be happy."

"But what do I do about the conservatives?"

"Maybe the problem doesn't lie with us, but with them."

"How am I supposed to rule without them?"

"Stop denying yourself. Be brave. Seize what is yours. Build a new government that takes care of everyone. Good rulers care for all their people, not just a portion. A population that is well-fed, educated, healthy, has proper living conditions and sanitation, is safe, and has opportunity will reach a peak production higher than one under a government that serves only its elites and chosen few. A population that has its needs met will support the government and work harder. Unrest and rebellion will be minimal, as will crime. The populace's patriotism and willingness to defend the government will be higher.

The cost to an inclusive government to support its populace is less than the cost to deal with problems created by not supporting the populace. It can be done and has been done. You cannot rule from a position of fear or hate. True compassion and understanding create a foundation of rule that will stand the test of time."

Kimmy's mouth fell open. "I thought you didn't go to college."

Kita blinked and shrugged. "Sometimes, stuff just comes to me."

"Do—do you think I can do it?"

"Do you want to continue denying who you are and forward an agenda that discriminates and treats people like second-class citizens? Because that's what I am. I don't have the same rights or protections in the government's eyes that a straight girl does. I'm scared for my life, and I live in Cali—a state that has done stuff to protect the LGBTQ community, even let us marry."

Kimmy frowned. "I'm sorry. It's my fault. I was just continuing what my father created. Please, forgive me?"

"You're one of us now, and you have the power to fix it. I know in Cali, conservatives are just a small part, and there are lots of people who disagree with them."

"Yes, the liberals are entrenched in Cali and the West. They're almost as big as the conservatives. Others can be persuaded to join."

Kita folded her arms. "Do you want to do it?"

"It's going to take time. Once we find the Axiom and we start hunting Neophormes, then I can turn my attention to it, but I promise their agenda stops today. Thank you for showing me what I was missing." Kimmy hugged Kita and put her head on Kita's shoulder. "This—this feels right."

Kita put her arms around Kimmy.

Kimmy looked up. "I'm sorry. I don't mean to be presumptuous. I know you're with Velositi."

"Ah, actually, I'm supposed to be looking for a friend."

"Velositi, are you sharing?" said Kimmy.

"Kita needs a healthy relationship beyond what I can provide. You humans are complex with complex needs—needs I cannot provide. What kind of relationship she has is up to her to decide."

Kimmy looked at Kita. "Do—do you want more...from me?"

Kita gulped. "Ok, but that was my first kiss."

"Oh, well, I can show you how to do it properly." Kimmy wrapped her arms around Kita's neck and kissed her.

Kita gasped. "Slag. You—you know how to kiss."

"All that practice on boys trying to get something out of it. I knew I was missing something; I just didn't know it was you."

"I am glad to see that my hypothesis was correct," said Velositi.

"What was that?" said Kita.

"That Kimmy needed an opportunity."

"To be gay?"

"To find out who she is."

Kimmy put her arms around Kita. "To answer your question about your show, Velositi—it left me horny as hell. I've been squashing that feeling for fourteen years, thinking there was something wrong with me. It's the reason I became a doctor, but all my education and training said I was fine."

"You did not try a psychologist?" said Velositi.

"You know how bad that would have looked? And, if I'd been told the answer, I wouldn't have believed them."

"And you believe now?"

"I can't deny what I feel, and I won't deny who I am."

"Congratulations on your self-discovery."

"Thanks. If Kita's willing, I want to celebrate." Kimmy smiled at Kita and nuzzled her.

"Are you sure?"

"I am drunk enough and have waited fourteen years to find someone who makes me feel like you do. You've given me something to fight for. If I have to remake my entire government, I will. The only one who doesn't sound sure of what she wants is you."

*Ah, that's because I'm scared out of my mind. Acts of bravado are one thing. Sex is another.* "I just don't want anyone mad at me." She looked at Velositi.

"I will not be mad," said Velositi. "You do not want your first time to be with me. I am even more limited physically to what I can do than mentally and emotionally. Have fun with Kimmy and explore. Once you're done and if you are still interested, we can try something."

"I just don't want to leave you out."

"Just leave the door open, and I will be fine. I promise. Have fun."

Kimmy pushed Kita's hair aside and kissed the nape of Kita's neck.

All the hairs on Kita's arms stood up. *I'm beginning to think Velositi chose that witch show for more than just Kimmy.* Kita turned and kissed Kimmy. "Ok, just know I have no experience besides myself."

"My first-hand knowledge is old, but I do know what I've read from novels and medical journals."

"Read?"

"I've studied a lot of female anatomy trying to figure out what was wrong with me. Novels can be explicit as porn, and nobody cares what I read as long as it doesn't say erotica on the cover. Being gay would explain why, when I read, I imagine doing stuff to the girl, not being the girl." Kimmy planted a trail of kisses up Kita's bare shoulder and neck to her ear.

"What is in those books?" Kita purred.

Kimmy whispered into Kita's ear, "Lots of stuff I want to try. I bet you'll make awesome sounds. I know you have a set of lungs."

Kita giggled. "I don't want to wake the neighbors."

"The bunker's walls are ten feet thick. I can make you scream all I want, and no one will hear you."

Kimmy pulled Kita's halter-top off.

"That's a sexy bra," said Kimmy as she ran her hands over the pink lace and down Kita's sides.

Kita opened the fly of her jeans. "Panties match."

"Now, I'm glad I paid for your shopping trip to Victoria's Secret."

"You didn't like it?"

"I was jealous. You're not allowed to laugh at what I'm wearing."

Kita pressed herself against Kimmy. "Nothing can be as bad as the Air Force underwear I had to wear."

Kimmy laughed. She stroked Kita's hair. "You're like a beautiful angel, come to show me the light."

Kita blushed. "I'll be a fallen angel after tonight."

Kita awoke to Kimmy kissing her neck. She lay against Velositi, and Kimmy was curled up around her. With a yawn, Kita reached up and ran her fingers through Kimmy's hair.

"Meow," said Kita softly.

"Hey," said Kimmy. "I gotta go."

"Oh, but..."

"Sorry. If I'm not in my room when the Secret Service comes to pick me up, they'll lose their collective mind."

"You could tell them what you have been doing and had protection the whole time," said Velositi.

Kita giggled.

"I'll find time to do it again," said Kimmy. "Promise." She leaned over and kissed Kita, gently sucking on her lower lip.

A pleasant tingle ran up Kita's spine. Kita rolled over and hugged Kimmy. "You're welcome any time."

The two girls slid off the beanbag. Kita went to the bedroom and found a pair of pajama bottoms and a hoodie to wear. When she returned to the living area, Kimmy was dressed. Kita escorted her to the door.

"Thank you." Kimmy hugged Kita.

"Thank *you*. I had fun."

"So did I." Kimmy stroked Kita's cheek.

Kita captured Kimmy's hand and kissed the palm.

Kimmy hugged Kita fiercely. "I don't want to go," she whispered.

"I'm sorry. I'll see you at breakfast."

"I'll be working."

"Then, at the briefing."

"Ok."

Kita kissed Kimmy.

Kimmy opened the door, took Kita's hand, and squeezed it. Kita reluctantly let it go as Kimmy left. After closing the door, Kita climbed up the beanbag chair and curled up next to Velositi.

"She seemed both happy and sad," said Velositi.

"I no longer think I'm the one in the cage. She is," said Kita.

"I hope we showed her how to remove a few bars. How are you?"

"Oh, slag. I still can't feel my legs, and my hearing is muffled." Velositi giggled in reply. "Your fingers are incredible."

"I do have incredible dexterity and am ambidextrous."

"Did we do ok by you?"

"Oh, yes. You are both pleasurable to look at."

Kita yawned. "Oh, good. Ok. I'm going back to bed." She snuggled up to Velositi, putting her head on Velositi's shoulder, and fell back asleep.

Kita and Velositi arrived for the briefing early. Velositi would give the bulk of the presentation and wanted time to prepare her message. Kita hugged Velositi and left to find a place to sit in the audience. As Kita climbed the stadium seating steps, a whistle caught her attention. Adrestia waved to her. Kita moved to the second row and sat beside her.

"Hey," said Kita with a big smile. She hadn't been able to get rid of it all morning.

"Look at you," said Adrestia. "You're absolutely radiant."

"What?" Kita said, blushing, trying to hide her smile.

"I've been around long enough to know an afterglow when I see one. So, what was it like?"

"Attention!"

Kita remained seated as Adrestia stood. Kimmy entered and waved everyone to be seated.

Adrestia glared at Kita. "You're supposed to—"

Kita's eyes met Kimmy's. She gave Kita a smile and a wink. Kita smiled and waved.

"Oh...my...god," whispered Adrestia. "You didn't!"

"I didn't what?" said Kita trying to downplay her and Kimmy's interaction.

"Sleep with the princess!" Adrestia gasped in an excited whisper.

"How do you know that?"

"It's impossible to miss. She's glowing, too. How did you tame the shrew?"

Kita frowned. "She's not a shrew. She came to say goodnight, and she looked sad, so we invited her in. We discussed her politics, and I helped her find herself."

"I thought you and Velositi were an item?"

"We are. But Velositi wants me to find friends."

"So, it was the three of you?"

"Velositi just likes to look at us."

"So, how do I get invited to one of these parties?" said Adrestia with a grin.

"I don't know if we're going to be having parties. It just kind of happened."

"If it happens again, I'm available."

Kita gulped. The idea of sex with Adrestia was intimidating. Kita doubted the sex would be soft, sensual, and fun like with Kimmy. She envisioned a dungeon full of leather, latex, and weird devices. "I'll keep that in mind."

"Hey, I don't bite—hard."

Kita recoiled. "There was no biting last night."

"You don't know what you're missing. A little nip to the nipple will send a charge through you like a cattle prod."

Kita covered her nipples with her arm. "Ouch, no! That sounds painful."

"That's the point. You mix a little pain with pleasure, and it'll blow your mind."

"My mind was plenty blown last night. Velositi doesn't get tired."

Adrestia smiled. "I thought you said she liked to watch. You have to let me try."

"If you can convince Velositi, you're more than welcome."

"You don't want to come?"

"You scare me. I like Kimmy. She's sweet and soft."

Adrestia laughed. "You'll learn. I'm always available to teach."

"That's good to know."

Kita looked for Kimmy or Velositi. They were huddled together to one side of the stage. An officer stepped up to the podium.

"One minute. Please, take your seats."

Ryan hurried up the stairs and sat next to Kita. "Hey, what's up?"

"Nothing. Just waiting."

"Yeah. So, we finally get to learn the big secret—where is the Axiom?"

"I've heard some of it," said Kita. "I wonder where it will take us."

"Hopefully, somewhere cool."

"How are things with Sprokkit?" said Kita. "And how do you like the Air Force?"

"He and I are working on making the plasma converter more efficient and designed for manufacture so that it's not made out of spare parts. The Air Force is cool. I got my commission. As long as I'm working with Sprokkit, I get to wear civilian clothes. I still have to complete officer's school at some point. Where did they stick you?"

"I am a Ward of the Emperor. Kimmy says it's like being part of the extended royal family."

"Wow."

"I get to be with Velositi. That's what's important."

"Group, attention," said an officer.

Everyone stood as Kimmy walked to the podium. "Please be seated." Behind Kimmy, faces appeared on screens around an image of the world map. "Ladies and gentlemen, thank you for being available on such short notice. As you know, for the last forty-five years, we have been fighting the Neophormes and their human allies, the Illuminati. Today, I'm proud to announce we have made a great step forward in our war. Thanks to several citizens of the Empire, we have found the Vehlixen—the enemies of the Neophormes—and allied with them. We have agreed to help them find the Axiom of Command. In return, they offer to help us defeat the Neophormes. I would like to introduce Leader Velositi, Science and Medical Specialist Sprokkit, and Warrior Bernoot."

The three Vehlixen walked on stage and stood behind Kimmy. The room applauded politely. Everyone in the room had seen the Vehlixen. Those on the screens which hadn't seen them were in shock and awe.

Kimmy looked into the camera. "I have requested you here today to help us take the first step in finding the Axiom of Command. Leader Velositi will give you the details."

Kimmy stepped back from the podium.

Velositi stepped forward. "Thank you, Your Highness. Greetings citizens of the Empire of the United States. I am Leader Velositi of the Vehlixen. My team and I are on Earth to find the Axiom of Command. The Axiom dates back to the dawn of the Morphicons. It chooses our leader and bonds with them to create a powerful Morphicon.

"Five thousand, three hundred and sixty-six cycles ago—approximately twelve thousand Earth years—war broke out between the Morphicons. We split into two groups, Vehlixen and Neophormes. Our differences are many, but our fundamental difference is over how we are to survive. Vehlixen wish to heal our planet. Neophormes want to bleed our world of its resources to make an army that will spread across the galaxy to conquer new planets and strip them of their resources.

"At the beginning of the war, the Neophormes ambushed Omegus Hexious and killed him. His lieutenants recovered the Axiom but were unable to return it to Vehlix control. To protect it, the lieutenants left or world, Chellexon, to hide the Axiom among the stars. Without the Axiom, our war has been a stalemate.

"The only hint to the Axiom's location was received three hundred cycles ago —a simple message with clues to its location. These clues have led us to Earth. Here they are."

The map of the world changed to display a simple message.

A YELLOW STAR CIRCLED BY A BLUE WORLD,
A notch at the center of a ring of fire,
Leads to the middle of a web.

"WE ARE NOT THE ONLY TEAM SEARCHING FOR THE AXIOM. THE VEHLIXEN sent over a dozen teams to blue planets orbiting yellow stars. I need your expertise in deciphering the rest of the clues."

Kita looked at Adrestia. "Any idea?"

"No clue, but they called in all the best scholars and scientists in the country. If any group is going to crack it, it'll be them."

Kimmy walked to the podium. "Ladies and gentlemen, you've heard the problem. What are your ideas?"

KITA LEANED AGAINST RYAN. SHE WAS BEYOND BORED. THE DISCUSSION seemed to be going in circles. A *ring of fire* meant different things to different people: particle accelerators, String theory, music, and so on. So far, nobody could link a *ring of fire* with a *notch*.

Kimmy approached the podium. "Thank you, everyone. We'll take a ten-minute recess."

Kita straightened up and stretched. "I think I prefer getting shot at."

Adrestia laughed. "It can't always be exciting. A lot of government is like this."

Kita stood. "Lucky me. Let's see how our Vehlixen are doing."

Kita and the others walked down to the stage. Velositi was talking to some professor type. "Hey," said Kita, hugging Velositi.

"Oh! Hi, Kita. I am talking to Doctor Lee. He has an interesting idea that the *ring of fire* was a solar flare."

"Hello," said Kita. "Sounds great. Anything I can do to help?"

"No. Sorry. I am sure this is boring."

"It was interesting the first time. Then you started repeating yourselves."

Kimmy stopped next to Kita. "Can I talk to you?"

*She sounds upset. What did I do? Did I look too bored? Am I not looking professional enough? Why are people looking at me, anyway?* "Ah—sure, Kimmy."

Kimmy took Kita by the upper arm and led her off stage, through a door to a small room with a copier, an empty table, and boxes of paper. She let Kita go and closed the door. When she turned around, an impish grin had replaced her angry expression.

"Sorry," said Kimmy. "I didn't want anyone to get suspicious."

"Of what?"

"This." Kimmy put her arms around Kita's neck and kissed her.

Kita kissed her back, wrapping her arms around Kimmy's waist. Kimmy's hand wandered under Kita's jacket to her breast while holding Kita's head with her other hand.

Kita was happy to let Kimmy explore. *I so wish I didn't have clothes on.*

Kimmy pulled off Kita's jacket, exposing Kita's camisole. She kissed down Kita's neck to where her neck and shoulder met, hitting a sensitive spot with her tongue. Kita gasped. Grabbing Kita by the butt, Kimmy picked her up.

Surprised, Kita wrapped her legs around Kimmy. *She's stronger than I thought.*

Kimmy kissed Kita's chest, then looked up. Kita bent down and kissed her. Gently, Kimmy set Kita on the table and pressed herself against her.

Kita wrapped herself around Kimmy, trying to get as close to her as she could, desperately wanting to feel all of Kimmy at once.

There was a knock on the door, and Ryan poked his head in. "Kita, are you in here?"

Kimmy's head hit Kita's chest.

"Shut the damn door," snarled Kita.

"Oh! Sorry. I—they sent me to look for you."

"Shut up and get in here."

Kita unwrapped her legs from around Kimmy and hugged her. "You ok?" Kita said to Kimmy.

"Yeah." Kimmy stood up, letting Kita off the table.

Kita retrieved her jacket and fixed her top.

"You can't tell anyone anything," said Kimmy firmly to Ryan.

"Yeah, ok. No problem. It's your business. General Striker sent me to find you...ah, Your Highness."

"Don't call me that. Right now, I am Kimmy."

"Whatever you want, ah, Kimmy," Ryan said with a gulp.

"You're not in trouble, but you will be if this gets out. If anyone asks, I was lecturing her on etiquette."

"Ok."

Kita gave Ryan a dubious look. "I will hate you forever if you say anything."

"What about Velositi? Aren't you supposed to—"

"She knows," Kita hissed.

"Oh, ok."

"Come on," said Kimmy. "Let's go."

Kita put her jacket on and took Kimmy's hand and squeezed it. Kimmy hugged her, putting her head on Kita's shoulder. Kita kissed the top of Kimmy's head. Kimmy let go, put on a serious face, and led them out.

KITA PLAYED ON HER PHONE WHILE THE AXIOM LOCATION CONVERSATION dragged on into the late afternoon. She'd given up trying to follow the conversation when the discussion turned metaphysical.

*How much longer can this go on? These are the smartest people in the country, and they can't even decide on what* ring of fire *means. I don't think I can do another day of this.*

Kita closed her game when her email dinged. She opened it. It was an order for a carburetor for a 1979 Pinto. She hadn't gotten an order in weeks. *That's because I'm not out hustling.* She pulled up her inventory but didn't have one on hand. She typed PINTO into her search box to check her vehicle inventory. *Searching—that gives me an idea.* She did have a Pinto, so she sent a message to Ralph to pull the part. *I wonder if they're still working?* She hadn't received anything from them. *Of course, I haven't sent them a note saying I'm alive. I guess we'll see if they answer.*

Kita went back to her idea. She typed RING OF FIRE into Google. *Almost a billion results.* Music videos were the top results. She scrolled down until she found a result by the National Geographic Society. The website had a simple explanation.

*THE RING OF FIRE IS A STRING OF VOLCANOES THAT RING THE PACIFIC OCEAN.*

LOOKING AT THE MAP, HAWAII WAS AT THE CENTER. ZOOMING IN ON THE state map, there were several notches in the islands' coastlines. *I don't know about a web, but it's better than what these so-called experts are talking about.*

Kita got up.

"Where are you going?" said Adrestia.

"To talk to Kimmy. I have an idea."

"Then, I'm coming." Adrestia reached over and tapped Ryan. "Come on. Kita's got an idea."

The trio walked down to the stage. General Striker's new assistant, Major Rhodes, met them.

"I need to talk to Kimmy—the princess," said Kita.

"You'll have to wait until the next break."

"Oh, don't give me that crap. She outranks you." Kita pointed to Adrestia. "And if she doesn't, I do."

"You can't interrupt the meeting. I will pass her a note that you wish to talk to her at the next break."

*At the next break, I plan to do more than talk to her.* "I don't have the patience for you. Get out of my way."

Rhodes stood firm.

"Major, let her through," said Adrestia. "On my orders."

"I don't know who you are, Ma'am."

"Colonel Adrestia, Majestic Twelve, EUS Air Force and liaison to Bernoot."

"Colonel, you, and just you, can talk to General Striker."

"Take your ego and go to the Crushing Depths," snarled Kita to Rhodes. "Hey, Kimmy!" Kita yelled so everyone in the room could hear her.

"I hope you're not wrong," said Adrestia.

"I'm sure she'll let me make it up to her."

Kimmy looked back at Kita and her group. "Excuse me," she said to the panel and then walked over to the stage stairs. "What's the problem, Major?"

Kita giggled as Rhodes did her best not to tremble. "Colonel Adrestia wishes to speak to you, Your Highness."

Kimmy looked at Adrestia, who pointed at Kita. Kimmy pushed past Rhodes, climbed down the stairs, and stood next to Kita. "What do you have?"

Kita pulled out her phone and opened the NGS website. "Take a look at this. Hawaii is at the center, and it has some notches in the coastline."

Kimmy took the phone and studied the website and map.

"I don't know about the web part," said Kita. "I mean, it might be nothing. I could be way off or...or..." Kita gulped when Kimmy didn't react. "I can go sit down. I was just trying to help. Sorry—"

"Kita, this is it!" Kimmy said excitedly. She threw her arms around Kita and hugged her.

"Are you sure? Because I just thought of it. It probably should be checked."

"Kita, angel, if it comes from you, it has to be right."

Velositi came over and knelt at the edge of the stage. "What did Kita find?"

"The *Ring of Fire*," said Kimmy. "It is a geological formation of volcanoes around the Pacific Ocean. At its center is the state of Hawaii. One of these notches is a lava tube that will take us to the Axiom."

"That sounds promising," said Velositi.

"Are you sure?" said Kita. She knew nothing of volcanoes or lava tubes.

"I'll double-check," said Kimmy. "But I'd bet on you. This is your destiny, remember?"

"I just googled it."

"Which none of us thought to do."

"It makes sense," said Ryan. "Those ancient Morphicons were here before human civilization. They would only have had geographic references to go by. But it's been recent enough that the geography hasn't changed."

"Striker!" Kimmy yelled. "Contact the University of Hawaii. I want to talk to someone who knows the geography of the islands and the surrounding waters. Also, get a geologist, a volcanologist, and anyone else who knows about Hawaii's lava tubes."

"Yes, Your Highness."

Kimmy let go of Kita. She rushed back up to the stage. "We have our answer. Thank you, everyone, for your time and your duty to the country. Have a pleasant evening." She stepped back, and the monitors went black.

"Looks like we're going to Hawaii," said Adrestia. "Get your bikini ready, Kita."

"I don't own one."

"I guess we're going shopping then," said Kimmy.

Adrestia groaned.

Kita looked up at Velositi. Her eyes glowed, and Kita chuckled. "I guess I did promise you."

"Do you think you're ready?" said Velositi.

"Hey, if they think I look ugly, they can always look at you. We might even find Ryan a girl."

"It has been a few weeks," said Ryan.

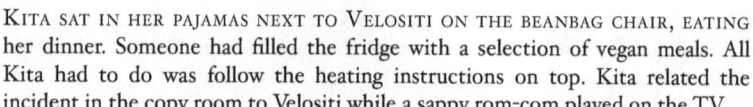

KITA SAT IN HER PAJAMAS NEXT TO VELOSITI ON THE BEANBAG CHAIR, EATING her dinner. Someone had filled the fridge with a selection of vegan meals. All Kita had to do was follow the heating instructions on top. Kita related the incident in the copy room to Velositi while a sappy rom-com played on the TV.

"Poor Ryan," said Velositi. "But you were late."

"I was a little busy to set a timer," said Kita as she stuck out her tongue.

"You leave it out there, and I will call Kimmy."

Kita laughed. "I don't know if I can do that tonight. I'm worn out from last night."

"But not too worn out to do it in the copy room?"

"That was just fooling around, not sex."

"According to the movies, you should be able to do it every night, all night. Is this not a typical male-female relationship?" said Velositi.

Kita laughed. "I have no idea. I don't think so. I think that is mostly stereotypes and dreams."

There was a knock at the door. Kita slid off the beanbag chair and answered it.

"Oh, hey, Kimmy." The princess was holding a bag.

"I'm not interrupting anything, am I?"

"Just dinner, but I'm almost done. Come on in."

Kita led Kimmy over to Velositi.

"Hi, Kimmy," said Velositi.

"Hi, Velositi. Is it ok that I'm here?"

"Of course. We are watching a movie and discussing its accuracy on the male-female relationship."

Kimmy smiled shyly. "I doubt my experience would be of any use."

"That makes three of us," said Kita. "The most experience I've had with boys was the pair that worked for me. If how they treated me is any indication, I'll take you and Velositi any day."

"Growing up as *the princess,* everyone treated me like I was made of glass, and my innocence was to be protected at all times."

"Your guards are not going to shoot Kita for ruining your innocence, are they?" said Velositi.

Kita climbed up the beanbag chair and offered a hand to Kimmy.

"I gave that to some idiot when I was eighteen. They treated him like a hero. I was disappointed. The big question now is, *why haven't I married?* They're not going to like who I want to bring home."

*Does she already have someone in mind? I guess she gets to meet famous people.* "Oh," said Kita quietly. "How did the meeting go with the university people?" Kita ate the last bite of food and took the plate to the kitchenette.

Kimmy sighed. "I learned more about volcanoes and lava tubes than I ever wanted to know, and they only know a little about the lava tubes that run under the islands. They did give us thirteen possible sites—most on the big island. Anti-Neophorm Team Five is flying out tomorrow to start scouting them. Most of them are in bays, but the experts said it is possible the volcano filled in a bay. Once they find a likely candidate, they'll let us know."

Kita climbed back up the bag with a pint of ice cream.

"I do have a question for you...both of you," said Kimmy wearily.

Kita took a bite of ice cream and looked at Velositi, who nodded. "Sure. What's up?"

"I...I...I wanted to know if you wanted to go over tomorrow...so we can hang out. I mean, you can have whatever time you want to yourselves, I just thought, we—I'm getting us a hotel. It's private and secluded, north of Kona. My staff is finalizing the details. It'll be private with a military staff so that Velositi can walk around. It has a beach. I was going to take all the Vehlixen and liaisons. I was just hoping to spend some time with you. I—I was hoping you'd be my...girlfriend." Kimmy slumped forward, staring at the beanbag chair.

"I just ask that Kita come when I want," said Velositi.

*Ah...what do I do? I just thought we were having fun...and this is becoming serious. Is Velositi right? Do I need more? I like Kimmy. She's fun. Can I do two relationships? And what does 'come when I want' mean? Why did this become so complicated? I was just eating ice cream and talking about going to Hawaii.*

Kita looked at Kimmy, and their eyes met. *She looks terrified. Is that over her question or what I might say? Can her life outside the bunker allow it? I'm just a junkyard girl, not a princess. And what if she gets bored with me? Then what? Where will I be exiled to?*

Kimmy whispered, "Please don't say no."

Kita gulped. *Oh, slag. What do I do? I tell her no, and I'll break her heart, and Velositi will never let me hear the end of it. Tell her yes, and what? I have a little fun...and maybe get exiled to live in the bunker for the rest of my life. At least I'll get free food.*

"Kita?" said Velositi. "Are you thinking or escaping?"

Kita wrinkled her nose. "What does *'come when I want'* mean? I'm not a dog."

"Perhaps that was bad phrasing. I want to know that if I want to spend time with you, you will."

"Of course I will. I love you. I like spending time with you."

*Velositi's not the only one who can make demands. I'm not getting stuck in the middle.* "Ok, ah, couple things. First, you two have to have some kind of healthy relationship—not just work. I'm not getting stuck in the middle if you have an argument. I will not choose sides. If you try to make me choose between you, I will hate you both. Second, if Kimmy and I break up, she's not allowed to exile us."

Kimmy laughed cautiously. "I wouldn't exile you. I'd make you my kept girl and have you live at the White House."

"I'll take exile."

Kimmy rolled across Velositi to face Kita. "You really want to...with me?"

"As long as we go slow. I'm not sure I'm ready for your world. Same as everyone else isn't ready for my world." Kita pointed to Velositi.

"I promise not to take you to any state dinners. I just want to have fun and be with someone who cares."

"You've got two people who care—me and Velositi. I hope you two will be friends."

"I look forward to getting to know her better."

"And I, you," said Velositi.

"Ok, good," said Kita. She grabbed her half-melted ice cream and put it back in the freezer.

Kimmy came up behind Kita, put her arms around her, and rested her head on her back. "Thank you. You seem upset."

Kita turned around. "No. A little shocked. I feel like I just got into a good place with Velositi. I don't want to screw it up with her or you."

"I understand. I promise if you feel like things between you and Velositi are slipping, I will back off."

"Thank you. I'm also terrified of life with you outside the bunker."

Kimmy grimaced. "I understand. My life is not easy, but I'm willing to make changes to accommodate us. Just know, there are things I have to do, but you don't have to come."

"Ok. I'm sure I'll grow into it."

Kimmy hugged Kita, and then hesitantly kissed her. "I haven't been this happy ever."

Kita smiled. "I'm happy, too...and excited. I always dreamed about what it would be like to have a girlfriend."

"Now, you have one. What do you want to do?"

"Cuddle."

"I like that idea. I brought my pajamas. I'll go change."

"Ok."

Kimmy retrieved her bag and went into the bedroom. Kita crawled up next to Velositi.

"Are you sure about this?" said Kita.

"You do not like the idea?"

"I do. I'm just scared to love two people."

"You were scared to love me and look how that turned out."

Kita nodded. "Fear gave way to happiness. The bars vanished."

"And they will again. Give Kimmy time."

Kimmy exited the bedroom and crawled up next to Kita.

"Ready to watch?" said Kimmy.

"Sure," said Kita. She settled in next to Velositi and put her arm around Kimmy. Velositi put her arm around them both and lowered the lights.

KITA ROLLED DOWN THE RAMP ON VELOSITI OUT OF THE C-5 GALAXY PARKED at the end of the Kona International Airport runway away from the terminals. They pulled to one side as Bernoot and Adrestia exited. Sprokkit came next with Ryan trailing. He was flirting with a crewmember of the C-5. Anytime during the flight she hadn't been busy, Ryan was in her ear.

The three vehicles clustered together as Kita dismounted, and Adrestia exited Bernoot.

"Found a friend?" said Kita, teasing Ryan.

"Ah, yeah. She's cool and told me how she's flown all over the world."

"Maybe you should ask her out?" said Adrestia.

Ryan rubbed the back of his neck. "I was going to ask Kita if she'd talk to the princess about it. I don't know if I'm allowed."

"Officers are allowed to date other officers."

"Really? I wonder if she can get some time off. Kita, do you think you can talk to the princess?"

Kita scowled. "Why do I have to ask?"

"Because you and her get...along...so well."

"Way to be smooth," said Adrestia. "Lucky for you, everyone here knows Kita is sleeping with the princess."

"You slept with her?" gasped Ryan.

"What do you think I was doing with her?" said Kita in a huff. "And she's my girlfriend for the record."

"Moving up," said Adrestia. "Guess this means I have to call you *Your Highness.*"

"That's the last thing I want."

"They do complement each other well," said Velositi.

"I'm surprised you agreed to this," said Adrestia. "You seem very protective of Kita."

"I am, and it was my idea. I have my reasons, and I believe it will make Kita and I stronger."

"I didn't know the princess was gay. She's never given any signals."

"She just needed an opportunity to understand herself better."

"You do make an imposing couple," said Ryan.

Kita looked over her sunglasses at him. "What's that supposed to mean?"

"She—"

"—Kimmy—"

"—Kimmy is *the princess,* and you're like fearless and don't take shit from anyone...including Kimmy."

The roar of jet engines made everyone turn as Air Force Three rolled by and came to a stop. A trio of motorized stairs were chasing after it. The tail opened, and a ramp extended. Three black SUVs drove out and parked next to the plane.

Kita watched the door in greedy anticipation. Kimmy had offered her a ride on Air Force Three, but Kita elected to ride with Velositi. Kimmy was disappointed, but Kita told her to get her work done so they would have the next two days free. Now, Kita wished she'd flown with Kimmy. She missed her.

The door to Air Force Three opened, and the Secret Service agents ran out and took their positions. Kimmy appeared and walked down the stairs. She ignored the SUVs and walked the hundred yards to Kita and her group.

Kita squelched the urge to run to Kimmy and kiss her. The airport was public, and Kita didn't want to ruin Kimmy's public image. So, she waited, a hand on Velositi.

When Kimmy was hidden by the C-5, Kita couldn't take it anymore. She hurried over to meet Kimmy and gave her a warm hug.

"Hey," said Kita. "Did you have a good flight?"

Kimmy giggled. "It's hard to get work done when I'm thinking of you. But I did get it done. I need to get a cute picture of you. Security footage and mug shots aren't the same."

"I'm sure those are fantastic pictures of me."

"Good enough." Kimmy squeezed Kita and let her go.

Together they walked to the Vehlixen and liaisons.

"How was the flight?" said Kimmy.

"Yo! No in-flight movie," said Bernoot, "or internet connection."

"Poor you," said Adrestia. "You had to talk to me the whole time."

"You ask, like, a ton of questions."

"And you don't know the meaning of a short answer."

"The flight was restful for everyone," said Velositi.

"Oh," said Kita. "Ryan had a question for you, Kimmy."

"M—Me?"

"You wanted me to bring it up to her, now's your chance."

Kimmy gave Kita a mischievous look. "What is it, Ryan?"

"I, uh, I wanted to know...if it...was alright...if..."

"What Ryan is trying to say," said Sprokkit, "is he has found a female he wishes to mate with and would like your permission and help, as the matriarch, to pursue her."

Ryan's mouth fell open as his ears turned red, and his face went white.

Kita giggled. "So that's what that face looks like."

"Are you saying I have embarrassed you?" said Velositi.

"Little bit."

"Who is it?" said Kimmy.

"Sarah—I mean Lieutenant Andrews," whispered Ryan.

"You're going to have to give me more than that. I have lots of lieutenants."

"She was a flight engineer on our plane."

"He talked her ear off," said Kita.

"I'm fine with it," said Kimmy.

"He wants you to give her some time off."

"Ah. If he asks her and she says yes, contact my assistant Daisy, and she'll get the time off worked out."

"Thank you, Your Highness."

Kimmy gave him a dirty look.

"Er, thanks, Kimmy."

"Everyone has today and tomorrow to do what they want. We're staying at the Mauna Kea Resort, and everyone has a private bungalow. We're the only ones there, and the staff is vetted so that the Vehlixen can walk around. There is a private beach so everyone can play in the water—"

"Radical!" said Bernoot.

"—Security will be tight, but they'll know you on sight. If you do change disguises, need anything, or have a problem, contact Daisy. There will be a tour of Volcano National Park tomorrow if you're interested. It does have lava tubes if you want to see what we're looking for. When we're ready, I'll lead us off the airfield, and you're then free to do what you want."

Kita and Kimmy walked over to Velositi.

"Do you girls want to go down Ali'i Drive," said Kimmy sounding uncertain. "It has food, shops, and several beaches. It runs along the ocean and...or if you want to go by yourselves..."

"Kimmy," said Kita. "Of course we want to spend time together with you. We took this trip so we could all spend time together. We're not going to leave you out."

"I know. I just have security and being me..."

"We'll have fun. Don't worry. Maybe we can ditch the Secret Service. It's not like you won't have the best security ever."

"That would be a vacation."

"Then we will find a way," said Velositi.

"Lunch first," said Kita. "Or breakfast. Whatever time it is."

Kita and Kimmy walked down Ali'i drive. They ate lunch at Quinn's, a local favorite, and were now exploring the nearby shops and galleries.

"Pretty picture," said Kita pointing to a line drawing of a seductive pair of woman's eyes with a flower in her hair.

"You like it?" said Kimmy.

"It...it reminds me of someone...I've seen those eyes before...maybe from a dream."

"Do you want it?"

"I—where am I going to put it?"

"Worry about that later. Let's get it."

Kita followed Kimmy inside. Kimmy didn't haggle over the price.

"Can I leave it here and pick it up later?" Kimmy asked the shopkeeper.

"Sure, no problem. What's the name?"

"Daisy King."

"All set, Miss."

"Thanks."

"Aloha."

Kita and Kimmy returned to the street. Kita fought the urge to take Kimmy's hand. She wasn't sure if she should in public. Kita settled for, "Thank you."

"Of course. I liked it, too. A very seductive set of eyes."

They window-shopped until they came to a swimwear store.

"You need a swimsuit, don't you?" said Kimmy.

"Yeah," said Kita with a sigh.

"You don't feel like modeling for me?"

"And me?" said Velositi from Kita's back pocket.

Kita pulled the phone out. "I guess," she said playfully, rolling her eyes over her sunglasses.

Following Kimmy inside, they browsed the bikinis.

"How about this one?" said Kimmy. She held up a black string bikini with pink hibiscus. "You'll match Velositi."

"Oh, let me see," said Velositi.

Kimmy held it up to the phone.

"Oh, that is cute."

"Ok, I'll try it on," said Kita. "Hey, dressing room?" she called to the clerk.

"In the back."

Kita navigated the racks and shelves to the back and found a single slatted half door. She went inside and struggled with all the knots she had to tie. Stepping out, she said, "Ta-da."

"Wow," said Kimmy and Velositi together.

"You look sexy in that," said Kimmy. She pushed Kita back into the dressing room and kissed her. Kimmy took the opportunity to kiss and caress other parts of Kita. "Yum."

"You like it that much?"

"So much I want to get one and go to the beach. Velositi, can you move closer to the shop so we can make our escape?"

"Sure. I am moving now."

"Come on." Kimmy grabbed Kita's hand and pulled her back into the store.

Kita browsed the bikinis, not sure what Kimmy would like.

"What do you think of this one?" Kimmy held up a red and blue bikini with white stars.

"Very you," said Kita.

Kimmy laughed. "It's patriotic without being overly so. I'll go try it on."

Kita accompanied Kimmy to the back and waited patiently for her to change.

Kimmy stepped out. "What do you think?"

Kita gulped. It didn't cover much. "You look fantastic."

"Good enough you want to take it off?"

"With my teeth."

Kimmy giggled and hugged Kita. "You know how to make me feel sexy."

"It's not hard when you are."

Kimmy gathered up their clothes. "Come on, let's pay for these and get out of here."

They hurried to the counter, giggling.

"These two bikinis and two sets of flip-flops," said Kimmy. "And do you mind if we leave our clothes here? We'll come pick them up in a little while."

"Ah, sure."

The clerk opened a pair of plastic bags, and Kimmy inserted the pile of clothes and shoes. She pulled out a credit card with a bald eagle on it and handed it to the clerk. After running the card, the clerk handed back the card and a receipt.

"Aloha!" said the clerk. "Have fun. The beach is just down the street, but if you don't mind walking, there's Pahoehoe Beach Park about three miles down Ali'i drive."

Kimmy put the receipt in her bag and tucked the card in her top. "We have a ride, so that will be cool. Thanks for the tip."

With a big grin, Kimmy took Kita's hand and pulled her out of the shop. Velositi waited across the street.

"We need to hurry," said Kimmy, "before the Secret Service catches up."

They hurried across the street and hopped on Velositi.

"Here, this will help hide you," said Kita as she passed her helmet to Kimmy. She tucked her phone into her top.

Kimmy put the helmet on and wrapped her arms around Kita. Velositi backed out, and they drove down the street. Ali'i Drive was beautiful and ran along the shoreline. Shops and restaurants lined the island side. A sidewalk and a lava rock wall ran along the ocean side. Waves crashed against the wall, throwing up showers of spray.

"No one mentioned traffic moved at a crawl on this road," said Velositi.

"It's a popular place," said Kimmy.

"I can see why. It's beautiful. I would love to live here," said Kita.

Kimmy squeezed Kita. "That can be arranged."

"What about you?"

"I'll build a summer White House out here."

"Just for us?"

"I want you happy."

"Oh, thanks." Kita reached down and squeezed Kimmy's hand.

"I am so glad you two are getting along," said Velositi.

"She makes me happy," said Kimmy.

"You both make me happy," said Kita. "You girls are going to spoil me."

Kimmy laughed. "I'll do my best."

"Here it is," said Velositi. She pulled off the road under a tall palm tree.

"Oh, I'm so excited," said Kimmy after she pulled the helmet off.

"Have fun," said Velositi.

Kita and Kimmy ran across the grass to the edge of the sand. They kicked off their flip-flops and tucked the phone and credit card in the helmet, then set everything next to a rock.

"Let's go," said Kimmy excitedly. She grabbed Kita's hand, and they ran across the beach into the water. They waded out until it was chest-deep. Kimmy dove in and swam a few yards away. "Kita! Come on. The water is *so* warm."

Kita waded a little farther out. "I don't know how to swim."

Kimmy disappeared underwater.

Kita looked around worriedly. Kimmy popped up in front of her. She slicked her hair back and put her arms around Kita's neck.

"I can give you lessons," said Kimmy. She kissed Kita. "Or we can do other things."

Kita pulled Kimmy against her and kissed her back.

"Oh god, I love kissing you," said Kimmy as she hugged Kita tight. "Do you believe in fate?"

"I never gave it much thought, but I guess so if what Velositi says is true."

"I didn't until you came along. It was like I was supposed to wait for you."

"You were going to send me home," Kita teased.

"I know. That's all part of it. It's like we were meant to be together, and nothing could keep us apart. No matter what we said or did."

*Does fate work like that? From this experience, I'm leaning toward we make our own fate and fulfill our own prophecies.* "I love being with you. I don't know how it happened, but I'm glad it did. We owe Velositi a big thank you."

Kimmy purred. "Another session with her sounds wonderful. I wonder if there's anything she wants?"

"I don't know. She hasn't said she wants or needs anything."

"Something like flowers. To show her she's appreciated."

"We could wave to her. Let her know we're thinking about her."

They turned and waved at Velositi. Kimmy kissed Kita on the cheek. Velositi's headlight blinked several times.

"I bet she's having a great time watching," giggled Kimmy. "Come on, let's play."

---

KITA BREACHED THE WATER'S SURFACE LIKE A DOLPHIN. SHE LANDED ON HER feet and pulled back her hair.

"Wow. I wish I could get a picture of that," said Kimmy from the beach.

"What?" said Kita shyly.

"You, looking super sexy. You belong on a calendar. Hang on, don't move." Kimmy ran and got Kita's phone. "Strike a pose."

*Ah...a pose? Uhm...* Kita tried to remember all the magazines on Mickey's desk. She stuck out her hip, twisted her shoulders slightly, cocked her head, and smiled. "Is that good?"

"Perfect. Turn around."

Kita did. She tightened her butt and put her hands on her hips.

"Nice. Now, I have something for my desk."

Kita laughed as she waded out of the water. They returned to the helmet and flip-flops and found two towels laid out.

"For us?" said Kita.

Kimmy sighed sadly. "Yeah. They're government issue."

"Come on," said Kita. "Grab your flip-flops, credit card, and the phone, and let's go ride. I don't see the SUVs. I bet they had to park far away. We should have enough time to get away."

"You don't want your helmet?"

"Traffic is moving slow, and I want to see the scenery."

"Ok."

They grabbed their stuff and hurried back to Velositi.

"Did you have fun?" said Velositi.

"It was awesome," said Kita. "Right now, we're trying to outrun the Secret Service."

"Oh, ok. Where do you want to go?"

"I dunno."

"I can take Kam III Road to the Hawaii Belt Road. That goes around the island. According to the website, there is a great ice cream shop to the south."

"That sounds awesome," said Kita.

KITA, KIMMY, AND VELOSITI FOUND THE ICE CREAM SHOP AND EXPLORED THE area, buying some shorts and tank tops from a shop that was a converted theater. The owner of the clothing store told them about the Kona Coffee plantation. Interested by the tale of geese, they turned around and headed north.

As Velositi rounded a bend, she passed a slow-moving car in a no-passing zone. With a clear road ahead of her, she sped up.

"Kita, there is an SUV behind us with a flashing light," said Velositi.

Kita examined their pursuer in the mirror. *Is it an actual cop or one of those rapists posing as a cop? There's no room to pull over, either.* "Velositi, find a public place to pull over. We'll see what he wants."

Velositi cruised for several miles and pulled into a McDonald's parking lot. She stopped next to the building.

Kita and Kimmy sat up and fixed their hair. The Hawaiian looking man stepped out of his SUV.

*The uniform looks official. He has a badge and a ticket book with him.*

"Aloha, ladies," the man said in a friendly voice.

"Are you a cop?" said Kita.

"Yes, Miss, I am."

"Undercover?"

"No. In Hawaii, police officers drive their private vehicles."

"Oh, ah, what's the problem?"

"Several things. You're not wearing helmets, you were speeding, and you passed in a *no-passing zone*. I need to see your license and rental agreement for the bike."

"We don't have that," said Kimmy.

"Then I'll need your names, the hotel where you're staying, the rental company for the bike, and your home addresses."

"Ah, well...her name is classified, the bike is classified, where we're staying is classified, and my name is Kimberly Roosevelt. I live at sixteen hundred northwest Pennsylvania Avenue, Washington, D.C., two-zero-five-zero-zero."

"That's not a new one," said the officer. "But, you're the first to give me the complete address."

"I don't know what to tell you," said Kimmy. "That's who I am and where I live."

"If you don't want to give me your information, we can take your fingerprints down at the station, and I'll have to impound the bike. So, do you want to tell me who you are?"

"My prints are classified, and my face is in every Imperial government building. You had to see me on TV."

"I know the princess' name. You kind of look like her, but she wouldn't be riding unescorted. Let's go. Get off the bike, and we'll go to the station."

"Can we call someone?" said Kita.

"At the station," said the officer.

Kimmy and Kita dismounted.

"Velositi, call Daisy and tell her where we are," said Kita.

"What?" said the officer.

"How about we wait five minutes and see who arrives?" said Kita.

"I'm not waiting. You can either go nicely or in cuffs."

"I've been in handcuffs a lot lately, and it's lost its appeal. You're about to find out how big a tantrum I can throw. We'll wait."

"Kita," said Velositi, "the Secret Service detail is on the way. The estimated time is eight minutes."

"You have eight minutes," Kita told the officer. "You can wait that long. Because, if you try to take me to the station, I'm going to be so pissed. And, if I'm pissed, she'll be, too." Kita motioned to Kimmy.

The officer sighed. "Turn around, please."

"No," snarled Kita. She ran to the corner of the building.

The officer spoke into his radio. He said something to Kimmy. She held up her hands, pointed at Kita, and shook her head. The officer ran toward Kita. She turned and ran past cars lined up for the drive-thru. Kita stopped at the window and grabbed a bag of food and a drink. Hurling the drink at the officer, it landed at his feet, splashing his shoes and pants.

"I told you to leave me alone!" Kita screamed. "I am not going with you."

The officer charged her. She reached into the bag, grabbed the burger, and threw it at him, hitting him in the chest and smearing him with ketchup and mustard.

Kita ran to the door and burst inside. Outside, two more cars with flashing blue lights arrived. Three officers exited the vehicles. One went to Kimmy and Velositi. The other two ran into the restaurant.

Finding herself in the middle of the seating area, Kita tried to watch all three officers at once. An L-shaped row of booths was between her and the two officers in front, and there was a row of tables between her and the officer pursuing her.

The two officers in front went opposite directions around the booths. The officer chasing her moved up the row of tables. Kita opened the bag and pulled out the remaining fries. She flung them at the officer chasing her. He took a step toward her and slipped on a fry. The other officers rounded the ends of the booths.

Kita dropped the bag, stepped on a booth seat, and then the table. The table tilted. *Oh, slag.* Kita crashed to the ground. The officers rushed her. Kita rolled onto her back, flailing her arms and legs. "Don't touch me!" she screamed.

Kita connected several times with the officers, but they persisted in turning her over and cuffing her.

"Let me go. I told you to wait!" she shrieked.

The officers stood Kita up and dragged her to the door as she fought them. In the parking lot were three black SUVs with flashing red and blue lights. *I've never been so happy to see those things in my life.*

"I told you!" Kita yelled. "Let me go!"

The Secret Service formed a perimeter around Kimmy. One of them was talking to the officer with her.

"Let me go!" Kita shrieked so loud she drew everyone's attention. She threw herself back and forth, trying to break free.

Kimmy ran over to Kita. "Kita! Calm down. Please." She looked at the officers. "Release her, *now*."

The officers gave Kimmy a dismissive look. A Secret Service agent and the other officer ran up behind Kimmy.

"Let go!" Kita snarled as she slammed her foot down on one of the officers.

The officer made a face, but he didn't release Kita from his grasp.

"Kita!" Kimmy snapped.

"Officers, I'm Special Agent in Charge O'Brien, EUS Secret Service," O'Brien showed them his badge. "Your prisoner is a Ward of the Emperor, and I request that you turn her over to me immediately."

The original officer looked at Kimmy. "You—you really are the princess?"

"Uh-huh," said Kimmy. "Now, let her go."

An officer produced a key and undid Kita's cuffs.

"You slagging bastards!" Kita yelled as she turned and took a swing at the nearest officer.

Kimmy wrapped Kita in a bear hug. "Kita, it's ok. They're just doing their jobs. I'm sorry. You're free."

"No one touches me!" Kita screamed as she fought Kimmy.

O'Brien and another Secret Service agent restrained Kita as gently as they could.

"Take her over to Velositi," said Kimmy. "See if she can calm her down."

The two agents nearly carried Kita to Velositi.

"Kita, please calm down," said Velositi. "It is over. You succeeded in buying enough time for the Secret Service to arrive. Take some deep breaths and relax. We're here to have fun."

"They threw me on that disgusting, nasty ass floor!" Kita yelled.

"We'll get you clean. No permanent damage was done—just a bruised ego."

"You be put in handcuffs."

"I am sorry. You just have a knack for ending up in them. I understand it is uncomfortable. Kimmy got you out as fast as she could. You are going to have to calm yourself. I cannot console you right now."

Kita shook off the Secret Service agents. "Go away," she snarled.

They backed off half a step. Kita huffed, turned around, and sat, leaning against Velositi. "I even smell like that damn floor," she muttered.

"We can go back to the hotel," said Velositi.

Kita grumbled. "Kimmy wanted to go to the coffee place. I don't want to disappoint her."

"I am sure she will not notice the smell."

"Someday, I swear, I will have the power so no one can hold me."

"You are well on your way," said Velositi.

"That's just trapped in a different prison. I will be free to do what I want when I want."

"That is a big dream."

"You told me to dream big."

"I did. I also said I would help you achieve it, and I will."

Kimmy knelt in front of Kita. "How are you doing, angel?"

"Grumpy."

"But you don't want to fight everyone in sight?"

"Yeah. I guess."

Kimmy giggled. "You're such a fighter. Are you ready to go?"

"Where are we going?"

"The coffee plantation."

"Ok. I guess I'm riding Velositi by myself?"

"Of course not, but we have to wear helmets and have an escort."

"So much for fun," said Velositi.

"I had to make compromises to ride with you and Kita," said Kimmy. "I thought that was better than riding in the SUV."

"Yeah, it is," said Kita with a sigh.

"What can I do to cheer you up, angel?" Kimmy said to Kita.

"She will come out of it," said Velositi. "A little time on the road will shake her black mood away."

"Does that sound good, Kita?"

"Yeah. Let's go."

"Just remember, my arms will be around you the whole way."

KITA AWOKE TO THE SOUND OF A PHONE RINGING ON KIMMY'S NIGHTSTAND. Kimmy let go of Kita, sat up, swore, and grabbed the offending device. Curious, Kita rolled over and wrapped herself around Kimmy.

"Do you know what time it is, James?" said Kimmy in a harsh voice.

Kita was close enough to the phone she could hear.

"It's eight-thirty. Do you know what I'm staring at?"

"It's goddamn three-thirty in the morning," Kimmy snarled. "I don't give a damn what you're staring at."

"You better. It's all over the news and tabloids."

*What news bridges those two things?*

"It's *too* early. I just went to bed. I don't care," said Kimmy.

"Too busy with your jailbird whore?" James retorted.

*Oh, slag.* Kita sat up, fighting the tears in her eyes.

"Don't you dare call her that," Kimmy hissed.

"What the hell are you doing, Kimberly? You're supposed to be allying with the Vehlix, not disgracing yourself with some local whore. You're supposed to be passed this."

"I'm finally living my life," Kimmy snarled. "You call her a whore one more time, and I will fire your ass."

"What would your father say?"

"If you can wake him up, feel free to ask. I'm no longer his to control. I make my own decisions. Not you—not him. I will choose whom I spend my time with."

"A goddamn slut, Kimberly? You said you were ready to be an adult. If you're so hard up, there are men lined up waiting to court you."

Kita burst into tears. *A slut? Is that what I am?* She didn't want to hear the rest and rolled across the bed.

"Kita, wait," cried Kimmy.

Kita rushed out of the bungalow right into Velositi's arms.

"It is ok, Kita," said Velositi. "Do not listen to him. He does not know you or care about you. He is just trying to get to Kimmy."

Kita wrapped her arms tight around Velositi and buried her face in Velositi's midsection.

"Kita, I know it stings, but it is not the truth. You cannot let it affect you." Velositi stroked Kita's back. "If you react, they win. And you do not want them to have that kind of power over you, do you?"

Kita sniffed. "No," she whispered.

"Then gather yourself. Kimmy will need you when she is finished."

Kita let go of Velositi and wiped her eyes. Velositi sat down and offered her lap. Kita took it and snuggled against her.

"No one has ever called me a slut before," said Kita.

"From my understanding, it is a word to describe girls who sleep around a lot, but there is no equivalent for men. The practice seems actively encouraged in men. It is a stupid double standard."

"What...what if they take her from me?" whispered Kita.

"I do not think Kimmy would allow that. I do think this is a test for her—the first step in consolidating her power, and Kimmy is fighting hard. I think whomever James is, his life is over. It does sound like a relationship with you will have far-reaching consequences."

"What do you mean? Am I too much of a problem?"

"That is up to Kimmy to decide. I think in her mind, you are not—from what she is saying. Oh, here she comes."

Kimmy came to the bungalow door. She was dressed in a cut-off camisole and shorts, similar to Kita. They had found Hawaii to be a very warm place to sleep.

"Who's on guard detail?" Kimmy called.

A Secret Service agent appeared out of the darkness. "Yes, Your Highness?"

"Dan, contact security at the White House and have James removed. Clean out his desk, his house, car, online accounts, everything. He's fired. Tell his deputy that he has the Chief of Staff job until I find a replacement."

"Yes, Your Highness."

Kimmy walked over to Kita and Velositi and knelt next to them.

"I'm sorry, Kita," said Kimmy.

Kita's heart fell. She blinked the tears away. "It's ok. I understand. I had fun. I can still be with Velositi, right?"

"What?" said Kimmy. "Oh! Oh, Kita, no!"

A lump grew in Kita's throat. "But...You said..."

"Kita! Kita, I'm not breaking up with you." Kimmy hugged Kita. "Not at all. I'm just sorry James called you those names. You're not any of those things. I blew up my father's finely crafted government coalition earlier than planned, but that's ok. I will find others willing to take over for the conservatives. I promise they won't see power again as long as I'm in charge."

Kimmy took Kita's hands.

"It's time the country moved forward, instead of remaining in the past. I love you, and I want to build a world where we're accepted. It's time for them to catch up and get off their plantations. There is more to my country than white males."

"You love me?" whispered Kita.

"Too soon?" said Kimmy with a grimace.

"No," said Kita. "I love you. I love you more because some little girl won't have to grow up like I did—alone, afraid, and questioning her existence."

"I'm so sorry you had to. Hopefully, our pictures will show them they aren't alone."

"What pictures?"

"There are several. Uhm, one not so flattering of you."

"Great. Let me see."

Kimmy showed Kita the photos of them at the beach—frolicking in the water and kissing. Another showed them on Velositi. A final one showed police officers dragging Kita out of McDonald's in handcuffs.

Kita sighed. "I like your expression of amusement."

"I warned them."

"And yet, you still love me."

Kimmy put her arms around Kita's neck. "It's one of the reasons I love you. You are such a fighter, and you never give up." She kissed Kita.

"Yum," said Kita.

"Since we're up, we can fool around...or we can go back to bed. The volcano tour doesn't leave until seven."

"Velositi, do you think you can slip through the door?" said Kita with a wink.

Velositi pulled into the no-parking zone across from the Thurston Lava Tube entrance. The black SUVs stopped, and six Secret Service agents exited. The SUVs and the rest of the Vehlixen drove on, looking for a place to park. Kita and Kimmy dismounted Velositi and took off their helmets and jackets. It was just before nine and already warm. They both wore shorts, flip-flops, and camisoles.

"Do you mind watching our stuff, Velositi?" said Kimmy.

"No problem. Though, I think I would terrify any potential thief."

"A Secret Service agent will be stationed at the entrance if you have a problem. When we see Ryan, we'll make sure he turns on the GoPro so you can see."

"Thank you. I am very excited to see a lava tube. Have fun girls."

"Love you," said Kita.

"Love you," replied Velositi.

Kimmy took Kita's hand. They crossed the street and followed a path until it intersected the trail down to the lava tube. They walked to the fence and looked out at the rainforest.

"Wow. It's pretty," said Kita.

"You're pretty," said Kimmy as she slipped an arm around Kita.

"I love you," said Kita. She leaned in and kissed Kimmy. "Yum," said Kita when they split after several exhilarating kisses. "I, ah, think we have an audience."

"Who?"

Kita turned Kimmy around. A young couple was standing a few feet away. A Secret Service agent was standing next to them.

"Can I help you?" said Kimmy.

"Your—Your Highness?" said the young woman.

"Yes?" said Kimmy curiously.

The couple knelt.

"Please stand. You don't have to kneel. This is not an official function. What can I do for you?"

The couple stood, and the woman took out her phone. "We're Jackie and Ian Bloomy from Ohio and were hoping we could get a picture?"

"Oh, sure. No problem."

Kita released Kimmy so she could stand with them.

"Oh, your girlfriend, too. We were so excited to see you had a girlfriend and were on the island, Your Highness."

"Just on vacation. You?"

"We're here for our honeymoon."

"Congratulations."

They arranged for the picture and took several selfies, and then passed the phone to the agent to take several more.

"Thank you, Your Highness," said Jackie, "and thank you...ah, the paper didn't give your girlfriend's name."

"Jane," said Kita with a dazzling smile.

"Thank you. Enjoy your vacation."

"Enjoy your honeymoon," said Kimmy. She smiled at Kita when the couple had moved on. "Jane? Are you Jane Doe?"

Kita laughed. "No, but you said my name was classified. Jane is a name I've always adored. I don't know why. But, don't look now, a line has formed."

Kimmy turned to see a line of four groups waiting. "Uhm, I guess we have some time."

Kita and Kimmy greeted each group and posed for pictures. They answered questions about the news story, and Kimmy assured the curious that more detailed answers about her new relationship would be forthcoming after their vacation.

A pair of women—a redhead and brunette, Kita guessed they were in their mid-forties—were next in line. They were dressed more like locals than tourists and knelt.

"You don't have to kneel," said Kimmy. "What are your names? Would you like a picture?"

The women stood. "Your Highness, I'm Jeannette," said the redhead, "and this is my partner Robyn. We live on the island. We want to know if the reports were true—that you were coming out?"

Kimmy smiled. "Yes. An official statement will be made, but the news reports are true. My girlfriend, Jane, and I met recently."

"Does this mean...things will change?" said Robyn.

"Yes," said Kimmy. "I promise there will be changes. My father's vision of what the country should be is not mine. It will take time to change hearts and minds, but I will champion the cause." She motioned to Kita. "I've already made a promise that no girl or boy will have to grow up scared and alone just because of their sexuality or gender identity. Everyone is a citizen and should be treated equally."

"Thank you, Your Highness," said Jeannette. "We know it will take time, and people will fight, but knowing the government supports us is like a light coming on in the darkness."

"I know it's been difficult, and I was part of the problem, but I will do everything in my power to promote change, understanding, and unity."

"Thank you," said Robyn. "Your coming-out means so much to us. It gives us a new-found optimism and hope."

Kimmy hugged both women. "It's taken me a long time to discover myself, and I'm sorry it did. But I'm much happier. Before you go, would you like a picture?"

Kita and Kimmy posed for a picture, and the couple left with a friendly wave. They took several more pictures before Ryan and Adrestia arrived. Kimmy halted the line and waved them over.

"What do we do?" said Kimmy. "This line is never going to end. I don't want to say no, but we have a schedule to maintain."

Kita tapped her nail against her teeth. "How about we invite them to the luau tonight? I'm sure not everyone will be able to make it. Also, invite some locals, first responders, military, and local leaders. We don't have to explain why the Vehlixen are parked around the area. We can do more pictures then."

Kimmy gave Kita an amused look. "When did you become an expert at public relations?"

Kita shrugged. "It just came to me."

Kimmy waved over Daisy and her Secret Service detail and gave them the change in plans for the night's luau. She stepped up to the line of people. "Everyone, I'm sorry, but I have to go. My assistant, Miss King, will give you passes and details to a private luau I'm hosting tonight. I hope to see you all there." Kimmy waved to them and then returned to the group. "GoPro on, Ryan?"

He hit a button on the camera on his chest and then tapped on his phone. "Sprokkit, Bernoot, Velositi, can you hear and see?"

"Yes," said Sprokkit.

"Yo! What am I looking at?" said Bernoot.

Velositi giggled. "You are pointing the camera at Kita's chest."

Ryan turned. "Oh. Sorry, Kita."

Kita rolled her eyes.

"Shall we go?" Kimmy took Kita's hand, and they walked down the path.

"How was your night, Ryan?" said Kita.

"I, ah, took Sarah to the beach, dinner, and saw the manta rays."

"Get a kiss for your trouble?"

Ryan smiled. "Yeah. Kimmy, can she come to the luau?"

"She's in the military. How much time off do you think I can grant her?"

"Well, I..."

Kita giggled at Kimmy. "You're so mean."

Kimmy smiled. "Her plane doesn't leave until we do, so I guess it's no problem. What did you do, Nicole?"

"My day wasn't as exciting as yours. I told you Kita was a handful." Kimmy laughed. "I took Bernoot to the beach, drove around the north side of the island, found a lesbian club, and got laid. Congratulations on coming-out. I think yours has got to be the biggest coming-out splash ever."

Kimmy blushed. "I didn't mean it to be my coming-out. I was just having fun. It is liberating. I feel like a weight has been lifted from my shoulders and can't help but think I wasted so much time trying to be straight, thinking something was wrong with me—how every touch and kiss felt wrong. And yet, being with a woman never occurred to me—not until Kita kissed me. It explains why I've been so bitchy for the last twelve years. I just wish I knew myself better and had the strength and courage to do it earlier."

"But, if you had done it earlier, you would not have met Kita," said Velositi from Ryan's phone.

"True," said Kimmy. "I wouldn't have her, and who knows where I'd be." She squeezed Kita's hand and hugged her arm.

"I don't know if things happen for a reason," said Adrestia, "but you seized the opportunity when it presented itself. That takes courage—especially something as life-changing as this. I know when I came-out, I was scared to death. I thought the world was going to hate me. And, some of it did. My parents kicked me out, and I lived with my girlfriend's family until I joined the Air Force. I still send them a Xmas card, even after she dumped me."

"That's awful," said Kimmy. "That shouldn't happen."

"You've got a lot of work ahead of you, Your Highness. Fighting the entrenched ideology of the conservatives is going to take a massive effort."

"I know," said Kimmy. "There is a lot I want to change. I started this morning by firing Mister Buchannan."

"Your Chief of Staff?" scoffed Adrestia. "He was an ass and a pig."

"He's the first of many, but I have to build a new coalition to fill the holes. I think if I pull the hawks away from the conservatives, I can align them with the liberals."

"The world is too dangerous not to have a strong military," said Adrestia.

The group reached the entrance to the park's lava tube and stopped. Amber lights lit the paved path through the tube.

"Wow, it's tall," said Kita.

"Sprokkit could easily stand in there," said Ryan. "Can you imagine the amount of lava that traveled through this? All the way to the ocean."

"What do you think, Velositi?" said Kita.

"It is impressive. It does not leave much room to maneuver or have much cover. We will have to be careful."

The temperature dropped as they entered the 400-foot-long tube. Water seeped in through the ceiling, and a drop hit Kita's bare shoulder. On the wall, lines of hardened lava showed the lava level over time, back when it had been flowing.

Kimmy's phone buzzed, and she read the text. "Kerr's team has found the lava tube," she announced to everyone.

"I guess we'll get to see a lot more of these," said Ryan.

The group exited the lava tube back into the warmth of the rainforest. They stepped aside to let a family with two kids pass. Kita pulled Kimmy in for a kiss.

"Goddamn dykes. Get out of the way and quit corrupting my kids. They don't need to see that shit," snarled the father as the family passed.

"What did you call me?" yelled Kita. She let go of Kimmy and charged the large round man.

"Kita!" called Kimmy as she turned around, revealing who she was. "Security!"

"You want to say that to my face?" Kita snarled, stepping up to the father.

"Get lost, bitch."

"You're not man enough to say it to my face? You slagging coward!"

"Know your place, dyke." The father slapped Kita across the face, knocking her to the ground.

"Back off, asshole," said Adrestia. She and Ryan stepped between Kita and the father.

Kimmy hurried to help Kita up, but it turned into holding Kita back.

*I'm going to bury him. I'll take him to the volcano and throw him. I will not be humiliated by some fat, bigoted man.*

"Back off, bitch, or you'll get one, too," said the father to Adrestia.

Three Secret Service agents ran up. Two took over holding Kita. Kimmy and O'Brien joined Adrestia. O'Brien produced his badge.

"I'm Special Agent in Charge O'Brien, Sir, EUS Secret Service."

"About time," said the father. "These dykes are being indecent in the park."

"I think we've met the only person who hasn't seen the headlines," said Kimmy with a nasty look. "Kneel."

"Who the hell are you?"

"Princess Kimberly Roosevelt—one of the ones you've been so affectionately calling *dyke*."

The father looked at O'Brien. "She is Princess Kimberly Roosevelt, Sir."

The father's face turned white as he and his family took a knee.

Kimmy took out her phone and tapped on it. She showed it to the father. "As of this morning, the world knows I'm gay. The girl you just assaulted is my girlfriend. Assaulting her is the same as assaulting me. I will not stand for this behavior. I ignored it before because I didn't understand, but now I do. I will not tolerate discrimination. We are all citizens of the Empire. Now, I will give you a chance to apologize to myself, my girlfriend, Jane, and Colonel Adrestia. You may rise."

The family stood.

Kimmy looked over at Kita. "Is she calm?"

"Yes, Your Highness," said an agent with his hand on Kita's shoulder.

"Come here, Jane," said Kimmy.

Kita, escorted by the two Secret Service agents, stood next to Kimmy and Adrestia. She folded her arms and glared. "I will not accept an apology from him."

"Jane, the only way things will change is if there are understanding and forgiveness."

"He *hit* me, Kimmy!"

"I know, and I am sorry. I promise to make it up to you. What will make the sting go away?"

*I want to watch him be humiliated.* "Where's he from?" Kita said with a growl.

"Charleston, South Carolina," the father said unhappily.

"*Your Royal Highness*," added Adrestia.

The father sighed. "Your Royal Highness."

Kita pulled out her phone and ran a search for gay and lesbian organizations in Charleston. She found three. "Four hundred hours of community service working with the gay youth of one of these organizations." She showed Kimmy the list.

"I'll make it two hundred hours," said Kimmy. "That sounds fair."

The father huffed. "You want me to work with a bunch of—"

"Don't say it," said Adrestia.

"Yes," said Kimmy. "You will learn these kids are no different than your own. Now, apologize so my family and yours can get back to their vacations."

The father looked at the ground. "I—"

"Look me in the eyes," snarled Kita.

The father looked up. He couldn't maintain eye contact for more than a second. "Your Highness, I'm sorry for my language and for disrespecting the throne. I'm a proud citizen of the Empire. I would never disgrace it. I'm sorry."

"That covers me," said Kimmy. "How about Jane?"

"I'm sorry for hitting you, Your Highness."

Kita sneered. She pointed to his kids. "You two, come here."

The two children looked at their mother, who pushed them toward Kita.

Kita knelt to be at eye level with the two boys. "How old are you?" she said in a friendly tone.

"Seven."

"Five."

"Do you know why your dad is in trouble?" said Kita.

"He hit you," said the seven-year-old.

"That's part of it. You both know you should never hit anyone, right?"

"Yes, Your Highness," they said together.

"You won't ever do that, right?"

"No, Your Highness."

"Good. Now, do you want to know why your dad's really in trouble?"

They looked at her curiously.

"Would you treat me any differently than your mom?"

"No."

"Your dad would never hit your mom, would he?"

"No."

"That's good. Now, unlike your mom, who loves your dad, I love the princess."

"That's bad," said the five-year-old.

"Why?"

The boys shrugged.

"A second ago, I was no different than your mom. Now, because I love a girl, I'm different?"

"You just are," said the seven-year-old.

"Ok. You're allowed to believe what you want to believe, and I'm allowed to believe what I want to believe. That's part of our freedoms. Fair?"

The boys nodded.

"Your dad is in trouble because he tried to force me to believe what he believes. He violated my freedom."

"Freedom is sacred," said the seven-year-old.

"It is," said Kita. "And it's wrong to try and take it from someone. Your dad is in trouble for trying to take my, Colonel Adrestia, and the princess's freedom. That's not cool, is it?"

"No," they said together.

"So, next time your dad tries to take someone's freedom from them, are you going to let him? It's your duty as a citizen to preserve freedom."

"We won't let him," said the five-year-old.

"Good. Enjoy the rest of your vacation." Kita waved the kids back to their mother. "I hope you learned a lesson," Kita hissed at the father. "And just remember, dykes are guarding your freedom." She pointed to Adrestia.

Kimmy let out a long breath. "Thank you, sir. Have a nice day." She waved for O'Brien to escort the father away. She looked at Kita. "That was brilliant and evil at the same time."

Kita shrugged. "It just came to me."

Kita and Velositi led the convoy of Vehlixen and military vehicles south on Queen Ka'ahumanu Highway through the lava fields. Dressed in her Air Force battle uniform, Kita's coat flapped in the wind.

*I like these military uniforms now that I have some that fit correctly.* "Ugh, it's boring out here," said Kita as they passed miles of lava.

"It has a beauty to it," said Velositi. "Did you know donkeys live out here?"

"How does a donkey survive out here?"

"Grass and rainwater. They are descendants of donkeys brought here to work the plantations. The state is trying to round them up and adopt them out."

"Huh. Don't hit a donkey, ok?"

Velositi chirped laughter.

Kita's phone rang, and she pulled it from her back pocket. It was Kimmy. The Secret Service had refused to let Kimmy go on the mission to recover the Axiom of Command. They tried to prevent Kita from going, but a fit and a promise that she would have a personal escort made them relent.

"Hey, love. Miss me already?" teased Kita.

"Hi, girls. I know it's only been half an hour, but it seems like forever."

"You're not missing much, just lava and donkeys."

"Donkeys?"

"I have been reading websites about Hawaii," said Velositi. "Several stated that donkeys live in the western portion of the big island."

"Fascinating," said Kimmy.

"What are you doing?" said Kita.

"I'm signing thank you cards to last night's guests and listening to the news. We're still the hot topic. All the experts are trying to guess what I'm going to do next, and even more are trying to figure out who you are. The heat's on from the conservatives. They're threatening everything from a congressional walkout to rebellion. The liberals are stepping up, claiming it's the dawn of a new era. Do me a favor and don't look at the news. They're somewhat respectful toward me, but it's open season on you."

Kita sighed. "I never paid attention to the news before, why start now?"

"Your identity has been scrubbed from the public record, and your employees and anyone who knew you in Reading has been sworn to secrecy. I, ah, what do you want to do with your yard?"

"I don't know. There's no use in me keeping it. I'm never going back, am I?"

"For your safety, I'd prefer that you didn't."

*What do I do? It's all I have left of Dad. But what good is it if I never get to see it again? I don't miss it. Like Velositi said, it's not my dream. It was Dad's. Is it time to cut the cord?* "Can you send someone to take pictures?"

"Of course. I'll send a professional photographer. Are there any personal items you want recovered?"

Kita frowned. *What do I want? Any of it? Most of it is junk, and what Dad did own belonged to the yard. There's nothing in the office. Is there anything? There must be something...* "I, ah...in the mechanic's shed is a small gray metal toolbox full of tools. My dad gave it to me. I hope Mickey didn't walk off with it."

"We'll find it," said Kimmy. "Anything from your apartment?"

"I haven't been evicted?"

"I paid what was owed and for another month. So, your stuff is still there."

"I don't think there's anything. You've given me way better stuff than I ever owned," said Kita.

"No pictures, stuffed animals, clothes...anything?" said Kimmy softly.

"All my pictures are on my phone. My favorite shirt is gone, but Velositi got me a better one, and I didn't have any stuffed animals. You can just junk the rest. I don't think it's worth donating."

"Ok, and your phone has been taken over by the Secret Service."

Kita grunted. "They're listening?"

"No. Sensitive numbers—like yours—are blacklisted, so unauthorized persons can't call you. We will get you a more secure phone."

"Ok..." *I suddenly feel like more bars are going up than coming down. But, it's not my fear that's building them. I understand Kimmy needs to be kept safe, but me?* "Is this necessary?"

"I'm sorry," said Kimmy. "But it comes with me, unfortunately. I promise they won't be overbearing or restrict you. It's there for your safety and comfort. The last thing you want is to be assaulted by reporters or angry citizens."

"Angry citizens?"

"The conservatives are upset. What's on the news is just the tip of the iceberg. What's flying around the internet is far worse."

"Oh, dear," said Velositi.

"What is it?" said Kita.

"I just checked the news and the comments on a few stories. Can they make death and rape threats, Kimmy?"

"They aren't supposed to, but we can't track down all of them, only the ones deemed credible by the Secret Service and IBI. They already have more than a dozen leads they're running down."

"Great," muttered Kita. "And there's nothing I can do?"

"Not right now," said Kimmy. "You'll just have to ignore it and let the Secret Service and IBI handle it. We'll release a statement and make some public appearances over the next few weeks so people can see you, and the tension will ease. Until then, just keep searching for the Axiom. How was dive class this morning?"

"Between the team and what you taught me—I won't drown."

Kita's morning started with dive training on how to breathe through a mask and swim with fins and an underwater scooter. An operator from Team Five would carry her tanks and control her air on the mission. According to the briefing Kerr gave, the lava tube was full of water for a thousand yards.

"You need to ask Velositi. She's the one who doesn't like water," said Kita.

"Is there a problem, Velositi?" said Kimmy.

"Morphicons do not swim, we walk along the bottom, and I do not like being in water over my head, but I will go where the mission takes me."

"Can you drown?" said Kita uneasily.

"No, but I can become stuck and not be able to reach the shore."

"I will alert the Navy divers in Honolulu to be on standby, in case we have to lift you out," said Kimmy.

"You can do that?" said Velositi.

"The Navy can recover large sunken ships. Getting you out of the water shouldn't be a problem—no matter how deep you go."

"That is a worry off my mind," said Velositi. "Thank you."

"Anything else?" said Kimmy.

"Nothing that we can prepare for."

"What's on your mind?" said Kita gently. She stroked Velositi's gas tank.

"I am concerned about what happens when we find the Axiom. How does it know whom to choose? Will it choose one of us, or will we have to take it back home?"

"You'd leave?" said Kimmy. "But, what about the Neophormes?"

"I have thought about that scenario. I would leave Bernoot and Sprokkit here and return with the Axiom. Once a leader is chosen, I will lead a group of Vehlixen here to fulfill my promise."

"How long will that take?"

"I do not know. The trip to Earth took ten cycles."

"That's a twenty-five-year round trip!" yelled Kimmy.

"I know. I am sorry. But I do not see an alternative."

"We could win with the three of you," said Kimmy. "Axiom or not."

"My mission is to retrieve the Axiom. I promise we will get rid of the Neophormes. It might just take longer than I thought."

"Goddamnit! We had a deal!"

"I will uphold my end of the bargain," said Velositi. "But the Axiom is vital to our success. I cannot win a small battle at the risk of losing the war."

Kita sniffed. She was annoyed that she couldn't wipe the tears from her eyes. "Why don't we get it first? Once we have it, we can decide what to do."

"Yes," said Velositi. "Conjecture is not helping."

"Kimmy?" whispered Kita.

"Find it," Kimmy snarled. "We'll take it back to the bunker and see what it is."

Velositi made an unhappy sound. "I need to take it—"

"It has taken you forty-five years. You can wait a few weeks!" yelled Kimmy.

"My planet could be dying."

"And mine is threatened. You said it yourself. The Neophormes want to conquer worlds. Are you going to worry about a threat far from you or in front of you?"

"I understand," said Velositi. "We can find a solution."

"All Dagger elements. Dagger Two. We have a Hind D gunship inbound from the east," came a report over the radio.

"Dagger Two, Dagger Six. Rodger. All elements take evasive action."

"Dagger Six, Dagger Skywatch. Scrambling air assets. Twenty seconds out."

"What is going on?" said Velositi.

"A Hind D is a Soviet gunship!" said Kimmy. "That's not human. That's Shelbak."

"Vehlixen, Neophorm Shelbak spotted to the east. Morph and engage," ordered Velositi.

Velositi morphed, cradling Kita in her arm.

"There!" said Kita. She pointed to a blob above the horizon.

Bernoot, Sprokkit, Adrestia, and Ryan ran up.

Velositi set Kita down. "Bernoot, Sprokkit, spread out and shoot him down."

The Vehlixen jogged into the lava field, firing at the gunship.

Adrestia grabbed Kita by the back of her uniform. "Come on."

"Where are we going?"

"To take cover." Adrestia led them down the highway's far shoulder. She motioned Kita and Ryan to lay on the embankment with her.

Kita didn't want to hide in the dirt. She took off her helmet and crawled toward the road.

"Where are you going?" said Adrestia.

"To see."

The military vehicles were in a wishbone formation—alternating pulling off at an angle on either side of the road—and the team moved into the lava field. From above came a roar. Four F-22s flew in from the west just above the ground. The lead pair fired a set of missiles that exploded on the slow-moving Shelbak. The other F-22s engaged their 20mm cannons. Shelbak morphed and dropped into the lava field.

A high-pitched motorcycle engine came from the south. Kita turned as a dark green Honda RVF1000 wove its way through the parked vehicles.

"It doesn't have a rider," said Kita.

The RVF1000 morphed and leaped into the lava field shooting at the operators. The F-22s came around and fired at Shelbak.

"What are we going to do?" said Kita.

"We're not going to do anything," said Adrestia, clutching her rifle. "Our job is to stay out of the way. They should be able to handle two Neophormes."

Kita's phone rang. It was Kimmy. "Hey."

"What happened? Why'd you hang up?" Kimmy said tersely.

"Easy. I had to take cover."

"Are you ok?"

"I'm fine. The battle is out in the lava field. We have two Neophormes—a light and a heavy."

"The light would be Ultranova. Can you see what's going on?"

"Ah...Sprokkit and Bernoot are fighting Shelbak. Velositi is taking on Ultranova. The operators are assisting, and so are the fighters."

Kimmy hummed. "Ok. I've alerted Schofield Barracks on Oahu. They're sending a flight of Apaches. Marine and Naval aviation units are en route and should be there soon."

Shelbak's chest exploded after a hit from Sprokkit.

"The two sides are close together. They won't hit the Vehlixen, will they?" said Kita.

"No. Team Five has two air traffic controllers assigned to them. They'll be directing fire missions."

"Oh, slag!"

"What?" said Kimmy.

"The two Neophormes just morphed into a much bigger Morphicon with more guns."

"I didn't know Neophormes could bond."

Kita shrugged. "I didn't know either, but it just picked up Bernoot and threw him."

Kimmy made an irritated sound. "Dammit. Kerr is not helpful. He thinks his team can handle this."

"The Neophorm just turned a set of cannons on the team," said Kita.

"I don't have any assets on the big island," Kimmy said in a huff. "They're all on Oahu. I'm scrambling the Marines and as much airpower as I can get. The Kitty Hawk carrier group is in the area. They can send more air assets. We can pound them to death from the air. I'll prove to Velositi that we don't need the Axiom to defeat the Neophormes."

Kita shrugged. "Whatever you say."

"I thought you'd object when she said she would leave."

"I—I was going to, but I didn't want to get between you. I don't want to be caught in the middle. That's what I was trying to prevent. You can work it out between you. I will help you find a solution. But, don't force me to choose."

Kimmy sighed. "I understand. But together we should be able to—"

"Just don't," whispered Kita.

"I'm sorry. I just can't let this opportunity slip away."

"I know. Just remember, I'm your girlfriend, not one of your subordinates."

"I expect you to support me."

"I do." Kita blinked a tear away and hung up the phone.

"Ok?" said Adrestia.

"No," said Kita.

Adrestia sighed. "Is there anything I can do to fix it now?"

"No."

"Then you're going to have to put it aside and concentrate on what's in front of us. You can't fix it if you're dead."

More fighters rumbled overhead and fired a barrage of missiles that slammed into the bonded Neophorm.

Kita's phone rang again. She sighed and picked it up, expecting it to be Kimmy, but it was Velositi.

"Hey," said Kita. "Is everything ok?"

"We are doing our best. A bonded pair can take more damage and has twice the system cores to destroy."

"Are the fighters helping?"

"Yes. They are keeping it off balance and preventing it from acquiring targets accurately. My concern is the team. They are not firing much, and Captain Kerr is putting them directly in our line of fire."

Kita grunted. "Ok. If Kerr isn't helpful, you can talk to the team directly. Tell them where to go. The ones talking to the fighters are called combat controllers. They tell the fighters where to shoot."

"That is helpful. If I can coordinate our attacks, we can do more damage," said Velositi.

"Kimmy said more helicopters and fighters are coming. How are you?"

"I am not wounded, but Bernoot and Sprokkit have sustained damage."

"Is it serious?" said Kita, trying to keep the worry from her voice.

"No," said Velositi, "but too many shots from a bonded pair can be dangerous. Their cannons are more powerful."

"Be careful. I love you."

"You sound unhappy," said Velositi flatly.

"I am, but we'll talk about it later."

"Did I do something?"

Kita rolled her eyes. "Yes, but concentrate on the fight. Not me."

"If you are not right, I am not right."

"You're going to leave me for twenty-five years. Do you know how old I'm going to be?"

"I have to return the Axiom," said Velositi firmly.

"Why you? Send Sprokkit."

Velositi didn't answer.

*She's never not answered me before. What's wrong with Sprokkit returning the Axiom? Doesn't she want to stay with me? I want an answer.* "Is the Axiom more important than me?"

"It will save my planet," said Velositi quietly.

"Then send Sprokkit!"

Velositi was silent.

"What's wrong with sending Sprokkit?" demanded Kita.

"I am sorry," said Velositi as she hung up.

"By the Crushing Depths," snarled Kita. "They've both lost their minds."

"What?" said Adrestia.

"Kimmy wants me to push Velositi to delay returning home with the Axiom. Velositi can send Sprokkit with the Axiom but refuses. She'd rather leave Sprokkit and Bernoot here. She's choosing the Axiom over me. I don't know why."

"Velositi does things to get noticed. I bet whoever returns the Axiom gets a lot of glory. I'd even wager some pay that she thinks the Axiom will choose her."

"Oh, slag," muttered Kita.

"You're not going to throw a fit, are you?"

Kita laughed darkly. "Not here. I'm way too pissed for that."

A pair of Apache helicopters rushed up from the coast. They fired a series of rockets and hellfire missiles at the Neophorm. They flew to the east, and another pair replaced them. Missiles from attacking fighters slammed into the Neophorm, and large areas of the fourteen-foot Neophorm's body glowed red.

*It can't take much more.*

Seahawk helicopters came from the north. Using the highway as a landing pad, they landed and disgorged a squad of Marines each. The Marines formed up and pushed out into the lava field firing at the Neophorm.

*I hope this is enough to take the Neophorm down.*

A set of explosions rocked the Neophorm. It morphed back into Ultranova and Shelbak. Shelbak morphed into the Hind D helicopter and took off, and fighters and Apaches engaged it. In a series of explosions, Shelbak fell from the sky and crashed into the lava field. More missiles and rockets hit him, and he didn't get up.

Ultranova rushed toward the highway on a damaged leg. Most of her torso and arms were glowing red. Velositi tackled her, and they rolled down a hill. A series of bright explosions lit the lava field. Ultranova flipped atop a mound of lava. Velositi landed behind her, dropped to her hand, and whipped her legs around, knocking Ultranova to the ground. Velositi backflipped over Ultranova and fired into her middle, then grabbed Ultranova's head, put her cannons to Ultranova's back, and fired. Ultranova's chest exploded outward. Velositi dropped the body and walked away.

Kita and the others stood up. She dialed Kimmy and handed the phone to Adrestia. "Tell Kimmy it's over. They can come to clean up."

"Why don't you do it?"

"Because I'm mad at both of them."

Adrestia nodded. "Sorry, Your Highness. Kita is upset...She says at both you and Velositi, but I think more at Velositi. The Neophormes have been destroyed. The team is checking them now, and they will be ready for retrieval...Yes, Your Highness. I can't promise she'll take it." She lowered the phone. "Kita, the Princess says she's sorry and wants to talk to you."

Kita wiggled her nose. She held out her hand, and Adrestia handed the phone over. "Hello?"

"Kita, I'm sorry. It was wrong of me to use you as leverage over Velositi. It's between me and her. I know you'll love us no matter what we do. Forgive me?"

"Yeah. I understand. After watching, I can see that you can't defeat the Neophormes without the Vehlixen. The Neophormes would have chewed up Team Five. The fighters are effective, but we can't match them on the ground. Velositi said Kerr wasn't performing as he should. The team wasn't firing and was in the way."

"I'll look into it. You still don't sound ok."

Kita huffed. "I'm furious at Velositi. I think she's choosing the Axiom over me."

"But, why?"

"Nicole says Velositi wants the glory. I plan on talking to her," said Kita grumpily.

"That makes sense. Velositi does strike me as the kind that would want the glory."

"Here she comes. I'll talk to you later. I love you."

"I love you."

Kita hung up as Velositi, and the other Vehlixen climbed onto the highway.

"Are you ok?" Ryan said to Sprokkit.

"A bonded pair contains a lot of firepower. It hurts, but I will be fine."

"You can still dive, right?" said Ryan.

"Yes. It won't limit my effectiveness."

"How are you, Bernoot?" said Adrestia.

"Yo! Big boy packs a punch, but I added a bonded to my kill count."

Kita looked at Velositi and turned up her nose.

"Kita, you must understand—"

"I understand just fine!" yelled Kita. "You're choosing the Axiom over me."

Velositi's eyes dimmed. "I have worked my whole life for this."

"I gave up my life for you, and you're going to leave me! Do I mean that little to you? You said you weren't using me, and you *are*! I'm nothing but a means to an end. Everything you told me means nothing. Do you even love me?"

Plasma leaked from Velositi's eyes. "Yes. Yes, of course, I do. I meant everything I said. I care about you. I adore you. I love you. But this *is* my chance to be great. You have to understand that. It means a great deal to me. Please."

Kita's eyes flashed with anger. "You said greatness chooses us. How do you know returning with the Axiom will make you great? It sounds to me like you're trying to be great. You don't even want to share credit with Bernoot or Sprokkit. You want to leave them here. How many more people are you going to use to get your shot at glory? That's three of us, plus the humans that have died this morning. You're supposed to be better than this."

"I told you it was my dream."

"And dreams change!" Kita shrieked. "You taught me that. You know what? I'll give you your slagging dream. I'll help you get the Axiom. Once you have it in your hands, you can decide what's more important—your dream or your friends. But I am not riding with you. I'd rather ride with Sprokkit. At least he's honest about his willingness to throw me under the bus."

Kita grabbed her helmet and hurled it at Velositi. She stomped over to a military vehicle and sat on the massive bumper. She wiped at the tears in her eyes. Voices startled her. "What?" Kita screamed at a group of Marines gathered on the other side of the truck.

"Marines, take it somewhere else," said Adrestia as she sat down next to Kita and put her arm around Kita. "I'm sorry."

Kita put her head on Adrestia's shoulder and cried.

BEHIND A MILITARY VEHICLE, KITA AND ADRESTIA STRIPPED OFF THEIR BATTLE uniforms down to their swimsuits. Kita wore her black and pink bikini, and Adrestia had a black one piece. They helped each other into the wetsuits and put their uniforms in waterproof bags.

Kita said little on the ride from the attack site on the highway to Kiholo Bay, the location of the lava tube. Her anger turned to melancholy. She was doing her best not to bring everyone down.

"Ready?" said Adrestia.

Kita nodded.

They walked from behind the vehicle to the beach. The team waited, ready to go. They still wore their uniforms under their scuba gear.

"Ok," said Kerr, "we have a hundred yards of coral to cross before we reach the edge of the bay. The coral is flat, but *be careful*, there are six-foot crevasses that you don't want to get stuck in. Because of the delay, we missed the tide, so the water won't be deep enough to swim. We'll have to walk.

"Once we reach the edge of the coral, we'll dive. The tube entrance is to the northwest and twenty-five feet down, and then it's a thousand yards before the tube goes dry. Once in the tube, we stash the tanks, scooters, and fins, and prepare for combat operations. Petty Officer Reynolds will escort Colonel Adrestia. Petty Officer Jacobs will escort Captain Callaghan. Master Sergeant Boxer will escort Her Highness. Any questions?"

The team shook their heads.

A big man with arms the size of logs appeared in front of Kita. "Your Highness, I'm Master Sergeant Boxer. I have your mask and fins." He also carried two large air tanks, a small emergency tank on his hip, a rifle, the underwater scooter, and a rucksack on his front.

"You need a hand?" said Kita.

"No problem, Your Highness. Follow me."

"Hey, yo bro!" said Bernoot. "Me and Sprokkit will carry our peeps out. They won't slow the show that way."

Kita shrugged. That sounded preferable to navigating the reef. "Let's do that. I'll see you out there, Master Sergeant."

"No problem, Your Highness."

*He looks relieved. I'm sure he'd never hear the end of it if I fell into a hole.*

Bernoot picked up Kita and Adrestia and waded into the water. He made a game of hopping from one set of corals to the next. The corals were six feet high, flat on top, and square. Some had grown into each other creating bigger blocks. Behind them, Sprokkit and Velositi picked their way forward, followed by the team.

"It's pretty out here," said Adrestia.

The water was a turquoise color, and a warm breeze blew. Palm trees and bushes grew around the bay, and lava fields lay beyond.

"It is nice," said Kita sadly.

"I'm sorry," said Adrestia.

"I just don't understand. I thought she loved me and wanted to stay."

"You gave her an option. We'll see what she decides. Give her some time. Maybe she'll come to her senses."

"Bernoot," said Kita, "what do you think of Velositi returning home with the Axiom?"

"Yo, our mission is to sniff it out and bringing it back."

"And if Velositi leaves you here?"

"She's the boss. I do what she tells me."

"Even if she takes all the recognition?"

"Why would she do that?"

"The most important thing is the Axiom returns home," said Sprokkit. "Recognition is secondary."

"Seems to Velositi it's the important thing," said Adrestia.

"Velositi will do what is right."

"I don't doubt that, but she's keeping you from getting the recognition you deserve. You all had a part in recovering the Axiom."

"Whatever Velositi's motives are does not matter as long as the Axiom is returned," said Sprokkit gruffly.

"And if the Axiom chooses her?" said Kita.

"She will make an excellent leader," said Sprokkit. "You will have to remain here. You cannot survive on our planet." his eyes brightened.

*He seems happy about that.* "Ryan has to stay, too."

"I am deciding if I want to stay. Ryan and I can accomplish much together."

*Great. Velositi leaves, and I'm stuck with Sprokkit. At least I have Kimmy...but, will she want me if I don't have Velositi? I'm not special or useful then. That's...That's not right. That's worst-case scenario thinking. Kimmy loves me for me, and I better get used to the idea. They already call me* Your Highness. *Who would have ever dreamed that?*

Bernoot stopped. "End of the line." He set Kita and Adrestia down.

Kita walked to the edge and looked over. It was a long way down, and she couldn't see the bottom making all the hair on the back of her neck stand up. Adrestia came up next to her. "So, all those dumb things I did before..."

"Yeah?"

"They don't look half as dumb as this."

Adrestia laughed. "This is probably the safest thing you've done."

The rest of the operators arrived and donned their gear. In twos and threes, they stepped off the knee-deep reef and sank into the dark water below. Boxer found Kita and helped her put on her fins and mask. He jumped into the water.

Kita gulped. *Oh, slag me.* She stepped off; her dry bag slung over her shoulder. Landing in the water, she did her best to float. Boxer motioned for her to dive. *I don't want to go into the deep, dark water.* Kita dove, kicking with her fins as bubbles from her mask rose to the surface. Boxer took her hand and guided her down the cliff face toward a group of lights.

Boxer turned his light on. The lava tube was a big black spot on the side of the cliff face. The lights disappeared into the opening. When they reached the opening, Boxer placed Kita's hand on the underwater scooter and started it. The device pulled them forward into the darkness.

———————⟩————————

BOXER HELPED KITA OUT OF THE WATER. CHEMICAL LIGHTS LIT THE DARKNESS revealing the black sides of the lava tube. The operators lined the walls as they took off their scuba gear and readied their combat load. Kita took off her fins and mask and followed Boxer to an empty spot. Adrestia and Reynolds joined them.

Adrestia shook the water from her M-4 rifle. "That was a wild swim."

*Not the word I would use.* "I think I'll stick to the pool." Kita ran her hand through her hair, feeling the saltwater. *Yuck. No showers around here, either.* Kita took off her dry bag and stripped off her wetsuit. Boxer took it from her and laid it out to dry. She put on her uniform, folded up her dry bag, and put it next to her wetsuit.

Bernoot emerged from the water, his eyes glowing in the dark. He walked over to Adrestia. "Pretty gnarly drop. You miss the grab, and it's a long walk back to Cali."

"Maybe Velositi will miss it," said Kita.

"Oh, dudette, harsh."

"She can use the time to think about what's important to her."

"The world is at stake! Nothing more important than that," said Bernoot.

"I'm not arguing that. I'm arguing she doesn't need to go. She could send you with the Axiom."

Bernoot's eyes lit. "We still have a rumble at home."

"And there's a fight here. She could lead, win, and get all the glory for it."

"She's an awesome fighter, and it's an awesome fight at home. Big players show up for big games."

Kita grumbled. "Do—"

Adrestia grabbed Kita's arm. "Leave him be. He doesn't understand. You'll just make yourself angry."

Kita nodded.

Sprokkit and Velositi emerged. Kita turned her back when Velositi walked by. A hand signal passed down the line.

"We're moving out, Your Highness," said Boxer.

"Ok."

Surrounded by Boxer, Adrestia, and Reynolds, Kita followed the dimly lit silhouettes into the dark lava tube.

KITA TRUDGED ALONG AND PULLED HER PHONE FROM HER POCKET. THE STEP counter she set said they were averaging eight thousand steps an hour. Kita calculated the distance traveled—almost twenty miles. *No wonder I'm exhausted. How does Boxer do it?* She guessed he carried seventy-five pounds of gear. *I'd ask, but I don't want to get told to shut up again.* Boxer and Adrestia had been polite about it, but the message was the same.

Up ahead, Kita saw a set of glowing blue eyes. *Too short for Bernoot or Sprokkit. What does she want?*

"Kita?" said Velositi when her group came close.

"I'm not supposed to talk," said Kita politely.

"Please, listen to me."

Kita shrugged. "Walk and talk."

"I am sorry I have to leave, but it is my mission to return the Axiom. When I return it, I will have the leverage with the Elders to send more Vehlixen back to wipe out the Neophormes. When the war is over, I promise to come back to you. The war will not last long once the Axiom selects a new leader. Please, you must be patient. Enjoy the time we have spent together."

"Damn," said Adrestia. "If that was supposed to make me want to wait for you, I'm turning around and walking the other way."

Velositi's eyes dimmed.

"I will do what I promised," said Kita. "I will make sure you get the Axiom. What you decide to do with it is up to you. Just know, if you leave, I won't be here when you return."

"Why do you refuse to understand?" yelled Velositi.

Kita put a finger to her lips. "Shhh. Operational security."

Adrestia rolled her eyes.

"Kita, please," whispered Velositi.

"As great as you are, you can't have it all," said Kita. "We all make sacrifices for what we want. You must decide what you want. No matter what you decide, I will be happy for you. You will be the hero you desire. I'll have what I want —love."

"I should never have let you be with Kimmy," hissed Velositi.

"It wouldn't matter. With or without Kimmy, I would never wait for you. I want to be loved, adored, and appreciated. Leaving me to be a hero and reap the glory, means you aren't interested in anything I care about. I want you to be the hero. You could do it here and share it with me, but here obviously isn't good enough. I'm sorry it's not. I love you. I always will. Now go away. You just break my heart."

Velositi's eyes dimmed as she moved back to the head of the column.

Adrestia put an arm around Kita. "I'm sorry. But, don't fall apart on me. I need you collected."

"I'm fine," said Kita. "Everything is cold and numb." Boxer looked relieved. *My reputation precedes me. You don't want to carry me, too?*

EVERYONE AHEAD OF KITA TOOK A KNEE. BOXER PUT A HAND ON HER shoulder and pushed her down. "What is it?"

"Something ahead is interesting, Your Highness," said Boxer.

"Let's go see."

"If they need you, Your Highness, they'll call for us."

"They may not know they need me." Kita ran forward in a crouch past the operators.

"Dammit," said Adrestia as she led Boxer and Reynolds after Kita.

Kita moved next to Velositi, Sprokkit, and Kerr. "Whoa, what is that?"

Spotlighted by the team's lights was a fifteen-foot-tall gray and green statue in the center of a large room. The statue's form was boxy, made of right angles and straight lines. Its head was square, with diagonal-shaped eyes and a mask covering its mouth. The legs were shoulder-width apart, and its outstretched arm held something shiny dangling on a chain from the clenched fist.

"It is an ancient Morphicon," said Sprokkit.

"What's it holding?" said Kita.

"I will not know without inspecting it."

Kita took two steps forward before Boxer and Adrestia grabbed her.

"Oh no you don't," said Adrestia.

"Someone has to look."

"Let the Vehlixen do it. You're here to help them if they need it. Otherwise, I'm keeping you as far away from danger as I can get you."

"Why?"

Adrestia poked Kita's chest. "I am not explaining to the princess how you got injured or killed." She pulled Kita back behind the others.

Bernoot came trotting up from the rear. "Yo! What do we got?"

"Let us go find out," said Velositi. She led the Vehlixen into the center of the room. The operators spread out around the room's perimeter, leaving the liaisons and their guards at the lava tube's exit.

"Any readings?" Velositi asked Sprokkit.

"Negative. He has been without plasma for a very long time."

"How old is he?"

Sprokkit put his hand over the ancient Morphicon's chest. From Sprokkit's finger, a cable attached itself to the ancient Morphicon. "His cellular structure is much larger than ours. I would say he is many generations older than us."

"Old enough to be one of Omegus Hexious' lieutenants?" said Velositi.

"Yes."

"What is this thing?" said Bernoot as he poked at the dangling object in the ancient Morphicon's fist.

Sprokkit inspected it using several instruments from his hands. "It has an energy reading I have never seen before. The atomic structure is configured in a lattice holding nucleotides."

"Sprokkit," called Ryan, "human DNA is made of nucleotides in a double-helix formation."

"Then this not human DNA. It is in a quad-helix formation."

"Is it Morphicon?"

"No. Our information is encoded in a binary system."

"What creature requires so much genetic information that it needs a quad-helix?" said Ryan.

"None that we have ever encountered," said Sprokkit.

"Is it the Axiom?" said Kita.

"If it is the Axiom, it is much smaller than I expected." Sprokkit tried to pull the object free. "The lanyard is stuck in his hand."

"How do we know who it chooses?" said Kita.

"Maybe they have to put it around their neck?" said Ryan.

"Sprokkit, we must get it free," said Velositi.

The Vehlixen tried to pry the hand open.

"It is a no-go," said Bernoot.

"Sprokkit," said Velositi, "what if we used a small amount of plasma to stimulate the cells in his hand, just enough to make his hand pliable?"

"That could work." Sprokkit opened a compartment on his chest and produced a small glowing glass cylinder. He took the top off and pressed the end against various joints in the ancient Morphicon's hand.

The ancient Morphicon's eyes lit green, causing the Vehlixen to take a step back. His extended arm retracted. "Who dares disturb me? Mighty Hexicron, second only to Omegus Hexious."

Velositi stepped forward. "Oh, great one, we have come to reclaim the Axiom."

"Then, the Star Bridge is complete?"

"No, great one. We received your message."

"No message was sent," said Hexicron. "The Star Bridge is to be our link between this planet and Chellexon."

"Great one, we need the Axiom."

Hexicron's eyes brightened. "Has a great leader been constructed?"

"Yes, great one. I believe I am that warrior. I will wield the Axiom of Command and lead us to victory."

Kita rolled her eyes. *I remember telling Sprokkit he was pompous. I changed my mind—the ego on this girl.*

"What is the Axiom of Command?" demanded Hexicron.

"The symbol of Omegus Hexious's fair and just leadership. It gave him the power to protect his people. The Neophormes killed him for it. You and the other lieutenants took the Axiom and hid it from them to protect it until a great warrior could find it and defeat the Neophormes."

Hexicron's eyes brightened. "You fool. Omegus Hexious held the Axiom of Evil. It gave him the power to destroy his enemies and enslave Chellexon. It was not the Neophormes that killed him, but the slaves. Omegus Hexious planned to build a network of Star Bridges to conquer and enslave worlds to build a glorious empire. You are not Neophormes, but the slaves that killed Omegus Hexious, and you will die."

"Oh, this just took a bad turn," said Adrestia as she flipped the safety off her rifle.

"Your Highness, get down against the wall," said Boxer. He pushed Kita down and crouched in front of her.

A series of booms echoed through the tube, punctuating the sounds of the team firing. Flashes of light lit the darkness. Kita wished she could see as Adrestia crawled out into the middle of the tube and fired. Reynolds joined her.

*Why does she get to help and not me?*

On her stomach, Kita tried to see around Boxer's legs. She couldn't see Hexicron, but she could see Velositi flipping and twisting while firing her cannons at an accelerated rate. She didn't seem to attract much fire, which eased Kita's mind.

Kita wasn't sure why, but hearing Velositi get denied was satisfying. It made her feel justified. *Velositi's not as special as she thinks. She's special to me, and that should be all that matters.*

"Get down," said Boxer as he fell on top of Kita.

"Oof," grunted Kita.

There was a loud thud not far from Kita.

"What was that?" said Kita as she tried to weasel out from under Boxer. "Let me up!"

Boxer got off Kita. She sat up and gasped. Part of Bernoot's torso, head, and left arm was lying in the tube.

"Bernoot!" said Adrestia.

"I got him," said Kita. She crawled over next to the stricken Vehlix. "Bernoot! Hey!" she shouted while poking him. Crawling up next to his head, she found his eyes were out. "Bernoot!"

Ryan crawled next to Kita. "This looks bad."

Kita and Ryan crawled around to the damaged area. It wasn't glowing red, just a cold gunmetal color. *That's not good.* They inspected the damage. Ryan found part of a glass cube sticking out of the metal.

"I don't think this can be repaired," said Ryan.

Tears fell down Kita's cheek. She crawled back to Bernoot's head and gave him a hug and a kiss. Ryan put an arm around Kita.

"Poor Nicole," whispered Kita.

Adrestia wasn't paying attention to them. She was busy firing at Hexicron. Kita crawled up next to her but didn't say anything in fear of breaking Adrestia's concentration. Large portions of Hexicron glowed red, and his arms and left leg were moving incorrectly. *How much longer can he last?*

Velositi pummeled Hexicron with her cannon fire. Her shots didn't do much damage, but she fired at four times the speed of Sprokkit. Added together, she was doing a tremendous amount as she ran, flipped, and twisted around Hexicron. She had a few glowing spots, but nothing that looked serious.

Sprokkit had sustained the most damage as he was taking the brunt of Hexicron's aggression. A few operators were down. The anti-Neophorm claws lay on the ground unused. *Why did those not work?*

Hexicron turned from firing on Sprokkit to fire on Velositi, exposing his front. Velositi hit the hand holding the Axiom in rapid succession. Hexicron's fingers exploded. The Axiom fell from his grasp and landed at his feet.

*What if he steps on it and destroys it? Well, I'm not doing anything.* Kita jumped to her feet and sprinted toward Hexicron.

"Kita!" yelled Adrestia.

Hexicron turned toward Kita.

Kita didn't take her eyes off the Axiom. *What in the Crushing Depths?* The Axiom blinked a purplish-black color. As Kita drew near, it blinked faster.

Hexicron brought his cannon around and aimed at Kita. "Don't touch it!" he roared. Velositi slammed into Hexicron's side, making his shot go high. He wrestled with Velositi, picking her up and slamming her into the ground.

The Axiom blinked rapidly and twitched back and forth. Kita took two more steps, and the Axiom lifted off the ground and flew at her. She ducked and threw her hands up. The Axiom hit her hand and fell around her neck.

A bright flash lit the room and blew Kita off her feet. She hit a wall, and everything went black.

KITA AWOKE TO THE SMELL OF AMMONIA. "WHOA. YUCK." AN OPERATOR WAS waving a packet of smelling salts in front of her face. She pushed his hand away. "Ok. I'm awake."

"Relax, Your Highness," said Boxer. "Master Sergeant Lang needs to check you out. He's one of our medics."

"How are you feeling, Your Highness?" said Lang.

"Fine. My head hurts."

"Let me examine the back of your head."

Kita let him.

"No crepitus; You have a bump, not bleeding." He produced a penlight. "Can I check your eyes, Your Highness?"

Kita opened her eyes wide.

"Pupils equal and reactive. Any nausea, dizziness, ringing in the ears?"

"No."

"What's your name?"

"Kita Logine."

"Do you know where you are?" said Lang.

"In a lava tube somewhere under Hawaii."

"Ah, who's your girlfriend?"

"Kimmy."

"I would have accepted Princess Kimberly Roosevelt, too," said Lang with a smile.

Kita shrugged. *I'll call her Pookie bear if I want.*

Lang produced two pills. "This will help with the pain. If it lasts, come find me."

"Ok."

Lang packed his bag and hurried off to help the other wounded.

"Are there others injured? Why didn't he work on them first?" said Kita to Boxer.

"Because the way you hit the wall, we thought we'd be taking you out on a backboard," said Adrestia coming over and kneeling next to Kita. "But upon inspection, we didn't find any neck or back injuries."

"I feel fine."

"You've got the luck of fools. What possessed you to run into an active firefight?" Adrestia said sternly.

"I didn't want the Axiom to get damaged."

"Where is it?"

"I, ah," Kita looked down at her chest. She expected to be dangling from her neck. She pulled her coat forward to look underneath. There was a purplish-black glow through her tan T-shirt. Lifting her T-shirt, embedded in her chest, was the Axiom. *It looks like a feather.* "Uhm, Nicole?"

"Where is it?"

"Look."

Adrestia looked down Kita's T-shirt. "What the hell did you do? Get the medic back over here."

"Nothing," said Kita. "There was a flash, and then I was waking up."

"Take your coat and T-shirt off."

Kita wiggled her nose. It was a little cold to be wearing just a bikini top, but she did as instructed, draping her coat over her shoulders.

Boxer called for Lang, and the medic returned.

"Something wrong, Your Highness?" said Lang when he saw Kita undressed.

"Take a look at her chest," said Adrestia.

Kita opened her coat to reveal the Axiom.

"Does it hurt?" said Lang.

Kita shook her head. "It feels fine."

"Do you mind if I touch it?"

"No, go ahead."

Lang ran his fingers around where the skin and Axiom met. "There is no scarring, tearing, contusion, or any abnormality. It looks like you were born with it. Let me take your vitals and listen to your heart and lungs."

"I'll be right back," said Adrestia.

Kita nodded and let Lang conduct his examination. Adrestia returned with Velositi causing Kita to roll her eyes.

"We do not know if this is the Axiom or how it chooses someone," said Velositi.

"I think it is, and it has," said Adrestia. She pointed at Kita's chest.

Velositi's eyes lit. "Then this cannot be the Axiom. It is supposed to choose a Morphicon warrior."

"I don't think you know as much about the Axiom as you think you do. I think Sprokkit should examine her."

"Why?" said Velositi.

"Because I don't want any weird voodoo leaking into her system and changing her into some kind of monster."

"It is not the Axiom," said Velositi firmly.

"You have no idea what it looks like. Hexicron said it was the Axiom and was ready to give to a worthy Neophorm. Just because it didn't choose you, doesn't mean it didn't choose a great warrior. Kita fights her battles and is willing to risk everything to win. She may not carry a rifle, but that doesn't mean she's not a warrior. How many times has she fought for you?" Adrestia countered.

Ryan and Sprokkit trotted over from examining Bernoot.

"What's the matter?" said Ryan.

"I have a new decal," said Kita, pointing to the Axiom embedded in her chest.

"Whoa. How'd that happen?"

"That's what we're hoping Sprokkit can answer. Physically, I'm fine." She looked at Lang for confirmation.

"I don't know much about human anatomy or physiology, but I can determine if the Axiom is stable."

"What's unstable?" said Adrestia.

"I do not know what the Axiom does," said Sprokkit. "But I have the readings I took before it chose Kita."

"That is *not* the Axiom," said Velositi. "She is not a Morphicon."

"Yeah, but who's to say the host has to be a Morphicon?" said Ryan. "Hexicron said it was the Axiom of Evil. It contains DNA, unlike either human

212

or Morphicon. It might have a way of adapting to the host. I don't know why it chose Kita. Maybe the host has to be evil, or maybe it's evil potential."

"It could choose any human with that criterion," said Kita.

"Why would it want an evil creature?" demanded Velositi. "It is supposed to be a force of good."

"Did you even listen to Hexicron?" said Adrestia. "This thing was used to conquer and enslave your ancestors. Maybe someone thought they could discover how to use it against their masters. Over time, that idea became a legend of yours."

"Most legends are based on fact," said Ryan. "But reality never matches the legend."

Sprokkit knelt before Kita. Instruments from his hand examined her chest and the Axiom.

Kerr came over. "Colonel?"

"Yes?" said Adrestia.

"We have wounded we need to get out."

"Ok, Captain. We need to get Kita out as well. Get everyone ready to move." Adrestia turned to Sprokkit. "We don't have much time; just make sure she's stable enough to travel."

"I do not observe any changes in the Axiom. The readings are the same," said Sprokkit.

"That's good enough for now," said Adrestia. "We'll have to wait until we get somewhere else to see about removing it."

"If it is even possible to remove it. If the Axiom was able to embed itself like this on its own, removing it may be impossible."

"We will stop periodically so you and the medics can monitor her."

"It is no longer our concern," said Velositi.

"Are you serious?" said Adrestia. "You're going to cast Kita aside because a crystal didn't choose you?"

"The Axiom is not what we thought it was. It is useless to us."

Adrestia stepped up to Velositi. "After all Kita's done for you. She got you here, and because it's not what you expected, you're going to leave her when she may need you the most?"

"Kita was supposed to get me here. That was it."

"Velositi," said Sprokkit, "our mission is not a failure. Just because an ally controls the Axiom, it does not mean all is lost. We helped them, and they will help us. We have also denied it to the Neophormes, the intended host. That may prove to be the most important result."

Kita stood up, slipped her T-shirt on, and stood next to Adrestia. "I'm sorry it didn't choose you, Velositi, but at the same time, I am relieved. If this thing is to turn me into an evil monster, I'd rather it be me than you. Your courage, compassion, and conviction are a beacon of light across the galaxy. I'm just a junkyard girl. If my moment of greatness is to preserve you, then so be it. I love you." Kita turned and picked up her coat.

"You think you'll turn into a monster?" said Ryan, putting an arm on Kita's shoulder.

"I've seen enough anime to know what happens. I'll say goodbye to Kimmy and go someplace where I can't hurt anyone. Maybe I'll go chase snow leopards in Tibet." Kita slipped on her coat. "I'm ready to go, Nicole."

"I hope you're happy," Adrestia hissed at Velositi.

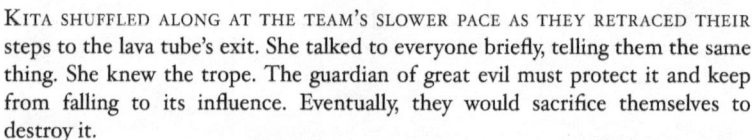

KITA SHUFFLED ALONG AT THE TEAM'S SLOWER PACE AS THEY RETRACED THEIR steps to the lava tube's exit. She talked to everyone briefly, telling them the same thing. She knew the trope. The guardian of great evil must protect it and keep from falling to its influence. Eventually, they would sacrifice themselves to destroy it.

At least, that's what she wanted someone to believe. Heavy footsteps came up behind her. *I wonder if someone's been listening? Yeah, I'm sacrificing myself for you. Do you feel bad yet?*

"Kita?" said Velositi.

Kita glanced over her shoulder. Velositi carried Bernoot's torso on her back. "Yes?" she answered sweetly.

"Are—are you going away?"

"I'll go somewhere where I can't hurt anyone."

"Kimmy might be able to get it off."

Kita shrugged. "I don't think so. What kind of creature do you think I'll become? It's shaped like a feather, so probably something with wings. What did Omegus Hexious look like?"

"We do not know."

"He could have been a Morphicon with wings. I'll probably grow large with fur, claws, a tail, giant teeth, and be ugly." Kita made claws with her hands and gnashed her teeth.

"You must give them a chance to remove it. There must be away," said Velositi sounding upset.

"I'll probably turn into a slime mold." Kita laughed.

"Do not say such things."

"Why not? I don't know what's going to happen. All I can do is laugh because otherwise, I'm too scared. The one person who might help they won't let me near. The other is upset her life plan fell apart and blames me for it. So, yeah, I'm going to laugh. Maybe I'll be an evil mouse."

"What—what can I do?"

Kita huffed. "I don't even know if you love me anymore. You hurt me—badly —and you're going to abandon me. You blamed me and accused me. You made me feel like I don't matter. I apologized to you, and you spurned me. Do you hate me that much? What did I do?"

Velositi's eyes went out for a long moment. They were dim when she opened them. "I do not hate you. I love you. I am sorry for my behavior. I was not fair to you."

"And you came back. Why? You didn't seem concerned when we left."

"I am concerned about your fate. You do not deserve to be forced into exile. You did not choose or even desire the Axiom. But you are the one paying the price for it. It is not fair."

Kita shrugged. "Life isn't fair."

"I do not want you to go. If you must go, I will go with you."

"The life plan fell apart, and suddenly I'm important again?"

"I am sorry. Yes, I let my hubris get the better of me. Finding out I was wrong was humbling. Not being chosen for the Axiom was even more so. It hurt, and I was alone. No one was there to help me. I was angry. Then, you said you were leaving. You are the best thing to happen to me. I could not lose you. I will fight for you, and I will not take *no* for an answer."

Kita chuckled. "So, after being a prima donna all day, I should forgive you and let you back with me?"

"Do I need to grovel more? Is there something you want or something I can do? I am sorry. I just wanted to be important."

"You're important to *me*," said Kita. "I care that you want to be important to other people, but I'm supposed to be the most important person to you. I'll make sacrifices for you and give you the time to do what you want, but I will not be left behind for twenty-five years waiting like a princess in a tower for you to return. You might not age, but I do. I want to enjoy you while I'm young. You can be famous after I'm dead."

"I do not like to think about your death. It is sad."

"Well, you have a while," said Kita.

"I am sorry," said Velositi. "Please forgive me. I promise I will not leave you. You are the most important thing to me. I love you."

"Even if I'm no longer pretty?"

"I will not leave you, but some adjustments might have to be made. I might request a bag, a groomer, or that you spend more time with Kimmy."

Kita chuckled. "And what if the Axiom makes me the most beautiful thing ever?"

"Then Kimmy will have to find someone else."

Kita laughed. "She might fight you. Ok, forgiven. Don't do it again, ok?"

"Ok."

KITA AND VELOSITI PASSED THROUGH THE GATE OF THE MAUNA KEA RESORT Hotel, leading the convoy of Sprokkit and military vehicles through the early morning light. A few vehicles had gone south to take the wounded to the airport for transportation to Honolulu. Velositi followed the narrow road around to the beachfront bungalows. A gray Charger sat to one side. The vehicles parked and everyone unloaded.

Kimmy waited at the edge of the parking lot on the path leading to the bungalows with her Secret Service detail. She hurried over as Kita dismounted. Kita took off her helmet, and Kimmy hugged her from behind.

Kita tipped her head back and rested it on the top of Kimmy's head. "Hey," Kita said tiredly.

"I missed you," said Kimmy. "And I think I gnawed through a box of pencils waiting for you to come back."

"It was a long day," said Kita.

"You sound exhausted."

"I'm ready for bed, but I have something I have to show you."

"Ok. I have one detail I have to take care of."

"I'll hang with Velositi then."

Kimmy let Kita go. "O'Brien, call the investigators over."

"Yes, Your Highness."

A man and a woman dressed in civilian suits exited the charger. Together with the Secret Service and Kimmy, they walked to the military vehicles.

"What's going on?" said Ryan walking over.

"I don't know," said Kita. "It can't be good."

The operators around the vehicles stopped what they were doing and turned toward Kimmy. Kita couldn't hear the discussion, but Kimmy was confronting Kerr. The investigators turned him around, cuffed him, and led him to the charger. Kimmy returned with her detail and Adrestia.

"Ah, what happened?" said Kita to Kimmy.

"After your report this morning, I had Captain Kerr investigated. We found a large cash payment to his account a few days ago. We traced it back through several shell companies to one the Illuminati like to use. Nicole told me how the advanced weapons didn't function during the engagements today. The Army Criminal Investigations Division will take over the investigation."

"That would explain the Neophorm attack this morning," said Velositi.

"Yes." Kimmy gave Velositi a nasty look.

Velositi took a knee in front of Kimmy. "I am sorry for the tone of our conversation this morning. My motivations were out of line and detrimental to our alliance. My behavior nearly cost me Kita. I do not wish it to cost me you."

"But you found the Axiom?"

"Yes, but it is not as we expected."

"What does that mean?" said Kimmy cautiously.

"It was not the Axiom of Command as in the legend. It is the Axiom of Evil," said Velositi.

"Did it pick a new leader? Where's Bernoot? Or do you have to take it home?"

"Bernoot was killed fighting Hexicron for the Axiom. Sprokkit is carrying him."

"Can we repair him?" said Kimmy.

"No," said Velositi. "A system core of his was destroyed. The Axiom—"

"Picked me," said Kita.

"What?" said Kimmy. "Isn't something supposed to happen?"

"According to legend, it is supposed to grant great power," said Velositi.

"I'm assuming it's an evil power?"

"Nothing has happened yet," said Kita. "But I'd like you to look at it."

"Of course. I'm not sure how up I am on trinkets."

Kita pulled down her T-shirt to show the top of the Axiom. "It's no trinket."

"Oh my god!" said Kimmy. "How did this happen? Come on inside so I can look. O'Brien, get my doctor's bag."

Kimmy led Kita by the hand into their bungalow. Everyone else followed.

"Take your shirts off and sit on the bed," said Kimmy to Kita.

"Sprokkit said it hasn't changed since before it chose me and after," said Kita as she took her coat and T-shirt off.

"The Axiom contains quad-helix DNA," said Ryan.

"Quad-helix? Morphicon DNA?" said Kimmy.

"No. Sprokkit says theirs is binary."

"So, we have an alien DNA trapped in this crystal?"

"Looks that way," said Ryan.

"We need to get you to a lab," Kimmy said to Kita.

"I just want to sleep," Kita whined. "It doesn't hurt."

"We don't know what that DNA is capable of."

"No, please, don't lock me up," said Kita as she jumped off the bed, putting her arms out. "I won't hurt anyone, I promise." Tears filled Kita's eyes.

"Kita, I promise I won't lock you up," said Kimmy as she corralled Kita in her arms. "We do have to get a sample and see how it's affecting you. We might be able to get it off you."

Kimmy held Kita while she cried.

"She's exhausted, Your Highness. Letting her sleep will help," said Adrestia.

"Ok. It'll give the labs some time to get set up. I need to keep you up a little longer, Nicole. I need a report on what happened today."

"I can add to it," said Velositi.

"Ryan, you're dismissed," said Kimmy.

"Ok. I'll help Sprokkit with Bernoot."

"If you need, put him in the back of one of the military vehicles. We'll fly him back to Area fifty-one. Maybe they can still fix him."

"Ok. Thanks, Kimmy."

Kimmy waved him away and guided Kita to the bed. She opened a drawer and pulled out a set of shorts and camisole. With Adrestia's help, they coaxed Kita into changing. Kimmy lay Kita on the far side of the bed, stroked her hair, and kissed her goodnight.

Kimmy sat on the bed and invited Adrestia to take a chair. Velositi drove through the door and parked next to the bed.

"I promise I won't keep you long," said Kimmy. "It sounds like a lot went down today."

"You're not going to lock Kita up, are you?" said Adrestia. "She's sure she's going to be exiled."

"Of course not. We will figure out what it is and if we can use it, or at least not make it dangerous. We'll fly to D.C. and take her to Walter Reed. I will figure out a way for the Vehlixen to be there."

"Sprokkit can continue to monitor the Axiom," said Velositi. "He will alert us to any changes in its structure or energy."

"I'm sure Sprokkit's help will be invaluable. I promise Kita will not be treated as an experiment. I won't send her anywhere I won't go."

Kita rolled over and wrapped herself around Kimmy.

Kimmy smiled and stoked Kita's hair. "I think that's what she's been waiting to hear."

Kita sighed and fell asleep.

KITA AWOKE WITH A YAWN, ROLLED OVER, AND THREW BACK THE BLUE comforter with the seal of the Emperor of the United States. She sat up on the edge of the comfortable bed. From the décor of the room, you couldn't tell you were on a jetliner. All the wood and metals were polished to a mirror shine. The carpet was lush, soft, and warm as Kita put her feet down. *Kimmy has the best of everything. I hope she never saw pictures of my apartment. It's embarrassing.*

After using the bathroom, she searched the drawers and found a hoodie with the Emperor's seal. She put it on, covering her cami and shorts. Kita tied back her hair and opened the door. An L-shaped desk sat in the corner against the wall with a high-backed chair facing away from her. Two more chairs sat on the other side of the desk.

"—Yes, Senator, I understand why you can't support the new government. Why you think what goes on in my bedroom will have any hindrance to my ability to govern is beyond me. Last week you said I was doing a fine job. And, now, because I kiss a girl, I'm suddenly unfit?"

Kita frowned, knowing Kimmy's problem was because of her. She tiptoed around the desk and sat in one of the chairs. Drawing her legs up, she covered them with the hoodie.

Kimmy turned, saw Kita, and smiled. "Well, Senator, I can promise you I will not change my mind, and you needn't worry about getting an invitation to the wedding…How long I've been with her is none of your business. I don't care how long you've been with your wife…That's too bad, Senator. I'm sure you'd like her if you met her…Sorry, her name is classified…Yes, even from you. Now, if you don't mind, I have people who are interested in my attention who don't care who I sleep with and are interested in moving this country forward, not keeping it a hundred years in the past."

Kimmy held the phone away from her ear and bobbed her head back and forth in a mocking manner while rolling her eyes.

"I'm sorry you were born a hundred years too late. I'm sure there is some third world country you can move to that will let you do that." Kimmy hid a giggle with her hand. "Senator, I plan on it, and I know she'll enjoy it…It sounds like you should talk to your wife about that. I don't do hotdogs, only tacos. Have a nice day, Senator." Kimmy hung up the phone.

Kita giggled into her hoodie as Kimmy came around and kissed her.

"Sleep well?"

"Yeah. My legs are sore. I can't imagine what the team feels like."

"I didn't realize you'd be walking so far. I'll rub them down if you want."

Kita purred. "That would be nice. Are—are you really in trouble?"

Kimmy smiled wickedly. "They want me to think I can't survive without them. It means nothing to my position as leader of the country, but the rubber-stamping of their legislation is over. I vetoed a bill this morning. The liberals smell blood and are pushing to get into power. The greens, socialists, and labor are all interested in a seat at the table. I'm not in trouble. It will take time to reshuffle the deck and learn how to handle these other groups. I want to split the hawks off the conservatives, and I think I can do that. It'll be an interesting couple of months. But, don't worry. I'm fine. We're fine. Ok?"

Kita nodded. "Ok. I don't want to be more trouble than I'm worth."

"Never. I love you. I adore you. Something I know you love."

Kita smiled and rested the side of her head on her knee. "Yeah."

"How's your chest?"

Kita sat up. "It doesn't hurt."

"Let's see it."

Kita stripped off the hoodie, and Kimmy examined the area around the Axiom.

"Nothing's changed. Good. Walter Reed and the Center for Disease Control are looking at the data and images Sprokkit sent them. When we get to D.C., we'll take some pictures and see how this thing is attached to you. A group is working on methods to get a sample of the DNA inside. If we can't get it off you, maybe we can remove all the genetic material. We need to go down to the medical suite and gather as much medical information on you as we can."

*That doesn't sound like fun.* "What can you do from here?"

"The plane's medical suite has an array of advanced equipment. We still have six hours until we land, so enough time to run some tests."

"Ok," Kita said sadly.

"I promise we'll take a break to have some fun. Let me draw your labs, and then we'll get some food." Kimmy bent down and kissed Kita's forehead.

---

KITA AND KIMMY PULLED UP TO THE CURB OUTSIDE WALTER REED ARMY Medical Center between three black SUVs. They dismounted Velositi and took off their helmets. Kimmy pulled a red, white, and blue bow from her pocket and clipped it in her hair. It was a warm morning in D.C., and Kita unzipped her jacket.

Daisy appeared and took their helmets.

"Wow, this place is big," said Kita to Kimmy.

"The original buildings date back to the turn of the last century."

Kita could tell from the white columns, red brick, and rows of windows. Kimmy took Kita's hand, and they followed the sidewalk toward the front door. A dozen patients and a few nurses lined the sidewalk getting fresh air.

"This hospital is for the Army," said Kimmy. "These are all soldiers or vets who come for treatment." Kimmy stopped to exchange a few words with each, telling them *thank you*.

The second to last patient was older than the others. *Must be a vet.* The vet had a nurse with him, and a blanket covered his hands in his lap. *A little warm for a blanket.* Kimmy knelt next to him. Kita stood to one side, trying to look pleasant.

"How are you, Sir?" said Kimmy.

The man withdrew his hands from the blanket.

"*Gun!*" yelled a Secret Service agent. The agents next to Kimmy grabbed her, threw her to the ground, and jumped on top of her. The flash of the gun was bright in Kita's eyes as three blows hit her in the chest, stomach, and leg. She collapsed to the sidewalk, staring up at the white clouds in the sky.

"Kita! Kita, are you ok?" Velositi yelled from Kita's back pocket.

"Kita! Get off me!" Kimmy shrieked.

*Ouch. That burns all the way through. What happened? Did I get shot?* Kita tried to lift her head and see.

"Kita! Don't move!" ordered Kimmy. "Dan, get the trauma bag from the SUV. Geoff, go inside and tell them we need a trauma team, gurney, and prep an OR for a VIP." Kimmy yanked open Kita's jacket. "Get pressure on those wounds. Xander, monitor her pulse and breathing."

A hand pressed on Kita's throat. She did her best to be calm, breathe normally, and relax. It felt like she was only getting half the breath she needed, and her pulse pounded in her ears. *Kimmy's a doctor. She's got this.*

"Your Highness, pulse is one twenty. Breathing is elevated but sounds normal. Only half of her chest is rising."

"What? Her pulse should be dropping, not going up. With that rate, we should have blood everywhere. Keep pressure on the wounds. Monitor her airway. She has a bullet in her lung and will start coughing up blood. I need some plastic to seal the hole."

The hand returned to Kita's neck. A face appeared in her vision.

"Hi," said Kita to the Secret Service agent.

"Pulse one fifteen, Your Highness. She spoke."

"She's conscious?" exclaimed Kimmy.

Kimmy appeared in front of Kita's face. "Kita, I need you to relax—don't speak. Help is coming, just stay calm."

*I'm perfectly calm. It doesn't hurt as deeply as it did.*

"Do we need more compresses?" said Kimmy.

"No, Your Highness. There's barely any blood coming from her leg or stomach," said a voice.

Kita broke into a coughing fit.

"Turn her head," said Kimmy.

A hand turned Kita's head. With one deep cough, she spat up a bloody mass on the sidewalk. *Oh, yuck.* Kita's lungs opened, and she sucked in a deep breath. *Oh, finally, I can breathe.*

People and a gurney arrived. They lifted Kita and placed her on it. A needle was stuck in her hand, and something was clipped to the end of her finger. With a sudden lurch, the gurney moved—the sky change to the ceiling tiles of the hospital. As the gurney turned corners and crashed through doorways, it jostled Kita. They stopped in a room with big lights.

"The surgical team is scrubbing in now, Your Highness."

"I need pictures! Vitals?" yelled Kimmy.

"Unbelievable, Your Highness. Her pulse has dropped to fifty-seven. Blood pressure is one thirty over eighty-five. Breathing is excellent."

"Compresses are holding. No leakage, Your Highness."

"Kimmy," said Kita. She didn't get a response. There was a new pain in her chest, like something digging into her. *Slag that hurts.* Kita tried to sit up, but the nurse pushing on her chest wouldn't let her.

"Let me up. That hurts," said Kita.

"Kita! Stay down!" yelled Kimmy.

"Move!" snarled Kita. She slapped the nurse's hands.

"She's becoming violent," said the nurse.

Kita grabbed the nurse's arm and dug her nails in. The nurse yelled and let go.

"Kita!" yelled Kimmy. "Calm down!" She grabbed Kita by the shoulders and tried to pin Kita down.

Kita pushed Kimmy aside. She sat up, pulled the compress from her chest, revealing the butt of the bullet. She pulled the bullet out with her fingers and dropped it on the table. "Oh, that's better."

"Kita, I need you to lie back down, there might still be more in there," said Kimmy firmly. She picked up the bullet.

"I feel fine," said Kita.

"Kita, bullets don't back out."

Kita pulled the compress off her stomach. The butt of the bullet was visible in the hole. "It barely hurts."

"Kita, you need to lie back down," said Kimmy as she pushed Kita back against the table. "There's still internal damage that has to be repaired." Kimmy probed the shallow hole in Kita's chest. "It's closed..."

"Kimmy, can you get the one in my leg?" said Kita.

Kimmy pushed the nurse applying pressure aside and removed the compress. "Forceps!"

Kita felt a slight tug in her thigh, followed by the *ping* of a metal object hitting a metal pan. A moment later, they repeated the process for the bullet in her stomach.

"We need to get her in for a CT," said Kimmy. "There might still be trauma underneath."

The medical team transferred Kita to another gurney and moved to a neighboring room. *I could have walked.*

The CT staff positioned Kita on the CT scanner table.

"Kita lay still. This will only take a minute," said Kimmy.

Kita sighed. "Ok. Is this really necessary?" *I feel fine.*

"Kita, please do as they ask," said Velositi from Kita's pocket. "Humans do not regenerate at such an accelerated rate or expel foreign objects. Give Kimmy time to check you over."

"Fine." Kita huffed.

Kita waited as the machine moved over her body taking x-rays. When it was over, she sat up. "How do I look?" she called into the control room.

Kimmy came out ghost white. "It's like nothing happened."

"That's good," said Kita. "I feel fine." Kita pulled at the IV in her hand. Kimmy stopped her and pulled it out.

"Kita, I wouldn't believe it if I hadn't seen it."

"Why not? Velositi regenerates."

"We're not like them."

"Your Highness?" said a tech from the control room.

"Yes?"

"The images from around the top of her chest are unreadable."

Kimmy went to the control room, and Kita followed. The tech showed them pictures of Kita's chest. The Axiom was a bright spot that obscured the surrounding tissue and bone.

"We'll have to try something else to see how the Axiom is connected," said Kimmy.

"Could the regeneration be part of the Axiom?" said Velositi.

"It's the only explanation," said Kimmy. She turned and gave Kita a fierce hug as tears ran down her face. "I'm not ready to lose you. I just found you."

"I don't think I'm going anywhere," said Kita as she hugged Kimmy.

"You better not. I was so scared."

"You did everything you could to save me."

"It's the first time I've worked on someone I care about," Kimmy whispered.

"Thanks," said Kita. She kissed Kimmy.

"I have a sudden urge to wrap you in bubble wrap."

"I think I am." Kita tapped her chest.

"We need to learn all we can about that. What else is it going to do to you?"

Velositi pulled away from the hospital with Kita and Kimmy. They had spent the rest of the day trying to get images of how the Axiom attached to Kita, but nothing except visible light imaging showed anything. The images they did get were lower quality than what Sprokkit had provided.

"Velositi, can you turn on the radio?" said Kimmy. "I need to know what's happening."

"Sure. What station?"

"Ah...not Fox News Radio—how about NPR? I might as well listen to what I pay for."

"This is NPR," said a pleasant but formal voice. "An attack on the royal family at Walter Reed Army Medical Center was foiled by the Secret Service this morning. The White House insists Princess Roosevelt was not the target, but rather her girlfriend, Jane Doe. Witnesses at the scene reported shots were fired, and Jane Doe was taken in for treatment. The White House released a statement saying the injuries were minor, and Jane Doe was treated and released. The Secret Service confirmed they have two people in custody.

"A conservative protection group calling themselves *The Minutemen* claimed responsibility on social media, stating members of The Minutemen would defend the American way of life at a moment's notice—even from the government itself.

"In other news, Princess Roosevelt's announcement that she is gay is having a chilling effect on the conservatives in Washington. Polls show a divided country. Ninety-three percent of opposition party members support the princess, while only nine percent of conservative party members support the princess' decision.

"Senate Majority Leader Mike McDonald and Speaker of the House Dick Paul released a statement suggesting this was another *phase* Princess Roosevelt was going through. They plan to schedule a meeting with the princess to discuss her social activities and, quote, *set her straight*.

"In economic news—"

"I wonder how they plan to set you straight?" said Velositi.

"I'm sure they think another stern lecture will suffice. But not this time. I plan to tell them to get out. I'm done with old men telling me what to do. I want to find people I can work with to make the country better. I fully believe I can achieve what Kita laid out. I just need to find the right people. There are some bright young stars on the liberal side. I need to get a coalition together so they can form a majority. I've already reached out to the hawks and have hinted that we have a new ally in the war against the Neophormes. I told them if they don't want control of the military being passed to the liberals, they need to get on board."

"Are they?" said Kita.

"They're thinking about it—which means yes. I'll see what I have to give them to come over."

"Give them what?"

"Oh, contracts for military hardware most likely. Stuff I don't mind. The world's a dangerous place. The more planes, tanks, and soldiers I have, the better. I wish I could harness what's in your chest. That would save a lot of lives."

*I don't know if I like the idea of giving it away. It's mine. I dared to reach out and grab it.*

---

KITA, KIMMY, AND VELOSITI SAT AT THE FAMILY DINING ROOM TABLE IN THE White House eating dinner. Kimmy ate while working on a tablet and talking.

"So, what are we doing tomorrow?" said Kita.

"You are meeting Eugene, Michael, and Carol to get you situated in the White House."

"I thought I was?"

"They want to go over stuff with you. I'm going to Capitol Hill—"

There was a knock at the door. Kita got up to answer it.

"Sit," said Kimmy. "Who is it?"

The door opened, and the butler entered. "Your Highnesses, I have Special Agent in Charge O'Brien here to see you."

"Thanks, Eugene. Show him in."

O'Brien entered, wearing his black suit and tie. He had a stern expression. He stopped in front of the table next to Velositi.

"What is it, Dan?" said Kimmy.

"I have my resignation for you, Your Highness, over my failure to protect Miss Logine." O'Brien reached into his coat, pulled out a letter, and gave it to Kimmy.

Kimmy opened the letter and read it. When she was done, she passed it to Kita. The letter was short and to the point. The Secret Service agents had responded appropriately to Kimmy, but due to personal misgivings, they had failed to protect Kita. O'Brien, as their leader, was taking the fall.

"What do you think?" Kimmy said to Kita.

Kita cocked her head and looked at O'Brien. "What do you think?"

"About what, Your Highness?"

"About us. You've been professional, courteous, and respectful. You're in charge but personally assigned to Kimmy, not me. I was not your failing today. It was the other agents. Do you agree with the others?"

O'Brien straightened. "I took an oath to protect the princess. It doesn't matter what I believe."

Kita tapped her nail against her teeth. "The others took that same oath, and obviously what they personally believed mattered more than that oath to the princess. If you don't like us, that's fine, say so. We'll have no hard feelings. I'm sure Kimmy can assign you to guard someone else."

O'Brien's eyes narrowed. "I've served the princess for fifteen years. She's like a daughter to me. I will support her in whatever choices she makes. It's her life."

"But you don't personally like us?"

"I don't care that she's gay. I don't personally like you. I think the Princess can do better."

Kita smiled. "I'm just trash rolling in from the Cali desert? Not a prim and proper girl from D.C.?"

"You're reckless, aggressive, and put the princess in danger," said O'Brien in an angry fatherly tone.

Kita laughed. "I never considered myself a bad girl, but maybe I am. You don't like me because I make your job difficult. I understand, but my job isn't to make your life easy or"—Kita patted her chest—"maybe it is. I'm a better bullet sponge than you."

O'Brien glared.

"I say *no*," said Kita. "Clean house on the others, but he stays."

Kimmy covered a giggle with her hand. "I think, Dan, you just opened yourself up to a challenge. I'm sorry, but Kita isn't going anywhere. I want you to find two female agents to be her shadow. Vet the other agents. If they don't like that I kiss a girl, then they can catch counterfeiters. I don't want a repeat of this morning. We were lucky they took shots at the girl with the magic stone in her chest. Next time, it could be me, and I don't have one."

O'Brien nodded. "Yes, Your Highness. I will find a detail for Miss Logine."

"Make sure they can ride a motorcycle," said Kita.

"Yes, Your Highness."

"Go home, Dan," said Kimmy. "Get some rest and tackle it in the morning."

"Yes, Your Highness. I can show myself out." O'Brien turned and left.

"He is going to be up all night searching for the perfect candidates for Kita," said Velositi.

"You're probably right," said Kimmy. "But he won't make the same mistake twice."

"You want to go hang gliding?" said Kita.

Kimmy laughed. "You can be more creative than that."

KITA SAT CURLED UP ON VELOSITI IN THE WHITE HOUSE LIVING AREA watching *My Little Pony*. The door opened. *Only two people can open that door without knocking.* Kimmy entered dressed in a red business suit with her hair tied up in a red, white, and blue bow.

"Hey, angel. How was your day? Give me a second to change, and you can tell me all about it." Kimmy disappeared into the bedroom and returned with her hair down, a sports bra, and yoga pants. Kita moved to the couch, and Kimmy sat next to her, putting her arm around Kita.

Kita snuggled against Kimmy, resting her head on her chest. She listened to Kimmy's heartbeat, letting the rhythmic beating relax her.

"You missed me this much, huh?" Kimmy chuckled.

"For all the people, it's a lonely house."

"I'm sorry. I know it can get dull around here. Did you girls have fun on the driving tour?"

"I did," said Velositi. "The National Park Service ranger was very informative. Washington, D.C. is an interesting city, and there is so much history for such a short time."

"She had lots of questions," said Kita quietly.

"You seem down. Are you ok?" said Kimmy.

"There were a lot of people staring at me."

"I believe there is more than that," said Velositi. "Even with the large Secret Service detail, she was the victim of many vicious verbal attacks and threats. The Secret Service arrested one man for telling Kita he would put a Jane Doe toe tag on her. I do not like that I cannot protect her."

"I'm sorry, Kita," said Kimmy. "It was supposed to be fun and introduce you to your new home. I promise they can't hurt you. I know you want to protect her, Velositi, but when she's out in public, you're going to have to rely on my people to do it. I will remind people that you are protected by the same laws I am. That will stop some of it. The rest we'll have to ignore. In time, it'll go away." She squeezed Kita right.

A knock came from the door.

"Enter," said Kimmy.

A butler opened the door. "Your Highnesses, I have Colonel Adrestia and Captain Callaghan to see you."

"Thank you, Eugene. Please, show them in."

Adrestia and Ryan stepped into the room, both in their battle dress uniforms. Kimmy and Kita stood up and hugged Adrestia.

"I'm sorry," said Kimmy. "I read the report. I wish we could do more."

Adrestia nodded somberly. "A team is going to try and recover the system core and extrapolate the damaged parts. It's a long shot and is going to take a while."

"I hadn't heard that. So, there is some hope?"

"Sprokkit instructed them on how to create a system core," said Ryan. "They have to build the machine, but they know the theory. He's parked outside if we need him." He pulled out his phone and made a call.

"Yes?" said Sprokkit.

"I thought you might want to listen in."

"Hmm, if I must."

227

"Come, sit," said Kimmy. "I'm sure you're tired from your flight. Are you hungry? We haven't eaten yet."

"That sounds good," said Adrestia. "Nothing too fancy, though."

Kimmy laughed. "Burgers and fries, ok? I promise they won't be from McDonald's."

Everyone agreed and sat. Kita cuddled up to Kimmy as she picked up the phone and put the order in.

"Getting used to your new home, Kita?" said Ryan.

"It's a big house," said Kita to everyone's amusement. "I spent the morning with the staff. They asked me a bunch of questions about what I like and don't like. I never get to make a choice based on what I like. I've always made do with what I have.

"And there are always people around. We had lunch with the senators from... Cali?" Kimmy nodded. "I had no idea what they were talking about, but they seemed happy and excited. Then I toured D.C. this afternoon, and I was followed everywhere. I made the news."

Kimmy unmuted MSNBC, which had replaced Fox News as the news source of choice. "There you are."

Kita and Velositi were at the foot of the Lincoln Memorial with a park ranger, surrounded by Secret Service agents, including two female agents. The headline read PRINCESS' GIRLFRIEND VISITS DC MONUMENTS. A crowd of cameras and people were on the perimeter watching. Some people were trying to get Kita's attention. A string of beeps covered a long phrase that ended in *bitch*.

"Not everyone is happy with Princess Roosevelt's decision to come out as gay," said the anchor. "But, this courageous young woman, whose name has not been released and is only known as Jane Doe, is braving the political and public shaming storm generated by a vocal minority in the country. She refuses to be intimidated by the rhetoric, hate, and divisiveness coming from members of the conservative party's base. Tweets from prominent members of the LGBTQ community are praising both the princess and this young woman, as are members of the liberal party—"

Kimmy muted the TV. "I like this station. It is much more supportive and less fear-mongering."

"Don't worry about it, Kita," said Adrestia. "You have lots of people supporting you. Kimmy, make sure she doesn't get stuck in a bubble."

Kimmy sighed. "I know. My communications director and I have been working on a plan to get Kita exposure. We have a stack of invites from Hollywood."

"Cali would be a good place to start. It's extremely LGBTQ friendly."

Kita sighed. "Except for my hometown."

"We can make San Fran your hometown," said Kimmy.

"I've never been there. I like Angel City. I had fun driving around there with Velositi."

Velositi's eyes lit.

"How's the mark of the beast?" said Adrestia tapping on her chest.

Kita rolled her eyes. "I didn't even get to the hospital before I was shot three times."

"What?" exclaimed Adrestia.

"How come you're not in the hospital?" said Ryan.

"My body spat the bullets out and healed itself," said Kita.

"I wouldn't have believed it if I hadn't seen it," said Kimmy.

"So, you're ok?" said Ryan.

"I'm fine," said Kita.

"Were they serious?" said Adrestia.

"One hit her lung, and another hit her liver," said Kimmy. "Everything is functioning normally. All of her levels are good. Better than good, they're perfect —every one of them. It's not the only thing that's healed. The damage from the Neophorm mini healed, leaving no scars. It's like it never happened. We also learned the radiation the Axiom emits blocks our imaging devices, except for the visible light spectrum. How the Axiom is attached is still a mystery. I would like Sprokkit to inspect the Axiom and make sure its structure and contents are stable."

"But the Axiom is changing her," said Ryan.

"It appears it *is* doing something. We don't know how, and only know what we've observed. I expect a call from the CDC any time on the DNA and pathogens tests."

"The Axiom maybe constructing a healthy vessel for itself," said Sprokkit, "to increase its chances of survival."

"Maybe it needs a healthy vessel to transform," said Ryan.

Kita wrinkled her nose. "I'm right here."

"Sorry," said Ryan.

"I think we have time to figure it out," said Kimmy. "We're still working on getting the DNA out of the Axiom. Sprokkit and Ryan, can you help with that?"

"Sure," said Ryan. "Just give us a place to work."

"A team at Walter Reed is working on it. I'll introduce you tomorrow and get you set up." Kimmy turned to Adrestia. "Nicole, I know you're still grieving, but do you mind escorting Kita around when I can't? I don't want a repeat of the last two days."

"No problem."

"I have spare rooms if you both want to stay here."

"Wow," said Ryan. "I never thought I'd get to stay overnight."

"I'll even give you a complimentary toothbrush that has the White House on it," Kimmy said with a wry smile. The phone rang. "That must be the CDC."

Kimmy pushed a button on the remote, and a man in his sixties wearing a lab coat appeared on the TV. "Yes, Doctor Casa?"

"Your Highness. Good evening. I have the update you requested."

"Good. What do you have for me?"

"We have sequenced patient zero's DNA. The DNA has several pairs of genes that we've never seen before."

"Mutations?" said Kimmy.

"No. These are complete, and unlike any we have on record. We're isolating them so we can discover what they do."

"So, patient zero's DNA is unique. It should make it easy to trace."

"No, Your Highness."

"What do you mean?"

"Patient zero's genetic ancestry does not match any on Earth."

Kimmy looked concerned. "Patient zero has a mother and father, from Earth. We have records of them. I'll have to check if we have their DNA on file, but I'll dig up the graves if I have to."

"Knowing patent zero's genetic history might provide a clue."

"We'll see about getting the samples. How about the other DNA?"

Casa cleared his throat. "Using the images provided, we encoded the unknown DNA."

"That fast?" said Kimmy.

"The unknown DNA is similar in structure to our own but has eight nucleotides. What the sequence means, is still unknown. But the unknown DNA isn't completely foreign."

"What do you mean?"

"The construction of the unknown DNA is a quad-helix. It has two dual helices set at right angles from each other. On one dual helix section of the unknown DNA, we found patient zero's complete DNA structure, including the unknown genes."

Kimmy's mouth fell open. "How's that possible?"

"What does that mean?" said Kita.

Kimmy muted the call. "Sprokkit, I thought those images came from before the Axiom attached itself to Kita."

"They did. I have some from after, but they are incomplete."

"Could they have gotten mixed up?"

"No," Sprokkit grumped.

Kimmy looked at Kita. "Did you touch it before it attached to you?"

Kita shook her head. "No."

"Kita was held at the cavern's entrance during our initial examination of the Axiom," said Velositi.

Kimmy bit her lip. "It's a statistical improbability that an alien DNA from light-years away is going to be the same as Kita's." She unmuted the call. "Doctor Casa, it is an exact match?"

"Yes, Your Highness. One hundred percent."

"How the hell does that happen?"

"We don't know, Your Highness. The combinations of DNA are infinite, and there have only been ten billion people ever. The chances of such a perfect match approach zero. We also looked at patient zero's blood and discovered an infection."

*Uh-oh. That doesn't sound good.*

"What kind of infection?" said Kimmy.

"We don't know, Your Highness." The screen changed to several images showing cells in the blood. They had circled several small cells. "We've observed them, but we haven't witnessed them doing anything. They don't look like any type of bacteria we've ever seen, but they are organic. We're trying to isolate some so we can get a closer look. We strongly recommend patient zero be quarantined until we know more. Patient zero is a high risk to public health."

Kimmy looked at Kita.

Kita gulped and shrank into Velositi's lap. "Please, no," Kita whispered. "You promised."

"I know," said Kimmy. She kissed Kita's head. "Doctor Casa, put together a team to fly to D.C. tonight. It will be faster and easier than shipping samples to Colorado. I have a theory on those cells. Patient zero can heal at an accelerated rate. I want to know if those two things are connected. We'll get the team some tissue samples when they're set up."

"Yes, Your Highness."

"Thank you, Doctor." Kimmy ended the call. She sat back down. "Well, that just got stranger. How does a trinket, over twelve thousand years old and from millions of light-years away, have a third-party DNA in it with a portion exactly matching someone alive today? Anyone have a theory on that?"

"To add to that, what about the message?" said Ryan.

"What about the message?"

"Hexicron said he never sent it. He was waiting on the Star Bridge."

Kimmy frowned. "This was never in anyone's report. What is a Star Bridge?"

"According to Hexicron, that is the way the Neophormes plan on invading planets," said Velositi.

"And this is somewhere on Earth?" exclaimed Kimmy.

"We have no proof of its existence," said Sprokkit.

"It could explain the jump in the number of Neophormes on Earth. I will make it a priority of the CIA and IBI. If Hexicron didn't send the message, then who did? The Neophormes followed the Vehlixen here."

Ryan shrugged. "Another of the lieutenants?"

"The message only arrived three hundred cycles ago," said Velositi. "If Hexicron was out of plasma, so would the others."

"Maybe—maybe the Axiom wanted to be found," said Ryan. "In anime, it's not unusual for a McGuffin to trigger an event when it's ready to be found."

"Why is it ready to be found?" said Adrestia.

"Maybe it knew Kita was coming."

Kita hugged Velositi tight. "I feel like a monster," she whispered.

"It's just a hypothesis," said Ryan.

Velositi's eyes dimmed as she looked at Ryan. "We are supposed to be helping Kita feel better, not scare her."

Kimmy knelt next to Kita and Velositi and stroked Kita's face. "So far, there have been no negative side effects, only positive ones. We'll keep monitoring and see what else happens. That's all we can do. We'll go to Walter Reed in the morning and get more samples."

"Kita might end up with superpowers," said Ryan with a grin. "You could be like She-Hulk, Wolverine, the Invisible Woman, the Human Torch—"

"I just want to be normal," said Kita as she wiped the tears away. "I'm already strange enough."

"You're perfect," said Kimmy, stroking Kita's face. "Come on, why don't we get dinner? Then I'll send out my orders, and we can go down to the bowling alley."

"This place has a bowling alley?" said Ryan.

"In the basement. My mother was a bowler."

Kita sat on the examining table in her underwear and a hospital gown.

"Ten down, two more to go," said Kimmy holding a circular scalpel. She rubbed Kita's thigh.

Kita felt only part of Kimmy's touch. A large section of her outer thigh was numb where Kimmy was taking the tissue samples.

"Amazing," said Kimmy as the current sample hole healed. "It's like nothing happened—in just over a minute."

"It's still me your taking chunks out of," said Kita.

"I know. I'm sorry, I don't mean to be insensitive. It's just professional curiosity." Kimmy leaned in and planted a set of kisses on Kita's inner thigh.

Kita shivered.

Kimmy's head popped up to kiss Kita. "Better?"

Kita giggled, and then her stomach growled, causing both girls to giggle.

"Someone's hungry, and you just ate," said Kimmy.

"I know," Kita whined.

"We'll get you something to eat when we're done. I think all this healing is taking up your energy. Now, hold still."

Kimmy pushed her circular scalpel against Kita's thigh and cut out a piece. After putting the specimen in a glass tube, she placed the tube in a cooler, kept cold by dry ice. She wiped the blood off Kita's thigh. "I'm going to take the last one from the same place. I'm curious to see if they're the same or not." She waited for the hole to heal, then placed the scalpel against Kita's skin and turned.

"Ouch!" cried Kita. "That hurts."

Kimmy jerked the scalpel away. "It shouldn't. You should be numb for at least an hour." She ran her hand over Kita's outer thigh. "Can you feel that?"

"Yes."

"Ok. No problem. I'll numb it again." Kimmy grabbed a needle of lidocaine and injected Kita several times. After putting the needle away, she tested Kita's thigh. "Numb?"

"Yeah."

"Ok, hold still." Kimmy extracted the last sample, packaged it, and put it in the cooler. She checked Kita's leg. Only a slight depression was left. "I think you can get dressed. We'll get you something to eat, then go visit Ryan and Sprokkit."

---

Kita lay with her top off on a plastic table in the middle of a temporary lab set up in an outbuilding of Walter Reed Medical Center. Sprokkit and Ryan worked on aiming a laser at the Axiom. Kimmy stood next to the table, holding Kita's hand.

"I'm hungry again," said Kita.

"You just ate!" said Kimmy.

"I know, but I'm still hungry."

"Girls are always hungry," said Ryan.

"She ate five servings before we came over here," said Kimmy.

"Wow. Careful Kita, you might get fat."

"I was told I need to put on weight," Kita said, making a face.

"Not like this," said Kimmy.

"I'm still hungry," said Kita.

"Do I need to get your digestive tract tested, too?"

Kita shrugged. "All I know is I'm hungry."

"Ok," said Ryan. "We're ready."

"Are you sure this won't hurt her?" said Kimmy.

"It shouldn't. We're aiming at the Axiom, not her skin. The laser should just scrape off the surface of the Axiom and let us get at the DNA underneath. Once we have a hole, we can pull the DNA out."

"I need to get you guys an air conditioner," said Kimmy as she lifted her hair.

Kita didn't notice the temperature. She was comfortable.

Ryan chuckled. "It is warm in here, but it should only take a couple of seconds to get through. The Axiom lattice isn't that thick. Ready, Sprokkit?"

Sprokkit squatted down next to the table and extended the instruments from his fingers around the Axiom. A screen showed the Axiom surface the laser was going to penetrate. "Ready."

"Starting it up." Ryan flipped a switch, and there was a hum. He looked through a viewer and aimed the laser. "Ok, aiming laser on." On the screen appeared a large glowing dot. "Target acquired. Turning on the etching laser." The dot on the screen glowed brighter.

Kita hissed as she felt the burn. "Ok, I can feel that."

Ryan looked at the screen. "Can you take a little more? We're not penetrating."

"Ok, I guess."

Ryan turned a dial.

"Ow! Ow! Ow!" cried Kita as she ground her teeth. She squeezed Kimmy's hand and the edge of the table.

"Kita! My hand," cried Kimmy.

Kita let go of Kimmy's hand and flexed her other hand. There was a loud crack.

"Stop!" yelled Kita.

"Ok," said Ryan. He turned the machine off. "Anything, Sprokkit?"

"Nothing. No material has moved."

"By the Crushing Depths," snarled Kita. She held up a piece of the table.

"Did—did you break that off?" said Ryan.

"It hurt."

"It shouldn't. There are no nerves or anything in the Axiom. How did you break the table?"

Kimmy took the piece from Kita. "She snapped it off."

"That would take a lot of force," said Ryan. "Sprokkit, the table wasn't damaged when we started, was it?"

"No. The table's integrity was excellent. Kita would need my strength to damage it."

"Well, she did," said Kimmy, "and she nearly crushed my hand."

"Sorry." Kita took Kimmy's hand and kissed it several times.

"Was it a pain reflex or something else?" said Ryan.

"I don't know," said Kimmy. "Even with a pain reflex, she shouldn't be able to damage the table."

"Let's see. Kita, see if you can lift the toolbox."

Kita slid off the table and stood in front of the four-foot by six-foot toolbox on casters. "That must way five hundred pounds."

"See if you can lift one end. This way, we'll know if it's you or the table."

Kita huffed and squatted on one end of the toolbox. She slipped her fingers under, using her legs and arms she lifted with all her might. The toolbox flipped in the air and landed on its top.

"Oops," whispered Kita.

"Oh my god, Kita," said Kimmy.

"Damn," said Ryan. "How hard have you been hitting the gym?"

"Yeah, in all my spare time," said Kita sarcastically. "It barely weighed anything at all."

"Hang on," said Ryan. He ran over to a corner full of junk and spare parts.

"Is this the Axiom?" said Kimmy.

"I wasn't this strong before," said Kita.

"Your increase in strength is unprecedented," said Sprokkit. "I know of nothing that can facilitate this rapid growth in strength, especially since you have shown no change in physical stature."

Ryan returned, carrying two lengths of metal. "This is one-inch bar stock, used for construction. Solid all the way through." He gave one to Sprokkit and one to Kita. "See if you can bend it."

Sprokkit took the piece and bent it in a shallow U.

Kita turned the metal over in her hands. *How am I supposed to bend this? They make giant machines that put out tons of force to bend stuff like this.* Kita grasped both ends and flexed her arms and chest. With little strain, the metal gave. Kita, feeling cheeky, bent the bar into a heart and presented it to Kimmy.

"Wow," said Kimmy. "That was incredible. How are we going to keep you from destroying things?"

Kita shrugged. "I seem to have excellent control over how much force I exert. I don't think it'll be a problem—as long as no one is *burning me with lasers*." She glared at Ryan.

"Sorry. I guess it's back to the drawing board."

A NIGHTMARE WOKE KITA. SHE CURLED UP AT THE EDGE OF THE BED, CRYING. Images of dead and dismembered bodies engulfed in fire drowning in blood filled her mind. The nightmare ended with her smiling face. The scene was so vivid. She couldn't shake it.

"Kita, are you ok?" said Velositi. She moved to Kita's side of the bed and put a hand on her shoulder. Kita buried her face in the comforter. Velositi reached over Kita and tapped Kimmy.

"Huh?" said Kimmy. She sat up, hearing Kita's muffled crying and scooted across the bed. "What's wrong?" she said to Velositi.

"She woke up crying."

Kimmy put an arm around Kita and snuggled her. "Hey, angel, what's going on? What's wrong? Why are you over here?" She stroked Kita's hair, soothing her.

Kita wiped at her eyes. "Will you both still love me if I become a monster?"

"Kita, did you have a bad dream?" said Kimmy. "You're not going to become a monster. I promise."

"A nightmare," Kita whispered.

"Your subconscious mind is processing the recent days' events," said Velositi. "You have experienced some amazing changes, and it is going to take time for your mind and body to adjust. I promise I will love you, no matter what."

Kimmy hugged Kita tight. "What did you see, angel? Telling us will get it off your mind."

"Blood, lots of blood...bodies and body parts everywhere—everything was in flames. At the end was my face, smiling."

Kimmy looked over at Velositi. "What does that mean?"

"It might be a reaction to her being shot, or maybe she thinks all the changes the Axiom has made will have a negative impact on her."

Kimmy squeezed Kita. "It was just a bad dream. You're still you. You've done nothing wrong. None of the Axiom's alterations have changed who you are. You just eat more. Where you're putting it, I don't know."

Kimmy had examined Kita's stomach and intestines, expecting to find a mass of food. Instead, they found nothing. Kimmy watched on an x-ray as Kita ate an apple. Kita's stomach broke down the food completely, leaving no waste. What happened to the food after it was broken down was a mystery.

"But you're healthy. There's nothing wrong. We'll figure out the Axiom, I promise. I won't lose you. I love you."

Kita sighed. "I don't want to hurt anyone."

"You won't. You have great control over your strength. You haven't broken anything. I'm impressed with how well you've handled everything. I know the changes are coming fast, but we'll keep studying it until we understand."

"I don't want you to hate me. I couldn't live without either of you."

"Why would I hate you?" said Velositi. "I knew you were special when I met you, and now I am being proven right."

"I could never hate you," said Kimmy. "We both care about you and will take care of you. We adore you." She kissed Kita's bare shoulder.

Kita relaxed and smiled hesitantly.

"That is what I like to see," said Velositi.

Kimmy squeezed Kita. "I love you. Nothing is going to change that."

Kimmy's phone buzzed. She rolled over and grabbed it.

The clock said six-oh-six. *We're starting late today.* Most days, Kimmy was up at six.

"The CIA has something for us on the Illuminati and Neophormes," said Kimmy. "We have a briefing in the Situation Room at eight-thirty."

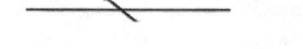

Kita, Ryan, and Adrestia followed Kimmy from the elevator through the basement of the West Wing of the White House to the Situation Room. Kimmy wore a blue business suit with her favorite bow in her hair. Kita, Ryan, and Adrestia wore their Air Force battle uniforms. Unlike the others, Kita's uniform was tailored to fit, with a patch of the Imperial Seal on her shoulder. She wore her hair in a low ponytail.

They entered a large briefing room. Men and women, some in military uniforms, others in suits, sat around the polished table. Everyone stood when Kimmy entered.

"Good morning, everyone," said Kimmy.

"Good morning, Your Highness," the group said in unison.

"Give us a few moments," said Kimmy. "We have some special guests joining us for the briefing."

Using a remote, Daisy turned on two screens, and Sprokkit and Velositi appeared.

"Sprokkit, Velositi, can you hear me?" said Kimmy.

"Yes, Your Highness," said Velositi.

The people around the table exchanged surprised looks.

"Daisy," said Kimmy, "please get chairs for Princess Kita, Colonel Adrestia, and Captain Callaghan."

"Your Highness, I have to protest," said a tall, thin man with a hawk face. "These three do not have the proper security clearance to be in the Situation Room, and what are those things on screen?"

"It's my room, Robert," said Kimmy, "and they have been working with the Vehlixen. They know more about the situation than you do. On the screen are Leader Velositi, and Science and Medical Specialist Sprokkit. I've spent the last week allying with them. They are Vehlix Morphicons—our new allies in the fight against the Neophormes."

"According to the news, you've been preoccupied."

"Nothing like a little misdirection," said Kimmy. "If the Empire is more interested in the new princess than a race from another planet, I have no objections."

"I understand the colonel and captain, Your Highness, but does she have to be here?" said a balding older man in a gray suit pointing at Kita. "She is not in the military and shouldn't be wearing a uniform."

"*She* is a member of the royal family, Daniel. The decree was made last week. She can wear whatever uniform she wants, just like I can. *Princess* Kita is the reason we know about the Vehlixen. She brought them to us and helped forge an alliance. It's because of her we found what the Vehlixen were searching for—the Axiom. Princess Kita is also in possession of the Axiom. Show them, angel."

Kita stood up, unbuttoned the first two buttons of her coat, and pulled down her T-shirt to reveal the glowing Axiom.

"Son-of-a-bitch, what is it?" said a stern-looking grizzled man in a Marine uniform.

Kita walked up to Daniel. "Pen." He handed it over. Kita took the bottom half in her fist and, with her thumb, bent the metal pen into a right angle. She dropped it on the table in front of him and returned to her seat.

"The Axiom is altering Princess Kita's body," said Kimmy. "She is under medical supervision, and we are monitoring the changes. I'm sure you saw the report that Princess Kita was attacked at Walter Reed. Not mentioned in the reports was that she was shot three times. Her body pushed the bullets out and healed the damage on its own."

"How do we get that into our soldiers?" said an Army general.

"We don't know enough about it yet," said Kimmy. "Right now, it only affects her."

"So, she being your girlfriend is just a cover?" said Daniel.

"Kita is very much my girlfriend. It was a pleasant perk from the trip to form an alliance with the Vehlixen."

"Your relationship will be detrimental to military readiness," said the Marine.

"Since when? The military has been one of the few places the LGBTQ community has been welcomed. Isn't that right, Nicole?"

"Yes, Your Highness."

"Are you saying you have a problem, General?" Kimmy asked tersely.

"It's one thing to have it go on in the ranks. It's another for it to go on at the top."

"So, you don't think you can keep the rank and file from mutinying?"

"It's bad for morale. Most will do their jobs. Some will leave."

"If you don't like it," said Kita, "just say so, and Kimmy will get someone to do your job for you."

"No one was talking to you!" snapped the Marine.

"*Your Highness*," Kimmy finished for him.

"She has not earned that title, nor deserves it."

"That's for me to decide," said Kimmy. "General Barker, you're relieved. General Mayfield will take your place until I chose a new head of the Joint Chiefs. I assume you can show yourself out."

"I was chosen by your father," said Barker angrily.

"Yes. And you served him well. But you do not wish to serve me well. I have a different vision for the future of our country than his, and I am the one in control. Good luck in retirement." Kimmy looked down the table. "Anyone else have a problem?"

A few heads were down, but no one said anything.

"Good," said Kimmy. "Now, Charlie, what does the CIA have for us?"

A squat-looking man with wire-rimmed glasses in a blue suit stood. "The CIA and IBI have worked closely on tracking Illuminati movements inside the Empire and around the world. When Majestic Twelve raided the Illuminati safe house in Angel City, we captured their hardware intact. This led us to a dark network, and we traced Illuminati activities around the globe. Everything leads back to the southern coast of Yonaguni, Japan. This location is known for ancient ruins believed to be ten to twelve thousand years old. We have tracked a steady flow of small vessels into the area. They aren't fishing but dropping and retrieving caches from the ocean floor. Anti-Neophorm Team Three and the submarine Utah scouted the area with underwater drones and passive sonar. We detected submersibles and one Neophorm using an entrance into the ruins. We believe this to be a major Illuminati base."

"Could it be the Star Bridge?" said Sprokkit.

"I don't know what that is. We haven't been inside farther than the dock area."

"A Neophorm was spotted. Was it a drone or a master?" said Velositi.

"I don't know what those are."

"Masters lead the Neophormes. Drones are mindless warriors."

"We couldn't identify it as any known Neophorm. We have some images of the outside and the dock," said Charlie. He displayed them on screen. Cut stone blocks, stacked to form tall, straight structures, rose from the seafloor. A long trench led to the largest structure and disappeared under it. "We followed this trench into the structure. It slopes upward to a pool. There is a ramp that leads out of the water."

"It looks like Neophorm construction," said Velositi. "They like simple, blocky structures that are well fortified."

"It fits the period for Omegus Hexious' lieutenants," said Ryan.

"It is possible the ancient Morphicons built it, and it was found by the Neophormes," said Sprokkit.

"With the available intelligence gathered by the CIA and military forces, The Pentagon has drawn up a series of assault plans, Your Highness," said General Mayfield.

"What assets will we need?" said Kimmy.

"The Enterprise battle group is in the East China Sea, ready to be the command and control node. SEAL Teams Two and Three will support ANTs One, Two, and Three."

"And you're sure this is a major base, Charlie?" said Kimmy.

"Yes, Your Highness. The signal traffic is high, and so is the surface traffic."

"Then, I want to move ASAP. Get the ships and teams in position."

"Yes, Your Highness. The jump-off point is Kadena airbase on Okinawa," said Mayfield.

"Good, then I will see them there."

"You're going, Your Highness?" said Mayfield, unable to keep the surprise from his voice.

"I don't plan on jumping in the water with them, but I will be on Enterprise. Wherever Velositi goes, Kita goes, and I go with her."

Kita raised an eyebrow. *You're not the one who regenerates.*

"We will plan extra security for you," said Mayfield.

"Whatever makes you happy," said Kimmy.

Kita, Kimmy, Ryan, and Adrestia sat on a picnic table overlooking the ocean around Okinawa. Velositi and Sprokkit were parked next to them. The sun was dipping under the horizon, leaving a fiery red trail on the water. Kimmy had her arm around Kita.

They and the Anti-Neophorm Teams had flown in an hour earlier. A black SUV pulled up, and Kimmy's head chef and sous-chef exited. They opened the back, pulled out four platters, and set them on the picnic table. Kita and the others turned to look.

"Your Highnesses, dinner is served," said the head chef as he and the sous-chef removed the domes revealing a spread of sushi.

"Wow, Francis, this is wonderful," said Kimmy.

"We are in Japan, Your Highness. It's all local fish. There are a variety of rolls, including vegan for Her Highness, Kita."

Kita smiled. "Thanks." She wasn't sure how much she could eat. After eating for two days straight, she suddenly wasn't hungry. But she would do her best to eat as much as she could. She didn't want to be rude to those who fed her.

"Bon appétit, Your Highnesses." The two chefs bowed and left.

"Wow," said Ryan. "I need to travel with you more often, Kimmy."

For the long flight, everyone had ridden aboard Air Force Three, including Velositi and Sprokkit.

"I don't know what *you* did the whole time, but *I* worked."

Kita spent most of her time in the vehicle cargo area with Velositi. Not the most comfortable, but she couldn't sleep, and Velositi made the time go by.

"Every time I saw him, he was talking to a girl," said Adrestia. "Most of them are enlisted, so off-limits."

"Oh," said Ryan sheepishly. "So, ah, what are we doing tomorrow?"

Kimmy swallowed a piece of sushi. "For the next two days, you and Nicole are going with Velositi and Sprokkit to work with the teams on underwater breaching drills and then the tire house to practice room clearing. Also, there will be classes for the SEALs on anti-Neophorm operations. Kita and I are flying to Enterprise with the tech people to make sure the communications work. We're going to tour the fleet as well. I need to be seen as in command, and Kita needs to be recognized as who she is."

"Moving Kita up fast," said Adrestia.

"The sooner she is established as legitimate in the minds of the military, the easier it will be to do it in the general population. I've informed the Pentagon that her rank is Princess."

Adrestia raised an eyebrow. "How does Kita feel about it?"

Kita shrugged. "It's not a state dinner, so I think I can handle it. I just have to nod, smile, and look pretty."

"Going to be a lot of jealous sailors," said Ryan.

"I think they'll be too intimidated to be thinking like that." Adrestia chuckled. "Kita's stature is quickly growing to match Kimmy's. And Kita was already a force."

Kita wrinkled her nose. "I thought I'd been pretty chill lately."

"That's because you've been getting your way."

"Well, isn't it much easier for everyone when I do?"

Everyone laughed.

Kimmy hugged Kita. "Humble isn't in your vocabulary."

Kita stuck her tongue out at Kimmy.

"Is that an invitation? Because I'm sure Nicole will."

Kita laughed. "Nope. She still scares me."

"You don't know what you're missing," said Adrestia.

"So, there is one person you're scared of?" said Ryan.

"A lot of people scare me, but I don't let them know it. I only tell the people I trust if I'm scared of them. I'm still scared Kimmy is going to exile Velositi and me."

"I told you, I'm keeping you at the White House. Like it or not." Kimmy kissed Kita's cheek.

"At least you'll feed me."

"And you eat a lot."

"Only for those couple of days. I haven't been hungry since. I've barely eaten."

"More of the Axiom?" said Adrestia. "What is it turning you into? Not a monster, but a superhuman."

"I wonder if it did this to those ancient Morphicons?" said Ryan.

"We only have stories," said Velositi. "Omegus Hexious was powerful, but they do not say how."

"But, I'm not a warrior," said Kita. "It's a waste. It should have gone to Nicole."

"It might not be done yet," said Ryan. "We don't know what the rest of that DNA does."

"Sprokkit's examination before we left showed the alien DNA hadn't moved," said Kimmy. "I'm sticking to my hypothesis that those new cells are behind her changes. The CDC just needs time to prove it."

"I guess I'll worry when I sprout wings," said Kita.

KITA AND KIMMY DUCKED THEIR HEADS AS SAILORS DIRECTED THEM OUT FROM under the Seahawk's rotors and escorted them across Enterprise's flight deck to the carrier's island where a line of waiting officers and senior enlisted waited. A man wearing a dress blue uniform with lots of color on his chest stepped forward and saluted Kimmy.

"Your Highnesses, welcome aboard the EUSS Enterprise. I'm Rear Admiral Ian Lindsey, Commander of Carrier Strike Group Nine."

Kimmy returned the salute. "Good morning, Admiral. It's a pleasure to be aboard. We look forward to seeing your command in action. I'd like to introduce you to Princess Kita Logine."

"Your Highness. It's a pleasure to meet you," said Lindsey as he saluted.

Kita smiled warmly and did her best to imitate the salute. "Nice to meet you, Admiral."

"Your Highnesses, I'd like to introduce Captain Allen. Enterprise is her ship."

After exchanging salutes, Kimmy said, "Captain, I look forward to seeing your ship. I'm also here to tell you that we'll need special accommodations in the hangar for two VIPs that will arrive the day after tomorrow."

"No problem, Your Highness. How much space do you need?"

"Just enough room to park a motorcycle and an ambulance—preferably someplace out of the way."

"We'll make sure there's room, Your Highness."

"Excellent," said Kimmy. "We're excited to see the ship. I haven't been on a carrier since Kitty Hawk during Fleet Week in Diego seven years ago. Princess Kita has never been on one."

"I think you'll be impressed with the Big E, Your Highness. She's the most advanced carrier in the fleet. Let me introduce you to my officers."

Kita followed Kimmy down the line, returning salutes and greetings with the officers and senior enlisted. They followed Allen into the island, toured the bridge, and watched several planes land and take off, before going to a dark room several decks down filled with electronics, workstations, and screens.

"This is the Combat Information Center," said Allen. "From the mission profile we received, this is where command and control will take place. We have room for the SEALs, Air Force commanders, and the equipment. The sensors from the strike group will allow for real-time updates. We are setting up a separate room for Your Highnesses to observe. You'll get all the same data, video feeds, and hear the commanders, but in a more comfortable environment."

*So, we'll be out of the way and not add to the stress. Like I'm going to second-guess them. I barely know what they're doing.*

Kita nudged Kimmy and whispered, "So, I'm not going down with them?"

Kimmy turned Kita around and huddled with her. "This mission is far too dangerous. We know there are Neophormes present, and it's deep underwater. This mission is for trained military only."

"What good is being *me* if I can't use it? What if they need me?"

"You are not indestructible. A Neophorm cannon could still blow you in half. If they need you, you'll go down after the area is secured."

"I'll have Velositi."

"Do you want Velositi worried about taking care of you or fighting the Neophormes?" Kimmy hissed.

"I'm supposed to go with her."

"Ryan isn't going, and neither is Nicole. You'll be here with me."

Kita huffed.

"I'm not budging on this," said Kimmy. "You don't have the training or experience. This is not the situation to go by your emotions. You can throw a tantrum if you want, but there's nowhere to go."

Kita snarled and stomped her foot, leaving a dent in the deck.

"Kita, your job as liaison is to work between Velositi and the commanders. You'll be more effective for Velositi here. The commanders will be here, not below. You'll still be able to talk to Velositi."

"If Velositi wants me to go, I'm going."

"I will fight her, too, if I have to. It's not safe, and I am *not* about to have a state funeral for you."

An image of Kimmy in black crying appeared in Kita's mind. *I don't want to do that to her.* Kita sighed. "Fine."

"I'm sorry, but it's for your own good." Kimmy kissed Kita on the cheek.

They turned back to Allen.

"That sounds good, Captain. As long as we can monitor events and have communications with the teams, it should be fine."

They continued to tour the ship, meeting sailors and exploring life aboard. In the bowels of the ship, they saw the nuclear control rooms. On the way back to the wardroom, they toured the hangar deck. Various planes had panels open as the crews performed maintenance.

"It's a busy place," said Kita as the crews went about their routines.

"Life never stops aboard Enterprise," said Allen. "We run around the clock."

There was a *thud* behind them. "Hey, look out! Holy Roller!" someone yelled.

"What's that mean?" said Kita as she spun around. Coming at her and Kimmy was a large 10-foot-long eighteen-inch diameter cylindrical tank with tapered ends.

"Your Highnesses, get out of the way!" yelled Allen.

Kita lifted Kimmy with one arm and stuck out her right foot to stop the runaway tank. After putting Kimmy down, Kita lifted the tank and carried it over to the fighter it came from. "Where do you want it, sailor?" said Kita.

"In—in the cradle, Your Highness." He pointed to a dolly with a scissor lift.

Kita placed the tank in the lift. "Like that?"

"Yes. Thanks."

"No problem. Don't drop it again. I won't be around to catch it next time." Kita walked back to Kimmy and the surprised faces of the ship's officers.

"That event is classified," Kimmy told Allen and her officers. "Princess Kita is special in more ways than one."

"Yes, Your Highness. Thank you, Princess Logine. A fuel tank is expensive, and we have to send it to port to get it repaired."

"It was nothing," said Kita. "You ok?" she said to Kimmy.

Kimmy giggled. "I'm fine, my hero."

Kita smirked. "Let's go see the rest of the ship."

KITA STOOD WITH VELOSITI ON ENTERPRISE'S DECK AS THE SAILORS HOOKED Sprokkit, in his ambulance form, to a helicopter. The sailors backed away and gave a thumbs-up. The helicopter's engine roared as it rose into the air, taking Sprokkit with it.

"My turn," said Velositi.

"Be safe," said Kita hugging her.

"I will do my best. The plan is solid, and this is the type of mission I excel at. Our chances of victory are high."

"Don't be a hero. Just come back to me." Kita hugged Velositi tightly.

"I will do what is necessary to win."

"Sacrificing yourself is not a win."

Velositi knelt and placed her hands on Kita's shoulders. "I am a warrior, and that means putting myself in danger. I love you. Nothing will ever change that."

Kita blinked away tears. "I love you. Just—just don't do anything foolish. Leave that to me."

Velositi laughed. "I will trust my training and instincts. They will bring me home safely."

"They had better."

Velositi stood, took Kita's hand, and walked her to the loading area.

"Right there's good, Your Highness," said a sailor to Kita.

Velositi morphed.

"Good luck," said Kita as she stroked Velositi's gas tank. She stepped back as the sailors rigged Velositi for the helicopter. The sailors hooked the helicopter's line to Velositi's rigging, gave a thumbs-up, and Velositi was lifted into the air.

Kita walked to the edge of the deck, following the helicopter. She waved to Velositi as the helicopter flew out of sight.

Kimmy came and put an arm around Kita. "She'll be fine. This is her specialty."

*It only takes one mistake. A bad bounce. An inch. And she won't come back to me.* "I know, but I can't help but worry."

"I know. Let's go inside, and we can watch."

KITA AND KIMMY STEPPED INTO ENTERPRISE'S WARDROOM. LARGE SCREENS and speakers sat on the table. A pair of sailors sat at laptops controlling the video and audio. A couch and some food sat on the other end of the room. Ryan and Adrestia stood watching a screen. Standing in a corner were O'Brien and three other Secret Service agents.

"How's it going?" Kimmy asked Ryan and Nicole.

"The SEALs have left the subs, the Anti-Neophorm Teams have jumped from the helicopters, and Velositi and Sprokkit are on the bottom. All teams are moving toward the trench, Your Highness," said Adrestia.

"Any signs of trouble?"

"Not yet. Drones are in position, watching the entrance."

"How do I talk to Velositi?" said Kita to the sailors at the table.

The sailor tapped on her laptop. "Frequency set. Just use this mic, Your Highness."

"Velositi, can you hear me?"

"Oh, hi, Kita. Yes. We're moving toward the entrance. I can see the teams moving in. Nothing else to report, other than the occasional spooked fish. Can you see my feed?"

The sailor pointed to a video feed on the monitor.

"Yes. I can see the trench up ahead."

"Good. I will check in once we are inside."

"Ok," said Kita. "Love you."

"Love you."

Kita put the mic down.

"Missions are always stressful," said Adrestia. "Especially when all you can do is wait."

"I don't like it," said Kita. "I don't like that I can't *do* something—anything—to influence the outcome."

"Angel," said Kimmy, "we've sent the very best on this mission. Highly trained and experienced people are leading it. We have to put our trust in them. They'll get the job done. I know you don't like waiting, but there is no other choice."

Kita sighed and sat on the couch. Kimmy sat next to her and put an arm around her.

"I know you worry about her," said Kimmy. "But this is what she was made for."

"I just don't like not having control."

"I know it's hard, but it comes with our job. Come on. Let's go take a walk and get your mind off it." Kimmy pulled Kita to her feet. "Nicole, I'll take Dan with us. Alert him when the teams enter the base."

KITA AND KIMMY ENTERED THE WARDROOM AFTER WALKING THE LENGTH OF the ship.

"The teams are moving up the entrance now," said Adrestia.

On the screens, everything was in monochrome green.

"Why is it green?" said Kita.

"Low-light vision."

On most screens, there wasn't much to see. On Velositi and Sprokkit's feeds, the sloping floor and walls were visible.

"There's the pool," said Ryan. There were lights visible through the water.

Velositi and Sprokkit used the ramp and emerged from the water. Crates in neat rows lined the area next to the pool.

"Neophorm spotted," said Sprokkit.

"All team leaders, Sprokkit and I will provide cover while you transition," said Velositi.

Kita ground her teeth as Velositi and Sprokkit engaged the Neophorm. The three ducked and dodged around the crates, exchanging fire. The SEALs and

Anti-Neophorm Teams engaged, many still wearing their scuba gear over their battle uniforms.

Two more Neophormes came from a passageway.

"They are drones," confirmed Sprokkit.

Commands from the squad leaders came through the speakers, directing the teams on how and where to engage. From the video feed, Kita couldn't tell what was going on. It was a blur of dark and flashing lights. Velositi's feed continuously rotated on various axes as she moved around the room. Sprokkit's was the best. He stayed mostly stationary while firing at the Neophormes.

One by one, the Neophormes went down. Velositi went around and checked each one, blasting each in the chest to make sure it was dead. The teams regrouped, dropped their scuba gear, and prepared to move deeper into the facility.

"All teams report *go* status," said the mission commander. "Teams proceed into the facility."

With Velositi and Sprokkit leading the teams, they moved down the passageway the Neophormes had come from to a room full of humans at workstations. The humans were frantically tapping on the keyboards.

"Anti-Neophorm Team one, clear the room," said the mission commander. "Save as much equipment as possible."

The firefight was one-sided as the teams killed the Illuminati personnel.

"Room is clear," a squad leader soon reported.

The teams' tech specialists hurried through the workstations, doing their best to undo what the Illuminati had started.

"Room is secure. The mission can proceed."

Velositi and Sprokkit exited the room down another passageway. It made a right turn, and light was visible at the end. Velositi stopped and let the teams catch up.

"We have a large room," said Velositi. "It has a table in the middle, and two Neophormes are visible."

Kimmy grabbed the mic. "The one on the left is Litsink. Try to take him alive."

"Velositi and Sprokkit will be primary engagement," said the mission leader. "ANT One you're to go left, ANT Two go right and support Velositi and Sprokkit with anti-Neophorm weapons. ANT Three and SEAL teams will hold in reserve. Velositi, on your mark."

"Go," said Velositi as she sprinted out of the passageway firing at the Neophormes.

The tall walls of the room led to a domed ceiling. At the cardinal points from the door were three statues sitting in stone thrones. The attack disrupted the Neophormes from clearing the world map on the table. They turned and fired at Velositi.

"Hey, those statues look like ancient Morphicons," said Ryan.

"Let's hope they don't get up," said Kita.

Velositi and Sprokkit attacked while the Anti-Neophorm Teams moved around the room's perimeter. Once the teams were in place, they opened fire.

"That statue just moved!" said Kita. She pointed to the statue furthest from the door. Kita grabbed the mic. "Set it to Velositi," she told the sailor.

The sailor tapped her laptop's screen. "Good, Your Highness."

"Velositi! Those statues aren't statues. The one in the back just moved."

"Are you—"

A light flashed, and Velositi went tumbling through the air. She hit a wall and slid to the floor. Across the room, the ancient Morphicons were on their feet, firing at the teams and Sprokkit. Each ancient Morphicon was fifteen feet tall.

An ancient Morphicon grabbed Sprokkit from behind and slammed him into the ground. His arm morphed into a giant sword, and he thrust it through Sprokkit's back. The other arm morphed into a cannon, and he fired. Sprokkit's video feed terminated.

"All teams engage," said the mission leader.

"We've got to get them out of there," said Kita to Kimmy.

"Give them a chance."

"They just took down Sprokkit."

Kimmy grabbed the mic. "All teams, free fire. Defeat them using whatever means necessary."

Kita fumed. *This is not a winnable fight. I know Kimmy wants to win, but not if it costs me Velositi.* "Why can't we withdraw?"

"The base has to be destroyed. I'm willing to pay the price to do it."

"What about Velositi?"

"She's doing fine." Kimmy pointed to Velositi's video feed. She was moving around, firing at a rapid rate.

The other teams had entered and were firing at the ancient Morphicons. Explosions hit them, but Kita wasn't sure of their effectiveness.

Velositi's feed spun wildly. Kita checked the other feeds. An Ancient Morphicon had caught Velositi and was slamming her into the ground.

"Velositi!" cried Kita.

The ancient Morphicon grabbed Velositi around the waist and shoulders and pulled.

"*NO!*" Kita screamed.

Velositi tore in half just under her chest. Her video feed went black. A giant lump formed in Kita's throat and her breath vanished as her heart broke.

"*NO! NO! NO!*" Kita wailed as tears ran down her cheeks.

"Get the subs online. Tell them to prepare to torpedo the base," said Kimmy.

"NO!" screamed Kita. "We can still save her. We have to save her."

"Kita! Velositi is gone. They tore her in half. We can't repair that. She's gone. I'm sorry."

"I won't lose her!" Kita shrieked.

"Kita, there is nothing we can do." Kimmy tried to hug Kita, but she turned away.

"There has to be something!" Kita yelled. "I won't—I can't—be without her."

"She's dead!" yelled Kimmy. "She'll go down as a hero. That's what she wanted."

"No," Kita sobbed as she sank to the floor. She curled up on her legs, holding her head in her hands. "I love her. I *won't* be without her."

Kita's chest exploded in pain. It radiated through her body. She screamed as her blood boiled. A pair of sharp stabbing pains between her shoulder blades took the air from her lungs. Everything from her hair to her toes burned. She shrieked, and then everything went black.

"BY THE CRUSHING DEPTHS, LEAF. I SWEAR YOU MAKE IT PAINFUL AS A WAY OF punishing me. What did I do to you?" Kita opened her eyes to see her black low-rise jeans and thigh pads with rows of throwing stars. She sat up and opened her vision to a full panoramic view. "Where am I?"

Two uniformed people sat at a table with some kind of equipment, a couch sat along a wall next to a table of food, and a group of people in suits with guns drawn stood in front of a distraught girl in a formal military uniform. A couple in different colored uniforms than those at the table looked more curious than scared.

A loading bar from the computer in Kita's head appeared in her mind. *About time.*

On the wall was a picture of a large seagoing vessel. In big letters, it said ENTERPRISE. *Hello, my old friend.*

The loading bar hit one hundred percent, and an indexing bar replaced it. *We're getting there.* Kita could feel the emotions of those in the room and the ship. The group of suits was getting anxious. *I hope they don't shoot me while I'm waiting.*

The upset girl tried to push past the suits, but they refused to let her. *She's beautiful. Who is she, and what is my relationship with her?*

"Kita! Kita!" the girl yelled.

*She knows my name. That's a start.* Kita floated upward and stood. *Isn't this an interesting era? It almost has all the creature comforts of home. Sure beats the Stone Age.* The indexing bar completed. Kita instructed her computer to load all the files from this lifetime's iteration. Her mind populated with all the knowledge and memories she had acquired during this time on Earth. *Well, isn't that interesting. I met a decent boy, and I fell in love with another princess and a bio-mechanical creature—a trifecta. Will wonders never cease?*

"Dammit, Dan. Let me go. She's not dangerous. We've proven that!" yelled Kimmy.

Kita chuckled. *I'm not dangerous to you, Kimmy. But I will devastate those that have Velositi.*

Kita turned around. "Hello, Kimmy, Nicole, and Ryan. Did I get that right?" She pointed to them in turn.

"Kita, are you ok?" said Kimmy.

"Never better. Dan, why can't I see my girlfriend? Never mind, I'll get her myself." The world shifted to black and white as Kita entered another dimension. She walked through the Secret Service agents and stood behind Kimmy. She exited the dimension and took Kimmy's hand. The world shifted back to black and white.

"What happened?" said Kimmy.

"We're phase-jumping by entering the fifth dimension. It looks instantaneous to those in the normal dimensions. It allows me to move around fast and get things I want. Like you." Kita led Kimmy back to where Kita had been standing. She held Kimmy in front of her and ended the jump.

"Put them away, Dan. I'm not going to hurt her," said Kita.

O'Brien and the other Secret Service agents spread out, trying to encircle Kita.

"Fine. Have it your way." Kita, with blinding speed, drew and threw four throwing stars into the end of each agent's pistol. "Now what are you going to do?"

"They're not going to do anything," said Kimmy firmly. "Dan, she's fine. I think if she wanted to kill us, she would have."

"What—what are you?" said Ryan.

Kita spread her black wings wall to wall and then wiggled the tips. "I thought it was obvious," she said as she closed her wings.

"An Angel?"

"Got it in one. Glad to see your powers of observation are as keen as ever."

"How can you see?" said Kimmy as she pushed the oversized hood off Kita's head. Kita's floor-length blonde hair spilled out and fell down her back.

"Oh my god," Kimmy gasped, looking up at Kita. "You're—you're breathtakingly gorgeous."

"Just makeup," Kita said with a coy grin.

Kimmy raised an eyebrow. "And when did you get so tall?"

Kita chuckled. "I forget as a human I'm only five-six. As an Angel, I'm five-eleven, plus the two-inch heels." Kita bent her knee to show off the heel of her black knee-high combat boot.

Kimmy placed her hand on Kita's chest. "Where's the Axiom?"

"It did what it was supposed to do—find me, protect me, and if called upon, transform me."

"Why?"

"It's here because I'm tired of dying horrific deaths. It transformed me because there is someone I want, and I need my power to save her."

"Velositi?"

"Yes."

"But, she's dead."

"Death means little. It's just a minor inconvenience."

Kimmy leaned back in Kita's arms. "What are you that *death* is only a minor inconvenience?"

Kita shrugged. "The simple answer is I am god."

Kimmy sputtered, "G—God?"

"What's God doing here?" said Ryan.

Kita's shoulders slumped. "It's lonely being god. There are only three Angels. We're trying to get the universes restarted, but we don't know how. We're learning as we go. As we test, we live."

"If the universes aren't running," said Adrestia, "then what are we?"

"You are trial run eight hundred and thirty-two. Leaf, one of the other Angels, and I came from the original universe, which your universe is based on. Our goal is to restart the original universe and finish what I started."

"What is that?" said Kimmy.

"Restoring the Emperor of the United Earth Empire to her throne and punish one of my former lovers for betraying me and the other Angels."

"If you were in the original universe, how did you become a god?" said Ryan.

"The universe you live in is not the primary universe, but a subset. A group of gods who inhabited the primary universe—called Infinity—made millions of subset universes—I came from one of these universes. They studied these subset universes to learn about concepts. The God of Murder studied me, and we had a child."

"How does a god have a child? Was it mortal at the time?" said Ryan.

"Science and it was complicated."

"I have a feeling that describes you a lot," said Adrestia.

Kita rolled her eyes. "Anyway, with the God of Murder's help, I earned my spot in Infinity as the God of Evil, but not all gods agreed I should be there. The God of Death made it his mission to see me eradicated. He killed many of the Angels, including my partner. I took revenge, destroyed Infinity, and discovered the nature of existence—it's nothing special, just a giant computer. I inserted myself into its programming and took control. I brought my friend Leaf back— she was the God of Light among the old gods—and we've been trying to get existence up and running ever since."

"So, what happens to us?" said Kimmy, stepping away from Kita. "And—did you say you were the *God of Evil*?"

Kita raised an eyebrow and shook her head, so all her hair hung loose. "Who else but the God of Evil destroys existence? I'm evil, but I'm not bad."

Kita's hair divided itself into nine parts, grouped into threes, and braided itself. "What you experienced with me is who I am. I just have more tricks now. I've never reached this point in a simulation before. I'm not sure when it ends. Probably when I say so."

The three braids plaited themselves into one large braid. Kita whipped her head, snapping the end of the braid up into her hand. She took a star from her thigh pad, held the center between her thumb and index finger, and melted a hole in the star. "I'm going down to get Velositi and take her back—that much is certain."

She braided the star into the end of her braid.

"That's not possible," said Adrestia.

"Braiding it by hand is impossible," said Kita. "The rest is physics."

"We just cease to exist?" exclaimed Kimmy.

"It's not painful or anything. You won't even know it happened."

"You're just going to leave me?" yelled Kimmy.

"You three are welcome to come with me."

"And be Angels?" said Ryan.

Kita scowled. "I host the most exclusive girls club ever. Girls become Angels. Boys become bears and know their place."

"What do Angels do?" said Adrestia.

"That's up to the Angel. I've had doctors, CEOs, researchers, pilots, soldiers —whatever the girl wants to do. I've designed Angels to be the apex predator of the universe. It's not just passive systems like what you've seen. We come equipped with some of the fiercest weapons and abilities I can think of." Kita's fingertips burst into flame. As the fire marched up her black leather and crystal bracers, she raised her other hand and pulled all the liquid on the snack table to her forming it into a ball. The ball changed to a hollow cylinder, and Kita blasted a lance of flame through it, causing it to boil. Kita snapped her hand closed, killing the flame, and with a flick of her wrist, she sent the liquid back to the containers on the snack table.

"How do you do that?" said Ryan.

"Physics and biology."

"We'll see combat?" said Adrestia.

"As much as you want. Angels are the best in existence and go on the most dangerous missions. But, if you want to go looking for a fight, I won't stop you."

"I'm in."

Kita floated over in front of Adrestia. "I wasn't kidding when I said the Axiom should have gone to you." Kita reached out and touched Adrestia's nose. "Boop!"

Adrestia screamed and fell to her hands and knees.

"What did you do to her?" yelled Kimmy.

Kita drew her sword *Dead*. A Secret Service agent lunged at Kita. She raised her arm and opened her hand. A gray sphere appeared around the agent. Kita cut two slits in Adrestia's coat and T-shirt between her shoulder blades and spine. Two long, thin fleshy growths sprang upward. They grew, forming joints and long bones. Fleshy buds covered the appendages and burst into blue feathers with silver edges.

Kita grinned. "Rise, Nemesis." She moved the agent back to the others and released him, then she helped Nemesis to her feet, keeping her from falling over backward. "Keep your weight forward."

"What happened?" said Nemesis.

Kita pulled a wing around. "Take a look."

"I didn't expect color," said Nemesis.

"Black is reserved for fallen angels."

"Let me guess. You're the queen?"

"I have, in the past, been as despicable as they come, but I am trying to be kinder and gentler."

On the ground in front of Nemesis appeared a large sniper rifle and a belt with a bullet maker and bullet cases.

"Thanks, Leaf," said Kita.

"This is mine?" said Nemesis.

"Yep. You'll find your body and mind has been changed to make you one of the greatest snipers in the universe."

"Why not the best?"

"The best was my former partner, and I would never hear the end of it if I made you the best. Instead, I made it so, if you put in the time, you could challenge her records."

"I'll spend years at the range if I have to," said Nemesis.

"Her standard is every bullet through the same hole at two miles."

"I can do that?"

"You have the tools—you just need to learn to use them."

"Agh!" Nemesis clutched her head. "Ow."

"Leaf gave you a head start by putting you through ten thousand hours firing the rifle."

"I feel like I've been holding it for years."

A suit, boots, and hood appeared. Kita picked up the armored bodysuit and shook it out. It was silver and blue made of a weave Kita recognized. Her daughter, Arial, had developed it to protect her biomechanical body. It was nearly indestructible.

"For me?" said Nemesis. "I thought I'd be getting something like you." She poked the exposed underside of Kita's breast. Kita's black short sleeve and open shoulder stretch top ran diagonally across her chest. Black pauldrons and pads protected her upper arms and shoulders.

"I dress in the grand tradition of thieves and assassins. But if you think you can pull it off."

"I don't have the stomach you do."

"You will."

"Can you cut the rest of this uniform off?"

Nemesis turned around, and Kita sliced the uniform off.

"You're not going to need your old clothes. The suit will have everything you need."

Nemesis ignored the rest of the room, stripped naked, and slipped the suit on. It sealed up her back and around her wings. She slipped the boots on, fashioned her hair into a low ponytail, and put the hood on. "Damn. I know how to use the hood, too. I need to change the voice. I don't want a man's voice in my ear."

Kita chuckled. "Girl after my own heart."

"All this to fire a rifle?"

"Missing means someone dies," said Kita.

"Roger that."

"If you're set, we can go outside, and you can fire a few rounds. Then we'll hit the water."

"How are we getting down there?" said Nemesis.

"Angels are rated for space and the deepest part of the ocean. We'll swim. It's like flying, except slower."

"What about me?" demanded Kimmy.

"What about you?" said Kita. "You didn't sound like you wanted to go."

"I—"

An Angel in a black uniform, boots, and short-billed cap appeared. Her blonde hair was reverse braided. She carried a rifle and large pack fitted around her wings. Her red feathers with white borders matched the sapper tab on her shoulder.

"Lizzy!" Kita squealed. She glided over and gave the new arrival a hug and kiss. "I missed you. I didn't think you'd be finished."

"I died attacking Carthage, so I punched out early. Leaf says she's got all the good data she's going to get since you found yourself. So, we thought we'd come in and have some fun."

"Roman Legion?"

"Hell yeah. Those are some hardcore mothers. They know how to fight and drink. Oh my god, can they drink. Roman food isn't too bad, either." Sapper stole a kiss from Kita.

"Who is she?" demanded Kimmy.

Kita slipped an arm free of Sapper. "This is Elizabeth Wallace or Lizzy. The universe knows her as Sapper. She is my girlfriend from a previous iteration. We died clearing a minefield in World War III, fighting a different version of the Soviet Union."

"Were you going to tell me?"

Sapper laughed. "Kita's the kind that has a girl in every port."

Kita playfully punched Sapper in the arm. "You're not helping. I didn't think it was a big deal because I love you and Velositi. You didn't seem to mind that arrangement."

"How many other girls are there?" said Kimmy.

"The rest are gone. It's just Lizzy and maybe Velositi. I was hoping you."

"What about my universe? My country? What am I supposed to do?"

Kita sighed. "You'd be free to do what you want."

"How is that fair to my people? We were setting up to do something—to make a difference. I have things I want to accomplish. People are counting on us. I'm not ready to leave."

"Leaf?" Kita whined.

A little Angel wearing a white sneak suit, mask, and hood appeared. Her brilliant white wings with gold tips shimmered. On her back were a katana, wakizashi, and bow.

"Wow, she's short," said Ryan.

The little Angel Aspen glared at him for a moment. "*Hey, Kita, what's up?*"

"Why is her voice in my head?" said Nemesis.

"Leaf doesn't use her mouth. She only uses the comm," said Sapper.

"You have a biological communications suite in your head called the comm," said Kita. "Think of who or what you want to talk to, and you'll connect."

"Are you going to kiss her, too?" said Kimmy darkly.

"Leaf was a student of mine," said Kita.

"Dare I ask of what?"

"Assassination." Kita grinned as O'Brien and the other Secret Service agents twitched. "Leaf, ah, is it possible to save this iteration?"

"*Sure. I can put it aside. Why?*"

"Kimmy wants to come back and govern."

"*It must be something about princesses. Gluttons for punishment. They like to rule, and they fall in love with you.*"

Sapper snorted, and Nemesis laughed.

"What's so funny?" demanded Kimmy.

"As usual, Kita," said Sapper.

"My love life is always fodder for everyone else's amusement," said Kita. "Leaf says she can save this iteration. So, we can set it aside, and you can come back to it whenever you want."

"You're coming too," said Kimmy. "You're the reason I'm doing this."

"What am I going to do? I don't want to govern. I've done that. It sucks. I get other people to do it for me."

"You can come to my state dinners. They're not that hard. Even you can do it."

Kita bristled. "Sweetheart, I grew up nobility, I was thrust into royalty, and I conquered and ruled a planet—not like your little constitutional monarchy—but with an iron fist. I know etiquette, protocol, and behavior that will make even the snobbish among you look like a beggar eating out a trash can."

"Easy, big girl," said Sapper pushing Kita backward.

Nemesis moved next to Kimmy and put a hand on her shoulder.

"What?" snapped Kimmy.

"I can't imagine making her mad is a good thing," said Nemesis. "Why are you fighting her? She's offering freedom. Otherwise, it's lights out."

"I'm the ruler of a country. How am I supposed to give that up?"

"She said you could come back anytime you want."

"And be subservient to her?"

"She's not looking for servants, she's looking for friends," said Nemesis.

"She's still in charge."

"Yeah, that is something most of us are used to. Few are in your position. But Kita hasn't ordered anyone to do anything, she asks. There is a big difference."

"And I don't like Lizzy," huffed Kimmy.

"You barely met her, or is it that you don't like Kita's relationship with her? Because it sounds like Kita has lived many lives and loved lots of people. She only keeps those who are special to her—Lizzy, Velositi, and you."

"What kind of relationship are we going to have with three of us?"

"I can tell you won't have any at all if you keep telling her *no*. Better to take the leap and figure the rest out later."

"Is that what you're doing?" said Kimmy harshly.

"No. I see the opportunity to make my dream a reality. I'll get to fight and be part of the greatest team ever."

"Doesn't sound like a great team if they all died."

"I once lost an entire unit to the man," said Kita. "I cried for days, even though we accomplished our mission. I remember every one of their faces. I learned that some days there would be fights where you have to sacrifice everything for victory. Go downstairs and talk to the commanders that just lost their teams and see how they feel. And we haven't even won yet. Sometimes great teams still lose. I'll make sure their sacrifice wasn't in vain—I'll get Velositi, grab the data, and destroy the base. The four of us can do it, no problem."

"Don't lecture me on sacrifice. I've been doing it for years!" yelled Kimmy as she jumped around Nemesis into Kita's face.

"Then act like it!" yelled Kita. "You can't govern if I turn off the machine. The only way the machine stays on is if you come with me. Coming with me has its perks. Loving me has its rewards. It means giving up your spot at the top to be higher up on a much bigger ladder. You don't sit at the top, but you're only a rung below."

"What good am I to you? I'm not a warrior. I haven't fired a rifle since officer's candidate school. What am I going to do? Stab them with a pen?"

"No," said Kita. "You just have to look them in the eye. Do you trust me?"

"I—I—yes." Kimmy's face softened. "You've never been wrong."

Kita reached up and touched Kimmy's nose. "Boop."

Kimmy fell to her hands and knees, screaming.

The Secret Service agents rushed Kita. With a wave of her hand, Sapper ripped the snack table from its mounts and flung it into the four agents. Kita sliced open Kimmy's bomber jacket and shirt as fleshy wing bones grew through the holes. The wings budded into red feathers with silver tips.

"Rise, Apocalypse."

Kita lifted Apocalypse into her arms.

"God, that hurt."

Kita chuckled. "A little pain for a great reward." She kissed Apocalypse.

"I have to get used to looking up at you."

"You can be taller if you want."

"I don't know if I'll look as good as you."

"You will." Kita pressed her nose against Apocalypse's.

Apocalypse groaned as she grew five inches. Her uniform became comically too small for her.

"I'll get you something that fits," said Kita. She walked over to O'Brien and the Secret Service agents and lifted the table off them. Picking O'Brien up by his coat, Kita put him on his feet. "You're sworn to protect Kimmy, right?"

"Yes."

"I assure you, she's fine. I've made your job easier, but I still worry about her. She isn't a warrior and should have a bodyguard." Kita pushed the tip of her finger into O'Brien's forehead.

Kita removed her finger, revealing a burn mark that burst into flame. The flame engulfed O'Brien burning the flesh from his bones until only a flaming skeleton in a suit remained, causing the rest of the sailors and Secret Service agents in the room to back into a corner.

"Hello, Bonehead," said Kita. "Firearms and flames are yours to command. You're charged with keeping Kimmy alive."

O'Brien grew a fireball in his hand.

"You got it," said Kita. "Grab the guns you'll need. You want to be normal, think human. You want to be flame-face, think demon."

O'Brien returned to normal.

"Good," said Kita. "Go protect your girl."

Kita led O'Brien over to where Aspen and Nemesis were helping Apocalypse into a bodysuit.

"That suit is programmable," said Kita. "You can form them into anything you want. You just have to think about it. It's what I wear."

"Why silver and red?" said Apocalypse.

"New colors for a new life. I thought red, white, and blue were too obvious."

"And you called me Apocalypse."

"That's your Angel name, what the outside will know you as—Lizzy is Sapper, Nicole is Nemesis, Leaf is Aspen, and you are Apocalypse. Given names are used among the Angels and deserving people. It's to help protect you and your identity. Not a big deal now, but it has been in the past."

"Why Apocalypse?"

"The end of the world is also its rebirth. You're a destroyer and a healer. Leaf can teach you how to heal and control the other goodies that come with being a healer. Outside, I'll show you the destruction part."

"Then, I'm ready to go." Apocalypse fashioned her bodysuit into a black business suit.

"How about it, Ryan?" said Kita.

"I, ah, think I'll stay here and watch."

"Ok. Let me know if you change your mind. Let's go outside, girls."

Kita followed the other Angels and Secret Service detail up the metal stairs to the flight deck door.

"Hey! What the hell are you doing?" yelled a stern voice from below. "We're at general quarters. Why are you practicing for the drag show and not at your stations?"

Kita turned around. "Do I look like a man?" she snarled at the man in a khaki uniform.

"Who the hell are you?"

Kita glared from under her hood. "You don't recognize your princess? Maybe you'll recognize this one." She moved a wing revealing Apocalypse.

"Can I help you, Chief?" said Apocalypse.

"Your Highness! I didn't know you were with them. Can I help you?"

"We're headed to the flight deck."

"The flight deck is for authorized personnel only during flight operations, Your Highness."

"I don't look like I'm ready for flight operations? Go to the bridge and tell Captain Allen that my friends and I will be on the flight deck. We won't interfere with anything."

"Yes, Your Highness. You'll need to stop by the locker room and get helmets and colored vests. They'll assign you an escort."

Kita rolled her eyes. "We come with all the color we need. Let's go."

Aspen flittered up the stairs.

"You can fly?" exclaimed the chief petty officer.

"Why do you think we're going outside?" said Sapper.

"Don't worry, Chief. It's all taken care of," said Apocalypse.

The Angels climbed the stairs and opened the door to the flight deck.

"Damn, man," said Sapper as she contorted to get through the door. "I thought the Army had small doors."

The roar of a jet engine momentarily drowned out all other sounds.

"*Not a lot of room out here,*" said Aspen.

Aircraft and the runway took all the available space.

"Over there," said Sapper pointing to an open area on the far side of the runway.

"We'll fly over," said Kita. "You help Nicole, and I'll get Kimmy."

"What are we doing?" said Apocalypse.

"Short flight to that open area. I'll help you fly." Kita put her hands on Apocalypse's waist. "Flap your wings and think up." She rose off the ground pulling Apocalypse with her.

"Oh, whoa...wow," exclaimed Apocalypse as she rose into the air.

"Keep flapping. Once we're high enough, think about moving forward, and we'll cross the runway."

Apocalypse flapped her wings, and they rose higher. Kita pushed her forward until she moved on her own. They crossed the ship and landed. Behind them, the Secret Service agents ran across the runway.

"Excellent," said Kita kissing Apocalypse on the cheek.

"That was incredible."

"Soon, you'll outfly the fighters. I'm going to go coordinate with the team

257

leaders. I need you to work with Leaf on learning your healing and defensive abilities. When I come back, I'll show you your offensive abilities."

"Ok. What are you going to do?"

"Rally the troops. I can feel emotion, and what I feel isn't good. I'm going to tell them it's not over yet."

"You think the teams are still alive?"

"I plan on bringing back everyone. Be prepared for a lot of swimming."

"I'm happy to help."

"Good. I'll be back." Kita stole a kiss. "Lizzy!"

"Yo!"

"Help Nicole with that rifle. Give her something explosive to shoot at."

"Ah! No problem." A red ball three inches across formed in her hand. "Sapper's my name, and explosives are my game." She hurled the ball out over the ocean. "Hit it." The ball was a small barometric bomb that, when detonated, gave off two shockwaves that caused a negative pressure between them, ripping soft targets apart. They were extremely effective in enclosed areas like caves.

Nemesis snapped her rifle to her shoulder, aimed, and fired. A massive explosion reflected off the water five hundred yards away.

Satisfied all was handled, Kita phased to the CIC. Inside, the darkness matched the sullen mood as the mission commander, team leaders, and Navy personnel went about winding down the mission.

"Everyone, listen up!" Kita barked as she swept her hood back. "The mission is not over yet. There's one more team to go down. We will kill the enemy, recover the data, and bring back the dead and wounded. I'm patching you in to my frequencies so you can talk to us." Screens around the room displayed what the Angels saw and heard. "My team's codenames are Kita, Sapper, Aspen, Apocalypse, and Nemesis. We'll need you to guide our insertion and watch our backs while we're there. Once we have the base secure, we'll need to work out the extraction of the dead and wounded. I only have two medics with me, so those not emergent will need to be treated in sickbay. Make sure they're ready. If it's possible to get this ship or another closer to the site once it's safe, that will make recovery faster. We won't have to fly as far. Any questions?"

"Your Highness, what the hell happened to you?" said a leader from the Anti-Neophorm Teams.

"You know that thing we recovered in Hawaii?"

"The Axiom?"

"I'm its owner."

"So, the legend is true?"

"I'm the greatest warrior to ever live, and I brought my friends. I'll signal you when we leave."

"Yes, Your Highness. We'll be ready."

"Holy shit!" someone exclaimed while looking at the screens. "They've got wings."

Kita chuckled as hers, hidden in the darkness, burst into flame. "Yes, sailor. Angels are real." Kita phased back to Apocalypse and Aspen. "How's it going, girls?"

"Kita! This is amazing. How's it possible?" said Apocalypse.

"Which part? Your shield and healing ability are thanks to an alien known as an A'ahegre. Don't be alarmed if you get a voice in your head. You can talk to it or ignore it. Leaf can tell you more about white A'ahegre. They like to connect to creatures with reason and intellect. I have a black A'ahegre who likes emotions.

"The medical viewer, barbs, and extractor are genetic modifications. The suite was designed by Nell, another Angel doctor."

"I get the barbs and viewer, but why an extractor when our bodies will push the bullets out?"

Kita chuckled. "Some Angels don't know the meaning of the word *dodge*. They just stand there and take the punishment. They can take dozens of bullets. Sometimes, it's nice not to have to wait. So, do you think you're proficient with them?"

"Yes, I think so."

"Let's see your shield."

Apocalypse stepped back, and a translucent pearly-white bubble appeared around her.

Kita rapped on it. "Good. Nice and solid. O'Brien!" she called.

He walked over. "Yes?"

"You are to remind her that she has this shield. It's impervious. If she gets in trouble, you tell her to activate it until I come rescue her."

"Yes, Your Highness." O'Brien looked relieved.

"I promise you I'm trying to make your job as easy as possible."

"You're still taking her into danger."

"If she doesn't want to go, I will not force her. But, it's her decision. Not mine, and not yours."

Apocalypse's bubble came down. "Of course I want to go. I want to be a member of the team."

Kita took Apocalypse's hands in hers. She kissed Apocalypse's knuckles, revealing slivers of ruby between them. Kita stood behind Apocalypse and held her arms up, pointing them out over the ocean. "You're not defenseless either. Think about beams coming from those rubies."

Apocalypse's brow furrowed, and there was a bright red flash.

"Good," said Kita. "Now, sustain it."

A bright beam erupted from Apocalypse's fists. She moved her fists around, and the beam moved with them.

"You can go full blast and melt through diamonds or be a big flashlight. Now, do the same thing with your eyes."

"My eyes?" Apocalypse looked out over the ocean, and a beam burst from her iris'. "I—Kita, this is amazing. How?"

"Something I've been saving for a special occasion. See if you can hit this." Kita grew a red ball in her hand and threw it out over the ocean.

Apocalypse's head followed the ball's arc. A beam shown from her eyes and an explosion announced she hit it.

"Excellent," said Kita. "You'll be a natural in no time."

"If she missed that would have been news," said Sapper sarcastically.

Kita frowned. "It took you a while to master your abilities—if I recall."

"I'm just saying if she missed, I'd be worried you were slipping."

"She'll be watching your back. You want her to miss?"

"I don't know if I want a cherry watching my back. That might be more dangerous than the bad guy. At least then, I'll know to look."

"Kimmy will do just fine," said Kita tersely. "If you don't want her watching your back, she can watch mine."

"She's a princess, not a shooter. She burns a hole in you, don't say I didn't tell you."

Kita ground her teeth. "I have every confidence in her, and I suggest you do too, or you'll find yourself watching the battle with Ryan."

"You're going to need me."

Kita grabbed Sapper by the jaw, kissed her, and shoved her to the ground. "You're a cocky kid. Remember, just because I sleep with you, doesn't mean I won't flatten you."

*"Remember—calmer and gentler,"* said Aspen.

Kita grumbled. "If we're ready, let's go. Dan!"

He trotted over. Kita opened a pocket dimension. "This is your way down to the base. I'll let you out when we get there."

"What is it?" said O'Brien.

"A pocket dimension. It'll feel instantaneous."

"You are going to let me out?"

"At the moment, you're not the one I want to shove in a hole and forget. Get in."

O'Brien stepped inside, and Kita sealed the dimension. She walked behind Apocalypse and grabbed her waist. "We're going high this time. Lizzy, help Nicole."

Kita flapped her wings and took off as Apocalypse flapped hers. They rose off the deck and circled the ship. There was some wild chatter over the ship's radio. "Everyone, watch for incoming fighters. The humans think we're going to hit one."

Kita circled the ship a few more times, so Apocalypse and Nemesis could get used to flying. As they flew, Apocalypse fired her beams into the water.

"I hope I'm not killing any fish," said Apocalypse.

Kita laughed. "We do need to find you some dead things."

Apocalypse gave Kita a questioning look. "Why?"

"Surprise. It'll make sure Lizzy doesn't get any ideas."

"What was her problem, anyway?"

"She's young and has to prove she's the best. She's got a lot of energy and thirst for adventure. I think she sees you as a threat."

"She doesn't strike me as your type. I guess I don't know anymore," said Apocalypse with a frown.

"Hey," said Kita gently. "I'm still the same person you knew two hours ago. I'm just more experienced."

"How old are you?"

"Ah, if you don't count the ten thousand years I was imprisoned, seventy? Maybe?"

"You don't look it," Apocalypse said with a teasing smile.

"I better not."

"I don't know if I want to share you."

Kita shrugged. "Not a problem at the moment. Lizzy is off doing her own thing. I've barely seen her since we were together in her universe. It doesn't bother me. People can come and go as they please. I love a lot of people, but I'm usually only with one person at a time."

"I bet you've loved a lot of people visiting all these universes."

"Nope. You, Lizzy, and Velositi. Being a lesbian through time is hard."

"So, you're always a lesbian? And you've never had kids?"

"I can't fight my DNA. I've never given birth," Kita shuddered, "if that's what you mean. I've raised kids."

"You said you included the Axiom in this universe because you were tired of dying?"

"I was tired of dying horrible deaths. Rarely did I die of old age or even an accident. I've been stoned, drowned, burned at the stake, died of exposure, mutilated, disemboweled, raped to death, and drawn and quartered—some multiple times—for being a lesbian throughout history. Though, I'm usually branded a witch, heretic, outcast, or something similar."

"That's horrible!"

"It's a control thing. You show a man he's not needed, and they get upset. The worst was the year I spent starving to death in a concentration camp. Talk about a horrific way to go. It takes your life an inch at a time, and they give you just enough to keep half an inch. You want to see humanity at its worst, put them in a situation where there's only the slimmest of hope. People will do anything to be the one to survive."

"Nazi?"

"American."

Apocalypse gasped. "What? That would—"

"Not all of history takes a similar course. The Americans are no better than any other group. They fall for the same lies like everybody else."

"You were in there for being a lesbian?"

"No. I was eight. My family didn't believe in God. How's that for irony?"

Apocalypse released from Kita's grasp and dropped. A lump grew in Kita's throat as she prepared to dive. Apocalypse caught herself, rolled on her back, and rose to hug Kita.

"Someone's confidence is high," said Kita.

"You sounded like you needed a hug."

"It is nice to find someone who cares."

"Leaf doesn't?"

"Oh, she does, and she listens, but even though she's my friend, she still sees me as Grandmaster and her as the student. She won't cross that boundary. She's a high angel, and as much as they look after the fallen, they tend to believe we get what we deserve."

"Do you?"

"I hope I deserve you."

"You've lost the innocent, junkyard girl charm, replaced by an experienced, tough as nails womanly allure. Yet, there's still a soft gooey center."

Kita chuckled. "I like to be loved by someone special."

"A few someone specials."

"I don't like to be alone. This way, I always have someone."

"And other girls go for this?" Apocalypse said, raising an eyebrow.

"Some did, and some didn't—once they found out there were others. It didn't mean I stopped loving them. I still saw them, but they lived their own lives. The others drifted in and out as they wanted. But I always had someone. It's good for my mental health. If you don't want to, you don't have to. The wings and everything I gave you are yours. I won't shut off this universe, and you can continue as you wish."

"Oh no, you're not ditching me to turn my country around by myself. It's because of you I'm in this position. I love you—that hasn't changed. I just have to get my head around you being god, and I'm the lowly princess, instead of me being *the* princess, and you being a junkyard girl."

"You're worried I might pull rank?"

Apocalypse laughed. "A little. I know the tantrums you can throw and what it takes to control them. I don't think I can throw my arms around a god and tell her to settle down. I like taking care of you. You don't need me to do that anymore."

"You would be surprised. I think the more powerful I get, the more I need someone to keep me sane. I'm pretty sure you will get tired of taking care of me. I don't throw the tantrums I used to. I try to be more rational and controlled. I love you, and that will never stop. I will attend your state dinners. They can't be as bad as my mother's estate dinners."

Apocalypse smiled. "I can't wait to hear about your life. It must be fascinating."

"A lot of fighting and the constant pursuit of knowledge that I could convert to power. There were a few quiet years when I was a mom. My favorite time was when I ruled Hades, and I had Jane and the girls. It was simple, and all I had to worry about was family. That lasted for four years."

"Would you settle down again?" Apocalypse said with a worried look.

"If I met the right person and the situation allowed it. We'd have to talk about kids. They're a lot of work—even for someone like you that has a staff to do the daily stuff."

Apocalypse giggled. "I can just see baby angels playing in the Oval Office."

Kita smiled warily. "They don't stay small for long. They grow into adults in a matter of weeks, and they're constantly hungry."

Apocalypse hugged Kita. "Thanks for talking to me. I feel better."

"Good. I would be sad if you left. If you're ready, I'll check on Nicole and alert command we're leaving."

Apocalypse kissed Kita, then let go, falling toward the ocean. She rolled right-side up and flew under Kita.

"*Nicole. Lizzy. How are you doing?*"

"*She can do it on her own, but she's not ready for the big time yet,*" said Sapper.

"*My girl is doing barrel rolls. What have you been teaching yours?*"

"*It's not my fault she's slow.*"

"*I know Nicole, and she's not slow.*"

"*She'll do well enough.*"

"*If she needs rescuing, you're going in after her. Everyone form up on me, and we'll head out. Command?*"

"*Yes?*" said the mission commander.

"*We're headed to the target. I'm sending you our position.*"

"*Roger. We have you. We'll guide you in.*"

KITA AND THE ANGELS GLIDED UP THE TRENCH TOWARD THE ILLUMINATI BASE. There was no sea life on the dark monolithic stones, and the precision construction left no gaps between them. *How do you quarry underwater?*

"*Command. Kita. Any activity outside the base?*"

"*Negative. All scopes are clean. You're clear.*"

Kita led the others into the darkened passage that led to the base.

"It's dark in here, but I can see," said Nemesis.

"Your eyes will adjust to low light levels," said Kita. "There are different lenses that let you see various other energy spectrums."

"There's an awesome one that lets you see electricity," said Sapper. "It's great for finding the remote."

"On your guard," said Kita as they came to the ramp that led out of the pool. The lights were on in the dock area. "We're here."

Kita walked up the ramp and out of the water. The teams' scuba gear remained undisturbed. She motioned for Sapper and Aspen to check the downed Neophormes.

"Dead," said Sapper.

"*Nonfunctional,*" added Aspen.

"Good." Kita opened the pocket dimension and let O'Brien out. "We're in the belly of the beast. Make sure Kimmy's taken care of."

O'Brien changed into his demon form. He picked up an assault rifle and a vest full of ECM ammunition. "All set," he said in a chilling voice as he stood next to Apocalypse.

"You two look cute in your suits," said Sapper. "Going to hide behind a desk?"

"Dress for the job you want, soldier," said Apocalypse. "Your job is to do and die. I *am* the reason why. I command more power from my desk than you can dream of."

"I can still kick your ass," snarled Sapper.

O'Brien stepped forward.

"I can kick his ass, too."

"Think you can kick mine?" said Kita. "Because that's who you're going to get."

"She's just lucky she's the new girlfriend."

"I should let her burn the skin off you, but I need everyone in one piece. So, shove it. If you have a problem with Kimmy, we can deal with it later."

"*I think her problem is with you,*" said Aspen. "*Lizzy is just picking on Kimmy because she's an easier target.*"

"Why are you projecting, Lizzy?" said Kita.

Sapper opened her arms and yelled, "She doesn't deserve to be here. She's not qualified."

"That's not what you're mad about. Why are you mad at me?"

Sapper withered under Kita's glare and looked at the ground. "You're choosing her over me."

Kita sighed. "I told you there would be others."

"I didn't expect you to make them Angels."

"Lizzy, you have shown zero interest in me since you found out what I was doing. All you've cared about is where you were going to fight next. I'm fine with that. I let you go. I still love you—that hasn't changed—but you expected me to wait for you? How is that fair to me?"

Sapper sneered. "You're so damn mushy with her; it's disgusting."

Kita rolled her eyes. "You're mad because I wasn't romantic with you? You never said you wanted that, nor do you act like it. You were always a love-hard-and-fast-type girl. I gave you what you thought you wanted."

"It might be a case of she-didn't-know-she-wanted-it-until-she-saw-it," said Nemesis. "You and Kimmy make me want to be soft and cuddly."

Kita chuckled. "Lizzy, I can be that way if you want. That's not a problem, but I'm with Kimmy right now. We can talk about dividing my time up later, but Kimmy gets first dibs."

"Just because she's a damn princess and I'm a soldier, she's better than me?" yelled Sapper.

"No," said Kita. "You chose to be a soldier. While you did, I found someone else. Now you have to wait your turn. That's how it works unless an arrangement is made, but I'm not going to do that here."

"*Glad to hear it,*" said the mission commander. "*As entertaining a soap opera as this is, the mission needs to move forward. People are wounded and need to be evaced.*"

"*Command, we're moving out,*" said Nemesis. "Kita, you're going to have to solve it later. Lizzy, time to be a soldier and put your feelings aside. The mission comes first."

"Roger that, Colonel," said Sapper with a grunt. She put her head down and walked down the passageway toward the command center, doing her job, and searching for traps and obstacles.

The others waited at the passageway entrance.

"*Passage is clear,*" said Sapper.

Kita and the remaining Angels entered the server room. The bodies of the Illuminati personnel lay where they had fallen. Kita walked to the first workstation. It was on and running a version of Linux. She put her finger to the USB port, and tiny fibers on her finger connected to the terminals. She scanned the computer. Satisfied the machine wasn't doing anything, she moved down the row, making sure they were stable, and she could recover the data later.

"*Command. Kita. Data is stable. I will come back and download it when the area is secure.*"

"*Roger. Ahead is the command room. Analysis of the earlier fight shows two normal-sized Neophormes—one codenamed Litsink—and three large ancient Morphicons.*"

"*Any status on the enemy's condition?*"

"*Our analysis shows Litsink and the other Neophorm have injures. The ancient Morphicons are unknown.*"

"*Thanks, Command. Get the recovery teams ready.*"

"*Assets are moving.*"

Sapper moved down the passageway, and the others followed at a distance. When the passage turned to the right, she became invisible.

"*How'd she do that?*" said Nemesis.

"*We can all do it,*" said Aspen. "*Just think invisible.*"

"*Don't do it now,*" said Kita. "*I'll teach you later.*"

As Kita turned the corner of the passageway, bodies of the SEAL and Anti-Neophorm Team operators littered the ground.

Apocalypse checked several. "Some are alive."

"Ok," said Kita. "We'll get them out as fast as possible. Lizzy, no red balls. We don't want to turn the humans to jelly."

In the command room, the ancient Morphicons—one red, one blue, one violet—sat on their thrones as Litsink leaned over a table. Bodies of SEALs and ANT operators littered the base of the walls. Sprokkit lay on the far side of the room, and Velositi's parts lay beside two of the ancients' thrones.

In a harsh voice, Litsink said, "I told you we are inoperable, human worm. The Vehlixen attacked and killed the server room slaves. Send extra slaves to get rid of these pathetic human bodies."

"Dan," said Kita, "use those ECM rounds and see if you can freeze Litsink's head. Nicole, Kimmy, target the drone. Lizzy, grab a claw launcher—they look like anti-tank launchers—and capture Litsink. Leaf, keep Litsink and the drone away from Kimmy and Nicole. I'll keep the rest busy."

"You're going to take on three ancient Morphicons by yourself?" said Apocalypse.

"Three? No problem. Four would be a problem," Kita said with a grin.

"Kita," said Nemesis, "if you look at a Morphicon with the electromagnetic lens, you can see their system cores."

"That'll make targeting them easier. If you think you can hit a system core, go for it." Kita switched lenses. Litsink's system cores were located in his chest and abdomen. The drone had two in his chest. The ancient Morphicons had three large system cores instead of five, located in their chest and protected by the extra mass. "Let's go."

Kita, Sapper, and Aspen charged into the room. Aspen vanished. Kita leaped at the violet ancient Morphicon, drawing her swords, *Dead* and *Buried*. She landed in the Morphicon's lap and slammed her swords into his chest, targeting his system cores.

The ancient Morphicon's eyes lit, and his hand reached for Kita. She yanked her swords out and backflipped off the Morphicon's chest. *I think I hit one of them.*

The other ancient Morphicons stood. *Great. I have to keep all three busy.* Kita aimed her fist at the red and blue ancient Morphicons. A purplish-black beam shot from her bracers into their chests, leaving deep, glowing scars. The three ancient Morphicons closed in around her. She launched herself at the red Ancient, plunging her swords into its chest. She pushed off, leaping backward toward the blue Ancient and thrust Dead and Buried into his chest in turn. Kita corkscrewed to her left and slammed her swords down on the violet Morphicon, cleaving halfway through the head and shoulder.

Something grabbed Kita by her wings, jerking her backward. It then slammed her repeatedly into the stone floor. She lost her grip on her swords, and they tumbled away. A blue foot came down on her; Kita caught it and pushed back. The battle of wills turned in Kita's favor when she twisted her arms, throwing the ancient Morphicon off balance. She jumped to her feet and slammed her shoulder into the blue ancient Morphicon's leg, knocking him to the ground.

Kita phased onto the red ancient Morphicon's back as a pair of cannon blasts from the violet ancient Morphicon scorched the floor. She put her fist against the metal body and fired her purplish-black beam. The front of the red ancient Morphicon's chest exploded, and he collapsed to the ground. Kita flipped off, landing next to Dead. She picked up her sword and faced the remaining two ancient Morphicons.

The sound of rifles firing caused Kita to open her vision. Around the room, wounded SEALs and Anti-Neophorm operators had joined the fight. Across the room, Kita found the reason. Apocalypse had her shield up while working on a wounded operator. O'Brien guarded her while firing at Litsink. Nemesis was calling out commands to the SEALs and ANTs. Litsink and the drone weren't down, but their attacks were wild and ineffective.

"*Lizzy!*" called Kita as she dodged a fist and sword strike.

"*Yo!*"

"*Try and catch Litsink in your magnetic field. I think that's what the humans use to hold the Morphicons.*"

"*They are metal monsters. I'll snap him up.*"

Kita rolled next to Buried and picked up her sword. She jumped into a double layout over the blue ancient Morphicon, slicing through its blocky head and shoulder. She flapped her wings, twisted, and slammed Dead into his chest. The ancient Morphicon spasmed, and his left half went slack. *About time I hit one.* Kita twisted free, dropped to the ground, and sliced into the blue Ancient's leg.

The violet Morphicon fired its cannons at Kita. She expanded her heat shield to block the attack. Her shield pushed against the blue ancient Morphicon, burning into his legs and back. The violet ancient Morphicon brought his sword down on the shield, causing the blade's edge to melt.

Kita collapsed her shield, jumped, grabbed the blue Morphicon by the head, twisting and throwing him into the violet Ancient. Kita fired her beam at the pile of ancient Morphicons, leaving deep furrows in their chests, legs, and abdomens.

"*Kita, I caught him. What do I do with him?*" said Sapper.

"*Just hold him. Nicole!*"

"*Yes?*" said Nemesis.

"*Do you have command and control of the operators?*"

"*Those that can fight.*"

"*Tell them not to shoot Litsink but finish off the drone.*"

"*Roger. Do you need help?*"

"*I—*"

A hand grabbed Kita around the waist and tried to squeeze her.

Kita cocked her head at the violet ancient Morphicon. "I've died that way before. You think I'm going to let it happen twice?" Kita snarled. She burst into flame and increased her temperature until she burned with dazzling white flames.

The violet ancient Morphicon dropped Kita, his hand glowing red. Kita pointed her fists, and lances of white flame hit the two ancient Morphicons in the chest. Sparks and chunks of living metal flew off.

Bullets and a red beam struck the ancient Morphicons. Aspen appeared and plunged her swords, Dusk and Dawn, into the blue Morphicon.

Seeing the others had killed the drone, and Litsink was securely in Sapper's control, Kita yelled, "Kill the blue one! Purple is mine!" She jumped and slammed her swords into the violet ancient Morphicon's chest. The heat of her flame melted the Morphicon's metal body. Kita swung back and kicked her feet into the violet Ancient's chest, burning a deep hole. She changed to her electromagnetic lens and found the ancient Morphicon's system cores. Slamming her fist into the violet metal chest, she melted her way to a system core, grabbed it and withdrew.

"This is yours," she said with a nasty grin as she held the two-inch cube up to the ancient Morphicon. The system core melted in her hand.

The violet ancient Morphicon stumbled while trying to grab Kita and fell. Kita withdrew her swords, backflipped, and landed a foot from where the ancient Morphicon's head landed. Kita sneered and brought her foot down in his head, squashing it like a melon. She walked on the ancient Morphicon to the other system cores and tore them out. "That is for Velositi," Kita hissed as she crushed the system cores in her fist.

Kita doused her flame, raised her fist, and fired her purplish-black beam into the back of the blue ancient Morphicon. His shoulder blew off. Aspen fired an arrow from her bow, shattering an exposed system core. The ancient Morphicon collapsed. Apocalypse fired her tri-beams into his chest, causing the liquid metal to boil. The remaining system core rose to the surface. It exploded when a bullet from Nemesis struck it.

"All clear?" called Kita.

"Secure," said Nemesis.

"Kimmy, Leaf, Nicole—help the wounded. Lizzy, I'll contact Command and tell them we have a prisoner. Get him to the surface. I'm going to secure the data."

Kita walked to the server room, where the workstations and servers waited to be downloaded. She went to the first and connected via the USB port. *Luckily, I don't need to know what I'm copying.*

"*Command. Kita.*"

"*Command. Go ahead.*"

"*Area secure,*" said Kita. "*One prisoner ready for transport. Wounded triage underway, and we will start sending them up shortly. Data retrieval in progress. Where do you want me to send it?*"

"*Normal standard operating procedure is to bring the hardware back to the ship.*"

"*Getting the data off the hardware is no problem. I prefer to send it as I'm pulling it. I'm plugged into the Defense Satellite Communications System. I just need a destination.*"

"*We'll have to contact the receiving agencies so they can make space. Do you know how much data there is?*"

"*Not much. Based on the machine I'm in now and querying the servers, about six petabytes.*"

"*I'd hate to see what you think is a lot. I'll contact you when I have a place. Surface ships are moving to your location. EUSS Stetson has the Morphicon containment system aboard. EUSS Stamos and Carlson will handle the wounded as they come up.*"

"*And the gear?*"

"*Deliver it to any ship.*"

"*Ok. We'll get to work.*"

---✕---

KITA LED THE OTHERS OUT OF THE ILLUMINATI BASE AND THROUGH THE trench. They carried the last of the dive equipment and computer hardware. Kita exited the trench, but instead of surfacing, she dove for the ocean floor.

"*Where are we going?*" said Sapper.

"*I smell death in the water,*" said Kita.

"*What do we want with a dead fish?*"

"*You'll see.*"

"*More Kita tricks?*" said Nemesis.

"*Actually, this was a trick of my daughter, Nina.*"

Kita led the others along the dark ocean floor, spooking the occasional fish. Soon, they were bumping into all manner of sea creatures. Out of the gloom came a giant blue whale carcass. Kita landed on the bottom and shooed a shark away.

"*What do we want with a dead whale?*" said Sapper.

"*You ask a lot of questions. I'm sure Kita has a reason,*" said Apocalypse.

"*Quit being such a suck-up before you choke on something.*"

"*Kimmy, come here,*" said Kita, ignoring the banter.

Apocalypse glided over. "*Yes?*"

"*Put your hands on it.*"

Apocalypse made a face. "*Ok. Ew.*"

"*Just wait.*"

Apocalypse's hands sank into the flesh. "*Kita, what's happening?*"

"*You need mass. Your body is absorbing what it needs.*"

"*You want me fat?*"

"*No. Your body will store the mass in special gravity wells. It needs the mass for when you transform.*"

"*And what am I transforming into?*"

"*You'll see.*"

"*How much do I need?*"

"*All of it,*" said Kita with a sly smile.

"*There is no way I can absorb all of this. It's two hundred tons. Are you going to transform me into a whale?*"

"*Nope. A dragon.*"

"*A dragon! You mean like a Komodo dragon—lizard type?*"

"*I mean scales, claws, teeth, wings, breath fire, horns and spikes, super huge, eat the knight-type dragon. But you can't grow big unless you eat...a whale.*"

---✕---

KITA AND THE OTHER ANGELS LANDED NEXT TO ENTERPRISE'S ISLAND AS corpsmen loaded Seawolf helicopters with the dead and wounded destined for Okinawa and the States. She was in the process of uploading the data she'd recovered to various government agencies, including the DIA, NSA, CIA, and IBI. Kita didn't plan on letting them have all the fun. She was already sifting through it looking for information on the Star Bridge.

"Good work, girls," said Kita. "Kimmy, Nicole, Lizzy—I usually don't break in new Angels against such heavy opponents, but you did excellently."

"What about you?" said Nemesis. "You took on the biggest three all by yourself."

Kita shrugged. "I'm nothing without you. And it's easy to kill; it's much harder to capture."

"Angel, you're incredible. You move like no one I've ever seen," said Apocalypse as she hugged Kita.

"I've been doing tumbling and gymnastics since I could stand—my mother insisted. She brought in acrobats to teach me. I just want you to know I'm proud of you for working as a team."

"*And, for once, Kita didn't need saving,*" said Aspen.

Kita smiled wryly. "You'd think you were the Grandmaster."

"*Even the great can stumble. That's all I mean.*"

Kita chuckled. "That's why I have friends. You mean the world to me."

"Ah," said Nemesis. "Quick, hug her before she gets sentimental."

The other Angels squeezed Kita and Apocalypse in a group hug.

"Ok," wheezed Kita. "I love you all, too. I can't breathe."

KITA, THE ANGELS, AND RYAN WAITED NEXT TO THE DOOR OF AIR FORCE Three. Outside on the tarmac of Edwards Air Force Base rain poured. Kita, Apocalypse, Sapper, Ryan, and Nemesis wore military parade uniforms. For the public event, the Angels turned their wings invisible.

"Umbrellas, Your Highnesses?" said Daisy to Apocalypse and Kita.

Apocalypse looked at Kita.

Pointing to the SEALs and operators standing in formation in the rain on the tarmac, Kita said, "If they're in the rain, we're also in the rain."

Apocalypse nodded. "No, thanks, Daisy."

From Daisy's sinking emotions, Kita gathered she would be in the rain, too.

"What are the chances it would rain in Cali today?" said Nemesis.

"Remnants of a hurricane moving up from Baja Cali," said Apocalypse. "The aid package from Congress just crossed my desk."

"Just curious if someone is setting the mood." Nemesis nudged Kita.

Kita shrugged. "I can't make that kind of change inside the universe."

"You were by yourself for a while," said Apocalypse.

"The power of pageantry *is* something I learned early in my career, but I haven't left."

A *thump* signaled the stairs' arrival.

The attendant opened the door, made sure the stairs were in the correct position, stepped into the rain, and saluted. "Your Highnesses."

"Everyone ready?" said Kita.

The other Angels nodded. Apocalypse stepped into the rain, followed by Kita.

"How many times have you done this?" said Apocalypse to Kita as they descended the stairs.

"More than I can count."

"I've never done one this large before."

"Just remember, you set the tone. They want to see respect, dignity, and honor. These are your soldiers, but to each other, they are friends and comrades —people they trained and lived with, and if need be, die with. It's a special bond of loyalty that you need to recognize. To many, the bond to each other means more than the oath they took to serve you. And, as of today, you are no longer just their princess, but one of them. They'll expect you to understand and honor that bond."

"I went to West Point. I thought I was."

"You've joined a limited sorority of those that have seen combat. You wanted to prove to the military you are worthy of command. By serving in combat, you've shown you know how to handle the pressure and work as part of a team. You've proven you are one of them, and that will gain you respect and loyalty no title can give you. I have images we can release showing you taking care of the wounded under fire. Wings removed, of course. No one will dare question your commitment and dedication to the Empire and the military."

"It seems a high price to pay."

"For victory, there is never a price too high, only those who lack the will to pay it. But you must know the difference between paying for victory and squandering your forces."

Apocalypse led the Angels to the left of the formation of SEALs and ANT operators. Twenty yards away on the tarmac sat two C-5 Galaxies with their noses in the air. Inside, rows of flag-draped coffins waited to be brought home.

The Angels and Ryan formed a line. A senior sergeant called the formation to attention, and the officers posted, moving to the front of their formations and taking command with a salute. A team of pallbearers, made of members of the different military branches, marched from the hangar, entered a C-5, picked up a casket, and marched out of the plane. As the first foot touched the tarmac, Taps played, and the formation saluted the casket as it went by.

Stone-faced, Kita added sixty-three more names and faces to her honor roll of those who died in her service.

---

TAPS ENDED AFTER THE LAST COFFIN ENTERED THE HANGAR. KITA AND THE others dropped their salutes. She took Apocalypse by the upper arm and whispered in her ear, "You need to talk to the soldiers."

"Why?"

"I can feel their loss and defeat. We can't have them feeling like that. They need to know they won today. If they see this as a pyrrhic victory, it'll affect morale and affect how they see you."

"Ok. Let's get them in a hangar where it's dry." Apocalypse hurried over to the formation commander.

"They're going to a hangar next door," said Apocalypse when she returned.

"Good."

Kita and the others fell in behind the formation as it moved into the hangar.

"Nicole, help me close the hangar doors," said Kita.

Once the doors were closed, Kita said, "Battle uniforms, ladies. Formalities are over. Wings out. Everyone hover in front of the formation. Ryan, wait in the back."

Kita and Apocalypse arrived last.

"What do I tell them," whispered Apocalypse to Kita.

"Remind them why they do what they do—and that we won."

"Ok."

Kita glided back and let Apocalypse take the stage.

"Men and women of the, um, Armed Forces, your service reflects greatly on our country...since our founding in, seventeen seventy-six, our military has fought to secure our freedom...and freedom is our most important ideal...um...and many have sacrificed for it. We are a nation built on freedom, and your duty is to protect it, and obey my father, Emperor...James Roosevelt. Service members die around the globe to protect the, um, Empire—"

Kita inwardly cringed regretted letting Apocalypse speak. Her lack of military experience and inability to speak from the heart showed. She tapped Apocalypse on the elbow. "Love, you want to inspire them, not bore them to death," Kita whispered.

"What do you want me to do?"

"Watch and listen."

Kita glided forward and drew Dead. She ran the blade across her palm, held her bloody fist in front of her, and let the blood drip out the bottom, hitting the concrete floor below.

Kita started in an even tone. "In our profession, our currency is blood. Victory is bought by taking it. It doesn't matter if you're the greenest recruit or the hardened veteran—blood is blood. Some days, victory is cheap—other days, it can bleed you white. These brave warriors"—under Kita appeared the SEALs and ANT operators that died or were too wounded to rejoin their units—"will not have sacrificed in vain." Kita raised her voice. "We went into their lair, grabbed them by the throat, and smashed their heads in. This is a defeat the enemy will not forget. We can hold our heads high. We are the finest warriors in the world, and we proved it. And now, they fear *us*!" she yelled. Her intensity increased as her voice rose. "We can reach out and attack them any time we want, and there's nothing they can do to stop us. We will drive the enemy from this world. Victory will be paid for in blood—*their* blood. We will extract it with interest for our fallen. We will never quit. We will not accept defeat. Defeat is for our enemies, and it will be swift and total. We will show them the *might* of the Empire and prove to the world—We. Are. The. Greatest!" she cried. "No one will dare challenge us. We will crush all who oppose us!"

"*Kimmy, Nicole, put your fist in the air,*" instructed Kita. She thrust her bloody fist in the air.

Apocalypse and Nemesis raised their fists.

"For the glory of the Empire!" yelled Kita.

"For the Empire!" the SEALs and operators boomed back, raising their fists in the air.

"For Princess Roosevelt!"

"For the princess!" yelled the formation.

"Never forget the fallen! Punish our enemies! Protect our freedom! Tomorrow is a new fight, and we will be ready!" roared Kita.

"Hooah!" the formation chanted.

"Come on," Kita said to Apocalypse.

"What are we doing?"

"These guys and girls have medals stacked to their ears, but what they don't have is a gift from a princess."

"I don't think they want a pen."

"A feather, love. Something personal of ours."

"Oh."

Kita took Apocalypse's hand and glided down to the first unit. The commander saluted. Kita and Apocalypse returned the salute.

"Commander, we have something special to present your unit for a job well done," said Apocalypse. She and Kita opened a wing and pulled out a feather. "*Ow! That hurts.*"

"*Wings are sensitive. I don't suggest cutting them off,*" said Kita.

"*You've done that?*"

"*On more than a few occasions. But the pain is a small price to pay for the loyalty and respect we're getting.*"

"Commander, please take these as a sign of our gratitude for your unit's service to our country," said Apocalypse.

"It's our gift to you for a job well done and a reminder of your duty, honor, and sacrifice," said Kita.

"Thank you, Your Highnesses. We will display them proudly."

"The meaning is classified," said Kita. "But, if anyone asks, they came from really big birds."

The commander nodded. "Understood, Your Highness."

Kita and Apocalypse repeated each presentation to the other four units. When they finished, they glided back to the other Angels.

"I know you want to go home," said Apocalypse. "So, we won't keep you any longer. You're dismissed. SEALs, have a safe trip back to Diego. ANTs, I will see you at Area fifty-one."

———————✕———————

THE GIANT DOUBLE DOORS ON LEVEL SIX OF THE AREA 51 BUNKER OPENED AS amber lights rotated. The head of Majestic Twelve's research, Doctor Paulson, stood to one side as the Angels carried Velositi and Sprokkit's bodies inside. Ryan trailed Sprokkit.

"We've cleared space for them by Bernoot," said Paulson. He couldn't keep the surprise from his face upon seeing Kita, Apocalypse, and the other Angels. "Your Highness, what happened to you?"

"I don't look good with wings, Doctor Paulson?" said Apocalypse.

"Are they a costume?"

Kita spread her wings wide then reached for the ceiling. "Quite real," said Kita.

"Is it the alien artifact?"

"*Your Highness*," Kita finished for him. "I know you live in a bubble, but do try and keep up. There's nothing alien about it, but it is classified. We don't need your help with it. And I'm not going to explain it to you."

Paulson looked at Apocalypse. "Your Highness?"

"She is a princess. And what the five of us are and what abilities we have are classified. Now, where are we putting our friends?"

"This way, Your Highnesses." Paulson led them down a cleared lane to where Bernoot lay.

Kita set Velositi's torso down next to Bernoot. Apocalypse placed the legs with the torso. The other Angels set Sprokkit down next to Velositi.

Paulson and his scientists examined Velositi and Sprokkit. Kita grew impatient and went to Velositi. Extending the barb on her left hand, she pushed it into Velositi's chest. She went down the line collecting a DNA sample from Sprokkit and Bernoot.

"What are you doing?" said Ryan when Kita sampled Sprokkit.

"Collecting DNA. If the eggheads can't fix them, maybe I can."

"Can't you wave your hand?"

Kita raised an eyebrow. "I don't have that kind of power inside the universe. *That* is a flaw I fixed. I seriously abused that power in the original universe."

276

"You don't want people gaining power like you did."

"I'm no fool, Ryan. I fought hard to control reality. I don't plan on giving it up. To force others to play by the rules means I have to play by the rules—to a point. Don't worry. I'll figure something out. Neither Velositi nor Sprokkit lost a system core—the damage is to their bodies. I'm hoping I can come up with a bionanite to repair them."

"What's a bionanite?"

"Remember that picture of my blood with the unidentified cells?"

"Yeah?"

"A standard nanite is made of inorganic material, performs a single function, and is made in a lab. Those cells are bionanites made of organic material. Bionanites can be made in the body, are native to the host, and can perform more than one function. I got my start with nanites. They were a gift from an AI. I created bionanites later. I'm looking to make healing bionanites. Their healing ability can be extensive—set broken bones, brain damage, spinal cord injuries, regenerate organs, and even reattach limbs."

"So, you think you can put Velositi back together?" said Ryan.

"Maybe. That's my plan for Bernoot. For Velositi, I have something different."

"You're going to make her an Angel?" Ryan said with a heavy sigh.

"Yep. This won't be the first time I've worked with alien DNA. Though, hers is simpler than any other. What's the matter? I offered to make you a bear."

"You also told me to know my place."

"That's right. Most men aren't decent like you. I like you. You're smart, caring, and intelligent. You've had your moments like all men do, but I forgive yours. But even you behave per the male-centric society you've grown up in. Males are more important, hold all the positions of power, and girls are expected to accept it."

"What about Kimmy? She leads the country."

"Yes, and for years they tried to get her to marry so she wouldn't be the leader."

"So, you want me to serve you?"

"Not you in particular. Men have served me in the past, and I don't treat them poorly, but I don't let them forget who's in charge. I just want you to continue as you have. You have a bright future in whatever you want to do."

"I want Sprokkit back."

"And I'll bring him back."

"I'm sorry I don't want to be a bear. I don't want to fight."

Kita shrugged. "That's your choice. I don't make anyone fight who doesn't want to."

"I'm curious to know how you make a universe."

"Maybe you'll get to see."

"Kita!" called Apocalypse. "Doctor Paulson is ready."

"Coming." Kita glided over next to Apocalypse and put her arm around her girlfriend, then stole a kiss. "What's the damage, Doc?"

Paulson cleared his throat. "Your Highnesses, the damage to Vehlix Sprokkit is severe. He has lost his plasma. We think if we introduce more to his system, we can stimulate healing. Vehlix Velositi is a total loss."

"You think you can fix Bernoot," said Kita tersely. "Velositi had the same type of injury—without the damaged system core."

"Her cellular structure is warped and twisted. We can't line up the connections."

"Kita," said Apocalypse, putting a hand on Kita's chest. "Don't get mad at him."

"I'm not mad." Kita pointed a finger at Paulson. "Extract her system cores and show me the machine you used to make the Morphicon body."

"We could put her system cores in the Morphicon body we built," said Paulson.

"I'm not putting her into that ugly thing. I will make her a new body. Where's the machine?"

"We don't have the material."

"Then get it!" Kita snapped. "Show me the machine!"

"This way, Your Highnesses."

Paulson led Kita and Apocalypse to a corner of the lab. The machine looked like a giant 3D printer. Paulson turned it on. Kita pushed him out of the way when it finished booting up. She found the USB port and copied the program.

"I have what I need," said Kita. "Get the material by tomorrow morning. I'll be ready by then."

Paulson looked around Kita at Apocalypse. Kita's anger skyrocketed.

"Why are you looking at me, Doctor?" said Apocalypse. "She's a princess and told you to do something. It's the same as coming from me. You have whatever authority and budget to get it here."

"Your Highness, it's a delicate machine. She hasn't proposed what she's going to do with it!"

Kita squashed the urge to grab him and shake him. *Calmer and gentler.* "I'm going to make a Morphicon. But I'm going to improve your software and make it capable of reading the DNA sequence I give it to build."

"That will take months!" exclaimed Paulson. "If not years."

"You don't have the computer or the knowledge I do. I only need a few hours."

"Doctor Paulson, if Princess Kita says she can do it, she will. I have every confidence in her," said Apocalypse.

Paulson deflated. "Yes, Your Highnesses. It will be done."

"How is the system core for Bernoot coming?" said Kita.

"The cube is finished. The etching machine is almost complete."

"Get it finished. I should also have a way to heal Sprokkit in the morning."

"How can you do the work that takes teams years in a night?" said Paulson, sounding exasperated.

"I'm used to working on a deadline. Morphicon DNA isn't complicated. Angel DNA is complicated. Get going, Doctor." With a wave of her hand, Kita dismissed him.

"I'll have to remember that gesture," said Apocalypse. "Something from your time as royalty?"

Kita laughed. "I learned it from my mother. I only use it when I can't kill a fool."

"What happened to calmer and gentler?"

"He's still breathing, isn't he?"

"Come on. Let's gather the others and go home. You're going to need some quiet time."

Kita seized Apocalypse's hand. "With you, that sounds wonderful."

"Will I even get to see you with all the work you have to do?"

"Most of it will be done in the background. You'll get most of my attention."

KITA AND APOCALYPSE CUDDLED ON THE GIANT BEANBAG CHAIR IN KITA AND Velositi's apartment. They had spent the night binge-watching *Black Pentagram*, pausing to add their own additions to the sex scenes.

A knock at the door caused Apocalypse to break her kiss with Kita. "Who could that be? It's not time for work, is it?"

"It's five forty-five. Maybe Paulson has my material."

"Are you ready?"

"I've been ready for two hours," said Kita.

Apocalypse rolled off Kita. They fixed their shorts and camisoles and fashioned them into Imperial hoodies. Kita glided to the door. "Yes?" she said as she opened it.

"Hey, Kita," said Sapper with a bright smile. "We thought we'd come over and hang out."

Kita looked around Sapper and saw Nemesis with Aspen.

"Ah, sure, come in."

"Not interrupting anything, are we?" said Nemesis with a wink.

"It's almost six, so nothing the Empire wouldn't be interrupting in fifteen minutes."

"Oh, good. I'd hate to ruin something for you."

Kita wrinkled her nose. *Lizzy is in a good mood, and Nicole is being snarky. What did they get up to? I can be snarky, too.* "You're too late to catch me with my legs too numb to walk. But we're going to need a patch for the beanbag chair. Kimmy took a bite out of it."

Nemesis bit her lip.

Kita gave Nemesis a mischievous look. "Did I fail to mention my previous partner, Jane, was an escort and had a voracious sexual appetite until she met me? I helped focus her energy into becoming a sex therapist. When it comes to sex, I don't think there's anything she didn't know, and she liked to teach." Kita glowered at Aspen.

*"Forgiven, but not forgotten?"* said Aspen sheepishly.

Kita nodded.

"Is that where you got the name Jane?" said Apocalypse.

"She left an impression on me that not even remaking the universe could remove."

*"Such a romantic,"* said Aspen with a twinkle in her eye.

"I like being in love," said Kita.

*"You like being adored. Which is a nice way of saying you have to be the center of attention."*

"What's wrong with that?"

*"Nothing. As long as Kimmy knows."*

"Oh, I know," said Apocalypse. "I'm surprised how gracefully she's shared the spotlight with me."

"I'm not trying to take your place," said Kita.

"I know, and I appreciate your wisdom and experience."

"Just don't ask me to craft legislation. I ruled by sheer will."

Apocalypse laughed. "I think you're better suited for PR and the military."

"I'm doing more as a princess than I ever did as Vicereine," Kita said with a playful sigh.

"Poor you, having to work," said Nemesis.

"I've been working all night."

"I believe exhibit one to that lie is the beanbag chair."

"My *computer's* been working all night, crunching DNA, creating nanites, rewriting software, and doing analysis on the data we recovered from the Illuminati. I do have to tell the computer what to do."

"*I don't think anyone has ever had her full attention*," said Aspen.

Nemesis gave Apocalypse a questioning look. "She gave me all the attention I needed. If she can do that and work at the same time, more power to her."

Kita put her arm around Apocalypse and kissed her cheek. "I did have to pause for a little while."

Apocalypse giggled. "What did you girls do last night? I doubt it was physical fitness." She raised an eyebrow at both Nemesis and Sapper dressed in Army and Air Force physical fitness uniforms.

Sapper shrugged. "Nothing."

"Oh," said Apocalypse. "That was a funny feeling."

"You can tell when someone lies," said Kita.

"Really?" She gave Kita a you-are-in-trouble look.

"Use the power wisely. Right, Leaf?"

"*It's a blessing and a curse.*"

"So, what did you do, Lizzy?" said Apocalypse with a twisted smile.

"I, ah, hung out with Nicole."

"You know I read emotions," said Kita. "You did more than that."

"I slept with her! Is that what you want to hear?" Sapper shouted.

Kita and Apocalypse cringed at the outburst. *Not the reaction I was expecting.*

"It's ok, Lizzy," said Nemesis. "It's no big deal. I told you if Kita can sleep around, so can you."

"I don't care," said Kita. "You're braver than I. I'm still not interested in getting bit."

Nemesis chuckled. "No biting last night."

"You don't have to tease me," snarled Sapper.

"Everyone was curious to know what I did last night," said Kita. "Fair is fair."

"You don't have to gloat about biting beanbags and sex with escorts."

Nemesis put her arm around Sapper. "Lizzy, calm down. We had fun, and so did they. That's what's important. And don't worry. I have a deep bag of tricks you haven't seen yet. Kita's not the only one that's been around the sex industry."

"To be honest, Lizzy," said Kita, "I was terribly uptight about sex for most of my life. It took me a long time to get comfortable with myself and others. It wasn't until I was free of responsibility and obligation that I learned to let go and enjoy the experience. Don't worry about what I'm doing. Have fun with Nicole."

"We were supposed to be battle buddies," said Sapper with a downtrodden sigh.

Kita wiggled her nose. "And I'm happy to fight with you."

"You know what I meant."

"I require *a lot* of attention and maintenance. You've never shown any indication that you want to give me what I want. Kimmy has. What happens when Velositi wakes up? I told you there would be other girls, and you said that was fine. You even told Kimmy. So, why are you upset? Were you expecting to be the primary over Kimmy?"

Sapper's frown and angry eyes didn't hide the hurt, rejection, and sadness she felt.

"Ok," said Nemesis, hugging Sapper protectively. "What you are and what she expected you to be after you got out of her universe are not the same. Did you tell her any of this? She's nineteen. You went from being her age to god. You can't expect her to know you."

"No," said Kita. "She didn't take the time—not in the universe or outside it. She jumped into the first universe when it became available."

"I was bored," said Sapper. "You and Leaf were always working. What was I supposed to do?"

"I wasn't always working. I don't expect you to wait for me, but if you're going to be gone all the time, don't expect me to wait for you."

"I don't plan on giving Kita up," said Apocalypse. "I share her with Velositi because I know the nature of their relationship. I trust Velositi, and I know she's good for Kita. I am not interested in sharing Kita with you, Lizzy. You're too young and inexperienced to handle someone like Kita, and I don't think Kita wants to take the time to teach you."

"You're barely older than I am!" yelled Sapper.

"I'm twenty-six, I am a doctor, and I have ruled my country for four years. Before that, I've been groomed to rule—be an adult—since I was five. I can connect with Kita on more levels than you can."

"You're just a dumb princess. You're nothing special."

"And I am the daughter of a duke," said Kita. "We may not be special, but we're made to be special. Unless you're one of us, you'll never understand."

"Don't gang up on her," said Nemesis, maneuvering Sapper away from Kita and Apocalypse. "Kita, you have made it clear you're not interested. That's fine, but you don't have to make it worse."

Kita shrugged. "If she keeps going after Kimmy, I will get nasty."

"Not sure I want to see your definition of *nasty*." Nemesis hugged Sapper. "Come and talk to me. You can cry on my shoulder."

"I don't want to cry!" screamed Sapper. "I want to knock Kimmy's teeth down her throat."

"That's not advisable. You won't win if you go after Kimmy, you'll get Kita. So come, sit." Nemesis guided Sapper over to the beanbag chair.

"I hate when they don't go easy," said Kita to Apocalypse.

"I know. Sometimes you have to be firm and mean."

*"Kita breakups usually result in people in the medical ward. 'Mean' is the least of the problems,"* said Aspen.

"I don't want to be mean. She doesn't deserve that. I can just be honest." Kita walked over and knelt before Sapper and Nemesis.

"What do you want?" snapped Sapper.

"Lizzy, I'm sorry. The truth is, I thought I could keep up with you, but I'm not nineteen anymore. I got caught up in your thirst for adventure. It was fun and intoxicating, but it's tiring. I'm past the point in my life when I need to prove myself. I know I'm the greatest. Now, I want to sit and cuddle and chew through a mountain of data searching for answers to unique problems that don't require a physical solution. I love you, Lizzie, and I always will. But I am not the one for you. I want you to explore and live—see the world—and you need someone who can keep up with you. Do you understand?"

Sapper took a deep breath. "You're telling me the girl I fell in love with doesn't exist?"

"She did—a long time ago. You're the girl I wish I'd met at sixteen. Life would have been so much better. I can't be her again. Time and experience have taken their toll. I don't see the world the same way you do. It's no longer bright and wonderful. I'm jaded. I don't want to ruin it for you with my cynicism."

"But you chose me!" yelled Sapper. "If you didn't want me, why didn't you leave me to die?"

Kita took Sapper's hand. "I did want you. I trust you, and you are my friend. I share with my friends, and you deserve to be an Angel. You excel at what you do, and you have the potential to go far. Regardless of if you're my girlfriend or not, you've earned the right to be an Angel. You don't have to stay if you don't want to. Every Angel is free to come and go as she pleases."

"I just fought giant robots. You think I'm going to walk away from that?"

"It's what is important to you that I care about."

Sapper ran a finger across Kita's palm. "It does look old, not like it did. I've never been dumped before."

Nemesis put an arm around Sapper. "It happens to all of us. Your heart is going to hurt, but I know how to make it forget."

"It's hard when I have to see Kita every day," Sapper said with a sniff.

Nemesis pointed to Kita. "Yeah, but is that the face you fell in love with?"

Sapper frowned. "It's too perfect and looks old."

Kita smiled. "I better not look that old."

"You look like you're thirty, which is old."

Kita looked at Nemesis.

"She doesn't act old," said Sapper.

"That's good. Our bodies stay looking and feeling like we're twenty-five to thirty. Your mind continues to acquire knowledge and experience."

"And how much has your mind acquired?"

"Enough to know that no matter how many lives I live, I wouldn't trade the one I have for anything. I'll take all the highs and hardships, sorrow and pain, anger and rage, and all the people who came into it because that's what made me who I am."

"You didn't say joy or happiness," said Nemesis.

Kita shrugged. "I don't feel joy or happiness. Regret or guilt. Right or wrong."

"That would make you a sociopath."

Kita smiled. "Who else becomes the God of Evil and destroys existence?"

"Did you know this?" said Nemesis to Apocalypse.

"I know now, but if I remember my course on abnormal psychology, there's little you can do about it. They"—she pointed at Kita—"don't think they have a problem."

"Of course not," said Kita. "I consider it a blessing."

Apocalypse chuckled. "You can be as mean and nasty as you want, as long as you're nice and loving to me—and you put a good face on for the public." Her phone rang. "Yes, Jeremy? ...No, I haven't seen the daily brief yet...I've been busy. What's wrong? ...Ok. She's here with me...I will not have her put under guard. She's not a *threat*...She knows how to motivate people. I was right there with her, and she was showing me how it was done...That's not for you to decide. I'm sure the Secret Service is aware, but I know Jane has been vetted by Dan personally...I trust Dan completely. There is no threat to the throne from Jane or anyone else. I don't care what the news says. I definitely don't trust anything from the conservatives...And you have to decide if your loyalty lies with the conservatives or with me. Make your choice...Uh-huh. I expect it on my desk on Air Force Three by noon. Goodbye." Apocalypse dropped the phone on the counter. "That is the second Chief of Staff in a week. I'm going to have to poach one from the liberal governors."

"What's the problem?" said Kita.

"A recording of your speech to the Special Forces leaked. The conservatives are convinced you're going to stage a coup for the throne." She picked up her phone, tapped a few times, rolled her eyes, and waved the other girls over.

The other Angels crowded around the phone to read the headlines Fox News screamed POWER GRAB! and The Wall Street Journal asked COMMANDER IN CHIEF DOE? Kita rolled her eyes. NPR claimed DOE RALLIES TROOPS, and CNN added THE PATTON FOR OUR GENERATION. MSNBC congratulated WASHINGTON'S NEW POWER COUPLE.

"How did this get out?" said Kita.

"I don't know," said Apocalypse. She made a call. "Alvin...What do we know about the hangar speech recording that was leaked to the press? ...No video? That's good...They didn't say where it came from or why? ...How nice of them to not compromise national security...I want to know who leaked it. Put the IBI on it. That speech was classified..."

Kita nudged Apocalypse. "The battle pictures of you."

"Oh, right. Alvin put together a press release for this morning. I accompanied the Special Forces on their mission as a medic. I have some pictures of the battle." She covered the phone and looked at Kita, "Do we have pictures of the SEALs and operators?"

"Yeah."

"Ok, Alvin, we'll have some of the Special Forces, too...I can't say what the mission was or where, but we were victorious, and it cost sixty-three lives...My photographer has pictures of me and Princess Jane returning with the caskets and the arrival ceremony at Edwards...Ok, put something together and get it to me to review. Thanks." Apocalypse hung up. "Hopefully, that will counter some of the conservatives' claims about you grabbing power. It'll show us working together. We need to go to D.C. and make a public appearance. I think it's time to introduce you."

Kita nodded.

"It was an epic speech," said Nemesis. "It made me want to charge the gates. I can see how you commanded armies and led nations. Your mouth is a weapon."

"Motivating people to do what I want is a skill I've perfected. I generate loyalty, and that allows me to project power."

"I spend a lot of money doing that for the Empire," said Apocalypse.

"No," said Kita, "loyal to me and me alone. Not to an idea, cause, or country. I had armies willing to do my bidding for no other reason than I wanted it. My country of Hades grew out of a city that I helped rebuild, and it was loyal to me alone. Loyalty goes both ways. You have to be loyal to those you lead and show you'll take care of them."

"You remind me of Senator Kennedy, Doctor King, and my great grandfather," said Apocalypse. "You have that charisma and mesmerizing quality to your voice that captivates the audience."

"Hitler had that, too," added Nemesis.

Kita rolled her eyes. "I despise genocide. I caught my youngest doing it, and I cast her out of the Angels."

"Yet, you snuffed out existence."

"That wasn't genocide. I just hit the switch. Do you have a problem with what I've done, or are you upset about something?"

Nemesis smiled. "You broke a nineteen-year-old's heart. You may not feel bad, but I don't want you sitting too comfortably."

Kita raised an eyebrow. "Then why don't you pick up the pieces? I can feel you like Lizzy."

"What about me?" said Sapper. She'd been staring off into space.

"I'm suggesting Nicole would be good for you," said Kita. "She wants adventure."

"Oh, yeah. Nicole, can we go back to your room?"

"Sure. We'll catch up with you girls later," Nemesis said to Kita and Apocalypse.

"We'll be in the lab."

Kita chuckled after everyone left.

"And what's on your mind?" said Apocalypse. "Happy you pawned Lizzy off on Nicole?"

"No. They'll do fine. I'm laughing about the Patton headline. He commanded my forces for both Arcone and Hades. He was a pompous, arrogant prick. His ego would know no bounds, seeing me compared to him."

"How did you and he come to be at the same time and place?"

"He was a computer construct with a hologram for a body. The United Earth Empire reconstructed great leaders for their expertise and kept them on file. I found them and used them to run my space station and armies."

"Really?" said Apocalypse. "That would be fascinating. Think of all the people you could meet."

"True. Josef Mengele was my personal physician for years."

"Of course he was. Now you have me. Shall we go to the lab…if you're ready?"

"I'm ready. Paulson better have what I need."

PAULSON INTERCEPTED KITA AND APOCALYPSE AS THEY WALKED THROUGH THE lab toward the Vehlixen.

"What do you have, Doctor?" said Apocalypse.

"Your Highnesses, the material for Velositi's new body has arrived and is being loaded into the storage tanks. We're still working on Bernoot's system core. We have to extrapolate the information, and that takes time. We've energized Sprokkit, but we've observed no change."

"Busy night?" said Kita.

"Teams have worked around the clock, Your Highness."

"So have I. You can rotate them out to get some rest. I'm finished with what I set out to do. I'll take over Bernoot's system core. Show me to the computers."

"Yes, Your Highness."

Paulson led Kita to a rack of computers and a screen running computations and a rotating cube showing where the program was in the etching process. It was sixty-seven percent finished. The estimated time to completion was three months.

Paulson withered under Kita's glare. "When you said you were 'still working on' the system core, I thought you meant you were close. Sixty-six percent of this cube is what you took off the original."

"The machine is using cloud computing. It's as fast as we can do it."

Kita interfaced with the USB port and copied the program and data. She ran the program and groaned. It required crunching numbers—a process Kita loathed. It inevitably seeped into her subconscious *and* conscious, so she dreamed, saw, and heard numbers. "I'll have this to you by the end of the day. Get the etching machine ready."

"No machine is that fast," said Paulson.

"I have a dimensional quantum computer linked to an organic brain. Your system works through the system core one point at a time. I'm working through dozens of points at once. You get to apologize to Kimmy why I won't be much fun for the next few hours as I think in numbers. Let's move on to Sprokkit."

Paulson led Kita and Apocalypse to the Vehlixen. Sprokkit lay on his front, the damage to his back exposed. Kita glided on top of him. The sword thrust was wide and went all the way through.

"Kimmy, come here," said Kita.

Kimmy glided up next to Kita. "Yes?"

"Extend a barb."

She did, and Kita extended one of hers and touched the tips together.

"I've given you the bionanite I've developed to heal Sprokkit and Bernoot. You should be able to disassemble it and reproduce it. When you're ready, we need to seed the damaged areas."

"Ok. I have it. I'm going through the DNA structure now."

"Paulson!" Kita barked. "Bernoot and Sprokkit need plasma. That's the food source for the bionanites. You won't see any change at first, but keep feeding them. Once they reach critical mass, they'll heal them."

Paulson frowned disapprovingly. "What is a *bionanite*, Your Highness? You can't use unapproved procedures and techniques in the lab."

"I've been using them longer than you've been alive," said Kita. "This bionanite uses Morphicon DNA, but it's not harmful. It will mutate until it works or dies."

Paulson turned to Apocalypse. "Princess Roosevelt, this is against regulation and very dangerous. We don't know what these things are or what she's engineered. She has no proof of concept. No tests."

Kita rolled her eyes. "I learned from two of the foremost experts on nanites: my ex, and my great grandmother. I surpassed them."

"You said they would mutate. You don't know what they will mutate into!"

"It's not random mutation. They have a stack of genes with different variations. When the bionanite decides it's not working, a protein is released, causing the bionanite to mutate and activate the next gene. It repeats the process until it works or runs out of genes and dies."

Paulson's mouth fell open. "That kind of genetic engineering is impossible."

"Yet, I have wings," said Kita as she knelt and injected the bionanites into Sprokkit's wounds.

"I have it, Kita." Apocalypse knelt next to Kita to help.

"Ok," said Kita standing up when they finished. "Paulson, plasma. Keep it well saturated."

"I can't allow this, Your Highnesses," said Paulson.

Kita made a face. "Then I'll find someone who will. So, be useful and amazed when it works, or pack your slag and get out."

"You have no authority here."

Kita grinned as she felt his uncertainty.

"She has what authority I give her," said Apocalypse. "Like I told you, if she says it, it's the same as coming from me."

Paulson stiffened. "Then you'll have my resignation."

Apocalypse raised an eyebrow. "This is a secret government lab working on a black program that you signed a contract and took an oath to join. You do not get to resign, Doctor. Nice try. Get the plasma, or I'll call Striker, and you can go to the stockade. Continue to resist—and with what you know—I'll send you to Guantanamo—where you'll be forgotten."

Paulson's eyes went wide. He hesitated and hurried off.

Kita and Apocalypse moved to Bernoot.

"Inject him, and then we'll align him," said Kita.

They completed the injections and moved the two halves as close as possible.

"How long will this take?" said Apocalypse.

"A couple of days? I don't know. It depends on if we get the plasma or not."

Apocalypse chuckled. "Give him a chance. Let's go work on Velositi."

They walked to the 3D printing machine. Kita checked to make sure the tanks were full. A quick volume calculation told Kita she had more than enough. She wasn't planning on making Velositi bigger, just better. Kita interfaced with the computer, loading the new software and design. She tapped the start button.

"It really is that easy?" said Apocalypse.

"Yep. I've changed the program, so instead of reading a 3D image, it reads in DNA. I don't trust Paulson to keep this on schedule, but I do know who I can trust."

"Who?"

"Ryan. This seems perfect for him. I'll call his room. He probably isn't up yet."

It turned out Ryan was out on a run. He arrived in the lab in his physical training uniform.

"Taking the military seriously?" said Kita.

"It keeps me looking good. What do you need?"

"Paulson's loyalty is questionable. He doesn't like my plans to fix the Vehlixen. I want you to take over. I also need Velositi's system cores extracted."

"You want me to take over for him?"

"Sure, at least the construction and healing of the Vehlixen. I don't care about the rest of their projects. You know more than anyone here about extracting, making, and aligning system cores and how Vehlixen function. I need Sprokkit and Bernoot kept in plasma until they heal, and Velositi's system cores extracted. Oh, and make sure no one messes with her body. I'll have Bernoot's missing system core ready to be etched in a few hours."

"You found a way to fix Sprokkit?" Ryan said excitedly.

"I think so. As long as he gets plasma."

"I'll make sure he gets it."

"I'll notify Striker that you're in charge of these projects," said Apocalypse. "You get priority for anything you need."

"Awesome. I'll get on it."

Kita took Ryan around and showed him what she had done. Afterward, Apocalypse and Kita gathered the scientists and researchers and told them which projects Ryan was in charge of and that he had priority.

"So, what's next for you girls?" said Ryan after the meeting.

"We're headed to D.C. while the Vehlixen heal. Kita's speech to the Special Forces leaked. A third of the country thinks she's trying to seize the throne."

"I see Kita more sitting in your lap."

Kita laughed. "We'll be back as soon as we can. If Velositi's body finishes, install the system cores but don't wake her until I get here."

"No problem. And Bernoot and Sprokkit?"

"Sprokkit should wake on his own. You'll have to install Bernoot's system core before you wake him."

"That's a lot to do, but if Sprokkit wakes up, that'll make it easy."

Kita put her hand on Ryan's shoulder. "You can do it, even if he doesn't wake up. I have faith in you. This is your Illuminati base. You've done this before."

"Yeah. Ok. I won't let you down."

"I know, and you can get Kimmy or me anytime if you need anything. Don't hesitate to call me if you have a question."

"Except for Velositi's body, it's all stuff I've done before. The bionanites just need plasma, and they'll take care of the rest, right?" Kita nodded. "The lab personnel have experience. Yeah, I got it."

"Good," said Kita. "We'll be back tomorrow night."

"I can't believe I'm in the White House," said Sapper as she entered the living area. "This is so amazing." She skipped over and jumped on a couch.

"Lizzy," scolded Nemesis, "this isn't your home. It's Kimmy and Kita's. You can be boyish at the apartment."

"It's ok," said Apocalypse. "Those couches are armored and weigh a ton. I don't think she could hurt them."

"Lizzy can control magnetic fields," said Kita. "She can crush them like cans."

"She'd be doing us a favor if she did. They're so ugly." The Angels laughed. "Make yourselves at home."

"I can't believe you call this place home, Kita," said Sapper.

"I've only been here a couple of nights. It's not very homey. I like the apartment better. But you will get to stay the night."

Sapper looked at Nemesis suggestively.

Kita laughed. "You can do whatever you want, just know there are people everywhere watching and listening."

"Have you?" said Sapper.

"No," said Kita. "For most of my time here I've been distraught."

"*The couches aren't made for wings,*" said Aspen as she twisted her wings forward so she could sit. "*This doesn't seem very Kita to me. It's not pragmatic enough. Too much wealth.*"

"I didn't decorate."

"My mother decorated," said Apocalypse. "I've never bothered to undo it."

"Maybe we should," said Kita. "That whole bit about holding onto the past and letting it weigh you down."

"True. We should at least redo the living area. The rest of the house is a damn museum. I think it takes an act of Congress to change something."

A knock on the door drew everyone's attention as they hid their wings.

"Yes," said Kita.

Eugene opened the door. "Your Highnesses, Mister Oliver to see you."

"Send him in," said Apocalypse.

A man in his mid-thirties entered wearing a blue suit with a power red tie. His slicked-back blond hair made him look greasy. His eyes twinkled when he saw the Angels, like a man picking out a prize horse. His arousal of lust, greed, inadequacy, anger, and vengeance spooked Kita. She'd been on the receiving end of a man like this growing up, and she wasn't about to expose the younger Angels to one.

"*Kimmy, he's fired. He can finish out the day, but tonight he's gone,*" said Kita.

"*What's wrong?*"

"*He has the profile of an abuser and rapist. The way he looked at you, Lizzy, and Leaf was disgusting.*"

"*He's always leered at me, and I make sure I'm never alone with him. He's on my list to replace, but I will hasten his departure.*"

"*If he tries anything with you girls, there won't be enough left to bury,*" Kita snarled.

"*Something I need to know?*"

"*I was raped at sixteen by one of my father's political friends. My father, the great politician, sided with his friend to preserve peace. My mother did nothing. I went and found another family.*"

*"I'm so sorry, angel. I won't give him the chance."*

Kita moved to intercept Oliver and keep him from going deep into the room. He was shorter than her, and she did her best to block his view of the others. "Can I help you?"

Oliver smiled like a snake. "I need to talk to the princess."

"You're talking to one. What do you want? She can hear you fine from here."

"I came to tell her that the news crews are set up in the Rose Garden and are ready. The story we released this morning of her providing aid to the troops has received positive feedback from the news sources and the internet. The pictures of her receiving the caskets of fallen soldiers at Edwards have also received positive reviews from military and veteran groups. There have been questions about why so many were lost. The media has been clamoring to know more about the mission objective and the enemy that killed so many Special Forces, and why Kimmy was in danger."

Kita crossed her arms. "That's Princess Roosevelt to you."

"Listen, Doe. I don't know what your problem is—you may be a princess, but you are not *the princess*. I've been working with Kimmy for years. Your power trip may work with the military, but this is the *White House*. You're just the girlfriend. You've no authority here. You'll be gone by next week."

Kita ran her tongue around one of her sharpened canines as she put aside old urges. She waited long enough that Aspen got off the couch and approached her cautiously.

Kita angled her head down, and flames lit in her eyes long enough to make Oliver question what he saw. "I know men like you. You can fool the young and innocent girls and use your status and charm to get out of trouble, but not with me. I have a nineteen-year-old and two twenty-somethings. If you think I'm letting you near them, you are sadly mistaken."

"I mean no harm to anyone. I'm a nice guy. Ask Kimmy."

Apocalypse's face darkened as she stood up from the couch. "Mister Oliver, Jane and I will be out as soon as we're dressed and done with hair and makeup. As soon as you leave that door, you are permitted to go where your duties take you, but nowhere else. You will have a Secret Service escort at all times. After the briefing, you no longer work at the White House. You're to clean out your desk. Don't leave town. The IBI will want to talk to you."

"Kimmy, you're going to take her word over mine?" Oliver protested. "She knows nothing of the White House or politics."

"My White House is now more than politics. I will not put up with corruption—monetary or moral. This country has suffered too long under the desires and greed of men like you. My father might not have cared, but I do. You're good at your job, Mister Oliver, but you need to be more than that. You can show yourself out."

Oliver opened the door. A Secret Service agent greeted him and escorted him out of the residential area.

After the door closed, Kita sank to a knee, leaning on a hand.

"Kita, are you ok?" said Apocalypse as she and Aspen rushed to her side and put their arms around her.

"I'll be fine," whispered Kita. "I just need to put the ghosts of the past away."

"Angel, I'm so sorry." Apocalypse hugged Kita as the other Angels huddled around.

"What was his problem?" said Sapper.

"Kita picked him out as a sexual predator," said Apocalypse.

"That explains the mama bird routine," said Nemesis.

"And he lied about it. I'll have the IBI turn him inside out. He has to have victims out there."

*"Or, you can let Kita out at night. You won't see her for a few days, but the problem will be solved,"* said Aspen. *"You might not like the mess."*

"We'll let the IBI handle it. Death is too good a punishment. Instead, he'll be someone's boyfriend in prison."

Kita stood up and received hugs from the other Angels. There was a knock at the door.

"Enter," said Apocalypse after the Angels had a chance to sit.

O'Brien entered. "Your Highnesses, I was told we had an altercation, and I received special instructions for Mister Oliver. Are you alright?"

"Kita is shaken, but I think she'll be fine Dan," said Apocalypse.

O'Brien looked at Kita with concern. "Even I have ghosts," she said. "But I'm more concerned about Oliver."

"I have a man with him."

"Add a female agent. He's a sexual predator, and that will upset him no end. He is a clear and present threat to Kimmy, Lizzy, and Leaf as long as he's on the property."

"Do you have proof?"

"I have what I felt, and Kimmy and Leaf know he lied when he said he wasn't a threat," said Kita.

"That's not enough for a warrant, but I only need suspicion of a threat against the princess to open an investigation."

"Use the IBI, Dan," said Apocalypse. "They have more resources. I don't think he's just a threat against me. I think he's a threat to Kita after she stood up to him. That's both of us."

"Yes, Your Highness. I'll double the detail on him until he leaves the property, then I'll turn him over to the IBI, and we'll look into his past activity."

"Thank you, Dan. That will make everyone feel better," said Apocalypse. "We need to get ready. I'll let you know when Kita and I are ready to go to the Rose Garden."

"I was hoping everyone would come," said Kita.

"Sure," said Nemesis. "It'll be fun watching you face the White House press corps."

O'Brien opened the door for Apocalypse, Kita, and the other Angels. The press corps gathered on the Rose Garden lawn. Behind them, official White House camera crews provided a live stream for the networks. The Angels exited the portico and gathered on the steps behind the podium.

Nemesis and Sapper wore their parade uniforms for their branch of service. Aspen changed into a traditional white assassin qipao with her hair pulled back with two combs. Apocalypse wore a fashionable white business suit with a flag on her lapel and a red, white, and blue bow in her hair.

The Angels debated what Kita should wear. A business suit didn't seem right, and her suggestion of jeans and her jacket was deemed too casual. She offered to wear her qipao, but it looked too foreign and dark. Apocalypse settled on the military uniform from the casket receiving ceremony. *It's generic, and I have nothing to put on it—except my nametag and the Emperor's Seal. I guess that's one thing no one else has.*

"You girls will stand on these steps," said Apocalypse. "If anyone asks, you're honored guests for your role in the military mission. Kita, you'll stand to one side until I introduce you. We'll take a few questions and then go back inside. Ok?"

"Yes, Your Highness," said Nemesis with a teasing smile.

"Shut up," Apocalypse laughed. "Ok, here we go," she said as she put on a serious face.

Kita took up her position a few feet from the podium. When she was set, Apocalypse stepped up to the mic.

"Good afternoon. I would like to begin with a moment of silence for the Soldiers, Sailors, Airmen, and Marines that died securing our freedom two days ago." Apocalypse paused. "Thank you. Their sacrifice will not be forgotten.

"Today, I announce that the Empire of the United States faces a new global enemy, the Illuminati—a coalition of state-sponsored terrorists. They threaten our interests around the world and have for almost five decades. Our strike two days ago was our first at the Illuminati abroad. We attacked a critical command and control node off the coast of Japan.

"Two weeks ago, we discovered the Illuminati operating on Imperial soil. We have acted swiftly and decisively to eliminate the threat here at home and have detected no further Illuminati activity in the EUS. Government agencies and police stand ready to repel any intrusion, while our intelligence agencies and military work tirelessly to thwart them abroad. They will be found and destroyed. Our freedom and our way of life are secure.

"My duty as Princess Regent is to protect the country, and I will. To prove my commitment, I accompanied our forces as a medic. I helped care for the wounded under fire and after the battle. We must do our duty to preserve freedom and protect our country. I am no different from any other citizen. I will fulfill my obligations, and I urge all citizens to fulfill theirs. If we stand together and all citizens do their duty, we cannot be defeated. United, the Empire is strong, and I will fight to keep it that way. There are no shortcuts to victory. We will fight the enemy and win. We are the greatest nation on Earth, and no one can stand against the might of our empire."

Kita kept her face neutral. Apocalypse's reveal was more than she would have given, but she never had a nation to answer to. The speech was good—for prepared remarks— and while it did hit all the right patriotic propaganda, it still rang hollow and lacked conviction and passion.

Apocalypse's mood shifted as she smiled. "As many of you have seen in the news, I have recently met someone special. She comes from the small town of Reading, Cali. She attended Reading High School, and after her father died, she ran the family business Reading Auto Parts and Salvage. I met her on a trip to Cali and was taken by her tenacity, bravery, and commitment. She showed me what I had been missing after years of unsuccessfully trying to find my Prince Charming.

"For years, I thought there was something wrong with me. I buried my feelings and did what was expected of me. I was miserable. I didn't know what my problem was. I thought I was doomed to a life of unhappiness. With a courageous act, she opened my eyes to who I am and what I was missing. I am proud to announce that I am gay.

"My eyes have been opened to the social and governmental discrimination of the LGBTQ community. I have made a promise to her that no boy or girl will have to live in fear because of their sexual orientation or gender identity. No child should have to live in fear, period. She showed me the constant fear she lived in, just because of who she is. I was aghast that such hate and bigotry went on in *my* country. I didn't know what it felt like until I experienced it firsthand in Volcano National Park. The reason for this citizen's ire? I kissed my girlfriend. A simple expression of love that is shown by all couples. This dark undercurrent has gone on for far too long. My father ignored it. I will not, and I know he would not allow his daughter to be subject to the cruelty and hate that has been shown to the gay community. We can't claim to be a free nation if we treat any of our citizens as second-class. My father said we were the shining city on a hill, but his city was gilded and crumbling from the inside. I will rebuild it and make it strong. We will be a beacon of hope in a world of darkness. The country will change. It has to. We are all equal in the eyes of freedom. Straight citizens are not denied their love, and I will not be denied mine. I would like to introduce my—"

Kita stepped next to Apocalypse and took a knee. She reached into her pocket and pulled out a gold ring with a large emerald on it. "Marry me, Kimmy?"

Apocalypse turned, and her mouth fell open. "I—You—"

"Say *yes*," said Kita.

"Yes, of course, yes."

Kita slipped the ring on Apocalypse's finger. She barely had a chance to stand before Apocalypse jumped into her arms and kissed her.

"*I love you,*" said Kita.

"*Oh, I love you. This is why you wanted the others here?*"

"*Yep. I wouldn't do it without them.*" Kita waved the others over, and she and Apocalypse were buried in a polite group hug.

"*You don't wait, do you?*" said Nemesis.

"*I know what I like, and I know what I want. I want to make sure she doesn't get away.*"

"*Like I'm going anywhere,*" said Apocalypse.

"*Now, you can't exile me.*"

Apocalypse laughed and hugged Kita warmly.

"*You know, you can't get married in D.C.,*" said Nemesis.

"*If I can't get the law changed, I'll do it in Cali,*" said Apocalypse. "*That'll burn the patriots and traditionalists. The princesses have the wedding of the century in Napa Valley miles from San Fran. Cali will look like a rose.*"

"*We could do it in Hawaii,*" said Kita.

"*A wedding on the beach, hmmm.*"

"*I saw a place that had a big tree with a big bowing branch on a private estate next to the water. Not far from Ali'i Drive. It belonged to a Hawaiian king.*"

"*We'll talk. We might do two—a private ceremony and a traditional one.*" Apocalypse shook her head. "*Details. Not now. We're not done yet. Everybody back to your places.*"

The knot of Angels broke up.

"Sorry," said Apocalypse as she stepped up to the mic. "I would like to introduce my *fiancée* Princess Kita Logine."

Kita stepped forward and bowed. She stepped next to Apocalypse at the podium.

"Thank you, Kimmy," said Kita. She turned and stole a kiss from Apocalypse. "It's my honor and privilege to serve the Empire in any way I can. I'm here for Kimmy and to help her be the best leader she can be. Together we will make the Empire strong and preserve freedom for everyone. I don't have any plans for the future, except wedding plans. When my position has become clearer, I will let you know what I plan to do. Thank you."

Apocalypse leaned in with a smile on her face. "We'll take a few questions. I know you have some."

Apocalypse started with the major networks. Most questions were wedding-related, and Kita and Apocalypse didn't have any answers. There were questions about policy for Apocalypse's equality movement. Apocalypse made it clear the government would change—and so would the laws and policies. She deflected most questions about the new Illuminati threat, promising it would not affect the day-to-day lives of average citizens.

A young reporter from the foreign press pool took his turn. "Your Highnesses, you claim that Imperial forces won the battle a few days ago and only sixty-three died. How do you explain the pictures from the Soviet News Agency that refute your victory claims—displaying scores of dead Imperial soldiers? Pictures that also prove that Her Highness was not there? The Soviet News Agency claims you staged the casket ceremony and the speech to your military to cover up your defeat. Would you like to comment?"

Kita's lip curled. Litsink got something out during the battle's lull. She searched the internet for the pictures and found them. Bodies did litter the floor of the Illuminati command center. They were still photos, and there was no way to prove who was alive and who was dead.

Apocalypse glanced at Kita.

Kita stepped to the mic. "In battle, there are always two sides. All these images prove is that we were there. The images of Kimmy helping the wounded are from the same fight, but after the Soviet pictures were taken. Kimmy arrived with a second wave of soldiers. She helped the wounded and turned the battle in our favor."

"Follow-up question?" said the reporter.

"Go ahead."

"Reports are surfacing that you, Princess Logine, are not who you appear. The White House released a report that you were attacked at Walter Reed Army Medical Center and left with minor injuries. Later eyewitness accounts contradict that report, saying you suffered three gunshot wounds and were rushed to the operating room, where you miraculously healed. These same eyewitness' reports say you have an alien artifact in your chest and that you can eat more than is humanly possible—other eyewitness accounts from your own military state that they have seen you with black wings.

"Still other reports tell of you with giant creatures that can disguise themselves as a motorcycle and a Firebird on Cali highway one-oh-two and downtown Angel City. A CHP officer eyewitness report says someone matching your description was with a motorcycle that changed into a creature and destroyed a highway patrol cruiser.

"Who are you, Princess Logine? What are you and the government of the Empire of the United States hiding?"

Kita turned and looked at Apocalypse. She kept her face neutral, but snarled, "*Loyal, huh?*"

"*Kita, I'm sorry. Just deny it. We'll find the leakers.*"

Kita didn't like her options. Someone was looking to embarrass Apocalypse, push her government into turmoil, expose the Vehlixen, and make Kita too much of a liability. She wouldn't allow any of it. Apocalypse was still young in the political world. Someone thought they were clever. *Well, let's give them what they want and watch them slag their pants.*

Kita turned back to the press corps. "I learned an interesting statistic the other day reading the Washington Post. Did you know seventy-seven percent of citizens believe in Angels? How many of you believe in Angels? Come on, a show of hands."

About seventy percent of the people in the Rose Garden raised their hands.

"*Kita, what are you doing?*" said Apocalypse.

"*Someone thinks they're being devious. They think you'll be too busy trying to put out fires to retaliate. I'm going to give them something serious to think about and show them they've stepped up to play with the big girls. I don't play to lose. We're going to show them what kind of threat they've unleashed.*"

Kita looked at the foreign reporter. "What's your name?"

"Ruslan Khristich from the UNIAN, Your Highness."

"*That's not his name,*" said Aspen.

Kita ran her tongue around her canine. "Your hand didn't go up. Do you not believe in Angels?"

"Ah, no, Your Highness. I do not."

"You better start."

A bright flash emitted from Kita, which blinded the reporters and cameras. Kita and the other Angels appeared floating above the podium with wings extended.

"I am the fallen angel Kita. I have chosen Princess Roosevelt and Colonel

Adrestia to join us. The Angels are the new vanguard of the Empire of the United States. We will destroy anyone who threatens the Empire."

Kita burst into flame as Nemesis brandished her rifle, and Aspen drew her swords. Sapper raised her arms, creating a magnetic field, lifting the metal objects in the press corps above their heads. Apocalypse floated above the other Angels and grew into a hundred-foot red and silver dragon with a long, spiked neck and tail, silver belly scales, red armor plates on her back, red and silver wings, and large feet with claws on the toes.

Kita glided over the press corps heads to Khristich. "Come talk to me."

"I refuse."

Aspen floated up next to Kita.

"Do you want to know what I am by trade?" said Kita. "I am *the* grandmaster assassin. Do you know what assassins are trained for? Besides the obvious—we're spy hunters. We root out spies and destroy them. Now, you can come under your own power, or the master assassin Aspen will drag you."

Khristich looked between Kita and Aspen. "You have no proof."

"Aspen says you lied about your name. Apocalypse can confirm."

The dragon changed back to an Angel. "He lied," said Apocalypse.

"I don't suggest lying, they'll know," said Kita. "Aspen, let's take him up front."

Aspen grabbed Khristich by the front of his jacket and lifted him into the air.

"*Prick him,*" ordered Kita.

Aspen and Kita flew back to the podium—giving Khristich the truth serum Kita had learned as a child from her adoptive mother time to kick in.

Khristich stood next to the podium, swaying slightly with a slack face. Kita put a hand on his shoulder. "Who are you?"

"Ilya Datsyuk."

"Who do you work for?"

"*Komitet Gosudarstvennoy Bezopasnosti.*"

"The KGB!" exclaimed Apocalypse as her eyes flashed in anger.

Kita pricked Datsyuk with the antidote.

"Dan, take him away," snarled Apocalypse.

Aspen and Kita handed Datsyuk over to a pair of Secret Service agents.

Kita turned back to the podium. "I'll answer one question before we finish. What do you have MSNBC?"

The woman looked startled to be called on. "Your Highness? Is that appropriate?"

"Is that your question? I think it still applies. I don't think Kimmy is dumping me."

"Yes, ah, what does this mean for the Empire?"

"The citizens of the Empire have nothing to fear from us. We will be their protectors, go after threats, and perform missions that Kimmy deems warrant Angel participation. Otherwise, we have other skills to offer to make the People's lives better. We're a friendly group and look forward to meeting people."

"What about Princess Roosevelt? These missions sound dangerous. She won't accompany you, will she?"

"Kimmy's now as hard to kill as I am. If she goes, it's up to her."

"Was she an Angel before you fell in love with her?"

"No. I fell in love with her when I was human. She became an Angel after."

"As a reward?"

Kita wrinkled her nose. "I shared my power with the girl I love. Simple as that. I want her to be able to go where I go and do what I do. Any more questions?"

"How will you fit into the power structure of the White House? You seem to lead the Angels."

"Kimmy is in charge of the Empire. I will only take what she gives me. I have no wish to rule. I want to help her as best I can."

"Are all the Angels gay, or is it just you and the princess?" yelled someone.

Kita sneered. "You'll have to ask them. I don't care what they do in bed. Who are you?"

"Fox News Radio, Miss Logine."

"You don't recognize my position?"

"You have no recognized relationship with the princess."

"Yeah? Hey, Kimmy, Fox News Radio no longer has a spot in the press corps." Apocalypse pointed to a White House staffer. "Ok, I've had enough. Kimmy, anything?" She shook her head. "The Angels will grant an exclusive interview later this evening with NPR. Come on, girls. We've made enough news for the day."

"Hey, you girls need to come check this out," said Sapper while looking out the window.

Kita and the others wandered over from the living area where they were watching *Black Pentagram*.

"What's going on?" said Nemesis.

"It's a bunch of people with candles gathering at the fence."

Kita looked over Sapper's shoulder across the south lawn of the White House to the sea of candles. It reminded her of her candle-filled sanctuary that was destroyed in her youth.

"*What are they doing?*" said Aspen.

"I don't know," said Apocalypse. She made a call. "What's going on by the south fence? ...Vigil? For what? ...For the Angels. What's that mean? ...Religious groups, ok...I haven't been informed of any calls from them. Mister Oliver no longer works for me. I don't know who has been handling the calls. Ok, thank you...No, don't have them removed unless they become violent."

"What is it?" said Kita.

"Religious groups holding a vigil. I don't know what that means."

"Let's go see what they want."

"Are you sure it's safe?"

"We can always fly away. Playing into people's beliefs is a great way to earn loyalty."

"Ok. Let's go."

After telling the Secret Service of their intentions, the Angels exited through the south portico and glided over the lawn and fence to land among the gathered people.

"*What do we do?*" said Nemesis.

"*I don't know,*" said Kita. "*In the past, people saw touching an Angel as good luck. I've healed people. Sometimes they just want to talk.*"

Kita raised her hands. "Hello. What can we help you with?"

"Mother of God, you are real," said a woman.

Kita chuckled. Her original mother was no one special, just a coward and a liar. "Yes. We are real. You've come to us, and we're here to see what you need."

"We've come for the blessing of an Angel," said a man with two kids holding onto his legs.

Kita knelt before his kids. She glided a thumb across the little girl's forehead, leaving a fiery trail. She did the same for the little boy. "The mark of an Angel to keep you both safe."

"Thank you, Your Highness," the man said as he knelt.

"Be loyal to Princess Roosevelt, and the Angels will smile upon you," Kita announced so the gathered group could hear. "*Spread out and touch them. That's all they want.*"

The Angels dispersed along the fence, touching as many people as they could. The Secret Service arrived with the Capitol Police and formed people into lines. Several news crews interviewed the waiting crowd.

A man in a white robe, blue vestment, blue biretta with a pom, and carrying a staff with a circle and triangle inside cut through the line. Kita's two female Secret Service agents stopped him.

"Foul creature of black wings!" he yelled around the agents. "Begone! You fool the innocent lambs with your false blessings. You only mark them so you can devour their souls later." He took a vial from under his robe, popped the top, and threw it at Kita, hitting her in the chest, splashing her with water.

Kita howled in pain as flames burst from where the water hit her. The fire engulfed her, burning like an inferno. The crowd stepped back. Kita's howl of pain changed to harsh laughter. "You must have missed that part of the news story where I burst into flames. Fire and water are mine to command." Kita extinguished herself. "I am not the one to fear—you are!"

Aspen arrived, her skin glowing and her wings glittering.

"A fallen angel and a high angel fight for the preservation of the Empire of the United States and its citizens. The only people who must fear us are the enemies of the Empire. We bless the people so they may be happy, healthy, and prosperous. Your corruption and tainted beliefs are depriving the citizens of our blessing."

The priest brandished his staff. "You are the one who is corrupt and tainted, foul creature. You, who have tasted the flesh of a woman, have polluted the princess so she may never bear children. The Empire is doomed by your vile pride and lust. She must be cleansed by a man of the cloth. My seed will purify her so she may bear child."

"Oh, *hell* no," snarled Apocalypse as she glided over. "No man will ever touch me. I will stand in the presence of God herself and declare my love for Princess Logine. I know God approves and sent the Angels to us as a blessing. I will not allow a charlatan to ruin this gift for my people. Get out! Do not attempt to lead my people afoul of God. I know the truth of God's word, and the word of God is reserved for women—those made in God's image. Police, escort him out of here."

"*You presume that I had a plan,*" Kita said with a chuckle.

"*You do now.*"

"*True. Nice speech. I do care about you.*"

"*I know you do. That's why you let me abuse your power,*" said Apocalypse.

"*I live to serve my love.*"

Apocalypse laughed. "*I doubt that, but you do have to keep me happy.*"

Apocalypse and Kita returned to blessing the crowd when an elderly woman stepped up to them, holding a small limp child with a medical bracelet from a hospital in her arms. She lifted the child to the Angels.

"She sick. Doctors can't fix," said the woman in heavily accented English.

Apocalypse looked at Kita. "What do we do?"

"Depends on what's wrong. I'd find out where the kid came from and ask them." Kita pointed to the medical bracelet from George Washington University Hospital.

"I'll call them." Apocalypse took the information and went to a Secret Service agent.

Kita blessed the child and a few more people as she waited.

"Ok," said Apocalypse, gliding over to Kita. "She has an inherited autosomal recessive condition called Tay-Sachs disease. It attacks the central nervous system. There's nothing they can do."

Kita nodded. "Genetic diseases aren't hard to cure if you know how. It requires having the right tool to repair the genes." Kita extended the barb on her hand, causing the woman to jump. "It's ok," said Kita. "I need a DNA sample."

The woman hesitantly offered the child.

Kita took her sample, scanned the DNA, found the offending genes, and programmed a fix in a bionanite that would terminate after the repairs were complete. While she worked, she greeted and blessed a seemingly never-ending line.

"Ok," said Kita. She waved the old woman over and injected the child. "This will fix your child. You'll see results in a matter of hours, and she'll be fully healed in a few days—"

"There she is!" A couple ran up, followed by a pair of Capitol police officers. "Mother! What are you doing?" cried a distraught young woman at the elderly woman holding the child.

"Angels, child! They heal Alex."

"Mother! They can't heal him. No one can."

"You not believe," said the old woman. "You must have faith."

"Excuse me," said Apocalypse. "Are you the parents?"

"Yes, ah...Princess." The couple knelt. "I'm sorry. We received a call from the hospital that Alex was gone."

"It's ok. We've examined the child, and Princess Logine developed a cure for the Tay-Sachs disease. She says it'll just take time."

"Wendy! Faith, child! Alex's eyes are open!" The elderly woman held the child up.

"What?" said Wendy as she and her husband crowded around the elderly woman. "He moved his arm!"

"*I thought it would take a while,*" said Apocalypse to Kita.

"*Small kid; heavy dose.*"

"How's this possible, Your Highness?" said Wendy's husband as Wendy hugged Alex with tears in her eyes.

Apocalypse smiled at the husband, then into the gathered cameras. "Princess Logine is an Angel with incredible abilities, knowledge, and power beyond even my understanding. She's chosen to bless the citizens of the Empire with her talents."

"Thank you, Your Highnesses," said Wendy.

"Take Alex back to the doctors for observation, but do nothing," instructed Kita. "He'll be fine in seventy-two hours."

"I can't thank you enough."

"Tell your friends," said Kita, "that loyalty to the Empire will be rewarded."

"Of course. We're proud to be citizens of the Empire."

Kita lifted her head to expose her eyes from under her hood. "Good. The Empire needs more citizens like you." Flames lit in her eyes momentarily. "Have a pleasant night."

"Thank you, Your Highnesses," said Wendy's husband. "Thank you so much. Ah, and congratulations on your engagement."

"Thank you," said Apocalypse. She and Kita waved goodbye to the family. "We're going to have requests a mile high of patients for you to cure."

"I perform one miracle a day," Kita said darkly.

"How much longer do you want to stay out here?"

"It's a long line, and this is an excellent opportunity to win hearts and minds —especially in a demographic that hates that we're gay."

"Funny how their faith overrides their beliefs," said Apocalypse with a sigh.

"What seems easier to believe, the creature that looks like the messenger of God or some man saying he speaks the word of God?"

"From everything you've experienced, you can accept them dropping their prejudices?"

"They better or I'm taking my toys and going home."

Apocalypse frowned.

"I don't expect it to happen overnight. I once told someone if they want help from the powerful, they needed to accept the powerful as they are. I still believe that. I have limits, but I'm not going anywhere. They couldn't drive me away when I was human. They definitely will not as an Angel. But even I understand futility."

"Yes, I suppose there is a point..."

Kita put her arm around Apocalypse and kissed her. "Showing them is better than telling them."

Apocalypse giggled. "Are you going to propose we have sex right here?"

"I was going to suggest pay-per-view."

Apocalypse laughed. "How much would lesbian Angel princesses bring in?"

"I don't know, but I'm sure lots of haters would watch."

"Let's concentrate on blessing these people before we try to reach the masses."

A CIA AGENT OPENED THE HEAVY METAL DOOR. KITA ENTERED THE TEN-BY-ten room. Datsyuk sat shackled to a metal chair with a hood over his head. Kita walked around the table in front of Datsyuk and sat on it. She pushed his arms out of the way so she could put the soles of her boots on the armrests. Kita leaned forward and, with a swift yank, she pulled Datsyuk's hood off.

"Hello, comrade," Kita said in a mocking tone. "Having a pleasant stay?"

Datsyuk took a breath to steel himself.

"I'm sure a well-trained agent as yourself has been taught to resist torture and other means of interrogation. I understand the CIA, IBI, and Secret Service have had a crack at you. That's why I'm here. I offered my services, but my methods are extreme. Thanks to one of the Empire's vassal states, we were able to rendition you to a place where I can work and not break the law.

"I know what you've been trained to do, so I'll tell you what I've been trained to do. All assassins are taught human anatomy. I know where to poke to cause excruciating pain and not permanently injure you, where to poke to cripple you and not kill you, and where to poke to kill you agonizingly slow or instantaneously. Where I poke depends on you."

Kita drew her sword *Dead*. "This blade is perfectly sharp, down to the atom. I can cut a body in half, or I can be as precise as a surgeon and take a little."

Kita passed Dead over Datsyuk's hand, removing the skin. His face remained rigid.

"Hurts, doesn't it? I'm going to tell you how this is going to go." Kita removed a capsule from her belt. "This is a cyanide capsule. The kind KGB agents are given to prevent capture. You're going to swallow it so I can say you killed yourself. What I am going to do is give you something to keep the poison from taking effect...until I'm ready. In between, I'm going to poke and slice to my heart's content. You're going to resist...for a while, and then you'll tell me everything you think I want to know. I'm going to continue, and you're going to tell me everything you can think of, from your formative years to what you ate two days ago. You'll tell me anything to get me to stop. I'll keep going until—"

Kita pulled a mason jar from her belt and set it on the table.

"—You fit in this jar. Then I promise to drop it off at the Soviet Embassy so you can be buried in the motherland. When they test you, they'll find the cyanide. You'll have died like a good KGB agent. Any questions?"

Kita licked her lips as Datsyuk's face remained rigid, but his fear and dread washed over her like an ocean.

———————⟩

KITA GLIDED UP THE STAIRS FROM THE DROP-OFF AREA IN FRONT OF THE White House to the door. A Marine opened it for her.

"Thank you," she said with a slight nod of her head. She went up the stairs to the living area. "Anyone home?" she said as she entered. The room was silent. *Everyone must be out. I bet Kimmy's in her office.* Kita walked through the White House to the Oval Office. A Secret Service Agent stood by the door. Kita smiled at him and tried the handle. The door opened, and Kita poked her head in. Apocalypse sat at her large wooden desk in a low-backed chair, looking out the window while talking on the phone.

Kita entered the Oval Office, walking around the couches in the center of the room. The room was full of artwork, busts, and historical artifacts. It felt old and stiff. She preferred stark aesthetics. She liked having just what she needed. Beauty was not in objects but girls. She liked to collect pretty girls.

Apocalypse turned around and smiled when she saw Kita. "Sorry, Senator, but someone requires my attention...There is only one person I won't keep waiting. Yes, she's very special. Email me with your proposal, and I'll take a look. Goodbye." She hung up the phone and leaned back in her chair, opening her wings to keep them off the ground. "Hi, angel. I'm going to need a chair made for wings. I stole this one from a staffer down the hall."

Kita chuckled. "Wings have some minor drawbacks."

"I'll get a designer to redesign everything with us in mind. So, I understand you had a busy night after blessing the populace."

Kita shrugged. "Some agencies wanted my help with an intelligence matter."

Apocalypse looked at Kita coyly. "I understand you visited Japan, played Easter Bunny at the Soviet Embassy, and there are twelve dead at the East German Embassy." Apocalypse stood up. "We need to talk—someplace private."

Kita wrinkled her nose. *How did she find out?* Kita walked around the desk and touched Apocalypse, phasing them a thousand feet into the air above the White House. "Private enough for you?"

"Unless a passing bird is a reporter." Apocalypse sighed disappointedly. "Angel, you can't do stuff like this. My government doesn't send spies back in jars. I don't know why you slaughtered the East German Embassy's night shift, but it can't happen."

Kita folded her arms. "Premier Kryuchkov took a big shot at you. It goes beyond embarrassment. It could topple you and split us up. I won't allow that. By revealing us, his very favorable gambit just blew up in his face. Not only are we a threat, but I've also shown we're not afraid to use it. I sent him a message that we won't put up with his games."

"What is to keep him from retaliating in kind? What if he goes after an ally's embassy?" said Apocalypse in a scholarly tone.

"He won't dare. I penetrated and killed a hardened target, and I killed everyone while planting evidence it was one of their own. If I'm willing to do that over a single spy sent to embarrass us, imagine what I'll do if he pisses me off."

"I understand that's how you're used to dealing with adversaries, but that's not how we do it in *my* government. I know you got some inside help from people who would like us to play the game that way, but we are better than that. No matter what was said, it would not have broken us up. The Angel reveal was a positive show of strength. The Soviet Union acts and talks tough, and they have good spies, but that's all they have. Their military is large, but we have a technological advantage. My military is better trained and highly motivated. We are the best in the world. The Soviet Union knows this. They pick at me, but they can't do any real harm unless we do it to ourselves. That's why they are part of the Illuminati. With the Neophormes, they can do real harm. That's who our true enemy is. You didn't need to do this. I know you want to protect me, but not this way. Ok?"

Kita's shoulders slumped. *Did I misjudge the situation? Did I let my anger get the better of me and cloud my judgment? Or, is her way another way of doing things? It seems to have worked for her. I don't want to lose her. There are so many people wanting us to fail. I want to love her, protect her, and make her happy.* "I'm sorry. I just wanted to protect you."

Apocalypse flipped Kita's hood up. "I know you do. I'm not mad. I believe it when you say you're as good as you are. I'm not worried about the embassy, but I do worry the next time they catch one of our spies that we'll get them back in a jar."

"If they catch one, you tell me, and I will go in and get them out," said Kita.

"It doesn't happen often. I don't plant spies like they do. Most of mine are diplomatic." Apocalypse kissed Kita. "I love you. Talk to me if you're worried about something. I know you want to protect me, but I've claws of my own. I may not be a tiger like you, but I can be feisty."

"You're my snow leopard," said Kita quietly.

Apocalypse snuggled against Kita. "I like that."

"What's the plan for the rest of the day?"

"I've got work to do. You can join the other girls. They went to tour the Maryland veteran's home, or you can stand by the fence and bless the faithful. We leave for Area fifty-one late this afternoon."

KITA AND THE ANGELS WALKED FROM THE MORPHICON ELEVATOR TO THE LAB on level six of the Majestic 12 bunker. Apocalypse's phone dinged. She pulled it from her pocket.

"More trouble?" said Kita. A hardline conservative radio host had picked up the idea only humans should hold the throne, and Apocalypse should be removed.

"No, not that idiot. It's another offer from a Hollywood group to throw us an engagement party."

"Oh," said Sapper. "That sounds so cool."

"You don't even know any of the Hollywood stars," teased Kita.

"They're all the same. They threw awesome parties in my universe. They have to do the same here."

Kita chuckled. Sapper loved following Hollywood gossip when they were in high school and the army.

"It could be fun," said Kita. *It sounds better than what the White House committee is planning.*

"I'll have Jerome look into it. It could be good PR."

"Angels love to party."

"*Except for Kita,*" said Aspen. "*She sits in a corner and sulks.*"

"You better not," said Apocalypse.

"Parties are a reward for the loyal. I'm thinking beyond it."

"*Or getting blackout drunk and sleeping with your ex and partner,*" said Aspen with a teasing giggle.

"This is a Kita story I haven't heard," said Apocalypse.

"There are lots of them you haven't heard," grumbled Kita.

"Don't get grouchy." Apocalypse hugged Kita. "I'm teasing you. I'm surprised you were on such good terms with your ex."

Kita shrugged. "I loved her, but we were bad for each other."

The Angels reached the giant set of double doors. They entered the lab and glided across the room to where Ryan and Sprokkit were working at Sprokkit's workbench. Bernoot stood next to Velositi, positioned at the end of the workbench.

Bernoot tapped Sprokkit. "Hey, big dude, check it out. Humans with feathers."

Sprokkit and Ryan turned around as the Angels landed.

"They may explain Velositi's new appendages," grumbled Sprokkit.

"Hey, Bernoot," said Kita.

"Dudette! Is that you peek-a-booing under there?"

Kita swept off her hood. "It is."

"Woah! You got—like—so tall." Bernoot put a hand on Kita's head. "And wide." He opened his hands wings-width apart.

Kita raised an eyebrow and spread her wings the full twenty feet.

"Why are you sporting black when your girls are like, colorful? You should be a rainbow."

Kita chuckled.

"*Black is a warning to leave the fallen alone,*" said Aspen.

"Gnarly. Who's got the sweet and silky voice, and how did it get in my noggin?" said Bernoot.

"That's Leaf," said Kita. "She's a friend of mine. You know Nicole and Kimmy. This is Lizzy. The Angels are like Morphicons. We have a communications suite in our heads."

"Righteous. Any friend of dudette is a friend of mine."

Sprokkit stepped up to Kita. "Ryan tells me you are responsible for our miraculous healing?"

Kita crossed her arms. "I am. I told you I was useful."

"You have metamorphosed into something new. I did not know humans could change."

"I'll explain when Velositi is awake. How is she?" Kita looked between Ryan and Sprokkit.

Sprokkit's eyes dimmed. "You have that look like the world is yours to command."

"That's because it is. How's Velositi?" said Kita sweetly.

"Her system cores are inserted and aligned," said Ryan. "We started waking her when they announced you'd be coming."

"Excellent." Kita glided up to Velositi and put her arms around Velositi's neck. She pressed her forehead against Velositi's, and then hugged her. "Come back to me," she whispered.

Velositi's eyes glowed brightly, before dimming to normal. "Who? What are you?"

Kita floated back so Velositi could see her. "Hey, Velositi. Welcome back."

"Kita! What happened to you? How did you get more beautiful? And wings!"

Kita smirked. "The Axiom found its mistress. This is my true form—well, when I'm not in my other form."

"What is your other form?"

"I am god."

"I do not understand. You are an invisible friend in the sky?"

Kita laughed. "No. I am the creator of reality. Don't worry. I'll show you."

"We do not have a concept of god. We make ourselves."

"Someone had to make the first of you," said Kita. "I am what kicked off the chain of events through time and space that led to you. It doesn't mean much right now. What you see before you is what I am. We are Angels." Kita moved aside to show the others.

"Kimmy! You have wings!" said Velositi.

"I do. So does Nicole. Kita takes care of the ones she loves, including you."

"Me?"

"I rewrote your DNA," said Kita, "and made some improvements and upgrades—including these." She reached around Velositi and pulled a baby pink metallic wing with black covert feathers around so Velositi could see.

"This is me?"

"You can fly, too. Just spread your wings and think up."

Velositi found her wings, opened them, and lifted off the ground. "This is incredible."

"You said you wanted to fly," said Kita.

Velositi glided forward and hugged Kita. "Thank you. I am so colorful. Why are you not?"

"I have a surprise for you." Kita's covert feathers turned pink. "Now, I match you. Black denotes a fallen angel. I'll explain later. I made other changes—I upgraded your cannons. You can convert any energy source to plasma, your system cores now use dimensional and quantum computing, you feel emotions instead of emulating them, and you're completely grounded. Electricity is yours to control—like lightning."

Velositi's eyes dimmed. "How is that possible?"

Apocalypse glided up to Velositi. "What Kita means by god is she has knowledge of everything and how to manipulate it."

"I can't snap my fingers, but I can usually find a solution."

"What happened to little Kita? You do not sound or act like you used to," said Velositi.

"The *me* you knew is still here, but I've grown."

"You have gotten taller."

Kita grinned. "Yeah. I didn't like looking up to men, and making them look up to me intimidates them for some reason. I take whatever advantage I can get."

"Kimmy is taller, too."

"She got a kink in her neck kissing me, so I fixed it."

Velositi laughed. "How did you heal us and get us out of the base?"

"I created a bionanite that put Sprokkit and Bernoot back together. I used the human's machine to remake your body after altering your DNA. The Angels went down and got you. This is Leaf and Lizzy. You know Nicole."

"Hello," said Velositi as she waved to the other Angels.

"How did the five of you defeat the Neophormes?"

"A question I have been wondering," said Sprokkit.

"Angels are the greatest warriors in the universe," said Kita.

"*It's easy when Kita does most of the work,*" said Aspen.

"*Hello* voice in my head," said Velositi as her eyes brightened.

"Kita is the self-proclaimed greatest warrior in the universe," said Nemesis.

"Of course she is." Velositi chuckled. "I take it you have gotten over your self-confidence issue?"

"Depends on my mood," said Kita. "Come on. Let's go back to the apartment, and I can tell you everything."

"Ok," said Velositi. "Is that a ring on Kimmy's finger?"

Apocalypse held it up. "What do you think?"

"It is beautiful. Kita, are you afraid she is going to get away?"

"I'm not taking any chances. She could still exile us."

"I'm going to lock you in the White House if you keep it up," said Apocalypse.

"*They had their first disagreement, and no one ended up in the medical ward. I think Kimmy is a keeper for Kita,*" said Aspen.

"Medical ward?" Apocalypse raised an eyebrow at Kita.

"In the past, disagreements have been solved by might makes right. Not reason."

"Don't forget, I change into a dragon and will step on you until you see reason."

"Yes, there is a reason you're a dragon. My partner gets the unenviable task of taming me."

"Hmm, well, now I have Velositi, so you're in double trouble," Apocalypse said with a smirk.

———————✕———————

"YOU HAVE LIVED A FASCINATING LIFE," SAID VELOSITI AS KITA CUDDLED IN her lap on the giant beanbag chair in their apartment. Apocalypse sat next to them. The other Angels and Morphicons were gathered around the room.

"*Some scary stories I haven't heard,*" said Aspen.

"Even you came late in my life," said Kita.

"I do not understand why an entity that controls all of reality needs to come to our universe and disrupt it," said Sprokkit.

"When I took over, I copied myself exactly as I am—with all the power and all the problems. And, even I get lonely. I missed my flock of beautiful girls and their friendship. I like to be *alone*, but when all you have is *alone*, it's depressing. You have no one to go back to."

"If you can do what you say, why not just make your own flock?"

"We did. We created universes full of creatures. I just had to go in and find them. Snapping my fingers and creating friends wouldn't be the same. How can I have the imagination to create all the experiences, thoughts, and emotions that make up who you are? It's much easier to create a universe and set the rules."

"*Rules even she has to obey,*" said Aspen.

Sprokkit grunted. "Setting limits to your power is dangerous."

"Maybe," said Kita, "but that's what makes it interesting and worth doing. I've lived when I could snap my fingers and do what I want. It creates more problems than it solves."

"We are just a god's playthings," grumbled Sprokkit.

"Of course not. I don't care what you do. I'm just looking for friends, and after searching through hundreds of universes, I found some." Kita snuggled against Velositi. "I will do everything in my power to protect you and keep you happy."

"*As long as there are those willing to love and adore her,*" said Aspen rolling her eyes.

"What's wrong with that?"

"I will love and adore her," said Velositi. "I know she will reciprocate."

"*She's much more a taker than a giver,*" said Aspen.

"I do find her adorable and charming," said Apocalypse. "I'll have to get with you, Leaf, and get Jane's secrets from you."

"*It's not hard: be firm, don't give an inch, show you disapprove, and have a good rational and logical argument.*"

"At least she comes housebroken, and I have a staff to take care of her."

Kita looked at Apocalypse and pouted.

Apocalypse laughed. "You expect me to take care of you *and* run a country?"

"I'm not a child. I can take care of myself," said Kita.

"Your knack for finding trouble is legendary," said Sprokkit. "I can see where a full-time caretaker would be useful."

"You think I'd get more respect for ruling over reality. All I *want* is to be loved. Is that *too* much to ask?"

Apocalypse slid into Velositi's lap and kissed Kita. "Of course not. But I don't want you coming home covered in blood."

"I didn't," said Kita firmly.

"I know. But I saw the pictures of the room. I'm sure some of it got on you."

"I *cleaned* it off. Jane used to make me shower, brush my teeth, and sterilize my clothes before she'd touch me. I finally convinced her I was cleaner when I burned it off."

"Is that why you smelled like a cinder?"

"It's not perfect."

"Aren't you God?" said Ryan. "Aren't you supposed to be perfect?"

Kita rolled her eyes and stuck out her lip. "I told you when I copied myself into the machine, I kept myself the same—flaws and all. There is no such thing as perfect."

"You could have fixed some flaws," said Nemesis. "Like the sociopathy."

Kita scrunched her face in anger, jumped from Velositi's lap, and glided to the door, raising her hood when she landed.

"Angel, wait," said Apocalypse. She glided down after Kita and caught Kita's arm as she opened the door. "Where are you going?"

"*This is the real Kita,*" said Aspen. "*Moody, irritable, irrational, sensitive, angsty— drama queen.*"

"I already know!" snapped Apocalypse. "And it's only a small part of her. It's how she deals with being attacked."

Kita twisted away and walked down the passageway with her head down. *What did I do to them? I am not a monster.* "This is such a mistake," she grumbled. "I should just pull the plug and go back to being alone."

"Please, don't. I would be sad without you, and I know you'd be sad without me," said Apocalypse catching up to Kita.

"Why? Everybody hates me. They all think I'm some kind of monster—even you."

"Angel, I don't think you're a monster. I never said that, and I know you never felt that. I disagreed with you over diplomacy, but that doesn't change how I feel about you. I don't care that you're a sociopath. You love me—that's all that matters. I know who you are. You've been sweet, kind, and caring to Velositi and me."

Velositi picked Kita up and hugged her. "I know you are upset, Kita, but you cannot expect everyone to understand. They are going to have questions and not understand your motives." She shifted Kita to cradle her in an arm.

"They don't need to pick on me. I've never said anything mean about Nicole or Sprokkit," Kita whispered. "I don't know what Leaf's problem is. She seems determined to remind me of how bad I am."

"She says she thinks if you're no longer a fallen angel, she'll no longer be a high angel," said Apocalypse.

"That's not how it works. I'll always be fallen. No matter what I do," Kita said with a sigh.

"What did you do?" said Velositi. "You never said."

"Before I became Commander of the Legion of Yorq and Rose of Arcone, I was a serial killer. Including that night, I killed one thousand nine hundred and seventy-eight people. My father used his dying breath to call me a monster. Zidin, my new caretaker, said I had evil talents that could be used for good and called me a fallen angel. I'll never reach absolution. I keep piling the bodies on, but I like to think I make life better for those who follow me and understand it's not about the methods, but the outcomes."

"*Exitus ācta probat,*" said Apocalypse. "That sums you up perfectly."

"Doesn't that justify bad behavior?" said Ryan coming up with the others.

"It's all I have," muttered Kita as she buried her face against Velositi's chest.

"You're welcome to not approve," said Apocalypse. "and you've all voiced your opinion. That's enough. If you don't like it, you're free to leave."

"Is that what you want to be associated with, Kimmy?" said Nemesis. "The EUS has always claimed the moral high ground."

"I claim it in public and let it guide most of my actions, but that doesn't mean always. We have done some despicable things in the name of freedom. Someone is always going to be hurt by our actions. I've had this discussion with Kita and how it will affect me, her, us, and the Empire. She has agreed to respect me and the Empire's beliefs, but that doesn't mean I won't use her talents if I feel the need. If there is going to be a great evil in the world, I want it on my side where I have some say over what it does."

"And if a great good arrives?" said Sprokkit.

"There is no great good or evil in the universe," said Kita. "There is just Leaf and me. I like her, and she likes me. We have different philosophies. I want more people to be like her. The universe can only support so many people like me."

"I think Princess Roosevelt's judgment has been compromised by her affection toward Kita."

"Are you saying mine has been, too, Sprokkit?" said Velositi.

"Yours cannot be compromised."

"I am no longer like you, Sprokkit. Kita has modified me. I do not believe I am compromised. I love her, but she has no hold over Kimmy or me. We choose to accept Kita as she is. If you cannot—if you believe her methods are too extreme—that is understandable. I believe they are, too, but I think I can be a good influence on her—like Kimmy. I believe Kita when she says she is trying to be kinder and gentler. She needs help, and now she has me, Kimmy, and Leaf."

*Morality is such a waste of time. If they spent the time doing instead of preaching, they'd get more done. If the others don't want to help, I'll do it myself.*

Kita glided down from Velositi's arm and flipped her hood up.

"Kita, where are you going?" said Velositi.

"To do what was promised—save this world and Chellexon. I didn't become a legend because I worried about the ethics or morality of how—I just did it. The greatest good is not the one that helps the most people but helps the right people—my people. I will save them or die trying. What I gave you is yours to keep and to do with as you wish."

Kita phased down a floor to the Morphicon detention area. She followed the passageway lined with containment panels to a large metal door. Two airmen sat at a desk armed with rifles. A pair of claw launchers hung on the wall behind them.

"Princess Kita Logine to see Litsink and Nitstik," said Kita.

The airmen stood. "Yes, Your Highness. You can't interview them without a fast reaction squad and a containment squad. I can call General Striker and get them sent down."

"I don't need to talk to them. I just need to touch them. You won't have to deactivate the containment panels."

"I still need General Striker's permission and a containment squad."

"You do that. I'll get what I need." Kita dissolved into a dimensionless and featureless black cloud—an ability granted to her by her A'ahegre. It allowed her to pass through solid objects. She drifted through the door and down a hallway lined with six cells, each with a heavy metal door. Kita looked in each cell until she found Nitstik. She drifted to the Morphicon and returned to normal.

"Aren't you ugly," said Kita. Nitstik's angular face couldn't move, but his eyes lit up. "Do you remember who I am?" Kita removed her hood. "You and your little helper terrorized me—*twice*. But, I'm not here to terrorize, just gather information. First, I need a DNA sample." Kita extended her barb and thrust it into Nitstik's chest, extracting a sample.

"Now comes the part that's going to hurt. I need to read your system cores to find out if it's nature or nurture that creates a Neophorm." Kita changed the lenses in her eyes to the electromagnetic spectrum. Locating Nitstik's system cores, she heated a finger and pressed it against his chest, melting her way to the glass cube. She extended the fibers on her finger and read the core, then repeated the process for the other four.

"Interesting...comparing you to Bernoot shows differences. You're programmed to dominate, and the Vehlixen are programmed to serve—like good slaves. But it seems the Vehlixen programming was corrupted. I wonder by whom? Probably an answer lost to history."

Kita changed back to her cloud and drifted through the cells until she found Litsink. The Neophorm's eyes lit up when Kita appeared.

"Remember me, do you? I'm the Axiom you've been searching for. My birthright was wasted on the likes of you. No imagination. Instead, you've been a pain in the ass. My turn." Kita melted her way to his system cores, downloading and then analyzing them. She searched for a particular piece of information. "You do know where the Star Bridge is...more importantly, your leader is here—Savacron. You're closer to invasion than I gave you credit for. If I'm good at one thing, it's crushing hopes and dreams. Now, I have to find a way to Russia. I miss the days of shuttles...and space. The stars are so peaceful. Oh, well."

KITA FLOATED CROSS-LEGGED ABOVE THE CONCRETE SLAB OF THE RADIO tower. She pressed her fingertips together in her lap as she admired the desert landscape from atop the mountain. The desert had a similar deadly beauty as space. Though the desert took days to kill, and space took seconds. The Angels and Vehlixen pulled into the gravel parking lot down the slope from her.

"Kita?" called Apocalypse from fifty feet away.

"*Don't interrupt her,*" said Aspen.

"What is she doing?" said Sapper.

"*She might be meditating with her cloud. If you interrupt the connection, it can cause painful feedback.*"

"How do we get her out?" said Nemesis.

"*You have to wait.*"

"How long?" said Apocalypse.

"*Kita can meditate for days.*"

"Days!"

"If she can mediate that long, she should be the calmest person on the planet," Nemesis said with a huff.

"*Kita doesn't do it to find inner peace. She does it to find the secrets of the universe,*" said Aspen.

"I thought she knew the secrets of the universe," said Apocalypse.

"*Kita and I set the rules of the universe and set it off. We don't know what goes on inside it.*"

*Leaf is correct. My cloud's knowledge is only useful for broad concepts in this universe, not the details, leaving me to chug through Morphicon DNA and programming on my own to find an exploit to use against the Neophormes. Just because I'm not meditating doesn't mean I want to be bothered. The Pentagon should have contacted Kimmy about my intrusion.*

"So, we wait?" said Sapper.

"*I can try a cloud connection and see if I can bring her out,*" said Aspen.

The group moved closer, and Aspen flittered up to Kita. She went to put a hand on Kita's knee. With blinding quickness, Kita grabbed her around the wrist. Aspen stiffened but didn't fight.

"*Kita?*" said Aspen cautiously.

"If I wanted to be disturbed, I would have told you where I was going."

"Angel, we're worried about you," said Apocalypse. "You haven't told us what you're doing."

"The job of the fallen. To do what must be done, so the innocent remain pure. I will strike down your enemies with an unholy fury and cleanse the land of the scourge that pollutes it." *And to think I used to believe that. How naïve I was.*

"What the hell is she talking about?" said Nemesis.

"*The fallen are supposed to deliver the retribution of the innocent upon the wicked,*" said Aspen.

Kita chuckled. "Something I used to tell myself to justify my actions. But I discovered you couldn't save everyone. Someone, somewhere, will suffer that did not deserve it. In the end, I learned an important lesson. Life is sacred. Individual lives are not. Tell me, Nicole, Kimmy, Velositi—would you sacrifice half a planet's population to save the other half?"

"It is a heavy price to pay, but the outcome is worth the price," said Velositi.

"What are you planning?" said Apocalypse.

"Do you have the conscience to do it or not?" Kita mused.

"'A single death is a tragedy. A million deaths are a statistic,' said Stalin."

"Interesting you quote your enemy."

"All that comes to my mind is logistics. Like, how are we going to clean up and dispose of the bodies."

"Said like the true leader you are. Nicole?"

"There has to be another solution. Killing billions is never an answer. You said you despised genocide. You can't kill half the world's population. I won't let you."

Kita turned to face the group. She pointed at the Vehlixen. "Not your planet. Theirs. Are you ok with that? Neophormes make up half their planet's population. They are programmed not to surrender. The only way their war will end is when the last Neophorm falls. Now, you know who will die. Do they still deserve to live?"

"If you can destroy them, you must," said Velositi. "The war will be over."

"Nicole? Not so simple is it."

"You set me up!" yelled Nemesis. "I still believe there is another way."

Kita grinned from under her hood. "The eternal optimist, coupled with the belief that good will triumph over evil. I must be a shock."

"I've seen far eviler in the world than you."

"I am discussing wiping out half a planet's population. How much more evil do you want?"

"It is not evil," said Velositi. "You are doing what is right and saving our planet."

Kita smirked. "It seems evil is in the eye of the beholder."

"Are you waxing philosophical for a reason?" said Apocalypse.

"Mostly, I have nothing to do while I program my solution and plot the invasion of the Soviet Union."

"You're doing what!"

"I found the location of the Star Bridge. I've gathered intelligence and calculated what we'll need to hold the area while we destroy it. I think I have a viable solution that needs to be run by military strategists. Running wars has never been my strength. I prefer to be on the front lines."

"We can't attack the Soviets," said Apocalypse, aghast.

"It's the only way to get at the bridge, and I need it to deliver my solution to Chellexon. It's on the Kamchatka Peninsula. It's easier for us to reach than them. There are several military installations. So, we'll have to deal with those."

"What is your solution, Kita?" said Velositi.

"A virus. I have two options. I can kill all Neophormes—drones and masters —or kill the drones and reprogram the masters. Reprogramming is not guaranteed. I might kill them anyway."

"Killing them all would be a safer solution," said Sprokkit.

"But, if you can save some, wouldn't that be preferable?" said Ryan.

"We don't need them. The drones are not real Morphicons. They are toasters. The masters are dangerous and should be destroyed to ensure the safety of all."

"Nicole? Preference?" said Kita.

Nemesis glared. "Save as many as you can. If you kill them all, how are you any better than them?"

"I'm not. I'm not pretending to be. I just offer a solution to bring peace. Who benefits is up to you. I can wipe out the Vehlixen if you want."

Nemesis frowned. "You enjoy rubbing my nose in this, don't you?"

"I want you to understand there is no right or wrong, good or bad. It's all a matter of perspective. Both sides think they have a right to life and are willing to fight for it. If we don't protect ourselves, they will kill us. If you want to show mercy and incapacitate them, you run the risk of failing and being put into a position where it will be easier for them to kill you. Reprogramming them is not one hundred percent. It could kill them, corrupt them, or just not take. I know what I would choose. I've been burned several times for giving second chances. But, it's not my people or my friends on the line. It's the Vehlixen—the choice is Velositi's. I will do as she wishes. I just want you to know I don't get some macabre pleasure for killing on this scale. It's a calculation and impersonal. If I want joy from killing, it's up close and personal, so I can watch the life slip from my foe's eyes. You can call that evil if you want."

"I still say death should not be the first solution," said Nemesis.

"When you shoot, you shoot to kill, not to wound. Why?"

"That's different."

"It's the same—just on a different scale. You want me to shoot to wound. Sprokkit wants me to shoot to kill. It's up to Velositi." Kita turned to her.

"Kita, you should reprogram them if you can. We must prove that we are better than they are. We may have been their slaves, but we will not be their masters."

"Then, I will do it. I just hope the feelings you feel are worth it, and it doesn't come back to haunt us."

"How empty your life must be," said Nemesis.

"Why is it I am evil and wrong when I question you, but you are righteous and noble for questioning me? Because I am different from the rest of you, I am somehow bad. That my lack of feelings gives me a perspective you can't conceive of is somehow wicked? Are your prejudices so great you can't stand to be in the presence of someone different? If you can't handle having your beliefs questioned and must lash out to protect them, then the problem isn't with me, it's with you."

"I am *not* in the wrong," snarled Nemesis.

"Then you will have to accept our differences. You won't be the first who doesn't like me for being me. But I have gotten this far being me, and I'm not about to change. I don't expect you to change, and I respect you and your beliefs. I expect you to do the same for me. Now, I must talk to Ryan and Sprokkit about developing a delivery system."

"What is your method of infection?" said Sprokkit.

"Initially it will be airborne, then hop around the population. It can infect and feed on plasma. One cell will be enough to multiply and infect the host. This will infect all Morphicons but be dormant in Vehlixen. It will slowly kill drones allowing them to spread the virus. In masters, once they reach critical mass, their system cores will be rewritten."

"In a dense enough population, we should get enough saturation to infect the planet. I have some ideas. We will need to go back to the lab."

---

"THE VIRUS WILL BE PROTECTED BY A PROTEIN CAPSULE THAT WILL DISSOLVE when it comes in contact with plasma," said Kita as she stood on the briefing room stage with Sprokkit talking to Doctor Som—one of the Air Force's lead scientists on biological warfare—via a monitor.

"The protein capsule will add weight to the virus, limiting its airborne effectiveness. We would have to get it high into the atmosphere for it to travel," said Som.

"Long-range airborne distribution isn't meant to be the primary infection method, just the initial distribution. It's meant for short hops between subjects."

"How soon can you provide us with a sample?"

Kita wiggled her nose. "How much do you need?"

"A few gallons, at least."

*I can't produce it in that large a quantity.* "I will send a sample in plasma. You can harvest what you need. Do we have a plasma converter we can send them, Sprokkit?"

"We have the first-generation models. Not very efficient, but this does not require large quantities of plasma."

"That will allow you to grow and harvest as much as you need. Will that work, Doctor Som?" said Kita.

"Yes, Your Highness. We have several delivery systems I believe we can adapt for you. What kind of system are you going to mount the launcher to?"

"A vehicle. Like a Humvee."

"That would be too light for the needed missile system."

"Sprokkit and Bernoot are heavy and dense. They each weigh several tons," said Kita.

"I will look into the lighter delivery systems. I'm sure we can adapt something, Your Highness."

"I don't have a lot of time, but it needs to be push-button easy."

"Yes, Your Highness. We're used to that kind of design parameter."

"Thank you, Doctor. I'll be in touch and will have the sample sent to you today."

Apocalypse climbed up the stairs to the stage with her aides while talking on the phone.

"That quickly? Excellent, Your Highness," said Som.

"This needs to go as fast as possible. If you need anything, let me know, and I will get it."

"Yes, Your Highness. We have the orders signed by Princess Roosevelt."

"Good. Thank you." Kita killed the connection. "Satisfied?" she said to Sprokkit.

"It shows promise. I will wait for the prototype."

"The prototype is probably what we take to the field," said Kita with a frown.

"I will need time to examine it to make sure it will function in our environment."

"I don't think a C-oh-two atmosphere will be much different than an oxygen one."

"You will not be there to help."

Kita raised an eyebrow. "Says who? Angels need a breath once an hour. I don't plan on us being there that long. Even if we are, it takes days before we deplete the oxygen in our bodies."

"I forget you have no weaknesses," muttered Sprokkit.

Kita looked at Apocalypse. "I have a few, and they can be more devastating than not being able to breathe."

"I do not believe love is your weakness."

"It's as close as I'm going to get. I do feel sadness, and losing Kimmy or Velositi would make me sad."

"I think you are crazy for not fixing your flaws."

"They make life interesting. I do not wish to be the computer I inhabit." Kita glided across the stage and landed in front of Apocalypse.

"Yes, Senator...Thank you for your support. I don't think much will come of either. They are just rattling sabers...It would take years for that to happen...They can vote all they want as many times as they want, but they better hurry. Elections are soon, and I will back candidates who share my vision of the future... That includes the hawks, Senator. We need a strong military...The Angels are a force multiplier. We still need the hammer and shield...The hawks won't get everything they want, but neither will you. I do plan to increase spending on social programs...I plan to raise taxes on business and the wealthy to pay for it. Princess Logine is very adamant that we increase our social programs...Yes, she can be very persuasive...She's with me..."

Apocalypse muted the phone. "Senator Hernandez from Miami wants to talk to you."

Kita wrinkled her nose. "Why?"

"She's a leading member of the Labor Party. I'm trying to get her on board. I'm sure she just wants to get to know you."

Kita rolled her eyes. She connected to the phone using her comm and included Apocalypse.

"*Yes, Senator?*" said Kita.

"*Princess Logine. Nice to talk to you. I understand you're busy, so I won't take up much of your time.*"

*How generous of you.* "*What can I do for you?*"

"*The Miracle of the White House—*"

"*You're going to have to be more specific.*"

"*The curing of the child with Tay-Sachs disease. I claim it was a simple medical procedure. I wanted to know when you plan to make this technology available so it can be used to cure other genetic diseases.*"

Kita frowned. "*Simple is relative. For me, it is simple. You aren't even close to having the level of technology required for this type of therapy.*"

"*But, with your help, we could be.*"

"*Senator, you must have a wheel before you invent the car. You haven't invented the* wheel yet. *My level of technology far surpasses even the civilization I came from. I developed it, and it is mine to use and disperse as I see fit. I have already chosen two of your citizens to be elevated to Angels. I have given them gifts, and they are free to use them as they wish. If Kimmy wants to spend her life curing the sick, that's up to her."*

Hernandez made a *tut-tut* sound. *"I will remind you that you are marrying into our royal family. What you know becomes the property of the Empire."*

*"The Empire already has a copy of my DNA that contains many of my secrets. If they can decode it, the secrets are yours. But just because you have the plans, doesn't mean you can build the machine."*

*"I was hoping you would be more cooperative. People's lives are at stake."*

*"I can always take my toys and go, Senator. I've wandered the universe before and am not afraid to do so again. It will be up to Kimmy if she comes with me. I will make it clear you are the reason I took my gifts and left. You have gone from giving your people a chance to be healed to no chance."*

*"Ok, Kita, we're not going anywhere,"* said Apocalypse. *"But, the technology the Angels—specifically Princess Logine—possess are secrets of the Empire and belong to Princess Logine. No discussions have been made on distributing them. As Princess Logine has stated, we are a long way from her level. We will discuss moving our technological level forward at her direction. But it will be her choice. Currently, she is comfortable with sharing it with a chosen few. I will not push her. Thank you for your time, Senator. I look forward to working with you in the future."*

*"Thank you, Your Highnesses. I look forward to seeing your new platform."*

*"I'm sure you will find some planks to your liking."*

*"I hope there are many."*

*"There will be more than before,"* said Apocalypse.

Kita chuckled. *Which was zero.*

*"Goodbye,"* said Apocalypse as she hung up the phone. "I give them an inch, and they want a mile."

"She seems determined to play hardball."

"They're testing how hard they can push. The conservatives are pushing two new ideas today—a vote of no confidence and a constitutional amendment saying you have to be human to be on the throne."

"Technically, you are human. Like me, your human DNA is part of your Angel DNA."

"It'll never happen. Three-quarters of the states have to approve, and I've already received confirmation from fifteen states that don't support the idea. The vote of no confidence will be embarrassing. They have enough votes to get it through Congress, and I'll have to veto it. I'll have to wait and see if they have enough votes to override it."

Kita hugged Apocalypse and kissed her. "If that's the worst they can do, let them. It'll release some of the tension."

"I'm not too worried. They might think twice about it with this afternoon's poll numbers."

"Oh?"

"I'm more popular now than I've ever been. I used to hang around fifty-five percent. Since becoming an Angel, I'm at seventy-five percent. I'm not sure how long the bounce will last, but I've gained most of the liberals and lost only two-thirds the conservatives."

"It might be worth going to heal more kids," Kita said with a wry smile.

"You're not getting off that easy. I'm here to lecture you about usurping the Pentagon's computer systems and leaving a file entitled *Princess Kita Attacks the Soviets—Please Read* spammed across the servers. I've spent hours confirming it was you and not a hacker."

"Did they read it?"

"They are reviewing it. We have a conference call to go over it in the morning."

"Thank you," said Kita as she put her arms around Apocalypse and nuzzled her neck.

Apocalypse laughed. "You're lucky I knew it was you."

"*To Kimmy from Kita* with little hearts around it didn't give it away?"

"That was a little embarrassing to have the generals show me."

"I'm sure it was more embarrassing for them. They'll get used to it."

Apocalypse turned in Kita's arms. "I know you're used to the government being your plaything to cause havoc whenever you chose and expect others to clean up after you, but mine is not. We are the princesses, but they're not here to indulge our every whim. Everyone is expected to act professionally—even you."

Kita frowned. "No wonder you were miserable before you met me. This is soul-crushing if you don't learn to have fun. It might have been embarrassing for them, but they'll get over it. I know you liked it."

"I did, but they won't see me as a professional."

"Because you got a love note from your fiancée on a military strategic plan? You're the princess in charge of the greatest military in the world. What am I supposed to do? Run down to CVS and get a card? You're busy and don't have time for cards. I got to get my mush on when I can."

Apocalypse blushed. "I love you."

"I know. What are we doing for the rest of the night?"

"Nothing. I'm yours all night." Apocalypse hugged Kita and kissed her, tugging on Kita's lower lip. "I don't plan on letting you sleep, though. I went shopping and found something you can take off with your teeth."

Kita licked her lips. "Yum."

"I do have a surprise for tomorrow night."

"Oh?"

"We're going to Cali."

"For what?"

"That's the surprise."

Kita stood with the Angels and Vehlixen on the stage of the briefing room in the bunker at Area 51, watching the large screen in the center display a visualization of her attack plan. Around the large screen, Secretary of Defense Gary Lowman, General Brice Mayfield and the other Joint Chiefs of Staff's faces were on small screens watching rigidly.

"Well," said Kita, "What do you think?"

"We're asking for World War Three," said Lowman.

"Why? It's just one large military exercise."

"On every major border of our largest rival."

"They do it to us all the time. It's where I got the idea, but on a much larger scale. Turnabout's fair play."

Mayfield cleared his throat. "A coordinated exercise across the Atlantic, Europe, southwest Asia, Arctic, the Bering Sea, Sea of Japan, and Pacific will take months, if not over a year to plan."

"I want to go as soon as my weapon's launchers are ready. At most, you have two weeks."

"That's impossible!" yelled Lowman.

"Aren't you supposed to be ready at a moment's notice?" said Kita.

"Rapid response units are, not the broader military," said Mayfield. "We'll need time to move personnel and supplies, get unit readiness up, get the proper clearance from our allies—a military exercise requires lots of coordination."

"I don't want any of it. The more of a paper trail we create, the easier it will be for the Soviets to discover our intentions. Let our units be surprised, just like a real war. They'll catch up. I would put out a military-wide directive to make sure maintenance is up to date and provisions filled."

"Princess Roosevelt, this is preposterous," said Lowman. "It will start a shooting war. You can't be considering this."

"I've read Princess Logine's report, and I believe her simulation is accurate. The Soviets will be paralyzed by so many threats along their borders. We won't cross the borders, naturally, except where we mean to. They'll be so busy with our main groups they won't notice us penetrating a far corner of their country. Flexing our military muscle is good for us and reminds Kryuchkov who carries the bigger stick."

"I'm more interested in changes the generals and admirals have," said Kita, "than excuses about whether we should or can do it. I know you can do it. *Should* is up to Kimmy and me. I want to make sure it's done safely, and with the greatest impact."

"It's up to Princess Roosevelt," said Lowman. "You have not completed officer's school, been commissioned, or appointed to any civilian post in the military."

"Don't make me commission her," said Apocalypse.

Kita looked at Lowman and smiled. "I'll only accept my last rank—commandant. That is a system grade officer, Gary. I was in charge of planets worth of units."

"None of your claims have been corroborated."

"Of course not. You're in the wrong universe. But, feel free to ask Kimmy if I was lying."

"No, she's not, Gary. Leaf?"

Aspen shook her head.

Lowman's eyes narrowed. "Your Highness, this plan is ludicrous and will start a war. You want to throw away our carefully cultivated reputation around the world and heighten tensions with the Soviets? Princess Logine has already upset the balance enough."

*That's only what you know about.* "Gary, what military school did you attend?"

"I didn't. I was appointed after serving as CEO of General Dynamics."

"And this makes you an authority how? You are not a general or diplomat. You're a manager. The only thing you've been effective at is lining the pockets of your former company, and others like it. We need a SecDef who understands the military, not how to make money off the military. Kimmy, I suggest we fire Secretary Lowman and bring in the Inspector General to investigate all military contracts for terms unfair to the government. I've reviewed a few contracts and found exceptional language and unfair costs. I'm sure after a few reviews, the others will be willing to restructure and save us billions. Money we can put to other military programs and freeing money for Senator Hernandez's social programs."

Apocalypse scowled at Lowman. "Is that true?"

"Are you going to take a junkyard girl's word over mine?" snarled Lowman.

Kita smiled. "Do you trust me, love?"

"Yes," said Apocalypse. "Gary, you're fired. Don't touch anything." Lowman's screen went out. She looked at Kita. *"Who do I replace him with?"*

*"What's wrong with General Mayfield? He knows the military and the situation."*

Apocalypse nodded. "General Mayfield, you will take Mister Lowman's place as Secretary of Defense. Secure his office. Don't let him do anything. I'll worry about getting you confirmed later. I have a feeling we're going to have a mess on our hands with the contracts, but this operation takes priority. What are your and your staff's thoughts on Princess Logine's proposal?"

"I will let my staff brief you on our assessment, Your Highnesses," said Mayfield. "I will go secure the secretary's office."

"Very good, General," said Apocalypse.

———————————<———————————

"I THINK THIS DRESS WAS DESIGNED FOR A GIRL WITH BIGGER BOOBS," SAID Kita as she tugged at the top of her black and pink strapless mermaid dress covered in sequins.

"Sorry," said Apocalypse. "Jeanine only had your uniform measurements, not dress measurements."

Kita shrugged. *I don't care as long as I get to look at Kimmy in that dress.* Apocalypse wore a similar dress, but hers was silver and red. *Talk about something I want to take off with my teeth. Not that the lace from last night wasn't fantastic.* Kimmy had worn a red bra and panties set that had made Kita sweat. Kimmy had also discovered that the areas around the base of Kita's wings were super sensitive erogenous zones and attacked them mercilessly.

Kita answered a knock at the door.

"Your Highnesses, they're starting," said the party coordinator.

"Ready?" said Kita. The question was more for the hair and makeup team working on Apocalypse.

"One second, Your Highness," said the stylist as she sprayed Apocalypse's hair with something.

"Are you girls ready?" Kita said to the other Angels.

"This is so cool," said Sapper. She was vibrating in her seat. "We get to meet actual celebrities."

"We're celebrities," said Nemesis with a chuckle.

"Not like them."

"Hanging out with the princesses isn't enough?" said Apocalypse.

"But, they're—"

Apocalypse laughed. "They're more glamorous."

"You're glamorous," said Sapper apologetically.

"I'm regal."

"Finished," said the makeup artist.

"Thank you," said Apocalypse. She looked in the mirror. "I can't believe it's me."

"You look amazing," said Kita.

"I'll have to remember this one. I have to make sure my beauty arsenal is fully armed."

Kita chuckled. She wasn't as strict about beauty among the Angels as her old partner Sarin, but Velositi was quickly taking her place. Sapper and Nemesis grumbled, but Aspen, who was used to Sarin, had no problem picking up the routine. Kita found some new styles that were lighter and more reserved that she liked. She did wish this universe had better hair products. *If I'm going to improve their technology leaps and bounds, it'll be there. This stuff they use I wouldn't put on a yak.* She had the formula for Black, the product she used in her home universe, stored on her computer.

The Angels followed the coordinator through the Malibu mansion to a glass door. Outside, a large patio full of guests stood around a pool listening to a couple on a small stage. The Vehlixen were parked around the patio, giving them a good view of the festivities. Beyond the patio, trees surrounded a green lawn with tables of food, and the setting sun on the ocean provided the backdrop. The coordinator opened the door and gave Kita and Apocalypse each a microphone.

The couple on stage turned toward the door. "And welcome our guests of honor tonight: Aspen, Nemesis, Sapper, Princess Kita, and Princess Kimberly," said Chris Cooper.

The Angels glided to the stage with big smiles and waves.

"Thank you, Chris," said Apocalypse. "And thank you to you and Angelina for this wonderful party celebrating my and Princess Kita's engagement. We couldn't have asked for a more beautiful location. Please, everyone, a round of applause for our wonderful hosts."

The crowd applauded enthusiastically. It was full of Hollywood celebrities, executives, politicians, and a few military, first responders, and citizens who won tickets. Kita didn't detect any threats. Everyone was here to have a good time.

"Thank you for coming, Your Highnesses and Angels. We're honored by your presence," said Angelina.

"It's our pleasure," said Kita. "I couldn't turn down an invitation to my home state."

That was a lie; Apocalypse and her event coordinator had turned down several offers, searching for the right location, people, politics, and level of visibility.

"Your Highnesses, everyone is dying to know the details of how you met," said Chris. "It must be a true Hollywood whirlwind romance."

Kita and Apocalypse traded a shy smile, which received warm applause.

"Well," said Kita, "most of the details are classified as we were working on a government project, but I can tell you I started courting her by calling her a *bitch*."

There were some gasps and nervous chuckles from the audience.

Apocalypse laughed. "Yes, you did. But I had gone back on my word and called you a subject."

"I took that to mean *slave*—so, I stormed into the desert and pouted for three days."

Nemesis floated into the air. "It gets better, I swear. They do love each other," she said with a teasing smile at Kita and Apocalypse. "I've seen it. They're really mushy."

The crowd laughed.

Apocalypse faced Nemesis. "I *did* apologize to her after we rescued her and asked her to be my friend."

"Which I accepted," said Kita. "I realized when I wasn't mad at Kimmy, she was smoking hot. That night, she stopped by my apartment, and I asked her to hang out."

"So, we naturally talked about boys."

"I was *so* not interested," said Kita to the chuckles of the audience.

"Yes, but it helped you later after I told you all my problems."

"Somehow, we got onto politics," said Kita with a laugh.

"And you exposed the faults of the bigoted, hypocritical, and misogynistic government I led."

"As your friend, I thought you deserved to know the truth." Kita received a warm round of applause.

Apocalypse laughed. "Not only did she tell me the truth, but in the middle of my argument, Kita kissed me. Like that magical Hollywood kiss to wake the princess, my eyes opened, and my heart caught fire. I now know I've loved her since I met her. I just didn't know it at the time."

"I fell in love that morning in Hawaii when you fired your Chief of Staff. Kimmy chose me over everything else," Kita turned and faced Apocalypse. "I can't tell you how special that made me feel, love. You were willing to throw it all away for a junkyard girl from the Mojave Desert. I didn't think I deserved you, but I knew then I couldn't live without you, and I wanted to spend the rest of my life with you. I love you, Kimmy, beyond infinity."

Apocalypse dabbed at the tears in her eyes. "I love you. You showed me who I am and what I want to be. I would be nothing without you. You're my best friend, and I'd give it all up for you. But I'd rather make this the world you asked for, so no child—or anyone else—has to live in fear for being who they are. I made you that promise, and I plan to keep it."

The crowd erupted in loud applause as Apocalypse kissed Kita.

"Thank you, everyone," said Apocalypse. "Kita and I promise to make the Empire better—a place where all citizens are free and equal, and the government is for everyone, not just a select few. It will take time, but with people like you, we can make it happen! Thank you for coming and sharing this joyous occasion with us. Thank you, Chris and Angelina, for opening your home and your hearts —for putting on this wonderful celebration. We love you all! Now let's party!"

Apocalypse and Kita blew kisses to the crowd as they applauded. When the crowd dissolved, Kita and Apocalypse, the Angels, and Chris and Angelina walked across the patio. They passed Velositi, and Kita stroked her cowl affectionately.

"*Love you,*" said Kita to Velositi.

"*I love you too. I am so thrilled to see you confident and happy.*"

"*You made me this way.*"

"*I know. And I have that same feeling as when you came out of the salon. You are beautiful and a pleasure to look at.*"

"*I didn't know confidence and happiness were something you could see.*"

"*I see it in you. It makes me happy. And someday, I will get used to feeling emotions like you do. I am warm and fuzzy.*"

Kita laughed. "*I wouldn't know, but I'm glad you're happy. I should be free the next couple of days. We should go riding.*"

"*Yes, we should. That sounds wonderful. Enjoy the party.*"

"*You too.*"

"*I will. There are so many beautiful people to look at and so many people stopping to look at me.*"

THE CONVOY OF BLACK SUVS AND VEHLIXEN CLIMBED THE LONG TREE-LINED driveway from the Malibu mansion to the highway. Kita and Apocalypse rode Velositi behind Bernoot and two SUVs. Flashing lights from a highway patrol car illuminated the darkness as they approached the highway. As the gate opened, demonstrators with signs that read FAG EMPIRE and GOD HATES FAGS yelled anti-gay slogans as they attempted to block the driveway. A cameraman walked in front of the demonstrators.

*Slag. We should have taken the SUV.* "Hey, love, this is going to get rough. Hang on."

"Who are they?" said Apocalypse.

"No idea. Why are they allowed here?"

"They're on a public sidewalk expressing their right to free speech—as painful as it is."

"Ignore them," said Kita. "They can't hurt us. Velositi, do your best to stay out of reach of them."

"I will try, but they are on both sides of the driveway."

The SUVs pushed through the demonstrators and turned onto the highway. They slowed to wait for the rest of the convoy to make the corner. Bernoot turned as Velositi pulled into the crowd of demonstrators. Kita held Apocalypse's hand. Demonstrators crowded in close carrying signs and waving them in front of Velositi or at Kita and Apocalypse.

Kita saw the buckets too late. Demonstrators hurled liquid from both sides, covering Kita, Apocalypse, and Velositi.

"Velositi, get us on the highway," cried Kita.

"Ugh, what is it?" screamed Apocalypse.

Velositi stopped next to an SUV.

"Ew, it's sticky and thick, what is it?" Apocalypse cried on the verge of hysterics.

Kita licked her lips. *Blood.* "I think it's pig's blood." *It doesn't taste like human blood.*

"Oh, *disgusting*," wailed Apocalypse as she jumped off Velositi. "It's in my hair, on my face, and my clothes—why?" she shrieked. "Why would they do this? What did I do to them?" She buried her face in her hands and sobbed.

Kita put her arms around her. "It's ok, love. I can get it off. It's no big deal."

Apocalypse looked up. Her face streaked from tears. "Why? I didn't do anything. I just want to be happy. Why won't they let me be happy? I haven't done anything to them."

Seeing Apocalypse in tears caused an oily surge that ignited into rage and hate in Kita.

"Kita, are you girls ok?" said Nemesis gliding up with Sapper. O'Brien and his agents arrived with him.

"Take care of Kimmy. I'll be back," snarled Kita. She sucked the blood off Velositi, her, and Apocalypse. She formed it into two balls hovering above her hands and stormed over to the demonstrators.

"You disgusting, miserable maggots!" Kita roared. "You dare defile us with your filth? You will learn respect for your princess!" She hurled the balls of blood over the demonstrators, and they exploded downward, showering the people in blood. "Dan!"

O'Brien hurried over with his agents.

"Find out who threw the blood and any conspirators. I don't care if you take them all to jail. This is assault with a deadly weapon." O'Brien gave her a questioning look. "It's pig's blood. They carry all kinds of human-communicable diseases and parasites."

"A court will have to sort that out, but I'll charge them with it—and a few other things we can dream up."

"Good. I'm going back to Kimmy. I want to get her out of here."

"Let me know when you're ready, Your Highness."

Kita walked back to the others feeling calmer. *Had I been younger, I would have slaughtered them for making Kimmy cry.* Apocalypse was still sobbing when Kita returned. She pushed her way through the feathers and took Apocalypse from Nemesis. The Angels clustered around Apocalypse to soothe her.

Kita opened the door to the bedroom aboard Air Force Three. She'd been down in the vehicle cargo area with Velositi while Apocalypse slept.

"Hey, love. Feeling better?"

Apocalypse sat on the bed with the other Angels. She smiled, but her eyes told Kita something was wrong.

"What is it? What did I do?"

"Nothing...well, it's not your fault. It's how it's being presented."

"I don't like the sound of that," said Kita as she sat next to Apocalypse.

"I can't believe anyone would listen to this fat bastard," said Sapper.

Kita turned her attention to the TV. A large man sat at a desk behind a radio mic, blabbing nonsense about gays taking over the Empire while a video of Kita yelling and showering demonstrators in blood ran on a loop. *I notice they're not showing us getting covered in blood.*

"Sorry, Kimmy," said Kita sheepishly. "I didn't like seeing you upset."

"I know. I'm not mad at you, angel. Normally I'd ignore it, but Fox has picked it up and is playing it—even before the morning news cycle. Other networks are calling wanting a statement before they air it."

The Vehlixen appeared on the TV.

"Sorry, everyone," said Kita. "I hate to interrupt your downtime, but we have a problem."

"What is it?" said Velositi.

Kita explained the situation.

"Yo! So not cool," said Bernoot.

"Yes," said Sprokkit. "You did nothing to provoke them. Ryan, Leaf, and I witnessed them throw the blood on you. I have video footage of it and Kita's response."

"Yeah," said Bernoot. "I got the aftermath of you girls hugging it out."

"I have video, too," said Velositi. "I believe between us we have the entire event. We should put it together and make our own video to show the world the truth. What Kita did was not right, but they started it. I think they underestimated Kita's powers to give as good as she got."

Kita chuckled. "Had I been younger, I would have slaughtered them."

"Not the young Kita I know."

Kita smiled. "The original young me. No one disrespects my girl."

"I should have turned into a dragon and eaten them," said Apocalypse.

"That would have made it worse," said Nemesis. "We have to be better than them."

Kita tapped a nail on her teeth. "Maybe we should get out ahead of this."

"What are you thinking?" said Apocalypse.

"All the major networks have morning shows, right?"

"Yeah."

"We should crash one and tell our side of the story before the other gets too much traction."

"Ok. That means a trip to New York City."

"Sweet!" yelled Sapper. "There's so much to see and do."

"We won't be there long," said Kita. "But I'm sure Kimmy and I can spare some time out to sightsee."

"I'll get it set up," said Apocalypse, "if you'll work with the Vehlixen and get us some footage."

"If you do not mind us using the plane's computer system," said Velositi.

"Feel free," said Apocalypse. "I know Kita's already been in it."

"Just trying to make it more efficient."

"Uh-huh. The Air Force techs are having fits with unauthorized changes."

"They're coming from me. How much more authorization do they need?"

"Something more than DON'T TOUCH, K left on the desktop."

"Submitting the paperwork would have taken a year, and I'm right here."

Apocalypse grinned. "Just keep a changelog. That's all I want."

"Ok. Velositi, I'll be down in a minute."

KITA AND THE ANGELS FOLLOWED APOCALYPSE ONTO THE SET OF THE *TODAY Show*, the most popular morning show in the country. High stools replaced the usual couches to accommodate the Angels' wings. The hosts, Gary and Emily, waited on a set of stools. The Angels sat and made themselves comfortable. Kita swept off her hood and pulled out her long braid. The decision was made to go on TV in casual attire to be approachable and look normal.

"Any changes to the topic list, Your Highness?" Gary asked Apocalypse.

Apocalypse looked at Kita and the rest of the Angels. They shook their heads.

"We want to start by asking you questions about your engagement before we get into the clip. Afterward, we'll ask you some questions and then move into general questions for all the Angels."

"That sounds fine," said Apocalypse.

"And I have here your names are Apocalypse, Kita, Nemesis, Sapper, and Aspen?"

"Princess Kimmy is fine for me," said Apocalypse.

"I'm ok with Princess Kita."

"Nicole, please."

"Lizzy."

"I'll be answering for Aspen, and she says Aspen is fine," said Kita.

"Does she need any special assistance?" said Emily.

"No," said Kita. "She can speak but chooses not to."

A light came on.

"Thirty seconds," someone announced from the stage.

Kita was impressed with the small army behind the cameras to produce the show. Through the lights, the control booth was filled with video monitors and people.

The light went out, and Gary and Emily welcomed the audience and introduced the segment with their special guests. *I wonder what happened to the people we bumped.*

"Good morning. Your Highnesses and Angels," said Gary with a bright smile.

The Angels said hello and waved.

"We are so excited to have you this morning," said Emily. "I know you've come from a long cross-country flight to be here in New York, but you look like you're relaxed, rested, and come from the spa."

"We haven't been to bed yet," said Sapper. "I don't think anyone's slept in days."

The Angels laughed.

"What she means," said Kita, "is Angels only sleep every two to three weeks. When we do, we sleep for an entire day. We get a lot done."

"Wow, that's amazing," said Gary. "It gives you lots of time to catch up on Netflix."

The Angels giggled. "We're usually more productive," said Apocalypse, "but we have been watching *Black Pentagram*. I think we're on season four. We met Charlotte and Rachel last night and exchanged mementos."

"Yes," said Emily, "the nation is dying to hear about your engagement party in Malibu last night."

"We have pictures of you and your guests," said Gary.

"Kita and I, and the rest of the Angels, had a wonderful time at Chris and Angelina's house. It was a small affair for friends. We will do something for the public later."

"That is some cake," said Emily.

On the monitor was a picture of a four-tier engagement cake in black, pink, silver, and red decorated with flowers and feathers.

"That cake was provided by Long Beach Cakes," said Kita. "It was amazing. Four different flavors and everything was edible."

"It looks like a fabulous evening, Your Highnesses," said Gary. "Everyone at the *Today Show* is happy for you and wishes you the best."

"Thank you," said Apocalypse.

"I understand there was an incident when you left?" said Emily.

"That's right," said Kita. "There is a clip floating around showing part of what happened, but not the entire incident. We've provided the entire clip to all the networks, but you get to show it first."

"Why don't we show it, and we'll ask you questions afterward," said Gary.

The Angels nodded, and the video showed the demonstrators throwing blood on Kita and Apocalypse and Kita's reaction. The clip ended with the Angels clustered together comforting Apocalypse.

"I'm so sorry, Your Highnesses," said Emily when the clip finished. "Are you alright, Princess Kimmy? You looked very upset."

"I am better, thanks to Princess Kita and the other Angels. I was in shock, to be honest. Recently Princess Kita introduced me to the violence experienced by the LGBTQ community. I thought I had experienced the worst of the bigotry in Hawaii when a fellow citizen called us names. This was an entirely new level of hate. Princess Kita and I did nothing to provoke the demonstrators from the Eastborough Holy Church. We were simply driving by.

"A month ago, when I was miserable and straight, no one would have dreamed of doing this to me, and I was fit to rule. Now that I'm gay and happy, I'm unfit to rule, and it's deemed acceptable to assault the crown. I understand some people disagree with my choice—and that's fine. I won't take anything away from them. They are allowed to live and associate with those they wish, but they are not the only people in the country. Only thirty-five percent of Americans identify as conservative. For years, the Imperium has represented them and their allies exclusively. No more.

"My new government will represent everyone equally. It will not be a liberal government or a conservative government, but an inclusive government for the people. I am working with members of the various parties to put together an agenda to increase social programs that will benefit all Americans. We are going to restructure military spending to improve our readiness and our size, so we maintain our place in the world. The government is no longer here to make a select few rich and make a small minority feel important. Everyone in my country is important. Citizens will be educated, their healthcare needs met, given the opportunity to succeed, and protected. I want this to be the last violent act against a gay person in our county. We are better than that. No child, gay or straight, will grow up in fear in the Empire. This is not a country for gay, straight, liberal, or conservative citizens, but a country for all Imperial citizens.

"I'm not blaming anyone, but that is the path forward I am charting. You are either on board, or you will not have my support for the next election. It's the dawning of a new age in the Empire. The gilded age of my father is over, and the new Imperial golden age is going to begin."

"That is an exciting declaration," said Gary.

*And was not given to you ahead of time.* "Princess Kimmy and I have big plans for the Empire," said Kita. "But first, I must apologize to the members of Eastborough Holy Church. I lost my temper over what happened to Princess Kimmy. I felt the need to protect her. I am sorry for spraying you with the blood you threw at us. We will pay for any dry cleaning or other damages. I will be doing twenty days of court-ordered community service at a local pet rescue in the Washington D.C. area. I sincerely apologize for any inconvenience I have caused you or any harm done."

Over the Angels' comm, they were laughing hysterically.

"*Next time I'm packing red balls in the middle,*" said Kita.

"*You will not,*" said Apocalypse.

"*Dan's face was awesome when you made him write you the court summons,*" said Nemesis.

"*I think waking the judge was even better,*" said Sapper.

"*No one can say I wasn't punished. When those protestors each get two hundred hours helping at gay youth organizations, they can't complain,*" said Kita.

"*While you get to play with kittens,*" said Nemesis.

"*I'm sure I'll clean a litter box or two.*"

"That is quite the apology, Princess Kita," said Emily.

"I admit I was wrong."

"I'm sure the rest of the Empire is with me when I offer our condolences for what happened last night," said Gary.

"Thank you," said Apocalypse. "We're not going to let one bad moment ruin our night. We had a wonderful time."

*You better believe the image of Kimmy covered in blood and sobbing is going to go viral.*

"That's wonderful, Princess. We're excited the rest of the Angels could join us. People around the Empire are interested in getting to know you better. The number one question is: How do *I* become an Angel?"

Kita chuckled. "Friend, need, reward, or potential. The Angels are my friends, and I take care of them. If I need a specific skill, I'll find a girl with it. I have, in the past, rewarded girls who have been loyal to me by making them Angels. Sometimes, I find girls with potential, and I want to help them be the best they can be. It takes a special kind of girl to be an Angel."

"Your number of friend requests is going to skyrocket," said Gary with a chuckle.

"You talk about women, no men?" said Emily.

"Men don't become Angels, but I do make them into something special—usually bears..."

"Bears?" exclaimed Gary.

"Shapeshifters," said Kita. "We do have a man with us I rewarded for his service to Princess Kimmy and myself. Dan?" Kita waved O'Brien on stage.

He walked out from behind the cameras and stood before Kita and Kimmy.

"Special Agent in Charge O'Brien has served Princess Kimmy for fifteen years, and we gave him everything an Angel has, except wings. He did get something else, but it's a secret. I don't suggest messing with Princess Kimmy or Dan will light you up."

"Congratulations, Special Agent. That is an honor."

"It's been my honor to serve Princess Roosevelt. I do my utmost to keep her safe."

"Thank you, Dan," said Apocalypse.

"So, Princess Kita, we couldn't help but notice your amazing stomach. I'm sure those at home want to know your workout routine."

Kita rolled her eyes. "I've been a gymnast since I was two..."

———————————⟨———————————

KITA AND VELOSITI SPED ALONG THE TWISTY TWO-LANE ROAD THROUGH THE mountains of western Virginia. Her Secret Service detail followed on bikes doing their best to keep pace with Velositi. An SUV trailed, and a helicopter flew overhead.

Velositi blasted through some golden leaves on the road. "Wee! What fun!"

Kita laughed. "It's beautiful out here. We didn't have autumn on my planet."

"We do not either. It is all metal and rock."

"I have a question for you," said Kita hesitantly.

"Of course."

"I wanted to know...I mean...I'm planning on staying here a while with Kimmy, but not forever."

"You are so cute together and complement each other well. You are going to leave her?"

"We are—I'm not leaving her! I mean, I don't want to stay in this universe forever. I will take Kimmy with me. I wanted to know if you would come. I don't want to leave you behind."

Velositi was quiet for a moment. "You would leave me?"

"I don't want to. I would stay here a long time for both of you, but if I wanted to leave, would you come with me?"

"And go where?"

"I don't know. You would come to the primary plane of existence, where Leaf, Lizzy, and I came from. It's not much, but I'm working on making it a home. I just need to make the ceilings taller. I can make it whatever you want. I thought we might explore other universes, and I want your help when I return to mine."

"I would happily go where you go. I am flattered you want my help," said Velositi. "I know you do not need it."

"That's not true. My strength comes from those around me. I lost sight of that when I became a god. Power is nothing if you don't have someone to share it with."

"You are most generous to those you care about."

"I don't want you to leave me," said Kita.

"I am not going to leave you. I love you, and you provide me with pretty things to look at."

Kita laughed. "Yeah, the girls are pretty. I used to have a flock of thirty. I miss them."

"Can you bring them back?"

"No. When I recombined the sub-universe with the main, I lost those who died. Most of the Angels with me at the end were deleted—their entire record wiped from the computer. A few died before that, but I think it would be selfish to bring them back. They died. Let them rest in peace."

"Then we will have to find new ones. You still have many more iterations to run before you reach your goal of a thousand, right?"

"Yeah, over a hundred."

"Plenty of time to find beautiful girls."

Kita sighed. "It took me eight hundred and thirty-two times to find you. Before that, I found Lizzy."

"There must have been others."

"None that captivated my heart the way you and Kimmy do."

"Maybe, with my help, we can find a better time and place in the universe to meet people."

"I was going to ask Sprokkit if he would come. I think he would like to work on universes," said Kita.

"He might find it an interesting challenge. Ryan, too."

"Yeah. I'm going to have to expand the dorm wing."

"Somehow, I think you have rooms ready and waiting."

"*Hey, girls. How's the riding trip?*" said Apocalypse.

"*It is beautiful,*" said Velositi.

"*Yes, she likes driving through leaves,*" said Kita.

Apocalypse laughed. "*The language of the no-confidence bill landed on my desk.*"

"*What does it say?*"

"*I'm keeping it a secret as I work on my response. I have a question: Could we produce an heir?*"

"*I can engineer a child. But you're going to veto this, right?*"

"*Of course I am. But you can make a child of you and me?*"

"*Sure, but I'm not carrying it.*"

Apocalypse sent an image of Kita pregnant.

"*Oh, by the Crushing Depths, NO!*" Kita yelled.

Apocalypse snickered. "*You said Angels grow faster than humans. How long would the pregnancy be?*"

"*I don't know. I've never done it. Are we considering this soon?*"

"*No. It's just nice to know. You don't want a child with me?*"

*Groan. Now I know how Jane felt.* "*It means rearranging life, but if you want to, I will.*"

"*Not right now, but someday. The signing ceremony is tomorrow morning. Can you be back by then?*"

"*Sure.*"

"*Ok. See you girls then.*"

"Oh, slag," whined Kita.

"That we have to be back tomorrow?" said Velositi.

"No. She wants a kid. I was hoping to stave that off a few years."

"Would you find a baby and give it wings?" said Velositi.

"No. I can combine our DNA and put it in an egg. One of us will have to carry it." Kita shuddered.

"You do not like the idea of reproduction?"

"I've never dealt with babies. My youngest was eight when I found her. But no. I never planned to do that. Not even when I was human."

"You might have to get used to the idea of a baby."

Kita rolled her eyes. "The first time it screams, I'm bringing it to you."

"You are lucky Kimmy comes with a staff."

"True. I could give it a proper Yorqian upbringing and only see it at dinner and special occasions until it's twelve."

"I do not see how that creates the proper bonding between mother and child."

"Which might explain a few things about me."

"Are you saying all your problems are rooted in childhood?"

"I don't know—maybe. But I promise the kid won't have that kind of childhood. All my girls, save one, turned out fine. I'm sure the next one will be fine, too."

KITA, IN HER FORMAL MILITARY UNIFORM, STOOD BEHIND APOCALYPSE AS SHE sat in her new chair behind the massive wooden desk in the Oval Office. Around the desk were leading members of the Liberal, Labor, Hawk, Green, and Socialist parties, along with several congressional dissenters from the Conservative Party. A camera crew was waiting. Other members of Apocalypse's staff hovered around as a photographer took pictures.

*I didn't know this was to be live.* Kita underestimated how big a deal the conservatives' declaration was. Apocalypse made it sound like it would be a simple signature. No one told Kita anything about what was going on, other than where to stand. From the pieces of conversation she'd overheard, the other parties were furious. Apocalypse was calm and relaxed when Kita talked to her when she arrived this morning, but the anger, hurt, and resentment Kita felt from her was staggering.

*There must be some underlying fundamental that I'm missing for them to be so mad. Had someone the power to do this to me, I would have had my secret police arrest the leaders and made it illegal for the party to exist. I don't think Kimmy can order the IBI to do that.*

"Are you ready, Your Highness?" said the director of the broadcast.

"Yes, whenever you are."

The director spoke into a radio. "When the light on the camera goes green, Your Highness."

The red light went out. *They must be coordinating with the networks.* The director tapped the cameraman and held up three fingers. He dropped them one by one. The light turned green, and the director pointed at Apocalypse.

"Good morning, my fellow citizens. I'm coming to you live from the Oval Office to share with you a bill that reached my desk for signature. This bill was drafted by Speaker of the House Dick Paul and by Senate Majority Leader Mike McDonald. The bill did not go to committee, was not open for public comment, or debated on either chamber floor. The votes in both chambers took place yesterday in closed-door sessions, and the language of the bill was not released to the public. Other members of Congress and I feel that you, citizens of the Empire, need to know what was voted on yesterday in your name. The bill states:

"THE EMPIRE OF THE UNITED STATES HOUSE OF REPRESENTATIVES AND THE Empire of the United States Senate hold Princess Kimberly Roosevelt in no confidence in her ability to govern the Empire of the United States. Her status as an Angel poses a conflict of interest that cannot be rectified. Her relationship with the Angel Kita is against the will of God. Her desire to live and promote a morally questionable lifestyle is unbecoming of the Emperor of the United States of America. The inclusion of the Angels at the highest levels of government poses a clear and present danger to the sovereignty of the Empire of the United States. We demand the immediate removal of Princess Kimberly Roosevelt to be replaced with a viceroy elected by the Empire of the United States Senate before Election Day, November 3, 2019. Princess Kimberly Roosevelt will retain her position as Princess but must forfeit claim to assets held by the Empire of the United States. The viceroy is to be elected every four years by the Senate until a suitable male heir is presented by the Roosevelt family."

AS APOCALYPSE READ, THE TENSION AND ANGER IN THE ROOM ROSE. KITA DID her best to look grumpy. On face value, this was insulting to Apocalypse, her, and the Angels, but it was meaningless bluster by a party that lost favor and was going to lose power. It should have been an annoyance, nothing more. Kita waited for Apocalypse's explanation.

"My fellow citizens, Speaker of the House Paul and Senate Leader McDonald did not think I would have the courage to share this bill with you. They thought I would be too embarrassed. The only thing I'm embarrassed by is how little they think of me. I am proud to be gay and am proud to have myself and Colonel Adrestia elevated to Angels. Princess Kita grew up in Cali and has proven her loyalty to the Empire. She is a proud citizen willing to fight for our freedom. That Princess Kita revealed her true form as an Angel is a blessing upon the Empire. What she and the other Angels offer will guarantee our sovereignty and our way of life. My relationship with Princess Kita has brought me the personal happiness that I wish for every citizen.

"The reason Speaker Paul and Senate Leader McDonald drafted and voted for this bill behind closed doors was they did not want the citizens of the Empire to know their plan to usurp power from my father by replacing me with a viceroy of their choice. This viceroy would hold power for four years and be elected by the

Senate, not the people. A viceroy would reign until I produce a male heir. They make this demand knowing I am gay. Even if I do produce an heir, they must find him suitable, whatever that means. They intend their viceroys to rule forever, usurping the power and trust placed in my family almost a century ago. I will not let this happen. Under normal circumstances, I would veto the bill and send it back to Congress, where they would try to override my veto.

"However, that will not happen. I have met with Chief Justice Logan and the rest of the Supreme Court. They agree with me that this bill is unconstitutional and violates Amendment Thirty of the Constitution. Only the citizens of the Empire have the right to remove my family from the position of Emperor."

"Therefore, I will not sign or veto this bill. It is to be struck from the public record. This bill will go to the Attorney General as evidence that Speaker Paul and Senate Leader McDonald conspired to commit treason against the Emperor. By attaching the date of November 3, 2019, they guarantee the citizens of the Empire will not have a say in who the Senate elects for the position of viceroy. Their goal is for the Conservative Party to remain in power indefinitely, usurping the will of the People when you elected my Great Grandfather Franklin D. Roosevelt Emperor. I have ordered the arrest of Speaker Paul and Senate Leader McDonald. The Supreme Court and I find Congress as party to the conspiracy. This is the first time a branch of government has tried to usurp the power of another. Because the Constitution has not foreseen this type of event, I am invoking Article Twenty-nine of the Constitution in the face of this national emergency. For the next six months, I have absolute authority over every aspect of the Imperial government. The Congress and Supreme Court surrender all authority to me.

"My first decree is to dissolve Congress and put the body into recess until the people can elect a new one in accordance with the Constitution. My second decree is to increase the Supreme Court from nine judges to nineteen. I will appoint these new Justices in the coming weeks.

"I have worked closely with these party leaders here with me over the last few days to produce a new budget that will meet the needs of the Empire. It increases spending for social programs, education, healthcare, infrastructure, military, and homeland security. To pay for these programs, the tax rate for large businesses will be raised to thirty-five percent. The upper tax bracket, for citizens making over fifty million dollars each year, will be moved to seventy-three percent. We will restructure government contracts to save billions. The days of the government making a select few rich are over. This government is for the people, not corporations.

"In addition to the budget, I have introduced a new set of laws to protect all citizens from the institutionalized bigotry and hatred that has plagued the Empire for too long. I made a promise that no child would grow up in fear in the Empire. I'm going to make good on that promise—for Jeanine, Robyn, Nicole, and Princess Kita. Everyone is equal in my eyes. No one will be denied freedom because of age, gender, ethnicity, sexual orientation, sexual identification, nation of origin, or religion. This law will go into effect as soon as it is signed."

An aide handed Apocalypse a folder. She opened it, picked up her pen, signed the document, and held it up for the camera.

"We are all citizens of the Empire with an equal responsibility to it and each other. We must take care of one another. This country was founded for the people, by the people. No group is better than any other. If we are to succeed, we must work together. That includes our neglected territories.

"To make sure the new Congress represents as many Americans as possible, I am granting statehood to the following territories: Northern Mexico, Sonora, Oaxaca, Maya, Eastern Mexico, Yucatán, Southern Mexico, Haida, Alberta, Yukon, Saskatchewan, and Manitoba. These new states are to hold constitutional conventions and elections to send representatives and senators to Congress.

"I am charged with protecting the Empire, and I will. Attempts to subvert the will of the People will not be tolerated and will be swiftly punished. I am proud to be a princess of the Empire of the United States and proud to lead this great Empire. The dawning of a new golden age is upon us. It will take all of us working together, but we will succeed."

Apocalypse stood up and raised her fist. "For the glory of the Empire."

Kita was a split second behind the rest of the group raising her fist and mouthing the words.

"For Emperor Roosevelt!"

*She took my lesson and ran away with it.*

The light on the camera turned red, and Kita let out a long breath. *Wow. I haven't seen a power grab like that since...me. I underestimated Kimmy.*

"Thank you, everyone," said Apocalypse, turning to the assembled representatives. "I know you're anxious to get started on winning elections. I hope I've opened the door for you. I will be endorsing candidates later this week, so submit your candidates by tomorrow. If you want campaign appearances, please submit those by the end of the week. I will concentrate on swing states first."

"Will the Angels be available?" someone asked. "We'd like Sapper and Aspen for a young voter campaign."

Kita rolled her eyes. *I have a war to win. I don't need them stumping for you.*

"I will talk to them. If they are willing, my office will let you know," said Apocalypse. "Thank you. Please keep my office updated. Good luck with your campaigns." She politely shooed the party leaders out of the Oval Office and returned to Kita, hugged her, and let out a big sigh.

"That was impressive," said Kita. "I thought you were going to veto it."

Apocalypse smiled coyly. "What do you think I've been doing while you've been in the mountains?"

"I, ah..."

Apocalypse laughed. "I applied the lessons you taught me."

"I'm proud of you, but I didn't teach you to seize power. You remind me of me."

"I've been doing this for more than a day," said Apocalypse with a devilish grin. "The treason charges probably won't hold, but I'm sure I can come up with a lesser charge."

"It was Machiavellian. The Conservative Party is going to be in chaos for a while."

"I'm hoping I've disrupted them at the Imperial level. I doubt I've caused much damage to the state-level parties, other than turn off the swing voters."

"And twelve new states?" said Kita.

"That'll make sure the majority stays out of the conservatives' reach. The conservatives are hated for the way they've treated those territories."

"Sounds like you have it figured out."

"I couldn't have done it without you," said Apocalypse softly.

"What did I do? I just stood there."

Apocalypse giggled. "If it weren't for you, I wouldn't have had the courage to do it. Knowing you're standing behind me gives me confidence and the assurance I need."

"I'm glad I can help, but you don't need me."

Apocalypse winked at Kita. "I don't need you, but I want you."

Kita's eyes widened in surprise. "No one has ever told me that before. I'm always the fixed point, and everyone revolves around me."

"You never expected to find another fixed point?"

"I never expected to find someone I want to revolve around."

Apocalypse stroked Kita's hair and the side of her face. "You don't revolve around me. We're two fixed points pulling each other closer. Together we'll be unstoppable."

*I'm speechless.* "No one has ever been my equal...until I met you," whispered Kita.

"I'm no god. I'm just an Angel."

"You could be."

"One step at a time. I just took over a country. I don't know if I'm ready for a universe."

"Give it time."

KITA WALKED AROUND THE MISSILE AND LAUNCH SYSTEM THE AIR FORCE HAD delivered. "I'd hate to see what they consider big," she said to Sprokkit.

The missile was eight feet long and the launcher four feet tall and about as wide. Along the missile's body were compartments. The missile ejected the compartments as it flew dispersing the virus over a wide area.

"Technically, it would fit in the back of an Air Force Humvee," said Sprokkit, "which was the specification you gave them."

"Even if you changed to Humvees, we couldn't mount this to you."

"I would prefer you did not."

"Can you make a Morphicon friendly launcher?"

Sprokkit examined the system. "It appears to need an electrical signal to trigger the missile's launch and a guidance system to direct it for its initial flight period. This launcher is mostly comprised of material to support the missile and aim it. Bernoot and I can do that. It should not take long to turn this launcher into something we can use."

"Excellent. I'll tell Kimmy to send the warning order for the military exercise. We'll have twenty-four hours to get to Russia."

"Another long plane ride, my favorite. I need a recommendation for a new show."

*What? Sprokkit watches TV?* "Ok. What do you like? I'll ask the other Angels. Did you ask Ryan?"

"I have finished watching all ten seasons of *Friends*. Ryan says he only watches Reality TV. I am not interested in shows about human reality."

*Friends? Found it...a sit-com.* "I will ask the others."

"Hurry. I would like to download as many episodes as possible before we leave."

"I'll get on it."

Kita left Sprokkit's workbench to find Ryan. *"Ok, girls, new mission. Sprokkit wants a new show to watch. Something like* Friends.*"*

*"He watched that?"* said Nemesis. *"No one watches* Friends.*"*

*"No idea,"* said Apocalypse.

*"I'll talk to him,"* said Nemesis. *"I've got a few he might like."*

*"Thanks,"* said Kita. She found Ryan by the virus incubation tanks. "How are they?"

Ryan looked up from the viewing window. "Full. I can start filling the missiles any time."

"Good. You can start in a minute. First, I want you to talk to me."

Ryan looked surprised. "What did I do?"

"Nothing. I've been ignoring you, and I'm sorry. I don't like neglecting my friends."

"It's ok. I've been busy in the lab."

"I know, but I don't want you to be all work and no play. Come chat with me." Kita touched Ryan's shoulder and phased them on top of the building.

"That was incredible. How do you do it?"

"We shift dimensions, allowing us to pass through the normal dimension to a new location."

"What's the math behind it?"

Kita chuckled. "I'm willing to tell you that, and a lot more secrets. That's why I want to talk to you. Two things, actually. I know you declined, but I wanted to offer you the basic Angel package again. You don't have to fight—you can do whatever you want. It's my gift to you for being my friend. You can leave if you want to go pursue something else."

"I don't want to be like Dan or a bear."

"What if I made you a cute bear that the girls will love?"

Ryan gave Kita a dubious look. "I don't want to be a six-foot stuffed animal."

Kita laughed. "That would be cute, but no. I was thinking of a panda bear. You'd be bigger than a normal panda. It'll come with armor and guns. It's up to you if you ever change into it. But you'd be protected and nearly indestructible. Please, take it—for my peace of mind."

Ryan sighed. "So, I'll be like you girls? Eating, sleeping, healing?"

"Yes."

"I could get a lot more work done."

"And you won't need the forklift to move equipment around."

"Ok, but you have to talk to Kimmy about getting Sarah stationed here or— or at least, get her to stop here."

"Have you talked to her?"

"Yeah. I email and video chat when I can. I have to use one of the Air Force terminals when I'm out here."

"Didn't you get a phone?"

"Not a military one. Sprokkit always does the talking."

Kita rolled her eyes. "We'll get you a phone, so you can call Sarah whenever you want. Talk to Sarah and see if *she* wants to be stationed here. If not, we can put her nearby or on a plane that makes regular stops."

"That would be awesome, thanks."

"I'm a princess. I might as well abuse the rank."

Ryan laughed.

"The other thing I wanted to ask you is if you'd be willing to come with me when I leave?"

"You mean to Russia?"

"No. When I leave this universe, I want to take you back to the main plane of existence. I could use your help working on the universes. I'll show you everything Leaf and I know. I think you can do some amazing stuff."

Ryan's jaw dropped. "I don't even know how ours works."

"You will. We've learned the basics, but there's a lot we don't know how to do. You and Sprokkit would be a big boost."

"Sprokkit's coming too?"

"I'm going to ask him. I know he'll come if you come. So, please?" Kita fluttered her eyelashes and smiled playfully.

"I guess so. When are you leaving?"

"I don't know. Kimmy sounds like she wants to stay for a while, so not in the near future."

"And Sarah?"

"If you're in a long term committed relationship, I'll bring her along. No promise I'll make her an Angel."

"I know it's a long way off."

Kita smiled. "If you think she's the one, go for it."

"How do I know if I don't get to see her?"

"True."

"Congratulations, by the way—for you and Kimmy. You girls took me by surprise."

Kita raised an eyebrow. "Why?"

"I was sure you were going to kill each other, and suddenly you're making out."

"Reactive elements react a lot when placed together."

"I've never seen elements go from repulsing to attracting."

"We weren't repulsing, just trying to find equilibrium. There was an attraction from the beginning. Ask Kimmy."

"How does Velositi feel?"

"She's happy and approves. We love each other, that hasn't changed. I think she's happy she doesn't have to take care of me and gets to enjoy me instead. Kimmy is a bonus for her."

"A bonus?"

"Velositi likes pretty things, even more than me. Kimmy is another pretty thing for her to look at."

"I noticed both she and Nicole look prettier."

"You will, too." Kita extended her barb and pricked Ryan's upper arm. "Give that a few hours. If you want to become a bear, think *bear*. To be human, think *human*."

"Ok. Thanks."

"My pleasure."

"I EXPECTED MORE SNOW," SAID SAPPER AS THE ANGELS AND VEHLIXEN exited the C-17 onto Elmendorf Air Force Base in Alaska. They were on a brief layover to refuel and give their air wings time to catch up.

"It's early in the season," said Nemesis. "Wow. I've never seen a flight line this busy."

Across the tarmac, crews scrambled around lines of fighters. Pilots were in the cockpits or rushing to their planes. In the distance, Crews loaded B-1 bombers and prepped them for flight.

"They're supposed to be in the air ready to repel an attack," said Apocalypse. "Several air wings are already on station across the Arctic and the Bering Sea."

"Are these fighters coming with us?" said Sapper.

"No," said Kita. "The B-2s and F-22s escorting us are coming from the mainland. They're already on their way. We'll meet them over the Bering Sea."

"How much you want to bet those Soviet assholes are shitting their pants right now?"

Kita chuckled at Sapper. Old hatreds died hard, no matter the universe. "Reports say they're confused, moving units back and forth and back again trying to guess where the attack will come from. We're moving units and squadrons around threatening new locations to make sure they stay confused."

"We're finding out they don't have as many armored and mechanized units as we thought," said Apocalypse. "They have a lot of equipment, but much of it is still sitting in the motor pools. Reports say they're marching basic infantry to the frontlines."

"What does that mean?" said Sapper.

"They don't have the money or supplies to train their forces on the equipment they do have."

"You should attack them and wipe them off the map."

"That's what we're doing," said Kita.

"Yeah, but I want to go to Moscow and punch Lenin in the nose."

"How about a Neophorm?"

"Almost as good."

---

A ROTATING AMBER LIGHT CAME ON ABOVE THE RAMP OF THE C-17.

"One minute!" yelled the loadmaster to the Angels and Vehlixen.

"*Everyone good to go?*" said Kita.

"*Radical,*" said Bernoot. "*This is going to be a way sick ride.*"

Kita stroked Velositi's cowl.

Velositi revved her engine. "I am ready."

The back of the C-17 opened. A chute deployed pulling Bernoot, strapped to a skid, out of the C-17. He landed on the ground a few feet below and slid across the two-lane gravel road. The C-17 crew pushed Sprokkit to the door. His chute deployed yanking him from the plane.

"Our turn," said Kita to Velositi.

The C-17 crew moved to the walls of the aircraft. Velositi gunned her engine, slipped her brake, and raced out the back of the plane. She hit the end of the ramp, and Kita opened her wings. They glided to the road and touched down, Velositi's rear wheel throwing rocks into the air. The Angels followed. The plane's ramp closed as its nose rose at a sharp angle and climbed into the night sky.

Kita and Aspen cut Sprokkit and Bernoot free.

"That was so epic," said Bernoot. "Can we do it again?"

"The next time the Air Force needs practice, you're welcome to go," said Apocalypse.

"Gnarly."

"Come on," said Kita. "We need to get moving so we can meet up with the Anti-Neophorm Teams." The rally point was several miles away. The Anti-Neophorm Teams parachuted in closer to the objective. This road was the only viable insertion point for the Vehlixen. Now they had to catch up to the teams.

The Angels mounted the Vehlixen and drove into the night.

---

KITA, APOCALYPSE, AND VELOSITI LED THE OTHERS DOWN A NARROW DIRT road. An infrared strobe light blinked from the edge of the forest.

"That's us," said Kita.

Velositi stopped at the light. Kita and Apocalypse dismounted, and Velositi morphed. They glided into the forest.

"Halt," someone challenged from the darkness. "Torch."

"Wood," said Kita giving the countersign.

The operators appeared out of the darkened woods.

"Any problems, Captain?" said Apocalypse.

"Negative, Your Highness. Everyone made it down. We're locked and loaded —waiting for your order."

"Good. Let's move out. The rest of the Vehlixen and Angels are waiting on the road."

The operators followed the Angels to the road. Forming into columns on the edges, the Anti-Neophorm Teams escorted the Angels and Vehlixen toward Shiveluch volcano.

In the distance, the sound of thunder rumbled.

"Right on time," said Kita. The Star Bridge was inside the volcano located in the middle of the Kamchatka peninsula. Satellite images showed a camp outside the entrance. To limit the number of enemies they would encounter cruise missiles were Pummeling the area. When they arrived, they would use laser-guided munitions from stealthy B-2 bombers and F-22 Raptors to finish off what was left.

"We need to hurry and get into position," said Apocalypse. They were a quarter of a mile from the encampment.

"The Angels will go first and clear the way," said Kita. "Anti-Neophorm Teams and Vehlixen follow when we give the signal."

The Angels turned invisible and glided up the road. Ahead, through a gap in the trees, fires caused by the cruise missiles lit the night.

"*Leaf, you go left. I'll go right,*" said Kita. "*Takedown any humans. Lizzy, spot for Nicole. Kimmy, call in airstrikes that Nicole lasers. Velositi, guard the others.*"

The Angels split up. Kita followed the edge of the forest, alert for any enemy on patrol. Moving shadows on the trees from the burning encampment said the camp garrison was active.

The first explosion caught Kita by surprise. More followed it in rapid succession. Kita scanned the flames and saw several Morphicon size objects moving among the wreckage. Another set of explosions rocked the encampment. *Kimmy's not messing around.*

Muffled voices came from the forest. Kita moved through the trees until she found the source. A quartet of soldiers watched at the edge of the woods. *You must have been the roving patrol, content to stand and watch.*

Kita flourished her swords, Dead and Buried, as she crept up on the soldiers. She turned visible, and with a double slash, she removed the heads of the first pair. She spun and brought her swords through the necks of the remaining pair before any of them knew she was there. Kita turned invisible and followed the tree line.

*"I found a patrol of four. Busy standing around and watching,"* Kita said to the others.

*"Nothing so far,"* said Aspen.

*"There are Neophorm drones in the encampment,"* said Apocalypse. *"We're bombing the hell out of them."*

*"The more the bombers get, the less we have to,"* said Kita.

The woods ended at a steep rocky escarpment that ringed the south side of the volcano. She followed the slope toward the encampment. A Neophorm near the cave entrance was yelling at the rest. *Who are you?*

More bombs fell. *"How many more bombs do we have?"*

*"I have another squadron, at least,"* said Apocalypse.

*"I think I've found a master."* Kita sent Nemesis her location. Kita saw the dot on the Neophorm's chest. She phased a hundred yards away as a pair of bombs exploded. She phased back and searched through the wreckage for the master.

The Neophorm pushed himself to his feet. His chest glowed red. Kita charged him and leaped. Turning visible, she plunged her swords into his chest. He punched Kita, sending her sideways into the dirt, leaving her swords in his chest.

Kita sprang into a corkscrew to dodge cannon blasts from the master. From the Star Bridge entrance, drones flooded out. They fired at Kita. She grew a pair of red balls in her hands and threw them. Snapping her fingers, the explosion knocked some back. Other drones charged.

*"Kimmy! I've got a problem. Drop the bombs."*

*"Where?"*

*"Right on top of me."*

*"I can't do that!"*

*"Just do it! I've got my shield."* Kita's shield expanded as the mass of drones crashed down on her. The drones fired at her shield while others smashed their fists against it, ignoring the damage the shield did to them.

The first bomb knocked Kita to the ground. *Ok. That was bigger than expected.* As she rolled to her feet, a second bomb struck next to her. The force of the blast collapsed her shield. The field around her was littered with drones, some struggling upright.

*"Kimmy, no more. My shield is down."*

*"Ah...Get out of there. Two more are inbound."*

*Oh, slag.* Something grabbed Kita by the wings before she could phase and slammed her to the ground.

*"Get out of there!"* cried Apocalypse.

*Trying.* A pair of drones Pummeled Kita as the third held her. Kita caught a fist and kicked up with her feet, catching the assaulting drone in the face, knocking him back into his friend. *I can't wait. I guess he's coming with me.* A blow to Kita's face made her see stars.

*"Kita!"* screamed Apocalypse.

*"I've got her,"* said Aspen. She appeared behind the drone that held Kita and plunged her swords into its back, flipped over the top, and sliced through the drone's arms. Aspen grabbed Kita as she expanded her shield, pushing the drones back.

A quartet of explosions rocked the area around them, blasting the drones to pieces. Aspen dropped her shield, and Kita got to her feet.

"Thanks, Leaf."

"*There are more coming.*"

"Perfect. *Kimmy, we've got more drones coming out of the Star Bridge.*"

"*I only have a few planes left.*"

"*Then we have to go through them the hard way.*"

"*You said Savacron was here,*" said Velositi. "*We should save those bombs and lure him out.*"

"*How do we do that?*" said Kita.

"*With us. To them, we are all that stands between the Neophormes and Earth.*"

"*Kimmy, deploy the Anti-Neophorm Teams. Vehlixen, make yourselves known. Angels, we need to put these drones in the ground. Time to go big. I have to find my swords.*"

"*Sweet!*" said Sapper. "*Time to hit the breach!*"

"*Anti-Neophorm rounds loaded,*" said Nemesis. "*Finding targets.*"

"*Scourge, coming up,*" said Apocalypse.

Kita and Aspen vanished as more drones exited the Star Bridge. Kita ignored them as she searched for Dead and Buried. Above her, Apocalypse roared. The dragon glided around the encampment attracting fire from the drones. She swooped low over a group of twenty, opened her mouth, and engulfed them in flame—those closest to her melted. The rest glowed red as she tore at them with her claws and teeth.

In the air, Sapper grew a giant red ball in her hands. She threw it in front of the Star Bridge entrance. The ball broke into a hundred smaller balls that would explode if something came close.

Nemesis fired as fast as she could acquire targets. With Sprokkit and Ryan's help, she had developed an Anti-Neophorm round based on the anti-Neophorm technology. The round's piercing jacket surrounded a capacitor that carried a charge of a million volts at twenty amps, enough to fry a Morphicon, and much stronger than the claw launchers which had held a fifty-thousand-volt charge released at half an amp. She moved from target to target, watching the other Angels' backs.

Velositi reached the horde of drones on the opposite side of Apocalypse. She fired with her cannons blasting through the drones, killing most in one shot. The mass of drones closed around her as she flipped, twisted, and glided around them. When a large group surrounded her, she reached a fist skyward. It crackled, and a lightning bolt crashed down on her. The bolt arced in all directions jumping through the drones, blasting them apart.

Bernoot and Sprokkit followed Velositi, watching her back while carrying Kita's missiles. They fired their cannons, blasting large holes in the drones.

"*Absolutely righteous,*" said Bernoot. "*My shooter's amped up.*"

"*Yes,*" said Sprokkit. "*I think someone did more than heal us.*"

"*I might have made some improvements. I wasn't going to let Velositi have all the fun,*" said Kita.

"*Yo! With that lightning, I need to get Velositi a hammer like Mike's comic books,*" said Bernoot.

Kita chuckled as she lifted a drone. *Where are my swords?* Kita glided around;

the flash of Velositi's lightning illuminated the hilt of Dead through the drone mob near the Star Bridge's entrance.

"*Kita, there are a lot more coming,*" said Apocalypse.

"*Yes, the tide is not stopping,*" said Velositi.

"*I'm thinking,*" said Kita.

A giant Morphicon exited the Star Bridge entrance. He was bigger than the Ancients the group had previously fought.

"*I think we've attracted who we're looking for,*" said Kita. She jumped into the air and streaked toward Savacron. Slamming into his giant chest, she knocked him off his feet. Kita's fists burned white-hot as she landed on his chest and pummeled him, throwing up sparks and slag.

"Wretched insect," Savacron snarled as he grabbed Kita's wings and slammed her into the ground. He climbed to his feet.

Kita sprang forward, grabbing Savacron's leg. She twisted, lifting him off the ground and slamming him into the dirt. Kita picked up a drone corpse and smashed it into Savacron's head. She punched a fist into him, melting his midsection while growing a red ball in her hand. When she had a hole big enough, she shoved the red ball in, backflipped, and snapped her fingers, tearing a beach ball size hole in his middle.

Savacron kicked his leg, sending Kita into the dirt. He jumped on Kita with both feet, slamming his fist into her exposed head several times. He grabbed her head and tried to crush it. His fingers tore into her skin, but he couldn't crush her skull.

"Hey, let go," said Sapper, flying up to the pair. She fired her rifle into Savacron's face. When he turned, Sapper grabbed his arm in a magnetic field and dragged him off Kita. She whipped the field around, waving him like a ragdoll and slamming him into the ground.

Savacron rolled over and fired his cannon, hitting Sapper in the chest. She released him and crashed into a pile of drones. Savacron charged her, but Kita slammed him from behind, knocking him into the dirt.

"*Somebody get to Lizzy,*" said Kita.

"*I've got her,*" said Aspen.

Kita fired a purplish-black blast into Savacron's back, creating a deep gouge. She dropped a series of red balls and backflipped into the air. Savacron snarled, twisted, and swung his arm, catching Kita before she could snap her fingers. Kita tumbled to the ground.

Savacron pounced on her, grabbing her by the wings and pulled.

Kita screamed.

The roar of Apocalypse as the dragon Scourge was deafening. She landed in front of Savacron, dwarfing the Morphicon. Velositi landed on her left.

"Let her go," said Velositi.

Savacron snarled. "Vehlix scum. I will bury you. This world belongs to us."

"You have to kill me first."

Savacron let go of Kita and fired his cannons at Velositi. She blocked the shots with her wing and performed a series of side-flips while firing, blasting big holes in him.

Scourge lunged, slamming Savacron with both of her front feet, driving him into the ground. She hopped backward, twirled, and drove her spike-covered tail into his front. She raised her tail with Savacron attached and slammed him back and forth on the ground.

When Savacron came free, Velositi jumped, firing into his back. Savacron bellowed, rolled to his feet, and his arms morphed into enormous cannons. He fired both into the side of Scourge, blowing through her scales and leaving deep holes.

Scourge roared and bit down on Savacron's arm. She blew a superheated flame melting through it. Savacron pointed his free weapon at Apocalypse's head and fired. Scourge recoiled, letting go of Savacron's arm. The scales and flesh from part of her skull were missing. Savacron slammed his arm into Apocalypse while she was stunned. She staggered backward and swung her head away to protect it.

Bernoot and Sprokkit joined Velositi firing on Savacron. Their hits left glowing red holes. Savacron raised his arm to fire at Sprokkit. Kita slammed into the arm, making the shot go wide.

"*Kita, look out!*" said Velositi as she raised her arm.

Kita phased away as a lightning bolt struck Velositi. With her arm, Velositi guided the lightning bolt at Savacron, hitting him in the chest.

Savacron pushed his way toward Velositi. "You are no match for me, Vehlix. I will tear you apart."

"Yo! Ugly! You got to get through us first," yelled Bernoot as he and Sprokkit fired, blasting Savacron in the chest.

"*Eat this,*" said Nemesis as she fired into Savacron's chest.

Scourge transformed back into Apocalypse and yelled, "I have not yet begun to fight!" as she appeared with the Anti-Neophorm Teams. She fired her beams as the operators opened fire.

Savacron roared as he lunged for Velositi. She jumped backward, firing at him. Kita appeared in front of Velositi with a wicked smile. She flourished Dead and Buried and slammed the hilts together to form the legendary greatsword Crypt, the reaper of souls.

"Ah-ah, she belongs to me." Kita twirled Crypt and swung, catching Savacron under the chin, knocking him back.

Kita rushed him, striking Savacron repeatedly in the chest, digging deep into the damage already there. Kita spun and slammed Crypt into Savacron's chest, destroying a system core. She withdrew, twirled, and slammed the other end of the sword into Savacron, destroying a second system core. She backflipped, kicking Savacron under the chin, sending him crashing to the ground.

Kita landed on his chest, thrusting Crypt into a third system core. "Not feeling too well, are you?" Kita yanked Crypt out and slammed it into a fourth system core. "Do you know me? I am the true mistress of the Axiom of Evil. I am the ultimate evil held within. This world doesn't belong to you. Your world doesn't belong to you. It never did. If it hadn't been for me, you would never have gained control. That is a blight on me, and I will set it right. Chellexon belongs to the Vehlixen. And this world belongs to her…"

Apocalypse landed next to Kita. "I'm going to drop your corpse in the middle of Red Square." Kita and Apocalypse floated off Savacron. Apocalypse fired her beams into Savacron's chest, destroying two more system cores. "All yours, Velositi."

Velositi glided up next to Apocalypse and Kita.

"Your tyranny ends tonight," said Velositi.

Savacron's eyes brightened. "You can't kill us all."

"I can," said Kita.

Velositi fired her cannons into Savacron's last system core. His eyes went out, and his head lulled to one side.

"One step down," said Velositi.

Kita and the others gathered around Aspen and Sapper.

"Lizzy, how are you?" said Kita.

"Stuff burns, but Leaf patched me up. I'm fit to fight."

"Good. Let's go see the prize we won."

"DAMN! THIS THING IS HUGE," SAID SAPPER AS THE ANGELS, VEHLIXEN, AND operators entered the cavernous room filled with generators, floodlights, equipment, and a three-story circular gate crackling with energy against the far wall. Through the gate was another cavernous empty room with black walls, glowing lights, and a large passageway led upward.

Kita drifted toward the portal. "Leaf, it's a rift gate."

"What is a rift gate?" said Velositi.

"Interdimensional travel. The universe has eleven dimensions. You know the four—space and time. The fifth dimension sits on top of the first four. That's what I use when I phase. The rest of the dimensions twist around each other as they hold the universe together while interacting on the subatomic level. These dimensions are flat and touch everything. If you bombard an area with enough subatomic particles, you can create a door through the dimension to another place in the physical dimensions. These doors can cover large distances and be huge. I had Angels that could open them."

"How did you convert this massive equipment to a biological process of a cell and miniaturize it to fit in an Angel?" said Sprokkit.

"It didn't happen inside a cell. The process is spread among many different types of organelles inside various cells. I can't take credit for figuring out how. That belongs to the AI Omega."

"You are admitting something is smarter than you?"

Kita chuckled. "Even I had to be educated."

"Can this thing be opened at another location?" said Apocalypse.

"Sure, but we need it to get to Chellexon. We just need to figure out how it works."

"Sprokkit?" said Velositi.

"I will study it and see what I can learn."

"Good. Hand me the missile. I will take it to Chellexon."

Sprokkit unslung the missile and handed it to Velositi. It was as tall as she was, but she slung it onto her back between her wings without protest. She floated upward, so she didn't drag its tail on the ground.

"Let us go," said Velositi. "The longer we wait, the more time the Neophormes have to react."

"Colonel," Apocalypse called.

The leader of the Anti-Neophorm Teams hurried over. "Yes, Your Highness."

"Your teams are to guard this location. If we don't come back or if Neophormes try to come through shut it down."

"Yes, Your Highness."

"Did you hear that, Sprokkit?" said Velositi.

"Yes. I hope I can get it open again if I must close it."

"Let's go," said Kita. She glided through the gate into the Neophorm side. The room's square and angular walls were a mixture of dull rock and shiny metal. There was no equipment on this side, just a glowing line in front of the rift gate.

"*What is that?*" Apocalypse pointed at the line.

"*It's a beacon made of decaying subatomic particles that are visible in the other dimensions. It allowed the Earth side to know where to open the gate.*"

Kita led the others up the passageway onto a walkway that went around the structure. A dim sun hung on the horizon of a hazy red sky. They stood on the tallest monolithic structure in a sprawling complex. Neophormes stood in formations or marched from one location to another. A giant mining operation was to the south and east.

"*Where are we?*" said Kita.

"*This is Dexthane—the largest Neophorm base in the north,*" said Velositi.

"*Good. Let's get the missiles oriented and launched.*"

"*We should fire one over the training grounds and the other over the plasma mines.*"

"*I thought plasma came from electricity,*" said Apocalypse.

"*Yes, that is the second step. On Chellexon, we mine plasma crystals and put them into a solution to unlock their stored electrons to create electricity. It's then converted to plasma.*"

"*That will be perfect,*" said Kita. "*It'll keep the bionanites fed forever.*"

The Angels helped Velositi and Bernoot take off the missiles and position the launchers on their shoulders.

"*It is too big,*" said Velositi as she tried to get the shoulder support to sit correctly.

"*Put it on,*" said Kita. Velositi lifted the launcher into place. "*Leaf, Lizzy, hold it.*" Kita heated her hands and bent the metal to fit around Velositi's shoulder. "*Is that better?*"

"*Yes, much.*"

The Angels lifted the missiles and placed them into the launchers fitting the control cleats into the firing receptacles. Kita went to each launcher and flipped a switch. "*Armed.*"

Velositi and Bernoot pointed their missiles out over the base and mining facility.

"*Letting her rip!*" said Bernoot.

"*Firing!*" said Velositi.

The missiles ignited and leaped off the launchers to streak through the sky, releasing their cargo.

"*That should do it,*" said Kita. "*Once they get into the plasma facility, it'll be over in a matter of weeks or months.*"

"*Excellent!*" cried Velositi in delight. "*I will send a message to the Elders and let them know.*"

Aspen put up her shield as cannon blasts splashed off it. "*Neophormes!*"

"*We'll take care of them. Keep Velositi safe so she can call her leaders,*" said Kita.

Aspen dropped her shield as the Angels and Bernoot assaulted the trio of drones. Nemesis raised her rifle and fired. A drone spasmed before collapsing to the ground smoking. Apocalypse fired her beams into the chest of another, punching a hole through him. The drone stumbled and fell off the structure. Bernoot fired three blasts from his cannon, blowing gaping holes in the last drone's torso. Kita and Sapper threw red balls at the damaged drone. Snapping their fingers, the drone blew apart.

"*That's going to draw attention,*" said Kita. "*We need to get out of here.*"

The Angels and Bernoot hurried to Aspen and Velositi. Aspen dropped her shield.

"*Velositi, we have to go!*"

Around the corner, more drones appeared. The Angels fired.

"*Screw it, get inside!*" Kita ordered. She extended her heat shield around her and Velositi.

The other Angels and Bernoot ran inside. Kita picked up Velositi as cannon blasts melted in her shield. Kita grew a large red ball in her hand as she flew down the passageway.

"*Lizzy, we've got to block this entrance,*" said Kita.

"*Hell yeah. I'm on it.*"

Kita collapsed her shield and tossed her red ball close to the entrance of the passageway. Sapper threw three more red balls that stuck to the ceiling.

"*Aspen, get your shield up around everyone. Lizzy, hit it!*" Kita extended her shield and snapped her fingers. The massive explosion blasted down the passageway. Three smaller blasts punctuated the large one. The shockwaves and heat went around the shields and dissipated against the walls. Kita left Velositi and checked the damage. They collapsed the roof, but she could see light trickling in through the dust.

"*We're not safe. Everyone back through the gate,*" Kita ordered. She flew to Velositi. "*Love, we have to go.*"

"*They do not understand the virus,*" said Velositi.

"*They'll get the idea once the Neophormes start dying and stop attacking.*"

"*They think we are killing the world.*"

"*You know that's not true,*" said Kita. Rubble rolled down the passageway. "*We don't have time to convince them.*"

"*They are threatening an all-out attack on the Neophormes to stop the virus.*"

"*Patch me through.*"

"*You are talking to the Elders,*" said Velositi. "*Gstex is the leader. Elders, this is Kita, the being the Axiom of Command chose.*"

"*Call it what it is—the Axiom of Evil,*" said Kita. "*Listen, I'm the legend you sent Velositi to find. She tasked me with saving the Vehlixen and as many Neophorm masters as I can. I've done that. There is no stopping it. But you have to be patient.*"

"*What you say is impossible,*" said Gstex.

"*Yet, I'm talking to you. Your choice, believe me or not, but I'm taking Velositi, Bernoot, and Sprokkit with me. I've done what I promised. Peace will be restored, and the Neophormes defeated.*"

"*Velositi was supposed to bring back the Axiom of Command. It will choose a leader to defeat the Neophormes.*"

"*Slag, you're supposed to be wise. Listen to what I'm telling you. Your legend does not match reality. It was never going to pick a Vehlix. It would only pick me, its rightful owner. I promised Velositi I would save Chellexon and the Vehlixen. All you have to do is be patient. Which, I can't be. I've got to go.*"

"*Velositi says you have unleashed death upon us.*"

"*I don't have time for a biology lesson. If you won't take the word of one of your best warriors, I can't help you. She and I are both telling you to do nothing and see what happens. There's nothing you can do to stop it. If you want to talk to us again, build this.*" Kita transmitted the plans for a rift gate beacon. "*We'll be looking for it. Come on, Velositi, let's go.*"

A drone appeared through the rubble and fired, hitting Velositi in the chest.

Kita cut the connection, grabbed Velositi's hand, and pulled her through the rift gate.

"Close it!" yelled Kita as she lay Velositi down.

"Kita!" cried Apocalypse. "What the hell took so long?"

"Vehlix logic is the same as Arconian logic. Velositi, are you ok?"

"I will be fine." A grapefruit-size hole was carved in her chest. "It hurts. I am sorry. I wanted them to understand."

"You shouldn't have told them anything," said Apocalypse.

Velositi's eyes dimmed. "I wanted them to be happy and be proud of me."

Kita knelt next to Velositi. "Don't worry about them. We're proud of you."

"Yes, you accomplished your mission and got rid of the Neophormes on Earth," said Nemesis.

Velositi's eyes brightened.

"If you want, I'll give you a parade and a medal," said Apocalypse.

"The gate is closed," said Sprokkit.

"Did you figure out how to reset it?" said Apocalypse.

"Yes, but I have no coordinates to give it, other than Chellexon."

"What kind of coordinates does it take?"

"It has a galactic map," said Sprokkit.

"Can it do my planet?"

"Yes."

The ANT colonel approached Apocalypse. "Your Highness, General Mayfield has sent a sit-rep."

"Ok."

"He says our forces in Europe and southwest Asia are holding enemy units in place. The strategic bombing force remains on station over the Arctic, holding the Soviet Air Force in place. The carrier groups in the North Sea, Mediterranean, Middle East, and the Indian Ocean are running practice sorties against Soviet targets keeping enemy aircraft in theater. The carrier groups in the Sea of Japan, Sea of Okhotsk, and the Bering Sea, as well as Air Force squadrons from Korea and Japan, have eliminated all Soviet airpower in the region. Eighteenth Airborne Corps, 173$^{rd}$ Airborne, and 4$^{th}$ Brigade have secured the Siberian provinces of Chukotka and Magadán. Marines have landed and are securing the cities of Magadán, Petropavlovsk, and Kamchatsk. Ranger forces have secured the airfields and sub pens on the Kamchatka peninsula. Operation Silent Slaughter has been a success, except for five Soviets subs in drydock and cruise missile strikes successfully eliminated them. Naval forces are moving against what's left of the Soviet Navy.

"General Mayfield says China and India are on alert but have made no moves against us. They, the UN, and NATO want an explanation."

"Excellent," said Apocalypse.

"That doesn't sound like what I suggested," said Kita.

"What is going on?" said Nemesis.

Apocalypse crossed her arms and gave them a look of defiance. "It was a good start, angel, but I decided even if we destroy the Star Bridge, the Soviets will rebuild it. The only way to make sure it stays in safe hands is if we control it."

"You're taking eastern Siberia! This was your plan?" exclaimed Nemesis as she stuck a finger in Kita's chest.

"Ah, no. I planned to put pressure on the Soviets and come here and destroy the rift gate. I knew nothing about the rest of this. I don't disapprove, but I don't know what's been done, either."

"Your Highness, this will start World War Three!" yelled Nemesis. "What happens when the Soviets pour into Europe?"

"They won't. Ninety percent of the Soviet military is west of the Ural Mountains. I haven't moved a soldier, plane, or ship out of Europe to do this. If they try to move forces to counter us here, what's to stop me from pushing toward Moscow? And now, they don't have a sub fleet or aircraft carriers. The Navy in the Atlantic is hunting down the rest of their surface fleet. The Navy and Air Force have devastated the Soviet Air Forces here, in the Far East, and the Navy has eliminated the Soviet Navy in the Pacific. Our technological superiority over the Soviets was greatly underestimated. Surprise was total, and I'm not done yet."

"Oh?" said Kita curiously. *What else does my love have planned for the world?*

"With this rift gate, I can move Army divisions anywhere in the world. I'm going to shove First Cav and First Armor all the way to the Urals. I'm taking Siberia as payment for forty-five years of war with them and the Illuminati."

"Winter's here," said Kita. "Waging war across the Russian steppe might not be the greatest idea."

"I just have to position my forces—like chess. Kryuchkov will have no choice."

"What about India and China?" said Nemesis. "They're Russian allies."

"I sent them a warning. Right, Colonel?"

"Yes, Your Highness."

"Whose head did you send?" Kita said with a chuckle.

"I sent a picture of Savacron and Velositi. Seeing their most powerful ally felled by mine should take the fight out of them. After seeing how bad the Soviets are being pounded, they won't commit their sub-par militaries when my mechanized and heavy forces in the States have yet to be committed. I'm sure Beijing is praying I don't decide to turn south."

"Impressive," said Kita.

"What if they all decide to attack? We'll be overextended!" said Nemesis.

"Nicole, calm yourself," said Apocalypse. "I'm not halfway through my deck of cards yet. I still have regular units, reserves, National Guard, and inactive reserves. That's an eight-million-person military. It's smaller than the Soviets, Chinese, and Indian combined, but better trained and equipped. They know this. For years they've been pestering this snow leopard with the Neophormes. Now, they don't have the Neophormes, and I'm hitting them with all my claws."

"Revenge isn't the Imperial way!" yelled Nemesis.

"It's not revenge. It's to preserve freedom. I'm going to make sure they can never threaten us again."

"The UN won't stand for this."

"They will once I show them the evidence. I already have the State Department working on it."

"You're not a dictator. This isn't right."

"Actually, as of a few days ago, I am. Did you miss the news? Currently, there is one branch of government—me."

"This is your fault," Nemesis yelled at Kita.

"What did I do?"

"You led her down this path."

"I did not. I was gone when all of this planning took place."

"You and your stories of being the powerful Vicereine ruling with an iron fist."

Kita shrugged. "Maybe. But Kimmy is doing it for the right reasons. She wants to keep the Empire safe. Sometimes you have to be the aggressor to assure safety. It's risky, people will die, but the reward for being victorious is peace. Kimmy is a great leader, better than I ever was. She's not an egotistical, self-centered, megalomaniac with delusions of grandeur. And Leaf, I was not delusional—"

"*I wasn't going to say a word.*"

"—Kimmy is a caring and pragmatic leader determined to do her duty to her country. This plan she's put together is a gamble—but no risk, no reward. The reward will be greater peace and security than what was before."

"And what if this blows up in our face?"

"Then the Angels and Vehlixen will work overtime to put it back together, and you get to say *I told you so.*"

Nemesis sighed. "I wouldn't do that to Kimmy, but I would hope she learned a lesson."

"I lose, and I could be out on my ass," said Apocalypse.

From the look on Nemesis' face that hadn't occurred to her.

"Yeah," said Apocalypse. "Everybody from the lowest private up to me is risking everything on this venture. I can't do it without you, Nicole. It's for the good of the Empire. And, think of the people joining the Empire—how much better their lives will be. The Soviets have left Siberia a backwater prison. The region has the resources—we have the technology. I plan to turn Siberia into the next Canada."

An operator sprinted into the chamber, holding a radio hand-mic. "Your Highness, new flash traffic code word PINNACLE/NUCBURST."

"What?" cried Apocalypse. "How many?"

"NORAD reports a single launch from Kazakhstan."

"That bastard can't lose with dignity," snarled Apocalypse. "Where's it going?"

"Eastern seaboard, Your Highness. Twenty-three minutes."

"D.C., Baltimore, New York, Boston, Atlanta, Miami, Philadelphia—we can't evacuate in that short of time. Alert the public to take whatever shelter they can. Tell General Mayfield to pick two targets. If D.C. or New York is hit, Moscow is one of the targets."

"Yes, Your Highness."

"What's going on?" said Kita.

"Kryuchkov has launched a nuke. He's not going without a fight. He knows he can't stop us, but he's going to make it cost us."

"NORAD tracks these?"

"Yes."

"Twenty-two minutes? I can catch it."

"Kita, there is no way you can get to it!"

"I broke the sound barrier when I was a young Angel. I can go faster now. Sprokkit, set the gate over western Russia."

"Hmmm, it seems improbable your wings can generate that kind of propulsion," he said as he set the gate.

"I just have to set a slider for my gravity wells to one hundred and," the rift gate opened, "berserk." A red aura formed around her vision as the world slowed to a near stop. She ran and jumped through the gate.

Kita appeared high above western Russia. She tucked in her wings, and the world went silent as she used her berserk state to push herself through the sound barrier and far beyond. Tapping into the EUS Defense Satellite Communications System, she connected to the NORAD computer system and located the nuclear weapon climbing into space.

The edge of space was beautiful—the curvature of the Earth, the blue atmosphere, and the blackness of space all in one picture. Ahead of her was the exhaust trail. She followed it and flew alongside the gray missile with *CCCP* painted on the side.

Kita stopped berserking and blinked tears from her eyes. Years of training turned the sobs following an episode into a few small tears. The emotional turmoil she felt hadn't lessened, but her ability to handle it had increased.

She searched for an access hatch to the navigational computer. *I don't want to have to push this thing out of the way.* She found several hatches—one was engine access, another was for fuel lines, a third revealed a receptacle with a twenty-pin port. Kita groaned. It was wider than her thumb. *Let's see if I can do this in parallel.* She pressed both thumbs against it and connected via the fibers in her skin.

*And, my Russian dictionary is six hundred years too late and from the wrong universe.* Kita translated enough to talk to the computer. She needed to break the encryption. Not a difficult task, but time-consuming. *I wonder how much time I have.* They were still in space, and the missile was level. She forced her way inside the guidance computer and ran through the flight instructions. *I could shut it down and let it fall or...*

The missile's coordinates couldn't be changed mid-flight. Kita needed to reboot the computer and restart the engine. *Luckily, I came with my own way to light this candle.* She shut down the missile, reprogrammed the destination coordinates, and restarted the computer.

Lights on a panel lit as the computer went through its startup sequence. Once it reached *launch*, Kita disconnected and dropped down to the missile's base. She lit a fireball and threw it into the engine nozzle. The missile ignited and lurched forward, leaving Kita behind.

Kita spread her wings and caught herself. She and the missile had fallen back into the atmosphere. Kita hurried after it.

"NORAD, Princess Kita. Can you hear me?"

"Yes, Your Highness. This is Colonel Hickman. What can we do for you?" said a male voice.

"The nuclear missile—did it change course?"

"It is deviating from the projected course, Your Highness. Should it be?"

"Yes, thanks. I'm going to watch it and make sure it hits the target."

"What's the target, Your Highness?"

"Write this down and get it to Princess Roosevelt. Are you ready?"

"Yes, Your Highness."

"*Kimmy, a special engagement gift from me to you, love, Kita.* You're to put little hearts around it and get—preferably a female officer—to kiss it, leaving a set of lip prints. Think you can handle that?" said Kita as she caught up to the missile. There was a click. *He hung up.* Kita called back.

"This is General Borland, Commander of NORAD."

"This is Princess Kita."

"What the hell is going on?" he snapped. "Why are you wasting my people's time in a crisis?"

"The crisis is averted," said Kita. "I retargeted the missile. Now, please give my message to Princess Roosevelt. If you ruin my gift, I'm coming to Colorado, and you get to explain to her why you felt so damn important that you would ruin my engagement gift to her, and I will make you write it out in front of her. I —Whoa!"

A white streak went by Kita and her missile and exploded. Kita rolled in the air to keep airborne. "Do it, General. I have some flies to swat."

Kita turned around. *Uh-oh. "Any EUS pilot on this band. This is Princess Kita. Any EUS pilot!"*

"*This is Commander Frazer commander of Strike Fighter Squadron One-Five-Four, EUS Navy.*"

"*Commander, if I wanted to shoot down a nuclear missile, what type of missile would you use, and how do I counter it?*"

"*A heat-seeking missile would be best to bring one down. To counter an HSM, we use flares that burn hot.*"

"*Right. I can become a giant flare,*" said Kita.

"*Do you need help, Your Highness?*"

Kita burst into flame and dropped into the wake of the missile. She turned up her heat to be hotter than the missile's exhaust.

"*I could use a hand if you're close. I have fifteen MiGs on the horizon, trying to shoot down my engagement gift. I'm built for speed, not aerial combat.*"

"*What's your location?*"

"*No idea.*" Behind her, coming up fast, were fifteen missiles.

"*Sky Fortress, do you have the princess' location?*" said Frazer.

*Who's he talking to? Never mind. Let's see what these missiles are following.* Kita curved upward away from her missile. Behind her, the Soviet HSMs followed. *Excellent.* Kita turned straight up, and the HSMs followed, gaining on her. *Ok, now what do I do?*

"*We have the nuclear missile location, Black Knight Lead,*" Sky Fortress said to Frazer. "*It is two hundred and fifty-three miles from your location. You don't have permission to enter Soviet airspace...but that was garbled. Go smoke some MiGs and help the princess. We'll vector you in.*"

"*Your Highness, we're on our way. Black Knights, kick it in the ass. Full burn.*"

*That doesn't help me right now. I've got to shake these things. I need my own flares.* Kita grew fireballs and tossed them to the side as she doused her flame. The HSMs followed the fireballs. Some exploded when they reached a fireball. Others lost the fireballs and streaked off into the horizon.

Kita dove and caught up to her missile. It was undamaged and flying on course. Behind her, the Soviet MiGs fired another round of missiles. *By the Crushing Depths. They're even closer.* Kita burst into flame and dropped behind the missile again. Her head swam, and she felt exhausted. *Slag me. I have to eat.* She opened a pouch on her belt and pulled out several energy balls. Each ball packed five thousand calories. It wasn't much, but it was enough to keep her going for a short while. She stuffed them in her mouth and swallowed them without much chewing.

The HSMs streaked toward her. Kita dove, taking them with her. She released a string of fireballs. Most of the HSMs followed, except for two. She doused her flame as they came close and made a hard turn upward. One HSM streaked under her, the other matched her turn and aimed at her. *Slag me.* Her heat shield expanded, and the missile detonated against it, sending her tumbling.

Kita entered a flat spin as she plunged toward the ground. *Uhm, I've never done this before.* Kita drew in her wings, and she spun faster. *Not helping.* Pain exploded in her thigh as a bullet took out a large chunk. Blood leaked into the air. She rolled her head, trying to look in the direction the bullet came from. A MiG was coming at her guns blazing. *Dive, dive, dive. I have to get out of here.* She arched her back, tilted her wings in the opposite direction of her spin, and somersaulted backward into a spinning dive. *This I can fix.* Kita adjusted her wings and stopped the spin. She turned her dive into a climb and raced to catch her missile.

Kita glided behind her missile as the Soviet MiGs tried to shoot it down with their cannons. Several fist-sized holes perforated her missile's skin, and something was leaking down the side. *I have to get rid of these guys. I'm glad they're not better shots.*

A MiG flew behind Kita. She twisted in the air, dodging the bullets. She drew her swords, pulled to one side, and slashed through the MiG's wing. Kita turned hard into the wingman. She landed on the canopy and thrust Dead into the pilot. She jumped into the air and raced after another MiG.

Bullets flew around Kita. Behind her, and from her left, a pair of MiGs bore down on her. A bullet slammed through her gut. *Ouch. A thirty-millimeter round hurts.* She made a ninety-degree turn and flew at the MiG that shot her. She dove underneath, slashing at the fuselage with her swords. She shoved a red ball into a hole she made, and dove. She snapped her fingers, and the plane disintegrated.

*Three down. Twelve to go.* Kita's vision grayed as she felt lightheaded. *Injury or energy? Both probably.* Kita made a wide turn and aimed at the side of another MiG. A fist slammed into the side of her chest as a bullet hit her rib and shattered. A few fragments punctured between her ribs. Kita couldn't catch her breath. A gray ring closed around her vision. *No, I can't.* A red ring overtook the gray one as she went berserk. She raced forward and slammed into the side of the MiG, sending it spinning out of control. She bounced into another, slashing through the fuselage behind the cockpit. The two parts fell toward the Earth.

Kita raced to her missile knocking the big 30mm rounds out of the sky with her swords. She landed near the base of the missile and knelt. Her vision returned to normal. *We're almost there. I just have to keep it together a little longer.* Kita summoned all her strength and extended her heat shield to protect herself and her missile. The 30mm rounds left long orange streaks through her shield as they melted.

*I have to stay awake. Help is coming.* She shoved the remaining three energy balls in her mouth. She swallowed them and felt the needed energy invigorate her. She focused everything on her shield.

Multiple explosions detonated on the side of her shield, knocking her off her missile. As she tumbled through the air, more explosions rocked her shield before it collapsed. The remaining HSMs streaked into the distance.

Kita tumbled through the air. *Today is not my day.* She flipped and opened her wings, righting herself. She took off after her missile, struggling to catch up. *I can do it. I can do it.* She pushed as hard as she could, slowly gaining.

A MiG pulled in behind Kita and fired. *Oh, no.* As Kita rolled out of the stream of bullets, one blasted through her pelvis, missing her spine. *Oh, slag me.* The MiG adjusted and came up on her. Kita collapsed her wings and dove. The MiG followed. Kita juked back and forth as the 30mm rounds flew by her. Kita flared her wings and made a hard-right turn. The MiG flew past her as she climbed higher. She used the speed from the dive to catch her missile.

To Kita's right, two more squadrons of MiGs appeared. *We still have a hundred miles to go. Or, I put it down here. Not as nice, but still a powerful message. I—*

Nine of the incoming MiGs vanished in fireballs. The rest broke formation. Kita scanned the horizon. From the west, she could see a squadron of twelve F-22s racing toward her.

*"Hang tight, Your Highness. We're coming in hot,"* said Frazer.

Kita landed on her missile and knelt. The F-22s engaged the MiGs, taking down four more in rapid succession before they broke into pairs to chase the MiGs around the sky.

*Ok. I can break the glass and heal.* Glands around Kita's body released healing bionanites. Special cells released her energy reserves to fuel them. She sat down hard and closed her eyes for a moment. When she opened them, a MiG was in front of her.

Kita jumped and opened her wings, flying directly at the MiG. Bullets whizzed by her. The MiG adjusted fire, clipping Kita's upper arm. She rolled and landed on the MiG's nose. Slamming her fist into the canopy, she ripped it off. The pilot ejected. Kita caught his seat as the chute deployed, pulling them toward the tail. She let go, turned, and thrust Buried into the plane's fuselage carving a hole in the metal then shoving a red ball in. Jumping into the air, she snapped her fingers, and the MiG exploded.

Kita's limbs went numb. *Uh-oh. I'm out of everything.* "I need a lift," she called to the F-22 pilots.

*"Hey, Your Highness. I'm Hedgehog. What do you need?"* said an F-22 that pulled alongside Kita.

*"I need a place to lay down for a bit. I took a couple of rounds."*

*"Do we need to get you back to the carrier?"* said Frazer.

*"Get the missile to Moscow. Then take me home. I'm just going to lie on the back of Hedgehog's fighter. Don't worry. I won't fall off."*

Kita glided above Hedgehog's fighter and landed behind the cockpit. She tapped on the glass and gave Hedgehog a thumbs-up.

*"Hold tight, Your Highness."*

*"No problem,"* Kita activated bionanites in her skin that let her stick to nearly anything. She rarely used them, but they were part of the original nanite package the AI Omega gave her. *"What's your name, Hedgehog?"*

*"Lieutenant Commander Karen McKnight, Your Highness."*

*"Call me Kita. Nice flying today."*

"*Thanks. I made ace! I bagged five today to go with my four over Iran.*"

"*Congratulations. That's impressive flying. Glad to know I'll be in good hands. So, why Hedgehog?*"

"*I had one as a pet growing up. They're feisty critters.*"

"*That they are. My daughter wanted to be named hedgehog.*"

"*There's nothing wrong with that.*"

"*No, but she wanted to call her sister porcupine.*" Hedgehog laughed. "*They were nine. We settled on Spike and Quill.*"

"*I haven't seen any report saying you had kids.*"

"*It was a long time ago.*"

"*Your Highness, the missile just launched ten submunitions,*" said Frazer.

"*Good. Then let's go home,*" said Kita.

The F-22s made a turn to the west. Kita settled in on the back of Hedgehog's F-22, resting her head on the canopy. As they flew back toward the carrier, colorful mushroom clouds grew on the eastern horizon.

———————————————

A HARD THUMP AND RAPID DECELERATION WOKE KITA. SHE SAT UP AS Hedgehog taxied across the aircraft carrier. Kita tried to stand, but couldn't put any weight on her leg, so she floated above the F-22 as it crossed the carrier and parked. She waited as Hedgehog shut down the fighter, and the flight deck crew placed a ladder against the cockpit. Kita glided down and met her.

"Thanks for the lift, Karen," said Kita.

"No problem, Kita. I've never had a VIP before."

"Congratulations on becoming an ace in a day. I have something for you." Kita placed her hand on Hedgehog's upper arm and injected her with the basic Angel package.

Hedgehog's eyes went wide from the poke.

"If you're up to the challenge, I want to reassign you to Angel School at Area Fifty-one."

"What's Angel School?"

"It's where you prove if you're worthy of these." Kita flapped her wings.

"You want me?" exclaimed Hedgehog.

"I want the best. You've proven you have what it takes in the field. Now, you have to prove you can hang with us."

"What do I have to do?"

Kita tapped the side of the F-22. "Prove you're the best in the world at flying one of these."

"You get me the flight time, and I'll out fly and fight anyone."

"Master this, and I'll see about getting you a custom fighter."

"A custom fighter?"

"Fly higher, faster, and harder than anything on Earth. Prove you got what it takes to hang with the big girls, and you might get wings."

"I'll do whatever takes," said Hedgehog.

Kita chuckled. "I know you'll master your plane, but can you master hanging out with a bunch of girls?"

"I...I'm liked among the pilots."

"I'm teasing you...I do have two military types, that should be easy, but what are you going to do with two princesses in the room? Come on. I need to eat."

Kita and Hedgehog crossed the flight deck to the ship's island. Members of the deck crew in their various colored shirts lined up in two rows for a *rainbow sideboys* salute. Kita glided between them, stopped, and waved Hedgehog to join her.

"You're an Angel in training," said Kita. "You go where I go."

They walked through the salute and stopped before the assembled senior officers of the carrier. They saluted, and Kita returned it.

"Your Highness, welcome aboard EUSS Abraham Lincoln. I'm Admiral George Keating. Commander of the Fifth Carrier Strike Group. This is Captain Mike Bowler, Lincoln's skipper."

"Thank you, Admiral, Captain. Glad to be aboard. I know you're busy. I need to eat and rest, and I need you to send a message to Secretary Mayfield to tell Kimmy where I am. Also, I'm assigning Lieutenant Commander McKnight to me. She's now an Angel and gets treated like one."

Keating raised an eyebrow at Hedgehog. "Commander Frazer radioed ahead and told us you would need medical treatment."

Kita shrugged. *I'm sure it would make Kimmy happy.* "If they can look while I eat, that's fine."

"I'll escort you to sickbay," said Keating.

———×———

KITA LAY ON THE HOSPITAL BED, EATING AND WATCHING THE SHIP'S TV station. It said little of what Imperial forces were doing, but it did report on the world's reaction. *Not as bad as I thought. They just want answers. No condemnations, but it doesn't sound like they know about eastern Siberia, either.*

The curtain giving Kita privacy jerked back. Apocalypse stood with a look of relief on her face. The other Angels crowded behind her. Apocalypse pushed the food cart out of the way, moved Kita's plate, and hugged her.

"They told me you'd been shot five times. I was expecting a mess," said Apocalypse. She was on the verge of tears.

"Then don't look at my insides," Kita said, trying to be funny. "Did you get my note, or do I have to skin a general?"

Apocalypse laughed and wiped away tears. "Yes, I got it—hearts and lip prints. The Soviets are in chaos. You took out the entire Politburo, Kryuchkov, and their military headquarters. The Soviet Ambassador has dropped off a request for a ceasefire and a meeting. He couldn't tell me with whom. I don't think they know."

"What did you tell them?"

"I told them I would only meet with them, the Indians, and the Chinese. I emphasized this was a war against the Illuminati, and they all had to answer for it."

Kita rested her head against the pillow. "I have no words for you, love. You truly are amazing."

"I'm not done yet. I haven't begun to squeeze the Indians and Chinese."

"I look forward to listening to them squeal."

"Hey, excuse me, Kita?" said Hedgehog from the back of the group.

"I'm here, Karen. You'll have to push your way through the feather fortress."

The Angels turned and let Hedgehog and Frazer through.

"Who are they?" said Apocalypse.

"This is Commander Frazer. His squadron saved me. And, this is Karen McKnight." She was wearing her flight suit with a flight jacket. A patch read ACE above her unit patch. She held another jacket. "Karen is our newest Angel-in-training."

"Awesome!" said Sapper.

Apocalypse raised an eyebrow. "You think she has what it takes?"

"She's shown she can handle herself in a fight. As an Angel, she'll blow them away. Next time I can send her to dogfight the enemy. I wasn't designed for that kind of aerial combat."

Apocalypse turned to the pilots. "Thank you, Commander. You and your pilots have my eternal gratitude for bringing her back." Apocalypse pulled a feather from her wing. "This is for your squadron."

"Thank you, Your Highness. We're most honored to fly with the Angels. The AWACS controller counted six enemy MiGs destroyed by unknown means. We watched Princess Kita take out two, and they attributed the other four to her, making her an ace. We wanted to give the princess her jacket."

Hedgehog presented Kita with a leather jacket with a unit and ace patches.

"Thanks," said Kita.

"The One-Five-Four Squadron is known as the Black Knights, but after today we'd like to change that to the Fallen Angels," said Frazer. "If that's ok with you, Your Highness?"

"I'd say you've earned it. You're welcome to fly with me anytime. You're now the elite squadron of the Navy. You're our honor guard, but you have to keep your combat skills sharp. As you know, I like to get dirty." Kita laughed, winced, and then sighed. "By the Crushing Depths, I hurt." A tear fell down Kita's cheek.

"Angel, I'm sorry. Where did they get you?" said Apocalypse.

Kita pulled off the sheet to expose the hole in her leg, the chunk missing from her arm, the two holes in her abdomen, and the mess that was her side.

"My god! Kita!" exclaimed Apocalypse. "They said the doctor checked on you."

"He did. I told him I needed to eat, and I'd heal on my own."

"And he believed you?"

"Why wouldn't he?"

Apocalypse rolled her eyes. "Ok, everybody out, except Leaf. Lizzy, find me the doctor and a nurse. Nicole, get in touch with General Mayfield and keep me updated. New girl, go with Nicole."

KITA AWOKE. SHE FELT BETTER. GLANCING UNDER THE SHEET, SHE LOOKED better, too. Nemesis sat in a chair next to the bed. *Not who I expected. Kimmy's probably busy.*

"Hey, Nicole. You didn't have to sit with me. I no longer need a bodyguard."

Nemesis looked up from the book she was reading. "That you're in that bed says otherwise, but I doubt I could have prevented it if I was there. Kimmy sends her best. I'm going to ignore the order to kiss you. I did that once, and I don't want to see the tantrum you'd throw now."

Kita chuckled. "I'm older now and much more gracious. As I recall, you were trying to worm your way into my bed."

"I wanted Velositi, not you. I would have worn you out and put you to bed within twenty minutes and spent the rest of the night with her."

"You think Velositi would be interested if I'm not around?"

"I'm not good enough for her? Not all of us can look as perfect as you," said Nemesis tersely.

"I'm not perfect. I'll show you perfect." Kita opened her hand, and a holographic image of Kita's former partner, Sarin, appeared. "She was genetically engineered to be perfect—physically."

"Not much for brains?"

"Not when I met her. I fixed that later. Some say I made her the perfect partner for me. She was smart, evil, ferocious, independent, and not afraid of me."

"Kimmy is a step down, huh?" said Nemesis with a twisted smile.

"Kimmy is a step up. Kimmy is all of those things. What sets her apart is her ambition rivals my own, and she doesn't need me to do it for her. I just have to be supportive."

"You dropped a nuke on twelve million people for her."

Kita shrugged. "Kimmy didn't need me to. She already won the gambit. That's why they launched the missile. The Soviets were going to extract a pound of flesh before they died. I protected our side and gave Kimmy an easier path to victory."

"Twelve million people are dead for your easy victory," snarled Nemesis. "You could have thrown it in the ocean."

"I thought about it. Do you want to know where that missile was going?" said Kita.

"The eastern seaboard."

"D.C., Miami, Boston, Atlanta, Philadelphia, Baltimore, and three to New York City. How many millions is that?"

"I understand saving our people. Why kill theirs?" said Nemesis.

"Because I wanted to make sure the Soviets would be incapable of retaliation—now or in the future. I wanted the world to see they took their best shot at the Empire, and it cost them—everything. The Soviets won't bother the Empire again. Yes, it cost twelve million, but World War Two cost Eighty-five million. I'll kill some to save more."

"No one had to die," yelled Nemesis.

"Maybe or maybe the Soviets attack Europe or unleash their entire nuclear arsenal. Sure, Kimmy has enough missiles to destroy the surface of the Earth, but that doesn't save the Empire. I don't know the cost of the alternatives. I *do* know the cost of my choice, and I'm willing to live with it. I'm sorry, Nicole. If I knew of any other less costly way with the same outcome at the time, I would have done it. I made the best choice at the time. It was not a good or righteous choice, but it was the best choice to protect my people, and that's what I swore to do."

"You could be so much better. You could be the hero the world needs."

"With the way Kimmy's going, I might be. What you don't understand is, I serve myself, not a higher calling. It's in my best interest to protect the Empire, not the rest of the world."

"Why not the rest of the world? What can't they give you?"

"Kimmy. I love her with an intensity I can't describe. It's deeper and stronger than anything I felt for Jane. I covet Kimmy. I adore her. I put her above all else, except me. I will be what she wants me to be. I will do anything to keep her by me. She is mine."

"Imagine if you felt that way about the world."

"I can't unless the world is going to be loyal to me," said Kita.

"It's always about you."

"It always is."

"When this is over, I'm leaving."

Kita winced. "I'll take you wherever you want to go."

"There are a lot of people in the world who need help."

"True. I hope you find what peace you seek, and that the world treats you far better than the others."

Nemesis cocked her head. "What does that mean?"

"You're not the first to not like me or my motives and not the first to leave, but they always return with a greater understanding of the world."

"Maybe I can repair the damage you've done." Nemesis stood up. "Feel better." She left her book on the table, pushed the curtain aside, and left.

*I wish you luck.*

THE EUS MOTORCADE FOLLOWED THEIR POLICE ESCORT OUT OF THE Leningrad traffic into Palace Square. It stopped in front of the Winter Palace—a giant mint green and white building built in the Elizabethan Baroque style that had served as the home of the Russian czars until the Russian Revolution. The Secret Service agents exited their SUVs and formed a perimeter as the Angels exited the Vehlixen. Kita and Apocalypse stayed on Velositi. Guards opened the ornate gate with a golden double-headed eagle in the side of the Winter Palace to allow Velositi and the others into the inner courtyard.

Once the gate closed, Kita and Apocalypse dismounted Velositi and let her morph. A group of Imperial diplomats stepped back in surprise as two Soviet soldiers raised their weapons.

"She's with me," said Apocalypse to the guards.

"*Убери оружие. Я не причиню тебе вреда. Я американец,*" said Velositi.

"You learned Russian?" said Kita, amused.

"I downloaded it. I thought it might be useful."

The soldiers lowered their weapons, and one made a radio call.

"Wow, I expected more of a garden," said Sapper, sounding disappointed. Cobblestones covered most of the inner courtyard except for neatly kept trees and bushes surrounded by a waist-high iron fence in the center.

"Few outsiders ever see this garden. It's leftover from the czars," said Apocalypse. "The Soviets don't believe in aesthetics unless it's to impress outsiders." Her diplomats approached and knelt. "Everything in order, Brice?"

"Yes, Your Highness."

"Good. Brice, meet Princess Kita and the Angels. Girls, this is Kevin Merithol, Ambassador to India, Mike Monsanto, Ambassador to China, and Brice Thompson, Deputy Ambassador to the USSR."

Kita mentally shrugged. The Ambassador to the Soviet Union had died in the nuclear detonation that destroyed Moscow. *I can't save everyone.*

"Your Highness, you haven't given any guidance on how we are to proceed with the negotiation," said Merithol.

"This will be a frank discussion. I'm going to show them my hand. I'll let them decide what to do after that," Apocalypse said with a mischievous grin.

Thompson looked at Velositi. "Is *it* part of your hand?"

"*She* is Velositi, a Vehlix Angel that has helped us defeat the Neophormes. Velositi is the tip of the iceberg. Come. Let's not keep the Illuminati waiting." Apocalypse took Kita's hand and motioned to inform the soldiers she was ready.

As they walked through the courtyard, Apocalypse swung her and Kita's arm playfully.

"You're in a good mood," said Kita.

"I feel like a kid in a candy store, and my dad owns the place."

Kita chuckled. "Don't celebrate too early."

"Nothing can stop me—only delay me."

"And what is it that my love desires in this candy store?"

"All of it."

"I can tell you from experience the chase is better than the catch. Ruling a world is hard."

"I have a plan. I don't expect to get the whole world today, just lay the foundation."

Kita raised an eyebrow. *It's not my show, but I'll do whatever she wants. I hope she can adapt well.*

Soviet soldiers opened a big set of double doors at the top of the steps into the Winter Palace. Kita, the Angels, and the delegation entered Armorial Hall. *Damn. Talk about impressive decadence.* The white and gold room radiated regal splendor. Golden pillars supported a balcony that ran around the room. Ornate statues lined the walls. Giant chandeliers hung from the ceiling. *Why haven't the Soviets torn this place down? It seems to stand for everything they're against.* A pair of Soviet officers escorted them through the room to a set of white doors with gold trim.

They entered the Military Gallery containing hundreds of paintings of Russian generals. The officers opened a set of double doors and waved Kita and the others into St. George's Hall. Evenly spaced windows between white columns trimmed in gold allowed light into the white and gold gilded classically styled interior. Chandeliers and candelabras lit the room. At the far end was an empty gold and red throne. A simple folding table with four chairs, three on one side and one on the other, sat in the middle of the room.

A group of men and a woman watched as Apocalypse led Kita and the others into the room. It was easy to tell who was who. Those in the ornate military uniforms were the Soviets. The Chinese looked like they were going to a board meeting. The Indians wore traditional dress—white Kurtas with trousers underneath for the men and a colorful sari for the woman.

"Thank you for coming," said Apocalypse. "I'm glad you got my message and understood the gravity it conveyed. President Patil, President Jintao, please be seated. Who is representing the Soviet Union?"

A man in a decorated Soviet military uniform, who looked like he hadn't slept in days, stepped forward. "I am General Alexei Malkin, ranking member of the Soviet Armed Forces."

"Please be seated, General." Apocalypse took her seat. It had a low back for her wings.

*At least someone knew enough not to be insulting.* Kita and the other Angels stood a few feet behind her. The ambassadors stood to one side. Daisy held an attaché case and waited on Apocalypse's left.

"So, why are we here?" said Apocalypse.

Malkin cleared his throat and said in a gruff, intimidating voice, "The Soviet Union demands the immediate ceasefire and withdrawal of American forces back to recognized international borders."

Apocalypse steepled her fingers. "I bet you don't know why we're here. Let me fill you in. For the last forty-five years, my empire has battled an international collective of countries called the Illuminati. This collective made a deal with an alien race, known as Neophormes. I don't know what was promised, but I do know the Neophormes have disrupted my empire's interests around the world. I have lost trillions of dollars, countless lives, and wars in the Congo, Iran, Australia, South Africa, and numerous small engagements due to their involvement. Most recently, I discovered the

Illuminati on Imperial soil attacking my citizens. You can imagine my displeasure.

"The reason my forces are on Soviet soil is the Star Bridge—an interdimensional gate between Earth and the Neophorm's homeworld, Chellexon. The Neophormes were going to use this gate to attack Earth and enslave it. Thanks to the brave actions of the Angels, Vehlixen—enemies of the Neophormes—and my forces, the Neophorm leader, Savacron, is dead, and the Star Bridge is no longer under Illuminati control. It is under mine. The Illuminati's power is broken. All that's left is to pay the piper—me."

"We will pay you nothing. You have no proof," said Patil.

"You're here, aren't you? I'm sure you are aware of the Illuminati base my forces raided and destroyed a few weeks ago. Princess Kita downloaded the data on the servers. I have so much evidence of your countries' involvement I could fill this room. Don't play stupid, Patil. Otherwise, I'll airdrop Savacron's body on the Taj Mahal."

Patil wrinkled her nose.

"We will never admit to anything," said Jintao.

"I don't care if you admit it or not. I know you're guilty," said Apocalypse. "This is what I want. Malkin, I'm taking everything east of the Ural Mountains, and your Middle Eastern and African colonies. Patil, I want your African, South American, and Middle Eastern colonies. Jintao, Australia, New Zealand, the Philippines, Indonesia, and all your Oceania colonies are mine."

Patil stood. "Never. You are a greedy child."

"Sit," ordered Apocalypse. She made a fist, and a beam burned a hole in the table in front of Patil.

The elderly woman looked at the hole, at Apocalypse, and sat.

"The wings—the abilities—are real. I am seeking forty-five years' worth of reparations. I think that what I ask for is fair. The Illuminati drove my empire out of Africa and the Middle East. We couldn't protect Australia and the rest of the Pacific from Chinese expansion. You invaded our zone of influence when you colonized Brazil and Argentina.

"You have kept the Empire of the United States from our rightful place in the world. In response to the Illuminati's threat, we were forced to adapt and innovate. I have the best-trained, most technologically advanced, well-led military in the world. Meanwhile, you have hidden behind proxy armies and the Neophormes, letting your militaries lapse. Now, the Neophormes are gone.

"I can project air power to any point on the planet. I have carrier groups sitting off your shores. With the Star Bridge, I can project my ground forces anywhere on Earth at a moment's notice. Can you imagine my 1st Cavalry appearing around the Forbidden City? How about 1st Armor rolling through New Delhi? Malkin—I can deliver units anywhere in the Soviet Union. How would what's left of the Soviet Armed Forces fare at being attacked from the front and rear?"

Kita kept her face neutral. She didn't think strong-arming the other leaders would work, but the threat of American forces appearing in the Soviet Union caused a wave of terror in Malkin. *He hides it well.*

"*Kimmy?*" said Kita.

"Yes?"

"You've scared the Crushing Depths out of Malkin. I suggest you divide and conquer. Make him an offer to avoid war, and then worry about the other two."

Apocalypse cocked her head. "Malkin, how would you like to avoid war? Because that is where your associates are headed."

"You can't defeat the three of us!" said Patil. "Our ground forces outnumber yours."

"You have the advantage of number of soldiers, but one of mine is worth at least three of yours," said Apocalypse. "When it comes to planes, tanks, ships, and nukes, you're nowhere close to me. How much of the Soviet Armed Forces are left, Malkin? I know your command and control disappeared with Moscow. You're who I'm coming after first."

Malkin's fear increased dramatically at the mention of nuclear weapons. *Once bitten, twice shy.* "Kimmy, I think Malkin fears we'll drop another nuclear weapon on him."

"I'm sure he doesn't know it was his side's missile that took out Moscow. He must think we struck first." Apocalypse opened her wings. "Malkin, I have what I want of the Soviet Union. Siberia's wealth dwarfs the rest of the country. I'll nuke the rest, spare my forces, and send them in to pick up the pieces."

Malkin pulled a handkerchief from his pocket and dabbed his forehead. "Let's not be hasty. The Soviet Union has much to offer. Soviet Armed Forces are strong. Next to yours, best in the world. War would be no good for either side." Malkin leaned forward. "What do you propose?"

"You can't be serious!" yelled Patil.

Malkin slapped the table. "Russian Soviet leaders are gone. Ukrainian leaders are in charge now. We will succeed where they could not. What is your proposition, Your Highness?"

Apocalypse smiled. "The Soviet Union signs a treaty to become a territory of the Empire of the United States. In ten years, your republics can apply for statehood. I am prepared to pump billions of dollars into the Soviet Union. I will upgrade the infrastructure, telecommunications, education, medical care, farming, and manufacturing. I will integrate and modernize the military. You and your soldiers will keep the rank they've earned, and they'll get paid what my soldiers get paid. Soviet officers will join American units to learn and lead. You will get a slot on the Joint Chiefs as head of Soviet forces integration."

Malkin's eyes lit. *These guys probably haven't seen that much money in their lives. Getting top billing helps, too.*

"One condition," said Malkin.

"What's that?" said Apocalypse.

"You make Kyiv capital of Soviet Union and build big palace. Make Kyiv bigger. Better city than pit Moscow."

"I will build a grand government complex in Kyiv. It will be the regional capital for my empire. I will make sure it rivals any city in the Empire."

Malkin stood. "Then we have a deal, Your Highness. The Soviet Union joins the Empire of the United States. The world will tremble at our might." He saluted Apocalypse doing his best to imitate an American salute.

Apocalypse stood and returned the salute. She motioned for Daisy. Her assistant reached into her case and pulled out a hardcover folder with the treaty and a set of pens. She handed the treaty and pen to Apocalypse and placed the other pen in front of Malkin. Apocalypse opened the folder and wrote at the bottom of the document. "I've added your request to make Kyiv a capital city to the treaty," she said to Malkin. "Sign at the bottom." She laid the treaty on the table.

Malkin read the treaty, nodded, and signed it.

Kita read it, too. It contained nothing of what Apocalypse had promised, except for the Kyiv part. Malkin wasn't swearing allegiance to the Empire of the United States, but Apocalypse herself. Kita didn't doubt Apocalypse would do what she promised, but who the Soviets were swearing loyalty to was a nuance they had missed. They didn't understand she wasn't the embodiment of the Empire of the United States but was an elected ruler, who could be removed. *Not anymore. Kimmy now has a country, slightly damaged, all her own that will do what she commands. And, the Empire of the United States will pay for it—at least until her emergency powers run out in six months, and she has to divulge these treaties to Congress. Kimmy must know this. What is her plan? And, can she pull off the other two?*

Apocalypse gathered up the treaty and set it aside. "Ambassador Thompson, please get General Malkin in touch with Secretary Mayfield. He knows what to do and is waiting for the word."

"Yes, Your Highness. General, if you will follow me."

As they left the table, Thompson's assistant handed him a phone.

Apocalypse turned back to Patil and Jintao and smiled pleasantly. "Anyone else want to join?"

"We will not be bullied," said Patil. "We have nuclear weapons and are not afraid to use them."

"All twelve of them," said Apocalypse with a chuckle. "I have more on a single sub. Yours aren't even as advanced as the Soviets—single warheads, not multiple —and can't reach D.C. I wouldn't waste the nuke. There are less destructive and more deadly ways to get what I want. You have a country of one point three billion people. That's a lot of mouths to feed, and I now control your number one supplier of foodstuffs. I can starve you out."

"We are not afraid of you. Our nation can support itself."

"You could force your colonies to supply you with more food and other raw materials. You have the world's largest commercial shipping fleet to move it. But, guess what I suddenly have? A large fleet of attack submarines with nothing to do." Patil's eye twitched. "How many weeks do you think it'll take me to sink your shipping fleet and blockade your ports? Your colonies will be useless. How fast will they strike allegiance once they realize you can't control them? Sure, China has an overland route to you, but they can't supply you with the food you are going to need. I'll make sure that the highway doesn't stay open for long. I have the aircraft to turn it into a moonscape.

"I can wait a year or two for your people to starve. In the meantime, with my technology, the amount of food the Soviets produce will skyrocket. I'll have so much food your people will beg for me to take over. If you sign my deal, I promise to keep the trade routes open around the world—no more pirates off Africa, South America, or southeast Asia. You will gain full access to all the markets of my empire. In Siberia, I have space for your people. And, I'll need people to settle it. I plan to make it the next Canada."

Patil's face remained hard, but her eyes and emotions betrayed her conflict. "We will not be a vassal for you to kick around like Japan."

"I'll give you the same deal I gave the Soviets. I will make India a territory. In ten years, your states can apply for statehood. You and your government will stay on to govern the territory."

Patil turned up her nose. "You did not treat your territories well, either."

"My father didn't. I just granted twelve territories statehood. I'm looking to add more."

A conflict raged in Patil. Her emotions were all over. *She must know she's beaten and is looking for a way out gracefully. Will Kimmy give it to her?*

"This will have to go before parliament. Why should they ratify it?" said Patil.

*Way to let Kimmy make your argument for you. I don't suggest you get in the habit of allowing Kimmy to do your thinking for you.*

Apocalypse's smile dazzled. "I have wealth, space, food, and I promise the people of India a better life. I want to work together to make a better world. I'm not looking to extinguish India's vast history or culture. On the contrary, I will expand it to all corners of my empire. Your influence will grow, so will your economy. Don't think of this as a conquest. For smaller companies to grow market share and increase their bottom line, they need the resources of a larger company. Consider this a merger. The Indian brand will flourish under my empire."

The argument eased Patil's conflicting emotions. *It's in a language she understands—familiarity soothes the soul. Good job, Kimmy.* "Fine. I will sign, but it must be ratified by my parliament before it takes effect."

"You have three days. Otherwise, a state of war will exist between us, and I will unleash hell." Apocalypse found the right folder and laid it out. She signed and then offered the pen to Patil.

Kita read the contract. It was the same as the Soviets. Kita approved of the tactic. She had done similar in the past. Having groups personally loyal to you gave you leverage and a way out.

Patil read the treaty and signed it. She offered her hand, and Apocalypse shook it.

"Talk to Ambassador Merithol," said Apocalypse. "He will get you into contact with the right people in my government and help you with yours."

"Thank you, Your Highness. I will do my best to ratify the treaty."

"I have the utmost faith."

Apocalypse motioned for Merithol to help Patil and moved her chair to be across from Jintao. "So, just you and me. You've heard my offer to the others. You know what I want and why I want it."

"The Chinese cannot be bullied or bought. China is stronger than the Soviets or India. We have stood for five thousand years on our own. We do not need you. If you want what is ours, you will have to take it by force. We will extract pound for pound."

"I assume the Illuminati agreed to some kind of deal with Savacron allowing them to bring an army here. In exchange, they would have promised to leave the

USSR, India, and China alone or let you be some kind of pet government. You know what the Neophormes are capable of. Let me show you what I'm capable of. Velositi?" Apocalypse waved the Angel over. "This is Leader Velositi. She is a Vehlix. The Angel Kita made her body in my lab after the original was destroyed." Velositi opened her hand, and a ball of lightning formed. It crackled and hummed as it arced to her. "Velositi is the first of many. I'm building my own Morphicon army. Soon, I will have many like her."

"*What?*" snarled Kita.

"*You left the plans for her body in the machine.*"

Kita roared, "*And you—*"

"*Easy, angel. I had Ryan delete it. Sprokkit donated his DNA, and we're making copies of him.*"

Kita relaxed some. "*Sorry.*"

"*It's ok. Your secrets are safe. But they don't need to know the difference between Morphicon and Angel.*"

Kita huffed.

"My formidable military will grow even stronger, and I can put them anywhere in the world," said Apocalypse.

A rift gate opened in front of the throne, and two Anti-Neophorm Teams with a full combat load marched into the room. The Soviets and Indian delegations moved out of the way in surprise. A single M-1 tank rolled in, its barrel moving back and forth menacingly.

"My forces won't be alone, President," said Apocalypse. "I will lead them." She stood up, stepped back, and morphed into Scourge. She filled as much room as possible. Her tail ended by the throne and her head on the far side of the room. She folded her wings on her back to keep them out of the chandeliers. Swinging her head around, she lowered it to be eye to eye with Jintao and blasted him with smoke.

Jintao fell out of his chair and scrambled backward. "You—you *are* the dragon god."

"You missed her on TV?" said Kita as she and the Angels floated around Scourge's wings.

"You can't believe everything you see on TV," said Sapper.

The Angels landed around Jintao.

"Can I help you up, Mister President?" said Kita. She pulled him to his feet as Scourge stuck her nose in his chest.

"She is real," said Jintao.

"Very," said Kita as she stroked the side of Scourge's head.

Jintao said something in Chinese, and he met with his delegation. They spoke rapidly, with a harsh overtone.

*They sound upset, but I feel they're excited and in awe.* Kita wasn't sure what that meant. *Dragon god* seemed positive. She didn't know what symbolism a dragon held in China. *Does Kimmy?*

The Chinese delegation split and Jintao stepped forward.

Scourge shrank back to Apocalypse. "What's on your mind?"

"Forty-five thousand years ago, the Yellow Emperor of China transformed into a dragon and ascended to Heaven. Since then, the Chinese people have descended from him, and the dragon has represented China's emperor. Only a true child of the Dragon God can take the form of a dragon. By right, China belongs to you, Red Emperor, Child of Yellow Emperor."

Apocalypse smiled. "*Who is the Yellow Emperor, angel?*"

Kita looked it up. "*A Chinese deity. He was the first legendary ruler of China.*"

"*I may not be a god of a universe, but I will be a god among men.*"

Kita chuckled. "*Another step closer.*"

"*I just need to ascend to Heaven.*"

"*You wanted to stay here.*"

"*I'm in no rush. I know you'll wait for me.*"

"*I don't know if the White House is big enough for two gods.*"

"*I'll have to build you that summer house in Hawaii.*"

Kita sent Apocalypse a video of a purring cat.

"I have an honored lineage and the mandate of Heaven," said Apocalypse to Jintao. "I will claim my right to rule China. I promise to bring wealth, health, and good fortune. It will be a jewel in the Empire of the United States. Come, let's sign the treaty, and my rule can begin." She guided Jintao back to the table.

*I will give her credit. She is a smooth operator—adaptable and unflappable. This must have been what it was like watching me.*

The two sides signed the treaty, and Apocalypse added it to the stack of others.

"Thank you, President Jintao. I don't think there will be an objection from the Chinese people to my rule. I will make China a territory, and you the first governor. In ten years, provinces can apply for statehood. I will integrate you as fast as possible into the Empire. Ambassador Monsanto will help facilitate and lead the transition."

"Thank you, Your Highness."

"Everyone," Apocalypse waved over Malkin and Patil. "Thank you for your cooperation. Together we will make the Empire of the United States strong and wealthy. Our people will thrive, and we will be the greatest nation on Earth. In the coming weeks, I will announce my plans for integration. It will take time, but construction and trade will begin in a few weeks, and food shipments will start immediately. You will be given secure communications to reach my staff or me if a problem arises. Most of my governmental laws and regulations are online. This time as a territory is to be the transitional period. I will send teams to help with the transition and to meet with your governments to help them understand how the Empire does things, what I require, and what you are allowed to do. Once the transition is complete, statehood will be considered. Any questions?"

The three leaders shook their heads.

"Excellent. I am flying back to D.C. tonight, and I will speak to the UN assembly shortly to announce our union. I hope you can be there."

Jintao raised his fist, and the others followed. "Glory to the Empire," they said together.

Apocalypse smiled. "For the Empire." She took Kita's hand and walked back to the Angels. "Daisy?"

"Yes, Your Highness?"

"Can you have them get that tank out of here? Its fumes smell. Tell the Anti-

Neophorm Teams to stand down and get some rest. They've had a long week. Then contact Secretary Mayfield and tell him dragons, tigers, and bears, and to prepare the military to send advisors and trainers to China and India."

Daisy nodded, stepped away, and pulled a phone from her bag.

"Does this mean you rule the world?" said Sapper.

Apocalypse laughed. "A large chunk of it. Getting them to join was the easy part. Now I have to make them part of the Empire." She led the Angels out of the hall.

"*I noticed those treaties said loyal to Princess Roosevelt, not Emperor Roosevelt or the Empire of the United States,*" said Kita to Apocalypse.

"*I wanted to make sure we have a place to go in case my plans for the Empire fall apart.*"

"*And what plans are those?*"

"*Cementing my power forever.*"

"*You could have a fight on your hands.*"

"*I've made it much easier for me. Congress and the Supreme Court are in my pocket. I want to rule like you—by my will alone.*"

Kita raised an eyebrow. "*You now have three countries that have sworn to.*"

"*I want the world. I will make it a better place and keep my promise to you.*"

"*You're taking me a long way from the junkyard.*"

"*You've been here before.*"

"*I hope it has a better ending than when I did it,*" said Kita glumly.

"*I won't fail.*"

*That's what I said...and I ended up powerless and in prison. But, it's not me this time. I can always take Kimmy away from here.*

KITA PACED BEHIND THE COUCHES IN THE LIVING AREA OF THE WHITE HOUSE. The other Angels sat waiting for Apocalypse's presentation to the UN to start. Kita was upset Apocalypse hadn't invited her and irate that Apocalypse had taken Velositi and the Vehlixen.

"Kita, sit down," said Nemesis.

"*What's wrong?*" said Aspen.

"I'm fine," huffed Kita.

"*You're pacing. You only do that when you're upset, but not upset enough to kill something.*"

Kita stopped pacing, folded her arms, and glared at the TV. "Why didn't she take me?"

Nemesis turned and leaned on the back of the couch. "She told you she didn't want to intimidate the other world leaders."

"I understand not taking you. But she could have taken me."

Nemesis shrugged. "Maybe she thought you could use a break."

"Kimmy's the one who needs a break. She's been working nonstop since we got back." That wasn't true. Apocalypse had taken a few hours out of each day to spend with her. But she didn't talk about what she was doing and deflected when Kita asked.

"*You can't stand not being the center of attention,*" said Aspen.

"To the Crushing Depths with it," snarled Kita as she phased above the White House, spread her wings, and flew to the south.

KITA FOLLOWED THE TWO-LANE ROAD THROUGH THE SWAMP. SHE WASN'T SURE where she was and didn't feel like finding out. A town of clapboard buildings appeared out of the trees. The mossy oaks gave it a sleepy feel. The main street was empty except for a couple of cars and a row of twenty motorcycles parked in front of a tired-looking bar.

A man with a scraggly beard, leather vest, dirty T-shirt, and heavy boots sat on a bench out front of the bar. Kita wasn't sure why he was there. A patch on his vest said PROSPECT.

Kita landed in the middle of the street and walked to the motorcycles. "You know it's illegal to block a fire hydrant."

The man looked up. "What the shit are you supposed to be?"

"Code enforcement." With a swift kick, Kita knocked over the row of motorcycles. "Oops. Sorry about your bikes."

"They're motorcycles, you dumb bitch. I'm going to knock your teeth down your throat. Then you're going to pick them up and go inside on your knees to say you're sorry."

"Yeah, no. But I think I found what I want to take my frustration out on." Kita glided over the motorcycles and landed in front of the man.

She drew back her fist and punched him in the gut. The man doubled over, and Kita brought her knee up into his face. As he went backward, she grabbed him by the face and heated her hand. The man let out a muffled scream as the smell of burnt flesh and hair filled the air. Kita slammed the back of his head against the building several times.

The rickety door opened.

"What the hell is going on out here, Nicky?" said a big man dressed like the man in Kita's hand.

"I'm supposed to apologize for your bikes," said Kita.

"Oh, shit," said the biker as he backed into the bar.

Kita threw the man she had after him, knocking both into the bar and to the dirty floor. She walked inside the dimly lit establishment. An iron cross with a skull in the middle adorned most of the surfaces.

A biker drew a switchblade from his pocket. "You walked into the wrong bar, you winged dyke freak."

"I'm going to save you for last," said Kita as flames climbed up her wings. She drew her sword Dead. "Meet the *real* Hell's Angel."

---

KITA LANDED ON THE SOUTH LAWN OF THE WHITE HOUSE. A GROUP OF people with candles stood along the fence. She ignored their pleas for attention and walked toward the portico. A Secret Service agent opened the door as she approached.

Apocalypse rushed out and hugged Kita. "Angel, where have you been? You wouldn't answer. You just disappeared."

Kita stood still, her mind blank, unable to process what was being said or the emotions she felt. She had shut her coping mechanisms down, so she didn't have to deal with emotions. It was better than being numb. There was nothing, just her fleeting thoughts.

"Kita, are you ok?" said Apocalypse.

Kita cocked her head. "I'm fine."

"What you said is technically true, but I've heard computers speak with more warmth and life."

Kita shrugged.

"What's the matter, angel?"

"I'm leaving."

"Why?" exclaimed Apocalypse.

"I'm not going back to prison."

Apocalypse sighed in relief. "Whatever you did, I can make go away. I just need to know what."

"A biker bar somewhere in the swamps in the south."

"Did you injure them—kill them?"

"Some were still alive when I left. The flames will have finished them."

Apocalypse nodded. "It's no problem. No one is going to miss a biker gang. But that's not why you left. What's going on?"

In Kita's mind, gears slowly turned. The mechanical animals she used to emulate emotions woke up. The assault on her empty consciousness was stupefying. It took effort to integrate what the animals were telling her into her thoughts. Her natural emotions caught up, dumping a healthy dose of anger, hate, and rage on everything. Caught in a balancing act of real and processed emotion, her mind tried to comprehend it all and put forth a cohesive thought.

Apocalypse took Kita's hand. "Kita, are you ok? You're worrying me."

Kita opened her mouth, and her thoughts nearly came out as a shrill shriek. She caught it, sorted back through the emotions, trying to temper her anger. She was angry, but she shouldn't be *that* angry. Apocalypse had no idea why she was upset. Kita had to be fair, even though her natural emotions were exploding. She leaned on her animals to process the emotions she felt from Apocalypse. *Kimmy's not mad, just concerned and depressed. I need to explain why I left. I'm sure she has a good reason for not including me.* "Why didn't you take me?"

Apocalypse frowned. "Angel, the UN is not the place to take my most intimidating weapon."

"You took Velositi!"

"Because I introduced the world to the Vehlixen. The world knows of Angels. I needed the world to know of the Vehlixen and their allegiance to me. It shocked them that Velositi was an Angel, too. Your power is so beyond their understanding. They can't conceive of what you command. I only do because I've seen it. I didn't include you because I wanted my offer to be genuine and not coerced."

"What offer?" said Kita.

Apocalypse made a disappointed face, but Kita felt relief. "You didn't watch?"

"I—no. I thought if you didn't want me there, it wasn't important."

Apocalypse bit her lip. "I guess I deserve that. I offered any country in the world a chance to be a territory with an offer of statehood after ten years. If the people wanted it and the leadership didn't, I would help them. I—I'm glad you didn't watch. They voted to condemn me for my actions over the Illuminati even after I made my argument. India is already trying to wiggle out of its deal."

Kita found the footage on CSPAN. Apocalypse stood in front of the UN assembly in a red business suit and a red, white, and blue bow in her hair. She looked like what she was—young and inexperienced.

"Let me show you what a dominating ruler looks like." Kita opened her hand. An Angel with black wings appeared dressed in a long sleeve black silk and velvet dress. A large hood hid her face. The back plunged to her butt, and the front opened to expose her chest and three bloody symbols carved in her skin. The front of the hooped skirt was raised to expose black knee-high boots. The dress' train pooled in the back.

"Is that your mother?" said Apocalypse.

"*That is the Vicereine,*" said Aspen.

"That's you?" exclaimed Apocalypse.

"If you want to rule the world, you have to look the part," said Kita.

"I wish you'd been there."

"How many countries took you up on your offer?"

"None."

"Today, the world leaders saw you as their equal or worse, a kid still learning. If you want to rule the world, you are *no one's* equal. They can't see you as a person. You must transcend and become something greater. You must inspire fear, awe, and wonder." Kita hugged Apocalypse. *"And you can't be a princess. You have to be an emperor."*

*"Who knows when my father will die."*

*"I'll worry about that. Until then, we'll worry about making you the part."*

<hr />

KITA AND VELOSITI FLOATED ABOVE THE SNOW AS THEY SUMMITED TRAIL Ridge Mountain. The other Angels and Vehlixen were admiring the view from the Alpine Visitors Center further up the road in Rocky Mountain National Park. The center was closed for the season, and Trail Ridge Road would be closing with the next storm.

The Angels, minus Apocalypse, and Vehlixen had spent two weeks on a goodwill tour crisscrossing the country and new territories drumming up support for Apocalypse and her expansion. Unlike the rest of the world, which denounced Apocalypse, the citizens of the Empire were enthusiastic, and patriotism was at an all-time high. Even the most hardened conservatives were giving their praise over the defeat of the Empire's enemies.

"It feels like we are on top of the world," said Velositi. "What a spectacular view."

"I think you can see Denver from here."

They had spent the morning in Denver. Every stop they made was a mob. Kita did her best to talk up Apocalypse and her achievements. The question on everyone's mind was: What would the young princess do next? A question Kita only had a vague answer for. Kita usually downplayed the question saying Apocalypse would be busy for a while organizing the new territories. India was proving to be the biggest headache. The Indian government ratified the treaties, but the Indian people were against it. Already civil disobedience was taking place in every major city. That was enough to satisfy the curious. Kita would let Apocalypse announce her agenda when the time was right.

"It's nice to be away from people," said Kita.

"You are not enjoying our tour?"

"The constant attention is draining. I'm not like you. I don't feed off it."

"You could skip some."

"I can't do that. I'm the princess and Kimmy's personal representative. I have to show the People I care."

"I am sorry it is hard on you." Velositi put her arms around Kita.

Kita sighed. "We're almost done. I can tough it out for a few more days. I'm glad you're getting some recognition. I know it's not the same as returning the Axiom to Chellexon. I hope you feel like you're getting some of the glory you deserve."

Velositi squeezed Kita. "This is so much better. I did more than retrieve a simple item. I helped save your and my planet. I could not have done it without you. If it were not for you, I would have nothing. I owe you a thank you."

Kita shrugged. "Just trying to help those I care about."

"You have always done that since I met you. You have come a long way from the girl I found cowering behind a dumpster."

Kita laughed. "I was human. What was I supposed to do? Now, I would throw the dumpster at Nitstik."

Velositi stoked the side of Kita's face. "You never quit fighting."

"It's what I know how to do. Never quit and die trying."

"You know what I am impressed about?"

"What's that?" said Kita.

"I am impressed by how much you are letting Kimmy take the lead. I was not sure you could."

"It's been hard, but she needs to learn on her own."

In the beginning, Kita had sat in on meetings and coached Apocalypse. They made a formidable team. Usually, those that could detect lies had scruples and refused to use the ability for personal gain. Apocalypse had no reservations and paired with Kita's ability to feel emotions they could outmaneuver any political opponent. Even though Kita rarely said a word during the meetings, after a week, the other politicians refused to meet with Apocalypse if Kita was present. Kita cheated by sitting in invisibly. When she thought Apocalypse was ready, she let her fly on her own. From the news she'd seen, Apocalypse was doing fine.

"I am glad she is such a good match for you," said Velositi.

"You're a good match for me," said Kita.

"I know I am. I was destined to be. I am proud of you—of what you have become."

"I don't know if you would have been proud of my past and who I was. I'm different now."

"Everyone comes from somewhere. Our experiences make us who we are. I like to think your experience with me has changed you."

Kita turned and kissed Velositi. "It has. I like who I am, and now I'm worried about going back to my universe."

"Why?"

"My universe requires a kill-or-be-killed mentality. I have to be mean, nasty, and cold. What if I can't do it?"

"You will have the rest of us. We will help you. Your universe cannot be so tough that we cannot win. And we still have more universes to explore to find help."

Kita nodded. "The new Angels will make a dark universe bright."

KITA SAT ON THE COUCH IN THE WHITE HOUSE LIVING AREA, HOLDING Apocalypse's hand. *Black Pentagram* was on TV, but the Angels were watching the election tracker crawling across the bottom of the screen.

"Labor wins a seat in South Carolina!" yelled Sapper. She flipped the channel and watched the name appear on the master list. "That's two hundred and thirty-seven to sixty-eight." The map wasn't so simple. There were lots of colors, each representing a different party. For simplicity's sake, the news channels combined all the parties in Apocalypse's Freedom Coalition under the color red and the conservatives as white.

"There's no way they're going to hold Congress," said Sapper.

*That was never in question. How many seats is the question.*

A knock at the door drew everyone's attention.

"Who is it?" said Apocalypse.

Eugene entered. "Doctor Henry, to see you, Your Highnesses."

"Show him in."

Henry was a tall, thin man with a hawkish face. He served as Emperor Roosevelt's physician. Entering the room, he glanced around at the Angels sprawled across the furniture and floor. His face hid his disgust well. *"Princess Roosevelt. I have come to inform you that your father passed twenty-five minutes ago."*

"What?" Apocalypse leaned forward and put her hands on her head. Kita put her arms around her.

"Kimmy?"

*"You picked tonight to kill him?"*

*"I thought it was a good night for him to die. You'd have a new government elect and could start fresh with them as emperor."*

*"I don't know if I'm ready."*

*"You are ready. I'll be by your side. You don't have to do much tonight. Announce his death and tell the country we're in a state of mourning. We can work out the details tomorrow."*

*"Ok. I guess I should see him and tell him what I think of him. I'll have to be polite in public. Call Daisy and tell her to get Chief Justice Logan over here so I can be sworn in."*

Kita helped Apocalypse stand and put an arm around her waist. "We'll be back, girls. We're going to go say goodbye."

KITA LEANED AGAINST APOCALYPSE'S DESK IN THE OVAL OFFICE. THE CAMERA crew busied themselves, setting up, checking lighting and sound, and testing their connection with the networks. *Where is Kimmy? It shouldn't take this long to change.* Kita finished hair and makeup twenty minutes ago. She wore her Imperial uniform, now with two medals—a Medal of Honor for redirecting the nuclear missile and another for the attack on the Illuminati base.

"Kneel!"

Around Kita, the crew took a knee. She remained seated on the desk. Her eyes met a crewmember, and he gave her a worried look. *Sorry, pal. I kneel to no one.* All the hair on Kita's arms and neck stood up as a painful tingle radiated in her nail beds and toes when she looked up. *An assassin, here?* She vanished, then realized the figure had a pair of silver and red wings. Kita gulped as Apocalypse crossed the room. *I've never seen a Victorian-style look like this.* The silver hooded leather and velvet calf-length jacket accented in red was stunning. Filigree dragons decorated the soft leather of the waist and cuffs, and dragons' heads adorned the lapel. A pauldron with a dragon's head on her right shoulder was similar in style to the one Kita wore. Kita became visible as Apocalypse navigated the cameras and crew.

When Apocalypse reached Kita, she said, "Rise," in sharp command tone. Everyone went back to work as Apocalypse turned to Kita. "How do I look?"

Kita raised an eyebrow looking down at the red-filigreed vest and silver button-up shirt with a popped collar open to reveal a silver dragon pendant. "My first instinct was to stab you in the back. I've never seen an assassin dress so elegantly."

Apocalypse twirled, revealing the back and coattails of her jacket were more ornate than the front with buttons and silk panels. A red silk half cloak with an ornate silver leather cap hung from her right shoulder.

Kita caught Apocalypse and pulled her in for a kiss. She felt the double belted sash around Apocalypse's waist. Kita ran her hands down Apocalypse's sides until she hit something hard. Pulling the jacket back revealed two tomahawks stuck in belts hanging from Apocalypse's hips. Kita pulled out a tomahawk. She never liked axes. They didn't have the agility or balance of a sword. "You know how to use this?"

"I'm proficient. I found a teacher." Apocalypse took the ax and threw it at the far wall. It stuck with a *thunk*.

"Nice," said Kita.

"I wanted something that said Americana and that you weren't an expert on. I won't be challenging you anytime soon, but I have time. Hey, you!" Apocalypse pointed to a technician. "Bring me back my tomahawk."

"You don't want me to teach you?"

"I've heard you're...not a patient teacher."

"I thought I was getting better."

"I'd rather it not get between us."

Kita shrugged and touched Apocalypse's lapel. "This wasn't in your closet."

Apocalypse smiled. "I found an unknown designer who specialized in Victorian attire. I told her I wanted something smart, classic, and intimidating.

I'm sure the reason it set your assassin senses tingling is the concept came from a game about assassins."

"Nice to know my life's work has been reduced to what you can do on a gamepad."

"Maybe we can license you to a developer."

Kita rolled her eyes as the technician delivered the weapon. Apocalypse put it away.

"Your Highnesses," said the director. "We're ready, and it's almost the top of the hour."

"It's Empress," Apocalypse hissed.

"I thought you were getting sworn in live," said Kita trying to spare the director.

"I decided people couldn't see me looking like a princess becoming Empress. I want a clean break and no connection between the two."

"You didn't want my help in this transformation?" said Kita curiously.

"It was something I had to do myself. You told me what I had to become. I had to decide how to get there."

Kita shrugged. She understood. Apocalypse wanted to grow into the role and not be told what to do. "I'll wait for you in the living area."

"No. I want you here standing by my side as the Vicereine."

Kita raised an eyebrow. "Wouldn't I be taking away from you?"

"I want the world to know that you and I are one. I may be Empress, but you are the only person who is my equal. I can do this without you, but I don't want to. You understand what it takes to get where I want to go. I've conquered my enemies, I'll conquer the world, and I won't stop there. I want the power to do as I please. I know you won't give it to me. I'll earn it—I'll take it if I have to. This is mine to do, but I want you by my side to share it with. I love you."

"I love you," said Kita. "I feel your ambition. I'll do whatever you want me to do. I can be anyone or anything. I'll stand there and scare them if you want."

"I like having you lurk in the background. It intimidates."

"You don't need me for that," said Kita with a smile.

"Having people wonder what you're doing makes it easier for me."

"I can help you, too."

"I need to do this myself."

Kita reached into Apocalypse's hood and stroked her cheek. "Love, if it weren't for my A'ahegre, I would still be commanding a Legion. I won't do it for you, but I will help you. It won't diminish your accomplishment, but it will hasten it." She stepped to the side, and her uniform morphed into the dress of the Vicereine. With her nail, Kita carved a dragon's head into the skin on her chest. Trickles of blood pooled against the edge of her dress. She stuck the nail in her mouth and sucked the blood off.

"You didn't have to do that," said Apocalypse.

"I only do it for special occasions," Kita said with a wicked grin.

"Empress?" the director stammered in a shaky voice.

"Yes?"

"Two minutes until the top of the hour."

"Excellent. Angel, you mind helping move my desk?"

"Isn't it traditional you give your address from your desk?" said Kita, more for the director than for her.

"The princess did that. We stand and look imposing."

"If that's the case, then let's get a better backdrop," said Kita as they moved the desk. "You can add a background over a neutral color, right?" said Kita to the director.

"Ye—Yes, Empress."

"I am the Vicereine," said Kita in a harsh voice. "Show me to the computer."

The director took Kita to a side table with several laptops. "I just need an image or video, Vicereine."

"Which one?"

He pointed. Kita pushed the operator out of the way. "Close the curtains." She dropped an image of three vertical black and white striped banners with a gray field and the Imperial Seal in the middle of the laptop's desktop. "Test it," Kita ordered the operator. She waited for him to show her. Apocalypse stood in the center with the banners behind her. Kita made one change. The Imperial Seal in the center, she changed to color. Finished, she joined Apocalypse.

The director tried to position them side by side. Kita ignored him and put Apocalypse in the center, and she stood to the side. *Pay attention to Kimmy, but know I'm important.*

"We're ready, Empress," said the director.

"Interrupt the feed. *Remind me, angel, that we need to be able to broadcast on all the channels, not just the major networks. No one should miss when we speak.*"

*She's learning.*

The director counted down and pointed at Apocalypse.

"Citizens of the great Empire of the United States, on this night when we celebrate one of our most cherished traditions, I bring tragic news. My father, Emperor James Roosevelt, has died. As is my right, I have claimed the throne. An hour ago, Chief Justice Logan swore me in as the next leader of the Empire of the United States. I am Empress Apocalypse, the Dragon God.

"My first official act is to put the Empire in a state of mourning for two weeks. This is a time for reflection on where we came from and where we are going as an Empire. At the end of two weeks, I will hold a rally to lay out my plans for the Empire.

"I have delivered us from our enemies, but there are those who still wish us harm. I will protect the citizens of the Empire at all costs. The military and law enforcement stand ready to protect us from any threat, foreign or domestic. We are not alone. Vicereine Kita has assured me the Angels' and Vehlixen's commitments to the Empire are stronger than ever and will help protect us from any who wish us harm.

"I am putting the world on notice. Anyone who wishes my empire harm will be met with force. This is the dawning of a new golden age for the Empire. We will become the greatest civilization in history, and the sun will never set on the Empire of the United States." Apocalypse raised her gloved fist as red energy sparked around her eyes. "For the glory of the Empire."

The director looked up from watching the feed. "And we're clear, Empress."

"Good. Clean up and go home. Get your team prepared to broadcast the rally. I want to be on every station and airwave."

"We can't—"

"I order it. Anyone who wishes to challenge me can come before me."

"Yes, Empress."

Apocalypse turned to Kita. "Shall we go watch the reaction?"

Kita nodded slightly. *"It should be interesting."*

Apocalypse led Kita out of the Oval Office back to the living area door. She stopped, turned around, brushed her hood back, and captured Kita around the waist, pulling her against her. Apocalypse pulled Kita's hood back and kissed her. Their kisses deepened, and Apocalypse shoved Kita against the wall with a *thump*.

Aspen's head appeared from the door. *"Called it in one. I swear raw displays of power turn Kita on. You do have a bedroom, you know."*

Kita chuckled as she adjusted her dress. "It's nice to find someone who's turned on by the same thing."

Aspen rolled her eyes. *"I doubt there will be a lack of sex in the White House now. Get in here. You're missing some of the greatest facial expressions."*

Kita giggled at Apocalypse. "Let's see how the world is reacting." They ducked through the door. All the Angels turned and looked at them.

"Am—am I supposed to kneel?" said Hedgehog.

"Don't be silly," said Apocalypse. "That message was for the average citizen. You're an Angel."

"You have got to see the reactions on TV," said Sapper as she hit the back button. She stopped a few seconds before the end of Apocalypse's announcement.

"Wow, angel, that backdrop is awesome," said Apocalypse.

"I thought it conveyed the right mood."

"Damn. We look more imposing than I thought."

"If you were trying to give the Empire nightmares, you succeeded," said Nemesis coldly.

"I'm not trying to terrify—maybe Kita is. I just want to be taken seriously."

"You called yourself *the Dragon God*."

"I am."

"You're not a god."

"Depends. I am not a god like Kita, but to over a billion and a half people, I am a god. Someday I will be like Kita."

Nemesis raised an eyebrow at Kita.

"Sky's the limit on her ambition, but I don't give it for free. You have to earn it. Conquering a world is a good start."

"These are people's lives. Not poker chips on a table. What happened to taking care of them? A new world that is inclusive, respectful, and equal?"

"I can't do both?" said Apocalypse.

"How can you be those things if no one is your equal?"

"Because people will never do those things on their own. If people think they are equal, they believe their ideas are equal—the good, the bad, and the ugly—competing ideas cause division and strife. That is how we got to where we are. The people have to be told by a higher power what ideas are good and which are bad. I cannot be equal to the average citizen. I have to be above them to create the empire I said I would. What does it matter if I spread my ideas to the rest of the world?"

"Whatever happened to freedom?" snarled Nemesis.

"There will still be freedom. My world will be freer than it ever has been. The difference will be everyone will have freedom, not a select few."

Nemesis pointed at Kita. "You created this monster."

"She's not a monster. In the military, your leaders are above you. You are expected to obey them. It's no different for Kimmy. No one will obey her if the rest of the world sees her as an equal. We already established that at the UN.

"Kimmy is the first person I consider my equal. She's ambitious, driven, and intelligent. What makes her different from the rest of you is scope. Leaf wants to be the best assassin. Karen wants to be the best pilot. Lizzie wants to be the best soldier. Nicole, you want to be the best sniper. Velositi wants to be the best warrior. Kimmy wants to be a god. That's what I wanted to be—I wanted to end existence. To get there requires not being the best at one thing, but the best at many. Kimmy is on her way. I'm proud of how far she's come, and this is only the beginning. If she wanted to destroy the world, she would have. She already has the power. I believe her goals are noble, and I will help her. If you help her, that's up to you. I know she'll help you achieve your goals."

"There is no going back to where we were, Nicole," said Apocalypse. "You didn't like that world. I didn't like that world, Kita didn't like that world. It can't change if the existing system is left intact. I can't rule like my father and expect change."

"So, you'll rule through fear?"

"My father ruled through fear—fear of those who are different. You, me, Kita, Lizzy—we are the people he taught others to fear. I will rule with compassion and understanding, but also strength. I want to inspire awe and wonder in my people. I don't want them to fear me, but respect me."

"What of her?" Nemesis pointed at Kita.

"The Vicereine is meant to intimidate my rivals, not my people."

"How many biker bars is she going to go through? What if the next one is a school?"

Apocalypse grimaced and hung her head. "I love her—the good and the bad. I'll deal with it as it comes."

Kita wanted to explode and pummel Nemesis for suggesting such a thing. She had more control than that. "Your self-righteousness will be your downfall, you pompous ass. I've seen such attitudes take down far better people than you. I've also known someone who mastered it and became one of my most beloved friends. Ask Leaf about Galina and Scarlett." Tears tumbled down her face as she fled toward the bedroom.

"*Way to show her the error of her ways,*" said Aspen.

"She can't be allowed to act that way," retorted Nemesis.

*"You can't stop her. It's who she is. You want any control of her actions you need to be like Scarlett."*

"Who is Scarlett?"

*"A high angel who used Kita's evil to further her philanthropic agenda and could influence Kita."*

"I don't need a lecture."

*"Just because I'm the size of a kid, doesn't mean I am one. I am way older than you, and I've been around Kita a lot. You're getting the lecture even if I have to drag you by your ear."*

Kita crashed through the door of her and Kimmy's bedroom. Her dress changed to a hoodie and pajama pants, and she landed hard on the bed. *I wish I had Sarge. I miss my cat so much.* She buried her face in a pillow instead.

"Kita?" said Velositi standing at the foot of the bed arms crossed. "What she said is not true, and you know it. But you rose to her bait, and she got a reaction out of you. It is not fair of you to manipulate the others into fighting your battle for you by being dramatic and crying. You are bigger and stronger than this. Because you are here crying, you are not out protecting Kimmy. Nicole only attacked you to get to Kimmy, and now she is alone with Nicole. Kimmy can hold her own, but you are not supporting her."

"I hate you," Kita growled through the pillow and her tears.

"I know that is not true. You do not like it when I force you to be an adult. I cannot believe the other girls let you get away with it."

Kita huffed. "Everyone else is scared of me. I'll always be human in your eyes."

"I will never be scared of you. No matter what power you possess."

Kita rolled over and hugged Velositi. "You'll never let me get away with anything."

"Not with your friends. I do not care what you do to the rest of the world."

"That is a popular sentiment," said Apocalypse from the doorway.

"Sorry," said Kita to the gathered Angels at the door.

*"That is the first time I've ever heard you apologize for an outburst,"* said Aspen.

"Good influences," said Kita.

*"The other Angels were bad influences?"*

"My old partner was an evil angel. My best friend and girlfriend were fallen angels. Not a lot of positive reinforcement. No one told me when I was wrong in a positive way. They just wanted to hang me."

"Did you feel like you had to compete with them?" said Velositi.

"I don't know if compete is the right word. I felt if I showed any weakness, I would lose everything."

*"The fallen are a subspecies of Angel and were always in competition with each other. They would fight for their spot in the pecking order,"* said Aspen.

"Kita is the only fallen angel now," said Velositi. "She has changed. Maybe it is time for all of them to change."

Kita nodded. "I no longer have a desire to control those around me. No one is threatening me or making demands of me like in the past. For the first time ever, I want to share not hoard."

"You have a dragon to guard it," said Sapper.

Kita took Apocalypse by the hand and pulled her in.

"I want my own power," said Apocalypse. "But I will guard Kita jealously."

"That's sweet and all, but the DVR is going to go live if we don't hurry," said Sapper. "And Nicole says she's sorry. So, let's go."

Kita laughed. "Ok. Let's go see how badly we spooked the world."

"OK GIRLS, HERE WE GO," SAID APOCALYPSE AS SHE TRANSFORMED INTO Scourge on the north lawn of the White House. She took flight with Sapper, Nemesis, Velositi, and Aspen. They turned east toward the Capitol Building. Kita, dressed as the Vicereine, placed a hand on O'Brien and Ryan's shoulder and phased them behind the Lincoln Memorial. The trio walked around to the stage setup halfway up the steps.

Apocalypse and the other Angels circled the Capitol Building dome and dropped low over the crowd. Ten million people packed the space between the Lincoln Memorial and the Empire's Capitol Building, spilling out into the streets. More people watched from giant screens in West Potomac Park and the Jefferson Memorial. To give the best view of the stage, large screens were positioned every fifty yards on both sides of the National Mall.

Apocalypse roared as she flew above the crowd. She circled the Washington Monument blasting flame into the sky. As she passed over the World War II Memorial, she dropped low and dipped her back claws into the reflecting pool, slaloming the braziers floating in the water. At the end of the reflecting pool, she turned south and made a loop over the people gathered in West Potomac Park.

She landed on top of the Lincoln Memorial, roared, and blew a long tongue of flame to light a pair of braziers on either side of the stage. The braziers burned through ropes unfurling large black and white striped Imperial banners. In the center was a blue field with a circle of stars and the Imperial Seal. Lines of fire raced down the steps of the Lincoln Memorial to the braziers floating in the reflecting pool. The flames burned through ropes, unfurling more banners. When the last brazier lit, teams unfurled yet more banners around the Washington Memorial, the National Mall, West Potomac Park, and the Jefferson Memorial.

Scourge transformed into Apocalypse. She glided to the edge of the roof, drew her tomahawks, and threw them at targets on her right and left. The tomahawks chopped through ropes, releasing large Imperial banners down the front of the Lincoln Memorial.

A flight of five black F-22s roared low over the crowd. Orange flames decorated the fuselage, and EUS NAVY was painted under each wing. The formation turned straight up, spiraling into the clouds. When they came down, four came from the cardinal directions, passing within inches of each other. The four planes turned to the east as the fifth plane flew over the crowd inverted. The solo F-22 turned to the northwest toward the Potomac River, and the other four turned south. The cameras followed the solo F-22 as it flew above the river going under and over the bridges. As it passed the I-395 bridge, it rolled over, turned on the afterburner, and with a *boom* broke the sound barrier. The F-22 dropped low, creating a wake in the river with its sonic boom. From the southeast, the other four F-22s raced up the Potomac River faster than the speed of sound. The solo F-22 passed through the other four. The five F-22s turned skyward and reformed on the single F-22. The flight turned and flew over Apocalypse and the crowd.

"*Thanks, Karen,*" said Kita. "*Excellent show.*"

"*No problem. I could never do that as a human.*"

"*It's just the beginning.*"

Apocalypse stepped off the roof and glided down to the entrance of the

Lincoln Memorial. She entered the marble temple, knelt at the foot of Lincoln, and bowed her head. When she emerged, she walked confidently to the stage. Kita fell in beside her. They stopped at the podium.

Kita took in the crowd. The wonder and anticipation from the crowd were at a peak. Apocalypse's display inspired awe. The air show was the opening act to get the crowd warmed up, and they were ready. *"They're all yours, love. They can't be any more receptive."*

*"I'm nervous,"* said Apocalypse.

*"You've practiced this. Speak from the heart."*

*"It's one thing to say it to you. It's another to say it to them."*

*"Conquer your fear. Use it to propel you forward, don't let it hold you back. You can do this. Seize your destiny."*

Apocalypse's confident expression hadn't wavered as she spoke to Kita. She opened her wings wide and rose into the air.

Kita made sure Apocalypse was connected to the PA system.

Apocalypse opened her arms to the crowd and spoke in a triumphant tone. "Citizens of the Empire of the United States, we gather today to celebrate our great Empire's triumph over our decades' long struggle. Not since my great grandfather, Franklin Delano Roosevelt, led us to victory over Nazi Germany and the Empire of Japan in World War Two have we faced so cataclysmic a threat to our way of life as the Neophormes. Our brave Soldiers, Airman, Sailors, and Marines fought them around the world—in the jungles of the Congo, the mountains of Iran, the grassy plains of South Africa, the depths of the Pacific Ocean, and finally in the Far East of the Soviet Union. We were dedicated, unwavering—defiant—as we battled these hostile aliens to protect *our freedom,*" her voice rose as she pumped her fist. Planted groups among the crowd cheered, causing the rest of the crowd to cheer and applaud.

"We have done more than hold this monstrous enemy at our gate. Our forces took the fight to them. We captured Neophormes and learned their secrets. Using the ingenuity and resourcefulness of our brilliant scientists, we developed weapons that let us fight back. With the help of our allies, the Vehlixen and Angels, we liberated the countries under Neophorm influence. As a final act of defiance, we delivered a bioweapon to the Neophorm's homeworld to make sure they will never threaten us again! I will do whatever is necessary to protect our *freedom,*" her voice rang out, like a rallying cry as she again pumped her fist. The planted groups in the crowd cheered and would each time she said the word freedom and would react differently to other preselected words.

She lowered her tone and spoke calmly and direct, "To show we harbor no ill will, I proposed the Soviet Union, India, and China join our great Empire. These noble nations agreed. Now, the sun never sets on the Empire of the United States. Our military is the strongest in the world. Our economy grows, creating wealth and prosperity for all. This is because of you, the great citizens of the Empire. Without your courage, perseverance, and dedication, the Empire would never reach the glory to which it aspires," when she finished, her tone was warm and endearing.

Her tone turned sober and serious. She clenched her hands and said, "But, let me speak frankly. Our great Empire is still under siege. When I brought news of our defeat of the Neophormes to the UN and the world, we were not met with jubilation, but condemnation. The world says we do not have the right to defend ourselves against threats to our *freedom*. The *world* says we cannot do what is necessary to prevent attacks on the Empire—to do what is necessary to keep us *safe!*" she nearly shouted the last line as she waved a hand over the crowd.

She spoke with authority as she declared, "The world sided with the Neophormes and has shown their true colors. The *world* is no friend to the Empire of the United States. We are on our own to protect our *freedom*. I, for one, am willing to stand up to the rest of the world and say, 'I will fight for the Empire.' Because the world does not support us, we *do not* support the *world*! We are withdrawing from the UN and seizing the United Nations complex in New York. They do not deserve to meet on our soil," she pointed at the ground as she angrily made her pronouncement.

Her anger continued, "Understand this, my friends, the rest of the world wants us weak, so they can dictate to us how we are to live. We will not let this great Empire built by my father, James Roosevelt Junior, grandfather, James Roosevelt, and my great grandfather, Franklin D. Roosevelt, be governed by the rest of the world. We reject the rest of the world's authority. I *am* Empress Apocalypse, the Dragon God, and the world will not tell me how to govern my proud citizens. We are a *free* people! We are a fair, just, and equal society! Our strength is in equality! If the rest of the world doesn't like it—too bad!" she shouted as she waved a finger and energy crackled around her eyes.

Her voice reflected the energy in her eyes, "And so, I say it is not enough for the sun to never set on the Empire of The United States—we must return to an idea that made this country great! I proclaim a new Manifest Destiny! We must expand our ideals of *freedom* and *equality*—truths that we hold self-evident —to all corners of the globe. The leaders of the world have shown they do not share our ideals. They choose to rule by tyranny and keep their people in oppression. We, as a just society, cannot ignore the plight of the people of the world. The Empire will be a shining beacon of hope to the world! Let all the people of the world join us and see what it is like to live in *freedom*! As citizens of our glorious Empire, it is our duty to take *freedom* and *equality* to every country of the world!" her words rang out over the crowd as spontaneous cheers erupted.

Her voice lowered, but she kept the same energy, "No doubt, the *tyrannical leaders* of the rest of the world will resist us. They will condemn us. They will sanction us, and even take up arms against us. We will not be *deterred*. We have the most glorious military in the world. But...the task will be long and difficult. There will be hardships, but nothing worth doing comes easily! For *freedom* and *equality* to spread throughout the world will take blood, sweat, and tears. Everyone will be asked to sacrifice so that we may make the Empire even more glorious!" she finished in a yell, raising both fists and shaking them.

She became somber and frank as she spoke, "What I am about to say I do so with a heavy heart and burdened soul. The Empire of the United States must be successful. A *strong hand* is needed to guide us. It cannot waver in the face of hardship. It must be above politics and cannot be swayed by the imperfections of men. It must remain true to our Manifest Destiny and always have the Empire's needs at heart. If we are to succeed, we must remove division and doubt. The fate of the world hangs in the balance.

Apocalypse raised her head and opened her arms. She spoke with authority and determination, "I, Empress Apocalypse, the Dragon God, am that guiding hand. I will guide our glorious Empire into the future. By the powers granted to me under Amendment Twenty-nine of the Constitution of the Empire of the United States, I am altering the dictatorial powers outlined in Amendment Twenty-nine from lasting a period of six months to a period of my lifetime, or until I abdicate the throne. At which point, the states of the Empire of the United States will become independent and able to form their own *unions*. I am also altering Amendment Thirty of the Constitution. The position of Emperor of the United States can no longer be changed by election. I proclaim that I, Empress Apocalypse, the Dragon God, am the rightful and only ruler of the *Empire of the United States*." Applause and cheering erupted that shook the leaves on the trees.

"We are a proud and glorious empire, and it is time to take our rightful place in the world. We will claim our Manifest Destiny! *Freedom* and *equality* will be the law across the globe!"

Apocalypse raised her fist. "For the glory of the Empire!"

The crowd raised their fists, and with a full-throated roar echoed Apocalypse's cry.

"*So, this is how democracy dies, to the roar of a crowd,*" said Nemesis.

———————✕———————

THE HAWAIIAN BREEZE BLEW THROUGH KITA'S CURLED HAIR AND VEIL AS SHE gazed into Apocalypse's eyes. She couldn't make the goofy smile on her face go away. She stood in front of a stand of tropical trees surrounded by flowers on the Hale Kai compound overlooking Keauhou Bay.

"Angel?" said Apocalypse.

"Huh?"

Apocalypse giggled.

"You can place the ring on Kimmy's finger," said Ryan.

"Oh, right." Kita turned and got the ring from Velositi. She took Apocalypse's hand and slipped the white gold ring with inlaid rubies on her finger. Kita kissed the ring and hand. "Sealed with all my love."

Apocalypse blushed.

"And Kimmy, you can place your ring on Kita's finger." Nemesis handed the ring to her.

Kita held out her hand and let Apocalypse slip the black gold ring on her finger. Apocalypse kissed the ring.

"You may kiss your bride," said Ryan.

Kita put her arms around Apocalypse's neck and kissed her as the small crowd cheered.

"I love you," said Apocalypse.

"I love you forever," said Kita.

"You better. You're stuck with me."

"May I introduce Kimberly and Kita Logine-Roosevelt," said Ryan as Kita and Apocalypse raised their arms and took a bow.

An upbeat pop-rock song played as they walked down the aisle. The harbor was packed with boats and canoes. People waved, and a few fireworks went off.

"*I know it's only been a couple of days, but what do you want to name the baby?*" said Apocalypse. "*Not Jane.*"

Kita chuckled. "*I don't know. All my previous kids came with names.*"

"*How about a family name?*"

"*Slag, no. I'm not naming my kid Marie.*"

"*What name do you want?*" said Apocalypse.

"*My best friend was into a football club called Chelsea. I always liked the name.*"

"*Ok, but you get to explain to our daughter why she's named after a soccer team.*"

"*What do you want?*"

"*I like Lynne. Chelsea Lynne Logine-Roosevelt has a nice ring to it.*"

SPECIAL THANKS TO THE FOLLOWING PATREONS!

Adam Dunsmuir
Jeremy Walker
K.V. Wilson
ParadoxicMouse
Adam True
Andre Matos
Joshua Le Tourneau
Kevin Colovos
Michelle Chambers
Javante Ferguson
Mark Gardner
Nick te Velde
Sarah Ilbrink
Sasha G

L. Fergus is an Amazon Bestselling author with Birthright, Razor's Pass, and Rebirth. All titles were #1 new releases in LGBT Science Fiction. Before Amazon, L. was a Wattpad Featured Author and #1 writer of science fiction. The Fallen Angel Saga has more than four hundred thousand reads. The books Birthright, BykeChic, and Rebirth have won over twenty awards, including Best Overall.

L. lives with four dogs: Rust, Moxy, Stormy, and Valor, and five cats: Nova, Jupiter, Crater, Pluto, and Forest Fire.

If you want the most up to date stories consider becoming a patreon at:
www.patreon.com/FallenAngelKita

Join L. Fergus' mailing list at FallenAngelKita.com for news about upcoming book releases. Follow L. on Facebook at Facebook.com/FallenAngelKita, Twitter @FallenAngelKita and contact L. at:
L@FallenAngelKita.com.

Did you enjoy BykeChic?
Tell the world what you think!

Leave a review on
Amazon or Goodreads